BEST OF FRIENDS

Cathy Kelly is a number one bestselling author. She worked as a journalist before becoming a novelist, and has published ten novels. She is an Ambassador for Unicef in Ireland, helping to raise awareness of the plight of 12 million children orphaned across Africa through AIDS. She lives in Wicklow with her family.

For more information on Cathy Kelly, visit her website at www.cathykelly.com

Visit www.AuthorTracker.co.uk for exclusive updates on Cathy Kelly.

Praise for Cathy Kelly:

'A must for Kelly's many fans; a warm, moving read.'
Daily Mail

'Totally believable.' Rosamunde Pilcher

'An upbeat and diverting tale skilfully told . . . Kelly knows what her readers want and consistently delivers.'
Sunday Independent

'An absorbing, heart-warming tale.' *Company*

'Her skill at dealing with the complexities of modern life, marriage and families is put to good effect as she teases out the secrets of her characters.' *Choice*

'Kelly dramatises her story with plenty of sparky humour.'
The Times

'Kelly has an admirable capacity to make the readers identify, in turn, with each of her female characters . . .'
Irish Independent

CATHY KELLY

Best of Friends

HARPER

Harper
An imprint of HarperCollins*Publishers*
77–85 Fulham Palace Road,
Hammersmith, London W6 8JB

www.harpercollins.co.uk

This paperback edition 2008
1

Set in Sabon by Palimpsest Book Production Limited,
Grangemouth, Stirlingshire

For Tamsin

PROLOGUE

Brush hair, brush teeth, forget about eyeliner, just go for mascara and a dust of bronzer. Squirt of deodorant ... blast, none left. Put that on the shopping list. Where is the shopping list, anyway ... ?

Sally Richardson had a million and one things on her mind as she hastily buttoned up her shirt and pulled on a pair of black trousers over skin still damp from the shower.

Friday mornings in the Richardsons' house were even more manic than usual because on Fridays and Saturdays, The Beauty Spot, the beauty salon that Sally owned and ran, opened at nine instead of half-past. That extra half-hour made a huge difference, Sally thought, every time Friday rolled round. She had to be out of the front door at eight forty-five on the nail to drop the boys at the day nursery instead of the rest of the week's more leisurely nine fifteen.

There was no time to dawdle over toast and coffee – not that much dawdling ever went on at the Richardsons', with two working parents.

Sally told her friends that she never had fantasies in which Jude Law ripped off all her clothes and told her she was the most beautiful woman he'd ever seen in his life. No, her fantasies were about the household running to a strict timetable, where she was perkily out of bed and showered by half-past seven (with make-up on, hair perfect and no snags in her tights), ready to drag three-year-old Daniel from his bed (four-year-old Jack would already be up and beheading a few Action Men). Dressing the boys and getting breakfast ready would happen without too much cereal ending up on the floor and without small boys squabbling, and there might even be time for Sally to share a cup of coffee with Steve before he raced out of the door at eight twenty. Of course, this was the stuff of daydreams, as Sally often admitted to her mother-in-law, Delia. (She nearly told Delia about the Jude Law thing but then thought better of it. Delia was more of a Sean Connery woman, anyway.)

'It can't be good for the image of a beauty salon when the owner arrives out of breath, without a screed of make-up on her face and her shirt buttoned up all wrong,' Sally had once pointed out.

But Delia, who knew how hard her daughter-in-law worked and thought she looked just as good with her creamy skin and flashing dark eyes free of cosmetics, laughed and said that early morning rushing was the working mother's daily marathon. 'I was as slim as you when Steve and Amy were young, and now look at me,' she said ruefully. 'Upholstered hips and arms like a weightlifter.'

'You look great,' chided Sally, who adored her mother-in-law and treated her like a surrogate mum. Her own had died of cancer when Sally had been only twenty.

Kids definitely kept you thin, Sally decided on this particular Friday morning in February. She'd been up for an hour and still hadn't managed more than a sip of tea because Danny had upended his Rice Pops all over his jeans and sweater, necessitating a complete change. The toaster had decided to have one of its off days and burned Steve's toast to charcoal, setting off the smoke detector.

'Damn!' came his muttered voice from the hall where he was attempting to silence the alarm.

'Damn, damn, damn,' repeated Danny happily, at the kitchen table, where he was having a good go at spilling more cereal.

'Damn, damn, damn,' joined in Jack, banging his spoon against his fortunately empty dish.

Sally, foreseeing days of 'damns' morning, noon and night,

2

sighed. 'Language,' she mouthed at Steve when he appeared a moment later, fiddling with his cuff.

'Sorry,' he said. 'Forgot. The button popped off while I was reaching up. Where's the thread?'

Sally prised the last bit of charcoal from the toaster. 'To be honest, Steve, you have a better chance of finding another clean shirt than of finding a needle and thread anywhere in this house. Will I iron you another one?'

'No, love, thanks. You don't have time. I'll do it.' Steve leaned over his tiny wife and planted a kiss on the top of her head.

Steve was six foot two while Sally was a petite five three. 'I never realised how ridiculous we looked together until I saw our wedding photos,' she would joke. Height aside, they made a handsome couple, Sally's elfin, dark-haired, dark-eyed looks a dramatic contrast to her husband's clean-cut features, fair hair and unusual rich brown eyes. The boys took after their mother, their inky black eyes, like hers, gleaming with mischief.

Steve was not a natural with the iron and he grumbled as he wrestled with another shirt. 'Today of all days, with the boss leaving, and I'm late as it is . . .'

'If the worst thing that happens today is your shirt button and this pair screaming "damn" when your mother comes to mind them this afternoon, then we're doing fine,' Sally pointed out.

Steve nodded, teasingly. 'You're right, Pollyanna.'

'I'm not Pollyanna,' protested his wife. 'It's just that Mum always used to say count your . . .'

'. . . blessings. I know.' Steve pulled on his ironed shirt and then drained his coffee.

'I don't want to be a pain in the you-know-what,' Sally went on earnestly, 'like some Goody Two-Shoes always looking on the bright side.'

'You're not,' Steve said, shoving the ironing board away with a clatter. 'But your optimism is one of the things I love about you. C'mere.'

3

They exchanged a proper kiss this time.

'Mummy, what's a pain in the you-know-what?' asked Jack innocently.

His parents laughed, then Steve picked up his jacket from the back of a kitchen chair. 'Bye, brats,' he said, kissing his beloved sons.

'Bye, Daddy,' they chorused.

'Bye, Pollyanna.' He ducked as though Sally might throw something at him.

'You're the brat!' she yelled good-humouredly.

The front door slammed and Sally glanced at the clock. Eight thirty-two. Blast. Late again and Danny was only a quarter of the way through his cereal. She sat down beside her younger son and urged him to hurry up, which inevitably made him slow down. Danny had a stubborn streak.

Ruffling his unruly hair lovingly, she thought of how lucky she was, having Steve and the boys. Steve might tease her about it, but her mantra had always been that you shouldn't take anything for granted in this life.

As her mum used to say: you never knew what was around the corner.

CHAPTER ONE

Abby stared into the cold hard depths of the hairdresser's mirror. As if she hadn't enough problems, now she was sure she could see fresh lines fanning out around her eyes. Ageing was like the San Andreas fault, she thought grimly: you never knew where the next crack was going to appear. Hitting forty had been the start of the slide, definitely. Since then – unbelievably *two* years ago – she felt her entire face had gone to pot.

Beside her, Cherise, who secretly thought Abby looked even more attractive in reality than she did on television, gazed critically at Abby's newly cut hair.

Cherise, like every member of staff in Gianni's Salon, was glowingly young, with dewy skin. She wore the hairstylist's uniform of black hipsters, slinky little T-shirt and belly ring. Abby whipped her envious eyes from Cherise's flat, toned stomach and smiled into the mirror. The wrinkles obligingly smiled with her. Despite her lovely new haircut, her smart Armani shirt, and the admiration of most of the salon, who had obviously recognised Abby, and watched her with interest, even though they pretended their eyes were glued to their copies of *Hello!*, Abby felt a chasm in the pit of her stomach. God, she was getting old. Old and tired-looking. Forty-two. It even sounded old. Other people said she was imagining it.

'Do you like it?' Cherise was anxious for some feedback.

'Thanks, Cherise, it's lovely,' Abby said kindly, instantly apologetic for not having said something nice sooner.

Abby was kind to everyone. That, said her producer on *Declutter: Your Home and Your Life*, was a huge part of her charm and, undoubtedly, the key to her success. It wasn't fake kindness: it was the real thing. Abby liked people and they liked her back. The ratings on *Declutter* had proved that. In just two seasons, Abby Barton had been transformed from a mum with a part-time small business into a TV hotshot.

Her fledgeling home decluttering service couldn't keep up with demand, there were talks about Abby writing a book to go with the programme, and the filming of a third series was due to start shortly. Both the TV pundits and the viewers loved her, the bank now sent the family Christmas cards instead of irate letters, and, occasionally, people she only vaguely knew waved at her hysterically when their cars passed in traffic.

She still felt the same underneath, though. As Abby said to her close girlfriends, she was waiting for people to realise that she was an impostor and that she didn't deserve her new-found fame or the money.

'Fame is transient – lack of self-confidence lasts for ever,' she joked, making everyone crack up with laughter.

'No one could ever say it's gone to your head,' her husband, Tom, said occasionally, huge praise from him.

Tom had unruly dark hair streaked with grey, a narrow, clever-looking face, rimless glasses and an elongated frame from never giving in to either the biscuit tin or too many glasses of wine (unlike Abby). There was a distinct puritan streak in him, an austerity that made him perfect deputy headmaster material, but also deeply disapproving of people who lost sight of ascetic values.

He'd have hated Abby to have changed from her old slightly scatty self into a full-blown celebrity obsessed with clothes, cars and holidays.

However, intellectually brilliant but unworldly, he'd never actually realised that Abby, despite being quite happy to find treasures in second-hand boutiques during their hard-up days, had always secretly liked to spend money on her hair and on ludicrously expensive cosmetics. And that one of the advantages of her new-found financial success was that Abby no longer had to hide the cost of hairdos and new clothes by buying cheaper cuts of meat and special offer vegetables. Certainly if Tom were given the slightest clue to how much today's jaunt to Gianni's had cost, he'd be scathing about the waste of money.

Money was a bit of a sore subject in the Barton household these days. After years of earning so little, Abby had imagined that her new, comparative wealth would make their lives much easier. Instead, in some ways it had made them more difficult, mainly because of Tom's vision of himself as head of the household and breadwinner.

At school, he might be viewed as a modern educator with plenty of innovative ideas, but at home Tom liked the traditional roles to be maintained. Despite her increased workload, Abby still did all the shopping and laundry, an arrangement that was beginning to grate. And she knew that he, like many men, did not feel comfortable about his wife earning more than he did.

'I think it suits you a bit more feathery round the jaw,' Cherise said now, fiddling with the fine ends and fluffing them up. 'It's kinder to the jawline.' Then she smiled and stood back to admire her famous client from a distance. 'Do you know, it takes years off you!'

Abby had a sudden vision of herself saying the same thing to her Aunt Sadie when Sadie had finally given up her five-decade red-lipstick habit in favour of a subtle warm pink. White-haired Sadie, squinting in the mirror in disapproval at the sight of her mouth without its narrow slash of crimson, had actually looked much the same. Still seventy-six, just with a more suitable lip colour. The youthful Cherise probably thought of Abby in the same way that Abby thought of Aunt Sadie: a tough old broad vainly trying to keep age at bay. But all the money and fame in the world couldn't do that.

Outside Gianni's with a bag of hair-care products, Abby slammed the rear door of her glossy black four-wheel drive – the purchase of which had almost started a war in the Barton household – opened the driver's door and swung herself into the seat. Her hair had turned out well, she thought, glancing critically in the rear-view mirror. Those much-discussed strands of rich chestnut really brought out the sea-green tints in her eyes.

A passer-by stared into the car and Abby saw the familiar quickening of recognition in the man's eyes. She shot him a brief professional smile and gunned the engine, hoping she'd have manoeuvred out of the parking space before he realised that he hadn't smiled at an acquaintance – which was what most people initially thought – but at Abby Barton, television celebrity and self-help guru.

Being recognised still shocked Abby. After eighteen months of it, she still wasn't used to complete strangers nodding to her in the supermarket, then their expressions changing as the truth hit them. That wasn't someone from down the road or the woman they saw daily at the school gates. It was that celebrity, whatshername, the one with that TV show telling everyone how to sort out their lives.

When Abby's daughter, Jess, was with her, the teenager would give a running commentary on the person's thoughts.

'What's *she* doing in the supermarket? Don't famous people have someone to do their shopping?' Jess would mutter, leaving her mother in fits of laughter as they hurtled their trolley away down an aisle. 'And look at the state of those tracksuit bottoms. I thought them big telly stars were loaded and she's out in trackies with a hole in them. Scandalous.' With a witty tongue and a great eye for a comic moment, Jess somehow managed to make being stared at by strangers fun. At other times, without the fifteen-year-old riding shotgun, it wasn't always quite so funny – especially, as Abby had discovered to her astonishment, since people felt that it was OK to say anything to famous people, even remotely famous people like herself.

Hovering by the tampons one day, wearily deciding which type she'd buy from the dizzying range, she'd jumped when a woman said: 'Wow! I thought you were much younger from the TV. They must use amazing make-up.'

For once, it had taken a lot of effort to summon up the legendary Barton kindness. 'They do. Truckloads of it,' Abby had said between gritted teeth, and picked up the first box of tampons that came to hand – the wrong ones, it turned out. Fame wasn't all it was cracked up to be, that was for sure.

As she drove out of the city, her mood lifted. It was impossible to remain miserable on such a lovely March day, when the promise of summer was in the air. Banks of daffodils brightened the edges of the motorway, all craning their long necks together as if to catch sight of a passing car. Between great grey clouds above the gently rolling hills that protectively surrounded Cork city, snatches of cerulean sky could be seen.

Leaving the sedate sprawl of the suburbs behind, Abby exited the motorway and took the road to Dunmore. Exclusive Dunmore was once a tiny harbour town nestling on the outskirts of Cork, but now the city was reaching out towards it. Abby could imagine giant tracts of housing estate would one day smother the lovely green meadows that encircled the town, remorselessly merging it with the city.

But for now it was still a perfectly self-contained place with its own banks, shops, industries, a recently restored pier and a strong sense of community among the five thousand residents.

It was six months since the Barton family had moved here, and Abby loved it. She adored the horseshoe harbour and the historic town square with its old courthouse (now a bank); the railway hotel, and the exquisite small, spired church set amid the big houses of the wealthy townspeople. A hundred years ago, Dunmore had been something of a holiday town for wealthy Victorians, who came to take the sulphuric waters. They built the big villas on Knock Hill from where they could look out over their rhododendron-filled gardens down to the jagged coastline. Now, these buildings were transformed into small hotels, conference centres and offices, with only a few still functioning as private residences. The spa water was sold round the world and the bottling factory provided massive employment in the area. The wealthy of Dunmore were no longer the idle rich but people who had to work hard to continue to live in this much sought-after area. Abby never drove through the pretty, well-maintained town centre without feeling a surge of gratitude that she had come so far.

Little Annie Costello of The Cottages, a misleading name for a pinched line of council houses in a country town many miles from Cork, had never hoped to have made it so far in life. The families who lived in The Cottages were lucky if they knew where their next meal was coming from. Now Abby Barton, née Annie Costello, could order in caterers should she feel like it. A healthy bank account, fame and respectability were hers, and the house in Dunmore was the icing on the cake.

Her parents hadn't lived to see her success. Mum would have been so pleased, Abby often thought sadly, imagining her mother's face filled with pride at how far her Annie had come. Her father, on the other hand, wouldn't have cared how successful his daughter had become, as long as he still had enough money in his pocket for his daily ration of booze.

Abby's next port of call was the supermarket. When they were first married, she and Tom used to do the weekend shop together, but these days, when she was busier than ever, he never offered to help.

She literally ran round the aisles, hoping to be ready in time to pick Jess up from the train station. It was only a ten-minute walk from the station to their home in Briar Lane, but Jess had looked tired from hauling her bag of books every day. Abby had had to bite her lip not to say anything. The last time Abby had offered to collect her, Jess had told her indignantly she was fed up with being treated like a child.

'I like having a bit of peace,' she'd snapped, raking her fingers through her sandy ponytail. 'I have to get the train to school on my own, so I can manage to walk home from the station.'

That had hurt. Jess was the one member of the family who hadn't wanted to move from the Bartons' modest four-bedroom city semi where they'd lived all her life. It had been close to Jess's friends and to her school, while the house in Dunmore was miles away, and Jess felt very cut off.

Today was Friday and Jess was sure to be very tired. She couldn't resent a lift today, surely, Abby thought. They could talk on the way home, perhaps, and it might be like old times. Before work had taken up so much of her time, and before they'd moved to Dunmore, Abby had often picked up Jess and her best friend, Steph, from school. The girls used to whoop with delight to see Abby's mud-caked old Fiat parked by the school gates, and after dumping sports bags, filthy runners and dog-eared library books into the boot, they would chatter merrily all the way home, telling Abby about how horrible Saffron Walsh in their year thought she was the bee's knees now she had a pink Guess watch, how the O'Brien twins were going to be expelled for smoking and how Miss Aston must have a crush on the new history teacher, Mr Lanoix, because her eyes turned dreamy every time she bumped into him in the corridor.

However, Abby's shopping done, the length of the queue at the check-out conspired against her, and then a woman with a huge trolley-load and no purse held up everyone for ten minutes. Once she had finally thrown her shopping into the car, Abby drove rapidly to the tiny station, looking out for a lanky, sandy-haired figure in a grey skirt and cardigan hauling a giant school bag. But, apart from a

11

couple pulling a huge suitcase up the station steps, there was no one there.

Knowing that Jess would take the shortcut home through the shopping centre and up the pedestrian-only backstreets, Abby drove off. Jess would be home before her and that meant Abby had lost the chance for a chat. In the car, Jess was a captive audience. At home, her after-school routine was to shut her bedroom door loudly and switch on her CD player. Abby wasn't sure if teenage hormones were to blame or if it was her own fault for somehow failing to bond with this new Jess, the argumentative girl who seemed determined to push her parents to the limit. But in some way she felt she was losing her.

Fortunately, driving down Briar Lane never ceased to lift Abby's spirits. As she bounced the Jeep over the speed ramps, she felt that faint thrill of pride that her hard work had brought them all here.

The previous house had been lovely, thanks to her skill at interior decoration. But Gartland Avenue had been a very ordinary road in a housing estate and with the unruly Milligans next door, screaming at each other at sixty decibels day and night, it hadn't been exactly anyone's dream location.

Briar Lane was a different matter. A winding road lined with stately sycamores and overgrown laurel bushes, it was a house-fancier's heaven – full of all sorts of different properties, from new Regency-inspired homes to low, sprawling old farmhouses, with some quirky cottages in between.

Abby had fallen in love with Lyonnais the first time she'd seen it. It had started life as the gate house to a big, now long-gone mansion and, after years of careful alteration, was now a large white-gabled family home with mullioned windows and rambling roses clinging to the stonework.

Even Tom, who wasn't at all given to sentimentality, had said there was a lovely atmosphere about the house as they'd wandered through it all those months ago with the estate agent at their heels.

Abby had squeezed Tom's hand in excitement. 'It's beautiful, isn't it?' she kept saying, despite his earlier warning that they weren't to appear too enthusiastic about the house, no matter how much they liked it. *This* was the sort of house a television celebrity should own – not a twenty-year-old semi that looked like every other house on the road, but this, this gorgeously unusual pile, with its large airy rooms and its nooks and crannies and the intriguing pantry with the hidden cupboard, and the rambling garden with the armless statue of some Greek goddess hiding shyly behind a gown of ivy tendrils. Abby could already picture what she'd do to the place, where she'd put things and what colours she'd paint the walls.

'It's way over our budget,' Tom had said firmly as they'd toured the attic bedroom, which, if the cobweb content was a reliable barometer, was home to an entire colony of spiders. It was certainly over any budget that his deputy headmaster's salary could manage and he found it difficult to look at the subject in any other way. It made no difference how often Abby said that his salary had kept them all for years, so what did it matter if hers was bigger now? It did matter to Tom. 'We can't afford this,' he'd reiterated later, his lips thinning into the disapproving line that made him look just like his crabby old father.

Abby hadn't cared. For once, she'd ignored Tom's disapproval and fought for what she wanted. They'd manage. She'd do more private commissions and there were sure to be other lucrative spin-offs from the TV show, like public appearances – even though Abby hated that type of thing. She was determined to do whatever it took to buy Lyonnais. They couldn't lose this house. They'd be so happy there, she knew it. All Tom needed to do was get over his strop about who earned the most money.

She sighed now as she swung the Jeep into the drive, admiring, as she always did, the magnolia tree to one side of the gate, now gorgeously in bloom. She did love this place but things hadn't been easy since they'd moved here.

Her relationship with Tom had deteriorated, while she and Jess seemed to be living on different planets. Just when life should be perfect for the Bartons, it seemed curiously off balance.

CHAPTER TWO

Earlier that afternoon, Jess Barton had glanced quickly at the classroom clock. Ten to three. Another forty minutes of science. Boring. Being a teenager was crammed with boredom, Jess felt, what with train-track braces, horrible exams and people constantly bossing you around, but double science was surely the most boring thing of all. Noticing Miss Nevin's gaze roaming over the class, Jess stared down dutifully at her science textbook, trying to appear as if her mind was firmly fixed on the knotty issue of what sort of chemical formula you came up with if you mixed sulphur, oxygen and hydrogen. Nobody acted dutiful interest better than Jess Barton. She was award-winning material, Oscar-nomination stuff.

'It's the angle of the head,' she often explained to her best friend and partner in crime, Steph Anderson, who was always the first person to be hauled out of her seat and left in disgrace outside the classroom door for not paying attention. 'And the pencil sucking. There's something about pencil sucking – it just makes you look riveted. You've got to lean over the book and look like you care, Steph.'

In Jess's opinion, all that any teacher required was a room full of students bent at forty-five-degree angles to their desks and sucking pencils thoughtfully. She knew this from her dad. He said that not everyone paid attention all the time but the kids he liked were the ones who actually behaved in class.

Jess behaved. She reasoned that your mind could be a

15

million miles away, or even four miles away at St Michael's School for Hot Guys down the road, but as long as you kept your head down, you gave the impression of being a good student. So far, this system had worked. Jess Barton had never been made to stand outside the door, a punishment that also merited ten black marks.

Naturally, chemical formulae were the things furthest from her mind. Ian Green was the focus of her concentration. Gorgeous Ian, with those piercing blue eyes and a hint of dark stubble on his perfect face. Steph said that stubble was so yesterday and the best guys were fuzz-free, but Jess had a secret yearning for the sensation of kissing a guy and feeling manly, grown-up stubble against her cheek, like in a passionate scene from a movie. Jess had enjoyed many happy hours daydreaming about herself and Ian, replaying such a scene. Ian was tall too. Tall enough to have to really lean down to kiss her, which was nice, because Jess was tall herself. There was only one problem. Well, two actually. The first was that he went to St Michael's School for Hot Guys instead of Bradley College, where Jess went. The guys in Bradley were mostly beyond boring. And the second: he had a girlfriend, Saffron Walsh, who was nearly sixteen, in the same class as Jess, and who was Ms Most Likely to Succeed.

'Most likely to succeed in becoming an airhead TV weather girl, more like,' Steph snorted resentfully. Some people might have thought that Steph was a rival of Saffron's, as they were both of the blonde hair, perfect figure variety. But Jess, who had been Steph's absolute best friend since kindergarten, knew that Steph's dislike came from the fact that Saffron was clearly not good enough for Ian. If Ian realised what a bimbo Saffron was, he might dump her and miraculously take up with Jess. Miraculous, thought Jess, being the operative word.

Jess was not blonde with a perfect figure. She was, she felt, more a 'reliable girl picked for netball' sort of person. Lanky like her dad, she had no curves, no need of a bra and she could never get jeans long enough for her skinny legs. Her eyes were nice – a thick-lashed, smoky bluey green like her mum's – but they were hidden behind boring glasses because she'd inherited bad eyesight from her dad. Her hair was boringly straight and the dull colour of wet sand, while the rest of her face was ordinary with a big O: ordinary nose, ordinary mouth, ordinary, slightly pointy chin. It all added up to the sort of person nobody noticed. Having a celebrity mum didn't help. People expected the daughter of the glamorous Abby Barton to be just as glamorous. 'And then they meet me,' Jess would say, grumpiness hiding the hurt.

Steph insisted that this wasn't true, and was always going on about how she envied Jess for being tall and slim, and for having great cheekbones and beautiful eyes that lit up when she was passionate about something.

'Now *I* have slitty eyes,' Steph would say, piling on another layer of Mac shadow to counteract this perceived failing. 'But yours are huge and your lashes are so long. Wait till you get contacts and get your train tracks off. Then the guys will be all over you like a rash.'

But Steph was only being nice, Jess felt. She knew that guys liked girls who looked like girls, meaning ones with actual boobs. Tall and lanky and not able to fill an A cup made her a non-runner, no matter how nice her cheekbones were.

Which led on to a third problem, actually. She'd never spoken to Ian. He went around with people from her school, of course, because he was going out with Saffron, but these weren't the sort of people who were interested in the likes of Jess. They were the glittering people who wore the right jeans, the right trainers and had money to go into the city centre at the weekends and hang round having fun, going for coffee and buying CDs. Jess didn't know how to hang around in that languid, I'm-so-cool manner that girls like Saffron had down to an art form.

Even worse, now that the Bartons had moved to Dullsville,

a.k.a. Dunmore, there was even less of a chance of her bumping into Ian.

'Ian & Jess,' she wrote on her notepad. Shading the writing with her hand, she drew a tiny heart around the words. Then she scribbled over the writing in case Gary, who sat beside her, saw it. Gary was good at science but bad at life, and was quite likely to announce Jess's doodle to all and sundry. Jess would just die if anyone but Steph knew how she felt about Ian.

'Homework,' announced Miss Nevin happily from the front of the class. 'I've prepared a list of thirty questions for the next lesson. They're not too hard – just to test you on what we've been learning this week. Hand these sheets round, would you?'

As the questions were passed down the lines of desks, there were a lot of sighs, mainly from the people who'd just suffered history and been given a huge essay on eighteenth-century wars to write for Monday. Honestly, all those eighteenth-century people did was have wars. What were they like? Had they never heard of the UN?

Jess opened her homework notebook and stared dismally at today, Friday. The class were doing exams in June, their first public exams, and the teachers were piling on the work like anything. Along with the history essay was an English assignment on *Paradise Lost* (from Mr Redmond, who obviously thought that fifteen-year-olds had nothing better to do at the weekend than analyse every single word Milton had ever written) and a note of the four chapters of geography to be revised for a test on Monday afternoon from Mr Metcalfe, more proof that he was criminally insane because they were the four biggest chapters in the book. There was also a huge tranche of maths homework, not to mention a page of French comprehension (not too bad) and some art history to read over (easy peasy).

Jess wrote down 'Science – 30 questions for Tuesday', and sighed at Steph as the bell rang.

'What are we? Baby Einsteins?' grumbled Steph as the two

friends shoved their science books into their rucksacks. 'Why did we do science?' Steph asked this question at least once a week. 'We could have done home economics and be making our name as fashion designers right now.'

'You don't get to make things in home ec,' Jess pointed out. 'You learn about the eight billion vitamins and minerals that keep you healthy, which is just biology, which is science, which . . .'

'. . . is why we did science,' finished Steph. 'I hate sewing, anyway. Look what happened when I tried to customise my jeans. Sequins should be glued, not sewed on.'

Jess nodded.

'What are you going to do tonight?' Steph asked.

'Telly, I s'pose,' Jess said miserably. She must be the only girl in the class to have a boring Friday night ahead of her. No, not the class, the *planet*.

'I'd love to be watching telly tonight,' Steph protested. 'Gran's party is going to be a pain – all the rellies telling me I've got so big and saying how they remember when I was a baby and they used to change my nappy. Like, how sick and twisted is that?'

Despite herself, Jess laughed. Steph had an enormous extended family and was very funny when she talked about them. Tonight was her grandmother's birthday and the entire Anderson clan were going out to the Hungry Hunter restaurant and bar to celebrate. Steph's mother was anxious that Steph wear this hideous royal-blue blouse and a sensible skirt to the gathering to please her grandmother, while Steph had personally earmarked a funky chiffon blouse with just a hint of bra peeking out underneath, and her skin-tight bootleg jeans. Her uncle's stepson would be there and he was 'in-cred-ible', as Steph drooled. She planned to look nonchalantly amazing, as if she always dressed like someone from MTV.

'At least you'll be out,' Jess said.

'Yeah, sorry.' Steph was apologetic. 'But at least we're going to Michelle's party tomorrow. You could work out tonight what you're going to wear. I'll lend you my Wonderbra, if you want.'

Jess was touched. Steph's Wonderbra was her most treasured item of clothing. It would be wasted on Jess, though.

'I better rush,' Steph added. 'I've got to do my hair.'

They parted, Steph turning left outside the school gates, Jess turning right.

She walked to the bus stop to wait for the station bus, fiddling with her Discman earpieces to fix the left one in her ear. She and Steph used to walk home together, when they still both lived in Gartland Avenue, before Mum had become famous and made them move. So what if Dunmore was chocolate-box cute? Jess didn't know anyone there and she had to take the train out of Cork to get home. She never saw any teenagers around Briar Lane. There were loads of kids, who all went to this cutesy school in the centre of town and played on roller skates all day long at the weekends or raced around on pink Barbie bikes. But there wasn't one single person her own age. She couldn't even hang around after school and talk to Steph, because if she missed the train there wasn't another one for an hour and a half. Moving to horrible Dunmore had ruined her life.

One other person from school got the train to Dunmore but he was in the year above, the longed-for, exam-free fifth year, and he was clearly far too cool to talk to her. Jess had sat near him the first few days she was commuting because he was the only familiar piece of this new landscape, but he never acknowledged her presence, just kept his dark head down as he played on his stupid Game Boy. So now she ignored him back and would stomp past his seat to sit in another carriage, deliberately tossing her ponytail nonchalantly as she passed to show him that she didn't care. He wasn't even waiting at the bus stop today.

On the bus, she turned up the volume on her Discman, pulled her school scarf over her mouth and nose, and felt miserable. Steph thought it was cool to have a mum who was on TV. It wasn't.

20

Her mum wasn't waiting at Dunmore station when the train pulled in, and there was nobody there when Jess arrived home. Nothing new, she sighed, conveniently forgetting that only last week she'd had a row with her mother over being treated like a child. Her mother never stopped worrying about where Jess was all the time, and Jess was fed up telling her that other people in her class were allowed miles more freedom, as long as they phoned to say where they were going. But Mum was like Interpol, and wanted details of every moment of Jess's day.

'Jess, I like picking you up from the station,' Mum had said in the you-are-my-baby-after-all voice that drove Jess insane. 'I'd worry about you if I didn't come and get you. There are a lot of scary people out there.'

This was a familiar argument. As if Jess wasn't clever enough to recognise weirdos when she saw them. *Honestly.*

'I'm nearly sixteen,' Jess had insisted. 'I'm not a kid.'

Dad had stood up for her, which had caused Mum to glare at him with what Jess called her 'laser eyes'. There was a lot of laser-eye action going on these days. So Jess had won and could come home from school herself. But still, it would have been nice not to have had to walk home today . . .

Now Jess looked at her mother's diary, forgotten on the counter beside the fridge, and flipped to today. 'Hairdresser 12 noon.' Lucky Mum, Jess thought. Imagine being able to swan off on a school day and get your hair done.

There was no sign of Wilbur either. Wilbur was Jess's cat, a ten-year-old tabby with unusual grey markings and a huge fluffy tail that shot up into the air if he was upset. His cosy bed on the kitchen radiator was empty and there was no point calling him. He was probably asleep somewhere he shouldn't be: snuggled up amid the towels in the airing cupboard, his favourite and forbidden spot.

Jess positioned herself at the bleached pine table in the kitchen, spread her schoolbooks out in front of her and then switched on the portable telly. A repeat of *Sabrina the Teenage Witch* was on. Jess picked up a pen, opened the book where she'd made notes for the Milton essay and began to watch the TV.

Ten minutes later, weighed down with groceries, Abby arrived home. As soon as she'd shut the front door behind her, she unzipped her high boots gratefully. The problem with being short was that she always felt the need to wear heels, but they killed her.

'Jess!' she called, shrugging off her jacket. 'Are you home?' There was no answer and Abby's heart skipped a beat. Dunmore was hardly crime central but you never knew. Anything could have happened to her . . .

Abby rushed into the kitchen in her socks to find Jess studiously working at the kitchen table, the television switched off.

'Hi, love, you're hard at it,' she said, smiling in relief at her daughter's bent head. Once, she'd have hugged Jess instantly, but recently Jess ducked away from hugs as though she couldn't bear to be touched.

'She's a teenager, what do you expect?' Tom had said sharply when Abby told him the first time it had happened. 'I see it all the time in school.'

'I know,' Abby had replied shortly, angry at the implication that just because Tom was a teacher, he knew more about teenagers in general, and Jess in particular, than Jess's own mother did. Abby knew the teenage years were going to be tough, she just hadn't expected her darling Jess to change from best friend to worst enemy in a matter of months.

Now she restrained herself from reaching out to stroke Jess's hair.

'Yeah, we've lots of homework to do for the weekend,' Jess said gloomily without looking up. 'And I've got to revise.' The more Jess thought about the exams, the more she felt like taking it out on someone else.

'I dropped by the station just in case you were tired,' Abby said hesitantly, not wanting a row. 'I thought you might like a lift. But I missed you.'

Jess raised her head from her books and focused on her mother at last. 'New hairstyle,' she remarked flatly.

'Is it OK?' Abby ran an anxious hand through her hair.

'Yes,' relented Jess. 'It's great. Mum, I wish I could colour mine again.' Jess's first home-bleaching experiment with Steph had gone terribly wrong. It had cost ten times as much to have the straw-like tinge toned down.

'They'd kill you in school,' her mother pointed out happily, thrilled that Jess seemed to be in a good mood with her. After a rash of pink-toned hair, the principal had banned all hair dyeing except for the fifth and sixth years.

'Subtle streaks,' begged Jess. 'I'd go to the hairdresser this time. Nobody would know. Mr Davies only notices punk black and bright pink. A few blonde highlights would get past him. Lots of people have blonde hair.'

'We'll talk about it,' said Abby, who'd have promised anything to keep the peace.

'That's what you always say,' Jess pointed out.

'Yeah, I'm your horrible mother, I know.' Abby began shoving the shopping into cupboards and Jess quickly reached back and put the remote control onto the worktop behind her. Her mother was pretty good about TV watching. Lots of her friends' parents nagged like hell now they were in fourth year and studying for their Junior Cert. But Mum did disapprove of working while the TV was on, and the price for tomorrow night's party at Michelle's was to finish her homework by Saturday afternoon.

'I got fresh pasta and I can make you garlic mushroom tagliatelle for dinner,' Abby said, deep in the fridge.

Jess's face brightened. 'Great,' she said. She'd been a vegetarian for over two years now and was always trying to convince her mother to become one as well. Didn't people realise that animals had rights too?

'Your father and I have to go out, I'm afraid,' continued Abby. She didn't see her daughter's face fall. 'It's a work thing. Beech's tenth anniversary. Probably cheese and bad wine,' Abby laughed. Beech, the production company who

23

made her television show, were notorious for not spending money on luxuries. 'We have to go, but if I cook the mushrooms now –'

'I'm not hungry,' Jess said in a monotone.

Her mother emerged from the fridge anxiously. 'You must have *something*.'

'I'll phone for pizza if I'm hungry.'

'If you're lonely, I'm sure Jennifer wouldn't mind staying until we get home,' Abby ventured. Jennifer was the twenty-two-year-old college student who lived four houses down and who was keen to babysit to earn extra cash.

'I don't want Jennifer! I'm not a kid, Mum. I thought we agreed. If Sally Richardson thinks I'm old enough and reliable enough to babysit for her, why don't you think I'm old enough to be on my own?' Jess was furious.

It was Abby's turn to look unhappy. She didn't like Jess phoning for pizza delivery when she was alone in the house. You read such dreadful things in the papers. Just because they had an alarm and Jess had been warned not to open the door to strangers, didn't mean bad things couldn't happen. What if the pizza delivery person was a rapist or murderer? Abby's mind raced over the frightening possibilities. Jess had refused to be babysat once she'd hit fourteen, and agreeing to that extra independence had seemed such a huge step to Abby. Now, she'd started babysitting for Sally's little boys. No late nights or long hours, just the odd hour here or there, but it still struck Abby as scary that her baby was now the babysitter.

'You know I don't like you ordering stuff when we're not here.'

Jess sat sullenly and Abby knew she was in a no-win situation. 'Could Steph's dad bring her round tonight?' she asked, knowing even as she said it that Steph couldn't come, otherwise Jess would have suggested it herself. It had been easier to organise Jess's social life when the family lived a few houses away from her best friend.

'She's busy,' Jess snapped. 'Her grandmother's birthday

is tonight. I don't know anyone else around this dump of a town.'

Abby shut the fridge wearily. She didn't need reminding. The guilt was enough to give her sleepless nights.

She sighed. Although she adored their new home, the fact that it made Jess feel isolated was definitely threatening their relationship. Or maybe it was just the teenager thing.

Abby left money on the worktop for a pizza and went upstairs to get ready. It was half-past six, they were due out at seven and there was no sign of her husband. Not that Abby was surprised by this. After nearly seventeen years of marriage, she knew that Tom had all the sense of urgency of an inhabitant of a desert island. Which probably made them a good match, she knew. She was fiery and wound up like a spring, while Tom was possessed of endless, monastic calm.

'You shouldn't get so hyper about everything,' was his standard phrase whenever Abby got in a flap about being late. Naturally, his saying this just made Abby even more hyper and irritated into the bargain. Could he not realise how *annoying* he was?

It was a relief to retreat to their room to get ready. It was a pretty nice bedroom, and one of the first she'd redecorated when they'd moved in. Floor-to-ceiling wardrobes ('essential for hiding clutter', as Abby herself said) and a bed with storage underneath. Everything was rich cream and cool apple green, and there wasn't so much as an out-of-place magazine to ruin the aura of classic calmness. It was hell to keep it like that. As Abby professionally advocated the use of trios of decorative storage boxes to hide everyone else's clutter, she felt she had to use them herself, but she could never remember which held what. She always ended up opening the wrong one for her jewellery and finding make-up instead. And she could never lay hands on a pen. It might be heresy to think so, but she almost missed the jam jar full of wonky biros that used to sit on her dressing table in the old house, before she'd learned how to declutter.

Abby's cupboards were where it had all started, really. Not her wardrobe – recently featured in *Style* magazine – or her bathroom – a shrine to Zen-like bathing that had cost a fortune to install – but her kitchen cupboards, where a simple rotation system of putting new tins and jars to the back meant that nothing ever had to be thrown out because it was months past the sell-by date. The list on the cork board also helped. Any item taken from the fridge, larder or cupboard was listed in the handy notebook with the pen attached, so that when Abby did her once-a-month stocking-up shop, she knew exactly what was needed.

A naturally tidy person, she'd hit upon the idea of offering her tidy mind to others in an attempt to help people organise their lives. Jess had just turned ten and Abby found she had time on her hands.

Originally, she'd started sorting out wardrobes: helping women with scores of identical black clothes prioritise and bin anything they hadn't worn for years. It had been a cottage industry, really – a few mornings a week in which she'd given her clients the courage to throw out much loved but threadbare garments and sell on those barely worn. She wasn't a stylist, she told customers, just a de-junking merchant.

'You can buy new clothes yourself afterwards – I'm just helping you let go of the old stuff.'

The breakthrough had come after two years of this when a customer had sighed at the pristine state of Abby's kitchen cupboards and said she wished she was as organised.

Abby offered to write down her system.

'No, do it for me,' begged the woman.

Soon Abby was organising clutter-free systems for home offices and sorting out houses stuffed with possessions where nobody could find anything any more. She was ruthless with old cards, newspaper clippings and letters from old flames, but gentle with the person reluctantly throwing out all their treasures.

'You're not using it, it's using you,' was her mantra. 'If it's not useful or beautiful, dump it! You'll feel so much better when your life is decluttered.'

When she decluttered the office of a magazine journalist, who wrote about the empowering experience of throwing out bin bags full of detritus, fame came calling.

At nearly seven o'clock, Tom's ten-year-old Volvo creaked to a halt outside.

'Sorry,' he called as he slammed the front door. 'I got stuck with drama club.'

Upstairs, fully dressed and clock-watching, Abby sighed. Typical Tom. Overseeing the drama club wasn't even his job. What was the point of being the deputy headmaster if you had to do all the extra jobs instead of foisting them on other people? At home he never hesitated to ask Abby to do things for him, but at work, he metamorphosed into Mr No, Let-*Me*-Do-It.

After another five minutes of waiting for Tom to come up and change, Abby marched downstairs. She wasn't going to say anything but she was ready and it was time they were out of the door.

Tom and Jess were in the kitchen together, laughing at some shared joke.

'Dad, you old hippie,' Jess was saying fondly. She had her chair pushed back and her feet up on another, black-stockinged legs stretched out comfortably. 'Go off and listen to your old Jethro Tull records, right? You are never going to be cool.'

'I can watch MTV with the best of them,' Tom retorted mildly. He gave his daughter a pretend slap on the wrist. 'I was just saying I like that Chad Kruger song. Don't send me into the old people's home just yet.'

'Next week, then,' grinned Jess. 'Shooo. I've got chemistry homework and you've got some posh do to go to.'

Tom ruffled Jess's hair. Jess didn't move her head away. She smiled at her father.

Abby watched them silently, half pleased that they got on

so well, half jealous that she no longer shared that same easy relationship with either of them. It was as if Jess and Tom were a tight little family unit and she was out in the cold.

Selina Carson slid through the throng with all the practised ease of someone who could throw a party for three hundred people in her sleep. As publicity director of Beech Productions, Selina knew better than anyone how to stretch budgets and coax favours out of people. Without her help, the tenth anniversary party would be above a grubby pub with sausages and chips to eat and one free glass of limp champagne each. Thanks to her, it was being held in a divinely proportioned new gallery with lots of outrageous modern art on the walls, including a modern version of Ingres's voluptuous ladies of the harem, which was being ogled by many of the male guests when they thought nobody was looking.

The wine was good ('Think of the publicity, darling!' she'd said to the beleaguered wine importer she normally rang when organising parties) and clearly the dim sum were going down a treat. She just hoped that nobody got food poisoning, because the caterers were new and scarily cheap. Still, you had to economise somewhere.

'Abby, darling, how lovely to see you. And Tom.'

Selina was relieved to see Abby, as she was running out of celebrities to introduce to the big advertisers and the company's backers there tonight. Abby would be the perfect person to feed into the slightly bored groups and make them feel like movers and shakers. Even better, Selina could quietly explain this to Abby and Abby would know just what to do. She was a professional down to her fingertips, a direct result, Selina thought, of being that touch older when fame hit.

'Your hair's fabulous.'

'Thanks, Selina.' Abby grinned. She never entirely believed it when people complimented her, a trait she'd unknowingly passed on to her daughter. They were just being nice, she felt.

28

Didn't they know she was just a forty-something housewife who'd struck it lucky?

'And, Tom, you look marvellous. Now, Abby . . .' Selina grasped her star's shoulder, whispered in her ear briefly, and then steered her round to a small group of men in suits. 'Gentlemen, you must meet Abby Barton.'

A cigar-chomping advertising mogul, who was fed up with having to make small talk to lesser beings, grabbed Abby's hand and shook it firmly.

'Lovely to meet you. My wife adores your show,' he said.

'How nice of you to say so,' cried Abby. Selina treated this like work but it wasn't at all. People were really so sweet.

Duty done, Selina grabbed Tom's arm and led him to the back of the gallery where small pockets of people stood on the edge of the crowd. To the left stood two very young women who were talking quietly together but eyeing the group as though they longed to be part of it but were too shy to approach.

'Do me a huge favour and talk to those two, will you?' Selina begged. 'The red-haired one is the MD's niece. She's coming in to work as an assistant next week but she doesn't know anyone yet and he wants me to keep an eye on her.'

'They'll want real TV people.' Tom grinned lazily down at Selina. 'They'll be bored with a dull old teacher.'

'Stop fishing for compliments,' Selina scolded, thinking how lucky Abby Barton was. With his ruffled greying hair, angular face and eyes like deep-set pools of midnight black ink, Tom Barton definitely did not fit the mould of a dull old teacher. Just because he was utterly without vanity and clearly never bothered about what he wore, it didn't mean that he wasn't an attractive man. There was, she thought, something sexy about all that intense brain power, and his other-worldliness reminded Selina of a patrician Knight of the Round Table, always choosing the hard path because suffering was nobler. Tom made such a change from the thrusting young things who worked in television and who wore much better suits than Tom's shabby grey one, but who could only talk about their new cars or their high-tech mobile phones. Tom could blind you with brilliance over the fall of the Byzantine Empire – Selina knew; she had hung on every word of that particular conversation, and, strangely, she'd never been interested in history before. He'd definitely grown better looking with age too. Lucky Tom. No, Selina corrected herself, lucky Abby.

She'd bet he was a darling at home. Those gentlemanly types were always rushing to open doors and carry in the shopping for you. Selina was unattached and had to drag her own shopping in from the car, more's the pity.

For three-quarters of an hour, Tom and Abby didn't catch sight of each other. Abby charmed her way through several groups of people, aware that her husband would be perfectly happy on his own. Tom said that years of suffering through parent-teacher nights meant there was no social occasion on which he was stuck for words.

It was nearly nine when Abby escaped from the final group, all of whom were nicely merry and already planning where they'd go next. She herself had stopped after one small glass of wine – it was her turn to drive home. She peered round the room and finally spotted Tom in a corner with two attractive young women. Twenty-somethings, dolled up in the high-street version of the designer suede skirt and cashmere knit that Abby was wearing.

The three of them certainly seemed to be enjoying themselves and were laughing as though they'd found more to talk about than television ratings and tax breaks for production companies. The blonde was nearly as tall as Tom and, from Abby's viewpoint, she was definitely giving him the come-on, angling her skinny pelvis towards him, smiling, even flicking her hair coquettishly.

Abby felt the mildest tinge of irritation. Not that she was worried about Tom – heavens no. Tom was quite genuinely immune to flirting. If offered a choice between a discussion on the intellectual concept of school league tables or a torrid session in bed with a supermodel, he'd plump for the discussion. But that girl should know better. If she got any closer to Tom, she'd be on top of him.

'Hello,' Abby said breezily, and slipped an arm through her husband's. 'Ready to go yet?'

'Oh, you can't go now,' wailed the blonde, her pretty face assuming a child-like petulance. 'We're having such a nice time. Nobody ever explained things to me in school like Tom can. He's telling us all about girls in harems like in that picture over there.'

Abby wondered who she was. Somebody's model girl-friend? A would-be TV star?

'My wife says we have to go and we have to go,' Tom replied, giving the blonde a warm smile.

Abby's irritation level ratcheted up another notch. Tom made it sound as if she was a martinet dragging him away from fun. All she needed was a rolling pin to hit him over the head and she'd be perfectly in character.

'Don't let me tear you away, darling,' she said, with heavy emphasis on the 'darling'.

'Yes, stay a bit longer,' begged the blonde leggy section of his audience. 'Just for another drink?'

'Yes, do,' said the other girl.

Tom shot a glance at his wife. His weakness was a captive audience.

'Of course, stay,' Abby said easily, her professional mask firmly in place. 'I have lots of people to talk to, anyhow. I just thought we should get home to Jess before too long. *Our daughter*,' she explained politely to the blonde.

Bright-faced, she surged back into the party and found Selina.

'Anyone else you want me to talk to?' she asked.

'You look very flushed, Abby,' said Selina in surprise. 'Are you all right?'

The journey home was silent. Abby, glad to have the diversion of driving, stared grimly at the road and told herself that she was overreacting. Tom had simply been polite. Selina had asked him to talk to the girls, he'd explained.

All he'd been doing was enjoying a relaxing glass of wine after a long day, Abby thought. Nothing more. And it was probably nice to have people listen to him when he talked: he was always saying that the pupils in the boys' school where he worked were so focused on exams that they only wanted to hear things they could use for the Junior or Leaving Certs.

'I'm tired,' he said, through a Grand Canyon of a yawn, without bothering to put his hand over his mouth. 'Those duty parties are always exhausting.'

Abby's anger resurfaced and she had to bite her lip so she wouldn't point out that he hadn't seemed in the least bit exhausted earlier. 'Mmm,' was all she said.

'You all right?' he asked.

'I've got a headache.' And that was more or less true, she thought. Irritation always gave her a headache because she clenched her jaw so tightly.

'Oh.' With that, Tom leaned back against his headrest and closed his eyes. He could sleep anywhere.

Abby gripped the steering wheel tightly and drove on into the night, thinking of all the smart remarks she *should* have made to put the blonde twenty-something bimbo in her box. If only Tom still gave her that kind of attention.

CHAPTER THREE

The weekend whizzed past with the whole family resolutely doing their own things. Jess spent most of Saturday in her room revising, then Abby dropped her off at Steph's to get ready for their friend's party. Abby had given permission for Jess to stay the night at Steph's, and she couldn't very well argue when Steph's mother phoned on Sunday to say the family were going out to lunch and they'd love to have Jess along.

Tom was caught up in rehearsals for the school drama group's play all day Saturday and didn't get home until late. On Sunday, he told Abby he'd have to spend the entire day marking homework, and he positioned himself at the kitchen table, his papers spread in front of him and a solemn look on his face. Feeling strangely abandoned, Abby retired to the living room with the papers and ended up dozing off in front of the television, only waking up later that evening when Jess slammed the front door.

'How was the party?' Abby asked eagerly, coming into the hall to greet her.

Jess shot her mother an irritated expression. 'Boring,' she said. Well, it had been boring. There were guys there, ones Jess didn't know, but they hadn't shown the slightest interest in talking to her. Steph had been a huge hit, though, which made Jess feel even more humiliated. She and Steph had done everything together since they were five, and now Steph seemed to be effortlessly admitted to this wonderful grown-up club, while Jess was outside looking in, like a kid with her nose pressed up against the sweet-shop window. Still, there was no point telling her mother that. Abby wouldn't understand.

'I'm going to my room,' she said, and stomped upstairs, leaving her mother in the hallway feeling miserable.

Monday rolled round and Abby woke up when Tom placed her morning cup of tea beside her alarm clock. It was his sole domestic gesture, but even after seventeen years he still did it.

'It's a quarter past seven,' he said shortly.

Comatose with sleep after a restless night, Abby groaned and thought about lying there for just five more minutes. But no, that would be fatal. She hauled herself up and took a sip of scalding hot tea. She preferred her liquids boiling and Tom was one of the few people who made tea the precise way she liked it. He was a morning person, and by the time Abby made it downstairs, he'd have made his toast, perked coffee and read half the newspaper. Once Jess had made people laugh by saying the reason they had such a happy family life was because Mum was a lunchtime person, she was a night-time person and with Tom on the alert from six a.m., the three of them never met up. She didn't say that any more.

Abby took another sip of tea and reached for the television remote. She loved breakfast TV but knew it was as dangerous as having just an extra five minutes in bed. Each TV segment ended with a teaser for something far more interesting, and it was so easy to lie there and plan to get up when the bit about spring fashion was over. Or the bit about Cajun cooking or, oh look, holidays in Austria, that's interesting . . .

She hauled herself out of bed and shuffled into the bathroom to brush her teeth. A woolly-haired woman with puffy eyes, tired skin and a pale mouth that seemed to have disappeared into her face stared back at her. Without her make-up, her new copper streaks gave her the look of Bobo the clown.

She badly needed a stint at Sally's salon.

*   *   *

34

Both Jess and Tom looked surprised when Abby arrived downstairs twenty minutes later, fully made up and wearing one of her best jumpers, a caramel angora polo neck, over her jeans.

'I didn't think you had a job this morning,' was Tom's only comment as he buttered his final piece of toast.

Abby shot him a glare but he'd retreated behind his newspaper.

'Thought you said you were working from home today,' Jess added.

'I am,' said Abby, smiling at her daughter brightly. 'But that's no reason not to look good. It's too easy to sink into dressing sloppily around the house when you're working from home.'

She hauled out the blender and began rooting around in the freezer for fruit for a smoothie.

'It's stupid dressing up for home, a complete waste of time,' said Tom absently, his eyes still on his newspaper.

'What if someone calls at the house? I don't want to look a mess,' Abby replied.

'Why bother dressing up on the off chance that someone calls in?' Tom asked. 'You always look OK.'

Abby's hand stopped reaching for the raspberries, her fingers as frozen as the fruit within her grasp. OK? She always looked *OK*? Why did that sentence have the ring of death about it? Why did Tom's tone of voice mirror his professional one? *'Your son's work is fine, Mrs X, not thrilling but OK.'*

Abby didn't want to look OK. She wanted to look bloody drop-dead gorgeous like that blonde bimbo who had been drooling over Tom at the Beech party. She wrenched a bag of raspberries out and slammed them on the worktop. Had her husband always been this insensitive or had it happened recently?

When Tom and Jess were gone, Abby spent an hour tidying the house and putting on washing. Then she sat down at the big cream desk in her study and leafed through her appointments diary. She had two diaries now: the official one Katya, her assistant, kept, which was a large suede-bound book; and her own smaller, floral version, in which she scribbled notes to herself on things she had to do and remember, like what to take to tomorrow's meeting at Beech with the new executive producer, a hotshot who would also be heading the company's new commissions division.

Katya worked only two days a week when Abby wasn't busy and three when she was. As a young mother with two small children, this arrangement suited her. When Abby was filming, Katya could be on call to help her and deal with phone calls, fan letters and new commissions. When Abby wasn't filming, Katya could work from her own house and pick up Abby's calls.

Today, Katya was at home while Abby was supposed to be working flat out on ideas for a talk at the Ideal House exhibition in three months' time. But for once, Abby's lively mind failed her. Usually, she could go into anyone's home and see instantly what they needed to do to sort themselves out. She had an unerring eye for the root of the problem. Only today, she wasn't in the mood. So she tried what she always did when she felt uninspired: opened up one of her notepads and wrote 'ideas' on it with a pale blue pen.

The creamy expanse of fresh paper normally invited creativity. Not today. Some doodling later, she gave up and flicked through a couple of recent copies of *House Today*, hoping for inspiration. In one magazine, there was a photoshoot of a television presenter called Candy, who worked on an afternoon chat show. Abby had met her once in Dublin and, innocently expecting some sort of camaraderie because they were both TV stars, had been startled to encounter frosty hauteur.

'You're from that sweet little programme on tidying houses, aren't you?' Candy had said bitchily to Abby. 'I do so love to see newcomers getting on. But you have to be in this business for the long haul. I see so many people come, and then go when the ratings drop.' And she went on to tell Abby all about her own successful career, clearly implying that the star of *Declutter* would not last the course.

Abby was far too vulnerable and unsure of herself to be a successful bitch, but she wasn't a pushover.

'It's true, you never know when a show will start to lose viewers,' Abby said, with some innocent eyelash-batting of her own. 'The ratings have been so high – better than *EastEnders* for the final show in the first series – but we can't sit on our laurels. Bye, so nice to meet you. I've always thought you're such a trooper for all those years in the business.' And she walked off, leaving Candy spitting at both the mention of mega ratings and the implication that she was getting old. Although she certainly didn't look old in the magazine, Abby reflected grimly.

'Candy welcomes *House Today* into her lovely home,' cooed the editorial, under two large photos of a kitchen and a bedroom, both of which must have been overhauled by an army of Filipino cleaners if the sparkle on the granite kitchen worktops was anything to go by.

For once, Abby's gaze didn't concentrate on the house, searching out things she hated, like the swagged curtains so beloved of everyone and their granny. She stared instead at Candy, who looked spookily young with her long caramel limbs, wide blue eyes and skin plumped up and dewy as a just-picked peach.

'She's forty-eight if she's a day,' Abby said crossly. 'They've touched up those photos.'

She unearthed her magnifying glass from a drawer and began to examine the pictures: Candy wearing low-slung denims with a saucepan in one hand; Candy, barefoot and curled up in a giant armchair. Abby peered closely but couldn't detect a line anywhere. Bitch. She must have had some work done, an entire renovation job from the foundations up, at that. Abby slapped the magazine shut and glared at the wall behind her desk. On it hung the big 'Star

Certificate' that the *Declutter* team had given her as a joke at the end of the last series.

'Thanks, Abby,' it said. 'We love working with you. You're a star.' A big gold star surmounted the words. She'd been so touched.

Abby stared at it dully. 'You're a star.'

'I don't bloody well feel like one today,' she said crossly.

On Tuesday morning, Abby was the first up. She wanted a head start on looking good because today she was going to meet Beech's just-hired executive producer and new commissions head, a woman called Roxie O'Halloran, who apparently wanted 'to toss around some new ideas for the show'. Abby had a bad feeling about that. She might not have much experience of this kind of meeting, but an instinct told her that 'toss around new ideas' was business code for 'change everything utterly'. She'd rung Flora, the show's director and a good friend, for inside information on the newcomer but Flora knew nothing and had blithely said that Beech were hardly going to change such a successful format, were they?

'Stop obsessing, Abby. We've got a winning formula and you're a big part of it.'

At the back of the bathroom cupboard, Abby found her highly expensive and rarely used Eve Lom cleanser and moisturiser. If it was good enough for superstars, it was good enough for her, she decided. Serious cleansing was the answer to holding back the wrinkles.

'What's got you up so early?' mumbled Tom, shuffling into the bathroom ten minutes later. His legs were thin under his oversized T-shirt, thin and pale. He had a long-distance runner's legs, he used to joke. She wondered if he'd be hurt if she called his legs 'OK' instead of sexy, which was what she always used to say if he moaned about how skinny they were.

She went back to rubbing scented body lotion assiduously into her shoulders and back. Tom didn't ask if she wanted help with the hard-to-reach bits. Once, he would have been only too eager to do so, slowly rubbing the lotion into more interesting places. Abby tried to tell herself this didn't matter.

'I've a meeting with the production team this morning to run through ideas for the show,' she said curtly.

Abby loved meetings. Nothing made her feel more business-like than sitting round the long table in Beech's modern office on the river-front, everyone with bottles of mineral water and clean pads in front of them, tossing ideas around, the creative buzz almost palpable. It made her feel like Melanie Griffith in *Working Girl* – beautifully dressed but a bit of a fraud. Hopefully, today's meeting would be enjoyable too. Flora was right: she probably *was* obsessing about the new executive producer.

'When you're in the shop later,' Tom said, turning on the shower, 'don't forget I need new razor blades – you know the ones I like – and we're low on espresso.'

He stepped into the shower.

Ridiculously, Abby felt like crying. It wasn't because her husband seemed completely unaware of the system that meant they never ran out of staples like coffee or razor blades, and that, ironically, underpinned her career success and therefore their comfortable lifestyle. It was because she finally realised what she'd turned into: his mother. The only difference was that occasionally – very occasionally – they had sex. She didn't even bother to cast her mind back to when that had last been. Apart from the sex, she was a *doppelgänger* for the late Mrs Beryl Barton, replenisher of razor blades and laundry angel, who required only the odd vague compliment to keep her running on oiled wheels.

OK. You look OK.

Fiercely, Abby began to apply her 'photo opportunity' panstick with the skill that came from watching the *Declutter* make-up artist work on her face. She might not be a twenty-something leggy blonde, but she could still do more than *OK*.

At least the perky young receptionist in the Beech office was pleased to see her.

'Hello, Abby!' Livia smiled from behind the wall of her sleek glass and chrome desk. 'They're waiting for you in the meeting room. Will I phone someone to get you or do you want to go up yourself?'

'Don't get anyone, Livia,' chided Abby. 'I do hate fuss.'

'I know,' sighed Livia. Abby was so lovely to work with, a rarity in their business. Honestly, she never demanded anything, not like some of the stars who rushed in and out of Beech's offices, rudely requesting taxis *immediately* and treating Livia like someone who could only hear if she was screeched at.

If Abby needed a taxi, she'd politely ask Livia if it wasn't too much trouble to call one for her. And say thank you. Abby always remembered to ask about Livia's mother, who adored *Declutter* and had been delighted to get a copy of the last video with a Beech compliments slip signed by Abby herself.

Abby rushed along to the meeting room, oblivious to anything but the loud swishing of her long leather skirt. The outfit had seemed like a good idea at the time – a sort of classy but modern look, worn with pull-on Lycra boots and a chic white shirt with big cuffs – but she'd forgotten how noisy the skirt was. Each step sounded like a legion of Russell Crowe lookalikes marching noisily into battle for the glory of Rome.

There were four people in the meeting room: Stan, the executive producer; Flora, the director; Brian, the MD of Beech; and Roxie, the new executive producer. Abby got on marvellously with the first three, but she instantly felt intimidated by the look of the new woman. Roxie, in an elegant Gucci suit, was sleekly glamorous with a pointed, clever little face, and she didn't look as if *she* felt like a fraud in the business world.

Abby was also somewhat woolly on exactly what Roxie's role in Beech would be and what she'd have to do with *Declutter*.

She wasn't long finding out.

After ten minutes of clapping themselves on the back for how well the last series had done, Roxie took the floor. Briskly flicking the switch to close the blinds, shutting out the spectacular view of the river, she touched a button and the widescreen TV lit up.

'This is an American show pretty similar to *Declutter*,' Roxie said, as the credits rolled. 'I think you'll all soon see my point.'

What point? wondered Abby, feeling a shade underbriefed.

The show was certainly the same format as hers, with people yielding up their homes for dejunking by the *Get It Outta Here!* team of experts. Only the experts were a trio of uniformly young and beautiful women – former cheerleaders by the look of them – and they didn't pull any punches. Instead of gently detaching the client from beloved piles of mementoes or clothes that belonged to a long-dead parent, the girls forced the person to jettison their junk by behaving like high-school bullies surrounding the class geek at her locker.

'Why would anyone want to keep *this*?' demanded one of them, holding up a faded stuffed toy that the tear-stained client had kept since her now thirty-year-old son was an infant.

Because it means something to her, Abby's inner voice said.

'What do we say to this?' said the US beauty, dangling the toy.

'Get It Outta Here!' chorused her two colleagues.

'This show is huge,' commented Roxie, fast-forwarding through the advertisements. 'It's bitchy, yes, but the ratings are big because everyone loves to see someone else getting it in the chops. This is the way forward.'

Abby watched Roxie's little foxy face with something approaching dislike. She couldn't imagine Roxie ever clinging on to a pile of old letters or a single broken earring because they had been given to her by a long-gone lover.

You couldn't dejunk anyone's life without having some vague understanding of what made people tick. Memorabilia was precious, and laughing at a person's precious things was plain cruel. Therapy by scalpel.

Roxie wasn't finished yet. She hit 'play' and the show started again. Abby began to write down what she didn't like about it.

Too hard on the people involved.
Very unsympathetic.
Difficult to get new guests once they'd seen the trauma
    caused.

She glanced at Stan, Brian and Flora, assuming they would agree with her. But the three of them were watching the show intensely and Flora was twirling her long black plait obsessively, her face rapt.

'That's the way to bigger ratings,' said Roxie. 'Not that I'm criticising what you've done up to now, but we've got to ratchet it up another level. Seventy per cent of TV shows have just two seasons in them, apart from the really successful concept quiz shows. We want to be in the winning thirty per cent with a show that runs and runs. Our new series is make-or-break time for us. We need to freshen it up.'

Abby sat rigidly in her chair, waiting for someone else to speak, to say, 'No, that's not what *Declutter* is about.'

But they were all nodding thoughtfully.

Abby felt the blood rush to her head. She never lost her temper at work but she felt perilously close to doing so now. They couldn't possibly expect her to become such a TV bitch. She couldn't do it – she wouldn't do it.

'I can't behave like that, I can't,' she said fervently, standing up and staring at the three people round the table she thought were on her side. 'People trust me; they know I've got their best interests at heart and that I want to help them simplify their lives. That's what the show is about – helping people move on, not destroying them or laughing at them.'

This show was her baby; she'd made it what it was. She'd walk if they wanted to ruin it. 'I'd leave before I'd act like a bitch to people.'

'Abby, we understand that,' said Roxie silkily. 'Part of your charm is how gentle and kind you are.'

Abby grimaced. Roxie made kindness sound as much of an asset as herpes.

'There's no question of you leaving,' insisted Brian. 'You *are Declutter*, Abby.'

'You make people feel warm and fuzzy inside, that's great,' added Roxie, 'but we have to move on. We need a harder edge. Someone with a harder edge.'

As quickly as it had come, Abby's anger departed and she stared stricken at Roxie.

'My plan is to recruit one or two new presenters to work alongside you, Abby. You'll be the host, of course, but we need fresh faces. I'm thinking young, maybe a male/female team,' she said, addressing Stan and Flora now. 'Abby will be the host and do the main links as well as being the primary de-junker, but we'll have the added interest of two new people. We could do a whole house per show with more people. And,' she ended triumphantly, 'this is the biggest change, make the show an hour long. The advertisers would love us.'

She didn't need to tell all of this to Brian, realised Abby with a sinking feeling. He was sitting back in his chair, watching his team's reactions. He knew in advance what Roxie was talking about and he clearly agreed with her.

'Think about it,' Roxie continued. 'We'll be broadening the appeal of the show, we'll be able to get some chemistry going with the two new leads, *and* we'll have more airtime plus more advertising revenue. Think of three ad breaks instead of just one.'

Abby felt like Coyote watching the huge rock fall on his head while Road Runner whooped happily in the distance. She wouldn't do bitchy, so they would find people who did – she'd walked right into the trap.

'I don't know,' said Stan. 'Would the show work in an hour-long format? And with regards to new presenters, shouldn't we get some figures on the appetite for this type of change? I don't want to mess up the formula. If it ain't broke, don't fix it.'

Of course, Roxie had an answer for that. 'We could always make some pilot shows, just to see if the idea works,' she said smoothly.

'Youth is the way forward,' philosophised Brian, sitting back in his leather chair and giving them all an even better look at his belly, which was straining against the buttons of his Charvet shirt.

He hadn't been able to afford handmade French shirts before *Declutter* had been so successful and transformed Beech's bottom line, Abby thought furiously.

'Definitely. Youth makes television magic,' he added. 'No offence, Abby.'

'None taken,' she said from between gritted teeth.

'Presenters are getting younger and younger,' Roxie put in.

'Youth is where it's at,' Brian repeated pompously. Everyone nodded sagely.

Abby glared at them. Youth? What did they know about youth? Brian was a childless man in his early fifties with thinning hair, and the nearest he got to exercise was propping up the bar after he'd watched a soccer match. Stan was a skinny single guy on the wrong side of thirty-five with a forty-a-day Benson & Hedges habit, a fondness for junk food, and the unhealthy pallor of someone whose arteries were furring up at the speed of a Formula One racing car. Flora had recently celebrated her fortieth birthday with a big, booze-fuelled party and had dramatically insisted that everyone wore black to mourn for her lost youth.

Being young was just a memory for all of them, yet they were able to pontificate to her about age. Only Roxie, who was twenty-five, max, and, with the hubris of youth, probably thought that old age happened to other people, could claim to understand youth culture.

After some discussion about casting new talent, during which Abby sat with a fixed smile on her face, the meeting ended.

'Great to meet you,' Roxie said to Abby. 'I love your work.'

'Thanks,' Abby said mechanically. She was too shattered to say anything else. She made her way to the ladies' room across the hall, and Flora followed her.

'I know it's tough,' said Flora, when she emerged from the cubicle to wash her hands, 'but Roxie has a point, Abby. Youth is in.'

'I know that,' said Abby, somehow managing to hide how desperately hurt she was.

'We'd all hate you to be upset. You're our friend, Abby – that goes beyond TV.'

'Course I'm not upset.' Abby's hands shook as she took out her make-up pouch. She daren't try to use her lipliner. Her face, pale and haggard with shock, stared back at her. Her new chestnut streaks looked ridiculously harsh against her pale face. Her previous all tawny tint had suited her colouring better.

Flora was watching her. Somehow, Abby recovered.

'This is a job, after all, and job descriptions change. I'm a professional, Flora. You should know that,' she said.

'Sorry.' Flora gave Abby's shoulder an affectionate squeeze. 'I forgot. They don't call you the most down-to-earth presenter on the box for nothing.'

Abby did her best to look down-to-earth, even though she felt like lying down on the tiled floor of the ladies, drumming her heels and screaming about the unfairness of everything.

'You know, I wasn't sure I liked Roxie at first, to be honest with you,' Flora was saying, redoing her plait, 'but she has some great ideas and she's all right behind that tough exterior.'

'Yeah, for sure.' Abby zipped up her handbag. 'Must fly, Flora. I'll talk to you soon, OK?'

She managed to leave the building without meeting Brian or Roxie.

'Oh, Abby,' sang Livia as Abby rushed past reception, 'Mr Redmond was looking for you.'

'Can't stop. Sorry, Livia,' said Abby politely. She could not face Brian Redmond now. 'Bye.'

She rushed to the car park, leather skirt creaking wildly. Only when she was in her car and past the security barrier did she allow herself to break into floods of tears.

CHAPTER FOUR

That same afternoon, in the doctor's surgery in the centre of Dunmore, Lizzie Shanahan searched the correspondence pile for a letter to the specialist. Mrs Pender stood in front of the desk, looking only slightly less shocked than she had the previous day when she and Mr Pender had emerged from the surgery with the gently delivered but nonetheless startling news that Mr Pender needed to see a specialist for further discussion on the results of his blood test for prostate cancer.

Lizzie found the letter and the attached Post-it note on which she'd written directions to the specialist's office.

She smiled warmly at Mrs Pender, doing her best to radiate both calmness and complete ignorance of whatever was in the letter to the specialist. Lizzie knew exactly what it said because she'd typed it and because the doctor's receptionist knew almost as many secrets as the doctor. But the patients were better off not really being aware of that.

This patient was too worried to go along with the sanctity-of-the-surgery façade. 'I haven't slept a wink since I heard,' Mrs Pender said weakly. 'Do you think it's bad, since they got him an appointment so quickly?'

Lizzie, who'd been told to plead emergency on the phone to the specialist's office because Mr Pender's blood test results signalled prostate cancer, felt a huge surge of pity for the woman but managed to look innocently surprised at the question.

'They may have had a cancellation, Mrs Pender,' she said

kindly, weighing up the merits of lying and deciding that the poor woman would possibly hear enough bad news from the specialist tomorrow without lying awake all night from anxiety.

Sleeplessness was a problem Lizzie knew all about. And she was aware that women worried five times more about their husbands' health than they did about their own. *Not* a problem Lizzie had any more.

'Yes, a cancellation, that could be it.' Mrs Pender brightened at the news and went off with her letter.

Lizzie scanned the reception room. It was a quarter to five. There were two people waiting. One was an elderly gentleman who'd looked uncomfortable on being told that Dr Morgan, the lady doctor, was on. The other patient was a weary-looking young woman with a small, red-faced baby on her denim lap. The baby cried non-stop, the tormented tears of teething that could reach ear-shattering decibel levels. The woman shot apologetic looks at Lizzie as the baby launched into another miserable aria. Lizzie had paid her own dues at the coalface of teething babies and gave the young mother an understanding grin in return. Lizzie had a very infectious grin. It was something to do with the combination of her wide, smiling mouth, rosy cheeks that shone through all cosmetics, and lively chocolate-brown eyes that sparkled beneath her shaggy blonde-streaked fringe.

It was ten to five when Dr Morgan opened the surgery door and called in the elderly man. Lizzie was due to leave at five and Clare Morgan, who was the most considerate employer Lizzie had ever encountered, leaned round her office door and said: 'Lock the door when you go, Lizzie. I'll let the patients out when we're finished.'

Lizzie smiled her thanks and began to tidy up, leaving a list of the evening's patients for Dr Jones, who'd be in at seven for two hours. There was no receptionist on in the evenings, and although Lizzie could have done with both the money and the time out of the house, she'd never suggested working at night too. Dr Morgan, who'd been kindness itself since the divorce, would have been shocked at the notion of Lizzie spending all her time working. Dr Morgan, divorced and the mother of adult children herself, was a firm believer that freshly single women had to make new, exciting lives for themselves. Lizzie outwardly agreed with all of this and inwardly wondered whether Clare Morgan planned her week's television viewing on a Saturday too, circling the programmes she wanted to watch in the TV guide, putting asterisks beside interesting documentaries. Probably not.

Lizzie locked the surgery door and, twenty minutes later, she was walking round the supermarket on Dunmore's Cork Road, a basket over her arm as she debated what to buy for dinner. That was one of the nice things about living alone, she thought to cheer herself up. You could eat whatever you wanted. Myles had hated tuna in tins, while Lizzie could have eaten it every night. He loved proper dinners too, not speedy suppers like beans on toast. Now, she could eat beans and tuna together if she felt like it. She rounded the frozen pizza corner and went bang into Josephine who lived four doors up. Josephine, a gossiper of professional standard, was wielding a loaded trolley that proclaimed to the world that she had a husband and four big sons to feed. Giant family packs of meat and many loaves of bread were packed precariously on top of each other. If her trolley could speak, it would have loudly said, 'I have a life.'

'Oh, hello, Lizzie,' she greeted. 'How nice to see you.'

Lizzie made a sudden decision. She couldn't face Josephine's gentle probing. Her single-person basket clearly said that she had no life and the carafe of red wine that had been on special offer would proclaim that she coped with this lack of a life by knocking back litre bottles of booze.

'Lovely to see you!' she said gaily, and kept walking. 'Sorry, but I'm rushing. I have someone dropping in and I'm late!' Lizzie smiled broadly to imply a busy, action-packed existence that left no time for concerned 'how *are* you doing?' conversations amid the frozen food.

From the corner of her eye, Lizzie could see Josephine's

garrulous husband amble over to the trolley. Thank God she'd made her escape. She couldn't face both of them. She rushed round another corner and hurried down the tea and coffee aisle, knowing exactly what Josephine would be saying: 'Poor Lizzie, isn't she wonderful, though?'

Lizzie knew that was what people said about her: 'Isn't she wonderful?', as if she was some simple soul who'd finally learned to tie her shoelaces. What they meant was 'Isn't it great that she isn't riddled with bitterness and with a long-term Prozac habit since Myles left her?' She had not been people-watching all her life for nothing. Her natural intuition told her what they were really thinking and she hated it. She knew that her friends and acquaintances had half expected her to slide into a decline when she and Myles had split up five years previously. But she had proved them wrong. She hadn't buried her head in the sand and told people they were 'taking time apart', like one neighbour who'd kept blindly insisting that her dentist husband was merely working a long distance away when everyone and their lawyer knew he'd set up home with a curvaceous female colleague.

Prevaricating wasn't Lizzie's style. When Myles had moved out, she'd told people the truth. Well, most of the truth. 'We're getting a divorce. It's over, I'm afraid,' she'd said brightly. What she hadn't said was how shocked and devastated she felt, how humiliated, at the abrupt end of their marriage.

Tellingly, nobody seemed surprised. Not her friends, not her family. *They* all seemed to have half expected it. Only Lizzie, who'd prided herself on being practical, hadn't.

'I know things haven't been right for years,' her elder sister, Gwen, said comfortingly. 'It's for the best.'

Lizzie, who was rarely speechless, was reduced to utter silence. Gwen had always been an old-fashioned advocate of marriage, and thought that women who didn't get married had a screw loose and were to be pitied. What desperate lack of harmony had been so apparent in Myles and

Lizzie's marriage that even Gwen thought they were better off apart?

Unfortunately, in the months after Myles moved out, Lizzie had a lot of time to think about this.

It was their younger child, Debra, turning eighteen and moving to Dublin that had been the catalyst. Until then, all appeared well in the Shanahan household. They had a nice home in a small housing estate on one of the older, tree-lined roads in Dunmore: a red-brick semi with four bedrooms, a dining room that, admittedly, was used less and less, and a small garden in which Lizzie spent an increasing amount of time. She had her job, her friends, her garden, and Myles had his work in the planning department in the council and his pals in the squash club.

If life wasn't exactly exciting, then Lizzie consoled herself that it would be once the children had both left home.

She and Myles were, or so she was led to believe, in the enviable position of having had their children early. Very early, she used to laugh, thinking of herself in maternity tights at the wedding. But that had its advantages. With twenty-one-year-old Joe in art college in London, and Debra starting nursing in Dublin, it was just Lizzie and Myles again. She could barely remember what life felt like without the kids.

But there was going to be no empty-nest syndrome in her house. No way, José. Not for her the resigned gaze at the empty places round the table. She adored the children, *adored* them, but they wouldn't thank her for turning into a resentful old woman just because they'd moved on and grown up. Lizzie and Myles Shanahan were going to live life to the full.

In this new, zestful frame of mind, she'd wondered if they could install a conservatory, maybe, or go on the sort of dream holiday they'd always promised themselves but had never been able to afford because there were always things to be bought for the children. A safari, she thought, wistfully imagining dawn Jeep rides into the grassland like the ones on the holiday programmes.

51

Lizzie looked after herself too. No sliding into slatternly ways for her. When tendrils of grey began to sneak into her shaggy light brown curls, she got streaks put in at the hairdresser's. Myles seemed pleased with all of this.

He hadn't let himself grow old before his time either, Lizzie thought approvingly. They were both forty-four. Some people were only just getting married or dealing with young kids at that age, and they'd done it all!

She got brochures for the conservatory and one day, just for the fun of it, picked up some safari ones too.

That evening, Myles sat in his armchair in front of the fire and looked mutely at the brochures Lizzie had left with such excitement on the coffee table. Then, in a quiet voice, he told her that he wanted a divorce, that he was so sorry but hadn't she realised? Didn't she agree that it was the right thing to do?

Lizzie, who'd already checked her husband's diary to see if he'd be able to take holidays during the best season for a safari, stood frozen beside the mantelpiece, one hand clutched around the china seal Joe had given her after a childhood trip to the zoo.

'I thought you knew; I thought you agreed with me,' pleaded Myles. 'You were getting on with your life and I was getting on with mine. We were only together for the kids and now they're gone, well . . .' His voice trailed off.

With terrible clarity, Lizzie saw that he meant what he said.

'We married too young, Lizzie,' he added sadly. 'We didn't have time to think about the future or whether we were really suited. If you hadn't been pregnant with Joe, we'd have never done it, would we?'

Lizzie gazed back at him. The shock of this made her remember another: the shock of discovering she was pregnant, standing in the loo of the restaurant where she was working and thinking that the test had to be wrong, it had to be. She'd only ever slept with Myles and she knew girls who'd slept with scores of men, so why did she have to be the

52

one to get caught? The slender streak of independence that ran through her shrivelled at the prospect of coping with this momentous happening on her own. Her parents were good and kind people, but they were locked in the morality of the past. Their beloved daughter becoming pregnant – pregnant and single. This would shake their world.

Lizzie would never forget the relief when Myles had said, with a lump in his throat, that they'd get married and he could support her and the baby on his salary from the council.

Now Myles was earnest again as if he could convince her by the force of his argument.

'Lizzie, I'm not saying I regret any of it but we *had* to get married. It seemed like the only option at the time. We did it and we've stuck together but we both knew it wasn't what we'd wanted. Didn't you always think there should have been more?'

She had never thought there should have been more. True, there were no violins playing in her head when Myles kissed her, but had there been violins in her parents' heads during their marriage? Marriage wasn't about that, surely? Did her happily bickering sister and brother-in-law share some secret hand-holding when they were out of the public gaze? No way. Violins were for soppy movies, not real life.

'We're still young enough to enjoy life,' Myles said, desperately trying to make her understand. 'We can make up for lost time.'

'What's her name?' demanded Lizzie, suddenly finding her voice. 'What's her name?'

'Oh, Lizzie . . .' The look Myles gave her was full of pity. 'There's no one else. Dunmore is too small to hide a secret like that. I just want out before I'm too old, before I lose the confidence to do it.'

And that was the most painful thing of all. There was no one else. No other woman had made Myles decide to leave his wife. The only woman involved was Lizzie herself. The spur was the nature of their marriage.

53

For months after he'd gone, she asked herself how she, who thought she was in touch with the world, missed what was plainly obvious to everyone else – that there was a magic ingredient to marriage and that hers lacked it?

She replayed Myles's words over and over again: 'Is that what you want, Lizzie? Us here, stuck together by necessity and children, unable to live full lives together but never having had the courage to live apart?'

Debra had been devastated and had arrived home from nursing college shaking and crying. 'How could you do this to us?' she'd shrieked at her mother. 'How could you?'

And Lizzie, who longed for Myles to stay but who wouldn't hold him against his will no matter what, had calmly told her daughter that people grew apart and wasn't it better to admit to it instead of living a lie?

'Life goes on,' she said with a serenity she didn't feel. 'This is still your home, but your father won't be living here any more. His home will be like another home for you.' Lizzie did not know how she managed to get that measured, 'everything will be fine' tone into her voice but she did it. Debra's sobs lessened, the way they had when she was a child and had a hurt only Lizzie could cure. Did mothers ever stop mothering, Lizzie wondered as she stroked Debra's head.

Joe had reacted differently. Then twenty-one and living happily in London, he'd come home for a few days, and when Lizzie had confided her genuine shock and bewilderment at what had happened, Joe was momentarily lost for words for possibly the first time in his life.

'Oh, Mum,' he said sorrowfully, 'even when I was younger, I knew you and Dad were staying together for me and Debs. I thought you'd both made a choice to do that.'

Lizzie stared at him. He looked so like his father: a wiry frame, the shock of receding dark hair that defied all brushing, the same gentle brown eyes. Even he had seen it.

She never told anyone what Joe had said to her. From then on, she was stoic about the break-up.

'People change and move on,' she said when anyone commiserated with her.

'Myles and I had our good times but you know we married too young and for all the wrong reasons,' she told her sister, Gwen. 'What did we know of love at our age? There should be a law against people getting married before they're thirty!'

'We should have split up years ago,' she said to Dr Morgan. She hid her misery and bewilderment from everybody.

Myles made it easier by moving out of Dunmore into the city and by virtue of the fact that there wasn't anybody else in his life – though, at first, nobody quite believed that.

'There *must* be another woman,' they said suspiciously, and all the single women in the squash club got fed up with being asked about Myles Shanahan.

'He wasn't the chatting-up sort of man,' they insisted time and time again. 'He was sweet and sort of lonely.'

But as time passed, and it became clear that he was genuinely happy but single, the chattering in Dunmore ceased.

Myles and Lizzie became the watchword for the modern world: they'd made brave choices and lived with them. They'd had the courage to swap two sets of slippers in front of the fire for the single life.

Myles had taken up sailing and, during a month's leave, had become one of a crew taking part in a big yachting race. Who'd have thought it? Quiet Myles braving the Atlantic and coming home full of energy, with a windburned face and his middle-age spread gone, looking ten years younger.

There was no problem talking about this to Lizzie either. She knew all about it. She, Myles and the kids still had their Christmas dinner together in Dunmore. They went to the hotel in the square for it and, the first year, people had stared at the family smiling over the turkey and wearing paper hats as if nothing had happened. Civilised was the word for it, and while everybody in Dunmore admired them, nobody had a clue how they'd managed it.

*   *   *

The house was silent as the grave as she opened the door. Look on the positive side, Lizzie told herself firmly. A quiet house meant she hadn't disturbed a gang of drugged-up-to-the-eyeballs burglars ransacking the place in vain for money.

The answering machine light was winking merrily and Lizzie felt her heart lift. Maybe it was Debra. She hadn't phoned for a couple of days but she never left it longer than a week before getting in touch.

Without taking off her coat, Lizzie hit the button and smiled as her daughter's light voice filled the hall.

'Hi, Mum. Oh God, you won't believe it, you just won't. Barry's sister is being *impossible*. She doesn't like the pattern I've chosen for the bridesmaid's dress. A-line suits everyone – I don't know what the problem is. She's just being difficult. She says she'll buy her own dress but we can't have that. It won't be what I want. I think I'm going to hit her. Can I come over and talk to you?'

Dear Debra.

It was wildly ironic that Debra, who wasn't pregnant and was of the generation who could have happily had a fleet of children without ever marrying the father or even introducing him to the rest of the family, was set on marrying her childhood sweetheart. The very words 'childhood sweetheart' made Lizzie shudder.

Both she and Myles had, separately, gently advised Debra that perhaps she should live with Barry for a couple of years first. Just because they'd been together since school and gone on holidays together for five years didn't mean that they were going to make it as a couple.

But Debra wouldn't hear of it. 'Marriage is fashionable now,' she told her mother, as if she was speaking to someone very elderly and very stupid. 'Commitment is important. I don't think older people understand that. What with terrorism and stuff in the world today, it's younger people who know what matters. Barry and I are committed to each other and this is the proof. We're trying to see if we can have doves at the wedding too because they symbolise peace. And just because you're jaundiced about the whole marriage thing, Mum,' she'd added tartly, 'that's no reason to put me off it.'

Lizzie, hurt at the idea that she was jaundiced about anything or that she'd harm a hair of Debra's head because of her own problems, withdrew her gentle objections and began to help plan the wedding.

'Commitment, commitment,' said Myles bitterly on the phone to Lizzie later. 'I've a good mind to remind her that she didn't have the commitment to stick with nursing.' Debra now worked in the offices of a double-glazing firm and shared a house with friends.

'You can't say that,' said Lizzie. 'She'd be upset.'

'I've a good mind to,' Myles went on, but he didn't, as they both knew he wouldn't. Debra was and always had been her daddy's girl.

Lizzie dialled her daughter's mobile.

'Hi, love, you can come over. I'm home.'

'I'm already on my way, actually,' Debra answered. 'I'll be just five minutes.'

'Great. I'll make tea.'

Lizzie hurried off to whisk cushions into place and to check if the house still looked like the welcoming home Debra had grown up in. She put on lipstick to brighten herself up too and was ready with tea and home-made shortbread biscuits (Debra's favourite and always ready for whenever she dropped in) when her daughter's Mini stopped in the drive. The car, an eye-catching dark red, was her pride and joy, and Lizzie never caught sight of it without feeling glad that she and Myles had been able to contribute to its purchase. Lizzie's part of the car had been money she'd saved to fix the leak in the roof in the kitchen, but there was plenty of time to deal with that. Debra's happiness was more important than a bit of damp.

Debra let herself into the house with her own key and went immediately to the kitchen.

'I shouldn't have any shortbread,' she said by way of

57

greeting. She put two sugars into her tea, added lots of milk, and took a biscuit.

'How are you, darling?' said Lizzie, not wanting to sound too like a concerned mother. Debra hated that.

'Fine,' said Debra through a mouthful of crumbs. 'Whatever am I going to do about Sandra? Fine bridesmaid she's turning out to be. You'd think she'd be happy to have a dress bought for her. Stupid girl's the size of an elephant.'

'Not everyone's skinny like you.' Lizzie felt sorry for Sandra, a sweet-natured girl who didn't share her brother's good looks or slim physique.

'That's not my fault,' Debra said with the disdain of one who'd never been less than pleased with her reflection in the mirror. She finished her biscuit and took another. 'I just don't want her to ruin my day because of this. We've only got a few months to go – you'd think she'd say something before this, wouldn't you? But that's typical of Sandra. Troublemaker.'

Debra's temper made her face flush, and Lizzie did what she'd always done when her children were upset: she reached out and comforted her.

'It'll be fine, love. Barry will talk to Sandra. He'll explain that this is your special day, that everything's got to be perfect and that you want to pick the dresses.'

A brief flash of memory reminded Lizzie of her own hastily arranged wedding where the bride wore a dress a size too large in order to hide her burgeoning belly and the bride and groom's parents wore stunned smiles. Times were different then, Lizzie reminded herself. Nobody had the money for big days out with three bridesmaids, a five-tier cake and an Abba tribute band at the reception. Mind you, nobody had the money for that now either. But Debra's heart was set on a big day in mid-July and neither Lizzie nor her ex-husband had the heart to say anything.

Just then, an idea hit her.

'Remember those lovely bridesmaid's dresses in the wedding shop off Patrick Street? We could go and have a look at them again,' she coaxed.

'But I thought we couldn't afford to buy the ones I liked.' Debra was suspicious, thinking of the compromise that had been reached when the cost of the reception had begun to spiral beyond the agreed sum. Something had to give and Debra felt that it wasn't any great risk to herself to have the bridesmaids wearing outfits from the dressmaker. Who would be looking at them? She was the star of the day. Her own expensive gown was worth the money but spending too much on bridesmaids was wilful waste. 'The dressmaker's doing a good job, really. It's just Sandra who's got a problem.'

'Well, maybe we could let Sandra get a dress from the wedding shop. All three bridesmaids are going to be wearing different colours anyhow –' began Lizzie.

'I don't know,' said Debra, struck again by the unfairness of her future sister-in-law's behaviour. 'I hate weddings, honestly. It's all a total pain. I've a good mind to tell Barry it's off.'

Lizzie sighed. Debra was so highly strung that she sometimes failed to see others' points of view. Unlike her mother, who saw everyone's point of view. They may have looked alike – the same big eyes and round, open faces – but in character they were very different. Lizzie used to wish that Debra wasn't so uncompromising but, in retrospect, she'd changed her mind. Being gentle and yielding got you nowhere in life.

Wednesday was manic in the surgery. First in the door on the dot of nine were Mrs Donaldson, a large, prune-faced pillar of the community, and her daughter, Anita, a shy, heavily pregnant woman in her late twenties, who would have been enjoying a perfectly normal pregnancy had it not been for her interfering mother. Mrs Donaldson, with five pregnancies behind her and a superiority complex, insisted on always seeing Dr Morgan because she thought male doctors knew nothing about female plumbing, but obviously felt that she herself was the expert on all things gynaecological.

She herself was 'delicate', she'd told a disbelieving Lizzie early on in Anita's pregnancy. 'My side of the family were all small-boned and pregnancy was such a strain,' sighed Mrs Donaldson, folding big strong arms over a considerable bosom emphasised by a silky blouse with an inappropriate pussy-cat bow. 'Dr Morgan won't see that poor Anita's the same. Poor lamb needs more ante-natal care and more visits. I can see it so why can't her stupid obstetrician?'

Through all of this, Anita smiled sweetly at everyone and followed her mother meekly into the surgery for each unnecessary visit.

Clare Morgan, normally the soul of discretion regarding her patients, confessed that she loathed the sight of Mrs Donaldson.

'Anita's perfectly fine and I'm convinced her mother's constant agitating is creating more stress for her than the pregnancy,' she said.

Today Mrs Donaldson was on high alert because next door's cat had been seen lurking in the vicinity of Anita's clothesline.

'Toxoplasmosis,' said Mrs Donaldson darkly to Lizzie. 'All cats should be put down.'

Lizzie's eyes instantly swivelled to the windowsill, where Clare Morgan's ginger cat, Tiger, liked to sit and mew miserably to be let in, even though he knew he wasn't allowed into the surgery. Luckily, there was no rotund marmalade shape there. Mrs Donaldson was quite capable of running out and hitting him with her handbag.

'The doctor is very busy this morning but I'm sure she'll fit you in,' Lizzie said, knowing that there was no point in saying anything else. Mrs Donaldson did not grasp the concept of people saying no to her.

By half-past twelve, after a hectic morning where the surgery had been packed with sneezing and wheezing patients, including one white-faced man who'd had to keep rushing into the loo to be sick, Lizzie felt as if she had only one unjangled nerve left. Every appointment had run late and there were always a few impatient patients who felt this was Lizzie's fault for overbooking and glared at her furiously as they waited. But somehow, the throng had cleared and the last person had just gone in to see the doctor. Lizzie got a glass of cranberry juice from the tiny fridge in the kitchenette and dosed it liberally with echinacea. She didn't know if it was the immunity-boosting medicine or the fact that she was daily exposed to every bug going, but she rarely got sick.

Luxuriating in the silence, she leaned back in her chair and stretched her aching back.

'Clang' went the bell over the surgery door. Lizzie straightened up to attention.

'Hi, Sally,' she said cheerfully, and relaxed again. Sally Richardson was a friend as well as a patient. She, Steve and their two boys had lived in the road behind Lizzie's for the past four years and Lizzie had come to know them both from the surgery and from bumping into each other in the tiny corner shop where they bought newspapers and emergency cartons of milk. She'd been to several of their parties, although she'd had to miss Steve's now legendary birthday party six months ago. And when Lizzie's funds ran to it, she'd enjoyed a facial in Sally's gorgeous beauty salon, The Beauty Spot.

'Hello, Lizzie,' said Sally, wearily pulling one reluctant small boy after her by the sleeve of his anorak. His younger brother was clinging miserably to his mother's neck and looking balefully at Lizzie. 'Tonsillitis again. They were both a little off form this morning, but now Daniel's started vomiting.'

From his vantage point in Sally's arms, Daniel stuck out his tongue to prove how sick he was, obviously used to doing it so people could look at his tonsils.

'Poor Daniel,' soothed Lizzie. 'Have you got a sore throat?'

He nodded tearfully, big brown eyes looking like a doleful puppy's.

'And are you sick too, Jack?' Lizzie asked his brother.

'Yes,' said Jack croakily, looking just as miserable.

They were both big children, too big for the petite Sally to carry any more, Lizzie thought. She looked exhausted.

From behind the reception desk, Lizzie produced the box of kids' toys she'd tidied up earlier. Jack wasn't too ill to fall happily onto the colourful jungle train, and was soon banging each animal, making it wail, roar or chatter. Daniel, however, clung to his mother and refused to be put down.

'The wait won't be long, Sally,' Lizzie reassured her.

'I feel terrible. I should have brought them first thing.' Sally's face was creased with guilt. 'I thought I'd stay home from work and see how they got on, and then Daniel began to be sick and every time I changed him, he'd be sick again, so it's taken us an hour and a half to leave the house. And Steve's in bits because work is a nightmare since his boss left last month, and he's got to do everything.' She looked so wretched, with her normally glossy dark hair tied back into a limp knot, and her grey fleece stained with dried sick on one shoulder. Lizzie decided emergency measures were called for.

'You need a cup of tea,' she said, hurrying to boil the kettle.

Then she produced the ultimate bribe of chocolate buttons, and Daniel grudgingly got onto the floor with Jack to play jungle train.

'They're soft, so they won't hurt your throats,' she said, dividing the chocolate between the two boys. Then she gave Sally a big mug of tea and an oatmeal biscuit.

'It's my medicine.' She smiled, sitting down beside Sally.

'You're so kind, Lizzie. I suspect that's why people tell you things,' Sally said, gratefully drinking the tea.

'They tell you things too,' Lizzie pointed out. 'The salon's like a confessional, with people revealing all sorts of stuff to you as they lie back being pampered.'

A faint grin touched Sally's wan cheeks. 'I think I'm too distracted this week to have anyone want to tell me their secrets,' she said. 'I'm worried about the boys and their tonsils, and I'm worried about poor Steve. He's working himself into the ground. I ought to make an appointment for myself too,' she added. 'I've been feeling a bit run down lately. Nothing out of the ordinary,' she went on, 'just I'm a bit weary. Mind you, isn't everyone?'

'It's good to hear you worrying a bit about yourself,' Lizzie soothed, checking the appointment book. 'You do too much, Sally. Running the salon, taking care of the boys and Steve . . .'

Sally laughed. 'I don't do too much,' she said. 'I don't do half enough. You want to see the pile of ironing . . .'

'You never stop,' Lizzie said firmly.

'Don't bother getting me an appointment yet, Lizzie,' Sally replied. 'I'll phone you for one when I've got time. Ruby's away so the salon is madly busy, and Delia, Steve's mother, is off on holiday soon, so she won't be able to look after the boys, so I'll be running round like a headless chicken for a few weeks. I'll come and see the doctor after that.'

'You have to look after your health,' Lizzie said, waggling a finger in mock disapproval.

'I promise I'll phone you when everything calms down,' Sally said.

The door to the doctor's room opened and the last patient emerged with Dr Morgan close behind.

Lizzie got up to see the patient out, and Clare Morgan led an eager Jack into her office.

'Thanks, Lizzie, you're a star,' whispered Sally as she got up to follow with Daniel.

On Thursday, Lizzie had a day off and Gwen arrived to take her shopping. They were not looking for clothes for Lizzie, who had already bought her wedding outfit – a lemon suit, which was the subject of much worry. She went to the spare-room wardrobe and looked at it every few weeks, hoping that the yellow colour wasn't quite as sharp and hard as she remembered. It had looked fine in the shop during the heady days of the previous year's August sales, when the thought of getting a bargain had outweighed all other considerations. Now, she wasn't so sure.

'Could I sell it in the small ads?' she asked Gwen idly. '"Mother-of-the-bride outfit. Never worn. Makes MOTB look like before picture in makeover article."'

'You wouldn't get the proper value of it,' advised Gwen. 'Sure, just plaster more make-up on for the wedding and you'll be fine.' Today's trip was to buy clothes for Gwen and Shay's cruise. Ten days on the *Star of the Mediterranean* in April would require lots of outfits, and Gwen, who wasn't usually even vaguely interested in what she wore, had entered into the whole cruising notion with great vim and vigour. She'd been scouring the local boutiques for nautical outfits, and had gone so far as to make a list of suitable evening clothes from her own wardrobe so that she could be sure of not doubling up on anything.

Lizzie thought this was unlikely. Gwen's life had not lent itself to cocktail gowns. A passionate knitter, she was far more likely to be remembered for her selection of oatmeal-coloured sweaters that could keep out even an Arctic chill. Unlike Lizzie, who could never resist colourful tops and flowing, gypsy skirts, Gwen preferred sensible outfits. Even her hair was sensible: cut short without any artifice covering the grey.

'Shay's giving out yards about having to buy a dinner jacket,' said Gwen when they were both settled in her car and driving at a sedate pace down Lizzie's street. 'I told him to shut his trap and stop whingeing. I said you'd come with me if he didn't. That shut him up.'

Lizzie grinned. Gwen and Shay had already warmly invited her to go with them, saying she hadn't had a holiday for years and she'd be welcome.

'You don't want me along,' Lizzie insisted. 'You've both been saving for this for years and it's special.' She didn't add that as well as being completely broke she hated to feel like the third wheel, and even Gwen and Shay, who hardly qualified for love's young dream and who bickered amiably twenty-four hours a day, could do without a gooseberry. The world seemed very coupley these days and Lizzie felt like a gooseberry a lot of the time.

'Did I tell you about the jumper I got in Marks?' Gwen continued. 'Pale blue ribbed cotton. The girl at the till said it was very Ralph Lauren, whoever he is when he's at home. I told her I was going on a cruise. She was dead jealous, I can tell you. Everyone is jealous!'

In the shopping centre, Gwen headed straight for the sort of glossy clothes shop she'd never stepped into before in her life. She bypassed sensible coats and tweedy skirts for the shimmering evening wear. Within minutes, she was wearing a royal-blue floor-length jersey that clung to her ample curves with the shop's three sales assistants standing around discussing how much the skirt needed to be taken up.

'I'm going on a cruise, you see,' Gwen informed them all gravely. 'This needs to be perfect.'

It took ten minutes and lots of humming and hawing to get it perfect.

'It mustn't be too long or you won't be able to tango,' Lizzie said, her face serious.

The three assistants' eyes widened.

'She's a marvellous dancer,' Lizzie added. 'And as for her husband . . .'

The blue jersey column began to shake with laughter. Shay had last danced at his own wedding and had refused to put a toe on any dance floor ever since.

'Don't mind my sister,' Gwen warned. 'She's a menace. Tango indeed. Who was in that *Last Tango* film? Burt Reynolds, wasn't it? And there was some furore about margarine, was it? How can a bit of margarine have caused so much fuss? I don't know. Although it's hard getting grease marks out of clothes . . .'

Lizzie kept her head down.

By the time they left, the sales assistants and Gwen had decided that the royal blue would be perfect for the captain's dinner, and that the silvery grey scarf would look great with the long black skirt and pale blue crepe blouse.

'Imagine me at the captain's dinner,' sighed Gwen. 'Who'd have thought Shay and me would ever be on a cruise?'

'You'll be the star of the ship,' Lizzie said fondly, linking her arm through her sister's. 'That royal blue will be gorgeous, just perfect.' And then she stopped. She and Myles had never been on a cruise. Now they never would together . . . Gwen was the one sailing into uncharted waters, the one who'd know all about tipping the staff on the ship and what the midnight buffet was like. Lizzie was left in the shadows.

'You'll have to tell me all about it,' Lizzie said, rallying. 'I want a detailed account of everything, from how big the cabin is to what the style is like at night.'

'You could have come, you know,' Gwen said again.

'Nonsense,' said Lizzie briskly. 'Haven't I so much to do here? Debra's wedding is only round the corner and the organisation takes up so much time.'

Gwen, who had two sons and had managed to get them married without any fuss from either side, held her tongue about what she privately thought about Debra. The truth, Gwen knew, was that Lizzie couldn't afford to go on a cruise with her daughter's extravagant demands to pay for.

A cup of coffee revived them both and Lizzie began to relate the latest tale of the wedding.

'I haven't spoken to Myles about the extra cost but know he won't mind,' Lizzie finished. 'We both want this to be perfect for Debra and if a different bridesmaid's dress makes it perfect, then so be it.'

Gwen regarded her younger sister solemnly. Their mother had been a great woman for what she called 'plain speaking'.

'Blunt as hell,' Lizzie and Gwen used to agree. Both had made conscious efforts to live their lives without resorting to such bluntness. In Lizzie's case, this had translated into a gentleness with other people and a sharp sense of intuition, although this was strangely lacking when it came to her own immediate family, her sister fondly thought.

While Gwen knew herself to be straightforward, she always made an effort not to hurt anyone with her remarks. But today, watching good, kind Lizzie making a fool out of herself with that spoiled brat of a daughter of hers, Gwen itched to speak plainly.

'I hate to see you both spend so much money on this wedding,' she said, trying to be delicate.

'If you can't spend money on your only daughter's wedding, then what can you spend it on?' said Lizzie easily.

'But, Lizzie –' Gwen broke off, not wanting to give a speech along the lines of her mother's: if Debra was a decent kid, she'd understand that her parents didn't have much cash to spare and would tailor her plans accordingly. Did Debra have any idea how much penny-pinching had gone on to give her this big, glitzy wedding?

'I'd love Debra to have a big day too,' said Gwen, trying her best to find some middle line without being too critical. 'But money does come into it, Lizzie, and maybe you should tell Debra that you can't afford to spend quite so much . . .'

'Stop worrying,' replied Lizzie equably. 'Course we can afford it. Debra deserves her big day.'

That was what was wrong with her sister, Gwen thought. Lizzie had so much time for other people that she neglected herself. She hadn't even noticed what was happening in her own marriage. Now, she poured her energy into the kids or, more realistically, Debra, since Joe was away and, anyhow, didn't need looking after. There was nothing else in her life.

'Why don't you come with us on the cruise?' Gwen said urgently. 'There's still time to book. They always have cancellations, and you never know.'

'No, Gwen,' said her sister firmly. 'This is your big holiday. And besides,' she pulled her coat from the back of the café chair, 'I can't afford it. Next year I'll have my holiday of a lifetime and scandalise you all by learning exotic dancing or something!'

'Shay has a bit put by for a rainy day,' insisted Gwen. 'You could pay us back. I'd love you to have a break.'

'Thanks but no thanks. I told you, Gwen, next year,' said Lizzie. 'Next year will be my year.'

She shot her sister a strong, happy smile but it took some doing. In her heart, Lizzie didn't think next year was going to be her year any more than this one was. She was so firmly in a rut that she'd need climbing equipment to get out. She had absolutely no idea how to solve the problem, but she *did* know that spending money she didn't have would not help.

CHAPTER FIVE

The other travellers boarding flight NR 706 from Chicago to Cork that Saturday morning watched the tall elegant young couple with interest. They were definitely both *somebody*, even though they wore comfortable faded jeans and didn't make a fuss or anything when there was a horrendous queue down the gangway because the plane was delayed.

Martine Brady, flying home to Cork after a colder-than-expected month in the States staying with her sister, watched them enviously. She hadn't seen a single famous person in all her time here. Not even a glimpse of Oprah, and she was supposed to be Chicagoan through and through. Martine, five people behind the glamorous couple in the queue, and bored, watched them with naked curiosity.

The woman was someone from the television, for sure. Her auburn hair was glossier than a Kentucky thoroughbred's coat, her fine-boned face was clear-skinned and subtly made up. And that camel overcoat she wore to keep out the Chicago chill was definitely cashmere. Martine would have loved a coat like that, though you had to be tall and slim to wear it well. And rich. A newsreader, that was it. She looked like a newsreader – all polished and intelligent, even though she couldn't have been but a few years older than Martine's twenty-five. She wasn't a movie star, Martine decided. Movie stars were always perfectly beautiful and this woman wasn't. Her nose was too big and her face was just a bit too long. She was more interesting-looking than beautiful. The man was good-looking but not quite as polished. His coat was a bulky navy greatcoat that would have dwarfed most men but he was tall and broad enough to get away with it. His hair was jet black and cut close to his skull. Maybe he was some famous sportsman Martine didn't recognise – a footballer or something. Those American footballers were all built like tanks. They were certainly Americans, that was for definite. Rich American women had a certain, unmistakable gloss to them, and Martine wondered how you could recreate it back home. All those manicures and visits to get your hair blow-dried every five minutes.

The queue moved and the couple boarded the plane. As they stepped on, the man smiled at his partner to let her go first, an excited smile that made it entirely clear to Martine that the couple weren't married at all but were business people going on a trip and they had more than business in mind. The woman's eyes gleamed as she smiled back at him. Bingo! thought Martine. She imagined dinner in fancy restaurants and then afterwards, the lure of the office romance would be too much for them and they'd end up in one bedroom, drinking champagne and trying not to answer the phone because it would be someone from home calling and the guilt would kill them and . . .

'Your seat number, please?' asked the stewardess.

Martine dragged her eyes back from the business-class section where the couple had just been shown to their seats.

'Fifty-six,' she said, returning to the real world.

'Right-hand side, down the back,' smiled the stewardess.

'Down the back,' repeated Martine. One day, one day, she'd be sitting up the front just like that woman with the gleaming copper hair and the gorgeous companion.

Erin took off her new cashmere coat and stroked it with something approaching awe. It was the most beautiful item of clothing she'd ever owned in her whole life and she still shuddered to think how much it had cost. Greg had arrived home with it the previous night, exquisitely folded in acid-free tissue paper in a huge Bloomingdale's box.

'A going-away present to say thank you for coming with me to Ireland,' he said, kissing her.

'This must have cost an arm and several legs,' Erin breathed as she slipped on the coat. 'It's gorgeous, Greg.' She looked at herself in the mirror of the wardrobe, which, being fitted, was one of the few pieces of furniture now left in the apartment since everything had been shipped the day before. The coat flattered her slim figure, transforming her instantly from an ordinary woman in jeans and a sweatshirt into a lady who looked as if she wore designer labels right down to her underwear.

'It's beautiful,' she said again, 'but we can't afford it.'

They weren't broke but they weren't far off it. They certainly couldn't afford cashmere coats. Erin's two-year-old black wool would have done her fine for a while yet.

'New coat for a new beginning,' Greg insisted. 'And you want to wow them at home, don't you?'

Now she began to fold the coat carefully so she could stow it on top of her carry-on bag in the overhead locker; but a pretty blonde stewardess appeared and said she'd hang it up.

'It's too beautiful to get creased,' the stewardess said.

'Isn't it?' agreed Erin ruefully, thinking of their bank balance.

'I recognise that accent. You and your husband are Irish?' the stewardess asked chattily, her own accent a gentle Northern Irish lilt.

'Yes, we are,' Erin said.

'Were you on holiday in Chicago? Wasn't it freezing? Chicago layover is the coldest there is.' The stewardess shivered in her chic green suit as though she could still feel the wind chill.

'We weren't on holiday. We lived in Chicago for five years, actually. And I was in Boston for four years before that,' Erin said, responding to the woman's friendliness. 'We're leaving the States and going back to Ireland because my husband's starting a new job in Cork.'

'Coming home,' sighed the stewardess as she turned in the direction of the long locker. 'Welcome back!'

'Thanks.' Erin sank down into the seat and stretched out her long legs. Even with her enormous handbag under the seat in front, there was still loads of space – a welcome change from economy class. Greg eased into the seat beside her and grabbed her arm tightly.

'Finally,' he said, face alight with pleasure, 'we're finally going. It all starts here.'

'Champagne or juice?' asked a different stewardess.

Greg's grin widened and he took two glasses of champagne, handing one to Erin.

'Let's hear it for business class,' he said appreciatively. 'Not just room for your legs but free booze too! Let's hope this is the only way we travel from now on. To our new life.'

Erin smiled back at him and took a celebratory sip. 'This certainly is the way to fly,' she agreed, thinking of their normal vacation flights with Greg's huge frame squashed into a tiny airline seat. 'If your new bosses weren't paying for our tickets, we'd be swimming to Ireland, which would ruin my fabulous new coat.'

'You look like a million dollars in it,' he said, 'and I don't mean all green and crinkly.'

'We still can't afford it,' she pointed out, squeezing her husband's hand.

'Actually we can,' he admitted. 'I sold my David Bowie special edition vinyl collection to Josh. He's lusted after it for years. The *Ziggy Stardust* album's one of only five hundred.'

'Oh, Greg,' sighed Erin, incredibly touched. 'You shouldn't have.' She knew how much he loved his precious record collection.

'What the heck, we've got enough stuff.' Greg took another gulp of his drink. 'This is good champagne,' he said. 'I think I'll have another glass.'

Erin fixed him with a faux stern glare. 'Greg Kennedy, if

you get legless and start blowing kisses at the stewardesses so the plane gets diverted to Newfoundland to have you arrested, remember, you're on your own.'

'Yes, ma'am,' saluted Greg. 'Just one more and then I'll stick to water. I promise not to disgrace you.'

Erin kissed him impulsively. Greg might look serious and the perfect corporate man, but underneath he was irrepressible. He loved silly jokes, chuckled for hours over Gary Larson cartoon books, adored comedy shows and could recite the Abbott and Costello baseball sketch in his sleep.

He was also fired up with a boyish excitement over their move. To Greg, this was an adventure, the same way helicopter skiing was an adventure. He loved the fact that usually Erin matched this spirit in him and was always just as eager to try white water rafting or whatever. Only this time, Erin didn't feel as thrilled about their new move: home to Europe after many years in the US. She was doing it for him.

She'd been fine about it all at first. This new job was what they'd both been waiting for ever since the shares scandal hit the company they both worked for and the firm's blue chip status wavered. There was talk of huge job losses and neither Greg, who was rapidly climbing the corporate ladder, nor Erin, who worked in human resources, could consider their jobs as safe.

It was a wake-up call, Greg said soberly as they sat up late in their not-yet-paid-for apartment and tried to work out what their financial position would be if the industry went belly up. Erin had known he was right. But that's when he started talking wistfully about going home.

Home for Greg was just outside Wicklow, a bustling large town where his father, who had run a post office, was recently retired. Although he hadn't been home for four years, his whole family had been to Chicago for the wedding. They'd been politely curious about the absence of any of Erin's family. But she was used to that.

'My grandmother brought me up and she's too old to travel,' was her stock answer. It was also untrue.

The reason Erin hadn't been home to Dublin for nine years and the reason none of her family made the journey to Chicago for her wedding had nothing whatsoever to do with her grandmother's age. Erin had left home and Ireland at the age of eighteen to get away from her family. She had never been back. Now twenty-seven, the guilt she felt at that abrupt departure had grown into a solid block of pain. When she'd cut the ties to her family, Erin couldn't have foreseen she'd feel so strangely adrift in the world. But it was impossible to explain that to the honest and genuine Kennedy family, although Greg knew. For his parents, roots and family were important. People who didn't appreciate family had to have something wrong with them.

Erin adored their son and wanted them to feel that he'd made a good choice in marrying her. She couldn't tell them the truth. 'Gran would love to be here but the trip would have been too much for her,' she said, feeling terrible for the lie.

'I suppose you'll fly home later this year, then,' said Mrs Kennedy hopefully, thinking that if the newlyweds visited Dublin, well, they'd certainly spend a couple of nights in Wicklow too.

'We'll see,' said Erin politely, privately thinking that there was as much chance of her being picked to play for the New York Yankees as there was of her flying home to the bosom of her family. They wouldn't want to see her now. Why would they? Yes, she'd been so hurt by them, but to run off and stay away – apart from those first few phone calls soon afterwards to let them know she was still alive – what family could forgive that, even a messed-up one like hers? And clearly they hadn't forgiven her. When she and Greg got engaged, the longing for home had become intense and she'd written several letters to her family. Nobody had replied.

Four years after the wedding, Erin and Greg's circumstances had changed.

The day after their heart-to-heart about their finances,

Greg heard from a head-hunter friend about a job heading the Irish division of a multinational telecoms company. They particularly wanted someone with his international experience. It seemed like a good omen.

The relocation fee would take care of their debts until they managed to sell the apartment, and their friend, the head-hunter, assured Erin that a human resources manager of her calibre would have no problem getting a job. Even better, the Cuchulainn Telecoms people, Greg's new bosses, promised to rent a beautiful home for the couple for the first six months.

The job sounded like the sort of challenge Greg loved, and he'd been told great things about his management team and particularly his recently promoted second-in-command, a guy named Steve Richardson. The final plus was the location: a heritage town outside the city of Cork that looked incredible when Greg and Erin checked it out on the Web. Neither of them had ever visited Dunmore when they'd lived in Ireland, but they'd certainly heard of it.

Greg told the company they'd have to think about it.

'It's a big move, honey,' he said to Erin. 'I don't want to force you to move back to Ireland because of me.'

'Oh yeah, and who said I was going to move back with you?' she teased. 'I might stay here and be frivolous with our money while you work your butt off in Cork.'

'Money? We have money?' he said, nuzzling her earlobe.

'The jar of quarters in the kitchen is getting awfully heavy. There's at least forty dollars in there,' began Erin.

'Forty dollars! You hussy. You could go wild with that, splurging on wine, men and song. I can't leave you here without me. You have to come. I'll pine without you.'

Erin looked at him affectionately. Whatever was wrong with the rest of her life, she'd struck it lucky when she'd met Greg. Other guys might bleat on about being the bigger earner and about how she had to go where his job took them, like women following soldiers following the drum. But even though Greg earned more than Erin, it had never made any difference, either to how they spent their money or to the balance of power in their relationship. If Erin insisted on staying in the States and the only job Greg could get was putting out the trash for McDonald's, then Greg would become the best trash man in the country – he loved her that much.

That love, and the sense that he would always be fiercely loyal to her, were the traits that had made her finally stop running. When she met Greg Kennedy, Erin realised that you could experience the sensation of coming home with a person too, and for her, wherever Greg was, was her home. It helped, of course, that he was utterly gorgeous. Erin was a tall woman but Greg could pick her up as if she were no heavier than a child. When he'd carried her over the threshold of the apartment on their return from honeymoon, she'd felt like a heroine in a fairy tale.

Erin made the decision. Nobody could ever accuse her of not being up for a new challenge. 'What the hell?' she said. 'That forty bucks might go further in Cork than it will here. And you've been talking about going home since I met you. Let's go for it.'

By the time Greg's new career move was sorted out, the job losses had started at their old company. Erin sold their car, which would, she said wryly, keep her in pantihose until she got a new job. They packed up the apartment, had lots of leaving dinners with friends, sorted out change of address cards and bank accounts. They were both wildly busy and neither of them had time to feel morose over leaving the city they'd called home for so long.

Then, a week ago, something odd had happened. Erin had been standing in Stuker's Dry-Cleaners waiting in line to get a pile of suits back. Her purse slung over one shoulder, she was ticking off items in her red Things To Do notebook when the enormity of it all hit her and she felt her lungs compress, as if all the air had been squeezed out of them. She'd stumbled and almost fallen as her legs gave way beneath her.

'Sit, missy, sit,' said the sweet Korean lady who ran

Stuker's. She eased Erin into a plastic chair, which, even in Erin's dazed state, seemed weird, because Erin was five feet eight and the Korean lady was barely up to her shoulders.

'You pregnant?'

Erin laughed in genuine amusement. Thankfully, there was zero chance of that. Before their marriage, Erin had been utterly straight with Greg and told him that she wasn't sure she'd want children after what her mother had done to her. It wasn't that she didn't like kids, but she wasn't certain she was mother material. And he'd said he understood. Another reason to love him, she knew, because she was sure it was hard for him to accept her decision.

Now she shook her head at the kind Korean lady. 'Not a chance. I'm just dizzy,' she said. 'Low blood sugar.'

The rest of the line, familiar with medical problems from lactose intolerance up, went back to waiting. Rendered almost invisible because she was slumped in a plastic chair like a well-heeled dope-head, Erin let the panic flow away from her body until she was able to examine the problem from a distance.

She was going home and she'd never really planned to. Oh yes, she'd talked about it. What person didn't? Home was like some magical and unchanging world of childhood for so many of her and Greg's friends. Scottish, Australian, Irish, Italian, every nationality possible – everybody talked about their homeland as though viewing it through misty, uncritical eyes. Not only was the grass greener at home but life was simpler.

'Different times,' everyone would sigh when they had enough drink inside them and the mournful music of home was playing on the CD player.

Erin had long suspected that those who did return home drove everyone in Italy or Australia mad by telling them how wonderful America was and how they missed it and how the roads/hospitals/coffee were better there.

She, on the other hand, never indulged in shows of nostalgia for the country of her birth. Not that anybody ever noticed. With a name like Erin and her swathe of rippling copper silk for hair, she seemed as Irish as they came. People *assumed* she quietly longed to be sitting in an Irish pub on Paddy's Day, proudly wearing a clod of shamrock and sighing mournfully into her Guinness. They didn't know she felt she'd recklessly thrown away her Irishness the day she abandoned her family.

When their friends heard that she and Greg were leaving the States, they all said the same thing: 'We knew you would.'

Erin felt like remarking: 'You knew more than I did, that's for sure.'

The line in the dry-cleaner's was gone but Erin didn't have the energy to leave the plastic chair and pick up her stuff. She was going home and she didn't know how to face the guilt.

Greg fell asleep halfway through the new Spielberg movie. Erin, who'd been watching the latest Nicole Kidman offering on her tiny screen, leaned over and gently removed his head-phones. She pulled the grey airline rug over his shoulders so he wouldn't be cold and moved his empty water glass onto her own tray in case he knocked it over, smiling at the realisation that she only gave in to her mothering instinct with Greg when he was asleep.

Conscious of getting dehydrated, she drank some more water, and settled back to watch the movie but her concentration had been broken.

As the plane flew through the night, Erin cast her mind back to her last hours at home. She remembered the stricken face of the woman she'd always called Mum but who was, in fact, her grandmother, when she'd shouted that she was leaving because they'd lied to her all her life. She remembered leaving many of her childhood treasures behind when she fled the house because she'd wanted to demonstrate the depth of her rejection. Most of all, she remembered the pain she'd felt when she found out that the most important people in her life – her mother, her father and her sister – weren't who they said they were. Thanks to Erin's shocking discovery, all her family relationships had shifted. Dad was really her grandfather, bolshy Kerry wasn't her sister but her aunt, and the long-absent sister Shannon, the wild one who never came home but sent postcards from exotic locations when the mood took her, was really Erin's mother.

The first thing that struck Erin as she and Greg followed the Cuchulainn driver out of Cork airport to the car park was how warm it was. There was no sign of the beating rain that was part of her memory of home. Instead, a soft spring breeze shimmied over her face, like a silky scarf just out of the dryer. The acid bite of Chicago's wind chill seemed a lifetime away.

'Lovely day,' said Greg appreciatively, filling his lungs with clean air after so many hours in the stuffy cabin.

The second thing Erin noticed was that the driver was refusing to fit the chatty Irish cabbie mould. There was none of the blarney she had expected, no third degree as he tried to work out where they were from, had they any family in Cork or did they know so and so in Chicago, which was the kind of thing Erin remembered from home. Oh well, she shrugged. She'd changed, so it was only fair to assume that Ireland had changed too.

Eager to see a bit of the place, Greg asked for the scenic route, so instead of taking the most direct road to Dunmore, which bypassed the centre of the city, the driver drove them along Patrick Street, pointing out places of note.

Erin tried to look at the sights but kept getting distracted by stylish people, who could have stepped off a Manhattan sidewalk any day. This, she didn't remember.

Sure, there were the usual few ould fellas in jackets so dated they could have taken part in a centenary of clothes exhibition, but for the most part, the citizens of Cork looked . . . well, marvellous.

When they finally drove through the hills to reach Dunmore,

it looked marvellous too: very cute in a picture-postcard way, like the upmarket towns she and Greg had visited in New England on their honeymoon.

'Dunmore looked lovely on the Internet but those pictures didn't do it justice,' said Greg, admiring the Victorian town square, which was dominated by a forbidding grey statue of some long-dead mayor. 'I can't wait to see our house.'

After the beauty of the buildings they had passed in Dunmore, the home the company had rented for them was a definite disappointment. The box-like terraced house on a shabby 1980s estate was so small that it was completely filled by their packing cases and their furniture, which had arrived the day before. Even a deeply apologetic letter from the agent on the kitchen counter top, explaining that due to unforeseen circumstances the house they'd been supposed to have was unrentable, didn't bring a smile to their faces.

'"I apologise to both you and Mrs Kennedy,"' Greg read from the letter,'"but if you could just bear with us for the next couple of weeks, we'll have other, more suitable premises for you then." I'd better get on to Steve Richardson about this. His office are supposed to have sorted the house out. Oh, the letter says there's champagne in the refrigerator as compensation,' he added, cheering up as he read the next paragraph.

Erin looked round the kitchen, which, although heroic last-minute efforts had been made, had clearly been rented out for years to people not familiar with basic cleaning equipment. One wall in the kitchen diner was obviously where the kitchen table had stood, for it bore a line of suspicious reddish stains that scrubbing hadn't been able to remove. The mustard-yellow cabinets and the pink-tinged walls hinted that at least somebody had a sense of humour, but wafting down from upstairs there was a definite hint of tomcat in the air.

'There'd better be two bottles of champagne,' Erin said, wrapping her arms round Greg's waist, 'because I'd hate to find out that the cat peed in the master bedroom and, at least with a bottle each, we'll sleep.'

Greg lifted her up effortlessly and sat her on the counter, so that her legs were free to lock round his waist.

'I vant to take you here, in ze kitchen, my Irish maiden,' he said, nuzzling into her neck. 'But I zink we bettair clean up first.'

'Good idea, Casanova,' said Erin, kissing him on the mouth. 'You wouldn't know what you'd catch here and I'm not taking off my knickers until this place is spotless.'

'Ooh, stop with ze durty talk,' moaned Greg.

'Later.' She held him close, loving the feeling of his heart beating next to hers. 'You open the champagne and I'll find the carton with the rubber gloves in it.'

Three days later, Erin was fed up. The day after they'd arrived, the weather had suddenly become unaccountably cold and the heating was either a very mysterious system that normal humans couldn't work, or it was broken.

Greg fiddled around with the timer for half the evening but he was so exhausted with the combination of jet lag and starting the new job that he failed to make any improvement.

'Sorry, honey,' he said. 'I know you're cold. Let's get on to the agency tomorrow.' Then he'd fallen into the deep sleep of the shattered, leaving Erin shivering in bed beside him, despite her bed socks and thermal shirt.

The agency said they would send round a maintenance man, but nothing happened. The next morning she phoned them again and they promised to send someone out that day.

Erin, who felt strangely out of sorts and still jet-lagged, wasn't amused. 'You said that yesterday,' she pointed out drily. 'Is there some kind of draw going on? You put all the names into a hat and when my name comes out, you actually send someone out. Is that it?'

The agency lady sounded quite sniffy and pointed out that two days of freezing weather had burst pipes in a few of their properties and that their maintenance men were busy.

'Burst pipes?' Erin enquired. 'If that's what it takes to get you guys out here, just tell me where they are and I'll burst them. OK?'

She hung up and glared round at the empty kitchen. It had been too chilly to unpack things since the cold snap. She had only opened the boxes for the living room because there was a gas fire in there. Besides, if they were going to be moving into a better house soon there was no point in getting out everything. She made yet another cup of coffee for personal central heating and stomped into the living room, pausing only to pick up Greg's old ski cap from the banisters and jam it on her head.

She was already wearing leggings under her track bottoms, two sweaters and an electric-blue padded ski gilet. All of which looked ridiculous, she knew. But who cared. She didn't know anybody in this town so there was nobody to wonder what had happened to the normally exquisitely groomed Erin Kennedy to turn her into such a slut.

Plonking herself down cross-legged on the floor, she tackled a box destined for the study. She was engrossed in a pile of newspaper clippings she was sure she'd thrown out in Chicago, when the doorbell rang.

Fantastic. Losing it with the rental company was clearly the way forward.

But it wasn't the maintenance man at the door. Instead, there stood a tiny Flower Fairy of a person, with round dark eyes, rippling ebony curls and a red hooded woollen coat that made her a dead ringer for Little Red Riding Hood.

'I don't know whether to invite you in or tell you that Grandma's sick and the big bad wolf is around,' said Erin before she could help it.

The woman laughed: a deep, throaty laugh utterly at odds with her Little Red Riding Hood image. 'I'll have to throw this coat out,' she cried, pushing back the hood.

'Sorry,' Erin said quickly.

'No, you're right,' insisted Red Riding Hood. 'Grown women should not buy clothes because they're cute. Then people *call* you cute and I hate that. Cute is an overused word. I'm Sally, by the way. Sally Richardson, Steve's wife.' When Erin still looked blank, she added: 'Steve Richardson works with Greg in Cuchulainn.'

Erin grimaced at her own stupidity. Greg had spoken every day about Steve Richardson, the hardworking second-in-command, who, to Greg's delight, did not appear to have applied for the top job, being newly promoted himself, and, therefore, who did not have a chip on his shoulder about a new boss.

'Sorry again,' apologised Erin. 'My brain isn't functioning these days. Jet lag. Or hypothermia, perhaps. The heating isn't working.'

'So I hear. Steve says Greg is worried sick because you're stuck at home getting frostbite.'

'I am wearing some fetching thermals.' Erin pointed down to her Michelin Man outfit. 'I didn't think it would be this cold.'

'It's freak weather, lowest temperatures for March in fifty years,' Sally said. 'We never usually get really icy weather because we're beside the sea. How about coming out to lunch with me? Steve phoned me to say he got Cindy in personnel to have a word with the rental company boss. Cindy loves a challenge.' Sally grinned. 'You'll have a maintenance guy out at half three.'

'I may offer to have sex with him in gratitude,' Erin deadpanned. 'Sorry, that was a joke. That's incredibly kind of you and Steve. Lunch sounds great.'

While Sally sat amid the boxes in the kitchen, Erin rushed upstairs to change into a less padded outfit. She hadn't washed her hair since the day after they'd left and she knew it was greasy. So she stuck a black felt beret on it, added mascara and lipstick, and was ready.

'Oh, I wish I could wear hats,' said Sally in genuine admiration when Erin arrived downstairs, willowy in a mocha corduroy coat, her long legs endless in suede bootlegs. 'I'm too short but you're so graceful and elegant, you can get away with it.'

And Erin smiled and said, 'This is the lazy woman's hairdo. It's been too cold to shampoo my hair, so a hat is the only option.'

'Well, if that's how you look when you haven't made an effort, you must be pretty amazing when you have.'

They went to a cosy pub and sat beside a crackling log fire to eat chilli wraps and fat chips.

Sally seemed to know without it being said that Erin didn't want to be cross-examined on where she and Greg had come from and why. Instead, she filled Erin in on Dunmore and Cork, explaining that the Cork people looked down their noses at Dunmore for being a sleepy country town, and the Dunmore people looked down on Cork for being a city.

'I was brought up in Cork, mind you, and I love it,' she said. 'There's a real buzz to the place. But I love Dunmore too. It's so tranquil here. You feel as if you're in a small community, yet the city is only a few miles away. The best of both worlds, really. We moved here because I had this dream of setting up my own beauty salon and we heard about some perfect premises on the Lee Road here.'

Erin, who had told Greg in no uncertain terms that she didn't want to cosy up with the locals until she'd found her feet, heard herself saying that she'd love to visit the salon soon.

'I haven't had a manicure for two weeks and my hands are chapped with the cold,' she said ruefully, examining her long slender fingers.

She regretted it as soon as she'd said it. Now Sally would leap on her and before she knew it, she'd book Erin in and take over.

But no. 'Come in when you're ready,' Sally said equably. 'Settle in first. You don't want to make lots of friends right away and then spend the next two years trying to shake them off!'

This was so much what Erin had been afraid of that she stared open-mouthed at her new friend.

'I know what it's like to move into a new area,' Sally added. 'People want to be friendly and you end up intimately acquainted with half the town and promising to have a drink with the other half by the end of the first week.'

'Now that sounds like the Ireland I know and love,' Erin said wryly. 'I'm originally from Dublin and in my neighbourhood, when a new family arrived, if the neighbours hadn't been invited in for tea and heard their life history within a week, the new arrivals were considered oddballs of the highest order.'

Sally grinned. 'Same as where I came from. They'd live in your ear. My mother used to say there was no need for a local paper, just take a trip down to the corner shop and you'd hear the news from the five nearest parishes.'

They laughed conspiratorially and were soon swapping stories of gossipy neighbours who could pick up a rumour faster than a submarine's radar could detect another vessel.

'When I met Steve, he had this clapped-out old van, and, the first night, he drove me home in it and we sat outside my house for an hour talking,' Sally explained. 'Next day, my mum's next-door neighbour leaned out her window when I was going off to work and said he looked like a lovely lad, wasn't he the image of a young, blond Rock Hudson, and was it serious?'

'A blond Rock Hudson, huh?' Erin couldn't stop smiling.

Sally nodded. 'She loved him, poor dear. Don't think she ever took it in that he wasn't the macho man she'd fallen for in the back seat of the cinema.'

'But wow, he was a looker. Is Steve really like him?'

It was Sally's turn to smile. 'Better looking, although he's got a bit of grey in the blond now, which I love teasing him about.' Without a trace of self-consciousness, she began to tell Erin how they'd met, fallen in love and got married.

Listening to Sally talking about her husband and her two adorable but utterly mischievous children, Erin realised that

85

it was a breath of fresh air to hear someone genuinely content with their life. Sally finished explaining about how Steve had hoped to make a living out of teaching art classes, but had ended up going back into the corporate world for financial reasons.

'He enjoys working in Cuchulainn,' Sally added, in case she'd made it sound as if Steve would give up work in a flash to go back to art. 'Making a living from art was his dream but we're both realists. We needed the money.'

'Hey, don't apologise to me,' Erin chuckled. 'I worked in human resources for years. Work is not everybody's first love, I can tell you. They weren't all buying lottery tickets for fun either. There were three big syndicates in my last company and if any of them had won, the office would've been wiped out.'

'I'm really lucky, then,' Sally said humbly. 'I love the beauty salon.'

Erin leaned back in her seat, her slim belly full of chilli and chips, and gazed at her new friend. 'It's great to see someone so happy with their life.'

Sally shrugged. 'When you're happy the way Steve and I are, people like to imagine that we both went through some awful torment to be together or had terrible childhoods and now, because of all of that, we're happy with each other. It's not like that at all. We both had great childhoods and lovely families, we just appreciate each other and are thankful for what we've got.' The sweetly smiling face was serious now. 'We know it's special. Not many people have that. You have to appreciate it when you have it. You never know what's round the corner, as my mum used to say.'

Erin studied Sally. She was an unusual woman: lively and warm, yet with an old soul in a young body. It was as if Sally had learned the secret to happiness and wanted everyone to share it. But despite her zest for life, there was an air of fragility to her. She was New York thin and there were defined violet shadows under the sparkling dark eyes.

'What about you? You and Greg, I mean. How did you meet?'

Erin gave in and opened the top button on her trousers. 'First, please tell me there's a good gym round here,' she groaned, looking down at her belly.

'There's two.'

'Tomorrow,' vowed Erin, 'I have got to join. OK, how I met Greg. It's not your average romantic story, for a start. He'd recently been appointed in the company I worked for and he came to my office to say he couldn't get on with his assistant, who'd been there for years and had worked for the guy before him. As I say, I worked in human resources,' she went on. 'I'd also just heard a rumour that a guy on his floor was sexually harassing his assistant but she was so nervous about her job that she was scared to report him and I put two and two together, made six, and reckoned mistakenly that it was Greg.'

'Ouch,' winced Sally.

'Ouch indeed. I gave him a very hard time about why he wanted to get rid of his assistant and when I realised my mistake he took it really well. Said he'd fancied me from the beginning and thought I was trying to put him off by playing tough cookie.'

'Oh,' Sally sighed, 'like a classic romance. First hate, then love.'

'No, first hate and then total and utter embarrassment,' pointed out Erin. 'I nearly died when I discovered my mistake. I didn't accuse him of sexual harassment but damn near it. I just cringed to think of how rude I'd been to him. Like, "And what is it *precisely* about your assistant that makes you feel you can no longer work with her?"'

'But he forgave you?'

'After a blow-out lobster dinner, yes.'

She went on to talk about how they'd got married, moved to a beautiful duplex and finally how the job market changed and brought them to Dunmore.

Although Sally noticed that, apart from the brief reference

to her childhood in Dublin, Erin's story was centred entirely on her time in the US and had no reference to life before that, she didn't say anything. It was as if Erin had blanked out the Irish part of her life, preferring to date her existence from her early days in Boston, waitressing and chambermaiding herself into the ground. There was, Sally reflected, a story to tell there with regard to Erin's upbringing. But Sally was a gifted listener who knew when to probe and when to stand back and say 'mm', and she felt that Erin would prefer the standing-back approach. As she'd learned from the years in the beauty parlour, people talked when they wanted to talk.

'It's disgraceful, you know. I'm here half a week already and I haven't sent my résumé anywhere or made phone calls to the head-hunters whose names I was given,' Erin finished. Her work ethic was as insistent as her pulse and she was surprised to discover that the upheaval of moving conti-nent had stifled her normal get-up-and-go. Worse, she felt almost . . . well, depressed or strangely anxious, which she was beginning to think was linked to being back home after all these years. The trauma of her departure from Ireland had come back to haunt her now that she'd returned.

'Give it time. You've only just got here. You need to settle in,' advised Sally, waving at the barmaid for the bill.

'We need to eat,' Erin pointed out. 'Moving wiped us out and I get scared when I'm not working. It reminds me too much of when I first moved to Boston and didn't have a cent.'

'Relax, you can be a powerhouse next month.'

'Power apartment block if I keep stuffing my face without working out,' Erin said ruefully. 'Thanks for lunch, Sally.'

'My pleasure,' Sally said. 'There's just one condition: we've got to do it again.'

'Deal.'

CHAPTER SIX

Three days later, on Friday morning just after nine, Abby pulled up outside a big house in a swish Cork suburb for a private decluttering job. Many people thought that Abby no longer took on private commissions since her television success but, in fact, the opposite was true. Although television paid well, it wasn't as lucrative as everyone imagined. The big sums of money bandied about in the who's-earning-what articles in newspapers were generally wrong and often represented what Abby would earn if she sold herself and her entire family into slavery for ten years. A successful television series meant a reasonable amount of money in the bank and the possibility of making more money if the series kept on attracting high ratings. It did not mean, as lots of people thought, that someone came round to her house with a Vuitton holdall stuffed with tenners. Private jobs were her bread and butter.

This morning's job was one she felt wary of: Tanya Monaghan, a local socialite much given to appearing in the gossip column photos, wanted Abby's help to declutter her life. Fair enough. Except that Abby had a sneaking suspicion that Tanya's house didn't need anything in the way of de-junking and that she merely wanted Abby's services because of the fame factor. It was like having your dinner parties catered by a famous chef or your garden landscaped by a well-known gardener.

'Abby Barton – you know, from the television – well, she sorts the house out for me,' Tanya would say airily.

There was an intercom built into the wall beside the electric gates of the Monaghan home. Tanya's husband, who was some sort of construction magnate, was clearly rolling in funds. Abby lowered the Jeep window.

'Abby Barton for Mrs Monaghan,' she shouted into the intercom.

'Come in,' said a gentle, heavily accented voice. Not Tanya's, Abby was sure. Therefore the voice of some hired help, which meant the whole house was probably spotless as it was. She parked on a flawless gravel drive and didn't have to ring the doorbell before the door opened. A shy, dark-haired woman in clumpy shoes smiled at her.

'Welcome,' she said in her quiet voice.

Tanya appeared from the top of the staircase. 'I'll take over, Manuela,' she said dismissively.

'Thanks,' Abby said politely to Manuela, who shot her a friendly look as though to say nobody in this household thanked her very often. Abby would bet her day's wages that Manuela could tell some stories about her employer. Perhaps they could compare notes afterwards.

'Nice of you to drop in,' said Tanya, waving a languid hand in Abby's direction. A skeletal blonde with size six hips in pink Versace jeans, she was coiffed to within an inch of her life and, from the studied bored look on her face, was clearly determined not to be fazed by her celebrity house declutterer.

Ms Size-Six-Hips lit up the first of many cigarettes and took Abby on a tour of the house. It was so big that Abby was glad she'd worn flat shoes. It was also as perfectly tidy as a house in a style magazine. They went upstairs.

'As you can see, I haven't any room in here,' Tanya said when they reached a dressing room roughly the same size as Abby's own bedroom. With clothes crammed into every space, it was definitely the messiest room in the Monaghan house, but still nowhere near the scale of disaster that Abby had encountered on the show. One family had lived for three years with all their clothes stored in plastic bin liners because their wardrobes were jammed full of really old clothes and nobody had been able to face tackling either the mouldy wardrobes or the moths. Compared to that, Tanya's dressing room was perfect enough to stand in for a clothes shop display.

'Do you think you can sort it out?' Tanya said, not looking at Abby but scrutinising an immaculate nail.

Abby thought of the endless perfect rooms, which required little work. It would be wrong of her to take on a job where there was none. Only this room needed anything doing to it, and judging by the labels hanging from many of the obviously unworn clothes, the main solution would be to take away Tanya's gold credit card. The money for the commission would be nice but Abby was intrinsically honest. Besides, she wasn't in the mood for spending much time with the self-obsessed and rude Tanya Monaghan.

'Tanya, there's not a lot to do here,' she said bluntly. 'This room needs a day's work but that's all. I couldn't take your money for nothing.'

'Well,' Tanya looked almost offended at the idea that her house wasn't suitable, 'can't you do *something*?'

'Tanya, it would be wrong of me to say the whole house needs doing. You've no clutter at all.'

'This room, then,' Tanya said eagerly.

'OK.'

'Great. I'll send Manuela up in case you want tea or coffee,' Tanya said, smiling now she'd got her way. 'I have to go out. I'll be back much later. Have fun.'

And she was gone, leaving Abby feeling decidedly irritated.

Working in Tanya's dressing room had another big minus, Abby decided when she'd finished the job and was pulling on her jacket: those floor-to-ceiling mirrors were as unforgiving as the ones in the hairdresser's, and magnified every line. She should have asked Tanya for advice on plastic surgery. Tanya would be the sort of person to know where to go to have eyebags miraculously lifted. The only problems with surgery, Abby decided, were that it hurt and there was always a risk of it going wrong. Look at all those women with lips that looked like inflated Lilos. No, Abby only wanted surgery if she could be guaranteed that she'd look herself, only younger.

On her way home, she stopped at a row of shops to buy a banana and some bottled water to keep her going. Emerging from the shop, she passed a glossy chemist's and the lure of shiny new lipsticks drew her in. She'd had a dull but lucrative day. She deserved a treat, like a new lippie or maybe some nail varnish. After an enjoyable ten minutes dawdling at the beauty counter, Abby decided to buy a new, even more expensive eye cream as well as a lip-plumping lotion, an ultra-moisturising face mask and, to cheer herself up, a mascara that promised spidery lashes like a sexy French actress. With huge jet-black lashes batting, perhaps nobody would notice Abby's crow's-feet. As her credit card was processed to debit a horrifyingly large sum, Abby decided that an eye lift would still be cheaper in the long run. Still, she signed the bill, turned away from the till and went whomp straight into the raincoated body of a man.

The impact winded her and she dropped her bag of make-up to the ground with a loud clank.

'Excuse me,' she muttered, not looking at the man but bending down to retrieve her package, hoping nothing was broken. Clumsy *and* wrinkly. Was there no end to her talents? No wonder her husband was bored with her.

'Abby Barton,' said an amused voice. 'Long time no see.'

Crouched down, she peered up at the voice and her stomach lurched the way it did when she drove the Jeep at high speed over bumps in the road.

The owner of the expensive-looking raincoat, staring down his long aquiline nose at her, was Jay Garnier.

A man she hadn't seen for what . . . eighteen years? Nineteen? At somebody's wedding, if she remembered correctly, when she'd wondered in advance if the old magic would be there and had been mildly upset when Jay had rolled up with an exquisite Brazilian girl with blue-black hair and a slim waist measurement which, even so, was undoubtedly a higher figure than her age.

'Typical,' everyone had said, watching them whirl round the dance floor, two tall lean figures moving in time to the music as if they were alone and just about to fall into bed. 'Jay always found the best-looking girls.'

And Abby had consoled herself that *she'd* been one of Jay's girls, once, and that everyone knew he moved on and the trick was not to be bothered by it. To show Jay exactly how not bothered she was by his not even coming over to say hello, Abby had flounced round the floor with her current boyfriend – the one before Tom – and got terribly drunk on pineapple daiquiris.

'Abby,' he said now, 'I can't believe it's you. It's so wonderful to see you – you don't know how thrilled I am. You've made my day!'

Abby melted. It wasn't just seeing him that made her feel twenty years younger, but the way he said her name. His voice had always been bewitching, low, husky. He never spoke loudly. Linda, her flatmate at college, who had never liked Jay, said he spoke softly simply to get women to lean closer to him, so he could pounce. But Abby disagreed. She could remember Jay talking to her as if she was the only person on the planet, his misty grey eyes locked with hers, passion smouldering.

'I've never felt this way about anyone in the world,' he'd said. She'd felt the same. Of course, it couldn't have lasted; they both knew that. Holiday romances didn't.

'It's so wonderful to see you.' Jay pulled her to her feet, and his arms were around her, and in that instant, Abby hugged him back tightly. He'd barely changed. The strong profile and the chiselled jawline were the same, the jaw only softened by the unexpectedly full lower lip that was now curved up into a delighted smile. He still looked fit enough to play a ferociously aggressive game of rugby and his hair was the same dappled chestnut, although shorter than it had been in college. He certainly didn't look forty-two, which was what he had to be – Abby's own age.

He held her at arm's length and stared appreciatively at her. 'You look fabulous, Abby. Do you have time for a quick drink and a catch-up?'

They sat in the bar of the hotel across the street and reminisced. Abby had kept in touch with some of the college gang, and, jittery with a strange excitement whenever he accidentally brushed against her, she kept up a stream of conversation about them, discussing how Peter and Fiona had got married after all and now lived in Stockholm, and how Denessa had lived near Abby in Cork until a few years ago.

Jay, who was in Cork on business, lived in Dublin and ran the sales division of a successful office supply company there. He was married to a woman named Lottie and somehow, Abby wasn't sure how, he gave a resigned impression that all wasn't well in the marriage. Abby's soft heart was moved at the way he shrugged and said wryly that even the best marriages went through difficult patches, didn't they?

'The boys are five and seven, and they're great,' he said. 'How about yours? You've got a daughter, haven't you?'

With relief, Abby talked about Jess and Tom, giving Jay the interview version of her life: how thrilled she was with the fame but that her family life was more important than anything else.

Jay told her about his two young sons, saying he'd married late and that the boys were keeping him young.

'I'm afraid I must go,' he said finally, when they'd talked for over an hour. 'I've another meeting.'

'Of course,' said Abby. 'Me too. Another meeting, I mean.'

His fingers brushed against hers as they both reached for the bill and Abby again felt the strangest sensation electrify her body. For a moment, she just sat and stared at Jay's outstretched hand.

'Let me pay,' he insisted. 'If you can't let an old friend buy you a drink, who can? And I'm a very old friend,' he added, laughing. 'Look at the grey hairs.'

Abby laughed easily. 'Not so old,' she said. 'You don't look a day over thirty-seven. I can only assume you have a portrait in the attic like Dorian Gray.'

'Look who's talking.' There was a relaxed, teasing quality to his voice and Abby smiled back as he leaned over and touched her hair. 'You look fabulous. Fame agrees with you, Abby.'

Their eyes met and, at that instant, she was able to identify the sensation she'd experienced when he'd touched her previously: the exquisite thrill of sexual attraction. Like the tail flick of an electric eel, desire rippled throughout her body, sending every nerve ending onto high alert. And just as quickly, Abby knew how dangerous it would be to admit this to Jay. How embarrassing to behave like that with an old boyfriend, a married old boyfriend at that.

The air of *savoir-faire* she'd worked on so hard for her television persona came to her rescue just in time.

'You charmer,' she said, her voice deliberately light. 'I bet you say that to all your old flames.'

'No.' Jay's easy smile was gone. 'I don't.'

'Well, don't say it to me,' she said, falsely stern. 'I'm an old married lady and I've forgotten how to flirt.'

'Bet you haven't,' he replied lightly. 'You were always a temptress.'

And they were back on safe ground, teasing merrily, two old friends delighted to see each other and happy to reminisce about the past.

'We must have dinner sometime,' Jay said, getting to his feet.

Abby, halfway through searching in her handbag for her keys, hesitated. Was he saying what she thought he was saying?

'I'd love to meet Tom, and I know you'd adore Lottie,' Jay went on.

'Fantastic,' Abby said heartily, relief mingling with disappointment. It would have been nice if he'd felt the same attraction she did, but it was easier that he didn't. Her life was complicated enough. 'Dinner would be wonderful. Here's my card and we can set it up.'

The thought of Jay filled her mind all afternoon. There was something wildly exciting about meeting someone who made her feel young and attractive in a way Tom just didn't any more. And Jay had been so focused on her, he'd given her his full attention, which was something she certainly never got at home these days. Dinosaurs had roamed the earth the last time she'd received anything like as much attention from her husband and daughter. Of course, old friends were always going to be interested in every detail of your life. Catching up, that's what Jay had been doing – she knew that. But it had been fun, Abby thought wistfully. Great fun.

Four miles away, Jess and Steph were not having fun at all, shivering like whippets in their thin Aertex shirts amongst a class of students on the school football pitch. Mr Hutton, the games teacher, stood at the front and explained that the afternoon sports session would be fun: relay races and five-a-side football to take the fourth years' minds off the impending exams. Whatever about the exams, nothing could take their minds off the cold wind, which was whistling up from the harbour with the malevolence of a nuclear-powered Jack Frost. Their track-suit tops were all piled on benches behind them because, as Mr Hutton said, 'You'll all be roasting after a few minutes of the relay races.'

'I don't know why he thinks this is going to help us relax,' growled Steph, rubbing her arms frantically to get warm. 'He's all right: he's wearing a bloody fleece.'

'I hate games,' muttered Jess. Her arms were turning blue and she'd got her period that morning in French – cramps with jaws like pit bull terriers were gnawing at her belly. She couldn't bear to think about running in a stupid relay race, never mind actually doing it. But she couldn't say anything to horrible Mr Hutton. How did they expect girl students to talk about period pains to male sports teachers? It wasn't on. Her mother had always moaned about having gone to an all-girls school but there had to be some advantages.

'Line up,' shouted Mr Hutton joyfully.

Shuffling miserably, the students lined up, with Steph getting shoved to the front of their group, three people ahead of Jess.

'Sorry,' Steph mouthed, peering back along the ranks.

Jess gave a resigned shrug.

In the team beside her stood Saffron, her shining blonde hair tied up in a jaunty ponytail, her skin clear and fresh. As if to remind Jess of its existence in the face of such glowing perfection, a pimple on her forehead started to throb. Great. Throbbing forehead and throbbing belly.

Hating everything and everyone, she stared stonily ahead and tried to ignore Derek and Alan on her other side ogling Saffron's high, jutting breasts, which completely filled out her tiny sports shirt. Jess shot the droolers a quelling look but they simply didn't notice her, their hormonally operated eyes glued to Saffron's chest. Ignored again. The story of her life, Jess thought miserably. Not that she wanted two Stone Age morons to look at her but still, it would be nice to turn heads the way Saffron did.

'GO!' shouted Mr Hutton and the first runners shot off. Everyone else shuffled up unwillingly in their lines. Only Mr Hutton and the insanely competitive guys from the football team were cheering. The rest seemed just as bored as Jess.

'It's going to be fabulous.'

Jess tuned into what Saffron was saying in a low voice to her cronies.

'The tickets are limited to fifth and sixth years but Ian says you lot are all welcome, he'll sort it out. I can't wait.'

If Steph had been with her, Jess would have rolled her eyes theatrically. The class blondes were always talking about some party or another. This time it was the dance on the night of the interschool soccer cup. Like, boring.

'. . . and it's boned, so it, you know, really pushes them up.' Saffron demonstrated having her boobs pushed up so high she could rest her chin on them. Jess didn't know which was worse: the hot gasps from Alan and Derek, or the thought of Ian's gorgeous face when he saw Saffron all wrapped up like a Christmas cracker for him, boobs spilling out of her dress and the 'Open' sign flickering in her eyes.

It all came down to tits, didn't it?

The guy ahead of her sprinted off and Jess tried to look ready for her turn. She stretched her stiff calves, aware that she hadn't limbered up properly. And what if she dropped the baton? She hated relay races.

Her team-mate reached the other end and turned back. More people were screaming support now and it was easy to see which team was winning: the footballers, whose line-up somehow managed to consist of the fittest guys in the class and no girls. Jess began to jog on the spot. Her team-mate was close, closer, he shoved the baton at her and she fumbled it. Then it went flying. Jess dived into the mud after it, grabbing at it frantically as it rolled out of reach.

'Come on, Jess, put some effort into it,' yelled Mr Hutton.

'Come on, Jess,' howled her team.

Her cold fingers grasped the baton and she lurched to her feet and into a clumsy run. The people she was running against were already on the return journey and Jess did her best. But the combination of embarrassment at her mistake and the rumbling ache inside conspired against her. Her legs felt leaden, like in a nightmare in which ghouls were getting closer but her feet were stuck in quicksand.

'Jess, Jess, hurry up!' shrieked everyone as she turned for home, to see the other runners nearly there. She put all her energy into the dash back and thrust the baton hurriedly into the final sprinter's hand. Panting, she turned to see that it was too late. Her team would be last. And it was her fault.

'Tough luck, babes,' sympathised Steph, patting her arm. 'I thought Hooty was going to have a heart attack when you couldn't pick up the stick. Somebody should give that guy a chill pill. Sports are so not cool.'

'Yeah, you said it,' muttered Jess, still feeling as if everyone was looking at her and mentally branding her a clumsy idiot.

The football boys won, to much wild screaming, particularly from Saffron's gang.

'Well done,' squealed Saffron, flicking her ponytail flirtatiously towards Tony, the best-looking of the winners. This husky-voiced giant sat near Jess in maths and had once picked up her silver gel pen when it had fallen onto the floor and handed it to her.

'Thanks, Saffron,' said Tony, giving the girl a smile of such promise that Jess felt scorched just by being near it. 'You were pretty hot yourself.'

Jess knew that if Tony had said anything so sexy to her, she'd be staring at him stupidly, mouth open to display the horrible inside of her train-track braces. Saffron merely smiled out from under darkened lashes – definitely covered with forbidden mascara, Jess thought grimly – and winked knowingly at Tony.

Jess watched them both surreptitiously. Despite hating Saffron on one hand, she had a grudging respect for her on the other. Somehow, Saffron had solved the mystery of guys. *She* didn't wait for them to throw her a crumb of conversation in the lunch queue. She didn't lie in bed at night wondering if they'd noticed her. She went out and got them, like a cowboy roping a bullock. What was more, she didn't panic that Ian would find out she'd flirted with Tony. For a brief, enjoyable moment, Jess imagined herself comforting Ian and hearing him say: 'I never thought I'd get over Saffron but she wasn't my true love. You are, Jess. I'm so glad she's going out with Tony. It's given me the chance to . . .'

'. . . pick up the baton without fumbling and run with it.'

Bewildered, Jess left her dream world to focus on the real one and found Mr Hutton loudly lecturing her about team sports, meaning team work. 'If you didn't want to be in the relay, you should have said something, Jess,' he added.

Stung by the unfairness of this, Jess was about to blurt out that the relay race would have consisted of five people in total if the class had any choice in the matter, but he barged on with his comments. 'That's what games are about. Joining in and doing your best for the team. You're tall and athletic – you ought to be as fast as any of the boys,' he went on.

'Yeah, Jess *is* nearly a boy,' sniggered Derek to Alan, staring meaningfully at her T-shirt.

Flushing with rage and misery, Jess looked down at her feet and realised that she was covered with mud from her frantic grappling for the baton.

If Mr Hutton had possessed even a single intuitive bone in his body, he'd have realised that Jess was staring down at the ground because she didn't want anyone to see the tears welling up in her eyes. But Mr Hutton wouldn't have known how to spell intuitive and decided that the lanky Barton girl was giving him cheek by her very attitude. She wasn't even *looking* at him when he was talking to her.

'Have it your way, Jess. Don't join in and see where that gets you in life. Nowhere, that's where. Well, you can stay late after class and put all the batons and line markers in the games shed. And leave the key with the caretaker.'

Games was the last class of the day and if she had to stay late, she'd miss her bus to the station. Mum would go mental.

'I'll do it with you,' said Steph, when Hutton had stalked off to organise the five-a-side tournament.

Jess shook her head, not trusting herself to speak.

'I will,' insisted Steph loyally.

'You can't. You've got your maths grind tonight,' Jess reminded her in a shaky voice.

'Shit, yeah. Lucky you for having a dad who can give you grinds.' Steph was falling behind in maths and had extra lessons, nicknamed 'grinds', with a private teacher to coach her for the exams.

Jess grinned for the first time that afternoon. 'Dad doesn't believe in grinds. He thinks they're a sign of bad teaching.'

'What did he send you here for?' demanded Steph. 'Without grinds, the whole school would grind to a halt. Grind, geddit?'

'Funny ha ha,' sighed Jess.

'How about we go to the movies on Saturday?' suggested Steph after a moment. She was desperate to cheer Jess up.

'I mightn't be able to get away.' Jess sighed again. 'I'm babysitting for the Richardsons on Saturday night and Mum says I've got to get my study done in the afternoon.'

'Tell her you'll study when you're babysitting.'

By the time she'd put away all the sports equipment, Jess felt utterly weary. She'd have a bath at home rather than a shower in the creepily deserted girls' changing room, she decided, pulling her coat on over her gym gear. At the bus stop, she rang home to say she'd be late but nobody answered and the machine wasn't on. She was about to try her mother's mobile when the bus trundled along, packed to the gills with rush-hour commuters. There was no way she was going to have one of those childish conversations along the lines of 'I'll be late, Mum, don't worry' with a packed bus listening, so she found the last seat upstairs, switched on her Discman and turned the sound up.

The train was packed too. Every seat was taken and bad-tempered passengers with briefcases, pushchairs and bags of shopping were crammed into every available gap.

With nowhere to sit, Jess squeezed into a space against the wall at the end of the carriage, her bag at her feet, and tried to drown out the boredom of the journey with music. When she looked up, she saw the guy from the year above pushing a path through the crowd to get a space and, incredibly, Jess thought for one minute that he smiled briefly at her. Tired, crampy and fed up, she wasn't going to risk smiling back and looking stupid, in case she'd imagined it. But then he made his way across the compartment and leaned against the last bit of free wall in Jess's section. This time she knew she

101

hadn't imagined the rueful smile, so she sent him a fleeting one back, before dropping her gaze again. Wow! It was the first bit of light in an otherwise horrible day.

But it was to be the only bit of light. When the train lumbered into Dunmore station, chugging even more slowly than usual with its enormous load of disgruntled commuters, Jess could see her mother standing anxiously on the platform, all wrapped up in that ridiculous chocolate fake-fur coat she loved. Her eyes were frantically searching every carriage as the train pulled in.

'Jess!' she shrieked, rushing forward to grab her daughter when Jess stepped wearily down onto the platform. 'I've been so worried. I tried to phone and there was no answer on your mobile . . .'

Jess glared at her to shut up, but Abby was far too relieved even to be aware that she was making a scene.

'Chill, Mum,' snapped Jess. 'I did phone to say I'd be late but you weren't there and the machine wasn't on.'

Trying to disentangle herself from her mother, Jess could see the guy from her school loping off down the platform towards the footbridge. He'd never smile at her again, that was for sure. Not now that her mother had made it plain that she was a kid who wasn't safe to let stay five minutes behind after school. Cool guys in fifth year didn't hang around with kids.

'Why didn't you answer your phone?' demanded Abby.

'Didn't hear it,' muttered Jess.

'You shouldn't have your Discman so loud that you don't hear the phone,' her mother said loudly. 'Have you any idea how worried I was?'

'For God's sake,' Jess said furiously, 'everybody's watching. You're not on bloody TV now.'

They drove home in frosty silence, even the lively banter from the drive-time DJ failing to crack the ice.

Abby, who'd felt guilty about her little detour into the past with Jay, and had been wondering if she should tell Tom, and who'd raced to the station after getting home and finding Jess hadn't returned from school, was furious with her daughter for not phoning to say she'd be late.

What had happened to Jess, she thought grimly. Her lovely, smiling daughter had been replaced by this sullen, angry teenager who bit her mother's head off every time she spoke. What had Abby done wrong? Or, she thought suddenly, was there something bothering Jess, something serious?

She tried again when they got home.

'So how was school?' she asked brightly.

Jess thought of the awfulness of the day and stupid Mr Hutton picking on her unfairly. Worse was what the boys had said to her. It wasn't her fault she was tall, lanky and flat-chested. She wanted to ask her mother how she'd been when she was a teenager, but then her mother was small and pretty and confident. How could she know how Jess felt? Mum was always going on about how she wished her boobs were smaller because she hated looking 'busty'. How unfair was that?

'We've got tons of homework,' Jess said, which was true. 'How are we supposed to revise anything when we've all this work to do?' she demanded, wrenching the fridge door open. She deliberated and then took out some cheese and made herself a sandwich.

Abby felt a surge of relief. That was the reason behind Jess's bad temper: nothing more sinister than too much homework.

'They wouldn't give you homework unless they thought you needed it,' said Abby, ever the deputy headmaster's wife. 'And you won't want to eat your dinner if you eat that sandwich.'

'I'm not going to have time for dinner,' snapped Jess. 'I'll be doing my homework.' With that, she stormed upstairs.

'Sorry, Jess,' Abby yelled in contrition after her. 'I didn't mean it like that, but the teachers know you have to get the courses finished before the exams, and I know it's hard right now but it will be worth it in the end . . .'

The only reply she got was the slamming of Jess's bedroom door.

Abby began to make Jess's favourite dish, a vegetarian lasagne that took ages to prepare. If Abby couldn't get through to Jess to tell her how much she loved her, she'd show her.

The lasagne was cooling, untouched despite many calls upstairs, and Abby had given up and gone into the living room to eat a forbidden packet of crisps and watch the soaps when Tom arrived home.

'How was your day?' he asked, throwing his bulging briefcase onto one of the armchairs.

'Don't ask,' she said, and was about to elaborate on what a precious little madam her client had been and how Jess was upset over her homework and how terrible Abby felt when she couldn't communicate with her, and guess who she'd bumped into today, but Tom didn't give her a chance to continue. He was just aching to talk about *his* day.

'I know the feeling,' he muttered, loosening his tie and throwing that onto the armchair to join the briefcase. 'Some joker in second year set the fire alarm off this afternoon and we couldn't turn it off. Seems the expensive new system we got in last year has a fault and we had to get a guy out from the company who installed it to deal with it. And then,' Tom sank onto the other armchair, 'Gina, you know, the new physics and maths teacher, tells me she can't cope and she wants to hand in her notice. She didn't think teaching boys was going to be as hard as it's turned out. Stupid cow. And I swear that Bruno always takes the day off just when there's trouble brewing. He must be bloody psychic. He gets the headmaster's salary and no trouble, and I get the deputy head package and every bloody disaster possible.' He shifted in the seat to get comfortable and began to look around for the television remote. 'What's for dinner?'

Abby counted to ten. 'Vegetable lasagne,' she said evenly. She went into the kitchen, cut Tom a portion and stuck it in the microwave with a loud clatter. Adding some limp lettuce from the fridge and a few baby tomatoes she couldn't be bothered to wash, she dumped the whole lot on a tray and plonked it on the table in front of her husband.

'Thanks,' he grunted.

Abby got herself a second glass of wine and another packet of crisps, and went upstairs. She knocked tentatively on Jess's door.

'Hi, Jess, it's Mum. Can I get you anything?'

'No,' came the reply.

Abby went into their own room, switched on the TV and settled herself onto the bed with her snack. So much for the moral dilemma over telling her husband about Jay. She couldn't believe she'd even worried over it. Clearly Tom wouldn't have cared less if she'd pushed Jay up against the hot-water bottles in the chemist's, wrapped her legs around his waist and French kissed him while the people queuing for their haemorrhoid prescriptions watched. So long as Tom got his dinner and had someone to listen silently to his moans about his day, he didn't need anything else. Why bother telling him about her chance meeting with an old flame? If Jay rang to set up the foursome for dinner, then she'd mention it. For now, she'd just keep it to herself, along with that disturbing sensation she'd felt when Jay had touched her.

CHAPTER SEVEN

That weekend, Lizzie couldn't resist the roses at the Saturday market. Their velvety crimson petals were just beginning to unfurl and she thought how beautiful they'd look in the old crystal vase standing on the polished hall table. Throwing caution to the wind, she bought two bunches and was rushing down Main Street to her car, face framed with the fat bouquets, when Mrs Hegarty, one of the surgery's most constant visitors, appeared from the post office.

'Oh, Lizzie, what beautiful flowers,' cooed the old lady.

'Aren't they?' said Lizzie, admiring them. They didn't smell, not like her own roses, but those wouldn't be out for ages and there was something so nice about coming home to that flush of rosy colour.

'From someone special, I hope?' continued Mrs Hegarty.

Lizzie grinned. 'You could say that,' she joked, but before she could point out that the someone special was herself, Mrs Hegarty had taken a wild leap to the wrong conclusion.

Her tiny wrinkled face, round as a crab apple, softened. 'Ah, dear Myles. Give him our regards. It's lovely the way you two meet up and stay such friends.' Mrs Hegarty's sloe eyes twinkled. 'We're all always hoping that you pair will see sense and get back together again.'

'Well, I am going to meet him,' began Lizzie because Myles had asked to see her urgently, and for once he hadn't said what it was about. They didn't meet that often, although they spoke on the phone about the kids, but today's meeting sounded different. What had he said? 'I've something I need to talk to you about.'

But Mrs Hegarty's mind had moved on to the absorbing subject of her husband's varicose veins.

'They're at him again and he's tormented with them. I said, if only you'd wear support stockings, Liam, I said, you'd be fine, but oh no, men don't wear them, he said. So I said . . .'

Mrs Hegarty's monologue went on and Lizzie waited patiently. Some of the people in Dunmore considered her on a par with the doctor, as if all Dr Morgan's years of medical training had somehow rubbed off and Lizzie was perfectly able to diagnose all manner of illnesses.

'He should call in to the surgery,' Lizzie said, as she always did. 'I should rush, Mrs Hegarty, I'll be late.'

'Ah.' Mrs Hegarty was all smiles at the thought of Lizzie rushing to see her ex. What with that and the confusion over the flowers, it would be all over town that the Shanahans were getting back together. Lizzie sighed. Chinese whispers was Dunmore's favourite occupation. But she was smiling as she bade Mrs Hegarty a fond goodbye.

As she drove out of town with the ancient Golf clanking gears noisily, Lizzie's eyes were drawn to the bouquet lying on the passenger seat. Myles had never been much of a man for flowers. He liked to buy either practical presents or gift vouchers.

'What's the point in me buying you a fleet of things you don't need,' he'd smile, 'when I can get you a voucher and you'll pick out what you really want?'

It had made perfect sense to Lizzie. Men hated shopping. The world and his wife knew that.

In a small Italian coffee shop scented with amaretti biscuits and freshly crushed coffee beans, Myles waited for Lizzie. He'd attempted to speed through the crossword but he was just too nervous. Throwing the paper down on the seat beside him, he fiddled with his Palm Pilot, counting how many months there were until Debra's wedding. Three and a half. Three and a half months to sort it all out and hope the whole family could come to terms with his news.

He hadn't planned for it to happen. Well, who'd have thought it would? Certainly not Myles. When he and Lizzie had split up, he hadn't thought he'd meet anyone else. That hadn't been on his radar at all and it wasn't why he'd left Lizzie.

Male friends all assumed he'd wanted out of his marriage because he was bored and wanted to be footloose and fancy free. But it wasn't that. Myles and Lizzie had had to get married and for all his married life Myles had thought of a time in the future when he'd have done his duty and could do what he wanted to in life. He didn't regret a second of his family life, it was just that he knew there were sides of himself that he could never express with Lizzie and he wanted to explore these while he still had the courage. Freedom to be his own person had been the spur – not the freedom to make notches on his bedpost. The very notion of that was ridiculous. Myles had no illusions about his chances of turning into Warren Beatty once he was no longer married. His appearance reflected his character: understated.

Joe managed to make the Shanahan male pattern baldness look interesting by keeping his receding thick dark hair short and wearing trendy black-rimmed glasses and casual chic clothes. But Myles would never be a trendsetter. He was a laid-back sort of man with an air of quiet intensity. And women, according to those male friends who'd tried to take him in hand when he and Lizzie had split up, were not mad for quietly intense, divorced civil servants with meagre wallets.

That was fine by Myles. He wasn't expecting wild passion. Despite all this, he'd met Sabine, thought she was gorgeous and, incredibly, it transpired that she was interested in him. He was fitter than he'd ever been, tanned from his time on the ocean. And the contentment he felt in his new life must have shown on his face, lending him an attractiveness he hadn't had in years. But he was still pleasantly surprised that she appeared to like him so much. He had acted as if they were just friends at first, like all the others on the scuba-diving course. For four weekends, the group of ten had driven in the minibus to Donegal to stay in the hostel and get their dives in, laughing and joking, retiring to the pub for song-filled evenings. He'd liked Sabine, was touched by her shyness and by how her light, pure voice wobbled with nerves when it was her turn to sing alone, but how she still entered into the whole thing with gusto. He'd liked the way her pale freckled skin looked almost translucent in the clear Donegal light, and he liked the way she smiled at him . . .

The door of the café opened and Lizzie whirled in, her cheeks flushed from running. Lizzie was always rushing. Myles's earliest memories of her were as a laughing school-girl hurrying to class, weighed down with an enormous schoolbag, her hair flying. She might have been a lot older now, but the hair was still the same, a shoulder-length mop of shaggy curls, and she still had a big bag, this time an elderly leather one she'd had for donkey's years. Lizzie's bag used to be a family joke.

'The kitchen sink bag,' Joe would tease her, hoisting it up and pretending to groan under the weight. 'No wonder you've good muscles, Mum, from lugging this around.'

'Sorry I'm late,' Lizzie gasped, reaching his table. 'Couldn't park the car.'

Now that she was here, Myles felt the desire to tell her his news and disappear. His stomach churned with anxiety.

'You've finished your coffee, shall I get you another?' she said cheerily.

Myles nodded.

When she got back with fresh coffee, he'd nervously rolled and rerolled his empty sugar packets up into two taut lengths.

'How are things?' asked Lizzie, licking her cappuccino spoon. 'I bet this is about the wedding. I had Debra on the phone last night raging over the band. It seems they've been asked to sing at a huge Abba convention in Germany and they're desperate to get out of doing the wedding. Luckily, Barry got a receipt from them when he paid the deposit and he says that's as good as a contract. Honestly, there's more drama in this wedding than in the Opera House!'

She looked up at Myles, her face still rosy from her hectic dash, her big chocolate-brown eyes shining and with a frothy line of cappuccino beading her upper lip. Myles felt like someone about to club a baby seal. He'd never forget how hurt and bewildered she'd been when he'd told her he wanted a divorce. He'd been so sure she'd be as eager as he was. But Lizzie, brave, resilient Lizzie, had dealt with it and now he was about to deliver another blow. He owed it to her to tell her about Sabine before all Dunmore rushed up to the house with the news that he'd been seen holding hands with a fair-haired, freckle-faced woman.

'I'm seeing someone, Lizzie,' he said, staring down at his rolled-up sugar packets.

'Seeing someone,' she repeated, as if she hadn't quite heard correctly and was hoping he'd contradict her.

'Yes.' Myles chanced looking at her. The merriment was gone from her face and it was as if she'd closed the shutters on her sparkling eyes. 'I met her at the scuba-diving course. I'm sorry but I had to tell you.'

'You don't have to be sorry. Why should you?' Lizzie said, shocked. 'We're divorced, you don't even have to tell me.'

Myles with another woman? She was more than shocked, she felt utterly stunned. When he'd left, he'd told her it wasn't for some middle-aged chance at fresh love and she'd believed him. Now this. But she wouldn't show Myles how shocked she was – no way. She'd hide her hurt.

'In fact, it's none of my business what you do any more,' she added tartly.

'I wanted to tell you before anyone else did. You know what Dunmore is like for gossip and if someone saw Sabine and me somewhere and told you before I did, well . . .'

'Well what?' she demanded, abandoning all attempts to hide how she felt. 'You were afraid I'd be embarrassed

110

or humiliated or upset? I've been all those things, Myles.' Lizzie's voice had become shrill and Myles could sense the other coffee shop customers watching them with interest. 'I was embarrassed and upset when you left me but I dealt with it. And now this.' She stopped talking, as though all the breath had left her lungs.

'It was bound to happen to one of us, Lizzie,' Myles said, hoping to comfort her, conveniently forgetting that he hadn't planned to fall in love again.

Lizzie's gaze caught his. 'It wasn't bound to happen to me,' she said fiercely. 'What did you say her name was?'

Myles hadn't meant to tell her the name, but he realised now that he had. 'Sabine.'

'Very exotic,' Lizzie said shakily. Grabbing her handbag from the chair beside them, she got up. 'I have to go. I hope you'll be very happy.' And she was gone, handbag banging off a table as she rushed for the door.

On the street, Lizzie allowed herself to slow down. Myles wouldn't rush after her, she knew that. He wasn't the sort of man who ran after people. Or perhaps he was, but only if Sabine was the one who'd left him sitting in a café so abruptly.

Her name sounded exotic, all right. Not like good solid Lizzie, reliable Lizzie who could be told anything and not lose her temper. But she wanted to lose her temper now. She wanted to scream and yell because it was so unfair. She'd been a good person. She'd behaved like a grown-up and hadn't raged or spread malicious rumours when Myles had left her. She hadn't become a paid-up member of the local ex-wives' group – nicknamed the Harridans by Clare Morgan – praying for famine, pestilence and penile gangrene to hit him.

She'd got on with her life with quiet dignity and where had it got her? Absolutely nowhere. Myles had someone else and she had no one.

She reached the car park and marched up to the automated ticket machine. Fumbling in her handbag for her ticket, she dropped it and her change purse, which was half open. Coins rolled off everywhere like freed lab rats making a dash for freedom.

'Bugger,' said Lizzie viciously. She never usually swore. She scrabbled around and found the ticket, and some of the coins. 'Double fucking bugger.' For good measure she kicked the ticket machine, not caring that it hurt her toe in her soft leather boots. Shock had left her beyond pain.

The couple of young mothers with pushchairs behind her gasped. Lizzie snatched her ticket from the jaws of the machine and whirled around, glaring at the women.

'Bloody fucking men!' she growled, and stomped off to the lift.

Lizzie's wild rage lasted for days. On the plus side, it meant that she cleaned out the attic and the spare bedroom the way local decluttering guru Abby Barton was always telling people to do. As she grimly went through the pieces of her life, Lizzie wondered did Abby ever envision people throwing out stuff because their ex-husband had just found himself a new love? Probably not, Lizzie thought, jettisoning whole bagfuls of precious cards and mementoes of her marriage, including the faded ribbon from her wedding bouquet.

'I. Don't. Want. You,' she said staccato as she held the once-pink ribbon over the bin bag, snipping it viciously into inch-long pieces with her kitchen shears. Photos of the wedding followed, along with a big pile of the cards Myles has given her over the years. Her courage faltered at the sight of one birthday card that wasn't even a 'To my darling wife on her birthday' one. Just a plain 'Happy Birthday' type with badly painted lilies on the front, the sort of card you'd give to someone you didn't like but who, inexplicably, always sent *you* birthday cards. The legend inside in Myles's writing read: 'Hope you like the saucepans.'

Saucepans. Lizzie remembered that birthday. Ten years ago, about. Her thirty-ninth, because Myles had bought her a clothes voucher for her fortieth, she remembered. She still had the saucepans. Heavy stainless steel with a lifetime guarantee, they were built to last. Unlike her and Myles.

For a moment, she didn't know which one of them she was angrier with: herself, for being so hopelessly unable to read the signs; or Myles, for daring to give her saucepans for a birthday.

The minus side of Lizzie's temper meant she was too wound up every night to sleep and ended up tossing and turning until she gave in, switched both the lamp and the bedroom TV on, and watched black-and-white cable movies until dawn.

Debra was no help. She hadn't known about Sabine but she didn't sound too put out by the news that her father had a woman in his life.

'Well, Mum, you've got to move on, you've got to forget the pain, haven't you? That's what I always say,' Debra told her in the misty tones of the oracle.

Lizzie, who'd never noticed even the faintest ability in Debra to forget pain and move on, had to bite her tongue to remind her daughter how long it had taken her to move on after the débâcle of leaving nursing college. For at least two years after she'd flunked her first year, Debra had burst into noisy tears at the first sign of a medical drama on television. Joe was the only member of the family who hadn't rushed in to comfort her, pointing out with great practicality that if Debra had studied instead of being out partying with junior doctors for the whole of her first year, she might have got through. Naturally, this wasn't a very popular theory with Debra.

'You don't understand,' she'd wail, reaching for a tissue. 'I did my best. It just got to me. You have to have a hard core to be a nurse. I'm too sensitive.'

Debra's much-vaunted sensitivity wasn't evident now her mother needed it.

'It's been five years, Mum,' she said matter-of-factly after Lizzie had sobbed her heart out while telling the story. 'You have to move on.'

How could her mother be so selfish, anyhow? She, Debra, was the one who needed support. She was the one who was organising a wedding, single-handedly almost, and coping with all sorts of crises. Barry's stupid sister had finally been persuaded into the expensive bridesmaid's dress but due to some frantic comfort eating, the dress – violet taffeta with a scooped neck edged with violet silk rosebuds – was now too tight. Sandra would need a shoehorn and Vaseline to get her into it. Debra had offered her some laxatives but Sandra had turned her snub nose up at them. Well, if she wanted to look like Miss Piggy in a marquee, that was her business. Debra vowed that the flower girls would station themselves in front of Sandra for the bridesmaids' photos. How could her mother be making such a fuss with all this going on? Didn't she realise that the most important day of Debra's life was in less than four months?

Gwen had been much more practical. 'Come on the cruise with me and Shay,' she'd urged again. 'We'll lend you the money. You might meet a tall, dark, handsome stranger. Although,' Gwen added thoughtfully, 'I hear the ratio of women to men is two to one on this cruise, so I might have to work hard to hold on to Shay!'

'Running away isn't the answer,' Lizzie said dully, not even amused by the notion of any woman other than Gwen being keen on Shay. The idea of running away was actually very appealing but she was terribly broke and the leaky roof in the kitchen was getting worse. 'I'm fine, Gwen, honestly.'

Although Gwen could see that her sister was anything but fine, she realised that Lizzie needed to be left to lick her wounds in peace.

In an unguarded moment, Lizzie told the truth to Clare Morgan, who couldn't fail to notice how miserable Lizzie was at work, and who'd asked if everything was OK.

'You mustn't let that get to you,' Clare said briskly when she'd heard. 'It's a shock when your ex moves on but I hope you haven't been harbouring hopes of getting back together, Lizzie. That never works. You've a busy social life, though, haven't you? You don't need him. Get out there and have fun. You're in your prime, Lizzie. Don't become old before your time just because it's easier to sink into lethargy.'

'Yes,' said Lizzie weakly, wishing she hadn't been quite so successful in her attempts to convince Clare that she too was a divorced, free and single woman. Clare was a go-getting sort of person and would never understand that Lizzie's life hadn't moved on since Myles had moved out. Everything was still exactly the same except now she cooked for one.

The phone in the surgery rang and Clare put her hand on it but didn't pick up the receiver. 'Lizzie, life's too short to waste it thinking about what might have been. Look at all the people who come through this surgery who aren't going to make it, like poor Maurice Pender. Things don't look good for him and he'd do anything to have life stretching ahead of him.' She picked up the phone.

'I know,' said Lizzie as she left Clare alone to talk to her patient, but she was only saying that she understood the doctor's point. She felt sorry for poor Mr and Mrs Pender but even that didn't dull her own misery.

At home that evening, Lizzie sat down in front of the soaps with chicken and pasta on a tray on her lap. Somehow, she couldn't concentrate on the television. Clare Morgan's words kept exploding into her consciousness like a nagging headache that wouldn't go away.

Don't become old before your time just because it's easier to sink into lethargy.

Lethargy was just what Lizzie was in the mood for. She felt too down to want to make any decisions, but perhaps it was time for decisions. A new life or the comfortable but lonely old one? It was like being a heroine at a crossroads in a weird fairy story. In one direction lay middle age with panty girdles, beige cardigans and big plaid skirts like the ones her granny used to wear. In the other lay a new life with men like Myles, the ones who'd been trapped in unhappy marriages and were only waiting for a quick sail around the harbour on a 24-footer before leaping into bed with someone new.

But in fairy stories, there was always a sign about which road to take. Cute elves would appear singing mystically and pointing their elvish fingers, or the only rabbit in the company would twitch its whiskers and refuse to go in the direction of the big dark tower with the flames pouring out of the top. In real life, the choice was murkier. And there were no signposts.

How did you know which road to take?

And if she took the one without the granny underpinnings, what hope did she have of attracting anything in trousers? Lizzie put her tray down and stared at herself critically in the big mirror over the fireplace. She'd never been able to do anything with her shaggy hair. Her face wasn't actually that lined, mainly because of the oily, olive skin that had tortured her with spots when she was a teenager. She liked her merry brown eyes, but hated the rosy cheeks that always made her look enthusiastic instead of pale and interesting.

And her boobs, once one of her best attributes, were no longer what could be described as perky. To cheer herself up, she thought of the joke of the ninety-nine-year-old woman who wanted to shoot herself in the heart, was told it was to the right of her left nipple and ended in hospital with a gunshot wound to her left knee. The same could be said for this forty-nine-year-old, Lizzie thought ruefully.

She sat back down and flicked through the channels until she came to a taut medical drama she liked. Lots of blood, trauma and pain. Other people's pain. Excitement was much easier to handle, Lizzie reflected, if you got it through the tube rather than in your own life. But sitting at home and box-watching did rather mean that you missed out on Life, with a big L.

CHAPTER EIGHT

Greg and Erin Kennedy were not the sort of people to let life pass them by – not when they could go out and grab it firmly with both hands.

When Greg's mum developed really bad flu and the planned Kennedy family reunion scheduled for Dunmore had to be put off for a few weeks, Greg and Erin decided to take advantage of the day's holiday Greg had taken.

They quickly booked a small hotel in Glengarriff, packed their walking gear in the suitcase along with some glad rags, and set off for a weekend of sightseeing and climbing mountains.

It was two years since they'd last done any climbing. Greg pointed out that a week's hiking along the Appalachian Trail didn't count. 'That wasn't a trek, that was an amble through the woods!' he said. The long weekend in the Rockies was their last serious trek, in his opinion.

Erin remembered the ache in her muscles after the trip to the Rockies and she hadn't expected the same level of sheer exhaustion in the beautiful Kerry mountains. But, somehow, she felt worn out before they'd even begun.

On Saturday morning, by the time Greg decided it was OK to stop for a break, Erin felt tired enough to lie down and sleep.

'Come on, slowcoach. You're nearly there. Just another few yards. I've got the chocolate opened . . .'

'If you eat it all, I'll kill you,' panted Erin as she hauled herself up the steep excuse for a path, side-stepping sheep droppings shaped bizarrely like tiny bunches of grapes, to arrive at the rocks where Greg was laying out their picnic.

'I am so wrecked. How high did you say this mountain was?'

She slumped down onto a small rock, stretching out her legs and leaning against a bigger rock, with her rucksack as a cushion for her back. This was ridiculous; she couldn't believe how exhausted she felt. Where was the athletic woman who used to daydream about the pair of them tackling something serious, like Everest?

Greg handed her a square of chocolate and then poured out a plastic cup of coffee from the Thermos.

'High enough to work off all this food on the way down,' he said, unwrapping the hefty cheese and ham sandwiches the landlady of the Mountain Arms Hotel had given them that morning before they'd set off. 'Just look at the view. Isn't it fantastic?'

Erin sighed with pleasure. They weren't at the top yet, but already acres of steep slope stretched out beneath them, covered with waves of pinky purple azaleas that flowered amid the gorse and bracken. To the right were the brooding shapes of more of the Kerry mountains, splayed haphazardly northwards towards Kenmare. The landscape below looked beautiful, untamed and desolate. Only the telephone poles and the odd house tucked away in the valley among the trees spoke of civilisation.

Far below lay the road where they'd parked the car – a rackety grey road just wide enough for two vehicles to pass, but from this great height, it looked nothing more than a winding dark line on a child's picture.

Despite the early April sunshine, which made everyone in Glengarriff insist it was 'a fabulous day for the time of year', it was cold on the mountain and Erin was glad of the steaming hot coffee. She was wearing a heavily padded skiing jacket, lined hiking trousers, thick socks with her walking boots, and a hat that was squashing her ponytailed hair, but she could still feel the chilly wind.

When they'd eaten everything in his rucksack, Greg sat beside Erin on her rock and put his arm round her. He hadn't bothered to shave that morning and when he rubbed his cheek against hers, she felt the spiky beard rough against her face.

The combination of designer stubble, a soft grey hat pulled down over his hair and the pale sun glinting against his sunglasses gave him the look of some glamorous French skier who'd just come down a black run.

'Wasn't this a great idea to come away for the weekend?' he said.

Erin kissed him on the cheek. 'Yes,' she agreed. 'We really needed the break. I'm sorry about your poor mum, but it's nice to get away all the same, isn't it? And we can have the big family reunion soon.'

'Erin,' began Greg, 'we've been here nearly a month . . .' He paused.

Erin stilled. She knew what was coming. Greg didn't disappoint.

'Don't you think it's time to visit your family or at least make contact?'

She said nothing but dug out another chocolate bar from the side pocket of her rucksack. Did he really think she could just phone up after nine years and think everyone would be thrilled to hear her voice?

'OK, OK, forget I said anything,' Greg apologised. 'I don't want to ruin the day.'

'No, don't,' begged Erin. 'We're here for the weekend to forget about everything: the pressures of your job, the non-pressures of my non-existent job and the horrible rented house. And I know you're on the rental agency's case and they're going to find us a mansion soon, but it is horrible.'

'Right, we're here to forget,' he agreed, and took a big slab of chocolate. 'I think we've been sitting here too long. I'm getting cold and stiff.'

'Me too,' admitted Erin. 'Can we phone mountain rescue and get them to helicopter us back?'

Greg pretended to think about this. 'I think they prefer to be called out in genuine emergencies and not to airlift lazy, fat tourists down to their cars so they can head back to their hotels for more Irish coffees.'

'Who are you calling fat?' Erin ripped the last piece of chocolate from Greg's hand and shoved it in her mouth with a wicked smirk.

'Oh, not you! But since you've eaten everything, we'd better go.' Greg got to his feet and put out a hand to haul Erin up. 'I'm afraid we've a bit further up to go before we're on the way down.'

They walked in silence, Erin reserving her energy for the hike rather than wasting her breath talking. As she climbed steadily, she couldn't help her mind slipping off the path in front of her and back to her estranged family in Dublin.

Greg didn't understand her reluctance to go home. He was a black-and-white sort of person. Families loved each other and no stupid argument, no matter how bitter, should stop people from being there for each other.

But a long time had passed since she'd left. Erin knew she'd changed beyond all recognition. She was a different person from the angry eighteen-year-old who'd packed her suitcase and stormed out of her home one evening. What really scared her was what if everything else had changed too in the years she'd been away? What if her grandparents had died? Erin wouldn't let herself think about that.

Kerry was eleven years older, so she'd be thirty-eight now, maybe married with kids, or maybe not. Kerry's love life had never run smoothly. She looked a lot like Erin, without the red hair but with the same long nose. Dad used to joke that Kerry, who had mousy hair dyed blonde, had got the red hair temperament. He'd been right. However the rest of the family reacted, Kerry would find it hard to forgive Erin.

The landlady of the Mountain Arms Hotel was attractive and middle-aged, with a genial manner and shrewd eyes. Meg Boylan had come to the Mountain Arms thirty years before when she'd married the proprietor's son, Teddy. Then, the hotel had been a family concern with just ten rooms and a small clientele who hadn't minded the shabby décor or the fact that the rooms were often cold. Thanks to Meg's hard work and drive, the Mountain Arms was now a thriving business with thirty rooms, a spacious, high-ceilinged room for weddings, a cosy bar named The Devil's Elbow and a small but elegant dining room called The Haven. Teddy, God bless him, was no help at all when it came to running the hotel, although it had taken Meg several years to discover this after his parents retired.

Nowadays, Teddy made an enjoyable daily circuit between the bookies and a small corner of The Devil's Elbow where he liked to peruse the racing pages and sip a couple of small ones.

'I like to make sure everything's run all right in the bar,' he told people cheerily when they enquired about his part in keeping the hotel running smoothly.

This left Meg free to run her empire, keeping a careful eye on the kitchens, not to mention overseeing the hotel's staff. She enjoyed being on the front desk and had long since realised that valued customers felt even more valued if they got a welcome from the proprietor herself.

She'd been on the desk when the young couple from Dunmore had arrived and found there was something refreshing about the way they'd laughed when she'd asked if they were newlyweds.

'We're married four years,' grinned the husband.

'And we can't afford the bridal suite this time, I'm afraid. The budget won't allow it,' added his wife. 'Not that that's going to affect our enjoyment.' She patted her husband's arm affectionately.

They had that glow of the just-married about them, Meg thought. And she admired them for their candour in admitting that they weren't in funds.

'Let's see what we've got for you,' she said, checking the hotel's computer, a machine she adored, even though Teddy wouldn't go within an ass's roar of it. The hotel had a bridal suite, which was the biggest room, with a pretty sitting room that looked out over the bay, and a four-poster bed draped with crimson and gold brocade decorated with medieval bower scenes, including maidens, unicorns and woodland glades. It wasn't booked until the following week when the Gerrard/O'Shea wedding party would take over the entire hotel.

Marriage to Teddy had long since drummed the romance out of Meg but the Kennedys had touched her heart.

'I have just the room for you,' she said. 'It's an upgrade but it's the same price as we originally agreed upon.'

The Kennedys grinned at each other. 'Thank you,' they said.

Meg's face softened as she smiled back at them. Wait till they saw the room.

Greg and Erin adored their luxurious suite, and when they got back from their hike they wanted to do nothing more than throw themselves onto the voluptuously soft bed, but they were both mud-splattered. In the bathroom, they stripped off their dirty clothes and Erin began to run a bath.

'I'll seize up if I don't soak,' she said, adding some of the hotel's lavender bath oil.

'Can I join you?' begged Greg.

Erin took a look at the bath. Greg was such a giant that most tubs were too snug a fit on him, and as for sharing a bath . . . forget it. But this elderly claw-footed creation was obviously built for large people who liked a bit of space to move around. It could have accommodated three at a push.

'We might go through the ceiling underneath,' Erin teased, as she tested the water with a toe, 'but why not?'

They lay back, luxuriating in the hot, scented water, feeling stiff muscles unknot.

'Is that your foot?' demanded Erin as she felt something prodding her ribs. 'No tickling.'

'Spoilsport.' Greg sank deeper into the water and Erin could feel his toes wriggling under her armpit, insistent and ticklish.

'We've got the bridal suite – we've got to do things like this,' he pointed out, still burrowing.

'Like this, you mean,' Erin retorted, sliding under the water, making him jerk upright when her big toe made contact with his groin. Laughing, her hair clinging to her like a water nymph, she sat up and shook the water from her head.

'You wanna play, missy?' Greg said, grabbing her ankles and hauling her through the water onto his lap.

'Is the periscope up?' Erin murmured into his neck.

'Nearly. Why don't we try dry land?' Greg said, his fingers finding the slippery nubs of her nipples.

Erin clambered out of the bath and wrapped a bath sheet around her, drying herself carefully. No point in drowning the bed too. Out of the bath, the steaming hot water began to have its narcoleptic effect. The bed, when they pulled off the coverlet, looking so inviting and so soft. Erin had suddenly never felt so tired and warm and soothed in her life.

'What a bed. Can we buy one like this?' Erin moaned as she lay down.

'Wouldn't it be wonderful?' yawned Greg, bashing his pillow a bit to get it right. 'It's so comfortable. I slept like a log last night.'

They curled up beside each other, bodies entwined, Greg's right hand gently stroking the curve of Erin's back.

'We could have a little snooze,' Greg muttered, his stroking slowing down, 'to get our strength back.'

'A little snooze,' agreed Erin sleepily. 'Ten minutes.' She somehow raised her head to look at her watch on the bedside table. 'Ten to four. We'll snooze until four.'

'Or ten past . . .' Greg said.

The room was dark when Erin woke up and for a few scary seconds she couldn't remember where she was. Then she

heard Greg's steady breathing beside her and she remembered. She still felt tired after their climb but mentally
alert. Lying in the dark, she let the forbidden memories
fill her mind.

It had all happened because Erin wanted money for her
eighteenth birthday. She wanted money because she yearned
to travel, to see the world, and if she got enough cash together
to buy a round-the-world ticket, she could work her way
across the globe.

Mum was anxious about giving Erin cold cash as a gift.
'I wish you wanted a proper present and not money,' she
said sadly. 'With Kerry and Shan—' She stopped herself just
in time. She'd been about to say Shannon, who was Erin's
older sister – not that Erin really knew her, and Mum found
it difficult to talk about her.

Shannon had left home to live abroad when Erin had been
a baby and there was nothing but the odd postcard home to
remind people she was still alive. Erin hated Shannon for
what she'd done to Mum. Kerry said Shannon was a selfish
bitch who'd never cared who she'd hurt and that she'd turned
Mum's hair grey overnight.

'What did you get Kerry when she was eighteen?' Erin
asked brightly, determined to get her mother over the pain
of thinking of Shannon.

'Earrings, those gold and opal ones she wears for good.
Your father and I would have liked to get you something
you could have for ever,' Mum said. 'Money is soon forgotten, Erin.'

'I know, Mum,' Erin hugged her mother, 'but I want to
build up memories I can have for ever, and if everyone gives
me cash, I can. There are so many places I want to see – the
Far East, Australia, America . . .' There was a far-off look
in her amber eyes and her mother sighed because she knew
that wanderlust was in Erin's blood, just as it had been in
Shannon's.

The family had held a small party in an upstairs room of

a local pub and it had been a huge success. Toasts had been made, many pints had been consumed and Erin had drunk her first legal vodka and tonic.

She did get cash for her birthday – not enough for a round-the-world ticket, but enough to book a trip abroad. She didn't know where she wanted to go, just somewhere. She'd never been abroad and the family visit to a caravan park every other year had been fun but not what you'd call exotic. No, abroad, with all its exciting connotations, was what she wanted. Australia was too far and would cost a fortune, but India . . . Erin was fascinated by India and could just see herself there, backpacking and sleeping in shabby hostels, being one of the people. And she wouldn't get sick, no way. She had the constitution of an ox, as Mum used to say.

There was lots to plan for her trip, but the first thing was to get a passport. She'd collected a form, but the paperwork was interminable. She had to get photos signed by the police and an official copy of her birth certificate – not a photocopy, but a real one. She'd asked Mum for that and there she ran into a problem. Mum, who kept all the family documents in a shabby accordion file in her and Dad's room, said she'd look and then came back and said she couldn't find it.

Undaunted, Erin sent off for it.

A couple of weeks after her party, the certificate arrived. Erin shuffled downstairs in her Snoopy T-shirt and knickers and picked the post off the hall carpet. She had the house to herself, as Dad and Kerry were at work and Mum had gone shopping, popping in to Erin's room on the way to remind her that she couldn't lie in bed like a big slug all day.

In the kitchen, Erin slopped cornflakes into a bowl and looked at the post. None of it was ever for her but today was an exception. 'Ms Erin Flynn' was typed at the top of an official-looking envelope. She ripped it open and for a minute thought they'd sent the wrong certificate. The name was hers all right but the rest of it made no sense. Under 'Mother' was written 'Shannon Flynn', and that couldn't be right, and under 'Father' was the word 'Unknown'. The date was fine and everything, but the civil service people had clearly mixed it up. Absently, Erin ate some more cornflakes, still staring at this confusing bit of paper. And then the truth clicked in her head, like those magic eye puzzles she'd always found mystifying until one day she learned how to 'see' them. The form wasn't wrong. Shannon, whom she'd always thought was her mysteriously absent sister, was actually her mother. Kerry wasn't her sister but her aunt, and Mum and Dad weren't her parents. They were her mother's parents. Her grandparents. Granny and Granddad not Mum and Dad. It was all such a shock.

But as she sat there, dumbfounded, she realised that by far the most disturbing part was the fact that Mum had lied to her. Mum was the most trustworthy person in Erin's world. The first time Erin's heart had been broken by a boy from her class, Mum had held her close and promised that it would feel better soon. And Erin had believed her, even though her heart was breaking, because her mother had never lied to her. Until now. Her spoon clattered onto the linoleum but Erin didn't bother to pick it up. No, she'd been lying before now. Mum had been lying to her for all Erin's life.

She ran upstairs and found the suitcase on the top of her parents' big 1930s wardrobe. It was heavy, and dust bunnies danced off the top as she hauled it down. Inside were old clothes, including a huge brown coat she remembered her father wearing for years, and a couple of old shirt boxes, their former bright blue faded with age. The first contained cards and mementoes belonging to Mum. Erin couldn't bring herself to look through them in case she found her own childish home-made cards, painstakingly painted and glittered in school.

The second box held a few documents of the sort that were usually kept in the big accordion file. There was the original of the birth certificate Erin had just been sent, much-folded, and a few letters with photos lying in between the pages. Shannon, who'd been so absent in the family album, was the star here. Now Erin could see the resemblance between her and her mother. Both had the same sheet of coppery hair and the same smile, although Shannon's eyes looked blue like Kerry's and Mum's. Erin must have got her eyes from her father, whoever he was. The sense of outrage at not knowing her mother or her father hit her forcibly. How could Mum have never told her the truth about her birth? Did Kerry know too? Erin sat among the photos and letters from her real mother and brooded on lies and deceit. Then she gathered together her papers and her newly acquired cheque book and left the house.

By the late afternoon, when Erin returned, Kerry was home from work and Mum was in the kitchen mashing potatoes for shepherd's pie.

'Hello, love. Where have you been all day?' called Mum when she heard Erin's familiar tread on the stairs.

Erin didn't answer. She didn't trust herself to speak. In her room, she threw down the papers she'd picked up from the au pair agency, along with the plane ticket to Amsterdam. The flight was in three days but Erin didn't plan on waiting at 78 Carnsfort Terrace until then. She'd pick up her passport at the passport office the following day, a privilege that came from having pleaded an emergency situation and showing the official her plane ticket, and she'd asked her friend Mo, who'd just moved into a cramped flat in Smithfield with two other girls, if she could bunk down with her until it was time to leave the country. Packing wouldn't take long. All she had to do now was confront her mother and Kerry about why they'd never told her the truth.

The kitchen smelled familiar: the scent of good food mixed with the comforting tang of the lemon cleaner Mum used diligently. Kerry was sitting at the kitchen table, shoes off and her feet up on a chair as she read the evening paper. Mum had laid the table for dinner and was now relaxing in her chair with a cup of tea, sorting out the receipts in her purse.

'Hello, lazy bones. What did you do today while I was

working my fingers to the bone?' asked Kerry, not raising her eyes from an article about celebrity diets.

In reply, Erin dropped her passport office receipt onto the table.

'What's that?' asked Kerry, scanning the document. 'You applied for your passport?'

She didn't get it, Erin realised. But Mum did. Her mother's eyes locked with Erin's and anxiety was written all over her face.

'Why didn't you tell me?' Erin asked quietly.

'Tell you what?' demanded Kerry, finally looking up.

'Tell me that Shannon was my mother.'

'Oh.' Kerry swung her feet to the floor. So she *did* know, Erin realised, and that realisation made her even angrier. Kerry knew but she, the person it most affected, didn't.

'I had to send away for my birth certificate.' Erin was caustic. 'You said it was lost,' she said accusingly to her mother. 'You knew I'd find out, so why couldn't you tell me the truth?'

'Erin, stop making it such a big deal,' said Kerry, going to the fridge and peering in to see if there was anything there to stave off the hunger pangs until dinner.

'Stop making it such a big deal?' said Erin incredulously. 'It's not big, it's huge. It's the biggest secret of my life and you all knew. Have you nothing to say about it?' she asked Mum, who'd stayed silent.

Mum shook her head wordlessly.

'It's not her fault,' snapped Kerry, temper rising. 'Your bloody mother created all the hassle in the first place by screwing around and getting pregnant –'

'Don't blame her!' shrieked Erin. 'Don't you bloody dare. You could have told me and I'd have found her. I was her child and you all kept if from me. How fucking dare you? What gave you all the right to act as God and only tell me what you wanted?'

Her grandmother sat quietly at the table, holding her head in her hands as if to fend off the hurtful words.

'Talk to me, Mum,' yelled Erin. 'Why won't you talk to me?'

Her grandmother looked up at Erin's fiery, hurt face. 'I don't know what to say, love. I'm so sorry we hurt you but there never seemed to be a right time to tell you when you were small, and then you grew up so fast and the chance had passed.' She reached out a tired, work-worn hand and beckoned for Erin to take it. But Erin stared stonily at her, refusing the gesture of reconciliation.

'That's rubbish. You knew I'd find out one day.'

Her grandmother's eyes filled with tears. 'I knew you would but I hoped you'd be able to understand . . .'

'Understand what? That you lied to me about the most important thing in my life?'

Her grandmother had started crying then and Kerry had lost her temper, yelling that everyone assumed Erin knew, and how the hell could she blame anyone else for her stupidity. Still Mum cried and Erin couldn't bear her tears but couldn't comfort her either. She felt so betrayed that she had no comfort left in her for anyone else.

She'd packed up and left, taking only her clothes and a few photos. Everything else – her gold bracelet she'd been given by Mum and Dad for her Confirmation, the precious earrings Kerry had given her years before when her sister got her first full-time job – she left on the dusty dressing table.

For three days, she stayed with Mo, half hoping someone from the family would find her, half hoping they wouldn't. Then she got on a plane. After six months travelling the world, working her way through bars and restaurants, she ended up working as an au pair to an American family in Greece when their own au pair left suddenly. When they went home to Boston, she went too.

A gentle knocking at the door woke Greg. 'What the . . . ?' He sat up, his eyes sleep-filled, his cropped dark hair flattened against his skull from where his head had lain on the pillow.

The door opened a fraction and a pair of blue eyes peeked in. 'Do you want your bed turned down?' said a voice.

'No, thanks,' said Greg. He couldn't see anything except the light coming in through the slightly opened door. 'What time is it?'

'Ten to seven.' The door shut quietly and Greg fumbled for the bedside light.

'We've booked a table for seven,' he said, climbing out of bed. 'We should get ready.'

Erin sat up in the bed, her hair in the same through-a-bush-backwards condition as Greg's. She felt tired now and had no inclination to get up and dress for dinner. She lay down again and felt the old familiar misery envelop her. She and Greg should have stayed in Chicago. When she was there, she didn't think about her family in the same way. Well, she thought about them, but she could deal with the pain because of the distance. Or maybe it wasn't that at all. Maybe the difference was in her – because she certainly felt unlike her usual self here. She didn't want to be here any more. She wanted to be home. But then, where was home?

CHAPTER NINE

Home was a decidedly miserable place for the Barton family. By the end of the first week in April, with the Easter holidays in sight, Abby decided she must put the arguments of the past weeks behind her and do her best to raise everyone's spirits. Unfortunately, the emotional barometer in Lyonnais still sat firmly at 'mostly cloudy/storms expected'.

Jess was monosyllabic, despite Abby's attempts to start mother–daughter chats.

'I know you're stressed about school, Jess, love,' Abby said carefully, afraid she'd say the wrong thing, 'but the exams will pass. Your dad and I don't want you to feel under any huge pressure, right? We want you to do well for your sake but we don't want you to crack up over it.'

Jess had looked at her mother with an expression that said 'you don't understand a thing'. Abby hated that expression.

At Tom's school, the headmaster came down with a bad dose of flu, leaving Tom to deal with both the crisis over the physics teacher, who didn't want to work out her notice, and the faulty alarm system, which was still going off at odd intervals, to the pupils' delight.

All he could talk about every evening was the difficulty of getting a substitute teacher at short notice and the endless but vain attempts by the alarm repair people to find the fault in their sophisticated system.

Abby began to wonder whether, if she got a robot to sit at her place in the kitchen every night and programmed it to mutter, 'That's terrible,' at intervals, he would even notice.

To cheer herself up, she went to Sally's beauty salon for what Sally called 'the works'. Since she'd moved to Dunmore, Abby went to The Beauty Spot once a month, a luxury unheard of in the pre-*Declutter* days, when a trip to a salon like Sally's happened a couple of times a year.

The works included a manicure, an anti-ageing facial, possibly an eyelash tint and sometimes leg waxing, all the while chatting with Sally and letting the relaxing gossipy atmosphere drift round her. Other posher beauticians were now keen to get Abby to patronise their establishments but Abby stayed loyal to Sally and her jewel of a salon. Their friendship actually went back ten years to when Sally was working in Cork as a junior teacher with Tom. When Tom had raved about this new recruit and spoke of how she was a breath of fresh air in St Fintan's, Abby had half expected an earnest do-gooder with mousy hair, jam jar spectacles, bitten-down fingernails and a crush on Tom.

Sally turned out to be nothing like Abby's imaginings, of course, and far from being keen on Tom, she was wildly in love with Steve Richardson, the dashing Zhivago to Sally's Lara. Sally had left teaching long ago to follow her dream of setting up a beauty salon. She and Steve had been idealists and when he'd left the corporate world to teach art, Sally had taken the plunge and given up teaching to do a beauty course. The Beauty Spot was the result. With its fifties-inspired décor, complete with raspberry-pink gingham curtains, the salon was certainly different from the normal temples to beauty. The women of Dunmore loved it and, from its humble beginnings, the business went from strength to strength.

'What colour would you like?'

Sally's pixie face stared expectantly up at Abby's from behind the manicure trolley. Her fingers hovered over the creamy beige Abby usually favoured, because she insisted that her fingers were too short to take rich shades of polish.

But Abby was in a wild mood. 'That one,' she said, pointing out a juicy cherry colour.

'Femme Fatale,' Sally read the label. 'Gorgeous and very different.'

'I'm in the mood for something different,' murmured Abby.

After an hour relaxing as Sally's sensitive fingers did their anti-ageing magic, Abby was feeling light-headed and prone to day-dreaming. There was something so sensual about Sally's facials: when her gentle fingers massaged the heavenly, sweetly scented oils into Abby's face, neck and *décolletage*, she found herself thinking of how wonderful it would be to have Jay touching her skin like that. His fingers trailing along the sensitive hollows at the base of her throat, and her beautifully manicured fingers touching him in return . . .

'Have you ever thought of cheating on Steve?' said Abby idly now.

Sally looked up from the polish she was carefully applying to Abby's fingernails. 'Why?'

'Well . . . just . . . you know, seven-year itch,' blustered Abby, feeling caught out. Whatever had possessed her to say that?

'It's the three-year itch these days,' interrupted Ruby, who was doing a French manicure beside them. Ruby was a statuesque thirty-something with hair the colour of a raven's wing, a warm, eager face, and notoriously bad luck with men. Her last boyfriend had thrilled Ruby when he'd murmured how he'd never felt this strongly about any woman ever before, and two weeks later he'd ended up in bed with a girl in his office. 'I wouldn't mind, but she's not even thinner than me!' Ruby had raged for at least a month afterwards.

'He wasn't the right one for you, Ruby,' comforted Sally now, knowing that Ruby was reflecting on her ex. 'If he'd been the right one, he'd have been able to resist other women. Oh, sorry, Abby.' She wet a cotton bud in nail varnish remover to wipe away the splodge of cherry-pink polish that had dripped onto Abby's finger.

Abby, who knew it was her fault because she'd jerked convulsively at Sally's words, shook her head. 'My fault. I'm jittery today. Hormones, I suppose,' she lied.

'Steve wouldn't want to cheat on you, Sally,' Ruby went on mournfully. 'He really does cherish the ground you walk on. Until I met you pair, I thought that was just a cliché – a sickening cliché at that,' she teased, 'but now I know it can be true.'

Sally flushed to the roots of her hair. She was one of the few people Abby knew who could blush prettily: that creamy complexion flushed a delicate rosy pink, unlike Abby herself, who developed a wildly unflattering scarlet fever circle in the centre of each cheek at times of stress.

'Steve has his moments,' Sally said sternly.

Both Abby and Ruby burst out laughing at this.

'What?' demanded Sally.

'You never say a bad word about him, do you know that?' Abby said affectionately.

'Well, you never say a bad word about Tom,' countered Sally, recovering.

Abby felt the scarlet fever hit her face with vigour. It was all very well for Sally, she thought as she sat with her fingers splayed to dry. She and Steve were only married eight years, not seventeen numbing ones. Nobody could be expected to feel passionate about anyone or anything after seventeen years. Where was the excitement, the thrill?

Seventeen years of watching someone leave their socks on when they'd taken off their trousers, so they stood there in underpants and socks. Not a pretty sight. Women made such an effort with their underwear, trying thongs and low-slung pants that bypassed comfort utterly, but try getting a man to wear anything other than the boring sort of jocks he'd worn since the year dot.

And that way he cleared his throat when they were watching television that made him sound like an elderly sea lion coughing up a fishbone. Abby was convinced he didn't even know he did it but it was so irritating.

Wait till Sally and Steve had been together as long as she and Tom. Then Sally mightn't feel the same way.

'Dry?' Sally checked Abby's fingernails for tackiness. 'A minute more, I think. Now, Steve and I are throwing an impromptu party on Saturday and we'd love you to come – all of you, Jess included.'

'Lovely. What's the occasion?'

'It's to introduce Steve's new boss and his wife to the area. They've lived in the US for years and they don't know anyone here. I thought it would be nice, and this is the only weekend we can do it. He and Steve get on like a house on fire and Steve keeps saying Greg is taking the company places.'

Abby perked up. Sally and Steve's parties were legendary. They'd thrown one for Steve's birthday six months before. The police had come at three and politely asked for the music to be turned down. One man had put his back out showing everyone that he could still stand on his head, while even Abby, who'd planned to take it easy because she didn't know any of the people of Dunmore, had joined the drunken conga around Sally's tiny alpine rockery. Tom had the photographic proof: a picture of a glassy-eyed Abby clinging to a dwarf conifer, wearing a hastily improvised Carmen Miranda headdress of two bananas and an orange all tied up with a tea towel.

Spur-of-the-moment parties, the type Sally and Steve were so good at, were always fun.

'Their names are Erin and Greg Kennedy and they're lovely. You're going to love her, Abby,' Sally continued. 'She's funny, very warm and absolutely stunning-looking.'

Abby, who'd had a mental vision of a glossy corporate wife determined to patronise the inhabitants of Dunmore, was even more turned off by this description. Stunning-looking women made her feel insecure. She wasn't entirely sure that she'd like this paragon.

'Does she work?'

'She used to be something big in personnel in the States but she's not working yet. They're both Irish, both glamorous. Ruby has a crush on him.'

'He's something else,' Ruby sighed. 'If I didn't know from experience how painful it is when another bitch runs off with your man, I'd go for Mr Kennedy in a big way. We're talking double chocolate chip with real chocolate sauce.'

'That good?' said Abby, impressed. She'd bet that no matter how cute Greg Kennedy was, he couldn't be better looking than Jay Garnier.

She paid the bill, hugged Sally goodbye carefully so as not to smudge her nails, and left the salon. There were three messages on her mobile phone when she switched it on. One from Tom: 'Can you pick up my grey suit from the cleaner's? I've got a parent-teacher tomorrow night and I'll need it. Oh, I'll be late tonight. Half seven probably. I won't have eaten. See you then.' Abby felt the kernel of dissatisfaction inside her swell. What was she – chief cook and bottle-washer or a career woman who was responsible for their financial success? Tom's bloody deputy principal's salary wouldn't have bought them a house in Dunmore, that was for sure, and yet she was still the one hauling her ass all over town, buying groceries and picking up suits.

The second message didn't improve her temper. It was Cheryl, the production assistant from Beech. 'Hi, Abby, it's Cheryl. Sorry to bother you but there's been a change of plan on the shooting schedule next week. Instead of shooting in Dublin on Tuesday, Wednesday and Thursday, we're just doing Wednesday and Thursday. I'll phone you later in the week with the details and we'll change your plane ticket and hotel reservation. Byee.'

Why did things change now? Abby had had to reschedule a lucrative private decluttering job from Monday and Tuesday simply so she could fit in the TV show. The client hadn't minded but Abby had to delay the work several weeks, which she hated doing. If she hadn't been so irritated by the first two messages, she might not have responded to the last one.

'Hello, stranger. I can't stop thinking about meeting you.'

The gravelly, late-night sound of Jay's voice was so seductive. Abby put a finger in her mouth and nibbled her nail nervously, uncaring that she was ruining her polish.

'Do you think there's any chance we might have that dinner we promised ourselves? We've a lot to catch up on, after all. Please call, Abby. I'll be waiting.' He'd never even said who it was, she realised, but he'd known she'd recognise him. For a moment, she gazed out at the traffic, possibilities running through her head. Then she took a deep breath, hit the message button, and clicked until she reached 'return call'. When the phone had rung six times, Abby decided it was fate. She'd leave a polite message and tell him, no, she was busy, but maybe they'd have that dinner for the four of them one day, her and Tom and Jay and Lottie . . .

'Hello, Abby.' It was Jay.

'How did you know it was me?' she asked stupidly.

'I've got you programmed into my phone. Your name appears on the screen when you phone and I'm so glad you did.'

A silly grin spread across Abby's face at the thought of Jay going to the bother of programming her number into his phone.

'So, dinner?' he said easily. 'Just you and me, I mean.'

Abby suddenly felt grateful to Cheryl and didn't stop to think about how the chatty dinner for four had suddenly become an intimate dinner for two. 'I'm going to be in Dublin on Tuesday of next week. I was supposed to be filming, but I'm not,' she blurted. 'I mean, we could meet or –'

'We'll think of something,' he interrupted silkily and Abby felt that exquisite quiver of pleasure ripple through her body. 'Where are you staying?'

'McGregor's Townhouse,' bleated Abby. McGregor's was a small but beautifully formed hotel in the centre of Dublin. All the Beech staff stayed there and since the show had become successful, Abby somehow got the best room. Last time she stayed, she'd been upgraded to a junior suite, complete with cast-iron four-poster – an extravagance that she knew Beech had certainly not paid for. She must ask Cheryl to keep the reservation unchanged.

'I'll phone you there on Tuesday afternoon,' Jay said, and he was gone.

Abby was left staring at her phone, unsure as to whether guilt or wild excitement was the primary emotion surging through her heart.

To save petrol – and money – Lizzie started to walk to work. The first week of April turned out to be so glorious that the two-mile walk to the centre of town was a pleasure. On Friday, the forecasters had predicted record temperatures for the time of year, and even at half-past eight in the morning, the sun was warm, reminding Lizzie of holidays in foreign climes. As she walked past the tiny town park with her sunglasses on and only a light jacket over her shoulders, Lizzie could almost convince herself that she was on holiday. Somewhere exotic, like the Adriatic coast of Italy, where men appreciated women with a bit of meat on their bones. Years ago, she and Myles had been on holiday in Italy, and Lizzie's confidence had soared at the admiring looks she received from all and sundry.

Gwen and Shay were off on their cruise in a couple of days and despite everything she'd said, Lizzie was sorry she wasn't going with them. Imagine real sweltering sun on her face and the scent of coconut sun lotion on warmed, relaxed skin. She tried to put holidays out of her mind on the grounds that she couldn't afford one, and turned her thoughts instead to the wedding.

Debra, in tactful mode, had mentioned that Dad would like Sabine to come to the afters, which was the informal bit following the reception, when the band would play and people who hadn't been invited to the main event turned up to admire the happy couple. Only if Lizzie didn't mind, Debra added.

Lizzie minded like hell, but her mothering instincts came

to the fore as usual. 'Do *you* mind?' she'd asked Debra, worried that the introduction of another person into the family dynamics might upset Debra's big day. After all, Debra had been devastated about the divorce, and, as a true father's girl, she might find it a betrayal too far to see Myles with another woman.

'Well, I don't mind her being there. She's not pretty or anything,' Debra said blithely, content as long as her father's new girlfriend wasn't in danger of stealing her thunder on the day. 'She's got mousy, reddish hair, mousy eyelashes and doesn't wear lipstick. I saw a photo of her at Dad's. And she's old. Certainly in her forties.'

Lizzie considered this information mournfully. Sabine clearly wasn't a red-hot mama, and if she appeared discreetly at the afters, nobody would faint into their gin at the sight of Myles Shanahan's girlfriend. They'd be pleased, probably, that nice old Myles had found someone.

The only problem was that then they'd begin to realise that Lizzie would be there on her own. The happy and civilised Lizzie and Myles partnership, which had survived the earthquake of divorce, was over. Myles had moved on. Lizzie hadn't.

Lizzie didn't like people talking about her and she certainly didn't like them feeling sorry for her. That was why she resented Sabine's existence.

Outside the surgery, Lizzie caught sight of Clare Morgan's indolent ginger cat, Tiger, delicately walking along the garden fence to find a hot spot to lie in.

'Hello, Tiger, you gorgeous thing,' she called.

Typically, Tiger pirouetted off the fence at just that moment and Lizzie was left facing Mr Graham, the solicitor whose office was joined on to the surgery and who was now standing open-mouthed on the far side of the fence, his car keys dangling limply in his hand. Lizzie hadn't seen him in time and she flushed at the thought that he'd imagined she'd called him Tiger. Mr Graham was as round as he was tall, and had both overwhelming halitosis and the misplaced conviction that he was something of a ladies' man.

'Sorry ... talking to the cat ...' she mumbled, before rushing into the surgery in a lather of embarrassment.

Oh Lord, how had she managed to do that? Next thing she knew, Mr Graham would be paying court to her, chatting to her if she sat in the surgery garden at lunchtime and winking at her at every opportunity. He'd tried it with Clare, who had given him very short shrift. Trouble was, Lizzie found it impossible to say no to people who turned up on the doorstep selling tickets, no matter what the tickets were for and no matter how broke she was. How would she say no to Mr Graham?

The other consequence of the beautiful morning was an empty surgery. It had always surprised Lizzie that the number of patients who wanted appointments was in direct proportion to the state of the weather. Perhaps the horrible flu that had seemed life-threatening in the rain magically transformed into a light sniffle as soon as the sun appeared.

Lizzie was tidying up before lunch when the phone rang. 'Cork Road Surgery,' she said pleasantly.

'Lizzie, it's Sally Richardson. Did I call at a bad time?'

'No, it's quiet here, Sally. What can I do for you? Is it for you or the boys?'

As she spoke, Lizzie opened the appointments book.

'No, the boys don't need an appointment, thank God,' Sally said gratefully. 'They're getting their tonsils out next month, as you know, and since we made the booking, they've been fine. I was phoning to ask you to a party tomorrow. I'm sorry it's such short notice – I meant to ask you last week but I was so busy it slipped my mind.'

'Lovely,' said Lizzie with pleasure. She hadn't been to a party for ages. 'Is it a special occasion?'

'It's fifty per cent a welcome party to these lovely new people who've moved in, and fifty per cent because we haven't had one for ages, not since Steve's birthday party with the drunken conga.'

'I'd love to come,' Lizzie replied.

'Great. Come around eight and there'll be food – a paper plate and a plastic fork each, mind you – and hopefully fun. Dress code is whatever you feel in the mood for. Bring someone or come on your own, Lizzie, whichever you want. See you then.'

Lizzie drew a big star on tomorrow's space in her diary, thinking that it was ironic how Sally could make it sound so normal when she said 'bring someone or come on your own', while all Lizzie and Myles's old friends either stumbled over the words with embarrassment or else made a big fuss about it.

Sally and Steve had never met Myles and clearly saw Lizzie as a single woman. Even better, they were perfectly happy to accept this, instead of either commiserating with her about the awfulness of life or trying to fix her up with single friends, who were uniformly so strange that it was quite apparent why they were still single. These two options were the most popular, Lizzie had found. The old friends she and Myles had seen when they were married didn't seem to know what to make of her. They never invited her to parties and only asked her to the occasional dinner when they had a man to spare, as though Lizzie was so desperate she'd launch herself on any roving husbands like a nymphomaniac cruise missile if there weren't any unattached men around. There was no point explaining that she wasn't interested in men, married or otherwise. Married women didn't believe her, preferring to behave like anxious medieval monarchs peering over the ramparts of their castles – always scared of invaders and always ready to whisk the drawbridge up.

She'd never widened her circle of friends enough to meet other divorced women, with one notable exception. Lillian, a woman she knew from the surgery, had invited her along for a night out with some other divorced friends, the ones that Clare Morgan nicknamed the Harridans.

It had not been the enjoyable bonding session Lizzie had hoped for. The night had involved plenty of good food, lots of drink and some harmless flirtation with the waiters, but had moved on to dark depressed rumblings about what 'He' had done now.

The worst venom was reserved for when a particular He appeared to be getting on with his life. Taking holidays, buying a new car, or, worst of all, enjoying himself, were top of the list of hate crimes. Lizzie was shocked. She'd expected the positive approach to singlehood that Clare Morgan espoused, not this outpouring of rage. She hated the venom with which the exes were discussed, and the malicious glee with which His failures were greeted. Myles had never been the sort of pig these women talked about, and even if he had been, Lizzie wouldn't have wanted to ill-wish him like one of the witches in *Macbeth*.

Clare Morgan hadn't been surprised by her reaction. 'I knew you'd hate it. Lillian has a PhD in bitterness. I've known her and her husband for years and it's a miracle the poor idiot stayed with her so long. Lillian likes to imagine that she's the victim but it's all her own doing. Keep away from her and those women she hangs around with,' she advised Lizzie. 'Bitterness is catching.'

Clare's advice on enjoying life did not mean either finding another man or grieving over the loss of a husband.

'Wash another man's dirty socks and worry over what to cook for his dinner?' she said scathingly, although Lizzie found it hard to imagine the clever, self-possessed Clare ever washing any man's socks. 'You'd want your head examined if you went back to that drudgery. I date men when I feel like it, but I don't need them in my life all the time. I've learned to enjoy my own company, Lizzie. This is the fun way to enjoy life and I don't intend to go back to the other way, ever.'

Fun. Lizzie flicked on the surgery answering machine. What was fun when it was at home?

CHAPTER TEN

On Saturday afternoon, the day of the Richardsons' party, Jess was studying the newsagent's window for cards to see how people advertised themselves as babysitters when she noticed the tall woman with the black and brown puppy in her arms. The woman's weathered face was thin and might have been stern but for the fact that she was laughing as the puppy did his best to lick her face energetically.

'He's lovely,' said Jess, the words out of her mouth before she'd thought about it.

'He is,' agreed the woman, smiling. 'He's just been in the vet's having his shots and he's so thrilled to be out that he's bouncing for joy. He wet the floor three times when we were there.'

'Ooh, poor darling.' Jess was stroking the puppy under his chin and he was responding deliriously, trying to chew and lick her fingers simultaneously.

The woman surveyed Jess, taking in the neat sandy hair, the pretty but understated face, and her tall, slim figure.

'Would you like to hold him?'

'Yes, please.' Jess snuggled the puppy in her arms, inhaling his lovely milky puppy scent and adoring the way he switched his ardent face-washing to her.

'His name's Twiglet,' said the woman.

'Lovely Twiglet,' crooned Jess. She wasn't really noticing what the woman was doing until she looked up and realised she had put up a notice on the newsagent's board.

Meeting to discuss fate of Dunmore Animal Refuge.
After twenty years in Dunmore, our local funding
has been cut and the refuge faces closure. We need
your help, please.
Come to the Parish Hall on Tivoli Road
on Wed 23rd, 7 p.m.

'Is that where you're from, the rescue centre?' Jess asked.

'Yes, Twiglet too. He and one of his brothers were rescued
from a refuse sack dumped on a building site. Some kind
person heard them yelping and brought them to us.'

Jess was horrified. 'How could anybody do that to a
puppy?' she cried.

'People do it all the time or else we wouldn't be so busy,'
the woman said wryly. 'They won't pay to spay their dogs
and then the refuse sack is their idea of a solution when their
bitch has a litter. It's worse with kittens. An unneutered tom
can father thousands and thousands of kittens, and a female
cat can start producing kittens when she's six months, a litter
every four months, the females of which can have kittens at
six months and so on. You can do the sums yourself.'

'But can't you tell people that if they don't want kittens or
puppies, then they should have their dogs – sprayed, is it?'

'Spayed,' corrected the woman. 'Education is the answer
but money is the solution. A lot of people say they can't
afford it.'

'There should be government funding to help.' Jess was
outraged at the thought of thousands of unwanted baby
animals being dumped.

'What's your name?'

'Jess.'

'I like the way your mind works, Jess. If you're keen on
animals, do you fancy doing a bit of volunteering at the
centre? We can always do with helpers to feed kittens and
pups, not to mention the less savoury parts of cleaning out
the kennels.'

'Oh, I'd love it.' Jess's eyes shone. The woman saw that

suddenly she wasn't understated at all, but very pretty, with a brilliant smile sparkling with vivacity and intelligence. 'I'm at school, though.'

'Dogs need feeding on Saturdays and Sundays, and maybe you'd have time in the evenings and holidays as well,' the woman said matter-of-factly. 'I'm Jean Harvey. The number's in the book and the address is too. We're on the Old Farm Road. Take the bus to Little Dunmore, but get off at the Snow Hill crossroads and we're up the left road about a hundred yards. Make sure your parents don't mind you helping out and they can phone me if they want.'

'I'll be there as soon as I can,' promised Jess, kissing Twiglet's velvety head goodbye.

Jean strode off to a filthy green Land Rover and Jess turned up the road for home. She felt a strange tingle of excitement at this new plan. She loved animals, and this opportunity to work with them was wonderful. She'd have to make sure that poor Wilbur wasn't jealous. He was her darling, but sweet, adorable Twiglet was so cute too. She idly wondered what would happen to him when he was older. Surely the centre found new homes for unwanted puppies. Wouldn't it be fabulous if she could take him home and care for him? Now that they lived in Lyonnais, they had loads of room for a dog.

Caught up in her dreams, Jess walked home with a smile on her face that her mother would have barely recognised.

Abby spent most of Saturday hacking back the undergrowth at the bottom of the front garden, screeching every time another horror-movie-sized spider appeared. Somehow, her hard-wearing garden gloves had vanished and she was stuck with flimsy cotton ones that were suitable for a bit of gentle bulb planting on a patio, perhaps, but not for Indiana Jones-style jungle-busting.

Tom was no help. He'd woken up that morning complaining of flu, and was now lounging in the kitchen, with the weekend papers spread out in front of him, wearing an expression that said *his* sniffles, headache and runny nose were undoubtedly symptoms of something much more serious than just flu.

'I've got so much homework to mark,' he said wearily, 'but my head aches, my muscles are weak and I just don't feel myself.'

Abby, who'd done the supermarket, dry-cleaner's and organic vegetable shopping trip that morning, and who'd have liked nothing more than to flop down with the papers and a coffee, managed to keep quiet. She'd nearly ruptured herself hauling grocery bags in from the Jeep and now she had to work on the garden because it looked so overgrown and she simply couldn't face another week of seeing the mess. It was Tom who'd insisted that having someone come in occasionally to do the garden was an unnecessary expense and that he would help out.

By half three, Abby was tired, scratched and dirty. Some steaming hot tea and a biscuit or three might give her the impetus to spend another couple of hours in the garden. Then she'd treat herself to a soak in a hot bubble bath and get ready for Steve and Sally's party.

Tom was no longer sitting at the kitchen table, although the papers were still strewn across it, while a dirty mug and blueberry muffin crumbs on the worktop were evidence that the invalid had felt well enough to enjoy a snack. Hitting the kettle switch with the back of her hand, Abby went in search of him.

She found him in the living room, with the sports channel on and no sign of the much vaunted homework anywhere.

Tom glanced around and noticed his wife standing at the door, arms folded and lips tight.

'Don't give me that look,' he snapped, turning back to the football.

'What look?' demanded Abby, marching up to the couch.

'Your "I'm working and you're lying around" look,' he replied. 'The martyred look.'

'Well, I *am* working.' She wouldn't lower herself by replying to the martyr crack.

'Nobody told you to,' he retorted.

Abby burned with the injustice of it. Nobody had told her to, for sure, but if she didn't tidy up or get the groceries, who would?

'I wouldn't have to work in the garden if you weren't such a Scrooge about having someone come in twice a year to cut back the undergrowth,' she snapped. 'Somebody has to tidy up this place.'

'Oh, that's it, is it?' he growled. 'It's all my fault. I said I'd help. I'm just not doing it this weekend.'

'Or last weekend or the weekend before that!' Abby said. 'The garden has looked like a disaster area for the past two months but you've done nothing.'

Tom finally gave up staring at the television. 'Can't you see that I'm tired?' he said. 'Tired of rushing round getting this house sorted out, tired of work, tired full stop.'

'And I'm not tired?' she demanded. 'No, I forgot, you have the patent on tiredness because you have a proper job, don't you, Tom? I only have my little television series and my house decluttering business, none of it as serious as being a precious deputy headmaster. Oh yes, and I have the housework and the grocery shopping and the laundry –'

'Mrs Regan does the housework,' he interrupted.

'Twice a week for two hours at a time,' Abby yelled back. 'She keeps the place ticking over but I have to do the hard grind. Inside and out! Do you have any idea how much work it takes to run a house, to do laundry, shopping, cooking, cleaning? Oh no, I forgot. You think Cooking and Cleaning are two towns in China.'

'Spare me the sarcasm,' he said acidly. 'Are you running through your answers for a newspaper interview on the successful working woman? Is that it? You're going to tell everyone how hard it is for the modern career woman because she has to juggle a job and housework, with a lazy lout of a husband who does nothing and doesn't appreciate her efforts?'

This was so precisely what had been running through Abby's mind that she could say nothing for a moment, but just glare at him. Finally, she found her voice. 'If you know what's wrong with me, why don't you do anything about it?' she snapped.

'It's not my aim in life to please you all the time, Abby,' Tom said with grim relish. 'They may do that in Beech TV studios, where you're queen of all you survey, but not here. Not in our home.'

'That's utterly unfair,' she yelled back. 'I'm not a bit like that and you know it! All I'm asking for is a little help around the house. You used to help, but now you do nothing. Since we moved to this house, I don't think you've done one week's grocery shopping or have loaded the washing machine once. It wouldn't kill you to make an effort.'

'You were the one who wanted to go back to work,' he pointed out.

'And you're the one who enjoys the benefits of the extra money,' she replied, without thinking of what she was saying.

'Oh yes, never let me forget that, will you? You're the successful one, the famous one, I'm only the boring old husband standing in the wings.' Abby was shocked at the bitterness in his voice. 'You love that, don't you, Abby? You love making more money than me. You love rubbing my nose in it.'

'No, I don't,' she said quietly, before walking out.

Her hands were shaking as she made a cup of tea. She'd never realised before quite how much he resented her job and the changes it had made. He might have liked living in a big and luxurious home, but he couldn't cope with the fact that her earnings had brought them there. Did he feel that her success had somehow emasculated him? He couldn't, surely. He was just being childish. Childish and lazy.

Abby flung the used teaspoon in the sink to join Tom's dirty cup and plate. If he couldn't be bothered to put things in the dishwasher, then neither would she. And when the house was a slum with no clean dishes and no clean clothes, perhaps *then* he'd cop on to how hard she worked.

Coming up Briar Lane, Jess realised that she hadn't thought about the exams for at least an hour. Which was good, because when she did think about them, she got this weird ache in the back of her neck that crept up into her head and sort of bounced against her skull. Nothing made it go away except lying in the bath, and you couldn't very well do that four times a day. But thinking about the animal refuge meant she hadn't time to worry about the exams. Tonight would help too. She was helping Sally Richardson with the boys later, so that Sally could get ready for the party. Jess loved the relaxed atmosphere in the Richardsons' house: there was always an air of laughter and good humour, not like at home.

A plastic bag of garden rubbish and a big gardening fork were sitting inside the gate when she got home but there was no sign of either Mum or Dad. Jess hoped she wouldn't be roped into picking up leaves or anything. She hated gardening, apart from that time in science class, when they'd all grown shoots from a bean.

Her mother was standing in the kitchen, dressed in old clothes and reading a newspaper laid out on the counter top.

'Oh, Mum, I met this amazing woman today who runs the animal rescue centre,' Jess began enthusiastically. 'She had this gorgeous puppy, Twiglet. Imagine, people dumped him and his brother in a refuse bag on a building site, but he's fine now.'

Her mother didn't respond, so Jess continued. 'They're trying to save the animal refuge because they don't have enough money, and this woman said if I wanted to, I could volunteer to help out. They always need people to feed puppies and kittens, and to clean up.' Jess felt a fresh surge of pride at the thought that this total stranger had trusted her enough to offer her a volunteer job. 'I can do weekends.'

'What about your exams?' said Abby, unnecessarily sharp. As soon as she'd spoken, she regretted it. What did exams matter when this animal refuge had brought a smile to her daughter's face for the first time in months.

But the shutters had already come down and Jess assumed the blank mantle of teenage indifference.

'Whatever,' she said, turning towards the door. 'Forget it.'

'I didn't mean it to sound like that,' Abby said but Jess was gone. Within seconds, she heard the thump of Jess's boots on the stairs and then the slamming of her door.

Abby gave up on the notion that if she read the papers standing up then she wouldn't get too comfortable to return to the wilderness that was the garden. She pulled out a chair and slumped down on it. She felt she was a failure – a failure at motherhood. If she was a failure at being a wife, then Tom had to shoulder a large percentage of the blame. But failing at being a good mother was all her own work.

Abby felt a huge desire to go upstairs, climb into bed and pull the covers over her head. But she couldn't. She had to finish the garden and go to the party. Sally had asked Jess to keep an eye on the boys, so the whole Barton clan would be there trying to pretend that they were playing happy families. Abby wistfully remembered when they had been a happy family for real.

Erin got cold feet at the last minute.

'Do we have to go?' She turned slanting amber eyes on Greg, who was shaving, while she lay up to her shoulders in a steaming bath, with her hair trailing down into a cloud of vanilla-scented bubbles. With candles all around the bath and a haze of vapour in the air, she could almost forget the nightmare pink bath and the awful purple paisley wallpaper.

'No, you stay. That's a wonderful idea, Erin. I'll go and chat up the local women,' Greg said firmly. 'I won't be late. Back by tomorrow lunch at the latest. You don't mind, do you? I won't have sex with anyone, I'll just mess around some . . .'

Erin flicked a splodge of bubble bath up at him with her right foot.

'You've a lousy aim,' Greg remarked, washing the bits of shaving foam from his face and splashing on Eau Sauvage. He perched on the edge of the bath and leaned down as if to kiss her but suddenly reached across to her toes and pulled the plug out.

'Creep,' wailed Erin. 'I was enjoying that.'

'I thought you liked Sally.'

'I do, she's great. It's just that I feel like slobbing out tonight.' Erin felt like slobbing out all the time these days, which was weird and very unlike her.

'Steve's been good to me,' Greg pointed out. 'I've got to go, but if you really don't want to, I can say you're not well.'

'Nah.' Rising like Venus from the foam, Erin pulled a towel round herself. 'Forget it,' she said in a fake schoolmarm voice as Greg reached a probing hand under the towel. 'You're on rations after that crack about flirting with the local women.'

CHAPTER ELEVEN

Delia pulled the last tray of savoury pastry squares out of the oven and dropped it on the kitchen table.

'Finished,' she said. 'If I never see another bit of pastry again, I'll be happy.'

Sally, who was sitting on a stool at the table constructing a pyramid of profiteroles with architectural precision, smiled. 'I know what you mean. The only fatal flaw with parties is the catering.'

'Absolutely,' agreed her mother-in-law fervently. 'But what I hate most is that moment just before everyone arrives when you've got the place beautiful, but you feel shattered and you wish you could cancel so you could spend the evening slumped in front of the box.'

Sally glanced up at Delia sharply. That was just how she was feeling but she didn't want her mother-in-law to know. Normally Sally had enough energy for ten parties and Delia would get suspicious if she noticed otherwise. However, Delia's face bore no awareness of that fact and she was busily using a palette knife to slide her just-cooked canapés from the tray.

Steve arrived in from the garden, having finished hanging lots of tiny white lights from the veranda and the apple trees.

'Smells good,' he said, picking up a pastry and wolfing it down. He reached for another but his mother rapped his knuckles with her palette knife.

'Stop it! We won't have enough, you big gannet.'

Steve grinned. 'It's nearly five,' he said. 'I'm going to collect the boys from that birthday party.'

Sally left the profiteroles and followed him out to the front door. Now that they were alone, Steve put his arms round her and held her tightly. 'How are you doing?'

'Fine,' she said brightly. 'You'd better get going. We've got a hundred people coming here in two and a half hours, don't forget. And we've got to do the glasses, give the boys dinner and get ready.'

'No problemo,' said Steve, his tone matching hers. 'Jess is coming at six to look after the boys, isn't she?'

'Yes, so we should be nearly ready but for last-minute things.'

'I still have to make the punch, but I promise, it'll be very mild,' Steve said with a wicked grin.

'I hope so . . .' Sally wriggled out of his arms. 'I'm warning you, one drunk partygoer this time and you'll be in big trouble.'

'Is that a promise or an idle threat?' he asked wickedly.

Sally shot him her most innocent look. 'You'll have to wait and see,' she said, and went back to finish making the dessert.

Erin and Greg's taxi reached the Richardsons' at exactly seven thirty. There wasn't a single car parked on the road outside.

'They did say seven thirty, didn't they?' Erin asked.

'They did.' Greg paid the driver, who sped off. 'Maybe everyone else is being fashionably late.'

'Or we're unfashionably early. I hope we didn't get it wrong. There's nothing worse than finding the host and hostess in bathtowels with no make-up on.'

'If Steve is planning to wear make-up, then we know we're in trouble,' Greg replied.

'You know what I mean, smarty-pants.'

'Hello!' Steve stood at the front door. 'Come in. Lovely to see you. Welcome.'

'We're not too early, I hope?' Erin proffered a china pot with an African violet, while Greg handed over a bottle of wine.

'Not early at all. I need some help to make a killer punch.'

'No you don't!' said Sally, hurrying to the door and fiddling with an earring. 'If you see him putting anything dangerous in that punch, call me. I want this to be a nice, non-plastered party.'

'Oh, no,' said Greg, deadpan. 'If that's the case, we'll go home. I've been looking forward to a bit of drunken debauchery with shades of the last days of the Roman Empire.'

Sally groaned. 'There I was, hoping that at least we'd have some friends who didn't know about our disreputable parties and Steve has to ruin it all.'

'He didn't tell me anything,' Greg said innocently. 'It was on the office bulletin board.'

'Oh, you two . . .' Sally pretended to take a swipe at Greg but kissed him hello instead. 'I can see why you and Steve get on so well.'

'They share a juvenile sense of humour,' whispered Erin as she hugged Sally hello. 'But don't tell them I said that.'

After that, the doorbell never stopped ringing as scores more people turned up, clutching wine and flowers. Music and conversation flowed and Erin and Greg were swept into meeting what seemed like the whole of Dunmore. Everyone was so charming and interested in the newcomers, and Greg was in his element, talking animatedly to their new neighbours. But for the first time in her life, Erin felt as if she just couldn't make conversation. Several times she caught Greg looking at her quizzically as she remained silent, as if to say what the hell was wrong with her. Erin wished she knew.

Lizzie wasn't sure about the new blouse she was wearing. In the trendy shop on the quays, with a sweet young sales assistant hovering, telling her it was 'really now', Lizzie had felt that she was perfectly entitled to wear a filmy chiffon top that was cut so low in the front, it could almost qualify as a handy-for-breast-feeding outfit in a mother-and-baby catalogue.

At home, with a sherry inside her for Dutch courage, it made her look modern and young, she decided. On the footpath outside the Richardsons', she peered down her front yet again and wondered if she had crossed the invisible style line between youthful chic and sinewy old mutton dressed as lamb. Home was only five minutes away; she could just nip through the laneway and change . . .

'Lizzie, lovely to see you,' yelled a man climbing out of a car.

'Hello, how *are* you?' shrieked his wife.

Lizzie rearranged the navy jacket she was wearing over the blouse, hoped she might get away with wearing the jacket all night, although it was a warm evening, and smiled.

'Margo and Ken,' she replied, 'lovely to see you too.'

What Steve and Sally's cottage lacked in size or luxury, it made up for in sheer homely style, Lizzie thought. A modest redbricked barn conversion with low ceilings, a dormer upstairs in one half, and a vast spacious floor-to-eaves room in the other, it looked fantastic decorated for the party. Outside at the front, scores of tiny white fairy lights were draped artfully over the apple trees and over the doorway, which had a tiny sloping roof like a house from a Hans Christian Andersen story. Inside, the whole of the big reception room was twinkling with fairy lights and candles. The French windows were open at the far end of the room, with its squashy old armchairs and sofas, and Lizzie could see candle-covered tables set up on the old flagstones outside and long garden tapers stuck into the flowerbeds, flickering among the frothing love-in-a-mist. At the other end of the room was the kitchen, with a scrubbed refectory table, an ancient cream-coloured range, and a collection of free-standing kitchen units that covered each of the past fifty years in furniture design. Steve stood at the table behind a vast collection of bottles of every colour, merrily doling out huge glasses of booze, while Sally's dark curly head could be seen as she flitted amongst her guests, chattering and hugging people, and telling everyone how delighted she was to see them. Enviably slim, in her iridescent dress she looked like a tiny butterfly shimmering in the candlelight. Goodwill hung in the air like children's bubbles. Despite her last-minute nerves, Lizzie was glad to be there.

'Lizzie, darling, I'm so glad you could come,' said Sally, instantly making Lizzie feel welcome. 'And Margo and Ken. Great to see you. Now, what would you like to drink?'

The problem with parties in small communities, Lizzie mused half an hour later, was that, after a few years, you never had the chance of seeing a stranger across a crowded room – you tended to know who everyone was. She knew, for example, that the tall craggy-faced man with the roving eye, who was standing at the French windows sizing up all the women, was unattached but a hopeless drip. Larry looked like every divorcée's dream but after two dates listening to his history of failed relationships, how he'd never bonded with anyone like he did with his mother and how his sciatica ached, even the most desperate of women went running. Lizzie knew this because Clare Morgan had told her. Lizzie didn't go out enough even to get on Hopeless Larry's radar.

She'd just come out of the cloakroom when Abby and Tom Barton arrived. The Bartons had clearly had a row if Lizzie's body language degree was anything to go by. They appeared to be trying to stand as far away from each other as possible, and both sported the clenched jaws of people afraid to open their mouths in case they said something they might regret.

'Hello,' said Abby brightly.

'Hi, Abby and Tom,' said Lizzie. 'Lizzie Shanahan,' she

reminded them. She didn't know either of them very well and never expected people to remember her.

'Of course we know you, Lizzie,' said Abby quickly. 'We met in the surgery.'

'Well, you must meet so many people,' Lizzie said, 'it's hard to remember names. I have a problem with that in the surgery and they've normally rung to make an appointment beforehand, so I've got their name written down and therefore have no excuse.'

'Oh God, names, don't talk to me,' groaned Abby. 'I am hopeless with names.'

Seeing the women doing that irritating female bonding thing they all seemed to be able to do after ten seconds, Tom smiled briefly at Lizzie, totally ignored his wife, and headed into the party proper. He needed a drink.

Abby glared at his retreating back.

'Husbands,' murmured Lizzie. 'Can't live with them and can't kill them.'

'You said it,' agreed Abby fervently.

'Sorry, I shouldn't have said that.' Lizzie wished her mouth wouldn't run away like that. Abby would think she was just chatting wildly to her because she was famous.

'No, you're right,' Abby said politely.

They stood there for a moment in stilted silence, with Lizzie feeling like an idiot for trying to start a conversation with someone like Abby.

'Sorry,' she said again. 'I hardly know you. It's just . . .' She trailed off, embarrassed.

Abby looked interested. Lizzie didn't know if she was being polite or not but she ploughed on anyway. What the hell, famous people must be good at walking away from conversations if they were bored, and all the magazine articles said Abby was very down to earth, so Lizzie might as well try.

'I got a sudden flash of memory of being married, having a row and convincing yourself that you can go out in public without screaming at each other,' Lizzie went on.

Abby felt the corners of her mouth lifting. So much for her theory that they could keep the row behind closed doors. 'You too?'

Lizzie grimaced. 'Not any more,' she said. 'My husband and I are divorced. We split up over five years ago, so we only row on the phone.' She considered this. 'Actually, we don't row at all now. Our daughter's getting married and Myles and I are ridiculously on the same wavelength about everything.'

God, why had she said that? Talk about spilling the beans to someone you had only just met.

'So you're saying divorce is the secret?' Abby said ruefully. 'We've got a teenage daughter and, well, it can be hard to cope with teenagers, can't it? Talking of Jess, here she comes.'

Jess, pretty in jeans and a sparkly turquoise T-shirt, her hair tied up in two jaunty pigtails with gorgeous violet scrunchies Sally had just given her, appeared with a tray of drinks.

'Hi, Mum,' she said sulkily. There had been no more rowing at Lyonnais that day but the atmosphere could have been cut with a knife, so Jess had worked out that her parents were fighting again. Not that *that* was anything new. It had been a relief to get to Sally and Steve's, where the atmosphere was tension-free and all she had to do was keep the boys amused while Sally, Delia and Steve finished the party preparations. Now Jack and Daniel were fast asleep in bed she'd offered her waitressing skills. 'I've done five rounds with the mozzarella rolls and the tapenade, so I thought I'd bring some drinks round too. D'you want some?'

'Yes, thanks,' said Abby, taking a glass of mineral water. 'Jess, this is Lizzie, who lives near us. Lizzie, this is my daughter, Jess.'

'Hi, Jess,' said Lizzie warmly. 'I love your sparkly top. Could we swap? I bought mine in HipBabe on the quays and it's definitely more your age group than mine. I feel I'm falling out of it.'

Jess giggled. 'It's lovely on you. Do you want something to drink? We've water, wine, fruit juice and this punch stuff.'

Abby felt a ludicrous stab of jealousy that her daughter could get on so well with this Lizzie person, and not with her. Jess had offered *her* a drink like the pest exterminator offering a rat some poison. But then Lizzie hadn't behaved like a bad, uninterested mother earlier, had she?

When Lizzie had taken a glass, Jess sailed off and Abby watched her go.

'She's a lovely girl but it's tough being mum when girls are teenagers, isn't it?' Lizzie said perceptively.

Abby nodded, so Lizzie continued.

'My daughter Debra is twenty-three now and we get on like a house on fire, but there were years when I thought of calling in Kofi Annan.'

At that, Abby laughed. 'I thought it was just me,' she admitted, then regretted it. She hardly knew this woman – why was she telling her such personal things?

'Oh, we all do. Women are programmed to think they're the only screw-up in the universe and men are programmed to think they're the smartest creatures in the universe,' Lizzie said, sitting down at the bottom of the stairs.

Abby plonked down beside her. 'That sounds like a book title.'

'Hey, you could do a TV series on that theme,' Lizzie said with enthusiasm. 'Millions of parents would watch it.'

Abby grimaced. 'I have enough trouble with the TV series I've got. Sometimes I feel like packing it in.' Before it packed her in, was the unspoken thought.

'But you're so good at it.'

Lizzie was genuinely admiring and Abby felt herself beginning to relax. Lizzie was so warm and easy to talk to, and after a week of nobody talking to anybody else at home, it was a relief to have a conversation that wasn't like picking her way through broken glass.

'You sound so clever and nice on TV, everyone I know loves your show,' Lizzie went on, and then felt embarrassed.

She never normally talked this much. It must be the sherry she'd had earlier. But Abby didn't seem to think she was being an idiot.

'Thanks, that's nice of you to say it,' Abby responded, 'but I don't feel clever. I feel as if I've taken all this stuff on and that everyone's just waiting for me to fall flat on my face.'

'But you're a big success.' Lizzie's shyness evaporated in the face of her incredulity. 'You've turned your life around – not like the rest of us who just think about doing it.'

'TV is easy if you're doing something you enjoy,' Abby explained. 'It's the rest of life that's hard.'

'Teenagers?' suggested Lizzie.

'And husbands.'

'Been there, done that, got the T-shirt, been handed the divorce papers.' Lizzie sighed. 'At least you've still got the teenager and the husband.'

Abby didn't want to think about her husband right now. She wondered why Lizzie had divorced hers.

'So, have you a significant other here tonight?' she asked instead.

Lizzie blushed. I wish, she thought. Abby would think she was hopeless. 'I haven't had a date since I first went out with my husband,' she admitted, blushing some more. 'How pathetic is that? I came alone tonight and, unless I get plastered and do fall out of this ridiculous top, I'll be going home alone too. Mind you,' she added, 'I can't imagine any man being overwhelmed with lust at the sight of me either in this outfit or out of it.'

'Don't say that,' Abby remonstrated. 'You're very attractive, and that's a sexy outfit.'

'You think so?' Lizzie sounded pathetically grateful for the compliment. 'I didn't think I knew how to do sexy any more. I'm fifty next birthday. Fifty and sexy aren't words you usually hear in the same sentence. Fifty is sadly linked to sensible skirts, beige cardigans and rubber-soled shoes.'

Abby burst into gales of laughter. 'You're a hoot, Lizzie. But come on, being fifty doesn't have to be any of those things if you don't want it to,' she insisted, conveniently forgetting how she felt as if forty-two was on a par with a hundred and forty-two.

'That's the theory,' Lizzie said earnestly, 'but if I dress like a teenager and start going to parties every night, people will think I'm in my second childhood, and if I head for the rubber-soled shoes and beige cardigans, they'll say I'm not trying.' She'd thought about this so often recently she felt ready to write a thesis on it.

'Is it being divorced, do you think?' Abby said interestedly. 'If you were still married, people would accept whatever role you went for, but if you're single, they expect more from you.'

'That's it exactly,' cried Lizzie. 'I feel as if I'm being judged all the time. If I buy a bottle of wine in the supermarket and someone I know sees me, I think they'll disapprove and decide that I sit at home drowning my sorrows in front of the telly.'

'I know what you mean,' interrupted Abby. 'People now recognise me in the supermarket and I can see them peering into my trolley as though to say, "Look at her buying frozen convenience food – she should be ashamed of herself."'

They grinned at each other, united in their dislike of people who judged. Lizzie was astonished at her own daring in talking so openly to Abby. If they'd met in a group, Lizzie would probably have just smiled shyly at her and not said a word, and now here they were, talking as if they'd known each other all their lives.

'It's probably our own fault, though,' Abby added. 'We wouldn't give a damn who looked into our trolleys if we were utterly sure of ourselves. We'd be proud of our frozen pizzas and bottles of Californian Zinfandel.'

'I'd love to be utterly sure of myself,' Lizzie sighed.

Me too, thought Abby, but didn't say anything.

'They have courses for that, you know: reinvent yourself courses,' Lizzie said wistfully. 'Trouble is, I'd feel stupid going to one.'

'You don't need a course,' chided Abby. 'You have to think yourself confident.'

'Tell me the secret.'

'You imagine how confident people behave and just do it. Smile, look confident and talk to people.'

'It sounds so easy.'

'It is,' insisted Abby. 'When you're nervous, put yourself mentally in the shoes of your most confident friend. And you need to practise. For example, if you want to date men, you've got to go for it. How about if you went up to that good-looking guy over there and began to chat him up?'

'Hopeless Larry?'

'Is that his name?'

'Not really. I've never talked to him before.'

'Go girl!' ordered Abby. 'He's only hopeless because he's never met you. Or if he is hopeless, you can practise your new confident-woman skills on him.'

'OK.' Lizzie surprised herself by saying this. Well, why not? Larry was single, she was single. He might not be as bad as Clare made out – he could be just the spur she was looking for to change her life. 'It's funny,' she revealed suddenly. 'I've all these old friends who knew Myles and me for years and if one of them told me to chat up a man, I'd be insulted at the idea.'

'Old friends know the old you,' Abby said sagely. 'Sometimes you need new friends to tell you new things.' She got to her feet. 'I shall go and circulate,' she said, wondering if she ought to see if Tom was in a friendlier mood.

'See you later,' said Lizzie, feeling strangely buoyed up by their conversation. She wasn't boring. She was interesting. She would go and talk to new people instead of sticking like a limpet to the 'safe' couples she knew.

The party was going with a swing but Erin wasn't. Steve and Sally had introduced Greg and Erin to lots of people but still she couldn't summon up the energy to chat. She wanted to go home but it was only nine o'clock, and now

Greg was embroiled in a heated political discussion and Erin was standing on the fringes of the group, not really paying attention and uncomfortably aware that she must seem cool and distant. Her eyes wandered round the room. Sally was perched on the arm of a chair, talking animatedly to a couple of women about children, while Steve was circling the room with a bottle of white wine and a jug of his lethal punch. Erin had had one sip of her glass of punch earlier and had quickly put it down. Greg said it actually wasn't that strong but whatever alcohol Steve had used tasted strange to Erin. Delia was circling in the other direction with trays of canapés, chatting gaily and forcing food on everyone. 'I cooked this, you have to eat it!' she would cry with good humour. She was being helped by a tall, fair-haired teenager, who offered food in a totally different way: shyly proffering her tray, a great smile lighting up her face when people talked to her.

Someone had turned up the music and the volume of conversation and laughter had increased accordingly – people were clearly letting their hair down. The television presenter person – Abby, wasn't it? – and her husband were locked in a fierce discussion in a corner of the kitchen.

Steve had introduced Erin to both of them earlier and Erin did not feel as if she'd met a friend for life. Abby had been perfectly polite but brittle.

'Nice to meet you,' she'd said, but her eyes weren't warm and her face bore an expression that Erin recognised: envy. Erin had experience of women being envious of her slenderness and her striking looks, but when they got to know her, the envy usually went. Was Abby one of those people who were threatened by other attractive women? Or maybe she was just in a strop with her husband, who'd seemed nice, if a little preoccupied. Erin watched them idly and wondered why some people didn't seem to mind arguing in public.

Oblivious to being watched, Abby glared at her husband, any thoughts of reconciliation forgotten.

'What's your problem?' demanded Tom, pouring another drink.

'You've ignored me since we got here,' Abby hissed. 'It's very obvious. Why don't you take out an advert in the local paper saying we've had an argument and be done with it? People will talk, and now that I'm well known, they'll talk even more.'

'Oh, you and your precious career,' he said snidely. 'We're among friends, people who knew you before you were famous. They don't give a damn if we have a row.'

'Well, *I* give a damn. I don't want our private life made public.'

'Is that right?' Tom shoved the white wine back in the fridge. 'Well, why do you talk about your private life when you do bloody interviews, then?'

'That's below the belt,' Abby cried. 'I don't talk about you or Jess. I do my best to protect you. I have to do some interviews: it's my job.'

'Spare me.' Tom was scathing.

'What's wrong with you these days?' demanded Abby loudly, totally forgetting there was a chance of them being overheard. 'You're in a foul temper all the time and you never talk to me any more, not talk properly anyhow, only to moan.'

'Moan? You're accusing me of moaning?' Tom sounded incredulous. 'You're the one who never shuts up moaning about getting wrinkles or how you've got cellulite and how all the TV stars are younger and doesn't anyone realise the pressure you're under –'

'Stop it! Everyone's staring at you.' It was Jess, speaking in a strangely high-pitched voice.

Both Tom and Abby were startled into silence and they looked around to see that many of the partygoers were indeed glancing in their direction, then turning away in embarrassment.

Abby felt scarlet spots of humiliation burn her cheeks.

'You never think of anyone else,' said Jess, 'just yourselves.

164

How do you think I feel when you fight all the time?' And she fled.

'Cheer up, folks. We all have the odd argument.' It was Steve, determined to defuse the row. He put an arm round Abby and another round Tom, drawing them close to each other. 'Either you've had too much of my punch or you haven't had enough.'

'We should go.' Abby was upset, both at the row and at having had it witnessed by poor Jess, not to mention everyone at the party.

'Don't go,' said Steve. 'It's only half nine. If you go now, you'll feel miserable all evening and mortified that people saw you having a tiff. Stay and relax.'

He understood how she felt better than Tom, Abby thought sadly.

'We'll stay,' said Tom. 'Won't we?'

Abby almost couldn't look at him but she did, and he appeared as upset as she was, which was something. He reached out and patted her hand. Still angry with him, she wondered if he'd touched her for Steve's benefit, because it couldn't possibly be for hers.

Forcing a smile, she agreed. 'Yes, we'll stay. Why storm out over a stupid argument?'

'Great.' Steve beamed.

Sally came in, her sweet face anxious. 'Are you all right?' she asked. Steve moved out of the way, letting his wife slip in between the Bartons. They were so in tune with each other, Abby realised with a pang. Steve knew that Sally was the comforter and they didn't need to communicate with words to decide that she could handle things better than he. Abby asked herself, had she and Tom ever had that silent affinity?

'We're fine,' Abby said brightly. 'I'll just check on Jess first.'

'She went upstairs. Shall I run up and see if she's OK?' asked Sally delicately.

Abby felt a rush of shame. Sally had seen how upset

Jess was and clearly thought it would be better if she, and not Abby, talked to her. She nodded, not trusting herself to speak.

Upstairs, Jess crept into the boys' room, drawn by the comforting soft yellow glow from Danny's beloved night-light. He'd had it since he was a baby and had refused to grow out of it, Sally said. The pretty light sat on a small white bookcase that was filled with the children's books. Soothed by the light and by the rhythmic breathing of the sleeping children, Jess settled herself on one of the tiny beanbag seats beside the bookcase and picked up the fairy tale she'd been reading to them earlier. Why did people tell children fairy tales? When she was a kid, Mum and Dad had read books to her in which everything worked out in the end. But real life wasn't like that. It often didn't work out. Ugly ducklings who wore braces and glasses didn't grow up into swans, and Cinderellas didn't have the prince fall in love with them.

A soft knock on the half-open door made her jump.

'Jess,' whispered Sally, 'are you in there?' Sally's dark head appeared round the door. 'You OK?'

Jess nodded.

'Do you want to talk about it?'

Jess shook her head. If she talked to anyone, she'd cry. And Sally would think she was just a stupid kid. Jess admired Sally so much. She was a grown-up and a mother and she worked and got stressed, but she was still fun. She and Steve laughed and joked with each other. Just as families should be, Jess thought, like her own family had been about a gazillion years ago. Before they'd moved to Dunmore.

'Call me if you need me,' Sally said, and closed the door gently.

Mum wouldn't have said that, Jess thought bitterly. Mum wanted to know what she was thinking and was everything all right all the time. She never knew how to back off, which was why Jess had to clam up or she'd never be able to have a private thought. Sally knew better. For a guilty millisecond, Jess wished that Sally Richardson was her mum, or even an older sister or something. Then, she'd have someone to talk to.

Larry wasn't hopeless, Lizzie decided. He was definitely good-looking, tall enough to peer down her blouse but gentlemanly enough not to. And he was at least her age so nobody could accuse her of cradle-snatching.

Imagine how a confident person would act, Abby had advised. Recklessly, Lizzie did her best.

'I can't believe we've never met before,' she said when they'd gone through the whole shaking hands and saying hello rigmarole.

'Nor me,' he said, again playing the gentleman. He had kind eyes, but his appearance was slightly marred by his tendency to stoop. The dreaded sciatica, Lizzie supposed.

'Lizzie!' She swirled round to find herself facing Mr Graham, the lawyer with the office next door to the surgery. Mr Pushy with Halitosis. 'Fancy seeing you here tonight.'

He kissed her on the cheek, a wet kiss that made her squirm and, somehow, he managed to squeeze her bum at the same time.

Lizzie's flesh crawled but she was programmed to be polite. 'Hello,' she said. 'Er . . . Larry meet Mr –'

'Ben Graham,' said the lawyer smoothly. 'I live two houses down. Lizzie and I work next door to each other.'

He made it sound so cosy, Lizzie realised with horror. Larry obviously thought so too.

'Nice to meet you, Lizzie, Ben,' Larry said, backing away.

Lizzie was stuck with Ben Graham, and his breath hadn't improved much.

'So, I've finally got you to myself,' he leered. There was no other word to describe it. Even his eyes gleamed wetly, Lizzie noticed with a shudder. It wasn't that he was a bad-looking man but he was so smugly sure of his attraction that he just made you want to back off. He was sleazy, Lizzie decided, and no matter how desperate she was, she'd never be that desperate.

'Larry wouldn't be your type,' he added confidently. 'Bit of a drip.' He leaned closer. 'No stamina.' He leered down her blouse. 'Tiger,' he said softly. 'I like that.'

Lizzie's stomach plummeted. 'I was talking to the cat that day,' she stammered, 'not you.'

'Oh, I see,' Ben said, still grinning as though he saw nothing of the sort.

He was so close to her that Lizzie took a step back and encountered the wall. Undeterred by this, Ben moved with her. He wasn't tall but he was still tall enough to keep his eyes fixed down her blouse.

'Great outfit,' he said, leaning one hand against the wall so he could get a better view.

Automatically, Lizzie's hand went up to try to pull the edges of the neckline together.

'Spoilsport,' Ben said.

It took a lot to rile Lizzie, but this did it. 'Does the concept of personal space mean anything to you?' she asked hotly.

Ben's confident expression faltered. 'Personal space . . . ?' he said.

'Personal space,' repeated Lizzie. 'I don't want you staring down my blouse. It's rude. And I don't want you standing so close to me that I can feel your breath.' She said nothing about the quality of his breath. No matter how horrible she was, she couldn't be that nasty to him.

'Nobody's complained before,' Ben said smugly, still not moving away. He reached out and touched her shoulder, with all the finesse of someone following a 'how to be sexy to women' manual written for and by fifteen-year-old boys.

As his oily fingers made contact with Lizzie's skin, she reacted instinctively, pushing him away from her.

'I said I don't want you standing on top of me!' she shrieked.

Startled by her actions, Ben stumbled and bashed into a small table behind him, sending a selection of glasses crashing noisily to the ground. Horrified, Lizzie stared at the chaos, then pushed past him and rushed into the cool of the garden.

Outside, the moon and stars were so bright that the garden was bathed in light, and even when she'd passed the candle-lit tables, Lizzie could easily find her way along the lawn and down to the little seat under the laurel tree. She'd hoped to be able to lick her wounds in peace but there were definite sounds of someone else there. Was someone being sick into the bushes?

Pulling a branch out of the way, she peered into the gloom to see the tall figure of Erin Kennedy hunched over, retching painfully.

'Erin?' asked Lizzie tentatively, not wanting to intrude upon the privacy of this woman she'd only just met. 'Are you OK?'

'No,' said Erin, retching again. 'I don't know what's wrong. I'm so sick and there was a queue for the bathroom.' Clinging to the sticky branch of a pine tree for support, she felt her breath come in short, shallow bursts. Was the nausea receding? Please let it be. She had nothing else to purge from her stomach because she had only eaten one piece of ciabatta slathered with olive tapenade. But as soon as she'd finished it, she had felt her stomach lurch.

The nausea was definitely easing off. She patted her pockets looking for a tissue but, typically, there was none.

'Here.' Lizzie reached out with a crumpled-up party napkin. 'It's all squashed up but it's clean.'

'Thanks.' Erin wiped her mouth, feeling so weak that she didn't care that a stranger had just witnessed her puking her guts up in someone else's garden.

She tried to recall Lizzie's name. She knew she was a friend of Sally's, and Erin remembered Sally saying she was very sweet but shy. That blouse was anything but shy, but then, Erin decided that it didn't look like the sort of thing Lizzie might normally wear, since Lizzie's hand was always checking the neckline. It was definitely a 'something to prove' outfit.

'I'm Lizzie,' the woman volunteered with a smile that was certainly sweet. 'Are you all right? Would you like to sit down on the seat? It might make you feel better.'

With Lizzie guiding her, Erin sank down on the rustic wooden bench. Lizzie sat beside her and put an arm round her. It was nice, motherly, and it made Erin feel ridiculously like crying.

'Thank you,' she said, sniffling. 'I don't know why I was sick. I've only eaten one canapé and I love tapenade.'

'Could you have food poisoning from something you've eaten within the past twenty-four hours?' asked Lizzie, switching into medical receptionist mode.

Erin shook her head. 'I had a tuna melt for lunch, and last night we had home-made lasagne.'

Lizzie racked her brains. Gastroenteritis, perhaps? 'Did you get sick earlier?'

'No, I've felt a bit nauseous all day but I never needed to actually puke before.'

There was one other possibility and Lizzie realised that Erin hadn't made the mental connection yet. Some women didn't. Highly intelligent and focused on their careers and the future, they missed the age-old signals from their bodies that had been telling women for millennia that something was happening.

'I don't mean to sound very personal, Erin,' Lizzie said slowly, 'but could you be pregnant?'

Erin's sharp intake of breath was audible.

'I'm sorry, I'm probably totally wrong, it was just a thought,' babbled Lizzie, fearing she'd said the wrong thing. 'I work in the doctor's surgery and, you know, I was just thinking of all the possibilities and ten to one, you've got a bug . . .'

'I'm on the pill,' gasped Erin.

Lizzie bit her lip. She'd probably intruded too much but she felt strangely protective towards this tall, red-haired girl. 'The pill isn't a hundred per cent effective,' she said. 'Lots of things can affect its efficiency: if you're ill with vomiting or diarrhoea, or some antibiotics can affect the body's absorption of it.' God, she sounded like a medical textbook. 'Look, Erin, it's none of my business but if you could be pregnant, it would affect what medication you can take for, say, your stomach upset.'

She gave Erin one last gentle pat on the shoulder and got up. 'Will I send your husband or Sally out to you?'

'Don't go,' said Erin, grabbing Lizzie's hand tightly. 'Talk to me. I was unwell before we came over to Ireland from Chicago – last-minute nerves, I suppose – and my whole system was messed up. Could that have done it?'

'When was that?' asked Lizzie, sitting down again.

Erin told her and Lizzie did the maths.

She could easily be six to seven weeks pregnant, which was when nausea kicked in.

'Please let me get your husband,' Lizzie said. It wasn't that she didn't feel able to cope with this drama, but he was the ideal person to comfort Erin.

'Hold on just a moment. I need to think about this,' Erin said. With the moonlight and the party lights shining on her face, she looked ghostly pale and shocked. 'He's having a nice time. I don't want to ruin it or have him rush out here at ninety miles an hour because he's worried about me. I'll be fine.'

She didn't sound fine, Lizzie thought. 'Have you ever thought about whether you wanted children or not?' Lizzie asked delicately.

'Children . . .' Erin said the word as though she'd never linked the notion of pregnancy with children before. 'This is all such a shock. I'm not a motherly person, to be honest. You have kids, do you?'

'Two, but they're not exactly kids any more,' Lizzie laughed. 'They're grown-ups. I was quite young when I got pregnant,' she added.

'Like my mother,' Erin said, looking down at her hands.

'Really?'

'She was seventeen.'

'I was twenty-two myself,' Lizzie said. 'I suppose those few years do make a difference. Did your mum find it hard to cope?'

She wondered if that was what was freaking Erin out – the memory of motherhood being a struggle for a teenage mum, who wasn't much more than a child herself.

Erin's pale face looked even more stricken.

'I must get your husband. What's his name again?' asked Lizzie anxiously.

'No,' begged Erin. 'Don't go. I can't face anyone now. I can't walk up past everyone looking this sick. When I feel a bit better, I'll get Greg and we'll go. But not yet. Please.'

Lizzie's mind was doing overtime. What if this baby wasn't Erin's husband's? Was that why she was so shocked by the news?

'It's not the end of the world, you know,' she said. 'Problems that look bleak now might not be later on.'

It was as if Erin didn't hear her comforting words. 'My mother didn't cope, you see. She was too young so my grandmother took me and raised me. I thought that my aunt was my sister and that my mother was another sister who'd gone away years ago. Nobody told me the truth until I was eighteen.' She hesitated. 'And then I left.'

Lizzie put her other arm round Erin's shaking slender body. 'You poor girl, it must have been such a shock. But it was a long time ago, wasn't it? And, of course, you're going to think about your mother at a time like this – well, if you *are* pregnant,' she added, seeing as they'd both taken this wild leap of faith. 'But you're an adult, not a child, and you've a husband. This could be a wonderful time for you.'

'You don't understand.' Erin sounded distraught now. 'I never went back home after I left. I wanted to hurt them by staying away. I sent some postcards so they knew I was alive, but I never went back, and then, when I began to think I should, it was too late. I can't go back now. It's all my fault.'

Tears began to fall down her face and Lizzie felt terribly

sorry for her. Earlier, when she'd been introduced to Erin, she'd thought the younger woman looked utterly confident and totally in control of her life. Now she appeared frighteningly out of control. Lizzie wondered if she should ignore Erin's request and rush into the house and find Greg.

'I'm sorry,' sobbed Erin, holding on to Lizzie's arm as if she'd float away without an anchor. 'I'm never like this usually. It's all just such a shock.'

Relieved that Erin was being more lucid, Lizzie abandoned her idea of getting Greg. 'Shock makes us think and do strange things,' she advised, 'and you might feel a lot different in the morning.'

'It's complicated,' Erin said, drying her tears on her sleeve as the napkin was now soaked. 'I really don't want children, I never did. I mean, my own mother couldn't handle having a child. She gave birth to me and ran away. She wasn't mother material and neither am I. Genetics strike again. That's the only thing I've inherited from her.' She laughed weakly at her caustic little joke.

'But your grandmother brought you up. She's your blood relative and she cared for you,' countered Lizzie. 'So you can't say that being unmaternal is part of your heritage.' She paused, suddenly wondering if the reason why Erin had stayed away from her real family for so long was because her grandmother hadn't been a good mother substitute. It would be understandable that Erin didn't want children if her own experience of childhood had been a painful one. 'Was she good to you, your granny?' she asked hesitantly.

For the first time, a real smile lit up Erin's face. 'Yes.'

It wasn't a story that Erin was used to telling, but she found it almost a relief to pour it out to Lizzie. And telling it stopped the tears because she'd trained herself not to cry when she thought about it.

'I phoned a few times to tell them I was all right,' Erin told Lizzie dully. 'Mum would cry when I phoned and one day Kerry took the phone from her and said if I was such a bitch not to come home, I could bloody well not bother them again.'

Lizzie winced, imagining the effect that would have had on the hurt and lonely teenager far from home. 'That wasn't fair,' she said.

'Kerry was protecting Mum, that's all,' pointed out Erin. 'She was very loyal and her loyalty was to Mum. After Shannon had run off and literally left Mum holding the baby, Mum was devastated. Kerry remembered all that. My doing the same must have felt like another horrible blow.'

What Lizzie still didn't understand was how Erin could have totally cut off contact. 'Didn't you try again?' she asked.

'When I met Greg, I wrote a letter to Mum giving my address and saying that I wanted to come back.' Erin used her sleeve again to wipe her eyes. 'There was never any reply.'

The only noise came from the hum of the party. Lizzie thought of how tragic it was that a family had been ripped apart by such circumstances. If only Erin had known who her real mother was when she was younger; if only she hadn't run away so impulsively; if only her grandmother had replied to the letter. There were so many 'if onlys' in the whole, sorry story. Just then, a figure emerged out of the darkness, and gave a gasp of surprise.

'Oh, I'm sorry, I didn't realise you were there.' Abby had come out for some air and wandered into their part of the garden. Seeing she was interrupting a serious conversation, she turned to go back to the house, but Lizzie stopped her.

'Don't go,' she said. 'Erin's just not feeling well.'

'Oh.' Abby looked down at the tall redhead on the bench. She looked drained and vulnerable in the moonlight, a far cry from the cool, distant woman Abby had met earlier. 'Can I get you something, Erin? Water?'

'Water would be great, thanks,' Erin said.

Abby returned with a glass of water and some baby wipes.

'People with young kids have these everywhere,' she said, handing them to a grateful Erin. 'Can I do anything else?'

Erin made a noise that was half laugh, half sob.

'Are you sure I'm not intruding?' Abby asked anxiously, feeling guilty over how cool she'd been when she'd met Erin earlier. Erin was so stunning and Abby, in her miserable mood, was reminded that she'd never be that young or that gorgeous again.

'No,' said Erin. 'I wasn't feeling well and Lizzie happened along and helped, and in return I told her all my problems.' She felt better enough to flash a small smile.

'Lizzie makes you tell her your life story the first time you meet her.' Abby grinned. 'We didn't know each other really until tonight and I've bored her rigid with chapter and verse on me.'

'Well, snap.' Erin laughed for the first time. 'How do you do that, Lizzie?'

Flushing, Lizzie shook her head. 'I don't,' she protested.

'You do,' insisted Abby.

'You're like Sally. People feel they can tell you stuff,' put in Erin. 'I've never talked about my family to anyone other than Greg until tonight.'

'I might get on well with other women, perhaps, but I'm hopeless with men,' Lizzie sighed. 'I originally came into the garden to hide from the solicitor who works next door to the surgery and who almost put his hand down my top! He wasn't interested in telling me anything, except that he was a man of stamina. He thought when I backed away that I was playing hard to get.'

'Told you it was a lucky outfit!' teased Abby.

She was nice, thought Erin in surprise, realising that her initial assessment of Abby had been wrong.

'Ugh, lucky,' said Lizzie. 'I'll never wear it again. Jess can have it if she wants. She's tall and slim enough to suit it, although that turquoise T-shirt suits her brilliantly too.'

'Oh, is the young girl in blue your daughter?' asked Erin with interest.

Abby nodded proudly. 'Jess is fifteen and a half and she's

very clever, but she's a bit shy. She babysits for Sally and she's helping tonight.'

Steve's silhouette appeared at the French windows, peering out, and he ambled down the path to where the three women were sitting at the end of the garden.

'So this is where you've all got to,' he said.

'We're having a good girlie chat,' Abby said quickly, sensing that Erin wouldn't want anyone to know she'd been ill.

Steve nodded. 'Sally sent me out to tell everyone that we're moving on to dessert now. Profiteroles with cream and real chocolate sauce. Sally's recipe and they're delicious.'

'We'll be in soon,' said Abby.

'Oh, and Greg's been looking for you, Erin. I'll tell him you're with good company.'

'They make you believe in true love, that pair,' sighed Lizzie as Steve went back to the house.

'I know what you mean,' said Abby, thinking of her own marriage again. She and Tom wouldn't make anyone believe in true love. They were more the anti-true-love lobby. Or the out-of-love lobby. Unbidden, the image of Jay Garnier came into her head.

'Coming in?' enquired Lizzie. 'We deserve something sweet, don't we?'

Abby smiled ruefully. 'I think we do.'

Greg and Erin left soon after dessert had been served.

'You were gone ages. I began to get worried about you,' he said as they got into the taxi.

'Oh, I was fine,' Erin lied. 'Making friends.'

'They're nice people, aren't they?' Greg said. 'I like this place, you know. It's homey.'

'Yes, it is,' said Erin absently, her mind a long way away.

Lizzie bundled up the chiffon top when she got home and stuck it on the top of her wardrobe, vowing never to wear it again. Then again, if she hadn't been wearing it, she'd never have rushed into the garden and been there when poor Erin was sick. Helping Erin was her good deed for the day.

Lizzie pulled on her nightie and wondered whether Erin had told her husband the news or not. It was clear that the other woman wasn't sure how she felt about being pregnant – if she was.

Lizzie thought wistfully of her own first pregnancy. She remembered the joy she'd experienced once she'd got over the shock and Myles had asked to marry her. She'd been so happy then. Myles had loved her, she was pregnant with a precious baby and she'd had her whole life ahead of her. And what had she now? Nothing but the ability to attract sleazy men. Feeling sorry for herself, she curled up in bed and tried to sleep. Hopefully, she'd feel better in the morning.

'We'll tidy up tomorrow,' Sally said to Steve and Delia as they surveyed the wasteland that was the house after a wildly successful party.

Delia stared at her daughter-in-law in astonishment. 'Are you sick?' she teased. 'I've never seen you be able to settle after a party until the place was spick and span.'

There was an ominous silence and Delia looked from her son to Sally. 'What's wrong?' she asked urgently.

'Nothing,' said Sally, 'probably nothing.'

Delia's hand fluttered to her chest and she sat down heavily. 'What do you mean, "probably nothing"?'

Steve took Sally's hand in his. 'Sally's found a lump in her right breast and she's going to see a specialist in the breast clinic on Wednesday.'

Delia felt her heart quicken. 'Oh God,' she prayed, 'please let it be all right.'

'It will be,' Sally said confidently. 'It will be.'

Delia and Steve exchanged a long look.

'Don't worry,' Sally said lightly. 'Dr Morgan says he's the best breast man in the business, and by Wednesday we'll be wondering what we worried over. I just have lumpy breasts, that's all. Nodular, Dr Morgan called them. I'm going to have an ultrasound, that's all, and I bet it's nothing but a cyst, honestly.'

This was a rerun of the conversation Steve and Sally had had every day since Sally's recent visit to the surgery.

'Yeah,' said Steve, 'you're probably right.' His arms enfolded his tiny wife tightly and she leaned her head against his chest, hating the fact that he was worried and wanting to comfort him.

Delia, who daily counted her blessings in having a loving family so close by her, closed her eyes and sent up a silent prayer to Daniel, her darling husband who'd died three years before. Sally had been so good to her after Daniel's death – even though she was recovering from the death of her own father at the time – as kind and loving as Delia's daughter, Amy.

'Yes,' said Delia firmly, 'we've got to be positive. I'm sure it will be fine.' After all, what else was there to say?

CHAPTER TWELVE

The next day, Sunday, Greg got up early and drove into Cork to the bagel shop that sold even better bagels than the ones he and Erin used to buy in Chicago. He also picked up some fresh roast coffee, the Sunday papers and a bunch of heady pink tulips from a small shop on the way out of the city.

When he got home, Erin was only just out of bed. She stood at the top of the stairs, tousle-haired and heavy-eyed.

'Morning, honey,' Greg said, climbing the stairs three at a time to hand her the flowers and kiss her awake.

'Oh, thank you,' she said, admiring the tulips.

'Thought they might cheer you up,' he said. 'Give me ten minutes and I'll have coffee and bagels ready, OK?'

She nodded and shuffled into the bathroom to shower. When she felt utterly scrubbed clean, she switched the shower from hot to cold and let freezing water cascade over her upturned face and body. It had been her favourite trick when she'd been moonlighting years ago and had only gone home to shower and change between jobs. Today, the icy blast had the desired effect. When Erin made it downstairs, dressed and with her wet hair sleeked back, she looked wide awake and her usual self. She didn't feel it, though. The shock of a cold shower couldn't remove the nagging sensation that Lizzie Shanahan was right and she was pregnant. She hadn't been able to check because pregnancy tester kits were not among Erin's normal health and beauty equipment, but she could buy one tomorrow after Greg had gone to work. Since she still wasn't sure what *she* felt about this turn of affairs, she wasn't ready for Greg's reaction. He loved her enough to deal with her not wanting children. That might change if they were presented with the *fait accompli* of an actual pregnancy. After all, the timing wasn't right.

'I've an idea about what we can do today,' said Greg, his back turned to her as he spooned freshly made scrambled eggs onto toasted bagels.

'Yeah?' Erin sat down at the table and pulled one of the papers towards her.

'Mother and baby supplement included today!' announced the strapline on the top paper. Was this a conspiracy? Erin covered the offending paper with the sports section of another one.

'We could look for a house,' Greg suggested. 'The company will pay for six months' rental but then we're on our own, and living in this house makes me realise just how much I hate rented houses, even if they do find us a nicer one.'

Erin agreed with him. A month of putting up with the cat pee (Erin had tried everything to get rid of the smell, to no avail) and décor from hell made her long for a clean, simple living space they could make their own.

'What do you think?'

He placed bagels and scrambled eggs in front of her, along with a mug of steaming black coffee. Erin never took sugar or cream. She tried a bite of her breakfast. 'Delicious,' she said with her mouth full. She actually felt ill at the thought of eating but didn't want to mention this to Greg. Morning sickness was another confirmation of what she now suspected.

'I meant, what do you think of the idea of buying a house here in Dunmore?'

'It would certainly be an investment,' she said thoughtfully, 'as everyone says house prices are going up round here. It's a desirable area and we'd get our money back if we sold . . .'

'That wasn't really the point,' Greg said gently. 'We don't want to buy a house just to sell it in a few years. I'm talking about putting down roots, settling here for good. I really like Dunmore and Cork, what do you feel about it?'

'I'm not good on roots,' Erin remarked.

'Yes you are, you're just as rooted as the next person,' Greg pointed out. 'OK, so you haven't seen your family for more than nine years but that's easily remedied.'

'Not so easily,' protested Erin, then stopped. Telling the story to Lizzie the night before had clarified it in some strange way. It was no longer a tale with a hopeless ending but a story of a family where simple misunderstanding had done its mischief. It wasn't tragic at all, but stupid. Yes, her grandparents should have told her who her real mother was earlier, but Erin understood how a simple secret could turn into a millstone when you'd kept it so long. They might have been trying to tell her for years but could never find the right time. And they'd always loved her – adored her, to be honest – and looked after her. Being upset was understandable, but in storming out and not coming back Erin had been silly, thoughtless and reckless. Kerry had been her usual argumentative self, and poor Mum had been stuck in the middle, too upset to do what she'd traditionally done and stop the fighting. Only Erin's real mother, Shannon, had got away scot-free, with no blame attached.

'You do like it here, don't you?' said Greg, moving swiftly on.

Erin grinned through a mouthful of bagel. He was so gentle with her, never pushing her about her family, even though she was sure it must seem so strange to him. 'I do like it here. And I don't deserve you, Greg. You're so good to me.'

'I'm not making scrambled eggs every Sunday,' he said, eyes smiling at her. 'This is a special treat. Next week it's your turn.'

'Next week we're going to your parents,' she reminded him. Greg's mother had recovered from her bad bout of flu, so the grand Kennedy family reunion was finally taking place. 'Your mum can coddle you with a full Irish breakfast next Sunday.'

Greg's eyes lit up. 'Rashers, eggs, spiced butcher's sausages, pudding and fried bread. Yes!'

'Would that be cholesterol-free fried bread?' laughed Erin. 'Oh sure, what else?'

They were not the first to arrive at the modern housing development four miles outside Dunmore. According to the paper, it had been launched the previous weekend and, already, thirty per cent of the houses were sold. A winding line of cars was parked along the muddy building site, with people trailing along to the showhouse. Erin and Greg took one look at the hordes of people queuing to get in and turned back to their car.

'They can't all be buying a house,' Greg said, astonished by the sheer volume of prospective purchasers.

'Sunday drivers amusing themselves, seeing what ideas they can pick up for decorating their own houses,' Erin informed him. 'Showhouse interior design is the hottest home study course there is.'

'Clever girl, you know everything,' Greg said, reversing out of the parking spot.

Not everything, Erin thought. Not that having a stomach bug could render the contraceptive pill useless.

The second development they stopped at was a small apartment block, the second block to be sold in a series of three. Settled in a natural hollow with trees all around and a bird sanctuary across the road, the complex was well designed, with lots of shrubbery, a tiny lake and plenty of discreet parking. The third block was already under construction but the builder's diggers and other machines were neatly lined up to the right of the construction site.

There weren't many cars outside the block where the new show apartment was situated.

'Does that mean everybody has seen this place already and it doesn't measure up?' Erin asked.

'Houses, not apartments, are the big sellers round Dunmore,' Greg said. 'There isn't as much call for apartments. The realtor told me that people like having their own patch of garden.'

'You *have* been doing research,' Erin teased.

'Well,' said Greg sheepishly, 'it's an idea I've been toying with. I did talk to a realtor but you know I'd never do anything until I knew how you felt about the idea of buying a place.'

Erin got out of the car and inhaled the fresh breeze. They were further away from the sea here, but the tang of salt water was still in the air, mingled with a woody scent from the trees around the complex. She liked Dunmore; she liked the people, the quaint town itself, the relaxed atmosphere. Nobody was too inquisitive – not like where she'd grown up – and there was a sense that you could find your own pace in Dunmore and live your life to that rhythm. Greg clearly adored it; he was happy in his job and happy with the fifteen-minute commute every morning. If Erin could sort herself out with a job, then it would be ideal. And at least she now had some idea of why she'd felt so lethargic about getting work, she realised ruefully.

'I do like Dunmore,' she said, as Greg wrapped an arm round her shoulders on the walk up to the apartment block. 'I like it a lot.'

She'd loved the anonymity of their life in Chicago and the way they were a tight little unit there with nobody else to consult about their lives. But she'd always known in her heart that Greg wanted to come home. And maybe, just maybe, so had she.

Until she walked into the show apartment, Erin had agreed with Greg's realtor that, if they were buying in Dunmore, a house would be the nicer option. She'd only lived in apartments in the US, and the idea of a bit of garden (as long as someone else got to do the actual gardening bit) sounded good.

But one step into the bright airy apartment and she changed her mind. It was as if an architect had consulted her personally on all the things she'd hated in every other apartment she'd ever lived in and had carefully fixed all the flaws. The hall (often a big waste of space in Erin's opinion) was compact but well designed, with a huge built-in closet perfect for coats, the vacuum, and even things like skis or bikes. The living-room/dining-room area was lit by a huge picture window and the south-facing balcony was like a mini garden, with potted plants and room for a tiny wooden table and chairs. A modern fireplace was set into one wall and Erin could instantly imagine herself and Greg curled up in front of it. The kitchen was bigger than the one in their Chicago apartment, although that wasn't saying much. There was a small bathroom with a corner tub, and the two bedrooms were good sized, with a decent master bedroom complete with a walk-in closet and a cosy en suite. The baby's room was big enough for a cot, a changing unit and a rocking chair.

Erin had to sit down on the bed in the second bedroom when she realised what conclusion her mind had come to. The bedroom wasn't decorated as a nursery but that's what she'd instantly thought of. A home for her baby – their baby.

She inhaled deeply to calm herself. She could give birth to this baby because what was there to stop her? Nothing, except her belief that she couldn't possibly be a good mother after her own mother had abandoned her. Self-fulfilling prophecies were for medieval peasants who knew no better. Erin didn't know why her real mother had run off but just because she *had*, didn't mean Erin had to follow suit. Excitement flooded through her.

Greg sat down on the bed with her. 'Nice, huh?' he said, scrutinising the built-in closets. 'A second bedroom is handy for guests, or we could turn it into a guest room-cum-home office.'

'Or a nursery.'

'If we got one of those sofa beds, it could be a pretty decent office and a guest room,' Greg went on, not taking in what she'd said. 'They've really designed it well. Even the hall is good, and I know how mad it makes you when half the apartment space is wasted in a big hall.'

Another couple wandered into the second bedroom, with a flurry of 'excuse mes' as they stepped past Erin and Greg.

'Did you hear me?' she asked, unable to keep the smile from her face. A baby, their baby.

'Sorry, I'm thinking about this bedroom . . . what did you say?'

'I said we could turn this room into a nursery,' Erin repeated, 'and if you want kids, you're going to have to get over this genetic inability to do or think of more than one thing at one time.'

The female half of the apartment-hunting couple sniggered.

'What?' Greg's face was a picture of astonishment.

The woman dragged her partner out of the bedroom and Erin could hear her stage whisper to him, 'She's telling him she's going to have a baby!'

'You're going to have a baby?' The way Greg said it, it was a question not a statement.

Erin nodded. 'I think so. I haven't done a test or anything.'

'Where can we get one?' Greg was off the bed in a flash.

'Would you be happy if I was?' asked Erin tentatively. This jumping into action wasn't what she'd envisaged.

'Hell, yes.' Greg sank back onto the bed beside her and pulled her roughly into his arms, kissing her passionately. 'Happy doesn't come close. I can't tell you how good I feel. But,' he pulled away and took her face in his hands, 'how do you feel?'

Erin considered this. 'Until five minutes ago, I didn't know, Greg. I felt confused by the whole thing and then I saw this room and thought it was made to be a nursery and . . .' The feeling of astonishment overwhelmed her again and she couldn't speak. She'd thought she didn't want a child and now she wanted nothing more in the whole world. She couldn't wait to have a belly that everyone would notice and she couldn't wait to feel baby kicks inside her.

'I'd love it to be a nursery,' Greg said. 'I couldn't think of anything I'd like more in the whole world. We could turn the spare bedroom in Cat Pee Towers into a nursery and I'd still be over the moon. You were always so anti-children.'

'Because of my real mum,' Erin reminded him. 'It wasn't that I hated kids or anything, but I believed I'd be the wrong sort of person to be a mother.'

'You'll be an incredible mother.' Greg's hand went to caress her still-flat belly. 'Have you got a bump, do you think?'

'If I have, it's not going to the gym and eating too much,' Erin pointed out.

'Well, come on.' Greg got to his feet and gently helped Erin to hers as if she was a fragile flower. 'Let's get to the drug store right now. We need a pregnancy test.'

'We?' she asked, unable to stop grinning at how delirious he appeared to be at the news.

'Yeah, we. If I'm going to be a dad, nobody's going to accuse me of not being there all the way. A father.' He looked so proud at the idea. 'Me, a father. I can't wait.'

The realtor peeped his head round the bedroom door. 'So? What do you think?'

'We like it,' beamed Greg. 'How soon could ours be ready?'

CHAPTER THIRTEEN

In the couple of days following the party, Abby and Tom made a huge effort to get on with each other in front of Jess. In private, they didn't discuss what had happened that night, but guilt over having upset their daughter made them at least outwardly polite to each other.

However, a smile delivered with 'Pass the broccoli, please, Abby' did not a reconciliation make.

In her heart, Abby was still furious with Tom for all the hurtful things he'd said to her. She knew that if she made the first move, the frostiness would be over. But this time she wouldn't apologise – *she* wasn't in the wrong. Tom was the one who'd insulted her and accused her of putting her family after her career. She worked so hard for this family, both in the home and outside it, that the notion of her putting them last enraged her.

In the face of this relationship breakdown, tricky questions kept slipping unbidden into Abby's mind. Were affairs always bad for marriage? Or, more accurately, would an affair hurt *her* marriage and was she mad to see Jay again before she could work out the answer, because seeing him was temptation?

These unanswerable questions went round and round in her head at times when she was least able to think straight. Like on Sunday night when Tom was slumped asleep in the den, piles of papers on his lap, his head lolling back open-mouthed. Or when she went into the bathroom on Monday morning and found the toothpaste left uncapped, his shower towel half in and half out of the laundry basket, and an empty loo roll hanging forlornly on the holder. If they'd been getting on, she'd have dealt with her doubts and reminded herself that marriage was the original roller-coaster ride with ups and downs.

But with marital war raging, it was as if she was being urged to have an affair. '*This* is your life and your marriage,' the whispery little voice in her head said. 'This is it, a man who treats you like Mrs Mop and who won't say sorry for the hurtful things he's said.'

By comparison, the memory of Jay was all glinting sexuality – the promise of something incredible when he touched her. It wasn't just about sex, Abby tried to convince herself. It was much more: the excitement of being alive, the thrill of being wildly attractive to someone else. When had Tom last spoken to her with such naked longing? He reserved his naked longing for the sixth years to do well in their state exams.

Long-forgotten memories of what it was like to be younger and in love rippled through her. And for Abby, who had felt so old and tired lately, the remembrance of youth was headier than any champagne.

If she did have an affair with Jay, Tom would certainly have to shoulder some of the blame, she decided in her wilder moments. If he'd bothered being a proper, supportive husband, then she wouldn't even have dreamed of meeting another man.

Nobody need know. It would be a little boost to her ego and then she'd go back to being a mother and wife, because she did love Tom despite everything. And Jay would go back to being in the past. They could still be friends, she hoped, once they'd got this attraction thing out of the way. They might even still have dinner as a foursome, with two of them sharing a secret that would always add a sparkle to their lives. Like a secret batch of love letters hidden in a drawer, there would be something for her to remember in the years to come: the time that she'd dallied with a man from her past.

As to what might happen if everything went wrong, Abby closed her mind to the very idea. Nothing would go wrong. Nobody would ever know. Anyway, she was only meeting Jay for dinner, she told herself.

On Tuesday morning, Abby prepared with care for the trip to Dublin. She packed her sexiest underwear and put on a silky jersey wrap dress in silver grey over a new, utterly beautiful bra-and-pants set for the journey. Lovely underwear would make her feel good, that was all. And anyhow, she had a meeting in Beech at ten before she drove to the airport, and when it came to meeting Roxie and hearing about her latest plans for the programme, Abby reckoned that she needed all the confidence boosters she could get.

The meeting was as tough as she'd anticipated. Roxie had made high-speed progress with her search for new talent for *Declutter*. In just ten days, she'd found eleven possibles and she had summoned the whole team in for a meeting to show them a tape of the candidates.

'Of course, you've got to feel happy with whoever we pick, Abby.' Roxie gave Abby her most caring smile.

Yeah, right, thought Abby grimly, convinced that Roxie didn't give a damn if Abby liked her on-screen partners or not. In fact, Abby believed it would suit Roxie down to the ground if she bailed out of the programme altogether. Then Roxie could hire a couple of twelve-year-olds to do the show and everyone would be happy. The candidates were uniformly young and gorgeous, all with teeth that must have involved second mortgages for their poor parents, and not a wrinkle anywhere. Abby didn't recognise any of them.

'Have they any television experience?' she asked when the showcase was over and Roxie was midway through extolling the virtues of the last girl, an ex-beauty queen who'd worn hot pants and a belly-revealing top for her audition.

'Good point,' agreed Flora. 'They all look wonderful but there's a difference between a simple to-camera test and doing a programme. I didn't see anyone who'd worked in TV before.'

Score one to the Help the Aged side of the table, thought Abby happily.

But Roxie had an answer for that. 'You didn't have any television experience when you started, did you, Abby?' she asked.

'Er, no,' admitted Abby.

'That was different,' said Stan, coming to her defence. 'The show was about Abby because she worked in de-junking people's homes. She was an expert rather than a presenter.'

Abby shot him a grateful smile.

'Yes, but the team at Beech, *you guys*,' Roxie enfolded Stan, Flora and Brian in the warmth of her praise and left Abby out, 'you all helped her learn how to become a presenter. You can do it again.'

'What if they aren't good enough, though?' insisted Flora. 'What do we do then?'

'We'll find more people for our shortlist,' Roxie replied as if it were very simple. And it probably was when you were someone like Roxie, Abby reflected gloomily. She'd bet anything that Roxie never had a moment's doubt in her whole life, about work, men, anything.

They sifted through the CVs with photos attached until they all agreed on five final presenters to be given studio auditions, three women and two men.

'As we're not sure which format to go for yet,' Roxie mused, 'we don't know if we'll need only one person, or two.'

'Time enough to talk about that when we've done the auditions,' Brian said, hauling himself out of his leather chair. 'Better fly, folks. We've got a meeting with some people about a new quiz show. Roxie's idea. Could make us a fortune.' He rubbed his hands together gleefully and smirked at his executive producer.

Abby watched dismally. She could see how valuable Roxie

must be to both Brian and Beech. Go-getting, ambitious, ruthless – she was what every television company needed. If there was a power struggle between Roxie and Abby, there was no doubt as to who'd win. The presenter of a show was always dispensable but an executive who could bring in millions in revenue from new programmes was worth her weight in gold.

As there was no point in hanging around any more, Abby said her goodbyes and left the conference room.

Roxie caught up with her by the lifts.

'Abby, there may be journalists phoning you about the new additions to the show. We've put the story out that we're looking for new talent and, naturally, people want to get your reaction.'

'Naturally,' said Abby. She wouldn't give Roxie the satisfaction of seeing how jolted she was by all of this.

'I'm sure you'll fill them in on how thrilled we are at this chance to give the show a boost because it was getting a bit tired,' Roxie went on, her sharp eyes travelling over Abby's carefully made-up face and stunning new outfit, making Abby hope that her new thick-lashes mascara hadn't got to the stage of sliding down her face like giant panda markings. 'If the new format bumps up the ratings, we're all happy, aren't we?'

Abby cast her mind back to the expression she'd used on the episode when trawling through one woman's shoe collection had yielded the furry corpse of a hamster that had gone missing many moons before. The trick was to look interested rather than disgusted.

'You can count on me, Roxie,' she said, her dead-hamster face firmly in place.

It was only when the lift doors whooshed shut that she allowed her face to reshape into an expression that showed her real emotion: anxiety.

Downstairs, Livia on reception had fan mail for her. A big A-3 envelope filled to the brim with letters.

'Thanks, Livvy,' said Abby, feeling suddenly close to tears

191

at the sight of this collected mass of approval. *Somebody* liked her, even if that horrible bitch Roxie wanted her out.

As she took the envelope a sudden waft of Livia's perfume made her legs feel weak. Livia was wearing Calèche. Abby had had a bottle of that once, just one bottle in her lifetime, but she could instantly remember when she'd worn it. There had been seven of them inter-railing round Europe, all with plans to split up and see different cities. Abby, her sister, Viv, and Linda from college wanted to see as much of Europe as possible in a month before ending up in Spain or Italy in a yet-to-be-discovered spot that fulfilled the twin requirements of being both cheap and very hot so they could spend two weeks on the beach. Jay, Colm and two other guys from university planned to relax first and then tour, ending up in Amsterdam so they could lounge around in the coffee houses, breathing in both the fuggy, smoky atmosphere and a bit of legal dope into the bargain.

Naturally, none of these great schemes went according to plan. Colm had a thing for Linda, so the guys followed the girls to Paris where they all spent a week, and then the groups split up with Linda, Colm, Jay, Viv and Abby taking a meandering journey towards Italy to sunbathe. Somewhere between Paris and Rome, Jay and Abby ended up sharing a room . . .

'It's exciting about the show, isn't it, Abby?' said Livia. 'Selina's out sick this morning – her sinuses, poor love – but she left a message to tell you she'd phone you on your mobile tomorrow to tell you which papers and magazines want to do a piece on the search for new presenters for *Declutter*.'

'That's great,' Abby said, taking her fan mail with her. She'd thought she and Selina got on well but perhaps that was changing too. The least Selina could have done was forewarned Abby about Roxie having put the story out publicly. Then, she'd have been able to smile politely when Roxie mentioned it. Abby's sense of anxiety notched up another level.

* * *

She reached McGregor's Townhouse at just after three, and as she stood in line to check in, Abby realised that she'd never noticed how quiet the lobby was before. When she'd stayed there previously, she usually rushed in and out far too quickly to notice, pausing only to collect her keys or order something at reception. But today, toying with the idea of meeting Jay there, she noticed the lobby was sepulchrally silent, with no musak to mask conversations and no lively chatter from other guests.

It was so quiet that if she and Jay tried an 'Oh hello! Fancy seeing you here,' everyone within a ten-yard radius would hear and no doubt instantly guess that there was some subterfuge going on. Worse, what if one of the *Declutter* team appeared suddenly and saw Abby heading off with a gorgeous man in tow, a man who definitely wasn't Tom? Why hadn't she arranged to meet Jay somewhere neutral for dinner instead of relying on his laid-back 'I'll contact you in the afternoon'?

Panic filled her. Abby checked in and fled to her room, too nervous to worry over what newspaper she wanted with her breakfast and whether she needed an alarm call or not.

She'd been given a junior suite again, but today she didn't bother cooing over the luxury of the king-size bed or the complimentary bottle of wine placed beside a fat basket of exotic fruit. Dumping her stuff on the bed, she rushed to the phone but its red message light wasn't lit. No call from Jay. And he hadn't phoned her mobile either, which had been her chief fear since she'd made the assignation. Every time her phone had rung during the past week, Abby had jumped with nerves. If it rang when either Jess or Tom was present, she ignored it.

'How can you do that?' had demanded Jess, who lived with her phone glued to her ear as she spoke ten times a day with Steph.

'I don't feel like answering it,' Abby had replied tersely as her mobile squealed insistently from the depths of her handbag in the kitchen.

'And you give out yards to me for not being able to hear my mobile when I'm on the train listening to my Discman,' Jess said accusingly.

Now, Abby sat on the bed and dialled Jay's number. It was switched off and she got through to his answering service. Nerves made her reckless and she left a message: 'Jay, sorry, I think this is a mistake. I know you said you'd get in touch with me in the hotel but it's too public. The team will be staying here, and what if one of them arrives early? I don't think I can go through with this. I can't have dinner with you. I'm married. I'm sorry, really . . . goodbye.'

She hung up, breathing heavily as though she'd just run up a flight of stairs. She'd actually done it. She'd told Jay she couldn't go ahead, and there was no doubt that this was the right move. She wasn't cut out to flirt, let alone have an affair. Practised adulterers probably didn't feel their stomachs leap with sheer anxiety at the thought of cheating on their husbands. They just jumped into bed with someone and got on with it. *Carpe diem* and all that. Abby, with convent-school morality drilled into her, was too nervy to *carpe* anything.

She slipped off her high heels and swapped her clingy grey jersey dress for the hotel's enormous towelling gown. Flicking on the TV, she began to unpack, half listening to a chat show as she hung up her clothes. Veronica from Beech's wardrobe department had provided two gorgeous new tops for this week's filming: a blush-pink fitted shirt that looked great over jeans, and a funky long-sleeved T-shirt with a fifties comic-strip illustration on the front. Now that she had nothing to worry about apart from the actual show, Abby could appreciate the new clothes.

She must have been mad to think of having an affair, she decided. Mad or off her head. Still, it was all in the past now.

When she'd unpacked, Abby got some orange juice from the mini bar, took some Toblerone as a treat, and sat down on a turquoise-and-white-striped couch to enjoy the

TV and the gossip magazines the hotel had thoughtfully provided.

She was halfway through the chocolate when the doorbell buzzed. She opened the door curiously and her breathing stopped. There stood Jay with a bottle of champagne in one hand and a small carrier bag from an upmarket deli in the other. His smile was wolfish and as he lounged against the door jamb, eyeing up Abby in her unflattering robe, she felt her resolve crack.

'May I come in?' he said in a low, dark voice.

'Of course,' she squeaked, scared someone would see him. Inside, he shoved the door shut with his foot, put the champagne down and took Abby in his arms. It was all happening so fast, his face close to hers, his body pressing against hers, and then he was kissing her. It was so different from kissing Tom, that practised dance of years of familiarity. Jay kissed her as if kissing was a form of sex all on its own, his big wolfish mouth devouring hers, his tongue flicking in and out of her mouth, one of his hands cradling the back of her head to pull her closer and closer. And Abby, who couldn't remember feeling such passion for years from mere kissing, kissed him back, her mouth locked on his, her body jammed up against his and the only thought in her head that they get out of their clothes and hold each other skin on skin before sinking into the bed and making love . . .

'You taste all chocolaty,' he murmured, breaking away from her to unfasten the belt of her robe. 'It's very nice.'

'Toblerone – I had no lunch,' said Abby, who'd felt far too nervous to eat before she'd called the whole thing off. Or *thought* she'd called it off.

'This is more than very nice.' Moving back so he could look at her, Jay's roving eyes took in the lacy grape silk knickers and the matching demi-tasse bra that left nothing to the imagination, the roseate peaks of her nipples visible through the delicate lace.

In that moment, Abby didn't care about stretch marks or keeping her poochy little belly sucked in. Her whole body throbbed with lust and she felt beautiful. His desire made her feel beautiful. Desire was definitely the greatest aphrodisiac of all.

'And very sexy. You always were a sexy woman, Abby. I don't think you knew it but you drove all the men in our year wild with that sexy walk of yours and the way you'd flick your hair back and lift your chin when you wanted something.' Jay reached out a long finger and lazily slipped it into one cup of her bra, pulling the fabric down so her breast was exposed, nipple erect. He didn't touch her, just looked at her breast, his breathing heavy. Then his eyes locked with Abby's and she could see the same expression mirrored in his eyes: lust.

'I want you so much, Abby,' he said, and his fingers brushed her nipple, making her arch against him with pleasure. 'But you have to want it too.' His fingers squeezed the sensitive peak, sending bolts of sexual electricity pulsing through her. When his mouth followed his fingers, sucking her nipple into the hot cavern of his mouth, making her gasp with wanting him, she was lost.

'Do you want it? Do you want me?' he demanded, his other hand moving down her silky skin to linger tantalisingly at the waist of her lacy knickers. Teasing, his fingers slipped inches inside the knickers, feathery strokes designed to drive her wild. He'd always been able to do that.

'Do you want me?' he repeated.

'Yes,' she moaned, 'yes, I want you, Jay.'

'Good,' he said, his eyes almost black as he stared into hers, his fingers delving inside her, making her know that there was absolutely no turning back now . . .

Afterwards, Jay opened the champagne without spilling a drop.

'To us,' he said, handing Abby a glass.

She drank deeply, the spiky taste of champagne bubbles reviving her from her post-orgasmic exhaustion.

The deli bag contained a mini picnic of tiny soft white rolls filled with cream cheese, a container of smoked chicken and another of soft prawns in mayonnaise.

'You certainly came prepared,' Abby joked as they sat on the bed, their picnic spread out before them on a hotel bath towel. She'd put her sexy underwear back on, not comfortable enough to sit there naked and not wanting to ruin the atmosphere in her giant, teddy bear robe. 'Do you normally bring a picnic?'

Jay shot her a quick suspicious glance and, instantly, Abby knew she'd said the wrong thing.

'It was a joke,' she said quickly. 'I know you don't do this type of thing . . .' And then her voice trailed off because how did she know what he did or didn't do?

'Abby, I want you to know that I've never cheated on Lottie before,' he said slowly, 'never. But you and I . . . we go a long way back, Abby. I've never forgotten you. I probably never got over you.'

'Honestly?' she said, eager to stop all talk about Lottie or Tom or the real world where real people would be hurt by what they'd just done.

'Honestly.' Jay filled up her glass. 'That summer was what fun and youth were all about. Do you remember that night on the train to Rome when we couldn't get a sleeper and we curled up on one seat, but kept sliding off?'

'And when we got to Rome we found a tiny hostel and went to bed and slept for a whole day?'

'We didn't sleep all the time,' Jay reminded her with a grin.

By the time they'd drunk the whole bottle, Abby felt sleepily sexy again, and this time it was even better. The booze had anaesthetised her conscience to that comfortable dull point where tomorrow and nemesis were both a long, long way away. Curled beside Jay in the comfort of a king-size bed with 250-thread-count Egyptian sheets cool against her skin, Abby felt strangely beautiful and utterly content. This was where she was supposed to be. Rules were for other people.

The shrill ring of her mobile phone jerked her into reality. Leaning over to the night stand, she plucked it up and automatically answered with a tentative, 'Hello?'

'Hi, Abby,' said a voice that rang a bell at the back of Abby's mind. 'It's Babs Lennon from the *Chronicle*.'

Abby remembered her. Babs was one of the first reporters Abby had ever spoken to, a TV-page veteran who'd written a glowing review of the show and who'd described Abby as 'the kind of woman you'd love to invite into your home to sort out your life'. Thrilled, Abby had kept the clipping.

'Hi, Babs,' she said warily, conscious of Jay lying naked beside her, the length of his thigh up against hers. Nobody could have seen her and Jay, could they? Oh no, what would poor Tom think? It would kill him. Remorse hurtled back with the speed of a steeplechaser. What had she done? And it was public knowledge now if the newspapers were phoning. She'd just have to say they were old friends having a drink in her room, that was all and . . .

'We're running a story on the search for the new *Declutter* presenter and I wanted a couple of quotes from you,' Babs went on.

'Oh, yes.' Feeling like a complete idiot for imagining that anyone would be interested in her private life, Abby was aware of the pit of fear in her stomach miraculously closing over. Who did she think she was – Nicole Kidman? She summoned up the energy to answer. 'It's a fabulous idea to get new talent on the show,' she said, trying to sound as if she actually meant it. 'We've been thinking of ways to revamp *Declutter* and this is one we all love. It'll be great fun working with another presenter.'

'Fantastic,' said Babs. 'So you don't have any objections to someone else working on the show?'

'Lord, no, why should I?' Abby's fake smile was stretched to breaking point. 'You can't sit on your laurels in the TV industry, Babs, you know that! It's vital that we keep the show exciting for the viewers and this is just the thing. The whole team are terribly enthusiastic about it all and we're looking forward to finding a new TV talent for Beech!'

'Great, great,' repeated Babs with the preoccupied tone of one scrawling quotes in a shorthand notebook. 'Thanks for that, Abby. See you around.'

'Yes, see you,' said Abby dully. Sober now, she felt unclean somehow, lying through her teeth. And then it hit her: she'd just done something she'd have to lie through her teeth about for the rest of her married life.

'Abby,' Jay kissed her bare shoulder, nibbling her playfully, 'I ought to go. I've a function this evening. We're taking some of our biggest clients out to dinner. Dull, but I've got to do it.'

He was off the bed and into the bathroom in one quick movement, and Abby heard the electric hum of the power shower kicking in. She sat motionless on the bed, hangover and guilt mingling together. What had she done?

In what seemed like moments, Jay was back in the bed-room, putting on his clothes. She watched him silently, marvelling at the speed with which he dressed. Tom dressed slowly yet still looked slightly dishevelled. Jay, in contrast, threw his clothes on at practised speed but looked immaculate at the end of it all. Nobody seeing the chic man in the exquisitely cut grey suit and darker grey open-necked shirt, his chestnut hair perfectly smoothed back, would have guessed that an hour before he'd been writhing on a hotel bed with Abby, skin flecked with sweat, hair rumpled as he groaned in orgasm.

'Please don't be upset, darling,' he told her, pecking a gentle kiss on her cheek. 'It has to be like this, we both know that. But I'll see you again. Soon, very soon.'

And he was gone, with only the empty champagne bottle, the deli carrier bag of rubbish and two condoms rolled up in tissues in the wastepaper basket as proof that he'd been there at all.

Abby looked round her hotel room with something approaching shock. She, sensible Abby Barton, mother to

Jess, wife to Tom, had just had sex with someone else in this room. In the cool light of day, without passion flooding through her veins, she knew she'd made a huge mistake.

'Abby, you poor love, you don't look like you've been sleeping,' tut-tutted Helen the next day, casting a professional eye over the presenter's wan face with its under-eye shadows.

Helen was Beech's hair and make-up artist, and she and Abby were sitting in the back of what Brian liked to call the outside-broadcast trailer, but which was, in fact, a big, rackety van fitted out with a lit-up make-up area, three chairs, a small red velour couch, a curtained-off rail for wardrobe and a tiny kitchenette for tea and coffee. The outside-broadcast convoy consisted of just three vans: two for equipment, christened AC and DC, and the make-up/wardrobe one, lovingly known as the Passion Wagon in honour of the red couch. On rainy days, the entire crew had been known to squash into the Passion Wagon to drink endless cups of tea, play poker and engage in some thoroughly enjoyable industry bitching.

Today was a gloriously sunny day and the team were inside Glete Cottage, a tiny two-bedroomed railway cottage in the centre of Dublin into which the owner had crammed the belongings from her previous house, a big family semi with five bedrooms and a conservatory. Abby hadn't been inside the house yet but she'd seen the photos and knew she'd have her work cut out, if only to decide how to remove the eight-seater dining-room table from the minute kitchen-diner. The movers would need a tin opener to get it out. The prospect of all this hard work wasn't made easier by the fact that she'd had two hours' sleep the night before, both hours being after five a.m., when exhaustion had finally overpowered guilt.

Helen dithered over base and finally chose the industrial strength version that would make Abby look strangely tangerine and caked in make-up in normal light, and healthily tanned under the cameras.

'Would you like a coffee, love?' Helen asked. Even though she was only in her early thirties, she mothered the whole crew like everyone's favourite granny. Lovers' quarrels, money worries and job difficulties were all aired in Helen's corner by the crew during quiet moments. Abby felt ridiculously like spilling her own drama out to Helen, but she knew that Helen liked her and she surely wouldn't feel the same way afterwards if Abby confessed that she'd just cheated on her husband.

'Coffee would be lovely,' she said, choking back a desire to cry. The Passion Wagon was blissfully quiet, and as Helen poured some fragrant coffee from the ever-perking machine, she asked: 'Is everything all right, Abby? You seem very down, not like yourself at all.'

'I've done something stupid,' Abby blurted out, and immediately regretted it.

'We all make mistakes,' Helen said calmly. 'Nobody shuffles off this mortal coil without a few mess-ups, but that's what makes us human.' She met Abby's gaze in the make-up mirror, her sweet brown eyes staring at Abby's anguished ones. 'You're a good person, Abby. Forgive yourself.'

Abby burst into tears. 'I can't.'

'How are you getting on?' called the newest runner from the back of the van.

'Another fifteen minutes,' replied Helen. 'Now shut the door, there's a good lad.'

The door shut quietly. Helen handed Abby a wad of tissues. 'Have a good cry. I'll keep everyone out for a minute and you can get it out of your system.'

'I'll look awful on camera, all red eyes,' sobbed Abby, mopping ineffectually.

'Hush,' chided Helen. 'I can make you look like Miss World in ten minutes.'

She bustled around, tidying up the make-up area, while Abby tried to compose herself. The desire to spill all had gone. How could she tell Helen what she'd done? She couldn't forgive herself so how could anyone else?

In the end, she didn't look quite like Miss World but she still looked pretty good, given the lack of sleep and the red-rimmed eyes.

Helen even had a solution for those – white eyeliner pencil used judiciously in the inner eye rim.

'I went through some supplies of that when I worked with Candy on the afternoon show,' remarked Helen, which showed she was trying to cheer Abby up – Helen was famously discreet and never talked about previous jobs. 'Candy was a great one for arriving with a raging hangover and eyes so red she looked as if she'd bleed to death if she opened them. She wasn't a nice person to work with,' Helen added with restraint.

No, thought Abby, but no matter what sort of a prize cow Candy was, at least she wasn't known to cheat on her husband.

A few hundred miles away in a small room in the breast cancer clinic, the doctor stared at the ultrasound results and thought briefly of the patient who was waiting outside with her husband. Waiting for news that was bad. The couple would undoubtedly suspect bad news now, after the combination of ultrasound *and* needle biopsy. When an ultrasound was being done, whichever member of his team was performing it would talk to the patient as they worked. Nine out of ten breast lumps were benign, they would say, doing their best to make the patient relax. The hundreds of women who walked through the clinic's doors every week needed that reassurance when they lay down for the screening test. Breast cancer were feared words, no matter what advances there had been in its treatment.

But the mass in this poor woman's breast looked anything but benign, hence the needle biopsy as well as the ultrasound. The biopsy results would tell him more, but a combination of instinct and long experience told him this was not a cancer caught in its early stages. And he had to break the news.

This was the part of the job he hated; not the long, arduous

202

days, the battles with bureaucracy for more money for the hospital, the endless reports or the arguments he had with his wife whom he hardly saw. Those problems he could handle. What was still heartbreaking, despite many years in the job, was watching people sit in his office with hopeful eyes and then see the hope flicker and die like a blown-out candle when he delivered his news.

He got to his feet and opened the door to his office to the Richardsons.

'Come in,' he said pleasantly.

Lizzie jerked up in bed when the phone began to ring. Grappling for the receiver, she looked at the alarm clock and fear ran through her. Twenty-five past seven in the morning. Nobody rang that early unless it was bad news.

'Hello,' she said, instantly wide awake, trying to ready herself for the blow.

'Hello, Lizzie,' said Clare Morgan. 'I'm so sorry to phone you at this unearthly hour but I wanted to be sure of getting you to see if you could arrange cover for me for this morning's surgery.'

Lizzie felt the fear ooze away. 'No problem at all, Clare. What's up?'

Dr Morgan bypassed the question neatly. 'I need you to phone Dr Jones and ask him can he fill in for me. I'd phone him myself but my phone battery's dead and I don't want to make too many calls from the hospital phone. Tell him I've been on call since four a.m. with a patient and I won't be home for a few hours. It was a kid with suspected meningitis. The parents were away and he was staying with his aunt, who didn't spot the symptoms. I wonder could we get more of those meningitis symptoms check lists from the health board and remind parents that anyone caring for their children should be up to date on this?'

'I'll handle it,' Lizzie said, thinking that her employer sounded dead on her feet. 'You should get some sleep, Clare.'

'Oh, I'm going to.'

'What about this afternoon's surgery?' Lizzie asked, sitting on the edge of the bed, looking for a pencil and a piece of paper to write notes on.

'Oh, I'll be there,' said Clare Morgan wearily. 'I don't know, I don't think I have the energy for this job any more, Lizzie. It's too painful and exhausting. I got a phone call yesterday evening when you'd gone to say that a patient of mine has advanced breast cancer. She's only thirty-four, Lizzie – thirty-four, and who knows if she'll see thirty-five. With young children and a husband and everything to live for. It's not fair.'

Lizzie knew better than to ask who it was. But she could tell that the doctor was shaken by it.

'Is there anything else I can do, Clare?' she asked. 'If you didn't take your car to the hospital, I could have a taxi pick you up so you can get some rest . . .'

It was as if the normally practical Dr Morgan hadn't even heard her.

'I can't believe we didn't find out sooner, Lizzie, not now when it's too late. And do you know, she says she can cope, all she's worried about are Jack and Daniel . . .'

Lizzie gasped. 'It's not Sally Richardson, is it?' she asked, not caring about patient confidentiality.

There was a pause on the other end of the phone. Then: 'Yes,' admitted Clare. 'It is. But please keep it to yourself, Lizzie. I think the family are going to need to come to terms with it before they start telling other people.'

Lizzie desperately wanted to ask how the cancer had developed so quickly without detection but she didn't. Clare was obviously tormenting herself with just the same questions – how could one of her patients become so ill without her knowledge? Lizzie thought back to all the time Sally spent in the surgery with the boys. She practically never made appointments for herself, and although she'd talked about seeing the doctor, she hadn't – not while Lizzie was on, anyway. She must have been in on one of

Lizzie's days off, and Iris, the covering receptionist, would have typed any referral letters to the breast clinic or a specialist.

'I've run out of money,' Clare said. 'I'll talk to you later. Leave any urgent messages on my mobile and I'll pick them up when I've recharged the battery.'

She hung up. Lizzie went downstairs to make herself a cup of strong tea. She felt so shocked. She remembered Sally and Steve's party the previous weekend and how Sally had graciously fended off compliments about how elegant and slim she looked in her shimmering sleeveless shift dress.

'I know it's annoying when people say they don't diet,' she'd said ruefully, 'but honestly, running round after the boys and working in the salon really does keep the weight off. Delia calls it the working mother diet!' she joked.

Sally had always been tiny but she'd looked as slender as a catwalk model that night, with ribs defined under the silky dress. Lizzie was ashamed to remember feeling envious. How wrong she'd been, she realised now. What kind of world was this when the thinness that actually came from a disease was prized by other women?

While the kettle boiled, she phoned Dr Jones and asked him to stand in for Dr Morgan. Then she drank her tea and stared blankly at a breakfast news show, anything to take her mind off the tragic news about Sally. But it was no good: she could think of nothing else.

Clare Morgan was not given to exaggeration. If she feared for Sally's life, then Lizzie feared too.

Of all the people she knew, Sally and Steve were happiest with their lives and with each other. They didn't bitch about anyone else, or moan that if only they had more money or a four-wheel drive or could win the lottery, their lives would be perfect. They were content with what they had. They were kind, loving, fun and they had their lives ahead of them. Now that was all being snatched away.

What would Steve do without Sally? What would it be like

for those two children growing up without the mother who adored them? Lizzie's own problems faded into insignificance in the face of these questions.

CHAPTER FOURTEEN

The seven days since she'd slept with Jay had been the longest of Abby's life. If she'd thought that presenting a television show with the weight of guilt hanging round her neck was hard, then having to fly home to her daughter and husband had been ten times worse.

With horrible irony, Tom seemed to have decided in her absence that he and Abby needed to make an effort at their marriage, and when she arrived home on Friday evening she'd been greeted by a big hello hug and a reservation at her favourite local restaurant.

'We've both been under a lot of stress,' Tom said. 'Can we put all that behind us and start again?'

Even Jess was in on it. 'I told Dad that you would have been working hard in Dublin and that you needed to get out.'

Inspiration struck Abby. 'Why don't we all go?'

Abby knew she was preoccupied at dinner but Jess made up for her mother's silences. She'd spent Wednesday evening helping out in the animal refuge and during dinner she chatted happily about the various dogs and cats there.

'Jean has just taken in two donkeys,' Jess said, when she'd given her parents the history of what sounded like every animal on the premises. 'They're lovely and they have to get homes together. Donkeys get very lonely . . .' she paused to nibble a bit of bread roll, 'and they have very delicate feet and shouldn't be left outside all the time. People are so cruel to animals.'

Because of Jess's enthusiasm, the meal was a success.

Tom drove home and occasionally put his hand on Abby's, squeezing gently.

As they drove up Briar Lane, Abby had to feign an attack of sneezing to cover up the tears that came to her eyes.

'You OK, Mum?' asked Jess in the sort of sweet concerned tone she hadn't used for a long time.

'Fine,' said Abby, hating herself. 'I must be getting a cold.'

On Monday, she left a message for Jay. She knew he was due to be in Cork that week and asked if he could meet her for lunch the following day, Tuesday. Then she switched her phone off. She didn't want to speak to him until she could tell him face to face that it was over. It was bad enough listening to his flirtatious message confirming the arrangement when she checked the mailbox later in the day.

Tuesday came and Abby felt sick with nerves. To complicate things, Tom's school were breaking up for Easter and he wasn't going in until lunchtime because he had some urgent paperwork to sort out.

'Where are you off to all glammed up?' he asked Abby as she got ready to leave at twelve. She was sitting at their dressing table, carefully fixing her make-up, while Tom was at the wardrobe, searching for a tie to go with his lilac shirt.

She could feel herself colour but somehow managed to answer. 'Oh, a work thing. Some boring lunch with Brian and some advertisers.'

'Where?'

She almost knocked over her small bottle of base. He never usually asked her where she was going to lunch. Was he suspicious? Had he guessed? In the mirror, she could see his expression. He looked perfectly normal, happy almost. The Easter break was upon them and he was due a fortnight off. He was just being friendly.

Abby forced herself to relax. 'Il Boccassio,' she said nonchalantly. 'It's such a media hang-out, I think that's why Brian likes it.' The lies she'd told Tom and Jess – Abby cringed at the thought. Cheating on Tom was about so much more than going to bed with Jay – it was about a tapestry of deceit between herself and those she loved best.

With ten minutes to go before she was due to meet Jay, Abby sat in the Jeep in the parking space and checked her lipstick in her compact mirror. Just one simple, totally innocent lunch. She'd tell Jay that the affair had been a mistake and that they had to stop seeing each other because they both had so much to lose. He'd be sure to understand after all, because he had Lottie and the boys and he adored them, even if there were problems in the marriage. She snapped the compact shut and went over her lines again. Abby had been mentally rehearsing the speech in her mind for so long now that she could recite it in her sleep.

'It was great, Jay,' (strictly untrue because any enjoyment had been ripped out of the whole thing by the gashing sense of guilt) 'but we have to think of our families, of Tom and Lottie.'

Abby hoped this line would make her plan seem the only sensible option. But then, maybe not. Maybe Jay was so consumed with passion for her that he couldn't stop, was hoping she'd divorce Tom, planned a future for them both . . . The thought made her blood run cold. What would she do if that happened, if Jay broke down and said he couldn't live without her?

Perspiration beaded her upper lip at the thought and her legs felt shaky as she got out of the Jeep. Pull yourself together, she told herself firmly. In a few hours, it will all be over and nobody will be any the wiser.

Il Boccassio stood out in the street of sedate office buildings because of its awning of periwinkle blue. She'd deliberately chosen the restaurant because it was so public that nobody could imagine meeting anyone for a furtive lunch there. Only a complete idiot would meet a married lover for an ongoing fling in the city's current hottest media haunt.

Abby thought she'd been doubly clever by choosing it. Before Jay, she'd have never thought she was capable of such subterfuge.

The restaurant was nearly full when she got there, jammed with beautifully dressed media types whose eyes scanned every newcomer to see if they were worth saying hello to. The famous long walnut bar was heaving with people having a drink before lunch, and the air was humming with greetings, laughter, the rattle of the cocktail shaker and loud orders for another bottle.

Abby tried to look nonchalant as she sailed in, following the maître d' past serried ranks of business suits and people much too important to wear formal business attire. She wore a black crepe trouser suit with a crisp red shirt underneath and her hair was styled in the exquisitely tousled, five-minute look that had taken three-quarters of an hour to achieve. Her make-up was understated in nude colours. She looked like she belonged. Jay was already at the table and Abby's confidence faltered when she saw that he'd somehow managed to snare the one table in the entire restaurant suitable for romantic dalliance: a two-place setting tucked cosily away behind a pillar with a potted plant further screening the table. If all the other tables in the restaurant were designed to scream 'Notice us, please', this was the one that murmured 'Leave us alone!'

'Abby.' He was on his feet and embracing her before she'd had a chance to casually say, 'Hi, Jay' in a colleagues-meeting-for-lunch manner. The maître d', who'd seen it all before and who knew where the bodies were buried, looked discreetly blank as the reasonably famous and married Abby Barton was hugged by a man definitely not her husband, a man who slid one hand round her waist in a very relaxed manner.

'Jay, we didn't need this sweet little table,' Abby said loudly, desperate to redress matters in the presence of the maître d'. 'What if anyone else from work pops by to say hello? They won't find us tucked away in here.'

'We don't want anyone finding us,' chuckled Jay in an innuendo-laden voice.

The maître d' slid off, no doubt to phone his favourite gossip columnist, Abby thought furiously.

'Jay,' she hissed when they were alone, 'this isn't a good idea. People know who I am. They'll put two and two together and make four if they see us cosied up in this corner!'

'Let them make four,' said Jay, still holding her hand. 'Let them make five, six and seven, for that matter. I don't care.'

Abby's discomfiture grew. She quickly slid into her seat, pulled her napkin across her lap and hid behind the huge menu. This was not working out as planned. It was as if Jay wanted people to see them being furtive together. At that moment, she wanted nothing more than to blurt out that the affair was over and then run out into the safety of the street, lunchless but relieved that the deed had been done.

But the soft streak in Abby's nature meant she couldn't do that to him. Jay seemed so thrilled to see her and he too had risked his marriage because he'd held a candle for Abby for all these years. He deserved a proper goodbye. Whatever the etiquette for these situations, Abby was determined to try to do it the kind way.

'How are you?' she asked, peeping over the top of her menu.

'Much better since I've seen you,' he said. 'I can't stop thinking about you. You've taken over my mind, Abby.'

'Well, let's order and we can talk,' she babbled, completely thrown by this line of conversation. Oh hell, how was she going to do this? If only they had food in front of them to toy with, then she could tell him the horrible truth while she pushed a salad around with a fork. But the waiters, no doubt primed by the maître d' to expect a leisurely, champagne-fuelled lunch where little dining but much gazing into eyes was the order of the day, were avoiding the romantic corner. Nobody came near them either to proffer bread rolls or to take their order. Abby stared round the restaurant in vain but no waiter caught her eye.

'I'm just a bit uncomfortable about this lunch, Jay,' she said nervously. 'It's so public.'

'You suggested we meet here.' He shrugged.

'Yes, but not this table. We look like . . .' Her voice trailed off.

'We look like we're having an affair,' Jay finished, shooting her a wicked look.

A waiter finally arrived bearing the inevitable bottle of champagne and an ice bucket. All they needed was an order of oysters and a sign saying 'Prelude to sex' to finish the picture. Abby sighed.

'Can we order?' she asked the waiter. 'I've got to rush back to work.'

'Of course, madame.'

She hurriedly requested green salad and steamed fish, while Jay dithered over veal with mushrooms, dragging the whole process out as he enquired about the type of mushrooms and how the veal was served. How could he want to eat veal? Jess's ethics had finally got through to her, Abby realised. Meat was murder but fish was justifiable homicide, as Tom joked. How had she ever wanted to sleep with a man who could order veal?

Once they'd chosen, the waiters were ever present, arriving with bread, butter, water and the correct cutlery.

Then the food arrived, and as Abby pushed her green salad around her plate, she realised that she'd never felt less hungry in her life.

'Settle down, my darling,' Jay said, pouring more champagne into her barely touched glass. 'I know you're nervous. We'll have to find somewhere more private next time.'

'There won't be a next time,' Abby said bluntly.

'Don't say that.' He didn't look shocked at all, just mildly irritated, as if this phase of the proceedings was to be expected but could be got round. 'You don't mean that. We all feel guilty at first but you'll get over it. Let's face it, Abby, marriage is never about happy ever after. Staying with one person for the rest of your life? What a load of old rubbish.' He sounded dismissive. 'Some people need more excitement in their lives and we're those sort of people, Abby. What's wrong with that? After all, nobody's getting hurt and my theory is that what they don't know can't hurt them.'

She stared at him, seeing him as if he were suddenly a stranger instead of the man she'd shared passion with in a hotel bedroom.

'Am I right in guessing that this isn't your first affair, Jay?' she asked coldly.

He grinned, the sexy charmer again with the glint in his eyes and an answer for everything.

'I've never been a monk, Abby,' he said. 'The ascetic life isn't for me – never able to taste the forbidden fruit because I'm married.' He shuddered. 'No, that's not how I am.'

A picture of Tom flickered inside her head. Tom, who'd never dream of having an affair even if he wasn't up for the Husband of the Year award. Reliable Tom, whom she'd betrayed. She'd make her marriage work, she vowed.

'You told me you didn't sleep around,' she said.

'So? You told me the same thing.' He shrugged. 'It's what people tell each other before they rip their clothes off: if you tell other people often enough, you might believe it yourself. I didn't believe you, by the way,' he added. 'You seemed to know what you were doing. I know I didn't imagine those vibes – you were looking for excitement in your life.'

'It was a mistake. I've never cheated on Tom before,' she said bitterly.

'There's a first time for everything,' Jay said glibly.

Abby stared at him with dislike. He'd made it all seem seedy and ugly. But that's what it was, wasn't it? Not a grand passion that had survived twenty years to resurface and consume them, but a tawdry fling powered by lust, boredom and reckless disregard for the people who really loved them.

Jay reached across the table and took her hand in his, sensually paddling the soft fleshy part of her thumb with his own. 'Come on, Abby, you enjoyed it, don't say you didn't.'

She looked down at his hand. Last week, she'd have melted under its gentle caressing. Now she felt nothing. But then again, last week she didn't know the sort of man he really was.

Honestly, did he really think she was going to hop back into bed with him after this? After he'd admitted that he was a serial adulterer and that he'd assumed she was too.

'Hello, Abby.'

Automatically, Abby looked up to see Tom standing beside the table, a shocked expression on his face, his eyes taking in the secluded corner, the bottle of champagne, the untouched food – and Jay's hand clasped lover-like around hers. Whipping her hand away, Abby stared horror-struck at her husband.

'I thought you were meeting people from Beech.' His speech sounded forced, as if he was having trouble remembering how to form words.

'I can explain,' said Abby, shoving back her chair and getting up. 'Tom, it's not what it looks like,' she gabbled frantically, not caring that she was lying again. She wanted to make everything all right, to put the pieces back where they'd been before.

'I'm not blind. I can see exactly what it's like,' Tom said in that same slow tone.

Abby looked desperately at Jay. 'Tell him,' she begged. 'Tell him we just met up for lunch. This is Jay, Tom. Jay from years ago, an old friend, we were just catching up, that's all. Tell him, Jay!'

But Jay was leaning back in his chair, distancing himself from the crisis, his expression saying that this was her problem and she was on her own.

Abby grabbed Tom's arm desperately. 'It's not what it seems,' she said again.

'I came to find you because I've had some terrible news,' he said.

Abby's hands flew to her mouth. 'Not Jess, oh, no, not Jess,' she cried.

'No. Not Jess, thank God. It's about Sally.'

For the first time, Abby registered the fact that now the shock had receded Tom looked grey. 'Sally . . . ?' she whispered.

'Steve phoned me shortly after you left. He's distraught. Sally's got breast cancer,' Tom said. 'Steve said he knew we'd want to know. It looks bad, he says. They didn't want to tell anyone she'd found a lump but she had a needle biopsy and it was cancerous, so they operated yesterday. It's spread to her lymph nodes, most of them, Steve says. They're calling it a stage three cancer. She could die.'

Abby stared at him mutely.

'I wanted to tell you before you heard it from someone else and I knew you were coming here for lunch. With Brian and all the people from work.' His eyes, dark and tortured, burned into hers.

'But how?' Through the shock of being caught out by Tom, Abby digested the news that there was something wrong with her dear friend. 'She's been fine. Wouldn't we know?' This was too strange to take in. How could a perfectly healthy young person be that ill without some symptoms?

'You don't necessarily feel pain with breast cancer,' Tom said. 'Like a lot of things, it all looks healthy on the outside and, on the inside, everything's been eaten away.'

Abby couldn't bear to keep looking at his hurt-filled eyes, knowing that he wasn't just talking about poor Sally's disease.

'Can we see her?' she asked.

'I don't know. She's in the hospital. I told Steve we'd drop . . . sorry. I'd drop in on him tonight when he gets back. He's devastated, doesn't know what to do. I've never known him like this. The boys are at the day nursery, then Ruby's going to fetch them so that Delia can be with Sally but I said they could come to us if Sally would like that. They love Jess and we've got lots of space.' The thought of Jess made his face harden and the pain was replaced by a look of loathing. 'So, now you know. You can go back to your lunch.' He spat the word lunch so venomously that Abby recoiled in the face of his hatred. 'I have to go.' He turned on his heel and left.

'Wait for me,' cried Abby, but he was gone.

'That wasn't ideal,' remarked Jay, picking up the bottle and pouring more champagne into his glass. 'No point in wasting good bubbly. It's eighty euros a bottle here.'

'Is that all you can say?' Abby glared at him. Her husband had found them out, one of her best friends was dying. Hadn't the man any compassion?

'What do you want me to say?' Jay sounded genuinely confused. 'It was nothing to do with me. You're the one who told your husband where you were going for lunch. That was a bit dumb, Abby. If we're going to do this again, you're going to have to learn how to lie a little better.'

She threw down her napkin and picked up her handbag. 'Do you honestly think we're going to ever see each other again, after this?' she hissed.

'You have my number if you change your mind,' Jay pointed out before turning back to his lunch.

As she stalked out of the restaurant, Abby wished she'd thrown his bloody glass of champagne all over his smug face. Not that it would have solved a single thing but it might have given her a smidgen of satisfaction.

For once in her life, Abby didn't know what to do. Shock numbed her. After leaving the restaurant, she sat in her Jeep and tried to work out where to go next. She thought of Tom's anguished face and his inherent kindness. He'd rushed to find her because he knew she'd be devastated by Sally's news. Only to discover her having an intimate lunch with another man.

And as for Sally . . . Dear Lord, prayed Abby, please let

it all be a mistake. Bright, vital, warm Sally could not be dangerously ill. It wasn't right. She was too young, she was a mother with two small boys – how could she possibly have breast cancer so advanced? There had to be some hope, didn't there?

People walked past staring into the car, and the money ran out on her meter. Abby didn't notice.

Her instinct was to find Tom and let him comfort her about Sally, and to plead for their marriage. But she was suddenly scared. They'd coped with so many other things but not anything like this. This was uncharted territory.

She couldn't imagine the pain and betrayal she'd feel if Tom had hurt her by having an affair. How must he be feeling? And Jess . . . darling Jess. Abby faced the fact that her actions would hurt Jess too, the child she'd done everything in her power to protect all her life. How could she have let her stupidity hurt Jess?

At that moment, the only person Abby hated more in the world than Jay was herself. She was to blame for all this. She'd callously pushed her precious family out of her mind just because she was bored and feeling neglected. She had believed her own television hype: she'd thought she deserved more than a faithful husband and daughter, and in doing so, she'd probably lost them both. Abby remembered the unyielding light in Jess's idealistic young eyes when she spoke about the people who hurt animals. She thought of that disgust directed at her, because it would be. Despite her protests to the contrary, Jess was still a child when it came to how she viewed her parents and she saw the world as black and white. There were bad things, good things and nothing in between. She wouldn't just disapprove of her mother's adultery, she'd be devastated by it. As bad, or even worse, Abby would have to tell her about Sally, and Jess adored Sally.

Sitting in a busy side street with people on their lunch breaks rushing past, Abby Barton burst into tears and didn't care who saw her.

*　　*　　*

In blissful ignorance of the news to come, Jess was stuck in the last lesson before the Easter holidays. She was trying to concentrate, really she was. But it was such an incredible day outside, with a shimmering sun that was burning the soccer pitch to the colour of straw, and Mrs Green's voice was droning like a swarm of bees, inducing narcolepsy in all but the most diligent pupils.

The teacher was going through essay possibilities for their English exam. She'd spent half the class discussing how to choose the topic and was now using an old exam paper to get the students to come up with five main points for each of the essay subjects. Nobody could think of very much to say on 'What Does Democracy Mean to You?' and there was a distinct lack of interest in the essay that had to begin with the sentence: 'The clock struck twelve and the door to the cellar creaked noisily open . . .'

Everyone, however, was keen on the question about individuality: 'Is It a Mistake to Follow the Herd?', which made Jess roll her eyes. How come the whole class were keen on the concept of individuality but not the practice? They didn't like Jimmy, who spoke four languages and was a maths genius; they didn't like Sian, the new girl from Wales, who'd showed absolutely no interest in the school and was haughtily indifferent to feeble attempts to intimidate her; and they all thought that Jess's idea of working in the animal refuge was oddball, therefore a waste of time. They didn't like people who were individual, so why pretend?

Saffron was haltingly telling Mrs Green that she liked the way Britney Spears had maintained her individuality in the world of music. 'Her clothes show that she is her own person, when it would be so easy to become like everyone else,' Saffron finished proudly. 'I admire that and would aspire to be individual in everything I do.'

Jess looked at Saffron with narrowed eyes. It was like watching the hundredth sheep in a field bleating that it was different before it trotted off obediently to join its pals.

Jess raised her hand.

Mrs Green smiled at her. Jess Barton was one of her favourite students: genuinely intelligent, thoughtful and aware.

'Yes, Jess.'

'Students say they want to be individual but they don't,'
Jess began. 'They actually want to be like everyone else, like
the same music as everyone else, go to the same concerts as
everyone else, wear the same jeans as everyone else. But they
want people to *think* they're individual because they've got a
pink streak in their hair or whatever. That's not individuality,
that's affectation dressed up to pretend it's individuality. And
when they come across anyone who's genuinely individual,
they gang up on them.'

Mrs Green was thrilled with this point but the rest of the
class stared sullenly at Jess.

'Weirdo bitch,' hissed a voice.

'Calling me "weirdo bitch" proves my point,' Jess went
on coolly. 'Because some of you don't agree with my point,
you react by ridiculing it and me, instead of appreciating the
individuality of it. You're threatened by individuality and by
anyone who doesn't follow the herd meekly.'

'Very good, Jess,' said Mrs Green. 'Class, that's an excellent topic for your essay for the holidays: to look at people
in history who've battled for certain rights even though the
general population hated them for it. History has proved
them right. I know there's some research involved but the
examiners want to see you using your brains and not trotting
out the usual clichés. Now, let's look at the final category in
the essay selection – the personal story piece: "Someone Who
Changed My Life". Fiona, we'll start with you. Can you tell
me how you'd approach this essay?'

'Have you got a bodyguard coming to protect us after
class?' Steph whispered as Jess sat down. ''Cos Saffron is
going to go for you big time. You ruined her "Britney is my
heroine" story and made her look dumb.'

'Tough. If she looks dumb, it's because she *is* dumb,' said
Jess with a defiance she didn't feel. It had seemed like a
good idea at the time to say what she had, but now that

the heat of anger was gone, she wasn't so sure. Saffron and her gang would have it in for her now and Jess wasn't sure she could withstand the sort of bullying they dished out to Sian. Until now, people like Jess went below the class bullies' radar. That could change.

On Tuesdays, the fourth years' timetables gave them the last two lessons free, ostensibly for extra revision for the forthcoming exams. Only the very diligent spent the free time in the library swotting. Everyone else left the school premises at high speed. Today, the start of the holidays, nobody was waiting behind to study, but despite the rush, Steph and Jess were still among the first out of the front gate.

'Tell Saffron to piss off if she says anything,' Steph advised, gasping with the effort of jogging while carrying a huge bag of books. 'She is a cow.'

'Unfair to cows,' panted Jess. 'I like cows.'

'Yeah, but you wouldn't want one as a pet, would you?'

'I'd like a dog, actually. They've puppies in the refuge and I'd love to have one but Mum says no.'

'What about Wilbur? Cats and dogs fight.'

'He's well able to cope with a dog,' Jess said confidently. 'He'd just swat it with his paw, show it who was boss and everything would be fine. Jean from the animal refuge says cats and dogs can be best friends. I've told Mum about the puppies and how they won't be kept alive if Jean doesn't get homes for them all soon, but she says Dad doesn't want a dog, which isn't true. It's just an excuse.'

'They're great with excuses, aren't they?' sighed Steph. 'If we use an excuse to say why we're home at ten instead of half nine, they go ballistic, but if they come up with one, it's a different matter. Hey, isn't that your mum's car?'

'Yeah, what's she doing here?' Jess wondered. They walked towards the Jeep and Abby hopped out, hugging Steph as if she hadn't seen her for months instead of just two weeks ago when Steph stayed over at the Bartons'.

'Hi, how are you?'

'Fine, Mrs Barton,' said Steph, bemused and making a what's-up? face at Jess.

'Hi, darling.' Abby turned to her daughter and held her tightly.

'Hi, Mum,' said Jess. Definitely something up. 'What's wrong?'

'Does anything have to be wrong for me to pick you up?' demanded Abby tremulously.

She'd been at some posh lunch, Jess vaguely remembered, and she'd obviously had something to drink, which was unlike her mother, who was very hot on not drinking and driving.

'Did you have wine at lunch?' she demanded. One of them had to be responsible.

Her mother's eyes filled with tears. 'Only a glass of champagne,' she said. 'Less than a glass, actually.'

Steph and Jess exchanged wide-eyed looks again.

'Well, bye, Mrs Barton,' said Steph, eager to be away from this mother-daughter twilight-zone scenario.

'No, I'll drop you home,' insisted Abby.

'OK,' said Steph reluctantly.

The girls hopped in the Jeep and Abby set off down the road in the direction of Gartland Avenue.

'Seat belt, Mum,' admonished Jess.

Abby nodded and obediently put her seat belt on.

Jess didn't glance back to look at Steph because she knew Steph would have her 'uh-oh, mad parent alert' face on.

At Gartland Avenue, Abby slowed down for the speed ramps and talked about how happy they'd been there. 'Remember when you were ten and some boys from the park tied you to that tree by your anorak strings?' she said mistily as they passed a stunted cherry tree halfway down the suburban street. 'Oh, and there's Mrs McDonald. Yoo-hoo,' she waved as they passed a woman walking a West Highland terrier.

'You hate Mrs McDonald,' Jess reminded her mother.

'Not really,' said Abby. How could she explain that the

nostalgia for her old simple life – before she'd slept with Jay and ruined everything – burnished the past with a golden glow. 'There's our house,' she sighed.

Jess, remembering the speed with which her mother had managed to get the family out of Gartland Avenue, groaned. 'What is it, Mum?' she asked, fed up with this magical mystery tour.

'I'll hop out here, Mrs Barton,' said Steph helpfully.

Abby pulled over and Steph climbed out, waving her mobile phone at Jess as a hint to phone her when everything was OK again.

'What's up, Mum?' asked Jess again.

'I'm so sorry, darling, it's Sally Richardson, she's very sick. It's cancer.'

Jess said nothing, just looked blindly out of the windscreen.

Abby's heart ached at the thought of how this would upset Jess. She and Sally got on so well. Sally treated Jess like a grown-up and had even given Jess a voucher for one of her favourite shops as an extra thank you for helping out at the party, and the girl had been as thrilled as if she'd been given a diamond necklace. If she found out about Jay as well . . . But she wouldn't. While she'd been driving to the school to pick Jess up, Abby had come to a decision: she'd beg Tom not to reveal the truth to Jess, she'd beg on her hands and knees if necessary. He would surely do anything not to hurt their daughter and he'd keep quiet for her, if not for Abby herself.

'Talk to me, Jess,' she said.

'What's to say?' Jess said dully. Cancer. Not Sally, it couldn't be right. Cancer was what old people got.

'I didn't want to treat you like a child and not tell you,' Abby went on. 'She might get better.' She crossed the fingers on her right hand. 'But you need to know, because it's very serious.' That sounded better than saying Sally might die.

'Have you seen her?'

'No. Steve told your father earlier. He's offered to let the

222

boys come and stay with us because they get on so well with you. I don't know if that's going to happen or not but we've got to be strong for them.'

'They're so small and sweet,' said Jess, thinking of the two chubby-cheeked little boys. 'Danny calls me Dess because he can't say Jess.' The tears came then.

Her mother began to cry too, tears speeding down her cheeks both for poor, dear Sally and for herself.

Dad was late home and, for once, the first thing he did was come upstairs to Jess's room. She was at her desk, supposed to be starting on her English work, but she had the radio on low and, hidden by her pile of school books, she was reading *The Little House on the Prairie*. The book was comforting and familiar – like having hot milk and toast in bed when she was sick. Nothing bad could happen when she was reading about Laura and Ma and Pa Ingalls.

'Hi, Jess.' Dad looked sombre; his face seemed older and thinner than usual.

'Hi, Dad.' Jess pulled her English notes over the book.

'How are you?' he asked, sitting on the edge of the bed beside the emptied-out contents of her school bag. He picked up her mobile phone in its purple furry cover and began fiddling with it absently. 'Terrible news, isn't it?'

Jess nodded.

'I phoned Steve on the way home,' he went on. 'He's left the boys with Ruby for tonight and he was going back into the hospital, but he says it would be good if we could take them for a couple of days from tomorrow until things settle down. Apparently Delia's so shocked she keeps crying and he doesn't want the boys to realise anything is wrong. I didn't know what to say to him, to be honest with you. What do you say to someone in that position? "I'm sorry" just sounds pathetic.'

Jess realised what was different about her father: he sounded the way he did when he talked to Mum in the evening, telling her about his day. But Mum was around, she'd been in the kitchen for hours cooking because Jess could smell it. She'd been at it so long, she must have been filling the freezer.

'Mum's downstairs,' Jess volunteered. 'She's really upset.'

For a second, her father's face hardened. 'Is she?'

'Yeah,' said Jess in surprise. 'She loves Sally.'

Dad reached out and touched Jess on the shoulder. 'I know, I know. I'm sorry, Jess, I'm upset. Everything's changed, it's all different and I don't know what to do.'

Pushing her work away, Jess threw herself at her father and hugged him. 'It's so horrible,' she said into his shoulder, wanting him to explain why it was happening. Dad could make sense of things like that; he always had in the past. Like when Granny Barton was sick and had died, and Dad explained that she'd been ill for such a long time and it was cruel of everyone to want her to stay on earth and suffer when she'd be happier in heaven. But this time, Dad had no explanation. He clung to Jess as if he was hoping for an explanation from her.

Jess snuggled deeply into her father. 'Don't worry, Dad. You've got us,' she said.

Abby looked at the foil containers filled with double helpings of vegetarian lasagne, chicken casserole and vegetable curry. Should war be declared, the Barton family could quite happily survive for two weeks on what she'd just cooked. Usually, after Abby had done a marathon freezer session, she felt ravenous and had to eat, no matter what spartan diet she was currently on. This evening, she didn't feel hungry. She'd cooked because it seemed like the only nurturing thing she could do without feeling like a hypocrite.

She'd heard Tom come home and had felt relieved when his footsteps had sounded on the stairs. Then, the relief turned to fear. What if he was going upstairs to pack and leave?

She assembled the last lasagne and was slotting on its cardboard cover when the kitchen door opened. Without looking round, Abby knew it was Tom. She closed her eyes to give her strength, then turned to face him.

To her surprise, he didn't look angry. Instead, he looked beaten, defeated, shrunk in stature almost.

'Tom, I'm so sorry . . .' she began.

'I have nothing to say to you, Abby,' he said. 'I mean it. Don't talk to me. *Don't talk to me*,' he repeated harshly.

'But, Tom –' she said.

'Did you hear me? Are you deaf? Don't talk to me.'

It was like listening to a stranger, not the man she'd married, the man she'd made love to, the man who'd held her hand through all the tough times. That Tom was gone.

'We've got to talk,' she said frantically.

'There's nothing to say.' He picked up his diary from beside the phone. 'I told Steve that we'd take the boys tomorrow for a couple of nights. He'll be here with them at ten. Will you be around?'

Abby nodded.

'Fine.' He left the room and, moments later, Abby could hear the front door shut quietly.

She waited up until midnight but he didn't come home. At one, she heard his key in the lock, but when he came upstairs he went into the spare bedroom and shut the door firmly. In the morning, he was gone before she got up.

It was nearly eleven the next morning when Steve Richardson arrived with Jack and Daniel and what looked like a car-load of kids' toys and clothes.

'I wasn't sure what to bring,' Steve said helplessly, 'so I brought everything.'

'That's fine,' soothed Abby, taking the boys into the den and plonking them in front of the children's channel with beakers of juice. Fascinated by the huge telly, and by all Jess's old cuddly toys that Abby had unearthed from a box in the attic, they were soon engrossed in a cartoon.

'I've made coffee, would you like some?' she asked Steve.

'Yeah, great,' he said absently.

By the time Abby returned with coffee for the two of them, Steve was staring at the television with the same intensity as his two sons. The only difference was that he was looking through it. Abby put milk in his coffee and handed it to him but Steve didn't drink it. He just held on to the mug and stared blankly.

Abby sipped her own coffee in silence, not knowing whether to say anything. She was almost too tired to talk. The little sleep she'd had the night before had been tormented by visions of both Sally and Tom dying, with her frantically trying to help them, only to have Tom shout at her to leave him alone, that it was all her fault in the first place.

'I don't know what to do, Abby,' Steve said suddenly. 'Last week, we thought the worst would be Sally having a cancerous lump, because they can do so much with cancer now. She was fine, we'd got it early, she hadn't any real symptoms although she'd lost weight. But now . . .' He looked bleak. 'The lump was the tip of the iceberg. She has what they call metastatic breast cancer, stage three advanced cancer. It's spread to nearly all her lymph nodes, which means it's moving. It could affect her lungs, her liver, her bones, we don't know. She's having a bone scan next, in fact.'

Abby realised he was fluent in this new language he'd learned: the language of breast cancer.

'What's going to happen now?' she asked.

'Chemotherapy,' said Steve. 'It's just that she has a very aggressive cancer and there's no guarantee chemo will work. I couldn't tell Sally that, I couldn't . . .' His voice broke off.

Abby put down her own coffee and took Steve's from his unresisting grasp, then held his hands in hers. She didn't say anything. What could she say? There were no words, no platitudes that could make it better.

'How do I tell her that there are no guarantees?' he went on. 'I'm supposed to protect her and I can't.'

Abby was silent.

'It's the fear I can't cope with,' Steve went on. He wasn't

looking at Abby. He was facing her but his mind was focused on some place and time far away. 'The fear of her dying and the fact that I have to keep going on without her for the boys' sake. I don't think I can do that. I can't.'

Abby tensed her throat, trying not to let the tears well up. He wasn't crying. Who did she think she was to cry when Steve was the one lost in pain and grief?

'Now is the eye of the storm, so to speak. She's here, I have her, I *still* have her,' he said, almost reverently, 'but what if she dies? I just can't . . .' He was trying to find the right words. 'I just can't picture that. I can't picture a life without her or a world without her.'

His voice was so calm. His eyes were still clear and dry, his thoughts far away in Sally's hospital room. Abby felt the first tear slide down her cheek, then another, faster and faster, following the same trail, dripping unchecked onto her shirt.

'I wish I was religious,' he was saying. 'Then I'd believe in all the things people say, like "When it's her time, it's her time", or "God has chosen her now". Or even find comfort in the thought that I'd see her again in another life.'

Abby realised she was holding her breath.

'But there isn't another life.' Steve's voice was flat. 'I don't believe in it. If Sally dies, it's over. I will never see her again. How can that happen?' For the first time, he looked directly at Abby. 'How can they say there's a God if He can let this happen?'

Abby shook her head mutely, tears still falling.

'She's so good and kind. The world is a better place with her in it.'

'I know.' Abby managed to rasp the words out. 'She's wonderful.'

Steve smiled at her, not a faint movement of the lips, but the broad smile of a man speaking proudly about the woman he loved.

CHAPTER FIFTEEN

Lizzie brought a bouquet of her own roses to the hospital a couple of days later. She didn't plan on trying to visit: she only wanted to leave some token to let Sally know she was thinking of her.

At the hospital, the reception desk staff told her to take the roses up herself. Lizzie walked up the stairs to Sally's ward and, at the landing, she bumped into Delia Richardson emerging from the lift. It was Delia's silvery blonde hair that she recognised, otherwise she would have walked right past without saying a word. Because Steve's mother had aged in the weeks since Lizzie had seen her. The lively, bright-eyed Delia from the party had vanished, and in her place was an old woman with a gaunt, worried face and red eyes.

Lizzie reached a hand out. 'Delia, hello, it's Lizzie Shanahan.'

Delia's eyes flickered with recognition. 'Hello, Lizzie.'

'I wanted to leave these flowers for Sally. I'm not coming in, I didn't want to intrude, but Sally always admired my roses . . .'

'They're lovely. I'll take them in for you.'

'How is she?' asked Lizzie, then hurriedly added, 'I'm not trying to pry, I just hope she's doing all right.' That sounded so lame, she realised.

The other woman shrugged. 'She's doing as well as can be expected. She's so frail, I hadn't realised how thin she'd got. It's in God's hands now.' She made a sign of the cross and then wiped away the tears that started to well up in her eyes.

'I'm sorry, I can't stop thinking of Jack and Daniel without their mother. It's not fair, Lizzie.'

'If there's anything I can do,' Lizzie begged, hugging Delia, 'anything, please call me.'

'Sorry.' Delia pulled away and tried to compose herself. 'I can't seem to cope with this at all. The doctors don't talk about curing her, Lizzie, they talk about giving her more time. It's breaking all our hearts.'

Lizzie fumbled round in her bag and found a pen and an old receipt to write her name and number on. 'Please, Delia, if there's anything I can do, please phone. I can look after the boys or make some food for Steve . . . anything. I'd just like to help.'

'Thanks,' said Delia.

Lizzie walked slowly back downstairs, the spring gone from her step.

She knew several women who'd been diagnosed with breast cancer and had come out the other side. Myles's older sister, Noreen, had had a mastectomy and, shortly after Lizzie and Myles had divorced, Noreen had celebrated passing the magical date of being five years free of the disease. There were so many success stories in the arena of breast cancer, so many courageous survivors. Why did it have to be poor Sally who was in the diminishing no-hope group?

When Lizzie arrived at Gwen's house, Gwen, just back from her cruise, took one look at her sister's face and said she'd put the kettle on.

'Are you all right, love?' asked Gwen gently.

'No,' said Lizzie, before she began to cry. No matter which way she told the story, it still hurt. Little Jack and Daniel could lose their mother, Steve would lose his beloved Sally, and there was nothing Lizzie could do to help.

Gwen was a good listener. She said nothing while Lizzie talked, but made sure the tea was strong.

'I feel so helpless,' Lizzie said finally, when she was all cried out. 'And it's all so unfair.'

'Life isn't fair,' Gwen pointed out, patting Lizzie's shoulder in comfort. She wasn't a person given to such gestures, so it made it all the more powerful when she was affectionate.

'Thanks,' sniffed Lizzie.

'You *can* help,' Gwen said. 'You can still be Sally's friend and help her through this. Don't run away from her. We all run away from death because we don't know what to say to the person who's dying.'

Lizzie nodded. Gwen was right. Sally had her family around her but she still needed her friends. Lizzie would be there, no matter what.

Greg was all for fundraising to send Sally to a clinic in America.

'Nobody can beat the US for medicine,' he told Erin. 'I'm not knocking the care in Europe, but the US is where it's at for cancer research. I told Steve I'd get the money for them somehow but he says they're going to put their trust in the doctors here.' Greg raked his fingers through his spiky hair in agitation. 'If it was you, we'd be on that plane so fast . . .' he said fiercely.

Erin curled into him on the couch, stroking his face for comfort.

'What would I do if it *was* you?' Greg said, closing his eyes and burying his face in Erin's soft hair. 'I couldn't cope with it.'

'You could,' she said. 'You'd have to. And Steve's coping in his own way. You have to let him and Sally make their own decisions. If the worst comes to the worst and she doesn't have much time left, then she probably doesn't want to spend it in another country going through more procedures, all of which might be futile. She'd want to be here with the kids.'

Their fingers entwined over Erin's belly.

'It's strange,' she said. 'I mean, I know I'm only ten weeks pregnant but it's terrible to imagine being sick and dying, leaving the baby.'

Greg kissed her, his lips gentle against the tender skin of her temple. 'That's not going to happen, right?'

'I know, I know.' In her head, Erin knew she was overreacting, but in her heart, the fear was still there. Sally had brought the idea of illness and death home. Erin knew people who'd died before, but they were generally much older than she. She'd never known someone like herself face a possibly terminal illness, a young person with everything to live for.

Steve had told Greg that he did his best to be hopeful and positive for Sally's sake, but every day he feared the news that cancer would be found somewhere else in her body and that the clock would start ticking faster.

'I won't leave you,' Erin promised the tiny bump in her belly. 'Never, not for anything.'

Abby hated hospitals. She remembered the grey room where her mother had lain battling with the pneumonia that eventually killed her before the cigarettes could. Maybe it was different if you were a nurse and the hospital was a place of work where there was bustling activity, an air of community and even fun. But as a visitor, Abby just felt a sense of impending gloom.

The boys had gone home for Easter – Steve's sister, Amy, had come to look after them – and Sally herself was due home in a few days. Steve had rung last night to say that she would like to see Abby.

'She hasn't wanted visitors until now,' he said, 'but she's asking for you.'

'Of course I'll come,' Abby said.

'I . . . she's . . .' Steve wanted to say something. 'She's devastated, so be prepared for that. Mum and I keep telling her she looks great, like she always did, but she doesn't. How can you look the same when you've had that sort of news?'

His warning meant that Abby managed to hide the shock when she saw her friend in the hospital bed. Physically, Sally didn't look bad – much better than Steve had led Abby to believe. It was the pain in her eyes that made Abby's heart ache. Sally's expression had always been so bright, so vital. Now, she looked as if someone or something had extinguished the light in her soul.

'Hello, Sally,' Abby said brightly, leaning down to kiss the dry cheek gently. 'I brought some books and magazines to while away the boredom.'

Privately, she didn't think Sally looked as if she had the energy to hold a book, let alone to concentrate on its contents.

'Thanks for coming,' Sally said.

Abby avoided looking at the paraphernalia of the sick-room: the monitors, the drip attached to her friend's slender hand. Perching herself on a chair, she arranged her gifts where Sally could reach them.

'How's Steve? I mean, really how is he?' Sally's voice was a whispery rasp. 'Delia says he's fine and he's coping, but I'm so worried about him. I knew you'd tell me the truth. I knew you'd give it to me straight.'

Abby smiled. 'You need a few straight-talking friends in life, don't you?' she said. 'You're the warm, cheering-up sort of friend and I'm the tell-it-like-it-is one.'

Even Sally smiled faintly at this. 'Having cancer makes people gild the lily when they talk to you. Not the doctors – they've been very honest.'

Abby gulped at the thought of what sort of honest things they must be saying to Sally.

'But Delia, God love her, keeps saying it's all going to work out fine because she is saying this novena to St Anthony and it's never failed. And Amy – she's come to take care of the boys this week when Delia and Steve are here – listening to her, you'd swear I was in to get my face lifted! She's so breezy and positive about it all.'

'Denial?' suggested Abby.

'Probably,' agreed Sally. 'Either that or she hopes that if *she's* cheery enough, then I will be too.' She changed the subject. 'How are Tom and Jess?'

'Fine,' said Abby quickly. Sally was the most wonderful person in the world to confide in but now was most definitely not the time. 'Steve is all right, Sally. He's keeping going, if you know what I mean. The first day he told me about you, well, he was devastated.' She remembered that awful day too well: Steve almost incapable of speaking about the notion of life without Sally. 'But he is coping for the boys' sake. Whenever I speak to him, he seems to be managing. And Jack and Daniel are great too.'

Sally's eyes misted over. 'The doctors didn't want the boys in here because of the risk of infection, but I insisted. They're my children, I can't keep going without them. I should be at home with them, not stuck here.'

Abby could see the tears pooling in the corners of Sally's eyes and her heart ached for her friend's pain.

'I'm going to start the chemotherapy soon,' Sally said, changing the subject. 'Steve's all fired up that this will cure me. He says we've got to believe it can, we've got to have hope.' Sally's little laugh turned into a sob. 'Oh, Abby, I'm so scared.'

Abby clung to Sally's hand to comfort her, willing herself not to cry.

'I have to be brave for Steve's sake because it's such a huge burden for him to carry, but I want to scream and cry and never stop. It's so unfair.'

Sally closed her eyes in anguish. She was too weak with grief to cry properly, Abby realised.

'If I don't get better, will you and Tom look after him for me afterwards? Please?' Now she was wild-eyed with desperation. 'He won't be able to cope without me. I know he's strong but we're a team. He needs me.'

'Don't talk like that, Sally,' begged Abby. 'You're going to get better, you've got to believe that.'

'You mean "think positive",' Sally croaked. 'That's Delia and Amy's motto. I've been thinking positively all my life and this still happened. You can think as positively as you want and you still die, Abby. I always thought that because it had happened to my mum it would never happen to me. Lightning doesn't strike twice and all that.'

'There's still hope, isn't there?'

'Of course there's hope,' Sally said fiercely. 'I'm going to fight for Steve and Jack and Daniel, you know I am, Abby. But fighting doesn't mean you're blind to the truth. I have to be ready for whatever happens. I won't be a victim, I won't hide. The cancer is like this evil presence inside me and it wants to be in control. I can't stop that, but I can change how I deal with it. It's taking over my body but it won't take over my mind.'

There was no noise in the room. Outside, Abby could hear the drone of the floor-polisher and the intermittent ringing of the ward phones.

'I thought that if you appreciated what you had, it wouldn't be taken away,' Sally said. 'I was wrong, wasn't I?'

'No,' replied Abby. 'You've always shown the people in your life that you love them. Steve knows that you adore him and the children, you never wasted a day of your life not telling them. Most people can't say that.'

'But I want more time to tell them,' Sally whispered.

There was nothing Abby could say to that, so she gently put her arms round Sally in the bed, holding her as if she was thistledown.

Tom was still sleeping in the spare room and the atmosphere between husband and wife was colder than the Arctic Circle. Abby wasn't sure what she'd thought happened when a marriage imploded, but she'd expected some sort of actual row. She could deal with a big showdown because she was desperate to apologise, to crave forgiveness on her knees if required, to do anything to put her marriage back together. But he wasn't giving her the opportunity.

Tom, thinner, gaunter, was playing according to his rules and that included ignoring Abby. Jack and Daniel had stayed with them for three days, and while the boys were there, the

Bartons had looked like a normal family – on the surface, at least.

Having small children around was a blessing because they gave Tom, Abby and Jess a focus. There were always games to be played, stories to be read or clothes to be changed, offering constant distraction. When Jack and Daniel had gone to bed, Jess retreated to her room to work. There was no time for her to notice what was happening between her parents. Or at least, so Abby hoped.

But the day after a shaken and dead-eyed Steve had fetched his sons, Tom was still ignoring Abby. With the place to themselves again, she'd hoped they could finally talk, but Tom showed not the slightest desire to do so and Abby began to feel quite desperate. She resolved to make her husband speak about it – she'd made a huge mistake, but that wasn't the end of them, surely.

It was the Saturday after Easter, a glorious day that hinted of summer with a balmy breeze that swept in through her bedroom window, lifting the filmy muslin curtains. From the open window, Abby could see Dunmore curling out below Briar Lane like an enchanting nineteenth-century village untouched by the modern world. Down to the left was the road where the Richardsons lived, and Abby sighed at the thought of their Saturday morning. Sally was home now, for the moment, and she imagined the two bundles of energy that were Jack and Daniel racing into their parents' room and not being able to jump onto their Mummy in case they hurt her. Steve would be stoic and cheerful, doing his best to keep Sally's spirits up, Sally would be doing the same thing and at the back of both of their minds would be the knowledge that only a miracle could keep their little family together.

When Abby thought of Sally and Steve and what they were going through, she felt the shame at her own actions overwhelm her. They needed a miracle but her family could work things out for themselves. She would make everything better between her and Tom, she would.

Dressed for battle in a particularly flattering amethyst shirt, she left her room and encountered Jess hovering on the landing, long bare legs topped by an oversized T-shirt.

'Morning, darling,' said Abby. 'Did you sleep well?'

Jess ignored the question. 'Why is Dad sleeping in the spare room?' she demanded.

Abby faltered. For the past week, Tom had been up and dressed before Jess, so she'd never have realised what was going on. Today, she had.

'He snores,' Jess went on. 'I thought we'd been burgled and the burglar was asleep in the spare room.'

Distraught, Abby thought of lying. But she couldn't. Jess deserved the truth – well, some of the truth. Abby couldn't risk her daughter's hatred.

'Tell me what's going on. I'm part of this family too, so tell me!'

'Come downstairs and I will,' Abby said. A great weariness invaded her body.

In the kitchen, Abby didn't bother boiling the kettle or putting on toast. She sat at the table and Jess sat opposite her.

'Your father and I are having problems,' she said. 'He's moved into the spare bedroom and we have some things to sort out. I'm sorry it's affecting you; neither of us wanted that to happen.'

'Problems about what?' demanded Jess with the ferocity of a prosecuting counsel.

'Just . . . normal things people who've been married a long time fight about.'

'Is it over you being on TV and having more money?'

Abby was startled. She'd never realised that Jess had been aware of those undercurrents.

'No,' she said slowly. 'It's nothing to do with that.' It might have *started* with friction over money but what happened next had nothing to do with who was earning the most. Abby was too honest to pretend that the blame lay elsewhere.

Jess, fidgeting on the edge of her chair, pulled a bit of

sandy hair into her mouth and nibbled it. 'Is Dad having an affair?' she asked hollowly.

Abby's heart bled. 'No, love, he isn't.'

Jess stared at her as if she didn't believe the denial. 'You'd tell me, right? Wouldn't you?'

Of course, that was the first conclusion she would jump to, Abby realised. In the world of TV soaps and teenage magazines, the male of the species was the one who cheated. Women were true and faithful, to their friends and to their men. She wondered if she had the courage to tell the truth to her darling daughter.

'Dad found me having lunch with a man I used to go out with,' Abby began, faltering.

Jess's eyes, over-bright, stared back at her, prompting her to go on.

'It didn't mean anything,' Abby added, 'but I hadn't told Dad I was meeting him and, well, he was upset and he hasn't forgiven me.'

'Having lunch?' said Jess. 'Why would that upset him?' She glared at her mother. 'It's more than that, isn't it?'

Abby knew that her guilty face gave her away but she said nothing, mentally begging Jess not to work it all out.

'How could you?' Jess cried. 'How could you, Mum? You have Dad; you're not supposed to see other men. He must have been so upset.'

It all sounded so simple the way Jess put it.

'He was but he won't let me say sorry,' Abby said. She gazed down at the scrubbed wooden table. It bore so many of the marks of their family life, she thought idly, withstanding years of abuse from hot saucepans being clattered down on it to craft knives being dug into it when Jess was younger and doing art projects. Abby ran a finger along one deep groove.

'I don't understand. Dad's not like that. He'd forgive you if you really were sorry,' Jess whispered.

Abby said nothing.

'You're not telling me everything.' Jess stared accusingly at her mother. 'You had an affair with him.'

237

Abby tried to say no but the word wouldn't come out. She couldn't lie, not to Jess, especially not to this Jess who suddenly sounded so grown up.

She nodded. 'It was only the once. I'm not proud of it and it was a stupid thing to do . . .'

'You're the one who tells me about love and not having sex with someone I don't love, and trust and respect and all that. And now look at what you've done.'

'I'm so sorry,' said Abby, in distress.

'Sorry?' Jess was incredulous. 'It's pathetic. Everything is going wrong in the world and you could do that? Mum, what were you thinking?'

It was as if a dam had burst and all the words Abby had wanted to say to Tom came rushing out. 'I don't know, Jess. I wasn't thinking. I never meant to hurt you or your dad, you've got to believe me! If I could turn the clock back and make it not happen, I would.'

'It was that day you told me about Sally, wasn't it?' said Jess. 'Dad had just found you out, hadn't he? I knew you were strange and it wasn't to do with Sally. How could you? She could be dying and you were upset only over being caught out.'

'No,' gasped Abby.

'Yes!' shrieked Jess, making for the door.

The roles had been reversed. Now Jess was taking the adult role and Abby was cast as the child, in trouble with no way out.

Tom stood at the door to the kitchen, dressed but with his hair wild, as if he had rushed down at the sound of the argument.

'Oh, Dad!' cried Jess, hugging him briefly before running upstairs to the safety of her bedroom.

Abby raised hurt, tear-filled eyes to his, expecting to see his face mocking and hard, but she was slightly comforted to read compassion in his expression.

'You didn't have to tell her,' he said.

Abby held her aching head in her hands. 'I didn't want

to but she knew it was something to do with an affair. She asked me if you were having one.'

'I'm surprised you didn't take the easy option.' The mocking was back.

'I wouldn't do that,' Abby said. 'You weren't the one who made the mistake so I couldn't let you take the blame.'

'Oh, it was a mistake, was it? Nice to know your screwing another man can be summed up in such a simple term.'

'I didn't mean it like that.'

'An accident, perhaps? You accidentally ended up in bed with him and all your clothes fell off. And don't deny it. That wasn't just lunch I interrupted. Where were you going next? A hotel, a love nest, a dive with rooms by the hour?' Tom rapped the questions out.

'No, I was ending it,' Abby protested. 'It happened once, that's all.'

'Well, I am glad to hear that.' Tom's voice dripped acid. 'Once is fine. Once is practically reasonable. I mean, everyone wants to screw around once, don't they? Who should I go for? Any suggestions?'

'Please, Tom, don't talk like that,' she begged. 'Can't we talk properly? We've got a good marriage, let's not throw it away over . . . over this.'

'Too late,' he said. 'You've already thrown it away. I feel I'm only here for Jess now. And I don't believe you about it being just once. You've known him longer than you've known me. He didn't just waltz back into your life, did he? He's been around for quite a while. Is he keen to hook up with Abby, the television superstar? Is that why you wanted this house so badly – because it was a fitting home for you and Jay?'

'No, no,' sobbed Abby. 'It wasn't like that. We – you and me – we weren't happy and I don't know what happened –'

'Yeah, blame me, why don't you? It's all my fault. God, Abby, you make me sick,' he said in disgust.

'What are you going to do?' she said frantically.

'I don't know, but when I do, I'll tell you,' he finished.

He left the room then, and Abby laid her head on the table and sobbed.

In her bedroom, Jess slammed the door so hard that one of her old stuffed animals fell off the top of the wardrobe. Poor Wuddly, she thought, grabbing the threadbare seal and hugging him close.

But hugging him didn't bring her any comfort. Nothing could. Jess had known that her parents weren't really talking, although at least it was a break from the constant sniping. But she'd never imagined this. Her mother had done the most awful thing. How could she have slept with someone else? Mothers didn't do that sort of thing. It was weird enough imagining her parents having sex at all, but for her mum to do it with someone who wasn't Dad – that was too . . . too terrible. She brushed Wuddly's tired old fur with her fingers. People got divorced when they had affairs. So that's what would happen next. The rows would change because they wouldn't all be living together, but there would still be rows, she knew. Lots of people in school had divorced parents and rows were part of it. The kids were stuck in the middle.

Robyn, a girl in Jess's year, used to pretend it was cool to have divorced parents because she got twice as many presents and stuff, but Jess and Steph had always known it wasn't. Robyn's dad never came to school plays or sports matches because Robyn's mother wouldn't let him anywhere near her.

Suddenly, she wanted to talk to Steph. Nobody made hard things seem easier the way Steph did.

Steph, how r u? call me. :-(

Normally, Steph – the speed-texting expert – would reply in, like, five seconds. But not today. It was Saturday, she was probably still in bed.

Jess got up and switched on her CD player. She wouldn't think about Mum and Dad, she wouldn't. She'd think about Ian. He was her favourite daydream and she even had a song she played that was their song.

Not that Ian knew it was their song. But it was the music she could imagine them dancing to, his arms round her, her cheek resting against his shoulder as they moved slowly. She sat on her bed, her knees folded up to her chest, and listened to the music. If she closed her eyes, she could just about imagine it.

And then they'd curl up beside each other on some squashy chair, and Ian would kiss her. The details were hazy because Jess couldn't quite imagine what it would be like to be kissed by someone she was in love with. Not the same as playing dares in second year when she and Steph were looking for tennis balls in the park near home. She'd had to kiss Jimmy Lynch and it had been awful. His breath was smelly, like that awful pong of hard-boiled eggs, and she'd wondered what all the big fuss about kissing was because it had been terrible. But kissing Ian would be different. She wasn't sure about the tongues thing. Girls like Saffron were so blasé about that. French kissing was no big deal, they said nonchalantly, implying that they'd done a lot more than kiss. If she'd had to kiss Jimmy Lynch again, Jess would die rather than use tongues. But with Ian, she'd try. And he was experienced so he'd know.

Maybe he'd realise she knew nothing about French kissing. That would be awful. He'd think she was a stupid kid. What if she did the wrong thing? Not that she knew what the *right* thing was, but there was bound to be a wrong thing.

It was all so confusing. And where would you put your hands? Jess had thought about this in bed at night, letting her pillow be Ian so she could try out how it all worked. If he put his arms around her, where was she supposed to put *her* arms? She didn't want him to get a dead arm where she'd lain against it.

The song finished and Jess flicked the remote to play it again. She closed her eyes and decided to forget about the annoying details. If she tried very hard, she could be back in that fantasy place where Ian was telling her he loved her and couldn't live without her before he kissed her. Then she wouldn't have to think about Mum and Dad and them getting a divorce.

The Easter holidays limped to a close with nobody in the Barton household communicating with anybody else. Jess had spent most of the time in her bedroom and made study timetables in her diary, using coloured highlighter pens to mark out sections of the day.

An article the school had photocopied for all exam-year students suggested getting up early every morning to start revising by half nine. Apart from lunch – which Jess preferred to eat in her room anyhow – the article suggested two fifteen-minute breaks every day. Jess took the breaks when she knew there was nobody else in the kitchen, so she could make a flask of coffee and take it back upstairs with her. Coffee was on the 'avoid' list in the revision guide, but Jess reckoned that nobody could put in an eight-hour day without some caffeine. Keeping her mind on studying wasn't easy, though. In the pit of her stomach, there was the gnawing awareness of all that was wrong in her family.

Tom, giving himself no time off, set up camp in the dining room, covering the table with the plans for the new school sports hall and having long phone conversations with engineers and architects. Abby, who sat in her study and tried to work on ideas for her decluttering talk at the Ideal House show, wondered if a school extension could really need that much forward planning, or if Tom was just keeping busy so he could keep out of her way.

The icy atmosphere continued after the holidays, with Jess revising non-stop and Tom home late every night.

The only time the three of them came together for anything approaching normal family life was for a lunch with Steve, Sally, Delia and Steve's sister, Amy.

It was Delia's sixtieth birthday and, in spite of her protests, Sally insisted that it be marked in some way.

'There'll be about twenty of us altogether, when you count Delia's friends,' Steve said when he phoned Abby to invite her. 'Sally would love all three of you to be there. We're going to the Hotel Dunmore because Sally says she won't hear of Delia catering for her own birthday.'

And Sally wouldn't be able to, Abby thought sadly.

Despite the wine flowing freely and the combined goodwill of all the guests, the party spirit at Delia's sixtieth was forced. The bravely smiling Sally drew people's eyes like a magnet.

'God help them,' said Abby's neighbour at the party, an old pal of Delia's. She said it so often that Abby wanted to beg her to stop.

'Ah now, there might still be hope,' said her other neighbour, another of Delia's old friends.

Abby didn't know which was worse: the woman living in cloud-cuckoo-land, or the man who still believed in miracles. Abby didn't believe in miracles any more.

CHAPTER SIXTEEN

It was the middle of May. The exams were just over two weeks away and Jess's life felt like a disaster waiting to happen.

'What sicko mind decided that exams should be in June when the weather's nice and every other sensible person is on their summer holidays?' Steph wanted to know.

Miserable and anxious, Jess didn't have the answer. All she knew was that she still had tons of revision to do and time was running out. She'd had to give up dropping into the animal refuge at weekends, school was a nightmare, home was an even bigger nightmare and she felt stressed out of her head.

Different people coped differently with stress, that was for sure. Steph, who was now dating Zach, the guy she'd met at Michelle's party months ago, distanced herself by spending hours texting her boyfriend on her mobile. She also now smoked the occasional cigarette, although Jess was sure it wasn't worth the effort involved in trying to hide the smell of smoke from Steph's mother.

'She will kill you if she finds out,' Jess warned. Steph's mother was pretty laid-back but she believed that smoking led to drug use, and would have ripped Steph's head off if she found her taking drugs. 'And smoking causes cancer.'

Steph was not worried about the long-term effects of smoking. 'Models smoke,' she countered Jess's argument.

Jess looked at her friend with exasperation. 'You sound

just like Saffron, do you realise that? Being thin and beautiful doesn't stop you getting cancer.'

'Oh, save it for the debating team,' snapped Steph. 'I promise I'll stop, OK?'

For Jess, cancer was no longer a word on a poster about the dangers of cigarettes. She had visited Sally Richardson at home after her first month of chemotherapy treatment. Sally was so thin, although her face looked weirdly bloated, and she had no hair.

'It began to fall out so we shaved it all off,' she'd said gaily, insisting on Jess touching her bare skull. 'Danny and Jack love my new hairdo!'

Jess had felt confused. Sally was obviously very ill so why pretend everything was fine? But then, that's what grown-ups did. Jess's mother was busy pretending to the world for some reason that everything was fine in the Barton household, so lying was clearly a vital part of adulthood. But then why had they spent so much of her childhood impressing on her the importance of telling the truth? Jess didn't want anyone lying to her any more. She wished her parents would be honest with her and with each other, and she wished they'd tell her the truth about Sally.

She'd overheard them talking – a rarity these days – and it seemed the cancer had gone somewhere else now. Listening outside the kitchen door, Jess had heard her mother crying but she knew Dad wouldn't put his arms around her and comfort her. He never did that now.

Dad slept in the spare room, ate his breakfast before Mum was downstairs, and managed to stay working late at school for hours every evening. Mum tried to pretend she didn't mind.

Mum watched TV in bed late into the night and drank too much coffee. Dad busied himself poring over the plans for the building work at his school. As soon as the exams were over, the builders were moving in to build the sports hall and Dad was in charge of it all. He was always out meeting architects and contractors, which was probably good, because the tension at home wasn't so bad when either Mum or Dad was out. Mum was never out at night. She'd arranged to avoid evening events until Jess's exams were over.

Jess would have preferred it if both parents were out all the time. She was so afraid that one day they'd call her into a room and break the news that they were getting a divorce. Even the icy tension was better than that.

Now, when Mum tried to talk to her, Jess made a beeline for her room, muttering that she had to revise. She didn't want to hear any more bad news.

That was why she'd decided to start studying in Dunmore library after school. She'd thought of using the school library but the trains from Cork to Dunmore were less frequent in the evenings, so she figured that the big Victorian library in the centre of the square would do instead. It wasn't old-fashioned inside, with computers lining one wall and modern furniture. In fact, the seats were far more comfortable than the ones in the school library.

Dunmore library was busy when Jess arrived there late one Tuesday afternoon, exactly two weeks before the exams, shoulders aching from hauling her bag of school books. Exam fever seemed to have gripped the whole town, for there were plenty of other students slumped at desks with giant textbooks spread out in front of them. Jess took out her pencil case, notebook, course books and writing pad, and left her bag in one of the lockers provided.

She chose a seat at the back of the main room and spread her books out in front of her. She closed her eyes and grabbed the first book she touched: history. She liked history but the syllabus was so huge that she'd never get through all the revision in time.

Glancing round, she saw people who'd come into the library to get books to read for pleasure. Jess longed to be able to sit down and lose herself in a good story, to lounge in bed at the weekends without the guilt of studying for the exams looming over her. In the summer holidays, which started for her in one month's time, she'd stay in bed late every day, and then spend the rest of the time in the refuge with the dogs. Lost in the daydream, she gazed towards the door of the library with a goofy smile on her face.

Gradually, she became aware of a dark shape moving towards her and then her eyes focused on a boy standing before her.

'Hi,' said the guy from the train.

'Hi,' she stumbled in reply. 'Oliver.' She'd found out his name by now. 'You here to study?' Doh, Jess! What else is he here for? To go swimming?

'I've got two more summer exams left,' he said, 'and this is quieter than school.'

Of course, she thought, people who weren't taking part in the public exams like the Junior Cert and the Leaving Cert finished their exams at the end of May before the big public exams started at the beginning of June. They began their summer holidays at the end of May when the fourth and sixth years were just about to go into exam rooms and sweat.

Oliver slipped into the seat beside her and Jess wondered what was happening. Cool guys like him did not seek out gawky girls like her. And Oliver was cool: he had spiky fair hair like that footballer all the girls drooled over, and he was wiry but athletic, like he played football himself, but wasn't a muscle-bound jock who spent hours in the gym. He had a nice face too, clever and expressive, with eyes that could speak without him saying a word. He probably had a girlfriend in his year. Jess had seen him in school with some of the football team and those guys always had girls hanging round them.

'That's sensible,' she said. Another clanger. *Sensible*. How lame-brained could you get?

'You studying for your Junior Cert?' he asked.

'Yeah, thought I might get more done here than at home,' she replied. Which was true. With the atmosphere at home, it was easier to stay away.

He looked at her history book. 'I liked history but the

247

course was way too long,' he said. 'I didn't choose it as one of my subjects this year.'

'What did you do?' asked Jess, thinking that talking to this boy wasn't as hard as she'd thought.

'Physics, chemistry and applied maths,' he replied, and then laughed at the appalled look on her face. 'I like them. I'm going to do science at uni, I hope. What about you?'

A girl at the other end of the table glared at them to keep quiet.

'I don't know,' whispered Jess.

'You know, erm, we can't talk in here. I was going to get a drink before I started. Would you like to come for a Coke or something?'

'Sure,' said Jess, as if it was the most natural thing in the world for her to be asked out by a guy. She gathered up her stuff at high speed but her pencil case hit the tiled floor with a clatter, earning her another fierce look from the girl at the end of the table.

Oliver didn't seem in the slightest bit fazed by this. He simply picked up Jess's pencil case, got his own stuff and they walked to the lockers to collect their things.

Outside, Oliver asked her where she wanted to go. 'I like the place at the back of the town hall,' he said. 'They play good music there.'

'I've never been there,' Jess said frankly.

'Really?'

She felt a bit embarrassed. 'I don't know anyone here to hang out with, and you can't go in on your own,' she muttered. She didn't mention that she'd gone into the coffee shop near Sally's once and had felt like such a dork sitting there by herself that she'd left quickly.

'I've lived here for years,' Oliver said as they walked along in the late afternoon sunshine, 'so I guess I know everyone, but it's hard to get to know people when you move.'

Jess nodded.

'Where did you live before?'

As they walked down the road towards the town hall, she

told him about Gartland Avenue and how it had been tough to leave Steph and her other friends.

'Steph – she's the blonde girl you hang around with in school?'

Oh yeah, here it comes. Jess came down to earth with a jolt. Oliver wasn't interested in *her*, he was interested in Steph.

She nodded, woodenly. 'Steph Anderson,' she confirmed.

'Do you and Steph ever go to Killian's disco in the city?'

'We do, but Steph goes with her boyfriend, Zach,' Jess said, emphasising the Zach part of the sentence. 'You know, I don't have time for a Coke, after all.' She turned and marched away from him, back towards the library. Who cared if she sounded rude, she thought, the tears pricking her eyes. If he wanted to go out with Steph, he should have asked her and not tried to go through Jess. It wasn't fair. Steph had a boyfriend and now Oliver was after her too, while Jess had nobody.

'Hey, Jess, hold on!'

So he knew her name. Marvellous. If you want to ask a girl out via her best friend, find out what the best friend's name is.

'Jess, stop. What's wrong?'

If there hadn't been so many things wrong in her life, Jess might have kept walking. Home was crap, school was crap, now this was crap. Somebody ought to hear how she felt.

'If you must know, I don't like being used to get to Steph,' she said furiously, eyes blazing. 'If you want to ask her out, ask her out. Don't expect me to do your dirty work for you.'

'What do you mean?' he asked, looking genuinely startled.

'You know,' snapped Jess. 'Asking me if Steph and I ever went to Killian's. Talk about feeble. I'll give you her phone number and you can ask her yourself.'

He looked uncomfortable. 'I'm not interested in Steph. I thought that if you were going, I could meet up with you, that's all. I didn't know if I should ask you straight out.'

'Ask me straight out?' Jess was astonished.

'You.' Oliver shrugged. 'That's why I went to talk to you in the library, to ask you out. But if you'd rather not –'

'No, no,' she said. 'I mean, yes, I'd like to go out with you if that's . . .'

They both stared at the ground for a moment.

'Sorry,' said Jess. 'I thought you were . . . and . . . sorry.'

'That's OK.' Oliver was smiling now and Jess found that she couldn't stop smiling too. 'Still want a Coke?'

She nodded. 'Yeah.'

They walked back up the road and Jess found herself stealing small glances at him. He wasn't as good-looking as Ian but then, who was? Ian was dark – 'brooding', Steph called him – while Oliver was fair-haired with a strong, intelligent face. She couldn't imagine him with lots of shadowy designer stubble but she could imagine him laughing with her, or going to the refuge and helping out with the animals. That wasn't the sort of thing Ian would be into, she knew that for a fact. Saffron was always going on about how Ian liked going out to pubs and clubs, even though he was underage. And Jess wasn't much of a club person.

'We don't have to spend long,' Oliver added. 'I know you've got to revise.'

Jess laughed. 'I'm fed up with revising,' she said. 'Let's never go back.'

Oliver's grey eyes sparkled. 'Fine by me,' he said.

Later that day, Erin and Lizzie met up outside the Richardsons' house. Erin carried an armful of magazines while Lizzie had a potted plant and a paper bag of delicate Italian pastries from the deliciously tempting Tucci Deli. They'd both visited Sally in hospital but seeing her at home was going to be different, particularly since it was known that Sally's cancer had spread to her bones and the hopefulness of the hospital was no more.

Lizzie had asked Clare Morgan what Sally's chances were

now, and Clare had sighed and said radiation would help to control the disease and relieve the pain.

'Control but not cure?' Lizzie had asked.

Clare had nodded.

'But what about the chemo? Won't that work on the bone cancer?'

'I'm not an oncologist and there are so many new developments in the field, Lizzie,' Clare said. 'I don't know what other therapies her oncology team have up their sleeves, but Sally's cancer is advanced. There may be nothing they can do for her now except keep the pain away.'

When Lizzie and Erin had bumped into one another in the supermarket earlier, they'd decided that visiting her together would be a good idea.

'What do you say to someone who's probably dying?' Lizzie had wondered. It was so different from pretending not to know in the surgery.

'I was hoping you'd tell me,' Erin replied.

On the way up to Sally and Steve's front door, Erin admired Lizzie's plant. 'I didn't know what to bring,' she said, gesturing to the magazines. 'I thought these would amuse her, then I've just realised that they're all about the fall fashions and new hairdos, and it's like I'm just reminding her that she's lost her hair with the chemo, and chances are she may not be around to wear the fall fashions.'

'Magazines are a lovely thought,' Lizzie said, touching Erin's arm. 'I've seen a lot of sick people come through the surgery and they generally don't want to be treated as if they aren't part of the normal world. If Sally was in bed after a run-of-the-mill operation, you'd bring her magazines, right?'

'Right, I guess.' If only this was a run-of-the-mill operation, Erin thought sadly. 'How are things with you, Lizzie?'

'Fine, fine,' Lizzie said automatically, then thought better of it. 'Actually, I'm not fine. I'm shell-shocked to be honest. This,' she gestured up at the pretty Richardson house where they'd all partied just over a month ago, 'seems all wrong.'

'I know,' agreed Erin sadly. 'It's terrible that it takes someone else's tragedy to do it, but I feel so ashamed of all the things I've been worrying over. This is real pain. Death, leaving Steve and her little kids behind, that's tragedy, not all the silly problems of my own making.'

'Snap,' said Lizzie. 'When I think of what's been bothering me . . .' She didn't run through the list because it seemed so trite: Debra's wedding; Myles managing to move on while she hadn't; her boring non-life – all stupid things that could be resolved with a little effort. There was no such quick fix for Sally.

Both women were silent for a moment before Lizzie sighed and remarked that they couldn't stand outside on the footpath all day. Somehow they had to go in and talk to Sally as if the shadow of death wasn't looming.

If anyone in the Richardson house looked ill, it was Steve. Erin remembered how Sally had described him to her when they'd first met – a blond Rock Hudson – and was shocked that Steve's handsomeness had worn away to reveal a gaunt face with hollow cheeks.

'Lovely to see you both,' he said warmly, embracing them. 'I was just taking some tea up to Sally, would you like some?'

'Sure,' said Erin. 'I'll help.'

'No, really.' Standing over the kettle, Steve looked almost fierce, a man pushed to the limit. 'I can manage perfectly well on my own.' It was as if this was the mantra he'd been repeating to himself endlessly, hoping that it would become true.

Lizzie had never been upstairs in the Richardsons' house and it was just as pretty as the rest of the place. Decorated with Sally's flair, the upper landing was a buttery parchment colour with a creamy orchid in a primrose pot dominating a small table, while one entire wall was dedicated to collages of family snapshots in various different-shaped frames. It was a wall of happy family memories and Lizzie could hardly bear to look at it.

'Hi, love. Lizzie and Erin are here to see you,' called Steve, pushing open the door with his foot and going through carefully so as not to spill the tea.

Behind him, the two women exchanged anxious looks and then followed him into Sally's bedroom.

'Lizzie, Erin, I'm so thrilled you're here!' cried Sally, sitting up in bed looking uncannily like an older version of herself. Her soft slenderness had become a scary thinness and somehow her teeth looked too big for her face. Her head was wrapped in a pink polka-dot scarf.

If they were both shocked by her appearance, they didn't betray it. She'd looked better in hospital, certainly, where you somehow expected people not to look themselves. But here, on her home territory, the contrast with the old Sally was horrible and the gravity of her condition was suddenly brought home to them.

Lizzie sat on a small stool on one side of the bed and hugged Sally gently.

'Sally, love, how are you?'

Erin sat carefully on a chair on the other side and grasped Sally's hand in greeting.

'I'm fine,' said Sally brightly. 'Steve, thank you for the tea, darling.'

Nobody said anything else until Steve had carefully put the tray on a small bare table next to Erin, and had poured for everyone. He handed his wife a cup, touched her cheek with a tender finger, and left the room. Sally waited until they could hear his tread on the stairs before she spoke.

'I'm OK,' she said. 'I know that's hard to believe but I am. I can cope because I have to cope for Steve and the boys.' She smiled ruefully. 'If I was single with no children, I'd rage against the world or God or whoever for doing this to me. But I have to be strong for them.'

Erin's hand shook as she handed Lizzie a cup of tea. 'I don't know what to say, Sally,' she admitted.

Sally shrugged. 'Nobody does. As long as neither of you tell me I'm going to a better place, then I'll be all right!' She smiled but the light and warmth everyone associated with Sally were absent from her smile. 'I had this wonderful plan to cut my hair and dye it blonde before it all fell out, but it beat me to it,' she added lightly, changing the subject. 'I've always wanted to go blonde and that was my last chance.'

Lizzie and Erin laughed uneasily.

'Blondes don't have more fun,' said Lizzie, touching her streaky tortoiseshell curls. 'Take my word for it!'

'Red, then?' Sally asked Erin.

There was a brittleness in her voice that had never been there before, Lizzie noticed.

'Too temperamental,' Erin advised. 'Stick with the Little Red Riding Hood look.'

And they were off on safer subjects, talking about how they'd first met and how Sally still hadn't got rid of that red hooded coat.

Lizzie remembered when Daniel had been a baby and they had come to the surgery for the first time.

'I thought you were some sweet little teenager with two kids. You looked so young, I couldn't believe you were in your early thirties.'

'Royal jelly,' laughed Sally. 'I swear by it. My mother used it and she had the most youthful skin.' Her voice softened. 'She told me that if I used it every day, I'd end up as a pensioner with baby-soft skin.'

A pensioner. The word hung in the air. Sally would never get to be a pensioner. Erin clasped Sally's hand again tightly. Every normal subject came inexorably round to the same awful conclusion.

When she and Greg had talked about Sally's illness he said that it was like a nightmare, but it wasn't: you woke up after a nightmare.

'You know my mother died of breast cancer when I was twenty? Steve never met her; that always upset me,' Sally continued, the tone of false gaiety now gone. 'I knew life wasn't always easy. That's why Steve and I were grateful for what we had. Funny,' she said, 'I was always scared of breast cancer but, in some ironic way, I never thought I'd get it. I thought it couldn't strike my family twice. Or that at least I didn't have to worry about it yet. My mother was forty-eight when she got it.'

Erin thought of her mother, her real mother. Shannon would be forty-five or six now. Was she well? And Gran, she would be in her late sixties. Had she faced serious illness?

'But your mother is always with you, isn't she?' Lizzie said gently to Sally. 'My mother's dead too but she'll always be part of my thoughts, my memories.'

'That's true.' Sally nodded. 'What worries me is that the boys are so young – how will they remember me at all? I had twenty years with my mother but they won't have that time. I can't remember things from when I was three or four, so how can they?'

Erin knew that it was wrong for her to cry. Sally was the one who should be crying, but instead Sally was composed and Erin was the one who felt like bursting into hopeless tears. It must be pregnancy hormones, she thought, and then she did cry.

Sally reached over and handed her a tissue. 'Don't cry, Erin,' she begged. 'I'm not. I mean, I did at first but I don't seem to be able to cry any more. There's nothing I can change about the disease. It's been terrible coming to terms with my powerlessness.' She looked at the two women. 'That's the irony of modern life. We think we are in charge, that we can change *everything* – our jobs, where we live, our lifestyles – but there are some things we just have to accept we can't do anything about. The only thing I'm in control of is how I deal with the cancer.'

She sipped more of her tea, needing both hands to raise the cup to her lips.

'Maybe I *haven't* come to terms with it, after all, and I'll go mad screaming in a day or so, but I have to make it right for my family. Steve will have the burden of bringing up our babies on his own. I can't leave him with the memory of my dying being a drawn-out horror story. We can enjoy what we've left, can't we?' She was pleading with them, hoping they'd say she was right, that being positive was a choice and not a way of hiding from the truth. But Erin and Lizzie were silent; neither of them could think of anything to say that wasn't a platitude. So Sally went on: 'I knew the cancer had spread even before they did the second bone scan. I just knew it. Every time I think I can beat it, it comes up with something else to throw at me. When they told me, it felt like being stuck in a lift with no air. I couldn't breathe. The hospital gave me a tranquilliser and I was like a zombie. I probably needed it at the time, but I don't want to be like that now; I want to know what's happening. Morphine makes you dopey at the end, not yourself,' she added. 'My mother was like that. It was horrible.'

'Is there anything we can do?' asked Lizzie.

'Come to see me, make me feel a bit normal, as if I'm not dying,' Sally said slowly. 'People get scared, you see. They did with my mother. Her friends didn't know what to do so they stayed away because they felt their visits wouldn't be any help. She wanted to see people, actually, but the ones she wanted to didn't come. I understood,' she added. 'What do you say to someone who's dying?'

'You're not dying,' cried Erin. 'There's always hope.'

'I am dying,' Sally said bluntly. 'We're all dying. Sooner rather than later for me, though. Treatment can delay it but I've discovered that accepting what's happening is the only way I can deal with it.'

They left soon afterwards, when Sally's pale face grew paler and she began to yawn. 'I know,' she smiled, 'I'm a great hostess. I can last an hour and then I pass out with exhaustion.'

'We'll come again,' Lizzie said. 'Promise.'

Outside on the street, they stood talking beside Lizzie's car. 'Can I drop you home?' Lizzie asked.

Erin shook her head. 'I think I'll walk. Fresh air might clear my head, but thanks.'

'How are you feeling?' Lizzie asked. 'I mean with the baby.'

'Fine but tired,' Erin admitted. 'I thought working two jobs when I was in Boston was exhausting but this tiredness is like nothing on earth, and I'm not even working.' She paused, thinking that her tiredness must be nothing to the weariness Sally was dealing with.

Lizzie smiled. 'I remember when I was pregnant with Joe, I had to go to bed every night at eight. I used to cry with tiredness. Poor Myles thought everything would be perfect because we'd got married but he didn't know what hit him, coping with a pregnant woman.'

'I haven't started crying with tiredness yet,' Erin said, smiling. Then she stopped. 'It feels awful to be able to smile, doesn't it? When Sally's so ill.'

Lizzie agreed.

'You know, I've been thinking, if I got news like Sally's got, I'd want to see my family again,' Erin went on, starting to cry again. She wiped her nose with a tissue. Pregnancy hormones were really something. 'It's like being estranged from someone but saying you'd go to their funeral – so the upshot is you'd wait until they died to make it up. Greg says, why wait until something bad happens? So the thing is, I've decided. I'm going to find them. And tell them about the baby.'

'That's wonderful,' whispered Lizzie, hugging Erin.

'I'd begun to think about finding them when I found out I was pregnant. Expecting a baby changes everything.' Erin's face lit up. 'I don't know why I was ever worried about having the baby. Shock, I suppose. I mean, I'm scared because I don't know how to be a mom but I wouldn't want not to have him or her. I can't deprive the baby of a family either.'

'You'll be a fabulous mum,' insisted Lizzie. 'And if you need a surrogate mum until you find yours, I'm here. Some-body needs to boss you around and make sure you're getting enough rest and are taking your iron tablets!'

Erin was too touched to speak, so Lizzie gave her one last hug and hopped into her car.

When she got home, it was to find Debra's Mini parked outside the house.

'I thought it was your half-day?' were the first words out of her daughter's mouth when Lizzie reached the kitchen. Today, Debra had made tea for herself and found some foil-wrapped chocolate biscuits. Dressed in an expensive-looking pair of suede trousers and a winter-white sweater, she was lolling elegantly against the sink unit. 'I've been here ages,' Debra said unnecessarily. 'I left work early on purpose.'

'Remember Sally Richardson at the beauty salon?' said her mother. 'Well, she's got cancer and she's dying, God help her. I was visiting her.'

'Oh. The cute salon with the pink and white gingham curtains?' Debra asked.

Lizzie nodded. 'It's so sad. Sally has a husband and two young kids. I can't imagine what they'll do without her.'

'Men are better at getting married again,' Debra said blithely, choosing another biscuit from the box. 'I saw an article in the paper about it. Although if anything happened to Barry, I know I'd have to get over it. Life goes on.' A thought occurred to Debra. 'Wasn't she going to do your nails for the wedding?'

Lizzie stared at Debra in disbelief. 'It hardly matters about my nails. It's not as if I have them done normally.'

'Well, Barry's mother is having hers done, and her make-up too.' Debra was shocked at this sign that her mother wasn't taking the most important day of her daughter's life seriously enough.

'This isn't about my nails,' insisted Lizzie. 'Who's going to be looking at my nails?'

'That's not the point.' Debra's pretty face flushed with irritation as she crumpled up her biscuit wrapper. 'People will be looking at you because you're my mother. There must be another beauty salon round here. Anyway, that's not why I came. Barry's cousin is organising the stag night and I thought it was supposed to be in Cork. It's not, it's in Dublin. Fifteen guys alone in Dublin. I'm furious. I told Barry, I said, "That is not what we agreed." And he said that it wasn't his fault. Imagine! Not his fault. His stag night and he's going to let them organise whatever mayhem they like.' She folded her arms. 'You have to start where you mean to go on, Mum. Men have to be shown that you're not a pushover.'

'That's not what marriage is about,' interrupted her mother. 'I hate the idea of wild parties where the poor groom gets stripped and tied to a tree, but you've got to let Barry and his friends do what they want, haven't you?'

'No.' Debra was adamant. 'No, I don't. I don't want him having that sort of stag night.'

'Well, it'll be over soon and you can forget about it,' soothed her mother.

'I thought you'd agree with me,' Debra retorted. 'Rita in work does.'

Rita was under Debra's thumb and would say that white was black if Debra wanted her to, Lizzie reflected.

'Why don't you tell him why you don't like the idea but let him make up his own mind?' Lizzie counselled. 'After all, you don't want to have a huge row now, do you? The wedding's less than two months away.'

'Oh, Mum,' groaned Debra in exasperation, 'you really don't understand men, do you?' She snatched her suede bag from the back of her chair. 'I should go. Talk later.'

Lizzie was left standing impotently in her kitchen, wondering why, when Debra was angry with Barry, it was her mother who somehow got all the flak.

She began to tidy up the kitchen and consider what to make for dinner. She wasn't very hungry, which was unusual. Lizzie's appetite was a hearty one, and no trauma had ever affected her ability to polish off a decent meal and possibly some hazelnut cluster ice cream for afters. But this evening, she had no inclination to eat.

Instead, she took the paper out into the garden and sat on the iron bench on the patio, letting the evening sun warm her bones.

The garden was looking good, proof of the weekends Lizzie had spent weeding, transplanting and burying bulbs where the ever-ravenous birds wouldn't find them. Yet despite her sense of pleasure at the result of her hard work, Lizzie felt sad. She wondered why it took someone else's misery to make people aware of how lucky they were. When the children had been young, she remembered a neighbour being killed in a car accident, leaving a wife and four small children under ten. Lizzie, exhausted with a teething Debra and a very naughty Joe, had suddenly felt very grateful for what she had.

Ten years or so ago, an acquaintance of Myles's had watched his family business go bankrupt and had lost his home. Lizzie, who'd once envied the man for not being a wage slave like her and Myles, had felt enormous relief at the humdrum security of their jobs. Of course, the relief and the gratefulness had worn off and Lizzie had forgotten about the widowed mother and the bankrupt man. But she shouldn't have, she realised. Tragedy could strike at anyone's lives.

She sighed. Debra was probably too young to understand that, she decided, and she was tied up with her wedding. That must be why her natural compassion was a little blunted and why she'd been so sharp with her mother. Yes, that was it . . .

CHAPTER SEVENTEEN

The day that Jess started her exams, Abby got a phone call from Beech about the new series of *Declutter*. She'd already filmed five shows on her own while the endless auditioning and reauditioning of new presenters went on, and had begun to hope that nobody else suitable would be found for the programme. No such luck. Two other presenters had been picked and Brian was keen for Abby to meet the new team.

'Can you come in this afternoon?' he asked, without so much as an 'if that's convenient' tacked on to the request.

'Well, this afternoon's not very easy,' began Abby, thinking of her plans to collect Jess from school after the English exam.

'You should try and make it,' Brian said querulously. 'It's your future too, Abby.'

Not so much a request as a command, Abby realised grimly. 'Fine,' she said crisply.

'See you at two thirty.'

Once, she realised, Brian would have suggested lunch before an afternoon meeting and she, Flora, Brian, Selina and anybody else they could round up would have gone off to enjoy a few glasses of vino and some enjoyable industry bitching, all the while congratulating themselves on how incredibly well *Declutter* was doing.

'You're the star,' Brian had told her on numerous occasions. 'You're the one who made it a success. People love you, they can relate to you.'

Ironic really, Abby reflected. For two seasons, she'd been

the star and the reason why the show was a success. Now, suddenly, on someone's whim, they thought she was too old to carry it on her own. Abby felt as if she was the only one who hadn't noticed her sell-by date slip past. She wasn't going to bother to change out of her faded jeans and little pale blue T-shirt or to do anything to her face except slick on more lipgloss. Tarting up was clearly a waste of time. Roxie and Brian had found youthful new talent and it didn't matter how many layers of Mac foundation Abby painted on, she was still forty-two with forty-three looming. They could take her or leave her.

'You look fabulous,' said Flora when Abby arrived in the Beech boardroom at two thirty on the nail.

Abby grinned. 'This is my casual look.'

'But it suits you,' Flora replied. 'You never wear jeans on camera. You should.'

Thinking of the fortune she'd spent on dress-to-impress clothes, Abby laughed to herself at the effect her old Levis were having.

Roxie, not wearing jeans, marched into the room and, after a perfunctory hello to Abby, clicked the blinds shut and rolled the video clip of the two new presenters.

'Identical twins,' breathed Abby quietly as two gorgeous brunettes hit the screen and introduced themselves as Linzi and Mitzi Devine. They were not a day over twenty-five and stunning, each grinning at the camera with utter confidence.

Abby couldn't find fault with their performance either. In a set-up de-junking scene they looked and sounded very natural as they sorted through tons of documents in an untidy office somewhere in Beech, gaily consigning reams of paper to a rubbish box, chorusing as they went: 'Shred it! Shred it!'

Their untrained style of de-junking wasn't like Abby's polished professional approach but she didn't doubt that they would be a success because of their attractiveness and their obvious good humour.

The short clip ended.

'Great, aren't they?' said Roxie, smirking directly at Abby.

With a blinding flash, Abby realised she wasn't nervous of Roxie any more. After all, what more could Roxie do? Only fire her, and being fired couldn't be any worse than anything else that had happened recently in Abby's life.

'They're excellent,' she said, matching Roxie's nasty little smirk with a grown-up expression of benevolence. 'I think they'll be a huge hit.'

She meant what she said and it gave her a rush of pleasure to see Roxie's self-satisfied expression falter.

'Yeah, well done,' said Flora. 'They got my thumbs-up the first time we met them. They're so enthusiastic.'

Abby tackled the remaining problem. 'It's taken so long to find suitable presenters, how do we fit them in with what we've already filmed?'

'That's sorted,' said Roxie stiffly. 'I know it took longer than I'd planned to find Linzi and Mitzi but they're worth the wait. And I know how we can segue their appearances into the show.'

Roxie's plan was simple: for the shows already in the can, the new presenters would de-junk a single room, and footage of this would be shown in cutaways from Abby's de-junking of the rest of the house. For the seven as yet unfilmed shows, Abby and the two presenters would continue to work separately, but link up at the end of each episode.

'Would you like to meet the girls?' Roxie added, with another smirk at Abby.

'Yes, very much,' she said, correctly guessing that everyone else had approved the new recruits already so that this meeting was purely cosmetic.

Stan's expectant face as Roxie went out to fetch them was a picture. Clearly he was smitten with Linzi and Mitzi. Brian even went so far as to readjust his tie in preparation.

In the flesh, the twins were even more lovely than on the screen. As tall as Jess, they looked like Olympic athletes: rosy-cheeked and glowing with health. Dressed up for the occasion in chic beiges and creams that complemented their sparkling blue eyes, they were beauty salon perfect. And they were dying to meet the famous Abby Barton.

'We're huge fans,' said one – Linzi or Mitzi?

'We love the show,' gushed the other.

Their eyes were wide with excitement and Abby couldn't help but respond to their friendliness and enthusiasm. 'Which is which, or is that a terrible question?'

'I'm Mitzi.'

'And I'm Linzi.' Linzi grinned. 'I have more freckles.'

'But that's no use in telling us apart unless we're together,' Mitzi pointed out.

Selina, who had come in behind her newest charges, raised elegant eyebrows at Abby, obviously delighted to see they were all getting on so well.

'Abby, do you have time to come for a coffee with us now? We'd love to talk to you and we'd really value your advice.'

'I'm sorry,' Abby said, 'but my daughter has just started her Junior Cert exams today and I have to pick her up soon.'

'Oh, of course,' the girls said respectfully, as if Abby had just mentioned that she was splitting the atom until Tuesday week. 'We'd hate to intrude; we know you're busy.'

'But then Selina's bound to be able to fix a lunch up or something soon,' Abby added quickly, 'although I'm sure you're going to be very busy doing publicity.' These girls were made for magazine photo shoots and Abby knew that Brian and Roxie wouldn't fail to capitalise on this fact. The new series wasn't due on air until the end of August but, by then, Linzi and Mitzi would be firmly imprinted on the nation's consciousness.

Selina wasn't going to lose a chance, and took Abby aside while everyone else chatted. 'How about coffee tomorrow morning?' she asked.

'If you've time, sure,' Abby said.

'The girls are genuinely keen to talk to you,' Selina whispered, 'and it would serve that Roxie bitch right if you all got on. She's dying to spread the story that you've stormed off the show because you can't stand the competition.'

'Coffee would be great,' Abby said loudly, patting Selina's arm in thanks. 'Say eleven, the patisserie in the Mall?'

'Brilliant,' said Linzi, or was it Mitzi?

Abby made it to the school in time to see Jess and Steph walking slowly out, talking nineteen to the dozen.

'I thought you might like a lift.' She smiled.

'I'd love one,' said Steph, opening the back door and throwing her school bag in as if it was contaminated.

'Thanks, Mum,' said Jess, giving her a rare grin.

The exams had been awful, dreadful, and as for that question on W.B. Yeats and imagery . . . there was no word to describe it.

'How can you answer a question like that in ten minutes?' wailed Steph. 'I don't know how they work out what time you need to spend on each question, but it's all wrong.'

'And I made such a mess of the modern novel question,' sighed Jess.

'Oh no,' interrupted Steph, '*I* made a mess of that.'

It was like old times, Abby thought happily as she drove to Steph's house.

After Steph got out, Abby was afraid that Jess would clam up but no, she seemed keen to keep talking.

'I know I should stay up all night doing maths but I've revised so hard now that I feel like I've no more room in my head for anything else,' her daughter said as they sped out of the city towards Dunmore.

Once, Abby would have instantly said that staying up all night was a nonsense idea anyhow, but she'd learned something in the last few weeks of family strife.

'I was never much good at staying up all night myself,' she revealed. 'And I've read that it doesn't do much good anyhow: you're too wrecked the next day to function properly.'

'Yeah,' Jess sighed. 'I'm wrecked enough as it is.'

'I got ingredients for a really nice wild mushroom risotto,' Abby said. 'Would you like that when we get home and then you can study, or do you want to work first and then eat?'

'Eat first,' said Jess. Then: 'Thanks, Mum.'

Abby told Jess about her day, with a light-hearted version of her meeting with Beech, leaving out the malicious intent behind every second word Roxie said.

'But it's still your show, isn't it?' asked Jess in concern, when she'd heard about Mitzi and Linzi.

'Sure,' Abby replied easily. 'But television shows have to move on and having new presenters is a part of that.'

'Oh, OK,' said Jess, not sounding convinced.

'Don't worry about me.' Abby smiled, squeezing her daughter's arm. 'I'm fine. Nobody's going to take *Declutter* away from me.'

'Good,' said Jess. 'You deserve your success.'

Abby decided that it was worth being sidelined at work if it brought her closer to her daughter.

Tom got home at the same time as they did and said he'd love some risotto. So, for the first time in ages, the Barton family sat down for dinner at the kitchen table chatting as though nothing had changed. Tom was too good a teacher to interrogate his own daughter about her exam, and instead cheered her up by recounting tales of students who'd left exams in tears, convinced they'd failed, only to get a decent mark months later.

'I hope that happens to me,' Jess said vehemently.

She got herself a yoghurt for dessert, smiled at both parents, and went off upstairs to tackle the next batch of revision. She also hoped there might be a text message from Oliver. She knew she didn't have time to see him in the middle of her exams, but he'd promised to text her every day and see her at the weekend. Thinking about him thinking about her gave Jess a warm feeling inside.

In the kitchen, Abby sank gratefully back into her chair.

Tom had been so friendly and normal. Was it too much to hope that things could get back to the way they'd been before?

Tom got up and began to clear the table, stacking dishes in the dishwasher. Abby watched, happy to have someone else tidy up for once. He'd changed out of his work clothes and was now dressed in an old sweatshirt and jeans. Out of the shirt and tie he wore to work, he looked younger, more like the man she'd married. He worked too hard, she sighed, up late correcting, and worrying about the new extension and the school's exam performance. They hadn't arranged a holiday this year and the plan had been to wait until summer to see what the finances were like, and book then. Jess would need a holiday too when her Junior Cert was over. They could take a cheap fly-drive to Florida, perhaps . . .

Tom's voice broke into her musings. 'Abby, I've been thinking. When Jess has finished her exams, it would be better if I moved out.'

Abby couldn't quite believe she'd heard him correctly. 'What?' she said.

He kept stacking the dishwasher and she realised that he hadn't been doing it to help: he'd been doing it to give him something to do while he dropped this cataclysmic news. 'I'm moving out. I don't want Jess to know yet, obviously.'

'You can't be serious?' She was stunned.

'I am.' He snapped the dishwasher shut and turned to face her, leaning against the worktop. He hadn't done the risotto saucepan, Abby thought wildly, then wondered why that mattered. Who cared about the saucepans now?

'What else can I do?' Tom demanded. 'Sit here and let you think it's acceptable to sleep with someone else? Play the househusband you want me to be? It's not enough that you rub my nose in your success, I've got to agree to an open marriage too. I don't want that sort of marriage, Abby.'

'Neither do I,' she cried, but he ignored her.

'Call me old-fashioned but I liked things the way they

were before, and now that everything's changed, we can't ever move back.'

'We can,' begged Abby. 'We could get counselling and you could learn to trust me again, please. Please. I'm so sorry, Tom. I never meant this to happen but we can start again. I thought we had,' she added softly.

'They might say you can start over in magazine articles, but it doesn't work like that in real life,' he said. 'Can you imagine us ever making love again without me thinking of him touching you?' He clenched his fists until the knuckles were white. 'You touching him . . . I can't think of anything else. It haunts me.'

Abby realised that she'd had no idea how much Tom had been hurting. She thought he'd been getting over it, that his pride had been dented as much as anything. Now she understood that she'd underestimated the effect of her thoughtless act. He was devastated by her betrayal. She felt ashamed to have imagined that he'd just come to terms with it and move on.

'Please understand, Tom, it meant nothing. It's you I love and it's you I've always loved. I was so stupid and lonely. You know we haven't been getting on, and –'

'Oh, so it's all my fault now, is it?' demanded Tom.

'No,' said Abby, thinking that Tom's coldness towards her had certainly contributed to her misery, but knowing he wouldn't see it as an excuse for her adultery. 'But you weren't exactly interested in me. I felt like your mother or your sister,' she added. 'We could be brother and sister for all the excitement in our marriage.'

Tom looked as though he might explode.

'I'm not using that as an excuse,' Abby went on hurriedly. God, was she making things worse? 'I was lonely, that was all. I thought having someone else flatter me would make me feel happier or younger or something, but it didn't.' She wanted to explain it as openly as possible, hoping he'd understand.

'You wanted to feel younger and flattered?' he said

incredulously. 'Is that supposed to be an excuse? Can you picture me jumping into bed with someone else because I felt old and neglected? Is that how little you valued what we had, that you'd abandon it for such stupid reasons?' He spat the words out.

'I *do* value our marriage, please believe me,' she pleaded. 'As soon as it happened, I knew it was a mistake. I hated myself for betraying you. Please listen to me, Tom!'

He didn't answer.

'And if you go, we'll never be able to get through it.' Abby felt the strength she'd had earlier slip away. She would plead with him, she'd do anything to stop him leaving. Didn't he care that this would destroy Jess too? 'Please, I beg you, please don't go. Let's try to work this out.'

'I can't,' he said flatly. 'I didn't want to involve Jess and I thought I could deal with it, but I can't. Like I said, Abby, I'm an old-fashioned man and when my wife sleeps with another man, my instinct is that something precious has gone and can't be replaced. If more modern men can cope with that, then good for them. I can't. And for the record, I never saw you as my sister, right? I thought we had a marriage; we don't any more.'

'But we could try and get over this . . . can't we? Won't you ever be able to forgive me?'

'I don't know,' he said. 'I wish I did. Right now, the answer is no. I don't want to talk about it any more. We don't want Jess to find out now: she needs to concentrate. But you had to know. I didn't want you to think that everything was all right because we shared one meal together.'

He left the room abruptly. Shell-shocked, Abby sat and stared into space.

She didn't know how long she sat there blankly. It was only the phone ringing that broke through her catatonic state.

'Abby, sorry to call so late,' said Katya, her assistant, breathlessly. 'The kids were sick and I totally forgot to tell you that *House Today* rang me earlier. They want to do a big interview with you for the cover of the magazine, to coincide

269

with the new series. They like to work well in advance, so if we do it now, it'll be on the cover of the September issue, which comes out at the end of August. Imagine! They want to photograph you at home because they've heard you've got this terrific house. I said we'd get back to them because we don't want to seem too eager, but, Abby, it's fabulous!'

'Yes, great,' said Abby, on automatic pilot.

'Now ideally they'd like Tom and Jess too, but I said you didn't involve your family in photos and they understand that. I mean, you have to have some privacy, don't you?'

'Of course,' murmured Abby, wondering how she was going to manage the interview. How could she talk blatantly about her happy marriage and how her family came first when her husband wanted to move out? She couldn't. It would be hypocritical.

'They'd like to do the shoot on Thursday or Friday of this week if possible. How does that sound?'

Abby thought about it. If she could save her marriage, keep Jess from finding out how close her parents had come to splitting up and erase the pinched, thin look from her own face by Thursday, then that would be fine. Otherwise, it would make the sorriest cover story *House Today* had ever seen.

'I'm a bit tied up this week,' she fudged. 'Jess is doing her exams. Can you check if they'll consider waiting for a couple of weeks?' It was the only excuse she could come up with.

'OK,' said Katya cheerily. 'I'll phone them tomorrow and see. Bye.'

Abby looked at her watch. It was half seven. Where had the time gone? She washed the risotto saucepan and left it on the drainer. Then she pulled a cardigan over her shoulders and wandered out into the garden. It was such a lovely evening, she thought as she walked, deadheading a rose here and there, admiring the peonies in their full-bodied pink beauty. She stooped to touch one, thinking that they were strangely old-fashioned flowers. Who'd planted them here?

Before she and Tom had bought it, Lyonnais had been owned by a developer who'd had great plans for knocking the old house down and building an apartment block in its stead. He hadn't got planning permission and had sold the house on to the Bartons. But before him, who'd owned it then? Who'd lovingly planted the peonies and tended the high-walled herb bed where rosemary towered over clumps of thyme? Who'd searched out the armless stone goddess that peeped out coyly from behind the ivy? Had a happy family lived here and laughed here, growing up and old together?

The wonderful garden had always calmed Abby, but of late she hadn't felt any comfort when she looked out at it. There had been too much going on in her life, too much anxiety. The garden represented her hopes and dreams when she, Tom and Jess had moved in. She'd imagined happy barbecues on the terrace, lazy sunny days spent on a lounger with a book in her hand and her family around her. Nine months ago, Lyonnais had symbolised a glittering new life for the whole family, but now it seemed as if those dreams were a thing of the past, and looking at the garden only highlighted the loss. If she and Tom divorced, this house and the garden would have to go. Another casualty of her stupidity.

Yet this evening, strangely enough, and despite the aware-ness that she might soon have to consider selling it, the calming quality of Lyonnais worked its magic. As Abby walked in the evening light, she felt the bizarre peace of having had the worst finally happen. Tom wanted to leave her. She was no longer scared out of her mind that he would. The fear had become reality. It was a nightmare, but somehow she would just have to cope.

She picked a piece of lemon balm and crushed it between her fingers, releasing the heady scent. Life would go on. She and Tom would separate. She would have to deal with it. This garden had, she guessed, certainly seen life's ups and downs: births, deaths, marriages, arguments, love and the death of love. Still the flowers bloomed and the herbs sent their fragrance into the evening. The cycle of life went on. Abby dropped the crushed leaf to the ground and went back inside.

CHAPTER EIGHTEEN

Dunmore experienced the hottest June on record. People who'd planned continental holidays began to regret not staying at home because the temperature hit the eighties every day. Proud gardeners watched glumly as their cherished lawns turned dry and scorched under a hosepipe ban, and the local garden centre sold out of parasols. People with children bought paddling pools and sat with their own feet in the cool water, while the electrical shop in the square had a run on electric fans. The Italian family who owned both an ice-cream parlour and a pastel-pink and blue ice-cream van made a fortune, enough to send the whole family to Florida for a month at the end of the summer.

Tom Barton, tied up with the school building works, found that he didn't have much time to look for a place of his own to rent. He viewed a couple of flats and a minuscule town house in Dunmore, but there was nothing he liked within his price range. Abby, who was working hard shooting the remaining seven *Declutter* shows with Mitzi and Linzi, and organising the hour-long talk she was giving at the Ideal House exhibition, was relieved when he did not leave Lyonnais as quickly as he had indicated.

Jess, having finished her exams and broken up from school for the summer, helped Delia with the Richardson boys, for which Steve insisted on paying her, and she also found a couple of evening babysitting jobs, so that, together with an advance on her birthday money from her mother, she saved up enough to buy a new mountain bike. A sleek metallic blue and grey, it could climb hills effortlessly and meant she didn't have to bother getting the bus on the days she helped out at the animal refuge.

She could also cycle to Oliver's house on the other side of Dunmore, although she didn't tell her parents about that. Oliver was her secret. They were just friends, really, she told herself, so it was nobody's business.

Never mind that Oliver had kissed her. That had been incredible and not at all like she'd imagined; it had felt right, and somehow she'd known what to do. They held hands a lot too.

Because Oliver was working with his dad in the family's market garden business, and because Mum was so nosy and wanted to know where Jess was every single second of the day, they didn't have that much time together. But when they did see each other, Jess, despite the trouble at home and her sadness at Sally's illness, felt happier than she had for a long time. Oliver liked her – no tits, train tracks, glasses and all.

At the end of the first week in June, Erin and Greg moved out of Cat Pee Towers and into their new apartment, where they felt immediately at home. They decided to leave the walls as they were painted until they knew what colours would suit, and Erin found she loved the peace of clean white after the hectic shades of the rented house. The only room they changed was the nursery, and they had great fun looking at wallpapers and borders featuring teddy bears, shy rabbits and loud cartoon characters. Erin veered between wanting and not wanting to know whether the baby was a boy or a girl. The knowledge would be handy when it came to decorating the nursery, she pointed out, but on the other hand it would be a wonderful surprise to find out when she gave birth. Greg, who was daily delighted by how her belly was swelling, said he'd prefer to wait and why didn't they decorate the room yellow? They could always add pink or blue curtains and blankets afterwards.

The one thing Erin hadn't tackled was the search for her

family. There was so much to think about, what with the move and her pregnancy, that it was easy to procrastinate.

Lizzie Shanahan got a stern letter from the bank about her overdraft and realised that she'd have to earn some more money somehow or she'd be in deep financial trouble. The cost of Debra's wedding was spiralling, and Lizzie was too proud to admit to Myles that she was struggling to pay her part of it. She scanned the jobs notices in the papers, but found nothing she was qualified for that would earn her any more money than she did already. Besides, she loved working in the surgery and it would break her heart to leave. Then, a tiny box ad caught her eye, telling her she could make a fortune selling beauty products at house parties. That was something she could do in the evenings after her day job.

Ladysmith cosmetics were Irish made, cruelty-free and the future of beauty products, the ad promised. Lizzie phoned up and discovered that working three evenings a week she could, incredibly, match the money she made in the surgery – if she sold enough Ladysmith products, of course. She'd also have to go on a short training course and buy her own starting kit for the beauty demonstrations. She was sent the registration form, then lost her courage and put it on the mantelpiece. She'd economise for a while to see if that helped and then, if necessary, she'd sign up. Lizzie didn't really want to have to work nights too, but unless she found some other way to save money, she might have to. It seemed like another symptom of how badly she managed her life.

One glorious morning, the second week of June, Sally and Steve Richardson met Sally's oncology team to hear what they already knew in their hearts: her bone cancer was frighteningly aggressive and spreading rapidly. Pain management and palliative care were all they could offer her now. Sally's favourite oncologist, the dapper Mr Patel, was so very sorry but he knew she appreciated hearing the truth. She would not recover.

Leaving the hospital arm in arm with Steve, Sally decided

that Jack and Daniel needed a paddling pool. She also wanted to get new tapes for their high-tech video camera. She'd been writing a diary for when the children were older, and it was nearly finished, and yet she still felt there was so much she wanted to tell them. About how much she loved them, how she adored their father, how she'd enjoyed life and, oh, so many other things. A video recording suddenly made perfect sense, because then the boys would see her smiling face and they wouldn't just see the tear-stained diary and imagine her sobbing with grief at leaving them. She didn't want their memories of her to be steeped in misery. If they had video tapes, her face, smiling and full of love, would stare at them from the screen and they'd remember the real happy Sally, their wonderful mum.

As they walked to the car, she broached another difficult subject. She and Steve couldn't hide her illness from the children any more. There was a therapist who specialised in bereavement counselling for small children. There was also, she added gently, a therapist from the same practice who specialised in adult bereavement counselling. Steve gripped her arm more tightly. He might think about it later for the children, but he didn't need it, he said.

Wouldn't a weekend away be nice? Just the four of them, somewhere romantic with babysitting services so that after the boys had gone to bed they could gaze into each other's eyes over dinner and talk.

It sounded wonderful, Sally said.

They went to a child-friendly hotel in Connemara and had a glorious weekend.

'No amount of counselling could improve on this,' Steve told his wife as they walked along the coast with their arms round each other, watching the boys search rock pools for tiny fish.

'You're right,' Sally agreed, her face lifted towards the sun. 'They should market the west of Ireland as a counselling alternative,' she added, clinging tightly to Steve's tall frame. 'Phone the tourist board and tell them when we get home.'

'Yes, ma'am,' said Steve. 'Your wish is my command.'

Afterwards, Steve said it was incredible how happy Sally had been for the whole of the weekend, playing with Jack and Daniel on the private beach of their hotel and enjoying romantic meals with him, as relaxed and calm as if they had a lifetime of such holidays ahead of them.

'She told me her guardian angel was watching over us all, giving us one final beautiful memory,' he said. 'She said that we were to remember the good times and not the bad ones to come.'

It was as if Sally knew the time was near. That glorious weekend was the last carefree time she got to share with Steve, Jack and Daniel. When they returned, Sally's condition deteriorated and only a few days after she'd played on a windswept Connemara beach with her family, she moved into a hospice.

Steve and Delia were at her side when she died in her sleep.

CHAPTER NINETEEN

Funerals, Lizzie thought, should be confined to wet, miserable days. It felt so wrong to bury anyone on a wonderful day at the beginning of July when the sun gilded the church spire and beamed down on the black-clad shoulders of sombre people hurrying through the church door. Burying vibrant, life-loving Sally Richardson on the sort of day she'd have loved seemed doubly wrong.

Lizzie slid into a seat alongside Erin and Greg, and nodded hello. Then, she glanced up the aisle and her eyes hit upon the solid, grim shape of the coffin. It was hard to imagine that Sally lay cold inside.

Like most people of her generation, Lizzie had been to many funerals and was familiar with the routines of death, but the sight of a coffin still had the power to shock her. A once-living person was lying there and would soon be in the ground, covered with earth, locked away in the cold. She would not want that for herself, she decided, then felt a wave of guilt at such a selfish thought at Sally's funeral.

She forced herself to look away from the coffin and saw a small boy sitting on the edge of the front row, feet dangling from the seat, already bored with this whole business. It was Jack, Sally's older son. His father's arm was around him but the boy didn't want to be held; he wanted to run up and down the aisle and explore. And from now on, his mother wouldn't be there for him to run back to.

Lizzie felt her breath catch in her throat at the thought.

What had Steve told the children? 'Mummy's gone to heaven but she's looking down on you'?

Sally had tried to tell them that she wouldn't be coming back and had worked so hard on that diary for when they were older.

'If I had daughters, I'd be able to include more advice,' she'd laughed wryly the day she told Lizzie what she was doing. 'I'd say, "Value yourself and remember you are beautiful and never leap into bed with a guy just because he says, 'You would if you loved me.'" It's harder to give advice to boys, Lizzie.'

Hard, Lizzie thought, considering Debra, wasn't the word.

She glanced up as the Bartons arrived and took a pew a few rows further up from hers. Abby, looking drawn and washed out in a charcoal suit, went in first and sank to her knees, followed by Tom and Jess. Lizzie had met Abby briefly in the bank earlier in the month and had been startled to see the change in her. Abby definitely looked thinner and somehow older; the planes of her face were more defined. Lizzie had overheard rumours in the surgery about Tom and Abby being on the verge of splitting up, but she hated malicious gossip and had ignored it. Abby had chatted merrily enough to her that day in the bank and, if there was a sad story of marriage break-up, she'd kept it well hidden. Now, seeing Abby's drawn face, she wondered if the rumours were true.

Sitting on the hard pew between her parents, Jess stared anywhere but at Steve and the children. She knew she couldn't bear to look at the boys' confused little faces.

She remembered months before, when Sally had first been ill and the boys were staying at Lyonnais, and Daniel had woken up early and crept into Jess's bedroom, delighted with himself for thinking up this new adventure.

'Story,' he'd demanded, dropping a book onto Jess and clambering into the bed beside her. 'Read me a story, Dess.' She had got so close to them. Those poor little boys.

Jess knew she'd cry if she thought about how they didn't have their mum any more. It was so sad. How could her stupid parents watch Sally's perfect family fall apart because of something beyond their control and still not understand that their own family didn't have to fall apart? Couldn't they see the difference? Sally and Steve would have done anything to stay together. Mum and Dad didn't seem to want to bother. They could have gone to a counsellor or someone. Lorraine in school's parents did that. Lorraine had even had to go once to a family session and they'd sorted everything out and made it work. Granted, Jess didn't know what had been wrong between Lorraine's parents, but you could sort most things out.

Mrs Lyons, the guidance counsellor and social studies teacher, said that at lectures on drugs and alcohol. 'Never feel there isn't anyone you can talk to. There is. Your parents care for you. If you imagine you're alone in the world, then nobody gets the opportunity to help you. But if you look for help and share the problem, then you'll realise that you're not alone.'

Steph hated Mrs Lyons. 'She looks straight at me when she talks about smoking being bad for you,' Steph grumbled.

Steph was smoking lots more now.

While Jess secretly thought Mrs Lyons talked sense, she also wanted to know why adults made such a big deal about how you could discuss anything and sort it out and then, in their own lives, refused to talk. It was one rule for teenagers and another rule for parents, she thought angrily. Like in everything else.

Sometimes, she wanted to scream at Mum and Dad to stop behaving like kids and make up. Didn't they know what this was doing to her?

The silence in the car on the way to the church had been stifling, but the atmosphere was almost as bad when they spoke to each other.

'Those boys are too young to go to the funeral,' Dad had said, almost as if he was daring Mum to contradict him, which she did.

'Sally would have wanted them there,' Mum replied sharply. 'She was their mother.'

'Mothers don't always do what's right,' Dad snapped back.

Shut up! Jess wanted to yell. This is a sad day. Stop arguing about stupid things! But she said nothing, and chewed a bit of nail on her index finger as she stared out the back window. Oliver had said he'd come to support her but she'd said no, she'd have enough trouble keeping the peace as it was and wouldn't have time to talk to him. Now she was sorry she'd said that. Oliver holding her hand would have been comforting. She'd finally told Mum and Dad about him, which was a relief. Dad had been cool about her having a boyfriend and seemed to like Oliver when they'd met. Mum, on the other hand, had gone all mental and paranoid, and now seemed even keener on knowing where Jess was every moment of every day. What did Mum think she and Oliver were going to get up to?

At the start of the ceremony, Jess coped by just not listening. She kept her mind elsewhere, thinking of how she'd go to the refuge in the afternoon and see Twiglet. There was something comforting about cuddling his wriggling little body, letting him lick her face before he'd struggle to get down so he could bite and pull at her socks. At five months old, he was addicted to worrying people's socks, and thought it was the best game ever, even better than getting an empty sock and having a tug of war with another dog.

'You love him, don't you?' Jean had said last time Jess was at the refuge, when she was exhausted from helping scrub down the cattery, but still found the energy to play with Twiglet and another, smaller puppy, Conker.

Jess nodded.

'He'll need to be rehomed soon,' Jean added, watching her face.

Jess said nothing, although she knew Jean was saying that she could take Twiglet home if her parents agreed. Her parents didn't want a dog. There was no point asking. They

281

didn't want a family either. Jess knew that when people split up, they had to move houses. If they could only afford a small house, there'd be no room for Twiglet.

At home, she sometimes pretended her toy sausage dog was Twiglet and she talked to him in her room at night.

'Are you cosy enough, Twiglet? Would you like another doggy biscuit?'

The sausage dog version of Twiglet would gaze up at her with its shiny black button eyes. He wasn't anywhere near as good as the real thing, but he still helped.

Four seats back, Erin cradled her hand round her growing belly. She loved doing this, reminding herself of the new life inside, a whole new being with a heartbeat. Despite her joy over this, it felt so unfair that she could feel this new life moving inside her and Sally's had been snuffed out.

Who decided who got to live or die? Why were good people taken away? What was the point?

She sniffed and realised that she'd forgotten tissues. Greg's big hand found one of hers and clasped it tightly. He knew how she felt: he felt the same.

'We've got so much and Steve has lost her. I don't know what I'd do without you, Erin,' Greg had said the night before as they lay in their new bed in the new-smelling apartment, curled close, his hand resting on her belly.

'I couldn't bear to leave you,' Erin said sadly. 'That would be the hardest thing of all: leaving you when I love you so much. It would break my heart.'

There was a certain peace to be had in the ritual of a funeral, Lizzie had usually found. The combination of the familiar prayers and the soft yet powerful way the words sounded when a large group of people chanted them was calming. Death was a part of life, the whole process seemed to say. We are burying this person but, one day, it will be you, and the people who love you will do you the honour of mourning you. The cycle of life goes on. But today, the prayers and the priest's words did not have the ring of truth for Lizzie.

Today, they felt all wrong. The old traditions could not do justice to Sally.

Then, Steve got up to speak.

Lizzie felt that tender ache in her heart that she used to get when Joe and Debra were little children and had to perform in the school nativity play. Her heart would swell with the hope that they were brave enough to get through it all. Now she felt exactly the same for Steve.

He looked broken, she thought as she watched him stand behind the pulpit, holding a few sheets of paper. Everyone else in the church was tanned and healthy from the superb weather, while Steve had the pallor of one who'd spent many hours inside. The sun had hurt Sally's eyes and, towards the end, in the sanctuary of the hospice, she'd been too frail to want to be wheeled outside to the tiny walled garden.

Lizzie had visited Sally there once but it had been a short visit. Sally, her eyes dulled with morphine, which in the end had been necessary, had only been able to remain awake for a few minutes. On the way back to her car, Lizzie had walked through the walled garden and sobbed.

Steve took off his reading glasses and laid them on top of his papers.

'I prepared something but I can't read it out. I don't know why I even wrote it down.' A faint smile touched his face. 'It's not as if I couldn't talk about Sally for hours without any script to guide me. I've always talked about her, I am so proud of her.'

There wasn't a person in the congregation who didn't feel his or her heart lurch at his use of the present tense.

'That's right,' he added. 'I *am* proud of her because she will always be with me. She's here in Jack and Daniel and she's here in my heart.

'Sally touched so many lives and it's a joy to me and the boys to see so many people here today. The hard part is that you're all here because she's dead. Sally loved parties and I just wish I was meeting all these old friends because we were having another party, laughing and drinking my awful punch.'

People around the church smiled at the memory of parties at the Richardsons'.

'We used to joke about it: how someone would end up drunk and she'd say she'd murder me if anyone was upset because of what happened at our party. That was Sally. She was the kindest person I've ever known, not fake kindness but the real thing. She wanted to help people and reach out to them in their pain. I'd never met anyone like her. When we fell in love, I felt so lucky to have found this precious, special person who loved me.'

It was a love letter, Erin realised, clutching onto Greg's hand so tightly that her wedding band crushed her finger. A love letter to Sally because soon she'd be in the earth and he wouldn't even have her cold body to say these beautiful words to.

All around them, people were searching in pockets and handbags for tissues. Somebody was crying nearby: little sobs they couldn't disguise.

Steve's eyes roamed round the church, then settled on his wife's coffin, and he went on, 'We knew what we had was special and Sally never wanted us to forget it. Count your blessings, she'd say, and it was never corny the way she said it. She meant it. She knew what tragedy was because she went through it when her mother died and she knew that life could be tough, so she wanted us to appreciate what we had. And we did – oh, we did.' He paused.

Abby found a crumpled, lipstick-stained tissue in the bottom of her handbag and ripped it apart to hand half to Jess, who was wiping tears away with her fingers.

'The hardest thing for Sally was leaving Jack and Daniel.' He smiled down at where his two small boys were sitting with their aunt and granny, distracted thanks to the bag of toys Steve had brought with him. 'I wanted them here today because it's a special goodbye to Mummy and when they're older, they'll be glad they were here. Sally left them a diary and taped messages because she wanted them to have happy memories, not just a trip to the graveyard once a year to put flowers on her grave. That's not how you should remember people, she said.'

The sound of sobbing increased.

'And she is –' Steve corrected himself – 'she *was* right. Sally touched so many people's lives and that's how she should be remembered: as a funny, beautiful, kind, loving, warm person and not as a mound in the earth. That's the person I want our sons to remember.

'She was brave too, so brave. Even when she was scared, having had the worst diagnosis a person could have, she was worried about us and how we'd cope without her. That's true courage.

'I miss her so much already and I know I'll always miss her, but I want us to celebrate her life too. Thank you.'

Stunned by the depth of his eulogy, the congregation sat motionless for a moment. Then the clapping started. The noise was deafening. Steve went back to the front pew and picked up little Daniel from the ground and held him tight. Those closer to the family could hear Jack's clear, loud voice: 'Is Mummy's special party over? Can we go now, Daddy?'

The final hymn was sung and everyone shuffled outside into the blinding sunlight. With Tom and Jess mutely following, Abby made her way over to where Erin, Greg and Lizzie were standing, facing the Richardson family. People milled around the bereaved, offering their condolences to Steve; ruffling the children's hair; saying, 'You don't know me but I was a friend of Sally's' to Steve's mother, Delia, and his sister, Amy, who both looked shell-shocked. Sally had no close family left to mourn her. Her side of the family was made up of aunts, uncles and cousins.

'It doesn't seem right,' Abby sighed, speaking for them all.

'I hate funerals,' Erin said tonelessly.

'Me too,' said Jess fiercely. 'It wasn't like the priest was talking about Sally at all. He didn't make it sound like he knew her. And how can that be God's plan, to take her away? That's all wrong.'

'It is all wrong,' Lizzie said gently, touching Jess's shoulder softly. Jess's bluey-green eyes welled with tears.

'I remember being a child and my mother taking me to all the local funerals,' Abby said dully. She didn't add that funerals were what passed for social life in a home where her mother was beaten down by poverty and sought solace in the old customs, such as holding a wake for the dead. Tom glanced at her but said nothing. It was unusual to hear Abby talk about her background.

The final wreaths were loaded into the hearse and Abby watched bleakly. She didn't want to go to the cemetery, although Steve had asked the family to go. If there was anything worse than watching a coffin being lowered into a gaping wound in the earth, then Abby didn't know what it was.

No, she contradicted her own thoughts. She did. It would be watching a burial and thinking that the dead person would have done anything to stay with her family, when she, Abby, had destroyed hers.

She felt as if she had been plunged into a nightmare where every old fear of her life was upon her: loss, poverty, fights, pain. Even worse was the fact that she'd been the architect of it all. But she had to cope – she had no option. And look at how bravely Sally had coped with tragedy. Abby drew strength from that.

By twelve, it was all over and a group of subdued people repaired to the bar of the Hotel Dunmore, where sandwiches and soup were being served for the mourners.

Jess followed everyone in silently and sat down beside Abby. She didn't know why, but she needed the comfort of her mother now, even though Mum seemed lost in her own private misery. Jess wasn't needed to look after Daniel and Jack; there were so many relations helping out that she knew they were safe. And she didn't trust herself not to hug them too close and sob into their soft shoulders about the unfairness of it all. Dad was nowhere to be seen.

Erin and Lizzie sat down at the table beside Abby and Jess, Erin grateful for a seat after all that standing. Nobody spoke as they drank their coffee and nibbled at egg sandwiches.

Finally, Lizzie broke the silence. 'Have you been having nice summer holidays?' she asked Jess brightly. 'I've seen you cycling around on a really cool bike.'

A shy smile transformed Jess's face. 'It's handy for going out to the animal refuge where I volunteer.'

'Oh,' said Lizzie, interested, 'is that the place out by the Old Cork Road? I read in the local paper that it might have to close.'

'Not any more,' Jess said proudly. 'We've been fund-raising.'

She began to tell Lizzie about the animals and her favourite, Twiglet, half hoping her mother might be listening. But Abby was staring over to the other side of the hotel bar where Dad was standing. Why didn't Mum ever listen, Jess wondered. From her position, she couldn't see the look of abject misery on her mother's face.

Erin saw it, though. Instinctively, she reached out and touched Abby's hand. 'Are you all right?'

Abby came back to earth. 'Yes,' she lied. She'd got a shock when she'd seen Tom talking to Leo, an old colleague who'd known Sally and whom Abby had never got on with.

Of all the people for Tom to meet, why did he have to bump into this guy? Since Leo's divorce, it was clear he thought marriage was an outdated institution. If he discovered what was going on in Abby and Tom's marriage, his advice was more likely to be 'leave her' than 'try to work it out'.

'You sure?' added Erin.

Abby had been about to mutter something mundane about how nobody could be all right at a funeral, but there was something genuine in Erin's eyes and Abby found that she didn't want to lie any more.

'No,' she admitted. 'But how could anyone be all right today?'

'True.' Erin looked over to where Steve was stoically talking to some mourners, holding stiffly on to a cup of coffee that he wasn't drinking. The cup was like a barrier, she realised. He wanted to keep people at a distance. 'It's such a shock. I know Sally was ill for a few months but I kept hoping that she could get better, you know, like when you read in the papers about someone who's given a few months and lives for years.'

'That's what Delia was praying for,' Abby said. 'But Steve and Sally knew for a long time that there was no hope.'

She changed the subject. 'How are you feeling? When is the baby due?'

'November.' Erin beamed, and Abby thought that she really was unusual-looking with those amber eyes and the long nose that saved her face from mere prettiness and made her striking. There was some dark mystery in her life, Abby knew. That night at Sally's party, when she had found them in the garden, Erin had been revealing some tragedy to Lizzie.

Lizzie was a bit like Sally in some ways – a million miles quieter and sweetly shy because she had no self-confidence, but she possessed the same innate kindness that made people confide in her.

'And how are you?' Erin enquired gently.

The moment for confidences had passed, Abby realised. Sally's funeral was not the place to recount the disaster she'd made of her life, even though she longed to tell someone, to find a shoulder to cry on.

'Fine,' she said, smiling her professional smile. 'Just fine.'

'None of us is fine really,' said Ruby, perching on a chair beside them. Her eyes were raw with crying.

'What will happen to the salon now?' enquired one of Sally's neighbours, leaning down to pick up some of the barely touched sandwiches on their table. She took a bite from one and spoke with her mouth full: 'Sally made it popular; it will hardly survive without her.'

Erin stared at the woman in astonishment. Had she no sense of timing and did she not realise how insensitive it was to say such a thing with Ruby present?

'I'm sure Steve will think of something,' she said with an edge to her voice.

Sally's neighbour flushed. 'I was only saying . . .' she said, and flounced off.

'Aren't you supposed to add something about her being the weakest link, and goodbye?' murmured Lizzie.

'Sorry,' Erin apologised. 'She just made me so mad and I saw red. What a tactless thing to say today.'

'Sally loved the salon,' Jess added quietly. 'We were talking about dreams one day and she told me that when she was my age, she always knew she wanted her own beauty salon. It was her dream.'

Abby put an arm round her daughter in remorse. When had she last spoken to Jess about dreams?

'I remember when she opened it,' Lizzie said. 'At the time, I didn't exactly have the money for beauty treatments. Still don't,' she laughed. 'But I did my best to go to Sally's. She didn't just give you a facial, she made you feel good, welcomed, among friends. Even total strangers came out of the salon feeling as if they'd known her for years.'

'I felt that about her,' Erin agreed. 'She didn't have to make such an effort to be friends with me when Greg and I moved back here, but she did. She was the first person to make me feel that I was part of Dunmore.'

'That was Sally all over. She was so friendly,' said Abby wistfully, the loss of her old friend aching anew.

'And funny,' Lizzie added.

'And kind,' Ruby put in. 'You've no idea how good she always was to me. When Dave dumped me, it was Sally who got me through it. The business won't be the same without her. Who could replace Sally . . . ?' Her voice broke.

'The business won't go under – we won't let it,' Erin

announced decisively. 'You're brilliant at what you do, Ruby, don't forget that. We're going to help.'

'But how?' asked Abby.

'By supporting it, I suppose,' Lizzie said.

'By making sure the customers don't go anywhere else,' Jess said sensibly.

'Staff is the big problem,' Ruby pointed out. 'Nobody could replace Sally, and while she was sick we relied on temporary help. Now she's gone, we have to face that and I can't bear to talk it over with Steve.'

'I can answer phones and tidy up and do all the things a manager does,' Erin said. 'Until Steve works out what he wants to do with it, anyhow,' she added.

She didn't have any other plans right now, and she'd love to feel that, somehow, she could pay Sally back for her kindness.

'That would be wonderful,' said Ruby tearfully.

'No tears,' Erin said firmly, determined to buoy everyone up. 'That's not going to help Steve and the kids – or the salon, for that matter. We're going to get through this as a team, right?'

The others nodded, doing their best to stave off tears too.

'OK,' muttered Lizzie. 'No tears.' Erin was right: they had to make an effort. If Steve could stand up in front of everyone at Sally's funeral and give that beautiful, loving eulogy with its message of hope, then they could all have hope for the future, couldn't they?

CHAPTER TWENTY

In the week after the biggest funeral Dunmore had seen for a long while, Lizzie felt as if she had the flu. Her head was heavy and her eyes watered at the slightest provocation.

'I know, take two aspirin and see me in the morning,' she said drily to Dr Morgan when she reported her symptoms.

'Actually, I was going to tell you to take some time off or go on holiday,' Clare Morgan replied. 'I know Sally was a special friend of yours but you won't do her or that poor husband of hers any good by getting sick yourself.'

'I'm too broke to go on holiday,' Lizzie said miserably, then felt even more miserable to be moaning about it. She might be broke but she was still alive. And she hadn't lost the person she'd loved most in the whole world, like poor Steve. She'd seen Steve in the supermarket the day before, wandering round like he was sleepwalking, but when she caught up with him, he hadn't wanted to talk.

'Sorry, Lizzie,' he said, his eyes glittering with unshed tears. 'I'm better off on my own right now.'

She'd felt helpless in the face of his pain.

'If you're broke, then go to London to see Joe,' said Clare in exasperation. 'You can get a cheap flight and, staying with Joe, you won't have any hotel bills.'

It wasn't a bad idea, Lizzie decided.

'Well?' demanded her boss.

'OK,' said Lizzie. 'I'll phone him.'

Joe was delighted with the idea and even offered to book the flights over the Internet. An hour after the suggestion had been made, Lizzie found herself in the strange position of having plans for the following weekend.

'See?' said Clare, when she heard it was all set up. 'I'm a holistic doctor – I deal with every aspect of your life.'

It was a quiet morning in the surgery and once all the filing, letters and chasing-up of test results was done, Lizzie made herself a cup of tea and unwrapped a chocolate biscuit from the luxury selection in the tiny kitchenette. She riffled through the magazines in the waiting room to see if there was anything new there. Clare's grown-up daughters gave their mother their old magazines for the surgery, so there were always plenty of fun-filled bright articles about how to clamber to the top of the career ladder, how to create a perfect capsule wardrobe, and how to seduce your man by taking him away for a sexy weekend.

Whizzing over an article on very intimate plastic surgery (Honestly, thought Lizzie, wincing, think of the pain. And whoever looks down there anyway?), she came to a double-page spread on 'Things to Do Before You're Thirty' – 'Things Every Woman Should Have on Her Wish List', cooed the drop headline.

Nibbling her biscuit to make it last longer, Lizzie began to read, half expecting it to be full of things she'd done, along with a scattering of wild things nobody in their right mind would want to attempt.

She was experienced, a woman who'd been through life and seen it all. Surely she'd be able to tick off lots of the sensible options on the list.

But 'get married, have kids and live in the same home for twenty-eight years' wasn't anywhere on the page. The further down the list she read, the more demoralised Lizzie felt.

- *Start an investment portfolio.*
- *Buy yourself a decent piece of jewellery.* Did a fake Moulin Rouge choker she'd got in Topshop count?
- *Go on holiday on your own and enjoy it.*

- *Try an adventure sport – mountaineering, skydiving, scuba diving.*
- *Stop talking about learning a foreign language and actually do it.*
- *Do something for charity.* Rattling tins for the children's hospital counted, didn't it?
- *Plan your career properly with professional advice.*
- *Tell your boss what you really think of him or her.*
- *Dance with somebody who knows how – ballroom, Latin, the choice is up to you.*
- *Own a car you've bought for reasons you don't have to explain to anyone.*
- *Make friends with your parents.* Well, she'd done that. Not that they'd ever fallen out in the first place, Lord rest them.
- *Throw out all your self-help books.*
- *Stop binge drinking – stick to 14 units per week total and don't have it all in one night.*
- *Get regular health checks – don't let silent diseases like chlamydia ruin your fertility.*
- *Spend an afternoon walking slowly round the Louvre.*
- *Learn how to use power tools so you can be your own DIY man.*
- *Flirt with a stranger just for the fun of it.*

Lizzie remembered lists from her youth when convincing the barman in an over-23s club to serve you a vodka and orange or having sex with a man you had no intention of marrying were considered the wildest things possible. Nobody had ever told Lizzie to buy jewellery for herself. Hell, no. Besotted boyfriends bought girls jewellery then, after being dragged past the shop endlessly and having the piece in question pointed out so they couldn't get it wrong. Any woman would have been ashamed to admit that she'd bought her own bracelet or ring.

Ballroom dancing was seen as boring as hell, the sort of thing everyone's parents had done in the fifties. Nobody could afford a car, although Lizzie remembered longing for a Volkswagen Beetle. And why would anyone go on holiday on their own when they had girlfriends to go with?

She shut the magazine with a resounding slap and picked up the morning newspaper. At least that could contain nothing to reproach her about wasting her life. Then she thought about Sally and felt the wave of sadness wash over her again. Sally hadn't wasted one second of her life and where had it got her? Lizzie went back to the magazine, ripped out the page and stowed it in her handbag.

The last time Lizzie had been in London to visit Joe, she'd been with Debra. It had been a short, frantic trip, with her daughter keen to see everything and to do it at breakneck speed. Lizzie, who remembered the buzz of visiting the city for the first time when she'd been nineteen, had been willing to rush around with Debra.

Now she was there by herself. Rattling along on the Piccadilly Line with her small suitcase squashed between her knees, Lizzie felt that old buzz of adventure. She was living that 'Things to Do Before You're Thirty' list, she thought happily to herself. She was going on holiday on her own – well, *almost* on her own. Visiting Joe meant she'd be with people she knew – he lived near his long-term girlfriend, Nina – but she'd travelled on her own and that was the big thing, wasn't it? There was nobody to say, 'I'll mind the tickets and the passports, you're not to worry about them,' nobody to stand with the bags while she rushed into the shop to buy a last-minute magazine for the plane. But she'd done it.

She'd smiled breezily at the airport security men in Heathrow, marched purposefully to baggage collection as if she did it every week, and had made her way safely to the tube station. This travelling solo was a breeze.

At Green Park she switched to the Victoria Line, joining the throngs of people swarming towards the northbound platform. And when she got off at Highbury and Islington, she didn't feel even a mild sense of panic when she didn't spot Joe instantly. He'd explained he might not be able to leave work in time and Lizzie had confidently said she'd just hop into a taxi to his flat, and could he hide a key under a flowerpot or something?

Pulling her case with determination, she headed for the Way Out signs. It might be nice to be at Joe's on her own. She could unpack, have a sit down and a cup of tea, perhaps pop out to the shop round the corner and buy a cake. Joe had never lost his fondness for sticky chocolate cake, which, once upon a time, Lizzie used to bake for him. It was years since she'd baked, she thought, panting as she hauled the case through the ticket barriers. She might get the ingredients in the shop and make one because Joe would surely never have flour or cocoa powder . . .

'Lizzie, Lizzie,' squealed a female voice.

Lizzie gazed about anxiously. Nobody could be calling her. It must be another Lizzie they wanted. But there, standing to the right of the barriers, her blonde curls shaking with the ferocity of her frantic waving, was Nina. Slender as a reed in a navy pinstripe skirt suit with T-bar shoes that matched the glossy red of her lipstick, Nina's narrow face was wreathed in a giant smile. Lizzie felt a rush of warmth for her. She didn't know Nina very well but had always thought her sweet, and she seemed genuinely fond of Joe. The only pity was that Nina had never come with Joe to Dunmore for a visit, so Lizzie felt she hadn't got to know her very well. That would change, Lizzie decided. There was nothing to stop her flying over to London more often.

'Hello, welcome.' Nina hugged Lizzie quickly and immediately launched into an explanation of how she'd hoped to meet Lizzie at Heathrow itself, but work had been manic and she hadn't been able to get away. Nina worked in a small art gallery off Cork Street, where her hours were anything but regular.

'I was so worried when I got here because I thought I might have missed you,' Nina added, trying to take over the wheeling of Lizzie's case.

'I'm fine,' Lizzie said, holding on, embarrassed at anyone having to feel the weight of it. Capsule holiday wardrobes had never been her forte.

'No, I insist.' Nina grabbed it from her effortlessly. All that shifting of canvases had given her surprising muscles for one so slim. 'Joe was worried you'd get anxious when he wasn't here and I said I could leave work early, so we thought it would be better if I picked you up. I know you haven't been to London for a while and we'd hate you to get lost and be wandering round not knowing where to turn.'

'I know how to get to Joe's flat,' Lizzie said mildly as they waited for a taxi. 'And my mobile phone works here, so if the worst came to the worst, I could always phone Joe.'

'I know.' A canary-yellow cab pulled up and Nina opened the door for Lizzie, helping her in like a dowager duchess with a leg in plaster. 'But it's not home, is it?' Having dragged Lizzie's suitcase in, Nina settled into the seat beside her. 'We all get a little nervous when we're away from home and there are young thugs around who prey on tourists. And it's not just visitors. An old-age pensioner was mugged in full daylight down the road here the other day. Joe and I would never forgive ourselves if that happened to you, Lizzie.'

All this was said in a kind tone that wasn't meant to hurt Lizzie in any way. But it did. It was clear to her that she was now cast in the role of aged parent. Lizzie felt herself to be a healthy woman in her prime, but in Nina's eyes she was on the slippery slope to Zimmer frames, stair lifts and not being able to work her mobile phone, while fit young thugs ran off with her handbag. It was a depressing picture – even more depressing to imagine that perhaps Joe shared this image of her.

'We've got lots of plans for your stay,' Nina went on, 'although we thought you wouldn't want to do anything tonight because you'd be tired.'

Lizzie tried to protest that she wasn't tired at all but it didn't seem to work. Nina, though kindness itself, refused to see that a short flight from Cork airport and a tube journey from Heathrow weren't quite the same thing as scaling the Himalayas, despite the novelty of doing it alone.

To get Nina off the subject of exhaustion in the elderly, Lizzie asked her about work and they spent the rest of the short taxi ride with Nina animatedly talking about new acquisitions and the figurative artist whose exhibition they were working on for next month.

At Joe's flat, the pampering continued. Nina insisted on hauling the suitcase up the stairs and even put it on the tiny single bed in the spare room 'in case you hurt your back lifting it'.

Lizzie, who hated unpacking, waited until Nina had left the room, then stuck the case back on the floor, opened it and took out her toilet bag and books. She'd take clothes out as she needed them. That way, she never really had to unpack, and she wouldn't have to feel guilty going through the endless unnecessary garments she'd brought.

'I've made tea.' Nina was bustling round the modern cube of a kitchen and she pulled out a stool for Lizzie. 'You sit there and have a rest. I was sorry to hear about your friend,' she added.

Lizzie sighed. 'She was so young. It's hard to deal with the death of a young person, isn't it?'

Nina nodded but Lizzie could see that she was preoccupied.

Lizzie remembered when she was twenty-six and it had seemed as if death was something that happened to other people.

A china cup and saucer were produced from somewhere.

'I didn't think Joe owned saucers,' Lizzie said in amusement, admiring the violet-patterned china.

Nina beamed. 'I knew you'd prefer a saucer,' she said. 'My mum is just the same.'

Since Nina was the youngest of five and her mother was in her sixties, Lizzie didn't feel too cheered up by this information. But still, Nina was just trying to be sweet.

They drank tea and ate ginger biscuits, chatting idly. Three years ago, on Lizzie's last visit to Joe, he'd just started seeing Nina and Lizzie had been delighted to meet her. Nina wasn't anything like the wildly arty girls with piercings and strange hair colours that Joe had favoured when he lived at home. Instead, she had a degree in fine art, wore beautiful fitted clothes, drank Earl Grey with lemon and had just taken out a mortgage on a flat in Archway. She and Joe made such a perfect couple that Lizzie kept expecting them to move in together but Joe, in an unguarded moment, said he thought it was a mistake to rush into such a big decision.

'I'm only twenty-six, Mum,' he'd said, 'too young to settle down. Nina and I like the freedom of living apart.'

Joe arrived home from work at seven, bearing a huge Indian meal from Marks and Spencer, with strawberries and vanilla ice cream for dessert.

'Lentil dhal and veggie pakoras,' drooled Lizzie as she took each fresh treasure from the bags. 'Balti chicken . . . fantastic. I love Indian food.'

'I know,' beamed Joe.

Dinner was wonderful, lubricated by Tiger beer, which Lizzie had never tried. She'd never drink wine with Indian food again, she said when they all sat back in their chairs and surveyed the commando raid that was the remains of their dinner.

'I wish I knew how to cook like that,' she sighed after she'd turned down Nina's offer of another cup of tea.

'You could take an Indian cookery course,' Joe said enthusiastically. 'Wouldn't that be great? It would get you out of the house and you'd have fun.'

Lizzie blinked. 'I do get out of the house,' she said in surprise.

'But you know, out to meet people,' Joe added.

Lizzie was diverted by the sight of Nina kicking Joe on the shin, in an unmistakable '*shut up*, you've-said-enough' gesture.

'We've got a lovely surprise planned,' Nina said, holding Joe's hand tightly. 'We'd both love you to meet my mum. We're taking you both out to dinner tomorrow night.'

'That sounds nice,' said Lizzie, thinking of her hopes of some wild nightlife to make up for her dull evenings back home. Maybe they could go to an exotic nightclub the following night.

Nina's mother was a rounded version of her daughter, with the same narrow, earnest face and the same mop of curls, although Edie's hair was silver instead of blonde. She was also at least twelve years older than Lizzie and although she didn't fit into any little-old-lady mould personalitywise, she was very stiff, thanks to arthritis, and seemed to appreciate being helped into taxis and having tea delivered to her in china cups with saucers.

She had a wry sense of humour too and was fun to talk to, which was just as well, Lizzie thought, since Nina and Joe appeared to think that the two older women would be content to sit together in the restaurant and gossip. Edie had seven grandchildren and loved talking about them, Nina said affectionately, clearly assuming that Lizzie, being of Edie's vintage, would be just as keen to discuss the sleeping patterns of two-year-olds. As Edie talked of her darling grandkids, Lizzie finished her first glass of wine and got well stuck into the second. Edie was sweet, but Lizzie had hoped for a bit more than this on her holiday. She could talk at home but she was here to enjoy herself.

With the added courage of the wine and no bread to mop it up inside her, she chanced a daring smile at the waiter as he placed her prawns in front of her.

'Thank you,' she said in what she hoped was a husky, sexy voice. Weren't men supposed to be mad for older women to initiate them in the pleasures of the flesh? She must get her legs waxed, though. And buy some of that oil the supermodels used to give their skin sheen. G-strings were in too, although Lizzie had never dared try one. But she might buy some here where no one in the shop would recognise her. Sacrifices had to be made for a new life.

Eyes shining with happiness at the thought of this life-altering plan and the new her that would emerge, butterfly-like, Lizzie had another slug of wine.

'Do you wear G-strings, Nina? I don't like them but they are sexy, aren't they?'

You could have heard a pin drop. Joe choked on his spring roll and Nina's face was a picture. Only Edie seemed unperturbed at this strange shift in the conversation.

'I couldn't be bothered myself, Lizzie,' she said seriously. 'I bought one once at an underwear party. They're not made for the ordinary backside.'

The waiter, back with more bread and some salad dressing, stopped in shock but recovered quickly. 'Anything else?' he enquired, looking slightly afraid of what these two mad women would ask for next.

Edie looked at the bottle of wine, which was now empty, mostly in her and Lizzie's glasses. 'Another bottle, love,' she said, and winked at him.

Lizzie giggled into her wine glass.

'You have to flirt, don't you?' Edie remarked. 'Reminds you you're still alive.'

The horrified gulp from Nina sent Lizzie off into another fit of giggles.

After that, Edie and Lizzie got on like a house on fire. Edie knew what it felt like to have close friends die, although these friends were older than Sally Richardson had been. But still, she *understood*.

'Young people think they're going to last for ever,' Edie said slowly as they drank coffees while their offspring chatted happily to each other. 'It's a shock when you realise that even you are mortal.'

Lizzie nodded. 'What's hardest to think about are the two small children she left behind,' she said. 'But, even though it was short, she had a good life. She had a wonderful husband

and family.' The wine made Lizzie tearful. 'Sally lived life to the full.'

'If I shuffled off this mortal coil tomorrow, I doubt if anyone would say that about me,' said Edie, patting Lizzie's hand in comfort.

'Nor me,' Lizzie replied. But that was going to change.

As she got ready for bed at midnight, Lizzie decided that a big glass of water beside the bed would be a good idea, after all that wine followed by two liqueurs. Not bothering to slip on her dressing gown over her ancient teddy-bear-patterned nightie, she padded barefoot down the hall and into the kitchen. Nina and Joe were still up – she could hear their voices from the small living room. The walls of the apartment were so thin, Joe said, that he could sometimes hear the woman next door's phone ring and think it was his.

Lizzie filled a glass with filtered water from the fridge, flicked off the kitchen light and went back into the small hall. Dinner had been great; she'd just pop her head round the door and say thanks again.

But standing at the door with her glass in her hand, Lizzie could hear clearly what Joe and Nina were saying.

'I'd love Mum to have someone in her life but I don't see it happening,' Joe said. 'She's locked in the past. I mean, she does her best to be brave about it all but it scares me that she's never got over the divorce – that she just *says* she has.'

Lizzie could hear what sounded like Nina kissing him and making soothing noises.

'It's not as if they had this great marriage anyway,' Joe went on. 'I knew it wasn't right, Dad did and even Debra did, but Mum said she had no clue. How could she not see it?'

'People hide from the truth,' Nina suggested. 'If they're scared of something, they pretend it's not happening. Your mum's lovely but she is a bit dizzy like that. I can just see her carrying on as if everything was OK – like she knew the marriage was dead but didn't want to admit it. Lots of women do that, apparently.'

'I don't know,' sighed Joe. 'That's why I find it hard to deal with it all. She should move on but she can't. She's stuck in this time warp where it's as if Dad's just gone out for the day and he'll be back. It's not healthy. She says she's fine but I can see she's not. She never dates anyone, she doesn't seem to have any sort of social life and now Dad's got Sabine, well, that must be hard on Mum. Stupid Debra was rattling on about Sabine all the time when she phoned last night and I warned her not to do it in front of Mum. I mean, Dad's so happy now. It would kill Mum to see him like that, as if he could be happy with someone else but not with her.'

Every word was like an acid-tipped dart shot into Lizzie's chest.

'Do you always remember the marriage being bad?' asked Nina conversationally. 'Even when you were a child?'

'It was never bad,' Joe said thoughtfully, 'but it wasn't wedded bliss, either. They never had anything in common, for a start. Dad was so into boats and sailing, and Mum's eyes would glaze over when he talked about it. Mum loved going out for meals and things, and Dad was perfectly happy to eat at home every night. They never had the money to pursue any interests either. They grew apart and if they hadn't had to get married, I doubt if the relationship would have lasted longer than a couple of years.'

'Let's hear it for contraception,' Nina said wryly.

'Yeah,' agreed Joe. 'Don't get me wrong, they loved us, and I suppose they loved each other in a way. They got on and there weren't many arguments in our house. But, you know, I get on with lots of people, though I wouldn't want to marry them. Apathy is just as bad for relationships as raging arguments. They were kids when they got married, that's the tragedy. Maybe if Mum hadn't been pregnant with me –'

'Don't say that,' teased Nina. 'Then I wouldn't have been able to meet you and fall in love. Anyhow, you can't blame yourself. They were responsible for their relationship, not you. I remember my mum and dad arguing all the time but they were mad about each other.'

'Mum and Dad didn't even argue much.' Joe was solemn. 'Arguing implies some sort of passion but they didn't have that. They were just married, married alive. Tell me we'll never be like that, Nina,' he said fervently, 'sticking together for the wrong reasons, not in love but fooling ourselves into thinking we are because it's easier than splitting up, staying together for the children or something.'

Lizzie felt a cool wet sensation on her skin and realised she was shaking so much that water from her glass was spilling onto her hand.

'Is this a proposal?' Nina said jokily.

Joe chuckled. 'I'm a bit anti-marriage, as you know,' he said.

'Makes two of us,' Nina replied. 'But I'm not anti-living together. We spend so much time together, we might as well just move in together and save on your rent. Not to mention the fact that my flat's much bigger.'

'Sounds good to me,' murmured Joe.

Behind the door, his mother turned and fled to the spare bedroom, terrified of being heard.

She shut the door and sat down on the bed, feeling prawns, pasta and all the booze churning uneasily in her stomach. Her hand was still shaking as she set the glass down.

That night, she lay in the narrow bed with the sounds of the city around her, and she felt lonelier than ever. She'd rushed off to be with Joe, hoping that he might cheer her up after the shock of Sally's death. But he couldn't. Worse, he pitied her for how she wasn't coping with life in general after splitting up with his father. He'd seen that she and Myles had a very mediocre marriage and now he was worried because she wasn't coping. She'd turned into the very thing she hated: a victim. Holding her glass of water to her chest like a talisman, Lizzie wondered where she'd gone wrong. She'd tried to change her life and be more adventurous but nobody seemed to want to let her. Nina and Joe carried on as if she was some little old lady who couldn't be trusted in London on her own, so how could they say she didn't make more of an effort?

CHAPTER TWENTY-ONE

Despite her brave words at the funeral, Sally's death affected Erin more than she'd thought. She'd felt so pleased with her plan to work in The Beauty Spot that she'd eagerly told Greg all about it, expecting the misery to be assuaged by the sense of doing something in Sally's memory. But still the loss hit her hard.

'I don't know why I'm so upset. It's Steve who's really suffering,' Erin said sadly, the day after the funeral, when she couldn't seem to stop crying.

'You're upset because an amazing woman has died and you'd want to be as hard as nails not to be affected by it,' Greg said.

'Sally was so brave,' Erin said miserably. 'I want to give her something back by helping out but all I can do is cry.'

'I'm sure she'd love to think of you helping,' Greg said. 'But you're shocked, love. And don't forget, you've got pregnancy hormones added to the mix.'

'I know,' sobbed Erin. 'I was going to phone Steve and ask him what he thought about my working in the salon with Ruby, but I can't. I don't want to cry in front of him.'

'I'll do it,' Greg offered. 'It'll be one less thing for him to worry about,' he added accurately.

By the time she was five months' pregnant, Erin's back was aching. Greg had found her a special chair for the days she worked in Sally's beauty salon, dealing with problems and answering phones, but Erin found, to her amusement, that she often stood with her back arched and one hand rubbing the aching place, in the classic pregnancy stance.

'How can one teeny tiny baby make my back ache so much?' she asked Lizzie when she dropped in at lunchtime one day in mid-July to ask Erin if she fancied going for a sandwich. Back from London, Lizzie was trying to forget the negative things Joe and Nina had said. Being cheerful was important, she decided firmly.

'It's got to be a boy,' pronounced Ruby, who had a few minutes' break before her ten past one appointment. 'Only a fella could cause a woman that much pain.'

'Ruby!' laughed Erin. 'You're terrible.'

'She might have a point,' Lizzie said. 'I went through awful back pain when I was expecting Joe, and with Debra I sailed through the pregnancy with no problems.'

'See?' Ruby said. 'I'm right. Men equal problems. That's what my poor mother always said, God rest her. There isn't a man born who won't hurt the woman who loves him.'

'That's rubbish,' laughed Erin, who loved Ruby to bits and found the days in the salon whizzed past, listening to her treating the staff and clients to her unique world view. The youngest of six, with five older brothers and a relationship history that made Ally McBeal's boyfriend problems look normal, Ruby's views on men were hilarious. Erin knew that Ruby was grieving for Sally like everyone else, but the girl had a gift for cheerfulness that was helping immensely. Even the glummest client left with a smile on her face after a bit of Ruby's personal magic.

'I'm just telling you what I know,' Ruby replied, unfazed. 'I swear, I'd become a lesbian at the drop of a hat if I could face . . . you know . . .'

'You know what?' asked Lizzie, enthralled.

'You don't want to know what, Lizzie.' Erin had to hold on to her belly when she laughed in case she hurt herself. The thought of Ruby – who adored men and dressed her statuesque body in figure-hugging clothes to impress them

– becoming gay was too hilarious. 'We've a new girl in the first treatment room doing a bikini wax and I don't want her to rip off too much with the shock of listening to you, Rubes. We're not insured against being sued for total deforestation.'

This time, it was Ruby who had to clutch her sides as she laughed. 'You're worse than me, Erin,' she screeched, flicking back a skein of jet-black hair. 'You're wicked!'

Erin grinned. 'I'm coming for a sandwich with you, Lizzie, if Ruby can promise not to empty the place in my absence with stories of her wayward sex life.'

'Don't knock lesbianism till you've tried it.' Ruby was sanguine. 'And you'd be able to borrow each other's clothes.'

Erin and Lizzie were still grinning as they crossed the road in the direction of the coffee shop. And there, walking towards them with her mobile phone glued to her head and her gaze unseeing, was Abby.

She hadn't been into the salon since the funeral. Erin knew because she checked the appointments book carefully to see if the client list was remaining healthy. But Abby didn't look as if she'd been spending millions in another salon. Her skin, used to the gentle nourishment of Sally's special facial, now looked tired. With her hair pulled back into an untidy knot, and wearing a black tracksuit that drained her face of colour, she looked nothing like the glamorous woman from the TV.

She noticed Lizzie and Erin outside the coffee shop, just as they were hoping to catch her eye.

'Oh, hi,' she said, clicking off her mobile.

'Hello, Abby,' said Lizzie warmly. 'Long time no see. Erin and I are just going for a quick sandwich. Want to join us?'

Erin expected Abby to make some sort of excuse and say no, but she didn't. In fact, she looked touchingly grateful to be asked.

'That would be nice,' she said. 'I've been rushing round going to the bank and stuff, and I never make time for lunch when I'm running errands.'

'I always make time for lunch,' Lizzie said ruefully. 'I suppose that's why you're slim and I'm not.'

Abby *was* looking very slim, Erin noticed, but from the strain on her face, it wasn't the result of careful attention to the Dr Atkins diet. Something must definitely be up *chez* Barton.

She, like most of Dunmore, had no idea that Tom had actually moved out. Abby, fearing that if one person knew, everybody would soon know, had done her best to keep the split a secret.

'Your daughter's wedding is soon, isn't it?' Abby said conversationally once they were seated with sandwiches and drinks.

'Next weekend,' said Lizzie. 'I can't believe it's nearly here. We've been planning it for what seems like a hundred years.'

'Is it going to be a big affair?' asked Erin.

Lizzie nodded. 'Huge. The burglars in Dunmore will have a field day because half the town will be whooping it up in the hotel on Saturday.' Then she felt embarrassed because neither Erin nor Abby were on the guest list. In actual fact, Debra and Barry hadn't left her much room to invite her own friends.

Gwen had given out to her sister over this. 'You've paid for the damn thing,' she had pointed out. 'The least you should be able to do is invite a busload of your own pals.'

Seeing Lizzie's embarrassment, Erin pushed on to show that she and Abby hardly expected to be asked. 'What are you wearing?'

'A lemon suit.' Even as she said it, Lizzie's face fell. 'I'll probably look like a big lemon in it.'

'It sounds lovely. You should come in and get Ruby to do your face in the morning,' Erin said. 'She's brilliant at make-up for special occasions.'

'That's a good idea,' Lizzie said quietly. She'd always planned to ask Sally to do her make-up. Sally would have calmed her pre-wedding nerves and made Lizzie feel good about herself. 'It feels strange to be talking about weddings and make-up when Sally's gone,' she added. 'When I'm doing normal things like grocery shopping and I get cross because I can't find a parking space or something, it hits me that I shouldn't complain because at least I'm here. Sally isn't.'

Both Erin and Abby nodded at this.

'I feel the same,' Abby admitted. 'Jess and I dropped in on Steve last weekend and he's really one of the walking wounded. He tries so hard for Jack and Daniel, but he looks like he's dying inside. It makes me feel ashamed of what I have and don't appreciate.' Or what she *had* and didn't appreciate, Abby thought.

Erin didn't feel hungry any more. 'What I keep thinking,' she murmured, 'is how do you get on with your life when you lose the person closest to you?'

It was a rhetorical question and the others didn't try to answer it.

'Do you know what the really awful thing is?' Lizzie said. 'That it takes someone else's tragedy to make you appreciate what you have in life. I look at Debra, for example, and think how lucky I am to be here for her wedding. Or I think of Joe and how he had asthma when he was younger, but he's fine now. And I'm lucky to have him.'

Lizzie was so rooted in her family, Abby realised. *She'd* never have risked her daughter or her husband's happiness for a stupid fling. She pushed her tuna sandwich away half eaten. 'More coffee?' she asked.

She was drinking too much coffee but she needed the kick it gave her. Nothing else gave her any energy any more. She felt drained most of the time and, in desperation, had started taking an iron tonic, which played havoc with her stomach.

The others said no and Abby got herself a cup.

Lizzie would have said yes to one of the fat cream cakes sitting under the glass case on the counter, but she was determined to be slim-ish for the wedding.

She wondered if she should mention the idea she'd been

toying with since coming back from London. Erin and Abby were the very people she wanted to share it with but would they think she was mad or had too much time on her hands? Abby had her TV show and she was bound to be busy all the time, as was Erin, who was doing so much to keep Sally's salon going, never mind cope with her pregnancy. Lizzie would have loved to know if Erin had done anything about getting in touch with her estranged family but she didn't want to intrude.

'I wish we could do something that Sally would be proud of, the sort of thing she'd do.' There, she'd said it. Lizzie looked at the other two for their reaction.

Abby was listlessly stirring sugar into her second coffee and Erin was wriggling on her chair, trying to get comfortable.

Lizzie tried again. 'Imagine if one of us had died, Sally would be doing something to remember us or make a statement about our lives or *something*.'

Erin was nodding now and, emboldened, Lizzie continued.

'Sally was one of the most special people I ever met. She got us together and made us feel part of something bigger. She deserves more than us feeling sorry for ourselves or for her. She'd hate that.'

'That's for sure,' agreed Erin. 'She didn't feel sorry for herself, even at the end. She was just worried about Steve and the boys and how they'd cope.'

'I don't know how she did it,' said Abby sadly. 'I'd have gone to pieces.' She was already in pieces, she thought, and she hadn't been given a diagnosis of terminal cancer. Even in the depths of her own misery, she marvelled at Sally's incredible courage when she was dying.

'So, what could we do? Have you any ideas?' asked Lizzie enthusiastically.

Neither Abby nor Erin said anything for a minute.

Then: 'It's a brilliant proposal,' Erin said, 'but what were you thinking of?'

'I was asking you two for ideas, really,' Lizzie pointed out. 'You're the creative ones.'

'Well, how about raising some money for a cancer charity?' suggested Abby lamely. She felt as creative as a plank of wood right now.

'Yes,' said Lizzie slowly, 'but I was thinking of something more special . . . I don't know what. Let's all think about it, OK?'

She picked up her jacket from the back of the chair. 'I ought to rush back to work.'

'Me too,' said Erin automatically.

'You will think about some ideas, won't you?' Lizzie asked both of them outside.

'Yes,' said Abby and Erin in unison.

Honestly, thought Lizzie, heading back to work, she'd hardly consider herself an ideas person. People like Abby and Erin were creative types, but they didn't seem to feel motivated. It would be up to her to think of a fitting tribute to Sally. There had to be an idea out there and she was determined to come up with it.

At home, Abby went into her study and filed the bills she'd paid in the bank. She hated filing with a passion. Tom used to tease her about it, joking that her *Declutter* fans should see the mess she kept at the bottom of the filing cabinet, a huge pile of paperwork waiting to be assigned a proper place.

'At least I do file,' she'd retort. 'I'm not like some people who have the school secretary do it all – yes sir, Mr Barton, no sir, three bags full, sir!'

'Are you jealous of Miss Peabody?' Tom had demanded, grinning.

'No, but she's definitely jealous of me,' Abby had replied sweetly. The school secretary had a crush on Tom and blushed from her pearl earrings to her toes every Christmas when he gave her whatever gift Abby had picked out during her high-speed present sweep.

She and Tom had had fun, Abby realised. Despite their

recent problems, their marriage had been a good one after all. Looking back made that obvious. It was too late to go back now, though. She hardly saw Tom at the moment. He had moved out a week after Sally's funeral and was living with Leo, the old colleague he'd met at the funeral. It didn't make Abby feel any better that she'd been correct in assuming that Leo would be keen to help Tom make the break from married man to separated pal about town. Recently, he'd been staying at Lyonnais for the odd weekday night while Abby was away filming. Then at the weekends, he came to see Jess, and Abby did her grocery shopping then, leaving them on their own because she knew Tom didn't want to see her. She'd tried to ask Jess how she felt about this split, but Jess didn't seem to want to talk about it.

'Leave me alone, Mum,' she'd said wearily whenever Abby had tried to raise the subject.

And Abby, who'd remembered what she'd been like as a teenager – self-contained, quiet, unwilling to talk about her feelings – knew that pushing Jess would not work. Time, she hoped, would be a great healer. She would do her best to make Jess feel loved, and wait for her daughter to come to her. Perhaps with time, she and Jess could become close again. Perhaps.

That afternoon, Abby wasn't the only one reflecting on the notion of appreciating what she had. Despite Ruby tying the entire salon in knots with her description of her latest blind date, Erin's mind kept drifting back to Sally, and Lizzie's observation that it took a tragedy for people to see what was important in life. She was right.

Sally's death had brought Erin and Greg even closer together, if that was possible, and now that she could feel the baby moving inside her, Erin felt even more aware of the fragility of life and how precious it was. But she still hadn't actually *done* anything as a result of this greater awareness. She hugged Greg more tightly than usual when he left for work in the morning, conscious that a freak accident could take him away from her. Yet for all her talk of doing so, she still had done nothing to seek out her family.

'You OK, Erin?' asked Ruby in concern. 'You look a bit wrecked.'

'I'm fine,' Erin said. 'Fine.'

Greg was due home late that evening. Perhaps she could start her detective work. A whole family couldn't disappear completely. They had to be somewhere in Ireland, and she'd find them.

CHAPTER TWENTY-TWO

Lizzie sat on the edge of Debra's bed and watched her daughter admiring her wedding dress in the mirror. Despite all the trauma over the colour of the dress and the shape of the tiny buttons down the back, the dress was glorious: fairy princess style in antique white silk, with a full skirt and a nipped-in bodice from which Debra's lightly tanned shoulders rose magnificently. Her streaked hair was coiled up into artful ringlets and she wore a headdress of white roses as well as a rippling lacy veil.

Debra had said she wanted to look like a princess on her wedding day and she did.

'It will be all right, Mum, won't it?' Debra said tremulously, half turning away from the mirror, anxiety on her face for the first time that day.

Lizzie dusted aside her misgivings about twenty-three-year-old teenage sweethearts getting married.

'Of course it's going to be all right, love. It's going to be wonderful. Barry is a special man and adores you. That's the best start there is for a marriage.' She handed her daughter a tissue before the threatened tears spilled over and ruined the carefully applied mascara.

'I know, it's just . . .' Debra dabbed her eyes with the tissue. 'What if we're making a mistake?'

Lizzie didn't need a degree in psychology to work out the unfinished bit of the sentence. What if we're making a mistake *like you and Dad?*

In her heart, she wanted to say that nobody ever knew for

313

sure what life would bring and that there were no guarantees. Look at poor Steve Richardson. But even as a child, Debra had seen the world in black and white. There were no grey areas, no maybes for her. Saying that she could learn from her parents' mistakes would not send Debra down the aisle with a smile on her face.

'You're not making a mistake,' Lizzie said gently, taking her daughter's hands. 'This is going to be a wonderful, special day and you're marrying a wonderful, special man. I only hope he realises what a prize he's won.'

'Oh, Mum.' Not caring if she crushed the delicate silk roses on the skirt, Debra sank onto the bed and clung to her mother. 'Thank you. Thank you for everything.'

And at that moment, Lizzie felt that every single second of worry over the wedding was worth it. Debra deserved a glorious day and she would have it.

The doorbell rang loudly.

'Dad's here,' roared Joe from downstairs, where he was providing tea and biscuits for everyone because it would be hours before they'd be tucking into the starter of filo prawns (with parmesan and mushroom tartlets for vegetarians).

'It's ten to two, we should go soon,' added Nina from Lizzie's bedroom where she was putting the finishing touches to her outfit.

'Yes,' Lizzie agreed. As the wedding was scheduled for two fifteen, they had a few minutes to drink their tea and head off in the wedding car for the five-minute journey to the church.

She stroked the bride's cheek gently, trying to drink in every feature so she'd remember this moment for ever. 'You look beautiful, Debra. I'm so proud of you today.'

'Thanks for everything, Mum,' Debra said. 'You're right, this is the most special day of my life.'

Lizzie felt the back of her throat constrict with emotion. She loved Debra so much. This mother love was the real love of life, she knew, not the other kind, the kind men and women had for each other. With your children, there was never any end to the love affair. Or the fear. Still holding on to Debra, Lizzie prayed a silent prayer that nothing or no one would hurt Debra or take away the innocent hopefulness of her wedding day.

'Dad!' squealed Debra excitedly as, over her mother's shoulder, she saw the door open and her father appear.

'I'm not interrupting, am I?' asked Myles, standing at the doorway.

'No.' Lizzie got off the bed and gave her ex-husband a brief smile. She'd made a vow not to let her own problems ruin either Debra's wedding day or her relationship with Myles. 'I was going downstairs to have a quick drink of tea before we go. You two don't have much time, you know,' she added.

'I know,' Myles said in a low voice to Lizzie. 'I didn't want to turn up too early in case I wasn't welcome because of . . . you know . . .'

Lizzie's grin was genuine this time. 'Don't be an idiot,' she said. 'You'll always be welcome here.' And it was true. There was nothing to be gained by cutting off her nose to spite her face. The relationship between herself and Myles was too good to squander simply because he'd moved on and she hadn't. 'Is Sabine coming to the afters?' Lizzie added, doing her best to sound as if this wasn't something she'd thought about night after night.

'If you're still OK about it?' Myles said.

'I'm fine,' said Lizzie firmly. *Carpe diem.*

'Daddy, what do you think of my dress?' Debra, tired of not being noticed on this, her special day, had got to her feet and was standing model-like with the tiers of her skirt spread out.

Myles touched Lizzie's shoulder encouragingly, and turned to Debra.

'You take my breath away,' he said. 'You look so beautiful.'

'Oh, Daddy,' cried Debra.

Lizzie left them to it. Nina had gone downstairs, so there

315

were a few minutes of privacy in which Lizzie could pat some more powder on her face, beautifully made up earlier by Ruby, and tweak her hair so that the wilder strands stayed down. The hairstylist had tried to tame the unruly waves and it now felt like a piece of sculpture thanks to all the hairspray. The lemon suit was still harsh, she decided, but it was too late to do anything about it now. She picked up her handbag and went downstairs, ready for the off.

'Settle down, Bradley, and stop fidgeting!'

The woman with the purple feathery hat and the hyper-active child obviously thought she was whispering but Lizzie was sure the whole church could hear her. Bradley apparently hadn't. He kept making 'vroom vroom' noises as he rattled a selection of toy cars noisily up and down the pew on the groom's side.

Up in the gallery, the organist was lightly practising tunes with the choir. The congregation, used to brides being late, were still arriving, doing their best to keep the squeals of greeting to a minimum in deference to the location.

'Hellooo, you look lovely,' could be heard in stage whispers every few moments, along with, 'Love the dress!'

In the front pew, Lizzie sat with Gwen beside her, over-shadowed by the size of her sister's hat, an edifice purchased with glee in Naples for the shockingly cheap sum of £5.50.

'Barry's mother's hat can't beat this one,' Gwen had said delightedly when she'd showed hers to Lizzie and crowed over the price.

'It's not a competition between the two families,' Lizzie had said, astonished.

'Yes, it is,' retorted Gwen.

And then the organist began to play and the congregation rose. Lizzie didn't know how everyone in the church didn't start crying immediately. Watching Debra gliding up the aisle, proudly escorted by Myles, gave her a lump in her throat the size of several giant toads.

Gwen clutched Lizzie's hand and squeezed tightly. 'She's beautiful, Lizzie love.'

As the ceremony rolled gently on, and Lizzie watched her daughter formally take a step away from her family and create a new bond with Barry's, Lizzie felt both a sense of loss and that the weight of responsibility had been partially lifted from her shoulders. Her children were grown up; it was official. They would always be her children and she'd always want to protect them but a subtle shift had taken place. Hers was not the advice they'd ask for first. She wasn't the most important person in their lives any more, as she had been for so many years. Joe had his life in London with Nina, and Debra had just married into a new life with Barry. It was time for Lizzie gently to let the reins go.

At the altar, looking like a fairy princess as she'd hoped, Debra giggled self-consciously when she stumbled over her marriage vows and the whole congregation smiled affectionately at the bridal couple.

'Sorry,' Debra said to the patient priest, a man who'd had to cope with so many fainting brides that one who merely got her words mixed up was a piece of cake. 'Nerves.'

'It's me who has the nerves,' whispered Barry so that only the first two pews could hear him. The first two pews laughed, and the rest of the church whispered, 'Whadidhesay?' loudly, keen not to miss a moment of the action.

When peace had been restored and the priest had cheerily told everyone that humour was an important part of marriage and it was clear this lovely couple could laugh at themselves, the ceremony continued. Lizzie found herself remembering Debra's christening, nearly twenty-four years before in this very same church. Debra had gurgled sweetly during the whole ceremony and had brought the house down that time too.

Lizzie kept her eyes on the bride and groom and fumbled in her handbag for a tissue. She'd been more sure of herself when she was the mother of the baby than she was as mother of the bride. Being a wife and mother was what she'd done for so long that it was hard to accustom herself to anything else. But perhaps she had been quietly clinging on to the past and her role in it to make up for the fact that she hadn't yet found her role in the future.

That would change, she vowed. In this holy place, she'd make a solemn promise to herself to change.

The reception went like a dream. Nobody's nose appeared to be out of joint over the seating arrangements, which had to be a wedding first, Lizzie decided, and the speeches were a hit, being both funny and short. Even the best man – adept at putting his foot in his mouth in real life – managed not to upset too many people. The cake, three elegant tiers decorated with hundreds of hand-made blossoms, drew delighted gasps from the crowd, while the happy smile on the bride's face as she and her new husband cut it made more than one person reach around blindly for a tissue to wipe their eyes.

Both Lizzie and Myles made heroic efforts for Debra's sake to look as if they adored each other despite being divorced. Etiquette decreed that they sat apart, with Lizzie beside Barry's dad, Stan, and Myles beside Barry's mum, Flossie. But they smiled at each other along the expanse of the top table, pleased beyond measure that their darling's day was going so beautifully. All the scrimping and saving had been worth it, Lizzie decided as she looked around the flower-bedecked room and watched people enjoying themselves.

'The mother of the bride is holding up well,' remarked Gwen as she powdered down the shine on her nose, her one concession to what she described as 'fannying around with cosmetics'. The meal was finally over and people were taking advantage of the lull to redo make-up or walk off some of the cake.

'Not bad,' Lizzie agreed, thinking for the nth time that day that lemon really wasn't her colour. But who was looking at her? Debra was the star of the show, and beyond checking that the MOTB was dressed in a reasonably sedate fashion, and hadn't gone all out to upstage her daughter as some did, nobody was actually that interested in what she looked like.

'Now Barry's mother's hat . . .' began Gwen, peering under the stall doors to make sure they were alone in the ladies', 'merciful hour, whoever sold it to her saw her coming. A red polka-dot veil indeed. She looks like she's got a bad dose of measles.'

'Gwen!'

'Well, she does. You look miles better.'

'You're very loyal but I have to say that yellow isn't my colour.'

'And polka-dot red is hers?' Gwen sniffed and fussed a bit with her hair, lacquered into obedience thanks to half a can of hairspray wielded that morning by the hand of Maurice, the blue-rinse artiste and doyen of Chez Maurice. 'I can't wait to have a dance. Shay really got into dancing on the *Star of the Med*, you know. We had lessons one day when the weather was bad.' Gwen still liked to reminisce about her holiday of a lifetime.

Lizzie was momentarily distracted from applying coral lipstick, the only colour that didn't look too bilious with her acid-lemon suit.

'Shay, dancing?'

'I know. Wonders will never cease. He loves it; even stops giving out about his dodgy hip when we're dancing.'

The Abba tribute band were warming up their instruments in one corner when Gwen and Lizzie arrived back in the ballroom. A sexily curvaceous Agnetha lookalike, who was squeezed into a skintight silver jumpsuit, adjusted the microphone to her height and eyed up the male talent, who eyed her back.

The ballroom was filling up as people invited to this part of the wedding had started to arrive and were joining friends at the round tables, now cleared of the remains of the wedding meal. Only the flowers and glasses remained. At the top table,

Lizzie overheard Barry and his father discussing the etiquette of the first dance.

'Now you dance with Lizzie,' Barry was reminding his father *sotto voce*, 'and Mum dances with Myles, and Tony dances with Sharon, but when the dance is over, don't ask Mum to dance unless it looks as if Myles and Lizzie are going to dance. You get to dance with Debs when her dad has danced with her, right? I only hope Lizzie does dance with Myles. He's invited his new girlfriend to the afters, and who knows what'll happen when Lizzie sees her. I think Debra was mad to invite her, and even though Lizzie said it was all right I have my doubts. You know what women get like at weddings. There's bound to be war.'

Hell, Lizzie thought. She'd worked so hard to be calm and collected and still people were expecting her to go for Myles with the wedding cake knife. Her ex-husband came back in from the bar looking harassed, and sat down. Lizzie took the empty seat beside him. 'I think poor Barry's worried that we might kill each other on the dance floor.'

'He's probably nervous that you don't approve of Sabine coming,' said Myles, with a look that said he shared his new son-in-law's apprehension.

'Is she here yet?'

Myles's eyes were classic bunny-caught-in-oncoming-car-headlights, which was all the confirmation Lizzie needed.

'Introduce me to her and let's get it over with,' Lizzie urged.

'Introduce you?'

'It's either that or avoid each other all night. So let's do it.'

Taking the bull by the horns was a heady feeling, Lizzie decided as she swept back out of the room to the hotel bar, which was where Sabine had told Myles she'd wait until he gauged it was all right for her to come into the wedding proper.

'She didn't want to come at all,' he said. 'She thought it would be more appropriate if she didn't because it's your day . . . and we didn't want you to get upset.'

'Oh, Myles, it's Debra's day. You and I are divorced. It's a bit stupid getting upset over that now,' Lizzie replied. And the great thing was, she felt as if she was almost speaking the truth. She was over Myles, honestly. Being piqued because he had a new partner and she didn't was another issue entirely and not befitting a woman in the prime of her life who'd decided not to waste another moment feeling sorry for herself. '*Carpe diem*,' she whispered softly.

Sabine was sitting quietly on a small couch and Lizzie's eyes quickly flickered over her. Sabine was definitely not a raver: soberly dressed in a navy suit, she looked pale and slim, having the sort of strawberry-blonde hair that came with white skin, freckles and blonde eyelashes. As Debra had reported, she clearly wasn't into make-up, having nothing but a faint sheen on her lips to hint at lipgloss that had long gone.

She'd brought a book and was engrossed in it, with an untouched glass of wine in front of her. Lizzie smiled at the thought that if *she* was going to a wedding where a possibly vengeful ex-wife was holding court with access to carving equipment, she'd have downed the wine in one already and be calling out for another.

'Sabine, this is Lizzie,' said Myles.

'Hello,' said Lizzie brightly. 'Lovely to meet you. But you mustn't stay out here. The dancing will be starting soon and you ought to see the first dance. That's special.'

Sabine's very pale face was almost translucent with astonishment but she didn't lack courage. 'Lovely to meet you too, Elizabeth,' she said. 'I thought I'd stay out here because I didn't want to upset you, to be honest. Weddings are very emotional occasions and I'd hate to cause a scene.'

'It's Lizzie, and you're not upsetting me,' Lizzie said truthfully, 'although we'll be giving Dunmore food for gossip for the next ten years if we all go back into the room together, which sounds like a good idea.'

Sabine roared with laughter at this and, eventually, Myles joined in.

'Has it been a good day?' Sabine tentatively began normal wedding conversation.

'Great. The weather's been fabulous. Debra looks wonderful and the best man's speech went off without a single cringe-worthy remark.'

'He went very near to the knuckle with that joke about what went on at Debra's hen night,' said Myles, every inch the outraged father.

'It was a joke,' said Lizzie, thinking of what the best man *could* have said if he'd been given full rein. 'The Chippendales haven't toured here for years, everybody knows that.'

'Mum, Dad . . .' The bride stood before them, the words dying on her lips as she found the odd threesome in the bar with no sign of blood.

'Darling, I was just meeting Sabine and telling her she mustn't miss your first dance.' Lizzie got to her feet, smiled at Myles and Sabine, and linked her arm through Debra's white silk-covered one. 'Are we all ready to go?'

'Er . . . yes,' said the bride.

'Yes,' said Sabine, getting to her feet and giving Lizzie a deeply grateful look.

As the four of them walked back to the wedding reception, Lizzie felt the heady sensation of triumph. She felt strong, free and powerful. Not only had she confronted her own demons, but she'd given Debra the best wedding gift ever by being a grown-up at her wedding.

On her mental check list of 'Things to Do Before You're Fifty', as she had customised it for her own use, Lizzie added another one: 'When your ex brings his new partner to your daughter's wedding, greet your replacement with dignity and style.' No thirty-something could say she'd done that, could she?

CHAPTER TWENTY-THREE

The third series of *Declutter* was nearly finished filming by the end of July, and Abby was wildly grateful for the fact. The schedule had been hectic in order to finish the editing by the first broadcast at the end of August. Abby had been away from home all too frequently, with Tom looking after Jess in her absence.

Hanging over Abby like a dark cloud was the knowledge that, soon, she and Tom would have to face up to the financial implications of their separation. Lyonnais would have to be sold so that they could each buy a smaller home.

Strangely, Abby found that she didn't care about selling her dream house. It wasn't as important as she had believed. The family who lived inside was the important part and now that was shattered, the house ceased to matter. Bricks and mortar did not make a home and she'd have been happy back in Gartland Avenue, noisy neighbours included, if she and Tom could have made their marriage work.

If the *Declutter* filming schedule had been exhausting, working with the twins was not. Despite her misgivings, Abby found that she liked sharing screen time with other presenters, particularly ones for whom the expression *joie de vivre* could have been invented. They were simply great fun, and she and the twins had become unlikely allies. Mitzi and Linzi were clever and eager to learn about television, and they appreciated both Abby's wisdom and her innate kindness. She'd begun by telling them that as she'd only worked on one TV show, she was hardly the best person to help them learn, but Linzi disagreed.

'You're a natural on telly, Abby,' she said. 'And you've learned the way we have to – by just doing it.'

'Yeah, learning on the job is the way to go,' Mitzi added.

Abby could tell the girls apart easily now. Linzi was the more serious of the two and her face was graver than Mitzi's, while Mitzi was incapable of talking for any length of time without smiling. They were both good-humoured and good company. Neither of them liked Roxie, although they were shrewd enough to hide the fact.

'What I don't understand is why Roxie doesn't like you?' Linzi asked Abby.

Abby shrugged. Roxie's opinion of her was unimportant in the grand scheme of things. 'I don't know and I don't care.'

'She's dangerous,' Mitzi cautioned.

'Me too,' said Abby wickedly. She had an ace up her sleeve, and it was all thanks to Selina, Beech's savvy publicity director . . .

'I know you've always felt you could handle your career yourself, Abby,' Selina had advised one day when they'd had a few moments together, 'but not any more, sweetie. You're not a housewife with a fledgeling TV show. You're a TV star and it's time you got yourself an agent.'

When Abby had first got into show business, she hadn't been keen on the idea of an agent, assuming she'd be able to manage her own career and hating the popular notion of the precious celeb who refused to so much as answer the phone without checking first with her agent. It was so *Absolutely Fabulous*: 'Darling, I must call my agent!! Order us some more Bolly, while you're at it.'

No, Abby didn't want to be that sort of person, so during the two years she'd been working on *Declutter*, she'd had a lawyer friend of Tom's check her contracts.

She pointed this out to Selina, who'd raised perfectly waxed eyebrows.

'That's naïve,' Selina said firmly. 'If you'd had an agent, Roxie wouldn't have been able to ride roughshod all over you when she hired the twins.'

'But I like the twins,' Abby protested.

'I know you do, sweetie.' Selina had been amazed at that because most stars of her acquaintance would have thrown a queenie fit at having two young beauties unceremoniously added to their television show without their approval.

But then Abby wasn't like most stars. She didn't put on the down-to-earth act that came over when she was on camera: she was genuinely like that. But the friendly, girl-next-door charisma had certainly suffered because of the trauma of her separation from Tom, Selina thought. Not that Abby had breathed a word of this to anyone, but Selina hadn't been in the business for twenty-nine years for nothing. She knew that Tom had moved out and she knew that soon the press would know it too. That was another thing she had to talk to poor Abby about, but another day, perhaps.

'Liking the twins isn't the point,' Selina said more gently. 'You need more power and you're too nice to demand it yourself. I have just the person for you, Mike Horowitz.'

'He's a superagent,' said Abby in awe. Mike Horowitz represented the biggest television celebrities, and she couldn't imagine that he'd be interested in her.

'Mike and I go way back,' Selina said. Way, way back, in fact, but she wasn't going to tell Abby that. Selina had remained forty-five for several years now and had no intention of getting any older. Botox was wonderful at holding back the years.

'He's asked me about you once or twice but I knew you weren't interested. Now you need to think about it.' Selina knew that as a Beech employee, her loyalty was supposed to be with the company, but she liked Abby and didn't want to see her shafted by the deviousness of someone like Roxie. She decided to spill the beans. 'There's nothing to stop Beech from firing you and running the next series with just the twins,' she said. 'They're cheaper and their contracts tie them up for the next two years to do every show Brian feels like, not to mention meaning that they have to show up to the opening of an envelope if Brian – or Roxie, more to the point – feels their presence might help.'

Abby stared at Selina in shock. 'They wouldn't fire me,' she said.

'They could,' Selina repeated. 'That's all I'm saying. The show is successful now, but if the ratings slip they could revamp it totally and you'd be out. You need someone to watch your interests. Mike is a brilliant agent and he's a rarity – he's honest, straight and decent. You'll love him. I hope.'

She'd set up a meeting between Abby and Mike Horowitz in his Dublin office on a day when Abby was filming in the capital.

Tom had arrived with his familiar overnight bag just as Abby was leaving for the airport that morning.

'Hi,' she said.

'Hello,' he replied shortly, and went inside.

Abby sighed and put her own suitcase into the Jeep, aware yet again of the huge gap in her life since the separation. Once, she and Tom would have talked about this meeting with Mike Horowitz. She'd accused Tom of not being that interested in her career, but that wasn't strictly true. He may not have been able to deal with the changes her success brought to their relationship, but he would have cared enough to have gone with her to meet the agent if things had been normal. If she and Tom had dealt with their differences better. If only they had worked harder at trying to understand one another's point of view. She would have loved him to be coming with her today.

Mike Horowitz's office was a suite in a plush glass monolith in the trendy docklands area of Dublin. Being a successful TV agent must pay well, Abby thought as she was ushered through thickly carpeted corridors to a huge office with floor-to-ceiling windows on two sides. Mike himself was not the cigar-chomping mogul in a white suit she'd expected, but instead a tall, casually dressed man with a bald head. Abby couldn't quite work out what age he was but he could have been anything from forty to sixty. He didn't look the type to pander to celebrity whims. In fact, he looked a bit like Abby's bank manager, with the same thoughtful stare. And there wasn't a bottle of Bollinger in sight.

'Good to meet you at last,' Mike said, shaking her hand and showing her to a very comfortable chair beside one of the stunning windows. He sat opposite, a low table between them. 'I've been following your career with interest.'

'Is it going up or down?' Abby asked deadpan.

Her joke broke the ice and soon they were talking rapidly, discussing Beech, *Declutter* and what the future could hold for Abby.

As they spoke, Abby realised that Selina had been right and Mike was just the man to sort out her career. She'd planned on being cool and reserved but now that she'd met him, she found herself warming to his straightforward manner.

Mike pointed out that most of the best-known TV stars had succeeded by knowing when to move on or to change direction. 'I think Beech have a very one-dimensional approach to your career and they haven't realised your potential. To be honest, I don't see you working on *Declutter* for ever,' he said bluntly.

'But that's what I know how to do,' protested Abby.

'That's true on one level,' he replied. 'You could have a whole spin-off career with books and TV specials about decluttering, but what made the show work in the first place is you. You have a warm and friendly screen presence and that's your USP. Unique selling point,' he added. 'That would shine through no matter what sort of show you were doing and, to be honest, I can see you being fantastic on a chat show.'

'Don't be ridiculous,' Abby said. 'I couldn't do that.'

Mike shrugged. 'Yes, you could. You should have more faith in yourself, Abby. Just because Beech don't see your skills because they're caught up in the youth-is-everything kick, doesn't mean everyone will feel the same way. But that's in the future. Right now, you have to go away and think about whether you want me as your agent.'

Abby, who'd planned to make no decisions today, changed her mind. 'I don't need to go away and think about it. I'd like you to take me on.'

'No, think about it,' Mike advised. 'Never make decisions quickly: that's my first bit of professional advice.'

'I don't,' Abby said, 'but I want you to represent me, OK?'

'OK. Welcome to the team,' he said, shaking her hand and smiling. He looked down at some papers on the table on which he'd jotted some notes. 'There's something we ought to talk about then. Something Beech could easily use against you in the future, both as publicity material and as a way to get you out.' He paused and Abby felt a twinge of worry. 'I know it's very personal but I'm talking about your marriage break-up,' Mike continued.

Abby felt her stomach lurch. 'What?' she breathed.

'Sorry,' he apologised. 'I know it's a tough time for you but people are beginning to work it out, Abby. Selina told me, and although she's very sharp and discovers things long before other people, this is a piece of news you'll find hard to hide.'

'Selina knows?'

The look Mike gave her was sympathetic. 'You're famous, Abby. People notice you. People notice if your husband is living somewhere else and never accompanies you anywhere.'

'But we don't live that sort of famous life,' Abby whispered.

'I know,' Mike said, 'and that's good. You can be very famous and very successful and never put a Blahniked foot near a première or a celebrity party. Lots of my clients live normal lives but they're still on the TV and people see them, even if they're only popping into their local shop for milk and a loaf of bread.'

Mike got up and opened the walnut cabinet where he kept supplies of booze, both for celebrations and as shock absorbers. 'As you're my client, it's my job to tell you where the next problem is coming from and try and protect you from that. When the new series of *Declutter* goes out next month, I bet you my first year's commission that Roxie O'Halloran will have primed some journalist with the news that you and your husband have split up. So she won't just have to rely on the twins to publicise the show, she'll have you as the sacrificial lamb. I can see the headline on every interview you do: "The private tragedy behind television's warmest star", "How Abby Barton's meteoric TV career ruined her marriage". Do you see what I mean?'

Sitting in the opulence of Mike Horowitz's office, Abby burst into tears.

Instantly, Mike handed her a box of tissues and the brandy he'd already poured into a crystal balloon glass. He'd learned a long time ago that in the entertainment business, timing was everything.

'Drink this,' he said gently. 'That's the worst-case scenario, Abby. You've got to be ready for it. We've got to be ready for it. And we will be. In fact, we can turn this to our advantage.'

'How?' sobbed Abby piteously, her mascara running down her face. 'How can we turn Tom leaving me into anything but a disaster?'

Mike allowed himself to smile. 'By letting you be you, Abby. What would you say if an interviewer asked you about it now?'

Abby blew her nose. 'I'd say it was a private matter; that neither I nor Tom would discuss our marriage.'

'Anything else?' probed Mike.

'I wouldn't hurt Tom or Jess by speaking about it,' Abby insisted furiously. 'You can't make me talk about it.'

'That's it!' Mike was pleased. 'Some television stars would have sex with their partners on live TV if it would get them any more coverage. You're not like that. That's what people relate to: Abby Barton being Abby Barton, not Abby Barton turning into a kiss-and-tell madam. You don't want to talk about it but you'll be ready when they start to ask you. Nobody is going to launch a surprise attack on you.'

'It's so painful,' Abby said quietly.

'I know.' Mike nodded. 'Been there. Twice. Which is why there will never be a third Horowitz nuptial ceremony.' He sat on the edge of Abby's armchair and patted her shoulder in an avuncular manner. 'You can get through it, you know. But you've got to stop thinking you're a bad person because your marriage has ended. You're normal, that's all. Sometimes it just doesn't work out.'

But it could have, Abby thought miserably, if only she hadn't slept with Jay Garnier. She might just be able to live with herself if only she hadn't caused the split.

'Come on, don't be so down on yourself,' Mike said.

'I had a wonderful friend who died recently and she was a good person. Compared to her, I'm a screw-up.' Abby threw back the rest of her brandy.

'Never compare yourself with anyone.' Mike sloshed more brandy into her glass. 'Learn from her and move on. You can't be like your friend because you've had different experiences in life. You can only be you.'

'I know, but she was good and kind and still she died, while I'm screwing up everything I touch and I'm still here. It makes you feel there's some truth in the cliché about only the good dying young.'

'Change the screwed-up bits of your life, then,' Mike said easily.

'It's not that simple . . .' she began. Then stopped. Maybe he was right. Instead of moaning about the past, she should face up to the future and change it. Sally would have had the courage to do that. Abby gave Mike a faint smile. 'That's all very profound. To think that I put off having an agent for years because I thought they were all shallow and full of "You were *fabulous*!" bullshit.'

Mike's tiny black eyes sparkled. 'I can do shallow, believe

330

me, I can do shallow. And people rave about my "You were *fabulous!*" But premium clients get the full Horowitz package, which includes poignant insights, relationship advice and brandy. Just don't tell anyone or my reputation would be shot to hell.'

Abby's faint smile widened into a grin. She liked Mike Horowitz and she'd been so sure she wouldn't . . .

'You couldn't be more dangerous than Roxie,' Linzi said now with a shudder.

'Watch me,' said Abby, thinking of Mike, her new secret weapon. 'Roxie's going to find that two can play that game.'

It was ten in the morning and the three of them were in a taxi, being driven to work. There was only one more show to film, and as soon as they arrived at the house, a tired semi in a sprawling commuter town in the midlands, the three presenters heaved a sigh of despair.

Abby, Linzi and Mitzi stared in disbelief at the mess that was the Lockwood family's house. They hadn't stepped inside the door and already the three of them wanted to drive away. If there was that much junk *outside*, what would it be like inside?

Bits of old cars were piled up alongside some old tyres, packing crates and a kennel so ramshackle that no dog could surely be sleeping in it. Filthy net curtains flapped from the open windows, and it was clear that nobody had felt like painting the house for the last ten years. The whole effect was that the house wasn't in need of de-junking so much as fumigating.

The Passion Wagon, AC and DC were already parked outside and when the women piled out of the taxi, they rushed into the Passion Wagon for coffee and reassurance that they weren't overreacting.

'You aren't,' sighed Julie, the assistant director, who was sitting on the red velvet couch comfort-eating her way through an enormous apple Danish. 'I don't know why this house wasn't ruled out in the initial stages. It's not just messy, it's squalid.'

'So, we don't have to touch it? We can find another location?' asked Linzi hopefully.

'It's too late for that, isn't it, Julie?' Abby said, selecting a Danish for herself from the box beside the coffee equipment. The high-speed filming of the end of the series meant that the system for weeding out hopeless cases from the hundreds of willing homeowners had gone by the wayside.

Julie nodded into her pastry. 'You're right on the money, Abby,' she mumbled through the crumbs. 'I'll kill someone when we get back to the office.'

'Don't worry, girls.' Helen, the make-up artist, was cheerful. 'I've got antiseptic wipes in my kit.'

Abby didn't know whether it was because she had decided to throw herself into her work, but she'd never enjoyed filming more. Meeting Mike Horowitz had cheered her up no end, and she'd decided that he was right: she could sort out the future. OK, so it wouldn't be the married-to-Tom future that she'd always seen for herself, but now that she'd faced up to that, she could mourn her marriage and move on. She wasn't a bad person, she was just a flawed human being and she could try and improve on that. Mike believed in her, so she still had a career. All she needed to do was repair the damage the separation had wreaked on her relationship with Jess. And she could do that. She adored Jess. Love had to count for something, didn't it?

So when she marched into the Lockwood family house, she felt invigorated and ready for action.

The twins, smirking like two naughty schoolgirls behind her, were doing their best not to giggle.

'Hello, Mr and Mrs Lockwood,' said Abby politely as she met the untidy couple responsible for the smelly disaster. Their children, three equally untidy teenagers, lingered sullenly in the background. 'Perhaps you'd show us the rooms we're going to be working on?'

332

CHAPTER TWENTY-FOUR

Lizzie's 'Things to Do Before You're Thirty' list was getting a bit battered.

She kept it in a zipped section of her handbag and took it out occasionally to remind herself that most of the tasks were still firmly on her 'to do' list. She had to stop wasting her life, she told herself.

So far, she'd gone on holiday on her own (Joe's in London *did* count), and she'd done one thing that wasn't on the list but was still pretty brave – welcoming Sabine to Debra's wedding had to merit some marks for courage. But that was it.

One evening in July, soon after the wedding, she sat in the living room with a glass of wine, unfolded the crumpled paper and looked at the list again. She didn't fancy getting checked for chlamydia – that would imply that she had a sex life in the first place. Learning about investments and setting up her own stock portfolio would be useless when she only had a tenner left at the end of each week. Surely investment broker people liked a bit more disposable cash than that.

She skipped hurriedly over the one about not drinking her entire week's alcohol allowance in one night. Not that she ever did that, but it wasn't wise to dwell on alcohol consumption when you were nearly at the bottom of a glass of wine and it was only ten to seven on a Tuesday.

Sighing, Lizzie looked to see if there was anything on the list she *could* do that would cheer her up and make her feel as if she wasn't ready for the scrapheap just yet.

The words 'adventure sport' leaped out at her. Adventure

sport. Rock climbing wasn't her thing and she never liked getting her head wet, so scuba diving wasn't an option. Besides, that was how Sabine and Myles had met, so she'd look like she was copying them if she tried that. Hmm.

In the background, the TV flickered. There was nothing on worth watching. There was never anything on. Lizzie decided that she'd go for a walk and burn some calories instead of sitting there all evening feeling sorry for herself. Reaching for the remote, she was about to click the 'off' button when she stopped. Another tampon advert was on. This time, the girl wearing white trousers was jumping out of a plane.

'Look at me – nothing is going to stop me doing things,' her lovely face said.

That was it, Lizzie decided. A parachute jump. She'd always wanted to do one and, years ago, she remembered some of Joe's pals doing one for charity. Joe, who didn't like heights, had said no thanks, but Lizzie had been wistfully jealous. She loved flying and the idea of leaping bravely from a plane somehow appealed to her. Of course, she hadn't actually done anything about the desire at the time. It wasn't the sort of thing she did. She was Joe's mum and that meant washing his horrible sports kit – not going skydiving with his friends. But why hadn't she? What had stopped her?

Her own vision of what a woman of her age did, that's what. Now, years later, she found that her own life vision was smothering her. It was time to change.

Skydiving – that would be her adventure sport. Yah boo sucks, she said to the 'to do' list. She'd get through it yet.

Enlivened by this new plan, Lizzie switched off the TV, pulled on her trainers, and went for a brisk walk. She knew that lots of charities linked up with parachute jump centres to raise money. The charity stipulated that a certain amount would have to be raised before the jump could take place, and the fee for the jump came out of that. Lizzie knew so many worthy charities from her work in the surgery, but suddenly one came to mind: a national cancer charity. Wouldn't it be great if she could jump for, say, Life Beats Cancer and make her donation in Sally's name? What a lovely tribute to Sally to do this life-affirming thing. Lizzie could imagine what Sally would say if she'd been alive and if Lizzie had asked her advice about doing a parachute jump. Sally wouldn't think she was too old or losing her marbles, she would say: 'Do it!'

Lizzie's previous experience of raising money for charity made her think that this would be the hardest part of her jump experience. She'd discovered that, yes, the LBC charity did organise charity jumps and she could jump at a local airfield. In fact, getting the promise of money turned out to be remarkably easy. The sponsorship cards she'd received from Life Beats Cancer said that Lizzie Shanahan was jumping for the charity 'in honour of Sally Richardson'. Lizzie had wanted that put in especially. This was her tribute to her friend.

The words 'Life Beats Cancer' and 'sponsored parachute jump' made most of the people of Dunmore who opened their front doors smile at Lizzie approvingly; the mention of Sally made them invite her in and offer her tea.

'Well done', 'Aren't you brave! I'm far too scared of heights to do that!' and 'Fair play to you for doing something to raise money,' were the most common comments, followed by sad conversations about Sally and how the person had known her. It moved Lizzie to find that her friend's untimely death had affected other people deeply too. And had saddened the most unlikely of Dunmore residents.

One burly neighbour who'd opened his front door with a wary eye that said he was fed up with charity collections had invited Lizzie in and spent ages talking about how kind Sally had been to him when his wife had died, baking big apple pies and phoning him at weekends to say hello.

'It made a difference,' the man said sorrowfully. 'I didn't feel so alone.'

Meeting the many and varied people who mourned Sally made Lizzie feel her loss even more acutely. Sally had been such a special person – not goody-goody or preachy, but genuinely kind, wanting to envelop everyone in her warmth. In her five or six years in the town, she'd become a part of it. Lizzie, who'd lived there for most of her married life and knew perhaps a quarter of the people Sally had, felt humbled by her dead friend's compassion and verve for life.

In the end, she raised the promise of almost twice the money that she'd aimed for, thanks to some last-minute support from some of the town's big businesses.

All she had to do next was actually jump from a perfectly safe plane and fall two thousand feet through the air with nothing but a parachute between her and sudden death. Easy, she joked to herself.

But skydiving was more complicated than Lizzie had imagined. She'd had a vague notion that somebody strapped you into a parachute, sent you up in a plane, and then shoved you into clean air, whereupon the chute opened instantly and you felt thrilled to be a part of the sky like a big, jumpsuited bird. According to the brochure she received from the training school, the reality seemed to be more complicated. First-time jumpers had to complete a day and a half's training course before they got to jump. Even then, the decision as to whether the novice parachutists could jump lay with the course instructors. 'We will have the final say as to whether a trainee is ready,' was the grim message.

Lizzie vowed that she'd be one of those jumping. She was doing this for Sally as well as herself, and it would be letting her friend down if she flunked at the first fence.

Her course started at nine on a cool Saturday morning in early August with clouds on the horizon and a nip in the air that was distinctly autumnal.

Undaunted, Lizzie arrived at the small airfield where the Santa Monica Flying and Parachute Training School was situated. It was a bare, flat place with several big plane hangars, a smaller breeze-block building and two runways stretching out behind the buildings.

There were several cars in the car park, and Lizzie climbed out of hers at the same time as two twenty-something women arrived in a funky little purple 4 x 4. She'd dressed in comfortable old jeans and a faded grey sweatshirt with runners on her feet, and her unruly hair corralled into a ponytail. The two girls, while also in jeans, wore the tight, butt-displaying variety, and showed off enviable figures in clingy little T-shirts and just as clingy zippy tops.

'Hi,' they said to Lizzie.

'Are you here for the course?' asked the girl with glossy short dark hair.

'Yes, for my sins,' said Lizzie.

'Us too. Isn't it an adventure?' The other girl, with silvery blonde hair worn loose over her shoulders, grinned. 'I'm Casey and that's Dolores.' The brunette smiled a dazzling, lipsticked smile, and Lizzie was sort of glad she hadn't bothered to do much more than slick on mascara and lip salve. In the glamour stakes, she wouldn't have stood a chance beside Casey and Dolores.

'Lizzie,' she said, holding out her hand.

The three of them walked across an expanse of cracking tarmac to the grey building where a sign read 'reception'. The two girls seemed very excited, and Dolores took out a compact as they walked and patted a bit of concealer on some non-existent spot.

'Want to look?' she asked Casey, who looked, squinted, then handed the compact back, secure in the knowledge that she looked stunning.

'We're doing this to meet men,' Casey revealed by way of explanation for all the primping.

'Isn't jumping out of a plane a bit drastic?' Lizzie asked. 'I thought nowadays people tried Internet dating?'

'That's just blind dating by another name,' Casey said dismissively. 'No matter how you hook up with the guy, Internet or whatever, you still have to arrange to meet him in a restaurant and hope he's not a serial rapist who's covered his tracks and has picked you as his next victim.'

'She's jaundiced about the Internet. She recently had a really bad blind date,' disclosed Dolores.

'Bad doesn't describe it,' sighed Casey. 'I sat there for two hours waiting for him and the waitresses had bets on when I'd give up and go home.'

'How terrible!' Lizzie could imagine the embarrassment of sitting there, watching every newcomer and feeling hope die as the time passed and nobody turned up.

'What's worse, I think he showed up, took one look at me and went home again,' the blonde girl added miserably.

'Don't say that. You're so pretty,' Lizzie said kindly.

Casey beamed at her. 'What are you here for?'

'Not the men, that's for sure,' Lizzie laughed. 'I'm doing the jump for charity.'

'Oh, us too,' Casey said hastily. 'And for the men.'

Inside, reception did not look like the sort of place where handsome men were likely to be lurking looking for dates. The walls were painted army green, and battered metal chairs made up the furniture, while a stocky man with a beard stood behind a desk and looked sternly at the assorted novices busily filling out forms. The majority of the form-fillers were, however, male, mostly young at that, and Lizzie saw Casey and Dolores exchange thrilled glances. The men noticed Casey and Dolores back and Lizzie felt a faint pang at how her age appeared to have rendered her invisible.

The three women checked in and were handed forms from the taciturn receptionist. When they'd filled them in, he collected the forms and took the novices, now number-ing twenty, down a corridor and into another bare room furnished with rows of chairs.

Two men with military haircuts were at the top of the room. One, Tony, was young and innocent-looking, with red hair and freckles. The other was older, with a lean weather-beaten face, shrewd eyes and a toned physique in his worn grey flying suit. Sitting on the edge of a desk, drinking from a mug of coffee, he watched the novices find seats.

338

Lizzie perked up. There was something about men in flying suits that sent a little shiver up her spine. He looked muscular and exciting, not the sort of man who'd ever look twice at her, but who cared? It was good to have something to admire to take her mind off the panic she felt at the thought of jumping. She located her strawberry lip balm in the front of her little bum bag, slicked a bit on her lips and listened as the man introduced himself as Simon, one of the co-owners of the centre.

Simon – nice name, she thought. And was she imagining it, or had his eyes flickered over her several times?

The training was repetitious and Lizzie could see how it worked. After a day and a half leaping from a bit of plane fuselage, counting 'one thousand, two thousand, three thousand, four thousand, check canopy,' she'd be doing the procedure in her sleep. And if she could do it in her sleep, she'd hopefully be able to do it once she exited the plane. 'This will save your life if for some reason your chute fails to open,' repeated Simon again and again. 'If that happens, you need to pull the cord on the emergency chute. I know it's repetitive but it will save your life. One thousand, two thousand, three thousand, four thousand, check canopy – if it's not open, go to plan B and pull emergency chute. That's the difference between a safe jump and death, right?'

Lizzie decided she must have been imagining that he was interested in her: he was so utterly professional about the training, giving each recruit the attention they needed, that she told herself she'd been dreaming. At least this meant he hadn't allowed his gaze to land on Casey too often, like the younger, red-haired trainer.

When the day was over, bonded by exhaustion and the thrill of what was to come, the new recruits took off to the pub.

'Isn't it fantastic?' said Casey, her make-up gone and her mane of silver-blonde hair flattened under a baseball cap. She looked even prettier with her face flushed from exercise, Lizzie thought.

'Wait till we have to do it tomorrow,' said Dolores, who'd hated jumping even from the second floor of the hangar wearing the harness.

What else was on her list, Lizzie thought happily as she drove back to Dunmore that night, tired but invigorated. Visit Paris? No problem. Buy jewellery for herself? A problem in the financial sense. Ask a man out? Easy peasy. Rock climbing the sort of wall Tom Cruise scaled in *Mission: Impossible 2* – now perhaps *that* was a challenge enough for her, after all. She could do anything, anything!

Debra's Mini was in the drive when she got home and Lizzie felt a bolt of pleasure. Wonderful. She hadn't seen that much of Debra since the honeymoon, although the newlyweds had presided over a family lunch in their new town house and Lizzie had felt proud of her grown-up, married daughter. The honeymoon in Mauritius had gilded Debra's skin, giving her a healthy glow, and she and Barry had looked lovingly at each other all during lunch, describing each other proudly as 'my husband' and 'my wife' until Barry's father had burst into laughter and told them how funny it was. Barry had laughed too, although Debra had not been amused.

'Hi, love,' said Lizzie cheerily as she threw her keys on the hall table and hung her bum bag on the newel post of the stairs.

Debra was in the garden, with a bottle of wine on the iron table in front of her and a cigarette dangling from her fingers. She did not look like the healthy woman who'd come back from Mauritius with her beloved husband. Her face was pinched and angry, and it was clear she'd been there some time because she was halfway down the wine bottle and there were six butts in the saucer she was using as an ashtray.

'Mum . . .' Debra's face crumpled and Lizzie automatically rushed to throw her arms around her daughter.

'What's wrong, love?'

'It's Barry,' sobbed Debra through a stuffy nose. 'He's a rotten bastard. I've left him.'

It took a pot of tea to get the full story out of Debra. Barry was a slob, for a start. He was perfectly happy to let the house descend into a tip before doing any housework.

'He has what he calls a system of using up every shirt in his wardrobe and not giving a toss where he throws them until the day before he runs out and then he does a wash. And only his stuff, not mine!' This was clearly the final straw. Debra had assumed that the washing would be done together and when she'd come home to find the clothes horse hanging with all Barry's clothes and not so much as a pair of her own knickers, she'd flipped.

'He did live in a flat with two other guys,' countered Lizzie, wanting to explain to her daughter that it took time for couples to sort out details like housework. Barry and Debra had, for some old-fashioned reason, decided not to move in together to their adorable town house until they were married, so there was definitely a culture shock for both of them in sharing now. Debra probably hadn't expected her female flatmates to be her soulmates, so had coped with messy domestic arrangements. Now, though, she seemed to expect perfection from Barry. True love equals everything perfect. Wrong, thought Lizzie.

'You'll have to talk to each other about this and come up with a proper system,' Lizzie went on. 'You know, you do shopping and cooking for half the week and he does the laundry, then you swap. Something like that.'

Debra wasn't having any of it. In not doing her laundry from the start, Barry had proved one simple truth: he didn't love her.

'Debra, of course he loves you,' said her mother, privately diagnosing post-wedding depression now that all the fuss was over. She thought of the tiny, beautifully proportioned house Debra and Barry had bought, and which Barry had moved into three weeks before the wedding. Then, their lives had been the whirl of the about-to-be-marrieds, full

341

of dress fittings, lively nights out with friends and obsessive worrying about the reception. There would have been no time to notice whether he was any good at washing up or cleaning the bathroom.

Yet, playing house when they were just married, when they were the most important people in their own small world, should be fun. Why had Debra failed to see that?

Debra lit another cigarette.

'You gave up,' Lizzie said reproachfully.

'I did, but if he doesn't love me what's the point of not smoking?' Debra said defiantly.

'It's just a squabble over silly things,' soothed Lizzie. 'I'll call you a taxi so you can go home and make it up.'

'Home! I'm not going home!' shrieked her daughter. 'We're selling that house and getting a divorce. I should never have married him. It's about more than just housework. I can tell you that I thought I knew Barry bloody Cronin but I didn't at all!' She shoved her tea cup aside and poured herself some more wine. 'And I'm going to take him to the cleaners in the divorce courts too! It's all his fault – that must mean something when the judge is working out who gets what.'

Lizzie began to think that she needed a glass of wine too. She collected some cheese and crackers from the kitchen, and returned with a tray of food and another glass.

'Now, tell me what else Barry's done,' she said.

'We were supposed to be going to Crete in October,' Debra sniffed. 'I know we've had the honeymoon but that was different and Barry said we'd need another break.'

Lizzie quashed the desire to enquire where they were getting the money for another holiday. Barry's job in car sales and Debra's in a double-glazing firm meant they weren't exactly in the highest tax bracket.

'But now he says we can't. He says we're stretched with the mortgage as it is, and if we don't go we can get a dining-room table and chairs. I don't know why we can't get both! I said if he hadn't spent so much money on his crappy stag night and on getting new tyres for that gas-guzzler of a car, we could have both and then he said I was spoiled and didn't I know you had to earn money before you spent it!' At this, Debra burst into noisy sobs.

'Oh, love, it's not always easy coping with financial problems,' Lizzie said, trying to be comforting. 'Most couples argue about money and you two have never lived together before, so it's going to take a bit of adjusting.'

'I don't want to adjust. I'm good with money! I've supported myself for years. *He* needs to adjust!' Debra sobbed.

Lizzie thought of Debra's Mini, to which she and Myles had both contributed because Debra's heart had been set on it. She remembered the deposit on Debra's second-last flat, which hadn't been returned because of some dispute, meaning Debra had needed a loan of money from her parents for the next flat's deposit. Like all loans to Debra – and there had been many – it had never been returned. And she thought of the wedding fund started by Barry and Debra – 'we want to pay for our own wedding' – that had never really got off the ground until Myles and Lizzie had got involved, at which point the plans for the big day grew more grandiose. Barry's parents, along with Lizzie and Myles, had even contributed whatever they could to the deposit for the new house, something all four would be paying for for a long time to come.

Lizzie didn't begrudge her darling daughter any of this but it would have been nice if Debra had ever been in the slightest bit grateful for it. But Debra's approach to money was that once it was given, it didn't need to be mentioned ever again. In Debra's book, parents did not wish to be thanked for their financial sacrifices. 'Eaten bread is soon forgotten,' as Gwen might say.

'Perhaps you should economise a bit,' Lizzie ventured. 'New houses are expensive and you've just been to Mauritius . . .'

'You're taking his side!' Debra was back to shrieking again, and Lizzie hoped her neighbours weren't earwigging on the other side of the garden fence. Then again, maybe it didn't matter if they were earwigging. Heaven knows, it wasn't as if they'd had anything interesting to listen to of late.

'I'm not taking Barry's side,' she said gently. 'All I'm saying is that marriage is about compromise and learning how to get on with each other. You've spent a lot of money lately and Barry's probably worried about the bills. Why don't you suggest a weekend away somewhere at home instead of a week abroad? There are great deals around if you book early, and that way you'd both get what you wanted.'

'I don't want a crappy weekend in Ireland,' snapped Debra. 'I want a week somewhere hot where I can get a tan, not a wet weekend shivering in this bloody country.' She drained her wine. 'I'm going to unpack. And if Barry phones, tell him I won't speak to him.'

She swept off, leaving the table messy and Lizzie with her mouth open. Unpacking. What did Debra need to unpack? And why?

Lizzie said nothing as she helped Debra drag three suitcases – newly purchased for the honeymoon – upstairs. She was Debra's mother, after all, and what was a mother for if not to provide comfort in times of need?

'What will we do tomorrow?' Debra asked cosily, once she had her former bedroom back to its usual glory, with the dressing table crammed with jars of far more expensive creams than her mother could afford, and a pile of precious cuddly toys staring from the bed like disapproving maiden aunts shifted from place to place without their say-so.

'I'm going to be out tomorrow,' Lizzie replied.

'Out? Where?'

For some reason, Lizzie didn't want to tell her daughter about the parachute jump until it was over. She had a feeling that Debra wouldn't understand or might even say she was mad to be doing it, and Lizzie needed to feel utterly confident to make the jump.

'Out with some girlfriends of mine,' she said, feeling terrible for lying.

'Oh.' Debra managed to invest that one syllable with myriad meanings. 'You won't be gone all day, will you?' she added.

'Well . . .'

'Goody. We could go out to dinner,' Debra said happily. 'There's this new place in town that everyone's raving about. I'll book.'

Lizzie wondered who was going to pay for this feast but said nothing. Debra just needed a little mothering and then she and Barry would sort out their problems.

'Mum, you shouldn't take her in,' Joe said that evening after Debbie had gone to bed.

Lizzie, who was beginning to regret phoning him for moral support, was more than a little shocked at his reaction. 'How could you say such a thing?'

'Because Debra has to stand on her own two feet and she's never going to do it if she can run to you all the time.'

'I hope I'm a good enough mother to be here for both of you, no matter how old you are,' Lizzie shot back.

'You're a great mother,' Joe said, placating her. 'It's not about you, Mum. It's about Debra. She wanted the big wedding that cost a fortune and she got it. She wouldn't listen to a word any of us told her about how there was no rush to get married yet, or why didn't she just live with Barry to see if they had a future together. No, it had to be the whole wedding extravaganza. Three bridesmaids, remember? And now it isn't working out. She should have to face up to her own actions. If they're going to split up, Debra should stay and face the music, not run home to you.'

'It's only a row,' insisted Lizzie.

'It's more than that,' snapped her son. 'Barry and Debs are totally unsuited. She's my sister and I love her, but she behaves like a kid who always wants her own way. Debs has some chance with a man who wouldn't take any of her crap and would make her grow up, but Barry isn't that man. He's not interested in hassle. He'll walk out on her rather than deal with the situation. This is serious, I'm telling you.'

'Don't overdramatise.'

'Mum!' Joe groaned. 'At the wedding when he had a few jars in him, Barry's father told me he never thought Barry would go through with it. Apparently he had second thoughts the night before. I think that only his mother threatening that she'd die of shame if he didn't marry Debra got him to the church in the first place.'

'Oh, Joe, I had no idea,' said Lizzie, shaken by both this new information and Joe's pronouncement that Debra's marriage was in trouble.

'Go upstairs now and tell her she has to go back to Barry and sort this out like an adult,' Joe ordered. 'Or you'll be drawn into it all and you'll never have your own life because you'll be babying her for ever.'

'But she's my daughter,' said Lizzie

'Yes, but you've got your own life,' Joe said ominously.

On Sunday morning, Lizzie woke early and crept around the house getting ready so she wouldn't wake Debra. She squeezed some oranges for Debra's breakfast and left a note saying there were eggs in the fridge and that she'd be back before five, hopefully. The night before, she had decided it wasn't yet worth advising Debra to go home to Barry and sort things out. It was easier not to. In the clear light of morning, she was sure that Joe had been exaggerating the problem between the newlyweds. Didn't every groom have a panic attack the night before his wedding? It meant nothing.

Lizzie was the first one in the training centre this time, and the reception door was still locked when she pushed it.

'Hold on, I've got the key.' It was Simon, a baseball hat pulled down low over his head.

He hadn't shaved and Lizzie felt her heart leap in an unfamiliar way at the sight of his lean, stubbly jaw.

'You're keen,' he remarked as he unlocked the door.

'It's fifty per cent fear and fifty per cent enthusiasm,' Lizzie laughed.

Simon grinned laconically. 'It's nice to hear someone being honest about it. Most of the people who come here feel the same but won't admit it. A little fear is healthy in parachuting because the moment you don't respect what you're doing, you're putting yourself at risk.'

'I never looked at it that way,' Lizzie said, following him into the grim reception room. 'I thought fear was the enemy of everything.'

'Only in the very stupid,' Simon said. 'I'm making coffee. Would you like a brew?'

'Yeah. Thanks.' Lizzie smiled. 'I woke up early today with nerves, so I could do with something to give me some zip.'

He led her to a small office where a coffee machine stood in one corner by a tiny sink. Two desks and plenty of elderly filing cabinets filled the room, and there were photos crammed on the walls, of planes with laughing happy people in front of them, some in full parachute harness.

'Remember that you don't have to jump if you don't want to,' Simon said, fixing coffee. 'Nobody's going to make you do it.'

'I'm going to make myself,' Lizzie commented, walking round to look at the photos. There was one of Simon, younger and with longer tawny hair, his arm round an equally tawny-haired woman in a flying jacket. 'I'm jumping for a breast cancer charity so I can't chicken out.'

Simon nodded but didn't enquire into why she'd chosen breast cancer specifically. He wasn't a prying sort of person. It was refreshing talking to him, she realised, because she didn't have anything to prove and because she knew there was no way in hell he could be interested in her. Therefore she could just be herself.

'You'll either love it or you'll hate it,' was all he said. 'A

347

lot of people jump once and never come back but if you get hooked, it's very addictive.'

'Will you be flying the plane today?' Lizzie asked shyly.

'No, I'll wait on the ground and see what you look like when you land,' grinned Simon. 'That's the true test.'

'If I look green in the face, don't think I'm a wimp,' Lizzie said. 'I've never done anything like this before.'

Simon handed her a mug of coffee. 'I don't think you're a wimp. You're brave.'

'For taking it up at my age?' Lizzie said wryly.

Simon gave her a considered look. 'Why did you ask that?' he said.

Lizzie flushed. 'You know, I'm the oldest person on the course.'

'So?' Simon shrugged. 'If you had to be under twenty-five to jump, I'd have been retired long ago.'

The door opened and Teddy, the bearded guy from reception, came in. He ignored Lizzie and spoke to Simon.

'Two cancellations already,' he said.

'Who?' asked Lizzie before she could stop herself.

'Dolores Moore and Louis MacNamara.'

Lizzie wasn't surprised that Casey's friend had chosen not to jump: she was clearly scared of heights, but Louis was the one who spent all day yesterday bragging about how he loved flying and was sorry he'd never done a parachute jump before. All clearly bullshit. Lizzie grinned, thinking that *she* hadn't chickened out.

Simon caught her eye. 'You turned up on the second day,' he murmured so Teddy couldn't hear. 'That's my definition of being brave.'

At half two, when she was suited up and in her harness waiting with three others to board the small plane, Lizzie didn't feel very brave. Her heart was pumping at high speed, there was no sign of Simon to give her fresh confidence, and Casey – who'd adopted Lizzie as her best friend now that Dolores wasn't there – was shaking like a leaf beside her.

'Why did we say we'd do this?' said Casey, teeth chattering with nerves and all her lipstick worn off from biting her lips.

'To meet gorgeous men,' Lizzie reminded her, giving Casey's hand a squeeze.

'I haven't seen any I fancy,' wailed Casey.

I have, thought Lizzie.

'Fantastic!' yelled a voice, and they all turned to look at the people coming in from the last jump. Everyone was smiling, great ecstatic smiles. Genuine enjoyment or sheer relief it was over, Lizzie wondered.

Four of them squeezed into the plane with Tony, the instructor, and a pilot. Their gear had been checked and rechecked, they had all been drilled to within an inch of their lives and if they didn't know how to jump safely now, they never would.

'Ready?' yelled Tony over the roar of the engine. Everyone gamely made thumbs-up signs at him.

What the hell am I doing? Lizzie asked herself as the small plane took off down the runway.

From the ground, it seemed as if the plane took ages to reach the site above the drop zone, but when you were actually in the plane, the trip was scarily quick.

'We're here. Ready?' Tony said again.

The thumbs-up were shakier this time.

Tony wrenched open the door and as the air rushed noisily in, Lizzie felt her stomach lurch. She was actually going to have to do this.

A big guy named Alan was seated nearest the door and Tony roared at him to get ready. In a moment, the pilot would cut the plane's engine and then the jumpers would take it in turns to have their static line attached, carefully put their feet onto the wing strut, edge themselves away from the door, holding on to the wing with their hands, then jump. One thousand, two thousand, three thousand, four thousand, check canopy, Lizzie muttered under her breath. One thousand, two thousand . . .

The engine cut out and Alan, his face white under his safety helmet, swung his feet out. Lizzie watched as he made his way carefully out onto the wing strut, then let go. Her stomach swooped in sympathy with his.

'Good jump,' roared Tony, marking a card. 'Next.'

Sergio hauled himself to the door, speedily clambered onto the strut and was gone.

'Oh shit, I can't do this!' Casey's voice was hysterical. She was next in line and she looked panic-stricken.

'Next,' repeated Tony.

'I can't,' said Casey to Lizzie. 'Don't make me. I'm so scared.'

'You don't have to,' said Lizzie, who was just as scared. Perhaps neither of them had to. Nobody would force them, Simon had said.

'She's too scared to jump?' Tony asked Lizzie, and for an instant she saw derision in his eyes.

'I think so,' Lizzie said, gritting her teeth, 'but I'm not.'

Squeezing past Casey in the enclosed space, she got to the door and waited while Tony fixed her static line.

'Good luck,' he said, and this time there was admiration in his face.

Lizzie shot him a smile that was far braver than she felt and swung her legs out onto the wing strut. Three thousand feet below her, the fields of Cork were laid out like exquisite squares of silk: olive greens and pale golds, with rich emerald patches bordered by tiny walls. The really teeny moving dots were cars. She would not think of how far away it all was. Instead, she took a deep breath and edged her way out until she'd gone far enough. All she had to do now was let go. The training drill clicked in and Lizzie let herself fall back into the sky as if she was falling onto a feather bed.

'One thousand, two thousand, three thousand, four thousand,' she screamed into the air. She felt a jerk and her body swooped upwards. 'Check canopy,' she roared. Looking up, there it was: the most welcome sight in the world at that precise moment, her own parachute canopy.

'OmiGod, omiGod, omiGod!' she screamed with relief and, suddenly, the fear was gone and in its place was delight at this incredible new sensation. She was floating on the wind, lifted by heat currents, flying over the world like a bird of prey. Now she let herself admire the countryside below her, her eager eyes drinking in the familiar sights from an unfamiliar angle. The training school looked totally different from the air and, pulling gently on the cords that controlled the parachute, she steered towards the big white X she'd been told to aim for.

She loved it, just loved it. Lizzie began to laugh when she thought of how scared she'd been. This was joyful, perfect pleasure, total sensation, and it was ending all too quickly. The only hard bit was gauging how far away the ground was. It was coming closer and closer but where . . . ? The ground rushed up to meet her and as Lizzie landed just beside the big X, she concentrated on falling correctly, letting her legs act as a giant spring to break her fall. Despite the jolt of coming into contact with the earth, she managed to roll with the impact and ended up with a better landing than she'd ever managed in training.

'Well done. You score ten out of ten,' said Simon, holding out a hand.

'That was the most incredible experience ever!' gasped Lizzie, eyes shining. 'I loved it.'

'Good.' Simon pulled her to her feet and, on impulse, Lizzie reached up and kissed him on the cheek.

'Thank you!' she beamed.

'Thank *you*,' grinned Simon.

'When can I do it again?' Lizzie couldn't wait to experience another jump. 'And higher. Can I jump from a higher altitude? That went so quickly, I want to spend more time up there.'

Simon helped her haul up her parachute. 'If you jumped tandem with an instructor, you could.'

'Please,' begged Lizzie.

'You could jump with me,' he said softly.

Excitement and the pride of her achievement raced through Lizzie's normally sedate veins. 'I'd like that,' she said, gazing at him.

It was after three by the time the whole squad of novices had jumped and the ones who'd enjoyed it stayed around to watch the local parachute club jump.

Casey had gone home as soon as the plane landed.

'I'm so sorry,' she mumbled to Lizzie, white-faced and red-eyed as she struggled out of her jumpsuit.

'Don't be,' Lizzie said, hugging the younger woman tightly. 'It's not for everyone. You were brave enough to get this far so don't be too hard on yourself.'

'But you did it,' Casey said.

'I know.' Nobody was as surprised as Lizzie herself. She'd been so scared and she'd beaten that fear.

The local club were all self-assured, joking and laughing, all in customised flying suits that looked miles better than the trainees' khaki ones. Their bright yellow, hot red and multicoloured suits turned the whole event into a gaudy festival. There were as many women jumpers as men, and as harnesses and chutes were checked and packed, the group laughed and joked with the familiarity of people who knew each other well.

Simon was piloting the plane for the first jump and Lizzie watched him surreptitiously as she sat on a bench outside reception, holding a mug of tea and munching on a biscuit. She was so hungry now that she'd jumped. It must be the adrenaline, she thought.

'Have another.' Teddy, the bearded receptionist, proffered the pack of digestive biscuits. The metamorphosis of Teddy was almost as astonishing as her enjoyment of the jump. Now that the real jumpers were here and the only novices left were ones who'd proved themselves, Teddy had unstiffened and seemed like a different guy. It was as if he could only communicate with people who loved what he did.

'It gets into your blood,' he said, sitting down beside Lizzie with his own mug of tea.

'Do all the club jump every weekend?' Lizzie asked.

'Some jump every weekend, others every month. It depends on your finances and your life. Now Samson over there,' he indicated a guy in an acid-green suit, 'would jump every day but his wife goes mad when he's gone all weekend. She's never jumped.'

To Teddy, the world was clearly divided into jumpers and non-jumpers.

'Does your wife jump?' Lizzie enquired.

'Not married, but my girlfriend does. She's gone up with Tony today.'

'And Simon?' she asked idly.

'Simon's divorced.'

'Really?' Lizzie took a big bite of biscuit and smiled to herself.

When Simon's plane landed, he sought Lizzie out.

'On Sundays, we often go for dinner after jumping. Fancy coming out with us?' he asked. The invitation was casual but the excitement that coursed through Lizzie was anything but.

'I'd love to,' she said brightly, then her face fell as she thought of Debra at home, waiting eagerly for her treat.

'But what?' prompted Simon.

'But nothing,' Lizzie replied, Joe's words resonating in her head. *You have a life too, Mum.* 'There was something I meant to do but it can wait until tomorrow.' Invitations to dinner with men she was attracted to didn't come round every day. Debra would understand.

There were ten of them around a long table in Jimmy's Seafood Shack, and somehow Simon had slipped into the seat beside Lizzie. When they'd got to the restaurant, she'd nipped off to the loo and done her best to tidy her unruly tortoiseshell hair without a comb, raking it out of the ponytail with her fingers. She didn't have a scrap of make-up apart from her strawberry lip balm, an ancient phial of Miss Dior of uncertain vintage, and some mascara, but she did her best with it. Anyhow, she decided, with her cheekbones burnished with freckles from the day's sun and a shine in her eyes from the sheer excitement of her jump, she had a healthy natural glow that suited her better than cosmetics. As a final sop to beauty, she took off her sweatshirt and wrapped it round her waist, opening a couple of buttons on her candy-striped shirt so that a hint of cleavage was visible. The *Vogue* model scouts would not stop her in the street to sign her up, but she didn't look half bad.

Her last bit of preparation was to phone Debra. Nobody answered the house phone so she left a message there.

'Hi, Debs, sorry I'm going to be late. We'll have to postpone our dinner until tomorrow. And if you've gone over to Barry's to sort things out, just leave me a note to say so. Love you.' She left a similar message on her daughter's mobile phone, which was switched off. Hopefully, Debra was making it up with Barry and would have had to cry off dinner anyhow.

Back in the restaurant, the proprietor himself, Jimmy, was listing the specials of the day.

The flyers interrupted him to whoop at Lizzie's appearance.

'Nice perfume,' roared Tony, as Lizzie squeezed past him.

'Nice shirt,' said the guy sitting opposite as she wriggled into her seat, giving him an unintentional flash of creamy skin.

'Open another button.'

'Oi, you yobbos, leave her alone,' ordered Simon.

'Ignore them, they're in their second childhoods,' a woman named Tash told Lizzie. 'They don't know how to behave with attractive women.'

'Kids, all of them,' added Lena, who sat beside Teddy. 'Apart from you, darling,' she added to Teddy.

'It's only a bit of fun,' Simon murmured in her ear, 'although the perfume is nice.'

'You don't think I should open another button, then?' Lizzie whispered back.

The answering gleam in Simon's eyes told her that he liked the shirt too. 'Not here,' he said, his mouth so close to her ear that she could feel the warmth of his breath against her. 'Tony and Ron would have to be resuscitated if you did and I don't want to give either of them mouth-to-mouth.'

'Simon, stop monopolising Lizzie,' Tony said grumpily. 'You don't have to annexe the only decent woman we've seen in months.'

'Well, thank you!' said Tash in mock offence.

'To go back over the specials for tonight,' droned the proprietor, Jimmy, who'd been standing with his pad during the whole rowdy conversation.

'Sorry, Jimmy,' said Lena.

'Yeah, sorry,' everyone chorused, not sounding a bit sorry.

Tony poured red wine into Lizzie's glass. 'Drink up,' he said. 'You deserve to celebrate a five-star jump.'

'Yes,' said Simon. 'Five star in every way.'

'Three cheers for Lizzie, our newest member!' announced Ron.

This was what she'd been missing, Lizzie realised with a happy lurch: the feeling of belonging, of being accepted. Here, in this disparate group, she wasn't the divorced wife of Myles Shanahan, mother of two adults, and a woman who hadn't had a date for over twenty-five years. She was Lizzie, a person in her own right, and she had a gorgeous man beside her, a man who seemed to think that she was attractive too.

When the taxi dropped her home at midnight, Lizzie felt a fluttering of unease because it seemed as if every light in the house was on. The unease rocketed to high anxiety when, before she'd even had the chance to find her key, the front door was flung open.

'Debra, what's wrong?' she asked as her daughter stood, fully dressed, in the doorway like an avenging angel.

'You're asking me!' yelled Debra. 'I'm not the one who's been gone all day without a word of explanation. Where the hell have you been?'

'Just out with some friends,' said Lizzie, trying hard to sound sober. She felt giggly after all the wine they'd consumed in the restaurant – at least five glasses, and she wasn't used to drinking that much.

She'd had such a lovely day and such a wonderful evening, and now Debra was glaring at her with undisguised fury.

'Out?' Debra yelled. 'And what about me, stuck at home waiting for you?'

Lizzie made the fatal mistake of laughing. She couldn't help herself. It was just that Debra looked so stern and this was such a bizarre reversal of the normal roles. She was the mother, Debra was the daughter, and yet it was Debra yelling at *her* for staying out late. It was funny . . .

The giggling really finished Debra off. 'How dare you stand there and laugh at me?' she said with rage. 'I've been worried out of my mind about you.' Lizzie plonked herself down on the chair in the hall and let her little bum bag drop to the floor.

'I phoned your mobile and left a message. Didn't you get it?'

'I got it all right,' screeched Debra, still at the same ear-piercing volume. 'But I wanted to talk to you. We were supposed to be going out together tonight. Didn't you think about that? And I've been in such a state about Barry.'

'Oh, Debra,' sighed Lizzie, the giggles turning to remorse in an instant, 'I'm so sorry. I was just having some fun with some new friends of mine and the parachute jump had gone so well and we just wanted to celebrate –'

'Parachute jump?'

Lizzie hadn't thought Debra could shout any louder but, somehow, she managed to. Lizzie was sure the people next door could hear.

'What parachute jump? What the hell are you talking about?'

'Oh, gosh,' said Lizzie slowly, 'I'd been meaning to tell you about it but I didn't want to say anything until I was sure I could go through with it.' She hiccuped, earning herself another furious glare from her daughter.

'You mean you did a parachute jump?' demanded Debra, the disdain in her voice making it clear she thought parachute jumps were anti-social behaviour on a par with skinny dipping in public places. 'At your age?'

Lizzie nodded tearfully. Suddenly she didn't feel like the brave woman any more, the woman who was going to work her way through that 'Things to Do Before You're Thirty' list with style and brio. She felt like a stupid forty-nine-year-old woman who thought she could reclaim her lost youth by jumping out of a plane.

'It was for charity,' she muttered. 'I thought it would be a nice tribute to Sally to raise money for breast cancer in her name, that's all. And a parachute jump is a good way of doing it because people are impressed and I would make lots of money.'

'But at *your* age,' Debra said.

'You can parachute jump at any age,' protested Lizzie.

'Well, I'm sure they *say* that,' her daughter said with a sniff, 'but they don't really mean it. They don't want older people like you jumping, do they?'

Utterly deflated, Lizzie stared down at her cleavage and the extra buttons she'd opened in a vain attempt to look sexy. Who had she been kidding?

'No, I suppose they don't,' she said miserably. Maybe she'd imagined what a wonderful evening it had been: maybe all the other parachute jumpers had been secretly laughing at her, this older divorced woman hoping to start a new life and make new friends with all the cool skydivers. She must have been crazy to think she could fit in or that Simon really liked her. Maybe he was secretly laughing at her too. In a flash, all the joy of the day was gone and Lizzie felt miserable, old and tired. Not to mention a little bit drunk.

'And you actually jumped?' asked Debra finally.

Lizzie nodded. 'Yes, I did.'

Just half an hour earlier, she'd been so proud of her jump, so proud that she hadn't been too terrified or chickened out when she was sitting in the tiny plane thousands of feet above the ground. She didn't feel very proud now. Debra had needed her and Lizzie had let her beloved daughter down.

'I'm so sorry, darling,' she said, desperately trying not to slur her words. She knew that would only enrage Debra more. 'We can go out tomorrow night, if you like –'

'No, thank you very much. I'm sorry if I'm such a burden on you,' snapped Debra. 'I won't intrude on your precious social life again. I thought you'd be glad to have me staying here with you, getting you out of the house. But seeing as I'm not welcome after all I won't stay a minute longer.' Debra picked up her handbag from the hall table. 'I'm going over to see Dad. I need to know I've still got one normal parent who isn't trying to recapture their lost youth!'

Triumphant after delivering her parting shot, she marched out of the front door, leaving Lizzie feeling thoroughly miserable and guilty. It wasn't bad enough that she felt like a useless mother, now Debra was going to race over to Myles's house and tell him the news too.

Totally forgetting her plan to drink a pint of water and take a couple of painkillers to ward off the inevitable hang-over, Lizzie went upstairs to her bedroom. Clambering into bed without so much as brushing her teeth or taking off her mascara, she fell into a heavy, miserable sleep.

She paid for it all the next morning. At five past eight Lizzie was lying in bed, knowing that she had to get up for work. But her head ached so much that she just didn't know how she was going to face another day – a Monday, worse luck. Just five more minutes in bed and she'd be ready . . . Then the phone rang. Was it always that loud? she wondered as the shrill noise beat a tattoo in her skull.

'Morning, Lizzie,' said her ex-husband's voice. 'How's your head?'

Lizzie felt about an inch tall. 'Oh, don't you start, please,' she begged. Who knew what Debra had told her father the previous night?

Myles always stuck up for Debra – she was his darling little daughter, after all. Even when she dropped out of nursing, Myles wouldn't hear a word said against her. He'd be annoyed that Lizzie hadn't been with Debra in her hour of need. She waited for the lecture and wished she had the energy to tell Myles where to get off. But no lecture was forthcoming.

'I suppose you know Debra's here,' Myles said heavily.

'She said she was going to see you last night,' Lizzie replied, and instantly went into apologetic mode. 'It's all my fault because she and I were supposed to go out and then something came up –'

'You don't have to apologise or explain to me, Lizzie,' said Myles quickly. 'You're your own boss, you're entitled to your own life. I'm just phoning to say what the hell are we going to do with Debra?'

If he'd said what the hell are we going to do about the situation in the Middle East, Lizzie couldn't have been more surprised. For once, Myles didn't sound like the doting daddy prepared to do anything to pacify his twenty-three-year-old daughter. He sounded – what was it exactly? – yes, irritated. That was it. He sounded irritated.

'She just landed here last night in floods of tears and Sabine was over and we were watching the new James Bond film, and suddenly, there's Debra in hysterics. I didn't know what to do,' Myles said. 'She bawled her eyes out and said it was all your fault and that she wasn't going back to stay with you ever again, that she hated you just as much as she hated Barry. Oh, Lizzie, it was a nightmare.'

Despite the thumping pain in her head, Lizzie couldn't suppress a grin.

'But I thought Debra and Sabine got on so well,' she said wickedly.

'They do,' acknowledged Myles, 'but not when Debra's

in floods of tears and won't listen to reason. I didn't even know she'd left Barry. I can't believe she did. To think of the money we spent on that wedding and now – after what? A month, two months? – it's all over. I was never so shocked in my whole life. Why didn't you tell me, Lizzie?'

'It wasn't my place to tell you,' said Lizzie. She sat up in bed to see if her head could take going vertical. Woozy definitely, but not too much pain. 'To be honest, I thought the argument with Barry was just a storm in a tea cup and it would all blow over. But Joe thinks it might be more serious than that. That's why I feel a bit guilty about leaving her last night,' Lizzie admitted. 'Joe seems to think that the marriage was doomed from the start. Did you know that Barry had to be begged to turn up at the church that day?'

From the silence at the other end of the phone, it was clear that Myles had no idea. Well, it was hardly what any parent would expect. They'd spent every penny they possessed – and some belonging to the bank – giving their only daughter the most incredible day of her life, so to hear afterwards that the wedding had the prospective longevity of long-life milk was a bit of a shock. For some reason, the leaking kitchen roof came into Lizzie's head. Myles wasn't made of money either. He was probably thinking exactly the same thing she was, imagining what he could have done with the money if it hadn't been gobbled up by Debra's princess dress, hundreds of exquisite roses and a huge reception.

And now he was stuck with a distraught daughter sleeping on his couch or probably borrowing his bed, knowing Myles.

Suddenly, Lizzie felt sorry for him. For all the fact that Myles had found a new life for himself, he still wasn't able to escape the old one.

'What are we going to do about Debra, then?' asked Myles pitifully.

'Where is she now?' Lizzie enquired.

'Still asleep,' Myles said. 'You know how hard it is to get her up in the morning. I just can't wake her. And I don't know if she's going to work or what. And Sabine and I are going to the theatre tonight, so I don't know what she's going to do then. And what about Barry and the new house and everything . . . ?' His voice trailed off.

'Look,' said Lizzie decisively, 'if I can get a couple of hours off work and come over, then perhaps we can sort all of this out. What do you think?'

'That would be great.' Myles sounded incredibly relieved. 'I can't just leave her here. She was so distressed last night. Do you think . . .' He sounded as though the idea had just occurred to him. 'Do you think we could phone Barry and get him to come over too and perhaps they might get back together and everything would be all right?' He was like a child hoping that Santa would bring the right toy for Christmas.

'I'd love to see Debra and Barry sort things out,' said Lizzie, 'but I think it might be a mistake to just bring him on over to your apartment. They both clearly need space. If Barry had wanted to talk to Debra, he would have known where to find her before now.'

Lizzie let that sink in. She'd hoped that Barry would storm up to her house, declaring undying love, and sweep Debra off to their home, but now that he hadn't she'd begun to think that the rift was serious. 'Perhaps we'd better let them cool off a little and then we can set up a meeting and be there to . . .'

'To referee?' Myles suggested.

Lizzie laughed. 'Yes, to referee.' She couldn't help thinking of what Joe had said – that Debra and Barry's marriage was doomed from the start because Debra was a spoiled child and would always want her own way. Lizzie felt Joe was wrong. Debra was just a sensitive girl. She wasn't spoiled – she was sweet and kind. She just needed delicate handling, and perhaps Barry hadn't figured that out yet. Lizzie resolved to talk to her son-in-law and explain to him just what sort of person Debra was. She wanted her daughter to be happy and she'd do anything to make sure she was.

'I'll see you in three-quarters of an hour,' she said to Miles, getting out of bed. Sitting up had been fine but standing up was another matter entirely. Lizzie felt the full weight of five glasses of wine hit her. 'Actually, better make that an hour and a half.' She'd need the extra time just to make herself presentable.

Then, she remembered that her car was still outside the restaurant where she'd had dinner last night. She'd have to get a taxi to pick the car up first.

'Make it three hours,' she said.

Clare Morgan was very sweet about giving Lizzie a few hours off that morning for a family emergency, which made Lizzie feel even worse. There wouldn't be a family emergency if she weren't such a hopeless mother who had gone out partying with a load of strangers when her own daughter needed her.

Hangover and guilt combined to make her feel utterly miserable as, only an hour and three-quarters later, she headed into Cork towards Myles's home. When they'd split up, she'd half expected him to buy a neat little town house nearby, but he'd gone for an apartment in the city centre instead and somehow that seemed to symbolise his new free life.

Lizzie wouldn't have liked an apartment herself, but she admired her ex-husband for choosing something so utterly different. He and Sabine were serious about each other, according to Debra, but Sabine hadn't moved in yet. Despite everything, she'd liked Sabine when they'd met at the wedding. It wasn't Sabine's fault that Lizzie felt old and frumpy. Lizzie had done that to herself. Nobody could be blamed for the pit of despondency into which she'd allowed herself to fall.

And her feeble attempts at making a life for herself hadn't been very successful, had they? Look at last night – doing something as wild as making a parachute jump had only managed to start a family row.

It was well after ten when she rang the doorbell of Myles's

apartment, and she got quite a shock when Sabine opened the front door. Maybe she had moved in after all.

'Lizzie, hello,' said Sabine warmly. 'It's lovely to see you. Come on in. I'm going out in a moment,' she added, 'so I won't be in your way.'

'That's OK,' Lizzie interrupted her. 'Don't feel you have to go out. We're hardly having a secret family conference. How is Debra?' she added in a whisper.

'Oh, fine,' Sabine whispered back with an overbright smile, leading the way down the hall.

Myles's living room was decorated with a nautical theme, complete with prints of ships, marine memorabilia and a huge brass clock made out of a porthole. Even the big couch was a deep ocean blue. Debra lay on it like Madame Récamier, looking wistful and miserable as if she was just about to shuffle off this mortal coil. A box of cereal, an empty bowl and some milk lay on the coffee table in front of her, showing that even if she was in the depths of despair, Debra had been able to eat some breakfast.

Myles sat on a matelot-striped armchair beside her, looking totally fed up.

'Hi, Lizzie,' he said enthusiastically when he saw his ex-wife. He got to his feet and was about to put his arms around Lizzie, the way he normally greeted her, but then he remembered that Sabine was there.

Etiquette books didn't exactly explain how to embrace your ex-wife when your possible future wife was in the room, Lizzie thought ruefully.

'Hi, Myles,' she said fondly. 'Hello, Debra,' she added.

'Hello,' said Debra in a weak little voice.

She looked so pale and exhausted that Lizzie felt a fresh blast of guilt hit her. Poor Debra. She'd been so upset about Barry, she needed her family around her.

Lizzie rushed over to the couch, got to her knees and threw her arms around her daughter.

'Oh, Debra, pet, I'm so sorry I was late last night. I just got carried away with these people I was with. It's not that

I forgot you – you know I'd never forget you. I love you and we can sort all of this out. Now, please won't you come on home with me and . . .' She racked her brains to think of some tempting treat to entice her daughter back home. Whenever Debra had been miserable as a child, chocolate fudge pie from Mario's in Dunmore's main street had always worked a treat. When she was a bit older, the promise of going shopping with Lizzie, using Lizzie's credit card naturally, had always worked. What exactly did you offer your grown-up daughter as a treat when she'd split up from her husband? 'We could go shopping,' Lizzie suggested. 'I'll take the day off work,' she added, crossing her fingers that Clare Morgan would continue to see this as a family emergency and not fire her. 'I'm sure you need lots of new clothes and –'

'Shopping would be great,' said Debra happily, sitting up brightly on the couch, all resemblance to Madame Récamier gone. 'I saw some fabulous sandals in BTs the other day. They were hideously expensive but they were just beautiful and I know they'd suit me. Oh, Mum, yeah, let's go shopping.'

'Shopping is all very well, but what about Barry?' asked Sabine in a sober tone. 'Don't you want to sort things out with him?'

Debra glared at Sabine. 'I think Barry is my business,' she snapped crossly. 'Family business,' she added, in case Sabine hadn't got the message.

Sabine managed to keep the calm smile on her face. 'It might be family business,' she said evenly, 'but because I was staying here with your father when you came over last night, I'm involved. I'm part of the family business. You can't run away from the argument, you have to face it.'

Both Lizzie and Myles looked at Sabine in alarm.

'Er, Sabine,' said Myles, wanting to ward off an argument, 'it's really up to Debs how she sorts things out with Barry. I'm sure they'll work it out in their own time.'

'Yes,' said Debra sharply. 'It's nobody else's business but mine.'

It looked as if Sabine might possibly say something to all of this but she managed to hold her tongue. 'Yes, of course,' she said.

'Come on, Mum.' Debra got to her feet quickly. 'Let's go.'

On the way downstairs, Debra could barely contain her rage. 'The nerve of her to say that to me,' she said with fury. 'How dare she talk to me like that? What does she know about marriage? What does she know about me and Barry? Just because she was at the wedding for five minutes, she thinks she knows all about us.'

At least, thought Lizzie, with Debra so fired up about Sabine, she'd forgotten she was supposed to be angry with Lizzie. That was a relief. Lizzie couldn't cope with Debra when she was on the receiving end of her wrath.

Debra was going on and on about Sabine and the nerve of her. Lizzie managed to tune out but found herself wondering, was it natural for a mother to be so nervous about her daughter's moods? Because she was, wasn't she? And so was Myles, to be frank. No, Lizzie decided. They weren't nervous of Debra's moods, not at all. That was the wrong way to look at it. They just hated her getting upset because Debra was sensitive, after all. And Sabine hadn't understood that.

They reached Lizzie's car, where it was parked beside all the shiny new cars in the apartment block car park.

'Jeez, Mum,' said Debra, 'this car is such an old wreck. Why don't you get a new one?'

'I can't afford to,' blurted out Lizzie, almost before she'd thought of what she was saying.

'Poor Mum.' Debra patted her mother on the shoulder. 'You need a new job. A new job and more money. That would be brilliant.'

'Yes,' said Lizzie weakly, thinking that she still had to ring up Clare Morgan and ask for the rest of the day off for the shopping expedition. She might be looking for a new job sooner than she thought. Still, she wasn't going to let that ruin the day.

'OK, Debra,' she said brightly, 'where to next?'

The sparkle had returned to Debra's eyes. 'The most expensive shop in town, of course,' she said happily. 'Let's burn some credit card plastic.'

'Right,' said Lizzie, putting the gas bill, the electricity bill and the mortgage out of her mind. She'd sort something out. As she drove out of the car park, Lizzie couldn't help but think about what Sabine had said. She'd been right. Debra *did* need to sort things out with Barry. It wasn't enough for her to put the argument with her new husband on some metaphorical back burner. But then, the argument had only just happened and poor Debs needed time to get over it. That was it.

Lizzie drove into the mid-morning traffic. She wouldn't tell Joe what Sabine had said, she decided, because she had an uncomfortable feeling that he'd agree with her. If there was a power struggle going on, somehow Debra had won round one.

Families – who needed them? Then, Lizzie felt guilty at such a thought as she remembered Erin, who had no family. Erin had been so fired up about finding her relations again and Lizzie wondered if she'd done anything about it. Lizzie hoped she had. Erin had obviously spent years trying to pretend that she could do without the love of her family, but Lizzie knew it had been pretence. Erin needed her roots, just like everybody else.

CHAPTER TWENTY-FIVE

The number for Erin's old home in the Dublin suburb of Kilbarrett had changed, the recorded voice told her sharply. Blast. She hung up and tried Directory Enquiries, but despite a lengthy conversation, there was no listing for Mary and Pat Flynn in Dublin and there was no way the operator would give her the current number for their old home.

Disappointed, Erin hung up. There must be another way. Then, she thought of the Gallagher family, who'd lived next door. Erin had always had their number when she was a child – Mum had insisted upon it. Mrs Gallagher was a good friend of her mother's and the logic was simple: 'If something happens and you can't reach me, phone Mrs Gallagher.'

In the tattered old address book that Erin had kept all these years, she found the Gallagher number. Her heart beating loudly, she rang it.

Mrs Gallagher didn't answer the phone. Instead, Erin got through to a friendly woman who'd lived there since the Gallaghers had sold up. The Flynns were long gone too, the woman said. But, no, she didn't know where the family had moved to. She'd love it if she could remember but honestly, it was four years ago and she couldn't recall what she'd done last week.

No, it was fine, Erin reassured her, but did Mrs Cora Flaherty still live next door on the other side? Mrs Flaherty was the nearest thing Kilbarrett had to the all-seeing eye of the oracle, as she knew everyone and everything. Mrs Flaherty would not only know where the Flynn family had moved to, but would undoubtedly have their phone number off by heart and would be able to relate in a flash what they'd had to eat last Sunday.

But Mrs Flaherty had died, didn't Erin know?

Oh yes, said the woman, it was terrible. Poor Mrs Flaherty had never got over those young thugs breaking into her house five years ago when she was at bingo and vandalising it. Pneumonia got her in the end, but that was the official story. Everyone said she'd died of a mixture of fear and a broken heart that her beloved home was no longer safe.

Erin felt sick. Had thugs threatened her darling Mum too, or jeered at Dad over the back wall as he'd tended his flowers? Kerry would have murdered anyone who'd looked crossways at her family but Kerry was almost a forty-year-old woman now, not a feisty tearaway. Erin knew from Chicago that young thugs took no notice of anyone, least of all women, and her family would have been sitting ducks for trouble.

Remorse and fear engulfed her. Anything could have happened to them and where had she been? Feeling sorry for herself in America and still blaming her family for doing nothing more than trying to protect her.

'It's terrible to lose touch,' the woman said companionably. 'What relation are you exactly, again?'

Erin couldn't bear to tell the truth but she felt that she couldn't lie either. 'Too close to have lost touch,' she admitted with shame.

'Well, you wouldn't know that many people round here now,' the woman said. 'We've had dozens of for sale signs on this road in the past year. The new industrial estate and the shopping centre have made it one of Dublin's up-and-coming suburbs, would you believe.'

'What about the Ryans or the O'Sheas or the Maguires?' Erin asked without much hope.

'The Ryans are long gone and I don't know any O'Shea family but the Maguires are still there.'

Erin's heart lifted. Vanessa Maguire had been a great pal

of Kerry's. She was sure to know where the family had moved to.

'You don't have their number by any chance?'

'Hold on, I'm sure it's here somewhere in my directory . . .' She found the number and recited it slowly.

'Thanks a million,' Erin said gratefully.

'No bother. Any time,' said the woman, and hung up after saying goodbye.

Although she was sitting in the cool sanctuary of her beautiful new apartment, Erin's mind was in the small hall of number seventy-eight, where the phone had sat on a low table under a print of an Irish country cottage. She wondered if the new owners had moved the phone. Probably. But Erin would never forget talking to her friends from school on that phone, perched on the bottom stair, the phone cord stretched across the old rug.

The country cottage print had been as much part of the scenery in the hall as the coatstand and the red and black floor tiles. The print had faded over time but Mum had always loved it and refused to move it. Erin could see the picture with incredible clarity: the cottage nestling in the crook of hills that loomed purple with heather. Mum had been brought up in a house not unlike that in a small village in County Wexford, that was why she loved it.

'Bet you couldn't wait to get out of the back end of nowhere,' Kerry said once, but her mother had looked wistful.

'There's more to life than city smoke,' she pointed out. 'One day, you'll see.'

Erin hoped that wherever her grandparents had moved to they were free of both city smoke and thugs, and could see mountains purple with heather in the background.

She dialled the Maguires and got an answering machine, so she hung up to think what she'd say. This would not be any ordinary message.

'Hello, this is Erin Flynn who used to live at number seventy-eight. I was hoping to speak to some of the Maguire family who could help me trace the whereabouts of the Flynns.' She reeled off her number and said that if the Maguires phoned and she was out, she'd phone right back. 'Please call. Bye.'

All she had to do now was wait.

The phone rang at four that afternoon as Erin was packing away groceries. She leaped for the receiver, or leaped as quickly as a pregnant woman can – Erin's waist had long since disappeared and she'd put on eighteen pounds, so her days of leaping were gone.

'Hello?'

'Is this Erin?' It was a woman's voice but not one she recognised.

'Yes.'

'This is Geena Maguire, I married Clark, remember?'

Erin could remember Clark all right, Vanessa's geeky older brother. Vanessa and Kerry used to predict that poor old Clark would never find a girlfriend because he was too weird, with his long dark hair and the earring, which he thought made him look cool but which the girls reckoned made him look even geekier. Geena, she didn't remember. Good for Clark.

'Of course I remember Clark, but you two must have got married after I'd left.'

'Well,' Geena said thoughtfully, 'we're five years married now because little Poppy is just four. We live here and Mrs Maguire lives with her sister in Liverpool. Vanessa's in Ballsbridge. She's got her own public relations firm now, did you know that?'

'No,' said Erin. There were so many things she didn't know.

'What happened anyway that made you run off?' asked Geena inquisitively. 'I always wanted to know but Vanessa wouldn't tell me.'

'Just a silly family row,' Erin said quickly. 'I'm in a bit of a rush, Geena – is Vanessa in the phone book or can you give me her number?'

'Lady Muck in the phone book? Lord no, but you can find her under VMPR. Vampire, that's what I call it. Get it? Ha ha.'

Vanessa's staff certainly protected her as if she was a descendant of Count Dracula who needed shielding from people wielding stakes.

Erin had tried explaining that she was an old friend who just needed a few words with Vanessa but the VMPR staff weren't giving an inch. Even Erin's ball-busting get-past-anyone routine didn't work. She left her number, expecting it to be filed in the black plastic filing cabinet. She'd have to think of some other way of tracing her family. Perhaps a trip to Kilbarrett would help.

Two days passed and July became August. Erin sat with a Dublin phone book and tried every avenue she could think of to track the Flynn family. She was sure they'd stay in Dublin and she was trying to work her way through the huge list of Flynns. The estate agent who'd sold the house didn't keep records of where people moved to and the Post Office wouldn't give out information on change of address.

'There must be relatives you could contact,' Greg suggested that evening as they sat on their small balcony beside the two azaleas in pots that made up their garden.

'There are,' Erin said, cursing the fact that she hadn't paid much attention to her aunts and uncles when she was a kid, 'but I don't have their numbers and there's no joy in the phone book. Dad's three brothers were all older, and Mum's sister lives outside Manchester, I don't know where, although we went there once on holiday.'

She thought that she could recognise her Uncle Larry's house in Phibsboro if she saw it, but she had no idea of the address and none of the Flynns listed in Phibsboro in the phone book had turned out to be Uncle Larry.

'I'm a moron,' she said dismally. 'How could I not know these things?'

'You're not a moron,' Greg said comfortingly. 'You're

normal. I mean, look at my Aunt Lily. I know her house like I know my parents' house but I don't know her phone number. I've an idea – why don't we hire a private investigator? Investigators know how to trace people properly.'

Erin considered this. The idea of using a private investigator to find her family was sensible but just highlighted what an utter mess she'd made of things. Hiring an investigator to trace a family you'd never met was one thing; hiring one to find a family you'd turned your back on was another entirely.

'I suppose you're right,' she said, staring out at the view of the estuary. Their second-floor apartment was situated on high ground from where they had a view of the harbour. The spire of Dunmore church and the faux battlements of the Victorian Hotel could be seen reflected in the calm smoky blue of the water. A pleasure cruiser on the water was dwarfed by a passing cargo ship chugging its way into Cork like a giant lorry labouring up a steep incline.

She and Greg were so happy here, Erin realised. The thought of sharing the rest of their lives with their son or daughter had made her so very happy. But being reunited with her family would close the circle, make life complete. Then she'd be content. But that might never happen, and if it didn't, she'd have to accept it.

Stretching out her hand, she found Greg's and held it tightly. They sat in comfortable silence.

When the phone rang, Greg uncurled his long body and went inside. Erin strained to hear who it was.

'Vanessa Maguire for you,' said Greg, leaning out of the patio doors.

'Hello, stranger.' Even Vanessa's voice was the same: faintly hoarse and husky, but definitely with posher overtones than could ever have emerged from Kilbarrett.

'Hi, Vanessa,' said Erin. 'Thanks for returning my call. I was afraid you wouldn't get my message.'

'Are you kidding? If anyone in work forgot to pass on a

message to me, they wouldn't be working for me for much longer.'

Erin grinned. Same old Vanessa. Improved vowel sounds couldn't disguise the feistiness she'd always possessed. When Kerry and Vanessa had teamed up, the local lads hadn't stood a chance.

'Where the hell have you been, Erin? Talk about vanishing off the face of the earth.'

Erin sat down on the couch. 'Don't have a go at me, Vanessa,' she begged. 'I was stupid, I know, but Kerry didn't help matters by telling me not to bother phoning again.'

Vanessa snorted. 'You know your sister. Her mouth works faster than her brain. She was angry with you, that's all, and she regretted what she said.'

'But how come nobody ever replied to my letters?' That was what had haunted Erin. She knew that Kerry was hot-headed and might easily have shot her mouth off, telling Erin not to phone back and regretting it later, but letters were different. Not replying to her letters was practically a sign that Erin had been cast out of the family.

'What letters?' demanded Vanessa sharply.

'The ones I sent afterwards.'

'Nobody told me about any letters and Kerry told me everything,' Vanessa said. 'When did you send them?'

'Over four years ago, nearly five,' Erin said, thinking back to when she and Greg had been getting married and he'd encouraged her to try to heal the rift.

'Well, that explains it then. The dozy cow who bought the place wouldn't have passed anything along.'

'So they probably never got my letters, then?' Erin couldn't describe the relief she felt. It was like having an enormous weight lifted from her shoulders. Her family hadn't turned their back on her; they'd simply never received the letters in which she'd begged forgiveness and told them about her new life and about Greg.

'They moved over five years ago.'

'Are they all OK?' Erin was afraid of hearing the answer.

'Fine. Your dad's great since he had the hip replaced, and your mother's fighting fit although she isn't as mobile as she used to be.'

Erin noted that Vanessa called them her parents and not her grandparents. Perhaps Kerry hadn't told her everything, then. But at least if she'd known, she might understand Erin's running away. Otherwise, she'd assume Erin was nothing more than a heartless bitch.

Vanessa went on: 'And Kerry, well, she's great considering what she's been through. She's a survivor.'

'What's she been through?' Erin asked rapidly.

'I forgot, you're out of the loop on that too. That's what she needed you for, Erin.' For the first time, there was genuine reproach in Vanessa's voice.

'What?'

'Breast cancer.'

Erin was glad she was sitting down or she'd have fallen to her knees. 'Breast cancer?' she repeated, knowing she sounded like the village idiot.

'Yeah. She's been clear for four years though, so fingers crossed.'

'I can't believe it. I should have known . . .' Erin felt so hopeless and helpless. That Kerry should have gone through this horrific disease that had killed Sally and she hadn't known . . .

'How could you know?' Vanessa was not the sort of woman to waste time on what might have been. 'So, I guess you want to see her?'

'Do you think she'd want to see me?' asked Erin hesitantly.

'Of course she would. She loves you; you're her sister. She's changed, Erin. Cancer changed her.'

'I can understand that,' Erin replied softly, thinking of the fear Kerry had gone through without Erin, her sister, to support her. Because that's what Erin was. They'd been brought up as sisters and that's what they were in their hearts, no matter that the actual bloodline was more

374

complicated. If only she'd been there for Kerry when she'd been sick.

'I didn't tell her you'd been in touch,' Vanessa said, 'not until I knew what you wanted to do.'

'I want to see her, and Mum and Dad,' Erin said. Please God let them want to see her.

'I'll phone her and give her your number, then,' Vanessa said matter-of-factly. 'Then it's up to her. Let her talk to your mum and dad – you don't want to give them a shock at their age.'

'No,' agreed Erin. 'Where do they live now?'

'Your mum and dad are in Wexford. They've got a cottage on the coast, it's lovely. Kerry and Peter live in Portlaoise.'

Erin didn't ask who Peter was. She'd asked enough. Kerry, if she phoned, could tell her the rest.

But there was one more thing she had to ask, even if it was a question that Vanessa couldn't really answer.

'Do you think they'll be able to forgive me?' she asked tremulously.

'If it had been my family, I'd say no,' Vanessa remarked. 'My mother wouldn't let me inside the door if I'd buggered off for nine years. But your mum and dad are cut from a different cloth. They'll be happy to see you.'

'And Kerry?'

'Well, she might give you a clip round the ear,' Vanessa laughed, 'but who knows with Kerry? Your sister's always been one mad mare.'

And with that, Erin had to be content.

Greg was waiting eagerly to see what had happened.

Erin sank back onto her chair on the balcony and told him everything.

'She'll call,' Greg said confidently.

'But when?' asked Erin. Now that she'd made contact she felt a strange combination of elation and anxiety. There were so many 'what ifs'. What if Kerry didn't get in touch? Or what if she did, only to tell Erin to get the hell out of their lives because she'd hurt them all enough already?

She moved uncomfortably in her chair, rubbing her back with one hand to try to banish the ever-present lower backache.

'Why don't I run you a bath and you can soak away for an hour?' Greg suggested.

She nodded. The bath was probably the best place for her. There she could sit and mope in solitude.

Fifteen minutes later, she was sitting neck-deep in bubbles with the bathroom door shut. Greg had lit the calming candles he'd bought her when she first knew she was pregnant. He'd spent ages buying them because he knew that some of the aromatherapy scents Erin loved were forbidden in pregnancy.

He was so good to her, Erin thought tearfully. He was a good person and was going to make such a good father. If only she'd listened to him in the first place and made a proper attempt to get in touch with Mum, Dad and Kerry, then she wouldn't be in this position. You could explain away three or four years of not getting in touch, but not longer, not nine. Nine was turning your back on people.

Their baby deserved to have a family on Erin's side, and through her stupidity she'd messed that up. When the tears came, they ran down her cheeks in floods. She never heard the phone, and when Greg came into the candlelit bathroom with the portable in his hand, he found his wife sobbing.

Taking a towel from the rail, he dried her tears gently.

'It's Kerry for you,' he said, holding up the phone.

Erin stared at it through wet eyes and then grabbed it. 'Hello, Kerry,' she sobbed. 'Kerry, it's Erin. I'm so sorry.'

'Oh, Erin, where in God's name have you been? We missed you,' said Kerry. 'We were so worried.'

The sound of her sister's voice set Erin off again, sobbing noisily into the phone.

'Jesus, are you all right? You're not in trouble, are you? In hospital? Prison?'

A half-sob, half-laugh escaped from Erin. Trust Kerry to

think of all the possibilities. *Midnight Express* had been one of her favourite films.

'No,' she said, snuffling. 'I'm fine, living outside Cork, and I'm married.'

There was a silence at the other end of the phone. Erin could imagine what was going on in her sister's mind: why the hell didn't you contact us before now?

'I wrote, Kerry. I wrote lots of times and nobody answered. After that time you'd told me not to phone again, I thought you all hated me and didn't want to hear from me.'

'You daft cow, course we wanted to hear from you,' said Kerry. 'I shouldn't have told you to stop phoning. I was angry, that's all. Mum and Dad were in bits about it all and you'd never given them a chance to tell you about Shannon, not properly.'

'I'm so sorry,' Erin repeated. 'I should never have run off like that . . .' She didn't know why she kept crying but she couldn't seem to stop.

'Are you all right?' asked Kerry.

'Yes,' said Erin, trying to stop crying. 'I'm a bit emotional. I've wanted to do this for so long and I thought you'd all hate me . . .'

'You sure you're not sick?' asked Kerry suspiciously.

'No. Pregnant,' sniffled Erin. 'My hormones are all over the place.'

'Pregnant, huh? To think of all the effort I went to when you were a teenager telling you how not to become pregnant,' said Kerry in amusement. 'Remember us going to the family planning clinic on Synge Street when you were going out with that Adrian bloke and I told you that you had to go on the pill or something?'

'And I didn't want to go because there was no way I was going the whole hog with Adrian.' Erin remembered it so clearly.

Kerry had been an incredible older sister, really. She'd done her best to protect Erin from everything. Looking back, Erin could see that Kerry hadn't wanted another member of the family going through the trauma of an unwanted pregnancy. But there had been more to it than just that. Kerry, for all her toughness and their daily arguments, had adored her baby sister and wanted to protect her from the world.

'You were so good to me,' Erin said softly.

'There you go. Water under the bridge.' She sounded like Kerry again: no time for crying over spilled milk. 'I suppose you'd better come and see me, unless you're the size of a house and can't travel.'

'I can travel,' mumbled Erin.

'You, pregnant, wow. I never thought I'd see the day. Peter and I have two daughters.' Kerry's voice was soft. 'They'll be thrilled to see an aunty from my side of the family.'

Meaning that Shannon still wasn't around, Erin realised.

'Can I come to see you tomorrow?' she asked.

'Same old Erin,' teased Kerry. 'Still the wild, impatient one with the red hair. It's still red, isn't it? You swore you hated red and wanted to be blonde.'

'Still a redhead,' Erin confirmed, then, going for the old family joke: 'No hair, just a red head. And you?'

'Ah, it was costing a fortune keeping me platinum,' laughed Kerry. 'I'm back to my natural mouse, or rather rat, with the odd blonde streak to remind me of my former glory.' She paused. 'It'll be good to see you, Erin.'

'Are you going to tell Mum and Dad I've been in touch?'

'We'll talk about it tomorrow,' promised her sister. 'I better give you directions to here.'

Erin climbed out of the bath, pulled on her dressing gown and took the phone into the bedroom to write down all the details. After Kerry had said goodbye, Erin remained sitting on her and Greg's bed, staring at the bit of paper on which she'd written the directions. After so long, she was finally going to see her family. Kerry, Mum, Dad. She felt a surge of emotion at the thought of hugging her parents and having them forgive her, because they would, she knew it. And maybe she'd even meet Shannon. Or maybe not. Shannon had never been around but perhaps that was the way the family wanted it in order for the deception to work. Erin hoped that was the reason why Shannon had never returned. The alternative was too painful to consider.

For the first time in years, Erin allowed herself to think about her birth mother and her real reasons for leaving. There was no way that Shannon could be called her real mother: that had been Mum; Shannon didn't deserve to be called that. After all, she'd left her child and had never come back. And she could have come back. It wasn't like the story of countless women who'd been forced to give up children and regretted it for ever. They'd never known where their children were, they could only remember birthdays and tearfully wonder who their baby looked like as she or he grew up.

But Shannon could have known what Erin looked like, she could have shared in her life. She simply hadn't wanted to.

Erin reflected on what sort of person Shannon must be. Had she been too emotionally immature to cope with a child or had she been the sort of free spirit who thought babies were burdens and someone else would have been better taking care of her?

Erin tried to remember the woman in the photographs: she'd had the same red hair as Erin and the same shaped face, but her eyes had been blue like Kerry and Mum's. Erin wondered if she'd inherited her startling amber eyes from her father. And who had he been? There were so many questions. But, Erin promised herself, she was going to find the answers. Years before, she'd run away and she regretted it deeply. Now, she was going to find out the truth about her birth, no matter how long it took.

Greg wanted to take the day off work to drive her to meet Kerry but Erin said no. She had to do this on her own.

'Are you sure?' he asked, and Erin hated to see the hurt in his eyes.

'Sure.' She pulled him close to her and kissed him. 'If and when we go to see Mum and Dad, I'd love you to come with me, to introduce them to their new family,' she added, putting one of Greg's hands on her belly. 'But today I have to go on my own.'

She was still unsure about her reception from Kerry. There was nobody in the world with more fierce loyalty than her sister. In Kerry's eyes, Erin had let everyone down. Nobody had spoken of Shannon much when Erin had been growing up, but Erin knew that Kerry had hated her sister for what she'd done to their mother. Erin prayed that Kerry wouldn't hate her too for doing the same thing.

Kerry's directions had been precise. On the Dublin road outside Portlaoise, Erin took a small road to the left, followed it for exactly three miles, turned right and drove for another mile, past a hamlet with two shops, a garage and a flower-bedecked pub. Kerry's house was the third house down from the pub crossroads.

She spotted the place instantly. Kerry had described it as a renovated old two-storey house with a windmill in the garden. She hadn't mentioned that the garden was a beautifully tended riot of colour. The whole place was so very not Kerry, a woman who'd said she'd die rather than live anywhere without access to twenty-four-hour shops, and who'd only notice flowers if they came in an expensive bouquet in the arms of a boyfriend.

Erin parked and got out of her car. She hadn't even reached in for her handbag when the front door of the house opened and a woman emerged.

Kerry might have been thinner, older and her trademark blonde bob was now a feathery short cut, but the sight of her still moved Erin to tears. In Kerry's arms was a squirming, vanilla-skinned child not more than one year old, and at her skirts, clutching a bit of denim fabric, was an exquisite little girl of perhaps five or six, her slanting dark eyes staring up at the stranger in wonder.

'Look at you,' smiled Kerry, gesturing at Erin's belly. 'Mummy.'

'And you,' said Erin, biting her lip to stop herself from having another crying binge.

'Say hello, Lianne.'

Lianne, the child hiding behind Kerry, said 'hello' in a barely audible voice.

'Hello, Lianne,' said Erin, bending briefly down to smile warmly at her.

'And this is Kaylin.' The child in Kerry's arms stopped squirming at the mention of her name and dimpled up at her mother.

'They're beautiful.' Erin gazed at the new additions to her family and felt the weight of shame again. Through her own stupidity, she'd missed years of their and Kerry's lives.

'I'm so sorry –' she began.

'It's all right, Erin.' There was no bitterness or resentment in Kerry's expression. 'Come on inside and take the weight off the floor,' she added. 'If you give me a craven apology, then I might let you have some of the chocolate-chip cookies Lianne and I made earlier.'

Emotion made Erin light-headed. She giggled. 'Craven apology, what's that?'

'I was going to ask for hands-and-knees stuff, but not with that belly,' Kerry pointed out. 'No, under the circumstances, it'll have to be a common or garden apology.'

'What's a pology?' demanded Lianne, hanging back to look at the stranger as Kerry led the way into the house.

'It's when you say sorry for doing something naughty,' Kerry said. ' "What" is her favourite word,' she added quietly to Erin. 'You wait till it's your turn.'

'I can't wait,' said Erin happily. She couldn't believe how well it was working out. There was no awkwardness, no hesitancy. Erin was home and Kerry was happy to see her. The past nine years might never have happened.

Kerry led the way into a small kitchen with a sun-filled conservatory at one end. Lianne's drawings covered the walls in the kitchen and a variety of brightly coloured pictures made with little palm prints were proof that Kaylin was getting in on the act.

'These pictures are lovely,' Erin praised Lianne.

Pride made the last of Lianne's shyness disappear. 'I can do horses too,' she said self-importantly. 'Want to see me do one?'

'Oh yes,' said Erin gravely.

Lianne rushed off to drag paper and crayons from a drawer and then sat at the kitchen table to begin her masterpiece.

Kerry settled Kaylin in a high chair and gave her a beaker of juice before piling up some cushions on a wicker chair from the conservatory and pulling it into the kitchen proper.

'For your back,' she told Erin, who sank into it gratefully. 'I noticed you looked a bit stiff.'

'I am,' Erin said. 'However did you notice that?'

'My new vocation. I give healing massages in the alternative health centre.'

'You do?'

'I had a career change a few years ago. There's only so much of your life you can spend in front of a computer typing reports, so I retrained.'

'Was this after the cancer?' Erin asked softly.

'Vanessa told you, huh? Big mouth.' Kerry put a plate of home-made cookies on the table.

'I should have been here.'

'It would have been nice to have you around,' Kerry admitted. 'It was hard for Mum and Dad. They felt pretty helpless, but then, so did I.'

'Vanessa said you're clear of it now.'

'Four years and counting,' Kerry said, crossing herself. 'I'm on medication and I have regular checks, but I was one of the lucky ones.'

'A friend of mine died recently from breast cancer,' Erin said.

Kerry shot a quick, anxious glance at her older daughter and Erin mouthed the word 'sorry'. But Lianne didn't seem to have noticed the talk of death and was busily colouring in a bright orange and yellow pony with four of the longest, skinniest legs Erin had ever seen.

'I work with people with cancer now,' Kerry said in a low voice, rescuing Kaylin's juice from where she'd flung it onto the table. She handed it back and Kaylin, delighted with this game, flung it again. 'One of the programmes in the health centre is the cancer therapy. Massage is hugely beneficial to people recovering. After I got cancer, Peter and I downsized. We moved here with Lianne, I trained in massage and Peter got a job in a big garage in town.'

'This from the woman who hated the country and was afraid of cows,' Erin teased.

'I know,' laughed her sister. 'But it's lovely here, we've a great life and the girls love it. We'd adopted Lianne before I got cancer and we were trying to adopt another Chinese baby, so that was put on hold for a while. Kaylin came to us six months ago.' Kerry looked down at her daughter with utter adoration.

'Mummy, look, I've finished,' announced Lianne, beaming as she displayed her drawing.

'Darling, that's beautiful, isn't it, Aunty Erin?'

'Fantastic,' Erin said.

After a while, they sat outside in the garden while Kaylin played in her sand box and Lianne rushed around showing her new aunt all her toys and how clever she was with them. She was particularly proud of her cycling ability, and whizzed up and down the grass.

'Dervla from my class still has to use stabilisers but I don't,' Lianne said, stopping beside Erin to let her admire the pink and purple bike.

While the children played, Erin told her sister about the missing years, of how much she loved Greg, of how thrilled they were about the baby – and how she'd always thought of home but had been afraid of her welcome. In turn, Kerry filled her in on how she'd met Peter ('I had this banged-up old car with a dodgy clutch and he worked in the garage down the road. I saw so much of him that we began going out and the rest is history.') and on her parents' decision to move house. She didn't mention the circumstances that led her and Peter to adopt their two beautiful daughters and Erin didn't ask. Kerry had been so welcoming to her, she couldn't expect to be let in on every secret yet.

'Mum always wanted to live in the country, and when Cora Flaherty's house was broken into, it was the beginning of the end for them. They never got the little bastards who did it,' Kerry said vehemently.

'And they're happy?' Erin asked tentatively.

'Very. But they'll be happier now they know you're back. I told them this morning.'

Erin gasped. 'And . . . ?'

'And I had to practically phone for a fleet of security guards to stop them hopping into the car and driving up here. They can't wait to see you, and Greg, and the bump.'

In true mummy fashion, Kerry had everything close by her, including tissues for baby emergencies. She handed a wedge of them to Erin.

'Why's Aunty Erin crying?' demanded Lianne, stopping for a moment in her cycling odyssey.

'Because she's happy,' observed her mother sagely.

Lianne, mystified by the strange ways of grown-ups, cycled off again. Why would anyone cry because they were happy?

'We could phone them, if you like,' Kerry said when Erin had managed to stop crying.

Erin nodded.

'You watch the little one,' Kerry ordered, and went in for the phone.

Erin watched Kaylin as if her life depended on it. Kaylin was fascinated by the notion of putting sand in a tiny striped bucket, then tipping it out again. Every time she did it, she giggled and looked up at Erin for approval.

'Aren't you clever?' cooed Erin.

Kaylin cooed back.

When Kerry returned, she was already speaking on the

phone. The butterflies fluttered in Erin's stomach. She'd waited so long for this but now that it was happening, she was nervous. What if . . . ?

There was no time for worrying. Kerry simply handed her the phone, saying: 'It's Mum.'

'Hello,' said Erin.

'Erin, my love, I knew you'd come home to us,' said her mother simply. 'I knew you would. We've missed you so much. If I had it over again, Erin, I'd do it differently . . .'

'Mum, me too,' said Erin earnestly. 'It was my fault. I shouldn't have run off.'

'My fault too,' replied her mother. 'I should have told you. I was wrong and it all came out badly. But we can move on, can't we?'

'Yes. I need a grandmother for my baby.'

'Oh, love,' sighed her mother. 'You'll have that. Here's your father for a wee word.'

'Erin.' Her father was choked with emotion and could barely speak. 'When can we see you?'

'Next weekend? Greg and I will come to you.'

'Greg's your husband?' asked her father.

'Yes. You'll have to vet him, Dad, see if he's suitable,' said Erin warmly.

'He's brought you back to us,' said her father. 'That's good enough for me.'

They had salad and Kerry's home-made brown bread for lunch. Then Kerry urged her sister to lie down.

'Kaylin goes down for a nap after lunch and I'll break the habit of a lifetime and let Lianne watch a video.'

'You don't approve of letting children watch television, then?' Erin asked seriously.

Kerry roared with laughter. 'I'm joking. All parents plan to keep their children away from the box until they actually have them and realise they'd never get a lie-in at weekends without resorting to *Postman Pat*. Video is a great invention.'

With Kaylin sleeping and Lianne wide-eyed in front of a Disney video, Erin lay down on a soft couch and Kerry sat in an armchair beside her.

'Rest for an hour, then I'll make you some tea and you should drive home so you miss the rush-hour traffic.'

'I wish I had longer.'

'Next weekend we'll have two whole days to talk and remember,' Kerry consoled her.

They reminisced some more, talking and laughing quietly about their past.

'Vanessa's done well for herself,' Erin said.

'Well, you know how driven she always was,' Kerry pointed out. 'She's a celebrity in her own right now, you know. Her photo's in the paper all the time at parties and she sometimes goes on radio for those Sunday-morning talks about what's in the papers.'

'Good for her,' Erin said. 'I'm glad she's happy.'

'Yeah, she is. Settling down with hubbie and kids was never on the agenda for Vanessa.'

'Like Shannon,' Erin said before she could stop herself.

'Vanessa is nothing like Shannon.' Kerry was firm. 'If Vanessa had got pregnant at seventeen, she'd have faced up to it, not run away and let someone else handle the hassle. That was always Shannon's answer to any kind of trouble – run from it and hope that by the time she got home, it would all be over.'

'When did you know that I wasn't your sister?'

Kerry grimaced. 'I always did. Shannon was pregnant when I was nine or ten and I remember her wailing about it all the time.'

'Wailing?'

'She was a drama queen,' Kerry said. 'Shannon never grazed her knee when she fell: she tore ligaments. She never failed an exam at school because she hadn't bothered studying: she failed because she had these blinding migraines and a person could hardly be expected to do well under such circumstances. There was always some excuse.'

'Didn't you get on?' Erin asked, although it seemed patently obvious that they hadn't.

'There was a big age gap; we didn't know each other.'

'There was a big age gap between us and we did,' Erin remarked.

'I don't know why, Shannon and I just didn't.' Kerry looked as if she did know but didn't want to talk about it.

'Why did you never tell me?' It was the one question Erin had been dying to ask.

'Mum said it was an important secret and it would hurt you if it came out,' Kerry sighed. 'She adored you and I think she was always scared that Shannon would arrive and take you away to live with her. Mum didn't want that sort of life for you – I mean, Shannon was barely able to look after herself. She'd have never been able to take care of you. Dizzy, that was the best way to describe her. Although she could be calculating enough when she needed to.

'And Mum was scared of losing you too. You weren't really her child and she had no legal hold over you. Shannon never hung around long enough to sort out adoption. That wouldn't have been her style.'

'Did you ever find out who my father was?' Erin asked hesitantly.

Her sister shook her head. 'Only Shannon knows that. She wouldn't tell us. Said it didn't matter. Typical Shannon, that was.'

'I'll ask her,' Erin said quietly.

'You're going to meet her.' It wasn't a question, more a statement of fact. 'I knew you would some day. But you won't find what you're looking for, Erin. Not with Shannon. She was always different from us.'

'What do you mean?'

'It's a horrible thing to say about your sister, but Shannon can be very selfish, for all her posturing about caring for the universe.'

'You could say the same thing about me,' Erin said guiltily. 'I left too.'

When she grinned, Kerry looked just like the wild girl Erin remembered. 'Yeah, well, there were extenuating circumstances with you. You're forgiven, just as long as it doesn't happen again. No, Shannon's different. When she had you, she could have kept you. Ireland wasn't stuck in the dark ages then. Yes, she was seventeen but Mum and Dad were supporting her, she could have managed. Instead, she couldn't wait to be gone and she never came back. I can't forgive her for that.'

'You were only a kid at the time,' protested Erin, 'you don't know what she was going through. She must have been scared and upset . . .'

'Yeah, I suppose.' Kerry looked thoughtful. 'Perhaps I'm so hard on her because I spent so long trying to have children and not managing to. I get annoyed thinking of someone like Shannon, who has a baby and blithely lets someone else bring it up, when Peter and I went through so much and couldn't have them.'

Erin's heart went out to her sister. Kerry had gone through such hell and she hadn't been there for her.

'Oh, don't mind me,' Kerry went on. 'I'm just being a grumpy old cow. I find it hard to forgive her for what she put us all through over the years.'

'Do you know where she lives?'

Kerry glanced at her sister sharply and appeared to be considering answering the question. 'Yes. She keeps in touch sporadically.'

'I want to meet her. I know I met her when I was a kid but I can't remember that,' Erin said. 'I have to meet her again, to talk to her.'

'And to ask her why she left?'

'Yeah, something like that.' Erin sat up on the couch and turned pleading eyes to her sister. 'I know you think it's a bad idea, but I have to see her.'

Kerry relented. 'She lives quite near to Mum and Dad.

Apparently, she was living with this guy and they ran a youth hostel for ages but they went bust. She moved last year. I have her address.'

'Do you ever see her?'

'Occasionally, although not for a long time.' Kerry sounded hard. She was perfectly capable of cutting her sister from her life, Erin knew. There was only one way for Kerry: you were either with her or against her. 'Last time she tried to contact me was when I was in hospital. She got talking to Peter and, God love him, he's too decent to understand our weird family situation. He thought she'd rush over to visit me when she heard I was sick.' Kerry snorted. 'Some hope. I haven't heard from her since, although I know Mum gave her some money before Christmas.'

'Is she broke?'

'Shannon always is and always was broke. She'll tap you for a few quid if you meet her.'

'Really?'

'Really.'

'I just wish I'd known all this,' Erin said slowly, 'so I would have had a proper vision of her in my head.'

'Did you think she was a perfect wonderful mummy figure who couldn't take care of you due to circumstances beyond her control?' Kerry asked bitterly.

'Don't sound so hard,' begged Erin.

'If I'm hard when I talk about her, it's because she made me that way. She hurt Mum so much when she left, and it's because of her that you left. And that wasn't a barrel of laughs either.'

'I know. But, hey, I wouldn't be here if it wasn't for her,' Erin added.

'True for you,' Kerry said, the bitter look going from her face. 'Let's have a cup of tea for the road and you can set off home, OK?'

The traffic was light as Erin started her journey back to Cork. It would take her perhaps two hours to get there. She switched her mobile phone on and left a message on Greg's voicemail to tell him that everything had gone well and to phone her when he got a chance. He'd already left several messages for her and she smiled as she listened to them.

'Phone me back if you're upset,' he said on one. 'If everything's OK, there's no need to phone. I know you want time to talk to Kerry without interruption, but remember, I love you. And Baby.'

Everything was working out so well, Erin thought as she drove out onto the main road between Cork and Portlaoise. She'd met Kerry and spoken to her darling parents. The baby, wriggling away inside her with little dolphin flicks, was healthy, and she was married to a man she adored. But she didn't have it all. Buried deep inside her was a core of pain, hard, cold and compressed like a lump of coal. No matter how much love there was in her life, the lump of coal was always there, reminding her that her real mother had betrayed her. Shannon had left her and had never come back. She could have but she chose not to. Erin was determined to get to the bottom of it all.

CHAPTER TWENTY-SIX

Lizzie knew it was wrong to be deliriously happy about going out to dinner with someone she'd only known a few days, but she couldn't help it. When Simon had phoned to ask her out on the evening of the day after her parachute jump, she'd been thrilled.

'It was a good night, wasn't it?' he'd said, while Lizzie's heart did somersaults of excitement at the thought that she hadn't been imagining it – Simon had fancied her.

'Wonderful,' she said, the stresses of the day forgotten. Debra had cheered up thanks to the shopping trip that had involved the purchase of an expensive pair of spindly sandals. When Simon phoned, Debra was upstairs trying them on with everything in her wardrobe, and the radio was blaring loudly, proof that all was well in Debra's world.

'I thought you might like to come out to dinner again, just with me,' Simon added.

'Yes,' breathed Lizzie, totally forgetting that modern women were supposed to play hard to get. 'I'd love that.'

Wednesday was the day picked for their date because Lizzie had to work late on Tuesday.

'Where will we go?' she asked with enthusiasm.

They thought about it for ages before settling on a lively seafood restaurant where a jazz band played on Wednesday nights.

'I'll pick you up at seven, if that's all right?' said Simon.

'Er, no, I'll meet you there,' said Lizzie, thinking of Debra, who wasn't used to the idea of her mother going on a date.

'Who was that on the phone?' asked Debra, coming downstairs to have her new sandals admired.

'Oh, er, just a wrong number,' Lizzie lied.

She spent Tuesday and most of Wednesday in a state of delighted excitement. She had a date! The girls who wrote those 'Things to Do . . .' lists would have disapproved of such enthusiasm.

'Make him beg' would undoubtedly be their advice, along with some helpful hints for getting him to improve his technique in bed so that she, the woman, had wildly improved climaxes before he even thought about his. Lizzie knew all this because she secretly flicked through the younger women's magazines on a regular basis now.

She also knew that in the highly unlikely event of her ending up in bed with Simon, she'd be too conscious of her own rusty bedtime technique to criticise his. Modern women were so strong and knew what they wanted, she thought wistfully. They were like Clare Morgan's cat, Tiger – aloof and careful about whom they favoured. She, on the other hand, was more of a bouncy sheepdog-type person – so thrilled with the companionship that she'd rush up and lick Simon's face. Well, maybe not lick his face but certainly act in a sheepdog, waggy-tail manner.

The only fly in the ointment was what she should wear. Lizzie, who'd spent years utterly at home in her traditional evening outfit of nice blouse and skirt or trousers, was suddenly wildly uncomfortable at the notion of such a rig-out. What would be suitable? After her disastrous purchase for the Richardsons' party, and the acid-yellow wedding suit, she didn't have the courage to go and buy something.

Debra was going out clubbing with her friend Frieda on Wednesday.

'Barry stifled me for a long time – I haven't been clubbing for ages,' she told her mother. She planned to race home after work to change before racing off again.

Great, thought Lizzie. This meant she'd have time to try

on everything in her wardrobe and parade in front of the landing mirror once Debra was gone.

But when she got home from work, Debra was still there and she looked sulky. 'Frieda called it off,' she said. 'And I was so looking forward to going out.'

'Oh.' Lizzie's mind did the computation: if Debra was angry that she wasn't going out with her friend, then she would inevitably expect her mother to stand in. Obviously Lizzie would not be suitable for clubbing but dinner would be acceptable. Lizzie now knew where her daughter and son-in-law spent all their money – on eating out. Debra and Barry had apparently been to restaurants at least twice every week, often three or four times. Debra obviously expected this to continue and Lizzie's finances couldn't stand it.

'I'm going out myself,' she said nervously.

'Where?' demanded Debra, fixing her mother with a basilisk eye.

'Out to Erin's,' said Lizzie, praying that a bolt of lightning wouldn't strike her for such lies.

'I might phone Mags and see what she's doing,' sighed Debra, now that it was plain that she'd be on her own.

By the time Lizzie was ready, Debra had rearranged her night and wanted a lift into Cork where she was going to meet up with Mags for a wild night.

'I'm getting a taxi,' Lizzie pointed out.

Debra sighed theatrically. 'I suppose I'll have to get one too, then. You're all dressed up,' she added.

Lizzie, who'd rediscovered a black jersey dress with a deep V down the front that was both slimming and sexy, flushed. 'I like to make an effort,' she said.

She was glad she had. She was a bit late by the time she made it to the restaurant, but her efforts at getting ready were worth it when she saw the glimmer of admiration in Simon's eyes.

'You look lovely,' he said, and it was clear he meant it.

'So do you,' she replied, and he did. His simple open-necked shirt couldn't hide his lean, muscular body, and

Lizzie felt a thrill ripple through her at the thought of being out with such a man. Myles had been nice-looking, yes, but he lacked the sheer male attractiveness of Simon.

'I didn't think women told men they looked nice,' Simon said, grinning.

'Haven't you worked out by now that I'm not most women?' Lizzie said, her eyes twinkling back at him.

She had worried that she wouldn't know what to say to Simon because it had been so many millennia since she'd actually had a date. But talking to him turned out to be easy. Lizzie didn't try to be anything she wasn't and neither did Simon.

Over lovely food, with a superb jazz piano band in the background, they talked about life, love, divorce, kids (Simon had a grown-up son who lived in Belfast), work and the pursuit of adventure.

'I'm boring compared to you,' Lizzie said, when Simon had explained about his days as an Air Corp flight instructor and how he'd co-owned the Santa Monica centre for the past ten years.

'You're not a bit boring,' he said, and the way his gaze held hers made her pulse quicken. 'Don't put yourself down, Lizzie.'

'Oh, I like to tease myself before anybody can get in there first,' she said lightly. Then she stopped.

Simon hadn't reached across the table but, strangely, she felt as if he was suddenly gently touching her.

'You shouldn't put yourself down,' he repeated softly. 'There's nothing a bit boring about you.'

'Old habits die hard,' said Lizzie.

This time, Simon did touch her – his fingers splaying out across the table to touch the tips of hers. It was such a small gesture and so electric. No open-mouthed kiss could be as tender as that touch, Lizzie thought in wonder.

When couples began to dance to the music in the tiny wooden-floored section, Simon shot her a questioning look. The pre-dinner Lizzie would have said no because she wasn't a wonderful dancer by any stretch of the imagination and, anyway, he might notice her huge bum on the dance floor. She could hide it sitting down.

The after-dinner Lizzie smiled and got to her feet. 'I have two left feet,' she whispered as they moved to the dance floor.

'Old habits,' murmured Simon, holding her close.

'No, really,' laughed Lizzie. 'This isn't a joke – I am hopeless.'

Only Simon wasn't. Lizzie had always hated dancing with someone she didn't know, but with Simon's body close to hers and his arms around her, she suddenly learned how to move. Leaning against him, utterly comfortable in his embrace, she danced as she'd never danced before, letting the gentle jazz melodies wash over her.

'Why did you say you couldn't dance?' Simon asked.

'I never could, until now.'

'You were with the wrong partner,' Simon said, his voice dark and husky in her ear.

Under the circumstances, she couldn't say no when he offered to drive her home. She'd ask him in for coffee, she decided. Just coffee. And it would be safe because Debra was out and undoubtedly wouldn't be back for hours.

At home, Simon seemed relaxed and Lizzie allowed herself to relax too.

It was nice to bring a man home for coffee and be able to trust that he wasn't going to hop on her. But, as they sat on opposite ends of the couch, talking and laughing, Lizzie found that *she* was the one who kept thinking it would be nice if something more happened.

She kept looking at the way Simon's strong fingers held his coffee mug and she kept imagining those fingers sliding tantalisingly down the V of her dress.

Stop it, Lizzie, she told herself.

It was nearly twelve when Simon reluctantly said he ought to go.

'I've an early start,' he said.

'Yes, of course,' Lizzie said, thinking that she couldn't remember when a night had gone so quickly. She put her coffee mug down too and stared at him over the Siberia of the middle of the couch. 'Well, you don't have to go just yet.'

'I should, Lizzie,' Simon said.

'Yes,' she said, crestfallen.

'You're too tempting in that dress,' he went on.

'It's a long time since I've had an occasion to wear it,' she said happily.

'You don't get out enough,' Simon grinned, getting to his feet.

Lizzie got up too and then, she didn't know how it happened, but they were touching and kissing, and it was like when they'd been dancing, only this time, there weren't other people around. Simon's hands moulded her body to his and she clung to him, kissing him as though she'd die if she stopped. And then, they were sitting on the couch, with Lizzie curled up against him, and she wondered if she'd left the heating on by mistake because she felt so hot and –

'Mum! What the hell are you doing?'

Lizzie shot out of Simon's arms like a guilty schoolgirl caught behind the bike shed. Straightening her dress rapidly, she saw Debra standing at the door with an expression of utter disgust on her face.

'Who is this?' Debra asked, in much the same tone as she'd ask about the provenance of some muck on her shoes.

'I'm Simon,' he said calmly, getting to his feet.

Lizzie supposed that skydiving made you calm under any circumstances.

'This is Debra, my daughter,' Lizzie said, hoping that civility would rule. It didn't.

'You're bringing strange men back to the house!' said Debra furiously. 'What can you have been thinking, Mum?'

'I'll go, if you'd like,' Simon said, standing close to Lizzie. 'Or I can stay.'

'Go,' she said, feeling like a coward. She couldn't face Debra's disgust, not even for someone as lovely as Simon. He kissed her gently on the cheek, while Debra made audible sounds of distaste. 'I'll phone you tomorrow,' he said, and made his own way out.

'I can't believe you did that!' shrieked Debra when they'd heard the door shut gently. 'Bringing a strange man back to the house. He could have been a rapist or anything. Are you stupid? Have you totally lost it? And at your age!'

'My age has nothing to do with it,' said Lizzie, stung.

'Yes it does,' said her daughter. 'Who is this man? Where did you meet him?'

She sounded so upset at having found her mother at home with a strange man that Lizzie didn't know how to calm her.

'I met him at the parachute jump. He's one of the instructors. He's nice,' she said.

'Nice!' Debra cried shakily. 'Nice isn't good enough. You've just met him. You don't know anything about him! You could have gone out with me tonight, you know, and you didn't. You obviously weren't at Erin's. Why did you lie to me? You lied so you could see some man. Why do you need to bring men home? I can't believe you'd do this to me!'

Lizzie didn't know how her bringing Simon home for coffee had turned into an attack on Debra, but that was clearly how Debra saw it. Lizzie had abandoned her for a man and Debra couldn't bear the idea.

'I didn't mean to lie to you, darling,' Lizzie said.

'But you did,' wailed Debra. 'I thought we were there for each other. I never thought you'd lie to me.'

'I'm so sorry, love,' said Lizzie, falling into the familiar pattern. She could see tears welling up in Debra's eyes, and she knew that when Debra felt threatened, she became upset.

'He's gone now,' Lizzie said helplessly.

'You've got to be careful, Mum,' said Debra, sniffling. 'Don't tell me that Lothario tonight didn't see you as a soft target. Older woman, living alone, divorced. He saw you as easy pickings, Mum.'

'He didn't!' protested Lizzie.

'Oh, Mum, get real,' said Debra. 'I'm thinking of you, you know. These types pick a certain type of older woman, that's the scam. And you fell for it. After a week, he'd have been borrowing money off you.'

'Simon's not like that,' said Lizzie quietly.

'How do you know? And did you ever think about me, Mum, coming home to the sight of my mother on the couch with a strange man. I got such a shock. What would Dad think?'

'We're divorced,' Lizzie said, but the fight had gone out of her. She sat down on the couch suddenly, feeling weak and weepy.

'Oh, Mum,' said Debra, contrite. 'I do love you. I worry about you, that's all. I'd hate to see you getting hurt and that's all that would happen here: you'd get hurt. You need someone to look after you and isn't it lucky you've got me and I've got you? We can look after each other.'

'Yes,' said Lizzie quietly.

Debra sat beside her and put her arms round her mother. 'We can go out and have fun ourselves; we don't need men, do we?' she said, sounding like a child.

'Yes,' repeated Lizzie.

'And men just complicate life and we don't need that, do we?'

Her mother shook her head. 'No, we don't.'

Sally's grave, over in the windswept far corner of Angel Gabriel's graveyard, had that raw and lonely look of recent graves. It was too soon for a headstone for it, too soon for the earth to have settled over Sally's coffin. No grass grew on the mound of earth, although there was proof that Steve visited from the small, well-tended pots of flowers edging the grave.

A small china vase filled with roses sat amid a cluster of

flowerpots. The roses were red – roses from Sally's garden – and they'd clearly only been placed there a couple of days ago. It broke Abby's heart to imagine Steve carefully cutting the blooms and placing them in the vase, keeping the water topped up, all as a tribute to his darling Sally.

Would anyone tend *her* grave with such loving care when she was gone, Abby wondered sadly. Probably not. She felt bad at giving in to such personal misery at her friend's grave. She was healthy, she didn't deserve to feel sorry for herself. She should feel sorry for Steve instead. Abby kept phoning to say hello but the answering machine was always on and Steve didn't return her calls. Abby was torn between wanting to respect his privacy and feeling the need to see if there was anything she could do.

She knew that he needed time alone to grieve but she had promised Sally, after all, that she'd look after him. She wasn't even doing that properly.

Abby closed her eyes and said a few prayers for Sally. She hadn't been to the graveyard since the funeral, but today, driving past on her way out of town, she'd suddenly been struck by the desire to visit her friend's resting place.

Somehow, Abby had thought that the peace and serenity of the graveyard would be the perfect place to talk to Sally and ask her, should she beg Tom to try again with their marriage? It was strange because, when Sally was alive, Abby wouldn't have had to ask her this question. Sally was too aware of appreciating what you had in life and would have done anything to reconcile her two old friends.

Abby put her flowers carefully on the grave beside Steve's. She prayed that Sally was somewhere good, somewhere where she could look down on everyone, happy, contented and loved, as she deserved to be.

Abby's mood was sombre as she left, despite her efforts to perk up to meet Tom. They'd decided to meet in a neutral place. Lyonnais was private but too full of bad memories. Tom had picked a pub on the road between Cork and

Dunmore and he was already there when Abby drove into the car park.

She parked beside his car and hurried in, knowing she was a few minutes late.

'Hello, Abby,' said Tom. He was sitting at a small table with a pint of Guinness and the newspaper crossword in front of him. Tom hated to sit waiting anywhere without something to read. He must have been there quite a while if he'd read the paper in its entirety and was now on to the crossword.

He looked good, Abby thought in surprise. She'd always assumed that once men left the marital home to sleep on a friend's couch, they ended up with badly ironed shirts and strange stains on their ties. But Tom, who'd never been exactly a natty dresser before, looked really good in a denim shirt and a pair of perfectly ironed and pristine chinos.

'What do you want, Abby?' he said without preamble or even offering her a drink.

Slightly taken aback by his tone, Abby sat down and launched into the speech she'd prepared earlier.

'I didn't come to talk to you about lawyers or a divorce or selling the house,' she began. 'I came here to see if we could make it work again. Please hear me out, Tom. I think we should try again for Jess's sake. And for mine,' she added. 'I've missed you so much – you've no idea how much. I'd do anything if we could start again.'

He stared at her across the table but didn't say anything and Abby took this as an encouraging sign.

'We could go for counselling,' she suggested. 'In fact, we *should* go for counselling because I know it's going to be hard for you to get over what happened, and hard for you to trust me. But it won't happen again.' She was getting into her stride now, the words she'd practised flowing easily. 'It was a one-off, a stupid, *stupid* moment when I wasn't thinking about you or our marriage, or Jess or anything . . . And I'm so terribly sorry, Tom, can't you see that?' Her eyes pleaded with his and she reached out to try and touch his hand. But Tom jerked it away before they could actually touch.

'So that's what you came here for,' he said bitterly. 'To beg me to come back, to make it all perfect again. I can't believe you're even attempting this, Abby. Do you really think it's that simple? Do you really think we can go back to the way we were?'

'No,' she said hurriedly. 'I know we can't go back to the way we were but we can try again. Things hadn't been good between us for quite a while – you know that, Tom. We'd both have to work at it but we have a marriage that's worth saving, don't we?'

His face was incredulous. '*We'd* have to work at it?' he said. 'What's all this *we* stuff, Abby? I didn't do anything wrong. I didn't sleep with anyone else. You did. If anybody has to make an effort, it's you, and I don't think you can. You sound just like some first-year student who's standing in my office whining that they didn't mean to turn the fire alarm on, and it won't happen again, honestly, sir.'

His voice was full of barely concealed anger and Abby knew she was wasting her time. But she'd had to try. She wouldn't have been able to live with herself if she hadn't made the attempt to get their marriage back on track. The failure of their marriage *had* been down to both of them. Yes, she'd been the one who'd slept with Jay but Tom had been instrumental in driving her to it. She knew that now. Nobody went out and slept with someone else if their marriage was working. And Tom must know that too.

She tried again. 'Tom, I'm not saying what happened was your fault but I'm saying we were equal partners in our marriage, and we both let it go wrong. I was the one who committed adultery but that doesn't mean that the whole thing is my fault, do you understand that? I know it's hard to face up to that but you must –'

'I must what?' he demanded. 'I must take responsibility for you screwing another man? Oh, fuck off, Abby. I didn't come here today to listen to this crap. I thought you wanted

401

to talk about lawyers and what we were going to do with the house. I can't believe you have the nerve to come here and ask me to come back – and then pretend that it was all my fault.'

'I didn't say it was all your fault,' protested Abby furiously. Really, he was so annoying. Couldn't he see that she was just trying to sort things out, not put the blame on him?

Tom sank the rest of his pint of Guinness quickly. He still hadn't attempted to order anything for her. Once upon a time, he would have had a drink waiting: a glass of white wine was his staple order for her. She used to joke that he never gave her the chance to order anything different.

'If that's all you came here to talk about, then I'm going,' he snapped. 'I don't have time to hang around. I've another life, Abby, the life you pushed me into.'

He left without another word and Abby sat in the pub for a while, staring at all the other customers who laughed and joked and chatted as if they hadn't a care in the world. If only she could go back to being like them; if only she could go back to her old life where she'd been so happy and had everything, if only she'd known it.

On Friday morning, Erin stood in the flower shop beside the supermarket and dallied over fragrant Star Gazer lilies, exotic arums and pretty yellow freesias with the most glorious scent imaginable. Mum had never been one for grand flowers, she decided, choosing the freesias. As the florist wrapped up a large bouquet, Erin idly stared out of the shop window and noticed Lizzie Shanahan walking past looking dreamily into the distance.

'Lizzie,' she called, hurrying to the door. 'Hello.'

'Hi,' said Lizzie brightly, 'how are you?'

She looked down at Erin's bump but didn't move to touch it, like so many other people. Lizzie was very intuitive and had seen how uncomfortable Erin was when people did. 'How's the baby?'

'Wriggling like a maniac,' Erin said proudly. 'It's either a footballer or a ballet dancer. Greg gets such a thrill when he feels it too. How are you?'

'Great,' said Lizzie, although not so brightly. Debra had got over her hurt at her mother wanting a life apart from her one with Debra, and was now really getting Lizzie down, what with all the caustic little remarks about older women and boyfriends. It was as if Debra thought Simon had been after Lizzie for her money. What money, Lizzie wanted to know.

Erin felt there was something going on but didn't want to pry. Ruby from the salon suspected that it was hard on Lizzie having her daughter living with her, although Lizzie was not the sort of person to volunteer such a thing.

'What makes you think that?' Erin had asked Ruby, unable to imagine anyone connected to Lizzie who wasn't just as lovely and warm.

'I've met her daughter and she's a right little madam,' Ruby had said, unimpressed. 'I don't think it's a barrel of laughs with her at home. I'd say she runs rings round poor Lizzie.'

'I haven't seen much of you lately, Lizzie,' Erin said now.

'Sorry. Some surrogate mum I've been,' Lizzie replied guiltily. 'It's just that –'

'No, don't apologise,' insisted Erin quickly. 'We're all busy. I'm only saying that I miss our coffee and chat. Abby's been very busy too: she's only been in the salon once recently, so I don't know how she is either. We must all get together to talk about our fund-raising for cancer.'

'I'd like that,' Lizzie said gratefully. That was the nice thing about Erin. She wasn't one of those high-maintenance friends who went into a total sulk if neglected. 'I've already done a teeny bit of fund-raising,' Lizzie added. 'I did a parachute jump for a cancer charity.'

'Fantastic!' Erin was impressed. 'I've been talking about it, but you've really done something. Well done! And I've some news for you,' she added, eyes sparkling.

'Your flowers are ready,' called the florist from the depths of the shop.

'Hold on just a minute,' Erin said, and rushed inside. Once she'd got her bouquet, she resumed her story. 'I've met my sister, Kerry, and I'm going to meet my parents later today. These flowers are for my mum. Greg's leaving work at lunchtime and we're driving to spend the weekend with my family.' She beamed.

'That's wonderful!' Lizzie was so thrilled for her friend that she reached out and hugged her, flowers and all. 'I knew they'd be thrilled to hear from you – didn't I say that?'

'You did and you were right,' Erin admitted. 'It just took a leap of faith to contact them again.'

'Family never forget the people they love,' Lizzie said warmly, 'and how could they forget someone like you?'

'Well, my real mother forgot me,' Erin replied ruefully. She could talk about it to Lizzie, who somehow managed to understand.

'I bet she didn't forget about you at all,' Lizzie said. 'You don't know what her life has been like. You've got to give her a chance.'

Erin thought about this. Lizzie had such belief in people. Nobody was ever a bad person in her book. Circumstances just forced them into corners where they made bad decisions. 'I wish I was more like you,' she said, smiling. 'You do see the best in people. I've spent ages feeling bitter about my real mother because she left, but you're right, I need to cut her some slack.'

Lizzie flushed with pleasure at the idea that someone like Erin would want to be more like her. 'Bitterness gets you nowhere,' she said. 'I've found that out.'

'Lizzie, you couldn't be bitter if you tried,' Erin said fondly.

'I have my moments,' the other woman replied. 'So, are you excited?'

'I'm nervous more than anything, I have to admit. And,'

she paused, 'a bit sad. I've missed so much of their lives. I guess I'll always feel sad about that.'

Lizzie's eyes took on a faraway look. 'We all carry a bit of sadness in our hearts, Erin. It makes us grateful for what we have.'

Erin had initially thought the family ought to meet in the Wexford hotel where she and Greg were staying for the weekend.

'Don't be daft,' Kerry had said bluntly. 'Why would we do that? Mum and Dad are upset they don't have enough room for you pair to stay with all of us, but they only have three bedrooms and, believe me, it's a squash getting the girls into that boxroom. Mum and I are going to cook dinner on Friday night, so you'll come there and you can go back to the hotel later.'

There was no arguing with Kerry when she was in that mood. So Erin and Greg drove to their hotel, checked in, then headed south of Wexford to the coastal town where the family lived. Erin had been like a cat on a hot tin roof for the whole drive, although she did her best to calm down for the baby's sake.

'This poor child will be born neurotic,' she fretted after yet another bout of 'I hope they're happy to see me but what if they're not?'

'She'll have my calm genes,' said Greg reassuringly. 'My mother is calm, Dad is so laid-back he's nearly horizontal, and all that genetic calmness will counterbalance any neurosis from your side.'

'The Flynns aren't neurotic,' insisted Erin, stung by this inference. 'I used to be calm, it's just there's a lot going on.'

Greg laughed. 'Told you I knew how to cheer you up,' he said.

Erin relaxed. 'Anyhow, who says we're going to have a girl?' she asked.

'Those determined little kicks,' Greg said. 'They remind

me of you, never wanting to sit still, so I know it's going to be a girl.'

Erin reached over and rested her hand on the back of his neck, gently caressing it lovingly. She didn't say anything; she didn't need to.

When they got to her parents' house, Erin was a wreck with nerves. 'I'm so glad you're driving because I'd never have been able to find it and I'd have been going round in circles for ages,' she gabbled as she checked how she looked in the visor mirror for the millionth time.

Greg understood her well enough to say nothing to this stream of conversation but tell her she looked lovely. Everyone must have been watching out the windows because Greg hadn't actually parked the car in front of the pretty little stone cottage before the front door was opened and the occupants streamed out.

'Oh God, Greg, look, it's Dad and Kerry, and Mum . . .'

With presence of mind, Greg stopped where he was and put the brake on not a moment too soon. Erin shoved her door open and clambered out into her father's arms, and suddenly her mother was there too, with Kerry and Lianne, and they were all hugging and laughing and crying at the same time.

'Let me look at you,' said Mum, holding Erin's face with both her hands and gazing at her as if she could wipe out the lost years by learning every new line or freckle on her beloved face. 'You look beautiful,' she said.

'Wasn't she always beautiful?' said Dad, still holding Erin's hand as tightly as a drowning man might cling to the lifeboat.

Erin had no idea what they had for dinner. She couldn't concentrate on something so mundane. Instead, she couldn't stop stealing glances at her parents, noticing the way her mother's frame seemed smaller and more stooped with age, and seeing that her father's grey hair had changed to silver. They looked older, there was no doubt. She would have done anything to turn the years back and be there for them for the nine lost years, and she knew she'd always feel a sense of loss for what she'd missed. But she thought back to what Lizzie had said: 'We all carry a bit of sadness in our hearts: it makes us grateful for what we have.'

Lizzie was right. Missing years with her family had made Erin appreciate them all the more. So many families fought and bickered all the time, never appreciating what family ties really meant. Erin was lucky because now she knew just what family meant.

She watched Kerry and Peter laughing at something Greg had said. Peter was a nice man, very quiet as befitted someone who lived with a live wire like Kerry, but very friendly to his wife's long-lost sister. He clearly adored Kerry and their children, and Erin spotted him touching Kerry with affection all the time, squeezing her hand tightly and stroking her arm.

They could have lost Kerry too, Erin realised with a jolt. Cancer could have taken her away just as it had taken dear Sally. And Sally had known just what family was all about, Lord rest her.

Suddenly a flash of inspiration came to Erin. Family and Sally. How many times had Erin wondered how the families of people with cancer coped? Trying to be brave, they had to hide their own fears and save their crying for when they were alone. But what if there was someplace where everyone could talk about the illness, where there was counselling for the person who was ill and for their family, children, everyone? That's what they could raise funds for. After dinner, Erin talked the idea through with her sister.

'You mean like a Life Beats Cancer centre?' Kerry said with interest.

'What's that?' Erin asked.

Kerry explained that the centre she worked at was affiliated with a national cancer charity that raised funds for complementary treatments for cancer patients.

'It's the holistic approach to the disease,' Kerry pointed out. 'They've got trained counsellors for the family and the person with cancer, and they offer all sorts of therapies, from visualisation and meditation to nutrition advice. And the help is really practical, too. For example, I went to the one in Dublin to get my wig cut. You know, so many wigs are hopeless but the LBC centre in Dublin has a panel of hairdressers who work on wigs to make them look better.' Kerry touched her short hair reflectively. 'They made my wig look fantastic, really natural, and when you're bald, with no eyebrows and a pasty face from chemo, you need all the help you can get.'

Erin felt a surge of emotion hit her. 'That's it then,' she said firmly. 'That's what we'll raise the money for – a centre like that for Dunmore.'

On Saturday, Erin left Greg in the hotel to do some work and headed off for her parents' alone. Peter was taking the girls out for the morning and it was to be just the four of them sitting in the cosy kitchen talking.

With the first of many cups of tea in front of her, Erin heard the story of Shannon for the first time.

'Shannon was so headstrong when she was younger,' Mum explained. She sat with the old white china teapot in front of her, like she'd sat throughout Erin's childhood. That teapot was part of the family, almost, and seeing them all gathered round it made Erin feel that time had stood still. There were more lines on her mother's face, naturally, and the arthritis had affected her hands, making the knuckles misshapen. But the warm light still shone from her clear blue eyes – eyes that missed nothing.

'She hated school, that was for sure. I used to dread those parent/teacher meetings because there was bound to be some drama over Shannon's behaviour, this class she'd missed and that bit of homework she hadn't ever bothered to do.'

Mum and Dad exchanged knowing glances, remembering.

'I'll go out and chop some logs for the stove,' said Dad, getting to his feet. He patted Erin and Kerry on the shoulders as he walked by. It was a warm day and there was certainly no need for a fire, but Erin knew her father was uneasy at emotional conversations. He liked the simple things in life: for his family to get on, for peace to reign and for there to be no need of grave family conferences.

When he was gone, Mum resumed her story. 'Your father never knew how to handle Shannon,' she said sorrowfully. 'He adored her but he didn't understand her. In your father's and my time, people would have been glad of a chance of education and the possibility of going to college, but Shannon was having none of it. She couldn't wait to leave school and go off travelling.'

'You must have hated it when I wanted to do the same thing,' put in Erin, wincing at the thought of how her mother must have experienced a feeling of *déjà vu* when she'd wanted money to travel for her eighteenth birthday.

'You were different,' Mum said kindly. 'Shannon wanted to go off and save the world and never come back; you just wanted a bit of excitement.'

'Look how it turned out, though,' Erin said slowly.

'Ah, get down off the cross, Ms Martyr,' grumbled Kerry. 'Somebody else needs the wood.'

They all laughed.

'And then,' Mum took a sip of tea that had to be cold by now, 'she came home one night and told us she was pregnant. It wasn't the news we were dying to hear or anything, but we said we'd stand by her. We loved her – what else would we do? Your father said we could add on a bit to the house for another bedroom – this was when we lived in Raheny and the house was small, to be honest, too small for four of us and a baby. But Shannon said no way, she wasn't having any of it. She wanted to travel and she would. She'd have the baby adopted; it wasn't going to tie her down.'

Erin felt a heaviness in her heart at this. It was painful

to hear how she hadn't been wanted, how her mother had planned to give her away.

'I know this is hard for you to hear, love,' Mum said to Erin, 'but I wanted to tell you the truth, the way it was. I owe you that much. I thought I could protect you with half-truths before and look how wrong I was, so this is the real story, warts and all.'

'I want to hear the truth.' Erin wasn't lying, but she hadn't thought it would be so painful.

'Are you sure?' Mum asked.

Erin nodded and glanced at Kerry, who was listening with the air of one who'd heard the story before and knew each and every twist of the tale.

'Your father and I couldn't bear for you to be adopted and we told Shannon we'd bring you up. That did go on, you know, love,' she added earnestly. 'There are lots of children in the world brought up by their grandparents, thinking their aunts and uncles are brothers and sisters. We just wanted the best for you both and that seemed to be it.'

'I know,' Erin said. 'You were wonderful to do it, Mum, honestly. It was just a shock when I found out.'

Her mother's lovely blue eyes clouded. 'I should have told you before, Lord knows, we talked about it enough, but as you got older, and we hadn't said anything, I didn't know how to broach it. And then when you asked for your passport . . . It's true what they say about making a tangled web when you start to deceive.'

Erin, afraid her mother was going to cry, and not wanting that, reached over and grasped her hands. 'Let's move on. Tell me about Shannon, what she's like. Let's talk about the good times and not the bad ones.' She could have talked for longer about when Shannon had become pregnant, and who her true father was, but she knew it would upset her mother.

'The good times . . . Lord,' her mother said, casting her mind back. 'I remember when she and her friend Lorraine made their First Holy Communion and they got all this money from the neighbours and they bought themselves so many sweets I thought they'd be sick, but they weren't. And Shannon had kept some chocolate bars she said she was sending to the poor people in the Third World because their children never got sweets.'

Mum's face shone at the memory. 'Oh, and the time she got it into her head that Father Ryan should get involved in the Campaign for Nuclear Disarmament because he was a religious man, after all, and she couldn't imagine why he wasn't rushing off to make placards and join her on marches. That was when she was fifteen. She met this local lad who was big into CND and that was when she got interested in campaigning for things that were important. Somebody has to think of the bigger picture, she used to say.'

'She liked the idea of campaigning more than anything else,' Kerry interrupted. 'When she got bored with CND, she moved on to the next thing. Remember that group who were going to travel to the States to protest about some secret military testing on Native American lands? She got interested in that because she wanted to go to the US. If they'd been based in the North Pole, she wouldn't have been so keen, would she?'

'Ah, don't be so hard on her,' pleaded their mother. 'Her heart is in the right place. She's an idealist, that's all.'

Kerry shot a wry look at Erin that said she didn't agree with this analysis but wasn't going to start a row by saying so.

Mum talked for ages about how kind Shannon was but that she'd always been a bit other-worldly and wasn't the most practical of people. That's why she'd known it was better for her and not Shannon to bring up Erin. 'With the best will in the world, she'd have had you living with strangers in some caravan on a protest site if we'd let her take you.'

'So she did want me, when she was older?' Erin asked eagerly.

'Not entirely.' Mum was cagey.

411

Kerry couldn't stand the edited highlights any more. 'When you were eight, she was going out with a guy and he had a three-year-old daughter, so Shannon thought you might live with them and be company for his kid. That's how much she wanted you.'

'That's when I remember meeting her,' Erin recalled grimly.

'Yeah, she came back because she thought you might be useful to her.'

'Kerry! Don't talk like that,' said Mum.

'It's the truth, Mum.' Kerry was unapologetic. 'She came back six years ago because she hoped we'd lend her money for that stupid hostel, and the only reason we know where she lives now is because she likes to think there's money on tap nearby. I hope you haven't been giving her any,' she added.

'I haven't,' said Mum, and both Erin and Kerry knew she was lying.

'Is she bad with money?' asked Erin.

'She doesn't understand that you have to earn it,' Kerry said caustically.

'Oh.'

Peter arrived back with the girls and Kerry went off to greet them.

'She's angry with Shannon for what she did to you and me,' Mum said. 'But I don't want you to think badly of Shannon; she's not a bad person at all. She's just what they call a free spirit; she doesn't want to be tied down. I longed for her to be like all my friends' daughters: happy to marry, settle down, have children, but she wasn't made like that.

'It was her choice and it's wrong of us all to punish her for that. Maybe I was the one who made a mistake. Maybe I should have forced her to take care of you and that would have changed her.'

'If she didn't want to, she didn't want to,' Erin pointed out. 'You can't make people do things.'

'I know. And we loved you so much, it was a joy to rear you.'

Erin's smile lit up her face. That was worth all the tales of how Shannon hadn't wanted her: Mum and Dad did and that was what mattered.

An hour after leaving her parents' house, Erin stood outside Shannon's apartment building and told herself that if she saw a woman in a television show doing something this mutton-headed, she'd change channels. But then, every part of her life connected with Shannon had the faintly unreal air of a television show. It was the Shannon effect, she decided.

She'd got the address from her mother, and when it was time to go, instead of driving back to Greg and the hotel, Erin had set off to find Shannon. She had some time to spare, as Greg was sure to be working in the hotel room, and the whole family weren't scheduled to meet again until seven, when they were going to have dinner. Erin knew that if she told Greg or Kerry that she was going to find Shannon, they'd want to come with her. But this was something she had to do on her own.

Shannon lived in Wexford town in an apartment in an old house with an imposing address. But somehow Rectory Lodge sounded much better than this place looked. On a busy street with shops and cafés all around, Rectory Lodge was a rambling old house that would cost more to tear down than it was worth. Erin stood beside the peeling black door and scanned the names under the doorbells. 'Shannon & William' was written in flowing script under bell number six. Thinking of how hard most people tried to hide behind the anonymity of initials on their apartment buildings, Erin thought it was sort of naïve of Shannon to trumpet her name so publicly. But perhaps William, whoever he was, was built like a linebacker and saved Shannon from men who tried to come on to her. Erin didn't know why, but she'd imagined that Shannon had lots of people do that to her. Men would like the glint in her eye and fancy their chances when the redhead smiled back in that knowing way. And Shannon probably spent her life saying, 'But I only smiled at him, that's all. It was just a laugh.'

Erin pushed the bell. It was so old that she had to push hard and, even then, she wondered if it had rung because it didn't look reliable.

'Oh, if you're looking for Shannon, she's out,' said a voice, and a girl dressed in a T-shirt and jeans, with her arms full of packages, pushed past breezily. 'You could wait on her landing if you'd like,' the girl added, taking in Erin's pregnant figure. 'There's no chair or anything but you could sit on a step.'

'No, thanks, I'll wait in one of the cafés,' Erin replied. 'You don't know when she'll be back, do you?'

The girl shrugged and shoved the door open with her foot on account of the packages. Erin marvelled at the notion of leaving the front door unlocked in this day and age.

'Dunno when she'll be back,' said the girl. 'But she went out when I did and it looked like she was going for groceries. Shouldn't be long.' She peered at Erin curiously. 'You're dead like her, though. You her sister or something?'

'Something,' Erin said.

In Coffee A Go Go across the street, she allowed herself a decaf latte and drank it deeply, thinking of the gorgeous lattes she used to get from a tiny coffee shop near the office in Chicago. How many times had she daydreamed away her lunchtime imagining this moment?

She kept watch on Rectory Lodge but, even so, she almost missed the slender figure who swept across the street and, despite the bags of groceries, ran lightly up the steps to the black door. The woman wore a long cream cardigan that covered her up, and Erin couldn't get a look at her face, but her hair flowed free in a long tangle of red. Erin would recognise that colour of hair anywhere. It was just like her own. Draining her coffee, she left money on the table and hurried across the street. She opened the door, ignoring the musty smell of old damp carpet. Up the stairs she went. The first landing contained flats three and four. One and two must be on the ground floor, she figured, going up again. The damp scent was worse on the second landing, and if Erin had looked she'd have seen that the carpet was tattered beyond repair. But she didn't look. Her eyes were fixed on number six, a plain green door that had been left ajar. Stopping to catch her breath, she waited a beat and then knocked.

'Hiya, Ciara, is that you? The door's open. Come on in. I got milk.'

Erin touched the door, waiting to wake up and discover that she'd imagined it and this was all a dream. But the door was real. She pushed and found herself in a big, high-ceilinged room painted apple green with an open door leading to what must be the bedroom. Postcards and posters for anti-war and anti-globalisation rallies decorated one wall and an old couch covered with several tatty throws dominated the room. Two peeling sash windows overlooked the street, and one section of the room had been turned into a shabby kitchenette where an elderly oven sat among a group of free-standing cupboards, painted a perkier French Golden Delicious green. A scarred foldaway table with three unmatching chairs was pushed against one wall and the two grocery bags had been dumped there casually. A small collection of vinyl records was stacked on a low shelving unit beside a portable record player of such vintage that Erin reckoned it must be antique. The room would have looked like a cheap student bedsit to Erin's eyes except it lacked the modern paraphernalia that students these days owned, like high-tech TVs, CD players and shiny racing bikes. By comparison with the student digs Erin had known, this room was cheaper than cheap. It was not what she'd expected by any stretch of the imagination. Unless her mother didn't have a penny to her name, this could not be her home, and such obvious penury didn't fit in with the picture of Shannon's hedonistic, free-spirited lifestyle. Mum and Kerry had said she wasn't good with money, but she couldn't be that broke. Who would leave their family for this?

A bustling from the open bedroom door told her that the occupant was in there and Erin had a moment's anxiety about being in the wrong place. She could see herself being thrown out of the flat with cries of 'Police!' echoing in her ears and . . .

A woman suddenly emerged from the bedroom and Erin's thoughts of being in the wrong flat vanished.

Standing there with a quizzical look on her face was a woman the mirror image of Erin. The same copper hair, the same almond-shaped eyes, the same narrow face with a proud nose over a full upper lip.

The girl outside the building had been right when she thought the two of them were sisters, Erin realised. This woman did not look anything like the mid-forties she had to be. Thirty-six at a push, but no more. Her skin was unlined and faintly freckled. Proof, Erin thought bitterly, that no responsibility was the ultimate in anti-ageing treatments.

'Hello,' said the woman in a friendly tone, remarkably sanguine about finding a total stranger in her home.

'I'm sorry but the door was open,' Erin began, and then felt angry with herself. What was she apologising for? It was Shannon who should be apologising. 'You're Shannon Flynn?'

'Yeah.' The woman smiled.

Erin delivered her bombshell. 'I'm your daughter, Erin.'

The smile widened. 'Wow, like, oh wow! Really?'

Whatever Erin had expected, it wasn't this.

'Aren't you surprised?' she asked.

'I figured you'd come some day,' Shannon said, unconcerned. 'Tea? I was about to make some peppermint for myself and ordinary for Ciara across the hall.'

'Tea would be nice,' Erin said weakly.

'I don't drink dairy, you see,' Shannon said, moving into the kitchenette.

She hadn't told Erin to take a seat or hugged her or

anything, but then it didn't take a genius to figure out that convention played a minor role in Shannon's life. Erin sat down anyway.

'Do you drink dairy?' enquired Shannon as airily as if they'd met at a bus stop and were chatting to pass the time of day. 'It's damaging, really. Soya's the way to go.'

Erin watched Shannon as she worked. Mum was the perfect example of how a woman could make tea, check the dinner in the oven, iron a shirt and keep a wary eye on the stock pot, all at once. Shannon, on the other hand, made a pot of tea like she was taking part in a complicated ceremony: utterly concentrating on the task in hand.

'Dairy gives you cancer,' Shannon rattled on. 'I've read about it. I've been on soya for years now.'

A flicker of anger ignited in Erin's brain. 'Kerry had cancer. Did you know that?'

Shannon kept concentrating on her tea bags. 'Yeah,' she said absently. 'She's OK now, though, right?'

'You didn't go and see her when she was ill, did you?' Erin felt guilty that she hadn't been there for her sister, but at least she had the excuse that she hadn't known. Shannon had. 'Why didn't you go to visit her?' Erin asked. What she really wanted to ask was why the hell had Shannon left her when she was a baby.

'Oh, you know, I'm not into all that family stuff,' Shannon said easily. 'I left it all behind years ago. You should make your own family, like in a commune.' At this, her eyes lit up. 'I lived in a commune for a couple of years when I was on an anti-globalisation protest. It was amazing.' Misreading the look on Erin's face, she said, 'Haven't you ever tried a commune? Oh, you'd love it.'

'How do you know what I'd love or not?' Erin said, her tone conversational. But Greg would have recognised the steel in her words.

'No, really, you can be yourself without all the boring structures of the settled, normal, semi-detached life.' Shannon said the words with distaste.

'Is that why you left home when you were young?' asked Erin, somehow managing not to add, 'when I was a baby'.

'I left to be free,' Shannon said, flicking back her long hair in a manner that Erin realised was her trademark. 'I knew I couldn't bear to be tied down, I'd have gone mad in that sort of life. Nobody has any principles in that world, you know? They just want to make money in some dull job and go home at night. They don't believe in anything.'

She brought two mugs to the table. One was chipped. Erin wanted to ask what sort of life Shannon had got in exchange for giving up her family: a shabby flat, chipped mugs and the memory of communal living once upon a time didn't seem like much of a bargain.

'I'll put on some music,' Shannon said, apparently oblivious to the tense atmosphere.

'Hiya,' said a voice at the door.

A tall, anorexically thin woman with coal-black dreadlocks arrived.

'Hiya, Ciara, the kettle's boiled,' said Shannon. 'This is Erin.'

'Hi, Erin,' said Ciara shyly, winding her thin body into the kitchenette to make her own tea.

'Oh, I love this music,' Shannon said, as the sound of Simon and Garfunkel drifted out of her record player. She did a little swirling dance by herself as though to prove the point.

'I'm Shannon's daughter,' Erin said to Ciara, determined to provoke some sort of response.

'Wow.' Ciara was jerked out of her shyness. 'You never told me you had a daughter, Shannon.'

Erin had been about to take a sip of her tea but, at that, she put the mug down. Shannon had never even told people about her. But what else did she expect?

'I have to go,' she said coldly.

'Ah, don't,' said Shannon. 'We have to catch up.'

Erin glared at her. To Shannon, she was just another person who'd dropped into her peripatetic life. They'd 'catch up' for half an hour, try to cram Erin's whole life into a single conversation, and then it would be over.

Shannon was lost in the world of hippie-dom, always ready to climb aboard the bus to an anti-war demo or a save-the-trees project. She didn't have many things, just posters she could roll up, her portable record player and whatever garments she could fit in her rucksack. Erin admired people who stood up for their principles, but in Shannon she wondered if the principle or the lifestyle surrounding it was the lure. And what about the principle of mother love? Where had Shannon's much-vaunted principles been when her daughter needed her? Were the trees more important than Erin?

Erin hadn't meant to get angry but, somehow, the rage boiled up in her like milk bubbling over in a pan.

'I think we've too much to catch up on,' she said bitterly. 'Twenty-seven years to be exact. You see, Ciara, I'm the part of Shannon's life that she wanted to run away from. The part she didn't think was worth fighting for. Not like anti-globalisation or the trees.' She glanced around at Shannon's posters advertising demos from all over the world. 'Save the Snails!' read one. 'Yes, my mother was more interested in saving endangered snails than in me. If I'd had a shell or if I'd had "Property of the US Defense Forces" stamped on me, would she have been more interested?'

Ciara looked anxious, as if she'd witnessed many bitter family rows and had hoped that living by herself was the way to escape them.

'It wasn't like that,' said Shannon mildly.

'What was it like?' demanded Erin.

Shannon shrugged helplessly. 'I was a kid, I wanted to feel free –'

'Free from what?' interrupted her daughter.

'You know, the structures of life.' It was all so obvious to Shannon. 'I didn't want to be tied down.'

'But what about me?' Erin rapped out.

Shannon shrugged. 'Mum looked after you. She loved

you. When you were small, I knew it was the right thing to do.'

'But how could you just leave and never come back?' demanded Erin. 'Didn't you ever want to meet me?'

'Mum said she'd say that you were her child. They moved house and everything so nobody would know and it would be easier for you. Sure, why would I ruin all that? People would have been asking questions and the usual. God, I hate that stuff. The parochial mind wanting to know who was the father and all that . . . That's what I wanted to escape from.'

'Responsibility, in other words.' Erin was harsh.

'You don't understand,' Shannon said easily.

'I understand how a teenager might want to walk out on her child because she was scared but I don't understand how a grown woman would never come home to see that same child, not ever.' Her voice shook. 'Even if you didn't want to bring me up, why didn't you ever want to see me, say hello, act the part of the big sister you were pretending to be? And coming back when I was a small child doesn't count. Where were you when I was growing up?'

'Oh, you're just like Kerry,' said Shannon, exasperated. 'Always harping on about the past. That was a long time ago.'

Erin stared out of the window, furiously blinking back tears. She hadn't meant this to happen but somehow all the years of wondering had exploded inside her. Shannon needed to hear how Erin felt. She was Erin's mother, for God's sake. Hadn't that meant anything?

'You gave birth to me,' she added harshly. 'I'm your child, you and whatever anonymous man you slept with. Doesn't that mean anything to you?'

For the first time, Shannon looked at a loss. She bit her lip, and Erin could remember seeing Kerry do just the same thing. Kerry had been right all along: she'd warned Erin that meeting Shannon was not a wise move. What had she said? 'You won't find what you're looking for,

Erin. Not with Shannon. She was always different from us.'

Erin got up, not caring that she'd knocked against the table and spilled her tea.

'Goodbye,' she said, and left Shannon and Ciara behind with their mouths open.

As she hurried down the stairs, she felt nothing but anger, which was a relief. It would have been terrible to have cried over someone like Shannon. She never wanted to see her again. What was the point?

Greg wasn't the only person to have figured out where Erin had disappeared to for an hour and a half. He, Mum and Kerry were all waiting in the lobby of the hotel when Erin returned.

'Never mind,' said Mum when Erin saw them all and her face crumpled. 'She doesn't mean to be hurtful, it's just the way she is.'

'Don't stand up for Shannon,' said Kerry crossly. 'Who knows what the bitch said?'

Greg hugged Erin tightly. 'I was so worried when you didn't come back. Kerry said she figured you'd gone to see Shannon. I'll kill her if she hurt you by what she said.'

'She didn't say anything,' Erin said wearily. 'She wasn't interested.'

'How could she not be interested?' asked Greg quietly.

'Shannon's only interested in herself,' Kerry retorted. 'I told you not to go on your own,' she said to her sister.

'I had to see her,' Erin said. 'I had to talk to her.' Not that it had done her much good. Kerry had been right – Shannon was only interested in herself. Everyone else was only a bit player in the drama that was Shannon's life.

A sudden squirming inside her made Erin reach down and touch her belly. The baby's movements fascinated her every time. Imagine, inside her, snuggled up safe and warm, lay her baby. The flailing arms and legs were signs that the baby was healthy and Erin couldn't wait to have her child in her arms, with those arms and legs wriggling in the outside world.

I'll never leave you, she told her baby silently. Never.

CHAPTER TWENTY-SEVEN

By the second week of August, it seemed as if everyone in Dunmore was on holiday. Except for the Barton family, of course. Given everything that had been happening over the last few months, Abby couldn't begin to consider going away. It seemed ridiculous to be thinking of sun, sangria and flip-flops when she and Tom had split up, Jess was barely talking to her and her career looked like it might be over. But eventually the lure of the brochures in the travel agents' windows was too much. Every time Abby ran past O'Callaghan's Travel on her way to the supermarket, she noticed special offers detailing trips to the Canaries, amazing fly-drive holidays to the States and long-haul flights to the exotic Far East.

Newspapers and magazines were just as bad. She couldn't pick up a paper or magazine without seeing another 'Diet yourself into a bikini' article or one of those 'Have you got your travel insurance sorted out?' features describing travel disasters where somebody had spent thousands in a foreign hospital getting their broken leg fixed all because they wouldn't shell out a few pounds on insurance.

While part of Abby longed to lie on a beach, feeling the sun baking her skin as she read novels and sipped boozy cocktails with impossible names, her heart just wasn't in it. Every holiday destination she could imagine would be redolent with the memories of other trips the family had taken.

France was out, for instance. They'd had an incredible camping trip to France when Jess had been a baby. Abby could remember it so well, even though it had been fifteen years ago. She and Tom had been thrilled with their new life, their new baby and the heady feeling of responsibility as new parents. Who cared that every insect in the Rhône decided to dive-bomb Tom, or that the camp showers left a lot to be desired? It had been a memorable time purely because of where they were in their lives.

That was the sort of trip that every new holiday would be measured against, and this holiday, this single-life holiday, would be so very different. There would be just her and Jess, two people rattling around in a holiday made for three. Tom would undoubtedly make his own plans and Abby had no idea what those would be. She and Tom spoke now only to discuss arrangements about Jess.

For Jess's sixteenth birthday in early August, Tom had coldly said he wanted to take her out to the cinema and to dinner and Abby, who knew he was doing this to punish her because there was no reason the three of them couldn't share this treat, had had to agree. That was the longest conversation they'd had in ages.

Since the day she'd pleaded with Tom to try again, they hadn't talked about the split at all. Which was easier in one way from Abby's point of view because she didn't have to face the naked anger in Tom's eyes when he looked at her, but harder in another way, because she knew that unless Tom changed his mind there was no hope of ever getting back together. The only plus was that at least nobody in Dunmore seemed to have cottoned on to the fact that they had split up. She and Tom had obviously lived such separate lives that nobody commented when they saw Abby on her own. But it couldn't last. One day, somebody would work it out. And if the split became public, Abby knew that her profile as a TV presenter meant the gossip writers would become interested. That thought filled her with dread.

Driving out of Cork one day after a meeting at Beech to review some early footage of the series, Abby decided to bite the holiday bullet. She parked outside O'Callaghan's Travel, ran in and grabbed a handful of brochures. She needed a break. In fact, after today's meeting, anybody would need a break.

Abby had gone into the office expecting a bit of back-slapping while the team looked at the video clip of the first show. What she'd got was the sensation of having the carpet pulled from under her feet.

Roxie had been charming to her, which should have given Abby a hint of what was to come.

'Great to see you,' Roxie had said with a smile that showed off pointed canines.

Definitely some fox in there somewhere, Abby decided. Or was it vampire? One of the nastier, flesh-eating creatures, that was for sure.

The blinds were drawn in the boardroom and the tape rolled. Even though Abby knew that this was only the rough cut, and that changes would undoubtedly be made, she was still shocked by what she saw.

She'd worked so hard on the series and it was clear that Roxie had been hovering in the editing suite, determined to see that Abby was sidelined. The twins were now the stars of the show. Abby was nothing more than a guest presenter – or at least that's what it looked like. Her scenes had been slashed to pieces so that for every minute of screen time she enjoyed, Mitzi and Linzi were given five. The de-junking segment she'd filmed was like the trailer to their feature presentation. She was devastated.

'Well, what do you think?' asked Flora nervously, as they sat around the boardroom table after viewing the footage.

'What do I think?' said Abby, enunciating every syllable slowly. 'What the hell do you think I think? This used to be my show, but not any more. Is the show going to be called *Declutter with Linzi and Mitzi* and you'll have my name in very tiny print down the bottom of the credits as a guest presenter? Or are you going to bother with my name at all?' She stared at everyone around the table with fury. She felt so betrayed. It had all happened exactly as Mike, her agent, had said it would. She'd half hoped that hiring him would make Brian and Roxie think twice about treating her badly, because Mike Horowitz was a name to be reckoned with in the business, but apparently not. Roxie was grooming the twins for stardom and Abby now had no place in the Beech line-up.

Perhaps it was her age, but she didn't think so. It was just that bloody Roxie hated her for some reason.

'Don't you like it?' enquired Roxie, with a nasty glint in her eyes. 'We all think it's wonderful, don't we?' She stared around the room, as if defying the other Beech executives to say a word. She had them exactly where she wanted them, Abby knew. Which meant that Abby was out of a job. Or soon would be. She got to her feet, glad that at least she hadn't bothered dressing up and was wearing the cool fitted white shirt and faded jeans of a veteran TV star who really couldn't give a shit.

'Well, we'll have to see what Mike thinks of all of this,' she said calmly, wishing she'd got an agent years ago and then she wouldn't be in this position now. Her contract with Beech was not precisely an industry boiler plate one and she had little comeback if the production company did decide to sideline her.

Mike had advised against any confrontational meetings with Beech over this. 'I've spoken to Brian, he knows I'm on board, now let's see what they do,' he said. 'Brian isn't stupid – he won't want to ruin his relationship with you, no matter how weak your actual contract is.'

Maybe Brian was stupid, after all, Abby thought. As soon as she left, she'd phone Mike.

'Bye.' She bestowed a cool smile on everyone because she wouldn't give any of them the satisfaction of knowing how rattled she was. Instead, she walked confidently out of the boardroom as if she hadn't a care in the world. It was only when she got back into her Jeep that she let the anger show.

Bloody bastards, she raged, hitting the steering wheel in

426

her temper. She'd come up with the idea for *Declutter*. It was her show. How dare they do this to her? Her fingers shook as she dialled Mike's private line and left a message for him. She wasn't sure what he could do in the face of this disaster, but he ought to know.

Mike somehow managed to calm her down.

'Legally, they can do this,' he said evenly. 'You should never have signed that contract in the first place without proper advice, but as you did you're stuck with it, and obviously Brian doesn't want to renegotiate. He's being very short-sighted, though. You have lots of talent, Abby, and just because Roxie only likes kids on TV, doesn't mean that the viewers agree. I need to see the rough cut – they were supposed to send it to me.'

'They knew better,' said Abby bitterly.

'Don't panic,' Mike said cheerfully. 'When I've got you a fabulous new job with another company, Brian will be crying into his cornflakes that he didn't appreciate Abby Barton when he had her. The plus side of your crappy contract is that they don't have any hold over you. You can walk at any time.'

Abby wanted to ask where to, but didn't want to appear negative. 'Yeah, right,' she said. 'Thanks, Mike. Somehow you make me feel better.'

In Dunmore, she'd got stuck at the traffic lights outside the travel agents'. Giant posters of people having a good time on holiday shimmered into view when she turned her head. What the hell, a holiday might not be the answer but it would certainly help. She definitely needed to get away and, after suffering through both her exams and her parents' break-up, poor Jess could do with one too.

At home, there was no sign of Jess. This was nothing new. Jess had been practically living at Steph's house for the past month of the holidays. Or at least, that's what Jess had said. She'd told Abby she couldn't see much of Oliver as he was working long hours in his summer job in his father's market garden business. He was also doing occasional shifts in the mineral water plant, he explained to Abby, so he could afford to pay to insure himself on his mother's car.

Abby knew that the plant ran twenty-four hours a day, so that a student trying to make money could indeed be worked off his feet. Nobody could say that Oliver lacked the work ethic, which was good. She also felt that Oliver was a decent lad who cared about Jess, but that didn't stop her worrying. She'd tried asking politely for Jess to ring her every day and explain exactly where she was, but when that hadn't worked, Abby had put her foot down and insisted that Jess phone in several times a day.

'If you don't call me, I'll phone Oliver and then Steph, and I'll keep harassing you until I know you're safe, right?' Abby had said fiercely. She hadn't wanted to fight with Jess, not after all that had happened, but she worried so much about her daughter. So, Jess was sixteen and Oliver was a nice lad. That didn't mean anything nowadays.

On impulse, she phoned Jess's mobile phone but got the busy signal. Oh well, she'd try again later.

Abby went to the fridge and poured herself a glass of cool white wine. She knew she was drinking far more than she used to when she and Tom were together. Then, they shared a bottle of wine a couple of nights a week. Now, she had at least two glasses of wine alone every single evening. She couldn't help it. What else was going to help her get through the bleak misery?

Taking the icy glass to the kitchen table, she sat down and started to study the brochures. She didn't want to look at the one for America. That had been where the Barton family had planned to go before it all went wrong, before Jay. She and Tom had been talking about a trip across the States for years. It was their dream family holiday, the one they were going to take if they won the lottery.

Tom had the itinerary planned: they'd fly to New York, see the sights, then rent a car and meander their way down south and across the country until they ran out of time or money, whichever came first. Abby had a longing to visit San Francisco but Tom had a childhood dream of seeing the Grand Canyon.

'It's a place you have to see before you die,' he'd told Abby. 'Wouldn't that be a fabulous trip? You, me and Jess, driving around seeing everything, living the American dream . . .'

Abby could remember how he'd looked at her when he was telling her all of this, that intense light in his dark eyes. That was the man she'd fallen in love with. She never saw that light in his eyes any more. Now, when he came to pick up Jess, his face was bleak and his eyes looked sad and somehow diminished. She had done that to him. She'd turned him from a vibrant, passionate person into a shell of a man who had lost his wife to another. Abby threw the American brochure onto the floor. She'd look at it later.

Maybe somewhere in Europe would be good. Yeah, Europe sounded like a good idea. Not France, of course. Remember the Rhône.

Spain, then. They'd never gone to Spain. She began riffling through the pages of the 'Discover Spain' brochure, feeling her spirits lift. There were beautiful villas in the mountains, fantastic apartments down in the south, and elegant hotels in the great cities where you could wander through art galleries and admire Spanish architecture all day. But perhaps Jess would be bored with that. Abby wasn't sure. She wasn't sure what Jess liked at all any more. That was another problem.

And what if Jess didn't want to go on holiday with her mother? When Abby had been a child, family holidays didn't exist. Not for her family, anyway. The Costellos had never gone abroad; they were lucky to have food on the table, never mind the funds to whisk everyone off on a plane for a week in a hotel. And now, when Abby finally had the money to take them all somewhere exotic, she had no family left. Her mother was long dead: she'd followed her husband into the grave within a year. Abby had always thought that was the final tragedy of her mother's life: when she'd finally been free of the drunkard who'd never properly provided for her or her two children, she'd become ill and died. Even in death, Frank Costello had had the last laugh.

Abby kept in contact with her sister, Viv, who now lived in Australia and had neither the time nor the inclination to come home. But they weren't close. Their upbringing hadn't been the sort to foster closeness.

Now Abby's family were Jess and Tom. Or *had been* Jess and Tom. It was unthinkable to ask Tom to go on holiday with her, and Jess might not want to.

Sitting at her kitchen table, in a beautiful house she'd worked so hard to afford, Abby Barton burst into tears. What had it all been for?

Three miles up the road, Jess Barton was busy cleaning out the dog kennels in Dunmore Animal Refuge. It was a filthy job and most of the other volunteers at the refuge hated it, but Jess never minded. She loved the animals so much and she wanted to do whatever she could to help Jean, who ran the place. Dressed in threadbare old denims with a too-big stockman's coat over her clothes to protect her from the dirt, Jess shovelled and scrubbed until she was sweating. There was something very satisfying about cleaning up after the animals. It was such a simple task. There were no emotions involved. Nobody asked you how you were feeling or were you upset or worried when you were shovelling out dog shit. Nobody was surreptitiously watching you to see if you were upset about the break-up of your parents. No, you just brushed and shovelled and scrubbed until you were sick of the smell of dog poo and the place was clean.

And afterwards, Jean would come out of the house with a tray of home-made coconut biscuits and cans of Coke. Jess loved the Coke breaks. They were so much fun, chatting to Jean and Olga, who worked full time in the centre, and hearing about the plans to rehome some animals, and discussing which ones needed to see the vet the next day. Listening to Jean and Olga, Jess didn't feel like a secondary-school student any more, she felt like an ordinary working person with opinions people were interested in.

Jess was good with the dogs and had noticed before anyone else that Lady, a nervy half-greyhound, was lame. She'd been in charge of Lady when the vet came, and holding the quivering, skinny body, Jess had felt as if she'd found her vocation in life.

It was so different from home. Jess could remember when home had been full of fun. But it wasn't like that now that Dad had left. The house was too big for just Jess and Mum, and they rattled around in it, lonely and miserable, each one pretending to the other that everything was OK. But it wasn't.

When Dad phoned, it was worse. If Mum picked up the phone, she instantly handed it over to Jess as if the receiver was red hot.

'How are you, Jess?' Dad would say each time, and Jess could tell he was on edge in case she cried or something.

'Fine, just fine,' Jess said breezily. 'I've been reading a review of a great new film. We could see it on Saturday.'

'I'd love that,' Dad would reply with relief.

They saw loads of films now, and yet they'd never gone to one together when Dad lived at home. But sitting in the dark of a cinema, with all emotion safely confined to the big screen, was easier than going for drives or long walks. Walking or in the car, Dad wanted to talk and Jess desperately didn't want to talk. She didn't want to talk to her mother, either, despite Mum's best efforts. If they talked, Jess wouldn't be able to stop herself asking why: 'Why did you split up? Why couldn't you have tried harder?' And that would be stupid, she knew.

Oliver was the only person she could confide in, and even then, she could hardly tell him everything, not like she would have been able to do with Steph.

Steph was so tied up with Zach that she didn't seem to realise what was going on in Jess's life any more. They

431

were still friends – God yes, they'd always be friends. But it was different. Now that Zach was on the scene, Steph had changed. She was slightly more grown up, not as willing to talk about all sorts of rubbish with her one-time best friend. And Jess missed that. They didn't see as much of each other as they used to, although Jess hadn't told Mum that. Mum would go mental if she thought Jess and Oliver spent hours together when he wasn't working. Mum seemed to think that everyone with the normal complement of teenage hormones thought of nothing but sex, so Jess found it easier to say she was with Steph.

She did think about going all the way with Oliver, though. Not that he'd asked her or anything. He wasn't like that. It was there, hovering in the background, but somehow Jess knew Oliver wasn't the sort of guy to push her.

He was great to talk to about most things but she couldn't really spill her guts out to him, how she could hear Mum crying at night when she thought nobody was listening or how Dad never seemed to pay attention to the films they saw, but just sat staring blankly at the screen, his mind a million miles away.

Oliver's family seemed so settled, his parents got on so well that he could never have understood what it was like to have your mum and dad split up. All she knew was that since her dad had moved out, everything was different and she hated it.

Coming up to the refuge and looking after the animals was a release from all that stress. Lady, Duke, Marmalade, Oscar and Smudge just wanted cuddles, biscuits and lots of sticks thrown for them. Twiglet, her favourite, was gone. Jean had kept him in the refuge as long as she possibly could, but when it came time for him to leave, Jess knew that there were too many things going on in her parents' lives to introduce a dog into the household.

He'd gone to a good home, she was sure of that. Jean never rehomed any of the animals without checking out thoroughly where they were going. But Jess had hated the thought of

Twiglet going, even though he went to a family with a huge garden.

'How's it going?' Jean stood at the door of the animals' quarters and peered in. Her shrewd eyes took in the fact that Jess had cleaned the whole area in about half the time that it took some of the other volunteers to do it. Nobody worked harder or gave more of herself than the sweet, shy schoolgirl.

Jean knew that something was going on in the Barton household, although Jess had never told her exactly what. All Jean knew was that in the last few weeks Jess had become even quieter, if that was possible. There was a sadness in her face that hadn't been there before. Jean would have loved to talk to Jess's parents about this, but she didn't know if she should intrude or not. In the beginning when Jess was working for her, Jess's mother had phoned up to talk to Jean and find out what kind of place the centre was and what sort of work her daughter would be doing. Jean, a no-nonsense individual, had found Abby Barton to be a very nice woman, in spite of the fact that she was on television and everything. Jean didn't have much time for celebrities but Jess's mother had sounded OK. She asked all the right questions and she was certainly interested in what her daughter was doing after school and at weekends. But she never came up to the centre itself. Jean found that a bit strange. What she didn't know was that Jess herself had resisted all attempts by her mother to visit the refuge.

'I'm not a child, remember,' she'd snapped at her mother. 'It's an animal refuge. Look, here are photos of it from the paper and here's their fund-raising leaflet. It's not a crack den in disguise!'

Mum had looked upset at this and, deep inside, Jess had felt sorry. But she didn't want her mother intruding in her place, and perhaps telling Jean what had been going on. She could imagine the conversation: 'Jess's father and I have split up, so I'm worried about her. Perhaps you could keep an eye on her . . .' Jess shuddered at the very idea.

433

'You've done a fantastic job, Jess,' Jean said approvingly now. 'I wish everyone knew how to work as hard as you do. Some of the people who offer to help seem to think it's all playing with puppies and kittens instead of bathing mangy, filthy cats and cleaning up after the dogs.' She was rewarded with a huge smile from Jess. 'So,' Jean went on, 'how are things?'

She left the question hanging in the air, hoping Jess would reply and perhaps open up a little. But Jess didn't. She began scrubbing at a non-existent bit of dirt on the wall. 'Yeah fine, everything's fine,' muttered Jess absently. 'How's Lady's limp doing?'

Jean knew better than to push it. She wasn't the sort of woman to pry into others' lives.

'She's doing fine. The vet was here this morning and he says she'll be right as rain in a few days. Come on, Jess. It's time for a break,' Jean said. 'Or Olga will have wolfed down all the cookies. She's just spent an hour washing that Shetland pony which just came in and she's worn out.'

'Oh, the Shetland looked so cute,' sighed Jess. She'd caught sight of the pony in the distance earlier, a tiny chestnut animal with a matted mane and tail that might have been palomino blond under all the dirt.

'Cute to look at, yes,' grinned Jean, 'but not so cute to wash. This one can bite. Olga's back is black and blue – the pony took chunks out of her each time she wasn't paying attention.'

'I'll just fix the dogs' beds and I'll be out,' Jess said.

She felt a bit guilty when Jean had gone. She knew the older woman was only trying to be kind but she didn't want to talk about what was wrong with her. She preferred to stay and think in silence. It was easier that way. And she had something nice to think about too. Oliver was meeting her later in town and they were going to go for a long walk along the beach. She couldn't stay out too late because then Mum would get suspicious and start worrying. Jess wondered if her mother would have worried so much about Jess and Oliver if

Dad had still been around. Then, Mum had been a worrier, sure, but Dad would have made her understand that it was normal for someone of Jess's age to have a boyfriend. Mum seemed anxious about the idea, but then she was anxious about everything these days . . . That was the problem with parents' break-ups, she realised. They touched everything in your life. Mum seemed to think that Jess was just a kid and worried about whether she cried at night or had nightmares over her parents divorcing.

It was more complicated than that. She wasn't a child any more for a start, and only a complete child would think there was any hope of her parents getting back together They talked to her about the importance of communication, and they couldn't see that for the past year they'd never talked to each other. Dad always thought he was right about everything and couldn't see any other point of view. Mum always seemed to put her foot in it with Dad, talking about her work, not realising that, for some reason, Dad hated her job. They were hopeless, really. Jess thought about telling them what she thought, but they never asked her opinion. She was the kid, right?

It was five thirty when she left the refuge to meet Oliver, and Jean watched her cycling down the rutted laneway to the main road at the bottom. Jean was worried about her. For the second time that day, she wondered if she should phone Jess's mother and talk to her. But maybe she shouldn't. Jess was a teenager and teenagers went through difficult years. Jean just hoped that she could talk to that nice young man of hers. Oliver – that was his name, wasn't it? He'd come to pick Jess up at the refuge a few times and he seemed a nice lad. Jess could just be going through those hormonal teenage years; yes, that could be it. And Jean was sure that Jess's family wouldn't appreciate her interfering. Whatever was going on in the Barton household was sure to sort itself out without her help.

*   *   *

Mum appeared so quickly when Jess opened the front door that she knew her mother had been waiting for her. It was half-past eight and Jess and Oliver had enjoyed a wonderful few hours walking on the beach, talking, laughing, holding hands and doing nothing in particular.

'Hi, darling, how are you?' Mum's voice was a little bit too bright and she was clutching a half-glass of wine. 'There's something I'd love to talk to you about.'

'Yeah?' said Jess reluctantly, not knowing what was coming next. She hated those 'I have something I want to talk to you about' conversations. They all meant trouble. Like: 'We're leaving the country on the next plane to live somewhere else and you'll never see your father again' type of thing. Just at the moment anything was possible.

'A holiday, that's what I want to talk about,' Abby said brightly. 'We both need a holiday – well, *I* do and I'm sure you do after your exams. So what do you think?'

She sounded so excited, so like a child, that Jess felt the positions were reversed. *She* was the grown-up and her mother was the kid. The only problem was, tonight, she didn't feel like being a grown-up. Tonight, she wanted to go into her room to lie on her bed, listen to music and think about Oliver.

'Yeah, whatever,' she said.

Her mother looked so downcast at this reaction that Jess felt a little guilty.

'I mean, we *could* go on holiday,' Jess pointed out, 'but you know it won't be the same without Dad.'

As soon as she'd spoken, Jess felt full of remorse. She hadn't meant to say it like that – it had just come out all wrong – and now her Mum looked as if she was going to cry.

'I just meant . . .' said Jess, embarrassed, 'I just meant it would be a different sort of holiday, wouldn't it?'

Her mother looked shattered. 'I'm sorry, Jess. I know this is hard on you.' Mum's fingers were taut around the stem of her wine glass. Jess noticed she wasn't wearing nail varnish or anything. Mum had always tried so hard with her nails; now she didn't bother. 'It'll be a very different sort of holiday but you need a break and we have to start a new life somehow.' Now she'd started, she'd better keep going. 'A holiday is only the beginning, Jess,' she added. 'We'll probably have to sell the house soon and move out.'

Jess said nothing.

'Anyway, back to the holiday,' Mum said, in overbright tones. 'What about Spain?' she suggested hopefully.

Jess looked at her as if Abby had just suggested a trip to Mars without oxygen. 'Spain?' she said in disdain. 'I don't think so.'

She remembered when Steph and the Anderson family had gone to Spain four or five years ago. Then, Jess had been mad to go, but not now. She didn't want to go anywhere because then she'd be away from Oliver.

The after-effects of her day were jangling Abby's nerves and she started to feel irritated. 'Where do you think we should go then?' she asked, finding it hard to hide her impatience.

'Well, I don't know,' replied Jess truculently. 'Why don't you ask Dad for his opinion?'

'You know I can't do that,' snapped her mother. 'This holiday is for you and me, not your father.' She took another big slug of wine and went back to looking at the brochures on the kitchen table. Jess was really being a complete pain.

'If you don't know where you want to go, why do we have to go anywhere at all?' Jess glared at her mother for a minute before turning around and leaving the room.

Abby heard her daughter stomp upstairs and then heard the familiar sound of Jess's door slamming shut. Sighing, she went back to the brochures. She needed a holiday and she'd better pick one soon.

Finally, she noticed the brochure detailing trips to Florida. One in particular caught her eye, a combination of a city break and a Disney extravaganza. Jess might say she'd hate it but in her heart she would love it, Abby felt. Florida it would be.

A few days later, the plans were ready. The tickets had arrived, a taxi was booked to take them to the airport and Abby had packed most of her clothes. For someone who specialised in decluttering other people's houses, she was notoriously bad at packing her own suitcase. She knew that at the other end of the journey she would face two suitcases with lots of creased clothes in them, but what the heck? She'd bring an iron.

There was only one other thing to do before they left and it was unfortunately the sort of thing Abby hated.

Selina from Beech had been on to Abby and said that a journalist at *Style* magazine was eager to interview her.

'Maria Carroll is her name and she loves the show,' said Selina. 'She's a tough cookie and she can be bitchy enough in print, but she wants to meet you and it would be worth it because everybody reads her stuff. I know you're rushing off on holiday, Abby dear, but please, pretty please, could you fit it in? It would be such good publicity for the show, and we need to launch with a splash.'

Abby was sick to the teeth of the show but she knew she would do it for Selina. And for her future career. 'Yeah, sure,' she said. There was just one problem. What if the journalist asked about her happy family life? Selina knew it was all a sham and that Tom had left home weeks ago, but nobody else did, and it was one of Abby's greatest fears that the journalistic world would discover her secret. She couldn't cope with the headlines. Imagine them: 'Abby Hides Secret Heartbreak.' Oh God, she could picture the stories all right, detailing every moment of her rise to fame and how she and Tom had done everything together in the beginning. Her success would be blamed, although in part it *was* to blame, she knew. And the articles would speculate on her future too, how she and Tom would probably have to sell their beautiful house. And what if they laid bets on her future love life too? Lining up lots of suitable eligible bachelors? She couldn't bear it.

'OK, Selina,' she said reluctantly. 'I'll do the interview but could you sit in on it, please? Just to make sure that Maria Carroll doesn't ask any horrible questions. Would that be all right?'

Once she'd got her way, Selina would have agreed to anything.

'Sweetie, I'd be delighted to sit in on it,' she said, magnanimous in success. 'But you know, the press are going to find out about you and Tom one day and you're going to have to talk then.'

Abby knew Selina was right but that didn't make it any easier. Breaking up was hard enough without having your whole story spread all over the pages of the newspapers. Tom resented her career as it was. He'd resent it a lot more if their personal story became gossip fodder.

'Now, I'll set this up and all you have to do is turn up and turn on that legendary Barton charm,' Selina said happily. 'That's what's so nice about working with you, Abby, you're such a pro.'

'Yeah,' muttered Abby, 'a real professional, that's me.'

The journalist from *Style* was a soignée, forty-something, who also wrote a lifestyle column detailing her working life as a mother of three. Abby had never met Maria, but she had read her columns several times and guessed that behind the amusing anecdotes about family life and getting cat fur off the couch, there was a tough career journalist with a heart of steel. Taking Bach's Rescue Remedy before such an interview could only do so much, so Abby decided that reinforcements were needed. The day of the interview, she nipped down to The Beauty Spot to have her nails and her make-up done.

It also gave her the chance to have a good gossip with Erin and Ruby in the salon. As she walked through the door, she was aware that she hadn't been to the salon very much lately. It wasn't the same since Sally's death. Ruby and Erin did a really good job keeping the place going but Abby never drove past and saw those jaunty pink gingham curtains without remembering Sally and thinking back to those fun days when Sally had been alive, when the Richardsons had thrown the liveliest parties, when Abby and Tom had still been a couple.

Abby had done her best to keep in touch with Steve but he'd become a virtual recluse since Sally's death, never wanting to talk for more than a moment on the phone and clearly uncomfortable whenever Abby dropped by. The week before, when she'd phoned to ask if he, Delia and the boys would come over for lunch on Saturday, he'd said no. He'd hired a nanny for the boys, he'd told Abby, and he wanted to be with them as often as possible because they needed him.

'Since Sally died, Daniel has been very clingy,' he'd explained. 'Every time I leave, he thinks I'm not coming back. Home provides some stability in their lives.'

'But you all need to get out,' Abby had said.

'I can't cope with going out,' Steve had said tellingly.

Today at the salon, there was no sign of Erin, but Ruby was thrilled when Abby walked in.

'Long time no see,' roared Ruby across the salon floor. Instantly Abby felt guilty. Honestly, if only she could remove the amount of guilt in her system and replace it with self-confidence – then she'd be a fabulous person.

'Yes, sorry, Ruby,' she replied. 'I haven't had a chance to come in for ages but I need the works this morning. I'm going to do an interview with *Style* magazine and I want to be stunning or drop-dead gorgeous or both, if possible.'

Ruby beamed at her. 'Drop-dead gorgeous is not a problem, honey,' she said.

'Is Erin around?' asked Abby.

'No, not today,' Ruby replied, then lowered her voice. 'She's off seeing her parents and sister. You did hear she got in touch with them, didn't you?'

Abby felt even guiltier. She had no idea that Erin had

caught up with her long-lost family. Vowing to contact her very soon, she sat down at a mirror in front of Ruby and sank back into the seat.

'Ruby,' she said, 'do whatever it takes. And if it takes industrial sanding equipment and Polyfilla, then go for it.'

Two hours later, Abby left the salon feeling like a new woman. Her nails were manicured and glossy, her make-up was perfect. And her skin shone with a sort of luminous glow that could come only from either a lifetime of careful cleansing – or one of Ruby's amazing half-hour facials. On the inside, Abby may not have felt like a top TV star, but she certainly looked it.

She was meeting Selina and Maria Carroll in a glamorous restaurant outside Cork city. The restaurant was newly opened and had been an instant success, thanks to fabulous food, exorbitant prices and the fascinating décor. Hollywood in the twenties and thirties was the theme, and the restaurant was decked out like a stage set from a majestic old movie. Abby had never been there but she had chosen it for the interview chiefly because it was reputed to be very dark – and the journalist wouldn't be able to see her face when she blanched every time she had to talk about her marriage.

She was the first there, so she sat at their table and drank a double espresso, which she hoped would sharpen her wits so she would be ready for even the toughest questions.

Selina and Maria arrived together and there was a flurry of 'Darling, how wonderful to meet you!' with lots of air-kissing and the fake bonhomie that Abby hated. Still, she went along with it. She knew that if she didn't, Maria's article would be bound to begin with something along the lines of, 'On TV, she's bubbly but, in real life, Abby Barton is one of television's more taciturn presenters,' meaning that Abby was square and dull in the flesh instead of flamboyant.

Champagne was ordered because, as Maria said, 'You can't beat doing an interview while sipping champagne, particularly when someone else, like Beech, for example, is picking up the tab.'

Selina and Abby exchanged a glance when Maria said this. It was going to be a long lunch, Abby thought. But Selina was well prepared for this type of behaviour. Throwing champagne into people in exchange for favourable publicity was what she did best.

'Sweetie, darling,' she said to Maria, 'champagne is the only way to go. What a clever idea.'

In the background Abby smiled as if she went along with this sentiment. Theoretically it would be easier to be interviewed by somebody guzzling booze, but Maria was probably not the sort of person to get legless after three glasses of Moët. Years at the coal face of journalism would have definitely upped her tolerance level and it would probably take three bottles to get her plastered. Even then, she was far too sharp to let anything slip by her, booze or no booze.

For the first twenty minutes, Maria, Abby and Selina chatted amiably about the industry and the latest gossip. They spoke as if they were best girlfriends having a slightly bitchy chat over lunch. But Abby was well aware of Maria's small tape recorder lying like a serpent on the table with the red record light on. To outsiders, it might look as if they were enjoying a girlie lunch. But Abby knew every word she uttered would be fodder for Maria's article.

By the time the first course arrived, a full thirty minutes had elapsed and Maria began the interview proper. Abby hated doing interviews over lunch – she could never concentrate on what she was saying when she was trying to eat a mouthful of salad or drink some mineral water.

'Tell me,' cooed Maria, 'about the latest additions to Beech's stable. I haven't met the twins but they sound just fabulous. Do you get on?'

Abby had just stuffed the last piece of butter-covered roll into her mouth.

'Well, yes,' she mumbled through the bread.

'You mean you don't get on?' enquired Maria sweetly.

'No, no, that's not what I mean at all,' Abby said when

she managed to swallow the bread and butter. 'I love Mitzi and Linzi, we're the best of friends and I think we get on brilliantly. It's just that I was eating.'

She knew this interview was going to be difficult, but she hadn't imagined that Maria was out solely to stitch her up. Maria was shovelling mozzarella ravioli into her mouth, still waiting for a good answer. Abby realised there was no way she was going to be able to eat any of her starter.

'The thing is, Maria, I love the twins,' she said with a smile on her face that Jess would have recognised as false. 'We get on fantastically well. In fact, the idea of getting new presenters into the show was mine,' she lied. 'I thought *Declutter* was getting a bit stale, do you know what I mean?'

She smiled the fake smile at Maria and prayed that the other woman wouldn't see through her. Abby did love the twins, that was true. But she'd originally hated the idea of them joining the team.

The true behind-the-scenes story would be an amazing scoop for Maria, but Abby had no intention of giving it to her.

'They're naturals on television. Have you seen the footage?' she asked Maria innocently.

Now that wasn't a lie. Abby really did believe that Linzi and Mitzi were brilliant on TV. But it was clear that Maria had expected a bitchfest, with Abby, the older television presenter scorned, subtly or not so subtly slagging off her co-stars the whole time. Well, Abby wasn't going to give her the satisfaction of that sort of interview. Maria would have to get her dirt elsewhere.

'No, I haven't seen the footage but I believe a tape's on its way to my desk,' Maria said. 'It's great that you all get on, though,' she added sharply, as though she didn't quite buy all this Abby-and-the-twins-bonding stuff.

'Get on?' Abby beamed at her. 'Honestly, we talk so much that the director says it's impossible to get a word in edgeways on the set!' A deliciously wicked new lie struck her. 'I'm going on holiday with my daughter soon and when I mentioned it to the girls, they were madly keen to come!'

Stick that in your pipe and smoke it, Maria, she thought with grim relish. However, Maria's next question made her realise she'd gone a step too far.

'But what about your husband?' asked Maria with a glint in her eye. 'I've heard you haven't been seen together recently. Do you go on separate holidays?'

Abby felt muscles clench somewhere in her solar plexus. 'It's a girls' holiday,' she explained hastily, as she tried to think of what would constitute a girls-only expedition and necessitate leaving her husband at home. 'A health spa in Arizona, actually. I shouldn't be telling you this, Maria,' she added, as though it was all of the utmost secrecy. 'Well, I can tell *you*,' implying that Maria was special, 'but we don't want it splashed in the magazine so everyone goes there, it's so exclusive.'

Selina, eating her green salad and out of Maria's line of sight, raised perfect eyebrows. 'A spa in Arizona? Not the one Sandra Bullock goes to, the one with the Native American healing ceremonies?' she enquired idly.

'That's the very one,' Abby said. 'The healing ceremonies are so soothing, I believe. And they've got this mud wrap they do at dawn that is the most incredible detox.' She was making this up as she was going along but Maria seemed to be buying it. 'Men hate that sort of thing, so it's strictly girls only but the twins are too busy to go.' She flashed a look at Selina that begged her to tell Mitzi and Linzi about this piece of fabrication to make sure they were all singing from the same hymn sheet.

After that, there was a lot of discussion of health spas. Maria had been to loads of them and Abby managed to hide the fact that she'd never set foot in one in her life.

From there, the interview segued into how hard it was to combine work with motherhood, and Abby – feeling like a total hypocrite – managed to talk about the difficulties without giving any of her real problems away.

'Oh, I know, it's difficult, isn't it, when you get home after a long day in the office and have to do laundry and everything?' sighed Maria.

Abby would have bet a month's salary that Maria had help coming out her ears and wouldn't know how to find the low-temperature wash on her machine, but she nodded gravely and said yes, wasn't it tough? People just didn't appreciate working women.

It hit her then that she'd been utterly convinced that Tom didn't appreciate her, and look how that had turned out.

Finally, it was over. Maria was nicely high on two bottles of champagne, Selina had that contented look that told Abby she felt it had all gone well, and Abby was relieved that she could escape.

'Bye,' she said, sounding suitably regretful, as if she'd have done anything to stay for the whole day, drinking champagne and gossiping.

Outside the restaurant, Abby left a message on Mike Horowitz's mobile.

'Mike, I need to talk to you. I've just done an interview with *Style* magazine. Maria Carroll, do you know her? She came very close to asking about me and Tom.' Abby paused. She hated talking about this, even to Mike, who had proved to be a tower of strength since she'd hired him as her agent. 'I'm scared the break-up's going to come out soon. Please phone me back. I need to talk about what we're going to do.' She hung up.

It was weird how Mike had become her confidant. Once upon a time, when she had any work problems, she would talk about them with Tom. Yes, he resented her career and he certainly resented the fact that she earned more money than he did, but he was always there to talk calmly and intelligently about whatever was bothering her. Sometimes he'd annoy her with his laid-back attitude. 'It's only television,' he'd say with a laugh. 'Come on, Abby, it's not that serious; it's not the end of the world.'

Mike Horowitz was a great person to talk to about show

business because he had been in the industry for so long and he knew everyone and everything. Mike didn't just know where the bodies had been buried – he'd been there *while* they were being buried. But inside knowledge wasn't the same as love. Tom had talked things over with her because he loved her.

She was on the way back to Dunmore when the car phone rang. It was Mike.

'Hiya, Abby,' he said cheerfully. 'So, the journalist from *Style* got a bit near to the knuckle. I hate to tell you I told you so but, well, I told you so.'

'Mike, don't,' groaned Abby. 'Please don't. I knew it was going to come out some day but I didn't think it would be this quickly. I mean, those journalists seem to know everything.'

'But she didn't know everything, did she?' said Mike with irrefutable logic, once she'd explained. 'She was just probing, that's all. Until they have some piece of concrete evidence that you and Tom have broken up, they won't print anything. But when they are sure, they'll phone you and ask straight out. You've got to be ready for when that happens. We've got to take action – action about your TV career as well as your personal publicity. You need to move on career-wise before Beech move you on. It's easier to look for a new job when you still have the old one.'

Abby sighed audibly. 'Oh, Mike, I've too much going on at the moment. I don't want to think about leaving *Declutter* or Beech. They have been good to me, honestly, they have –'

'No, they haven't been good to you,' Mike interrupted her forcibly. He'd been negotiating with Beech about the distressing rough cut of the series, but he'd wisely said that all-out war would be a mistake. 'You don't want to leave under a cloud,' he pointed out.

Secretly, Abby would have loved Mike to go to war with Roxie and Brian, but she had to trust his judgement.

'You've been good to Beech,' he said now. 'You gave them a hit TV series and it was all your own idea. Now they're ready to throw you on the scrap heap, if you let them. Trust me, Roxie didn't bring in the twins for fun. And that interview you did today, the journalist was a friend of Roxie's, wasn't she?'

'Was she?' said Abby. 'How do you know that?'

She could almost hear Mike smiling over the phone.

'I'm your agent,' he said. 'I know these things. Abby, I didn't want to tell you beforehand and neither did Selina. We didn't want to worry you.'

'Well, thanks a bunch,' said Abby furiously. 'I could have really put my foot in it. She shocked me when she asked about Tom. I could have messed up by blurting that we had split up.'

'She didn't know anything,' Mike insisted. 'Nobody knows for definite, not even Roxie. I wouldn't let you walk into an interview like that. That would be like throwing a Christian to the lions. But I bet Roxie had primed her to ask about how you got on with the twins.'

'Yeah, she did ask me that,' admitted Abby.

'That would be just Roxie's style,' Mike said. 'She wants to undermine you and the best way to do that is in print. If you come across in an interview like an embittered old hag, then it's much easier for her to fire you. And that is what we don't want to happen. When you leave Beech Productions, it will be to go to a better job. They won't be firing you.'

'What kind of better job do you have in mind exactly?' said Abby, feeling dispirited.

'I've been putting feelers out discreetly and the Seven Two Seven Network are talking about producing an evening TV chat show,' Mike said calmly. 'You'd be perfect for it. They're not looking for a twenty-something kid, they're looking for a mature and experienced interviewer with warmth and pulling power when it comes to the audience. You can do it.'

'I've never interviewed anyone in my life,' said Abby, shocked.

'And what do you do every time you go into some-body's house for *Declutter* and ask them what they want done to make their lives better?' Mike enquired. 'Isn't that interviewing? You interview people every time you're on the TV, Abby. You're a natural at it. You just don't realise that, and now,' he chuckled, 'neither do the powers that be in Beech Productions. When I've finished with your career, they're going to be so mad they let you go.'

Abby heard what he was saying but the words weren't quite penetrating her brain. She never believed she had any skills at all. In fact, she'd often thought she'd fallen into her TV career by sheer accident, the fluke of being in the right place at the right time rather than because she had any talent for anything. Being good at de-junking people's houses was hardly a skill. It was just something she was OK at.

It was lovely of Mike to say all those nice things but he didn't understand: if she was on a proper TV show where she had to interview people seriously, it would all come out. People would see that she was a fake, that she couldn't interview to save her life, that she wasn't the natural television performer she'd conned them into thinking she was.

Mike's voice interrupted her thoughts. 'I know what you're doing,' he said. 'You're giving yourself a long list of reasons why you can't do another TV show, why you would be totally useless at interviewing people and why you certainly don't want to go to an audition.'

'I'm not,' protested Abby. 'I'm ...' And she stopped, because he was absolutely correct. That's exactly what she was doing – talking herself out of the new job. 'So you want me to go and audition for this new show?' she asked tentatively.

'Yes,' Mike said. 'I've been talking to the producer over the last few weeks and he's very interested. I didn't want to mention it to you because I didn't want to get your hopes up but I think now would be a good time for them to try you out. You're just what they're looking for, Abby, believe me. Believe in yourself.'

'That's easy for you to say.'

'It's easy for you to do it too,' Mike pointed out calmly. 'You're a star, Abby, you just have to believe in yourself.'

'But I'm going on holiday in a few days' time,' she said anxiously. 'I can't do an audition before I go, can I?'

'Yes, you can. If you leave it till you come back, you'll be worrying about it all through your holiday. I'll set it up for the day after tomorrow. You can fly to Dublin in the morning and we'll do the audition in the afternoon. Then I'll bring you out for a fabulous dinner in the evening and we'll get plastered and tell each other our problems.'

'Dublin?' asked Abby, feeling stupid. Of course, the 727 Network was based in Dublin. 'If I got the show, I'd have to work in Dublin, wouldn't I?'

'The show would go out one night a week,' Mike explained, 'so you'd probably have to spend two days a week in Dublin, three max. That would mean two nights away from home. Would that be a problem?'

Would that be a problem? Six months ago, the answer would have been yes. Then, Tom would have been upset at her going away for two nights at a time and he'd certainly have felt that her career was interfering with their family life. It was different now. She didn't have to think about Tom. All she had to think about was Jess and how this would affect her. If, and it was a big if, she got the job, she would have to work out a way to have Tom take care of Jess when she was in Dublin. Jess might have thought she was a grown-up but she wasn't, not yet. She couldn't stay in the house on her own.

But then – another idea came to Abby. She and Jess could always move to Dublin. There was nothing to keep Abby in Dunmore, not any longer. She had her friends there, that was true, but the life had gone out of the place for her now without Tom. When the house was sold, there would be no emotional chains holding her there. Jess would certainly hate to leave her dad, Steph, Oliver and her friends from school, but she could stay with Tom at weekends and Steph could come and visit them in Dublin. Abby didn't think Jess was serious about Oliver, not really. She spent far more time with Steph than with him. And besides, Oliver planned to go away to college next year.

If they moved, she and Jess could get a nice apartment, somewhere central, somewhere near a good school for Jess. And she'd learn to love it.

Lots of couples move once they've split up, and suddenly, in a burst of excitement, Abby could see the sense of it. The more she thought about it, the more it seemed like a good idea: moving to Dublin – getting away from the memories of her life with Tom in Dunmore. All she had to do now was a good audition for the chat show role.

'OK,' she said to Mike. 'You're on. I'll do the audition. And perhaps you're right. Perhaps I do need to get out of Beech – and out of Dunmore altogether,' she added.

Mike spoke gently. 'Nobody said you had to leave your home.'

'I know,' said Abby, 'but all of a sudden, it seems like a very good idea. A new job and a new start. I suppose all I have to do now is actually get the job.'

'When they see you, they're going to love you,' Mike said confidently. 'Trust me.'

Abby laughed grimly. 'Why is it that when people say "trust me", I don't want to trust them?'

'That's because you have got a very jaundiced view of life at the moment,' Mike said calmly. 'You need a holiday, that's for sure.'

The night before the audition, Abby and Jess had a huge row. It started, like many rows, over something ridiculously simple. Jess being out with Steph, Abby had spent the day going around the house tidying up clutter. She figured that if they were going to have to sell up, she should make the place spick and span. It was amazing that, for a woman with a declutter-your-life series, there were so many excess belongings in Lyonnais: cupboards jammed with odds and ends, drawers filled to the brim with warranties and instruction booklets for bits of equipment that Abby didn't know they possessed.

Since Tom was still living in his friend Leo's house he had not cleared out his belongings from Lyonnais. He'd taken his clothes, or most of them. But the shelves in his wardrobe were full of junk, there were big file boxes at the bottoms of cupboards, all stuffed with papers and photos, and Lord knows what, all jumbled up in the drawers. Abby didn't feel it was right to throw out anything of his, but she made a big pile of all his belongings on the landing, intending to move it all tidily to the drawers and cupboards of a spare room. One day, when they'd sold the house, there would be enough money left over for them both to have a small home and then Tom would be able to take everything. This would have to do for now. It was a miserable job, but Abby gritted her teeth and forced herself on. It was amazing the things she discovered in Tom's belongings. She had never known he was the sort of person to keep old birthday cards and mementoes; he was always so good at throwing things out. But she had been wrong about that, as she had been wrong about so many other things.

In a big file marked 'school planning fund', she found every card and letter she had ever sent him over the years. There were even Valentine's cards. She remembered having arguments about Valentine's Day – Tom never seemed to consider the ritual a necessary part of life, while Abby loved getting sentimental messages and small bunches of flowers. She would never have believed that he'd have kept the cards that she gave him but there they all were, not tied with a romantic red ribbon, but kept all the same.

She didn't read any of these letters and cards. It would have been too painful. Instead she put the school fund file at the bottom of the pile on the landing. Perhaps Tom wouldn't realise that she had noticed them. She hadn't got as far as moving all of his belongings into the spare bedroom when the doorbell rang and she had to race downstairs and spend ages talking to somebody doing a charity collection. By the time the collector was gone, it was nearly six o'clock and Abby decided she'd just nip into the kitchen and put something on for dinner. She was rooting around in the freezer to see if she could get her hands on a vegetable lasagne when she heard the front door open.

'Hello, darling,' Abby said cheerfully. She found that this was the best way to get on with Jess these days: to seem bright and cheery, no matter how miserable or monosyllabic Jess was in return. It wasn't always easy, adopting the happy mother persona. 'How was your day, Jess?' she called out, trying to sound as if she wasn't interrogating her daughter to find out what she'd been up to. There was no answer. In the kitchen, Abby sighed. Another night of fun. Was she the only mother on the planet who couldn't communicate with her sixteen-year-old daughter? Or did everyone else have the same problem? If only she knew.

'Hiya, Mum.' Jess appeared at the kitchen door. She looked worn out and Abby instantly felt guilty for her earlier thoughts.

'Is everything OK?' she asked anxiously, abandoning her plans not to sound like an interrogator.

'Yeah, everything's fine,' said Jess, although it was obvious from her face that everything wasn't fine.

Abby was nervous of enquiring too far in case she pushed Jess away. Her instinct was to ask, but if something was wrong, Jess would tell her, right? Pushy mothers heard nothing but interested, non-probing mothers heard everything.

'You look a little bit tired, Jess,' said Abby tentatively. That sounded OK, didn't it? It wasn't prying but it was concerned.

'Yeah, I am a bit,' replied Jess. 'Steph and I went for a long walk,' she added. That was a lie for a start. Steph had never been that interested in going for long walks and certainly not nowadays, now that she was glued to Zach. Jess had actually gone for another long walk with Oliver but she didn't want to tell her mother that. If Mum knew how much time she was spending with Oliver, then she would be absolutely terrified that Jess was off having sex. Jess did not want to go there. It was bad enough having Steph asking her morning, noon and night if she and Oliver had actually done it yet.

'A long walk, that sounds nice,' her mother said in a friendly voice. Jess felt the faintest glimmer of guilt as she looked at her mother's face.

Mum was still looking at her. 'So, was it a very long walk?' Mum asked. 'How far did you go?'

Jess's feelings of guilt swelled. She really shouldn't have lied. It wasn't fair on her mum. 'We did about four miles,' she said and turned round. 'I think I'll go upstairs and have a hot bath before dinner, OK?'

Her mother looked so thrilled with this that Jess felt even more of a cow. She had been a bit of a pain in the bum lately. It wasn't fair. Mum was doing her best, it was just that Jess couldn't cope with her mother's full-on attention all the time.

'I'll just see if I can find a nice lasagne in here,' Mum said enthusiastically. 'Otherwise, I could phone for pizza?'

'Great,' said Jess. She ran upstairs and then at the top of the landing, she saw it: her dad's stuff. All those old box files he was always saying he was going to tidy up, and some of the reference books and magazines he used to keep in a pile in his room. Jess looked at it all with horror. What was it doing out on the landing? No, she knew exactly what it was doing – her mother was going to throw everything on the trash heap, just the same way she had thrown Dad on the trash heap. Dad wasn't wanted any more so he had to go and now all his belongings were going to have to go too. Jess felt tears pricking her eyes as she looked at his stuff. She walked past into her bedroom and slammed the door. How could her mum do this? How could she pretend to be so nice and friendly and all the time be making a big pile of Dad's things ready to dump them? Jess was furious. She threw her rucksack on the bed and thought about not ever coming down again. That would show Mum what she thought of her. But that was wrong. Mum needed to know exactly what Jess thought of all of this. She stormed out of her bedroom and ran down the stairs into the kitchen.

'How can you do that to Dad?' she snapped at her mother.

Abby looked up from the freezer bag she was defrosting in the sink.

'What?' said Abby. 'What are you talking about, darling?'

And then she realised: she'd never finished moving Tom's stuff into the spare room. Oh God, what would that look like to Jess?

'Darling, you don't understand. I was just tidying up –'

'I understand all right,' said Jess harshly. 'I understand everything. You want Dad out of your life for ever. Well, he's my dad and you can't take him out of my life. You stupid bitch.' She whirled around again and ran upstairs, slamming her door.

Abby slumped onto the kitchen floor and sat up against the freezer, her legs stretched out in front of her. She just couldn't do anything right, could she? Her husband wanted to divorce her and her daughter hated her. Perhaps that's what she should have told Maria at yesterday's interview. Now that would have made a hell of a story. But Abby didn't want to make wonderful stories for magazines. Right now, she'd settle for a reasonable relationship with Jess and her career going sort of OK.

It was no consolation to Abby to realise that when everything *had* been working out in her life, she just hadn't appreciated it.

Early the following morning, Abby drove Jess to Steph's house. She had decided to let Jess stay overnight with her friend's family while Abby was in Dublin doing the audition. It seemed more sensible than letting the girls stay by themselves in Lyonnais, which had been Jess's suggestion.

There was silence in the car on the way to the Andersons' house. Jess looked as if she'd had just as bad a night as Abby had. Abby herself had tossed and turned all night, barely able to get a wink of sleep worrying over Jess and Tom and the whole mess she seemed to be making of her life. Jess's eyes were as puffy as her mother's and she was pale and wan.

Abby turned the radio on loud, grateful for the early morning disc jockey's inane banter that meant that she and Jess didn't actually have to talk. They hadn't spoken at all since the row the night before. Jess hadn't come out of her room all evening until Abby had gone to bed. Then, she'd heard Jess's door opening and could hear her daughter's footsteps going down the stairs and into the kitchen. Abby had tried to console herself with the knowledge that at least Jess was getting something to eat. When she finally drove into Gartland Avenue, after an hour and a half in the rush-hour traffic, she thought she'd better say something to mend the quarrel.

'I'm sorry I'm going away and leaving you overnight, darling,' Abby said tentatively. 'And . . .' She paused. 'I'm sorry about last night. I wasn't throwing your dad's stuff out. I was just sorting it out so that he could come and take it whenever he's ready.' No matter how she put it, it still sounded all wrong. There was no easy way to tell your teenage daughter that her father would inevitably be setting up home somewhere else and that there really was no hope of him coming back to live a blissful family life.

Maybe that's what Jess had been hoping for, maybe that's why she had been so annoyed when she'd seen all Tom's belongings out on the landing. She must still be harbouring hopes that Abby and Tom would get back together.

Abby's heart bled for her daughter. She really didn't want to hurt Jess but she had to let her know the truth. 'Jess, you do know that Dad will have to buy another house and that we'll have to sell Lyonnais? You do understand that, don't you?' She turned to look at Jess's profile. Even sideways, she could see the exhaustion in her daughter's face, the baggy eyes and the drooping mouth.

'Yeah,' muttered Jess. She wished her mother would stop with all this touchy-feely, telling-her-the-truth stuff. She hated it. She wouldn't mind if they could have a grown-up conversation about everything, but it seemed they couldn't.

Staring out of the window, Jess looked at people walking along the footpath on Gartland Avenue: ordinary people going to work, walking dogs. Mums dragging small children off to day nurseries. They all looked like normal happy people with normal happy lives. Not like her horrible screwed-up family.

Abby stopped outside the Andersons' house.

'Please, Jess, don't be miserable,' she begged. 'After all, we're going on to Florida in a couple of days. Won't that be fun?' She looked eagerly at Jess, mentally begging her daughter to give her some sign that their lives weren't a total mess, that Jess could forgive her, some day. But Jess just stared stormily ahead. 'Come on, Jess,' Abby tried again. 'Florida will be fun, won't it?'

Jess's answer was to unhook her seat belt. She reached into the back of the Jeep and pulled out her bulging rucksack, stocked with her overnight things.

'Yeah, right, Mum,' she said sarcastically. 'A holiday is really going to solve everything in our horrible fucking lives.'

Abby stared at her daughter in shock. Jess never swore like that, certainly not in front of Abby. But before she could say anything Jess wrenched open the car door and was out. Without saying so much as goodbye, she slammed the car door shut and stomped off up the Andersons' driveway. Abby watched her go miserably. Jess was right. A holiday wasn't going to solve their problems, was it?

Normally, Abby enjoyed flying. She loved sitting at the front of the plane – since she had become a television presenter she travelled business class for work – and getting tea, coffee or even champagne from friendly stewardesses. She liked the feeling that her success and her hard work had given her the right to leave economy class behind. But today, she could have flown to Dublin tied onto the wing and it wouldn't have mattered.

She sat in her seat and stared blankly out of the window as the baggage handlers hefted huge packs of luggage onto the plane. Even when the stewardess recognised her – 'Hello, Mrs Barton. Lovely to have you on board again today' – Abby didn't cheer up. What use was being a recognised face when your life was such a disaster? Anyway, she didn't care to be recognised today. She hadn't had time that morning to put on any make-up except for a little mascara and lipstick, so she knew she looked pale and haggard. She accepted nothing but a cup of coffee and a newspaper from the stewardess and buried herself behind the broadsheet. She knew she ought to be psyching herself up for the audition later but, somehow, Abby didn't really care. So what if her career went down the toilet? The rest of her life was too.

At Dublin airport, a driver from the 727 Network met her at arrivals and, for the first time that day, Abbey began to perk up a bit. A driver, wow. Beech had never sent her a driver. Beech's idea of presenter relations was to phone for a taxi if she was very lucky. Normally she had to make her own way to and from airports but this new TV company certainly seemed keen.

'Ms Barton, lovely to see you,' said the driver, instantly taking her small overnight case.

Abby was just about to correct him and say it was Mrs Barton when she decided not to. He probably called every woman he picked up Ms because it was easier and you didn't want to offend anyone in the business by calling them by the wrong title. And she probably would be Ms Barton very soon. She couldn't go back to her maiden name. Abby Costello didn't have the same ring to it, but Ms Barton would have its own message, she thought.

In the back of the car – a sleek black Mercedes – Abby

began to apply some make-up. She didn't want to put on too much because she knew the make-up department in the TV company would plaster her up nicely, but she didn't want to go into the studio looking like Uncle Fester from the Addams Family.

She'd just finished the tricky job of applying eyeliner when Mike Horowitz phoned.

'How's my favourite client?' he enquired cheerily.

Abby laughed for the first time that day. 'You know, I hate it when you say that sort of rubbish, Mike,' she chided. 'It's insincere and you know it. If *I'm* your favourite client, what do you say to all the others? "Hello to my second favourite client, hello to my third favourite client"? I doubt it. Flattery gets you nowhere,' she finished.

Mike laughed. 'It doesn't get me anywhere with you,' he agreed. 'But that's why I like you – you're very straight and you don't want to be told how wonderful you are ten times a day. That's very refreshing in our business.' Sitting in the back of the car, surrounded by all her make-up, Abby allowed herself a rueful smile. Being straight with people didn't get you anywhere, either. She'd tried to be straight with Jess that morning and that hadn't worked, had it?

'What's the plan?' she asked.

Mike explained that he was going to meet her at the 727 Network offices, where they'd talk to the show's producers and generally shoot the breeze until it was time for the audition. It was all going to be very laid-back, he explained to Abby.

'It's nothing more than a simple pilot episode,' he explained. 'Nobody's expecting miracles, it's all going to be low-key and relaxed. They've got two guests lined up for you to interview. As you know, they were going to use staff to stand in for guests but I don't think that works, so we've got two proper guests, one an actor and the other a novelist. They know it's a pilot show but they're happy to be involved. On the basis, of course, that if the show *does* get off the ground, they're among the first guests.'

Abby was shocked. 'What do you mean – a pilot episode?' she asked in alarm. 'I thought this was just an audition to see how I looked on camera.'

'But my assistant emailed all the details to your assistant,' Mike said sharply.

Abby thought of the long-winded message that her part-time assistant, Katya, had left on the phone. Katya had definitely said something about checking emails but, what with all that had been going on, Abby hadn't even switched on the computer for a couple of days.

'They know what you look like on camera; they've watched your show,' Mike was saying. 'They need to see how you react when you're interviewing people properly.'

'Oh God,' moaned Abby. 'I knew this day was going to be a disaster. I'm not ready for that, Mike, I'm not ready at all. I didn't sleep last night . . .' her voice began to get higher with anxiety, 'and I had a huge row with Jess –'

Mike interrupted her. 'Don't worry about any of those things, Abby,' he said very calmly. 'You're going to be absolutely fine.'

'Yeah, absolutely fine,' repeated Abby as if the words were a mantra and could carry her through what was to come.

Afterwards, Abby never knew if it was because of her stress or despite it, but the pilot TV show went fabulously well. Once the cameras started rolling, she somehow relaxed, although she had no idea how.

She was suddenly struck by the blinding realisation that recording a pilot for a TV show didn't actually matter that much in the grand scheme of things. She could only do her best.

Free from the usual last-minute nerves of being on TV, she was able to concentrate on her guests rather than on herself or on her hair. She didn't have a moment to think, do I look fat in this outfit? She just got on with the job in hand. There were two guests for her to interview and she was going to switch on all the depth and compassion she possessed. The actor turned out to be a sweet but famously reserved man in his late sixties who'd starred in a TV soap for over twenty years before being unceremoniously dumped. Abby knew how that felt. Roxie would have her out on her ear if she could.

And that knowledge gave her an insight into exactly how to talk to him. Sitting on two squashy armchairs, she and the actor chatted as if they were old friends.

'It must have been very difficult to see your career on the show ending that way,' she said gently, 'particularly since you'd been instrumental in making it a success.'

'Yes,' he admitted, 'I felt that I had been dumped because I was over the hill and that I would never act again. You can't imagine what that was like,' he said.

'I think many people in the world can empathise with you on that,' Abby interrupted him with a smile.

The actor grinned wryly at her. 'It's not easy, is it?' he said. 'Your whole being is tied up in what you do for a living and for twenty years I had been playing Colin on *Family and Friends*, and, in an instant, it was all gone. I have to say I was devastated.'

'And it doesn't affect just you, does it?' Abby asked kindly. 'It touches everyone around you, especially your family.'

'Oh, you should talk to my poor wife,' said the actor. 'It was a complete nightmare for Eleanor because she was coping with me being depressed and miserable every day, and she was trying to keep her chin up for both of us.'

'Eleanor started out as an actress, too, I gather,' said Abby, casting her mind back to the brief notes she'd read moments before going on air. 'She's been a huge support to you during your career, hasn't she?'

'I don't know what I'd have done without her,' he sighed, and proceeded to talk about his wife and how they'd gone through the bad times together.

It was easy to talk to Abby, he found: she wasn't pushy, digging around for information, but she had such a warm, kind manner and she looked as though she understood.

460

Behind the cameras, the producers and Mike looked at each other in sheer delight. Abby Barton had it – there was no doubt about it. She could get blood out of a stone. The producers had only found the TV soap actor at the last minute and they thought he'd be a pretty hard person to interview, because he didn't like to give much of himself away. But under Abby's gentle probing, he was opening up in a way he never had before and it made fantastic television.

Mike watched his client with unalloyed delight. Abby might have said she wasn't his favourite client but if he was doing out a list, she came pretty high in the ranking. He loved her honesty, her sense of humour and the fact that she really didn't like the show business bullshit and flattery. As a professional, he also liked the fact that she was incredibly talented, although – a rarity in the industry – she didn't seem to realise it. She'd have to realise it now. This pilot would undoubtedly get the green light and it would make Abby Barton an even bigger star than she had been before. He just hoped that she was ready for what came with being a star.

On set, Abby wasn't aware of the grand plans going on behind the cameras. She was concentrating on conducting the best interview she could with this man she felt sorry for. She could remember seeing him in the soap series and certainly hadn't liked the hard-bitten character he played. But now, in the flesh, he seemed sort of soft and vulnerable, and she was drawn to him. She wanted to know what made him tick, what it was like to experience the huge fame he had known all through his life and then see it fade away. They talked about celebrity and how all it took was two seasons off the television for nobody to even remember your name any more. They joked about walking through the supermarket and having complete strangers smile at you and the actor told her how nobody ever remembered his real name, but everyone called him Colin, his character from the series.

Then they moved on to his family: his kids and his three grandchildren. Now he had time to play with his grandchildren for the first time in his life, and he loved that.

'So, if they asked you back on *Family and Friends*, would you go?' probed Abby carefully.

The actor laughed. 'Nobody's ever dared to ask me that before,' he said.

Abby could see the studio manager telling her to wrap up the interview. 'I'm only asking because I think I know the answer,' she said cleverly.

The actor grinned at her: the answer would be no, he said. He'd discovered too much else to enjoy in life.

Abby leaned forward and patted his hand in a warm gesture. 'I knew you'd say that,' she said.

The crew clapped when the cameras stopped rolling and the actor hugged Abby goodbye.

'I don't think I've ever done such an enjoyable interview,' he said genuinely. 'It really was great fun. You've got to get the job, Abby.'

She blushed. But before she could say, 'Don't be ridiculous!' the actor had been whisked away and the lady novelist was sitting on the set instead.

The second lot of filming was ready to begin and, yet again, Abby didn't have a chance for nerves. The novelist was slightly harder going. Abby began to see the wisdom of the director's words as she struggled in the early stages of the interview. Before the filming, she'd blurted out to him that, because of a communication breakdown, she hadn't known about the interviews in advance and that her preparation had been a quick glance through the two guests' biogs in make-up.

The director had said her secret was safe with him and added that she'd probably do a far better job if she just went with her instincts instead of having a mental list of questions from which she refused to deviate.

'There's nothing worse than an interviewer who can't

follow where the interview takes them,' he said. 'Look at it this way: if you can go in and interview someone with only ten minutes' preparation time, then you know that you are going to be able to work under any circumstances. That's what live TV is all about – expecting the unexpected. You've got to be ready if a guest shows up drunk or on drugs or doesn't want to talk about something he had previously agreed to talk about. It's the seat-of-your-pants experience. Good luck,' he finished.

He was certainly getting the seat-of-your-pants interview experience now, Abby thought to herself. This second interview wasn't going well at all. She fumbled around for something to talk about that would help her gel with this woman. Discussing literature hadn't worked because the lady novelist couldn't seem to grasp the concept that Abby hadn't consumed her books with something approaching joy. Not a mistake Abby would ever make again, if she was actually presenting the show for real. She racked her brains for subjects they could talk about and finally thought of one: children. Somehow she dragged the woman away from discussing problems with foreign tours.

'You've talked a lot about your family in the past,' Abby said, taking a huge risk because she could remember a mention of kids in the novelist's biog but was a bit hazy on how many children she had or if they were grown up or not.

For a moment, she thought the novelist was going to bleat that she didn't talk about her personal life but then as quickly as if Abby had turned on a switch, she started to talk. Yes, she had children, teenage children at that, and, Lord, they could be difficult. Her youngest had just done her Junior Cert and everyone was like a cat on a hot tin roof thinking about the results that would come in September. Relief flooded through Abby. Now she was on safe ground. They bonded over discussions about study timetables and the trauma of the exams. The frosty intellectual was gone and in her place sat a working mother with exactly the same problems as any of the other parents who'd be watching the show.

By the end of the interview, they were the best of friends and the people behind the cameras were again beaming from ear to ear. After another hug goodbye, Abby was finished, and she walked out to where Mike sat behind the cameras with a smile lighting up his face.

'Abby, I don't need to tell you that you were just fantastic,' he said.

And Abby could see that he really meant it.

'It was hard going, especially the second one,' she admitted, 'but I think it worked OK.'

'Worked OK?' demanded Mike. 'It worked brilliantly. They loved you. I don't know what you did to those people, but you got everything out of them. Talk about probing their inner secrets.'

'That's what I do when I de-junk somebody's house,' Abby explained simply. 'You can't go into someone's life and rip apart all their most precious possessions without knowing what makes them tick. That's what I tried to do up there today – to understand the people I was interviewing.'

'Abby!' shrieked a voice. It was the rather flamboyant executive producer rushing over to throw his arms around her. 'What a woman! You were incredible,' he said. 'This show is going to be a prime-time hit.'

Abby laughed. 'I thought we were just *talking* about making a chat show. I didn't know anyone had definitely decided to do it.'

'After today,' the producer said, 'we're definitely doing it. And you're the star.' He turned to Mike. 'We need to discuss contracts and see what your schedule allows you to do. We just want to facilitate matters for you,' he added to Abby. 'Whatever works for you, we'll do it.'

'Brilliant,' said the director, shaking Abby's hand. 'If that's what you do with ten minutes of preparation,' he whispered into her ear, 'I can't wait to see you when you're firing on all cylinders!'

For a moment, Abby basked in their admiration. It was a nice feeling, particularly after the last few weeks.

'Thank you,' she said sincerely. 'You and Mike can talk about the details, but first,' she grinned at them all, 'I could kill a cup of coffee.'

CHAPTER TWENTY-EIGHT

Florida was sweltering. Abby couldn't imagine how people lived all the time in the overpowering temperature. Heat rose in waves off the sidewalks and rippled in the air at ankle level. Even in her cool linen trousers and sandals, she felt roasting, her feet stuck to the sandals and her armpits glued to the little white cotton T-shirt she wore. Appropriately enough, Jess seemed to have ended the cold war for the moment, and mother and daughter groaned in unison about the heat.

'I mean, I can't believe it's so hot,' Jess said as they got out of the taxi in front of their hotel in Miami. 'How are we ever going to cope?'

'Turbo-charged air conditioning, I hope,' said her mother, fanning herself with her hand. 'If it comes to the worst, we can just stay inside the whole time.'

A movie-star-beautiful blonde girl on roller blades swept past, wearing the tiniest of tiny yellow shorts, long caramel limbs gliding effortlessly. Both mother and daughter turned to look at her go.

'Maybe we could learn to cope with the heat,' Jess said, staring enviously after the girl. 'I'd love to get a tan, and I'd love to have a go on roller blades. Do you think I could?'

Abby grinned. 'Yes, we could both do it. I've always wanted to roller-blade. Although if I go home with scabby knees and elbows, it's all your fault, right?'

'Oh, no, Mum,' laughed Jess. 'You're not going roller-blading with me. I have my reputation to think of!' But she was only joking.

For the first time since they got on the plane, Abby allowed herself to relax. This holiday might be all right after all.

'We'll check out roller-blading tomorrow,' she promised, 'but today let's just get into the hotel, relax in the air conditioning, unpack and then go somewhere absolutely fabulous for dinner. How does that sound?'

'It sounds brilliant,' said Jess, 'apart from the actual unpacking bit. I thought we could just live out of our suitcases.'

Abby looked up at the elegant hotel. 'Not in a place like this,' she said. 'They probably have maids to unpack for you anyway.'

She sighed as she thought of her badly packed suitcase. Oh well, who was she trying to impress anyhow? Here in America, she didn't have to pretend to be Abby Barton, TV personality, any more – she could just be Abby Barton, normal mother, a woman who didn't know how to pack. That would be much more relaxing.

Their hotel wasn't one of the grand art deco hotels for which Miami was so famous. Instead it was a giant modern complex with every luxury known to woman, from incredible designer shops in the lobby, to an Olympic-size swimming pool and spa on the top floor. When she read about the spa in the brochure as they checked in, Abby had a little laugh to herself, thinking of how she had fooled Maria Carroll into thinking she was going to a wonderful spa in Arizona. There was no mention of Native American rituals in this particular hotel, but you could have every sort of massage possible, including hot-stone therapy, and intense body wraps, which promised to take at least two inches off your thighs. Two whole inches! Abby decided she was definitely going to have one of those. Twice.

Jess was fascinated by the huge entertainment centre in their room. It wasn't just a TV – there was a DVD player, video, music system, you name it. *And* she could watch films that weren't even out yet in Ireland.

'Wow, Mum,' she said, looking at the on-screen list of films on the hotel's pay TV system, 'this is incredible. Steph and I said we were going to go and see this film at home but it's not going to be coming for months and I can see it here now. Steph is going to go postal!'

'Glad you approve,' Abby said, admiring the bathroom, an oasis of marble with towels so fluffy they must have been soaked in fabric conditioner for a month.

But Jess had moved on from the TV and was already deep in the hotel guide that listed all the huge shopping malls in the area.

'Look at this, Mum,' she said, sounding even more impressed. 'This mall has everything from Versace to DKNY.'

'So, what with the roller-blading and the shopping and the watching videos, we're going to have a pretty good holiday, don't you think?' her mother asked.

Jess smiled at Abby, the sort of sweet smile she used to give her mum before everything had gone wrong. 'Yes,' she replied, 'we're going to have a great holiday.'

And they did. It had been a brilliant idea to get away from Ireland and Dunmore, Abby thought many times during their ten days away. In the hot sultry atmosphere of Miami, the cold war really did end. It was like old times. In the mornings, they woke early and enjoyed a leisurely breakfast in their room, eating fruits they'd never heard of before and gobbling up the seven-grain low-cal muffins that Jess had developed a fondness for.

And they braved the sweltering heat of the day by slathering on sun cream and very cool shades, and joining all the achingly fashionable citizens of Miami meandering onto the beach. Of course, it was too hot to do much meandering, and they inevitably ended up in the air-conditioned shops, where Abby threw caution to the wind and got out her credit card. Not that Jess was a wild or greedy shopper. No, she'd never expected Abby to buy her wildly expensive goodies and that hadn't changed.

'Mum,' she said one day, shocked when she saw Abby

about to shell out $80 for a pair of particularly beautiful Calvin Klein sunglasses, 'you can't buy those for me! I'd be so worried about them all the time. What if I lost them or broke them or something . . . ?'

For some reason, Abby felt ridiculously like crying at her daughter's words. Despite everything, Jess was still such a good sweet kid and her mother loved her. It wasn't Jess's fault that horrible teenage hormones and Abby and Tom's break-up had messed up her life.

'Now, Jess, I want to buy you something nice and these sunglasses look really wonderful on,' her mother insisted. She'd worry about the credit card bill later. Anyway, if the 727 Network chat show worked out, money wouldn't be such a problem.

For the four days they were in Miami, they ate in out-of-the-way restaurants and tried to experience some genuine local culture rather than just heading to the big tourist spots.

They both had a go at Salsa dancing, although Jess was a tiny bit embarrassed when she was teamed up with a very good-looking young Cuban guy. Abby loved it, though. Tom had never been into dancing and it was such a joy to be whirled around the floor by somebody who really understood what rhythm was all about.

When it came to roller-blading, Jess was the expert. Abby was hopeless and gave up after a terrifying twenty minutes when she panicked non-stop that she was going to plough into a little old lady or fall over and break a bone. But Jess loved it. She adored letting the sea breeze blow her hair back as she bladed smoothly along the sea front.

'I'm going to get a pair of these when I get home,' she told her mum. 'Wouldn't it be brilliant? I could nearly get into school without going on the train.'

Abby felt guilty. She hadn't mentioned her plan about them moving to Dublin yet. If they moved, Jess might well be able to roller-blade into school, but she wouldn't be at school with Steph and all her other friends. Still, that discussion was a long way away. Abby decided to say nothing for the moment.

'You should definitely get a pair of roller blades,' she merely remarked.

At night they never stayed out too late because they were both tired after their early starts, but it was wonderful to wander back to their hotel along the lively streets, soaking up the atmosphere.

'Miami buzzes,' Jess said one night, and Abby agreed.

They were sad to leave when it was time to fly to Orlando. Repacking their cases was a nightmare because, somehow, they had acquired a lot more stuff. Jess even had to sit on Abby's case to get it to shut.

Disney World was a lot different from Miami. Even the most bad-tempered person in the world couldn't help but be cheered up by the wonderful fairyland, Abby decided. It certainly wasn't just for kids – it was for everyone.

Jess, who had said before they left Ireland that she was too old to go on stupid roller-coaster things, suddenly turned out to be madly addicted to the most dangerous rides in the theme parks. Abby, who was afraid of heights, made her go on her own.

'I'll just sit down here and wait until you're finished,' she said. Sometimes she felt sick just looking.

Jess liked Sea World best, but Abby loved the safari experience. In fact, their main problem was that there simply weren't enough hours in the day to do it all properly. The week sped past.

They spent practically no time in their hotel room, and when it was time for dinner, there were so many things to talk about, so many things they'd seen that day, that there was no time for introspection.

Abby had hoped that she might be able to have a grown-up, heart-to-heart talk with her daughter. There was so much to discuss: the break-up, selling the house, the new TV show and the possibility of moving to Dublin. She knew that, above all, Jess wanted to be treated like an adult, so the right thing for her to do would be to confide in Jess and tell her of all the plans. But there never seemed to be the moment for such a conversation.

At dinner on their last night, they sat in the medieval themed restaurant of their hotel and ordered pizza again. There wasn't an enormous choice of vegetarian dishes, and they'd discovered that the easiest thing for Jess to eat was pizza, so they'd had it practically every night. Once they'd ordered, Jess sat back in her seat and looked around the restaurant. As usual, it was full of exhausted-looking families with happy children. It really was the perfect place for small kids, Abby realised with a pang, thinking that she'd never have small children again herself. Another sign of getting old, she realised, astonished to find herself yearning for the days when she'd been looking after a toddler.

At the time, it hadn't seemed much fun. Between the ages of two and three, Jess had been into absolutely everything and her tantrums outdid anything covered by the phrase 'terrible twos' in the childcare books. Running around after her had been a full-time job. Abby had felt she couldn't look away for an instant or disaster would strike. Yet somehow, Jess had still managed to get the normal complement of kids' injuries, like bumps to her head and scraped knees. It was weird, Abby thought, to look back on those days with such nostalgia. Life was like that, though. Nostalgia was what happened when you remembered only the best bits, editing out the sadder times.

Maybe that's all this yearning was – nostalgia. She kept looking back over the past and thinking what an idiot she had been to mess it all up, because really it had been great. But what if it hadn't been great after all? What if she and Tom had really had a terrible relationship and it was only nostalgia that made it seem wonderful in retrospect?

'I'll never eat another pizza again,' Jess announced. 'You'd think they'd have some veggie options. I'd kill for a veggie burger. Or a veggie sausage,' she added dreamily.

Abby couldn't help but laugh. 'You always say you hate those veggie sausages I buy for you,' she pointed out.

'I promise I'll never say I hate them again,' Jess vowed.

Their drinks arrived: Coke for Jess and Diet Coke for Abby. She definitely had to go on a diet when she went home. Those enormous American portions had certainly added a few pounds to her waist, inch-reducing wraps notwithstanding, and she didn't want to go back to all the pre-*Declutter* publicity with a fat tummy.

The two small children at the next table were clearly bored and started roaring to get out of their high chairs. There was noise all around them and in the background they could barely hear Britney Spears singing. It might have been noisy but it was as good a place as any to have an in-depth conversation with Jess. Abby steeled herself for what was to come.

'We need to talk, Jess,' she said.

Instantly, the haunted look came into Jess's eyes. 'Talk about what?' she asked.

'Talk about the future and what's going to happen,' Abby said slowly. She felt terrible to be bringing this up, but she had to. Not for the first time, she wished with all her heart that she'd never slept with Jay. She was a mother and her primary job was to protect her family. In sleeping with Jay, she'd broken up her family and the end result was having to sit in a restaurant surrounded by happy families and talk to her beloved daughter about selling their home, about divorcing her father, and about moving away from everyone she knew.

'I feel guilty,' Abby said, 'because I've never spoken to you in depth about what happened and what's going to happen in the future. I suppose I was treating you like a child and you're not, are you?'

Jess resisted the impulse to stare down at the place mat in front of her. If her mother was going to talk to her like an adult, she'd act like one too. She looked at her mother's face, into the blue-green eyes so like her own. Oliver loved

Jess's eyes: he was always saying how beautiful they were. When he said that, Jess never really reflected on the fact that she'd inherited her eyes from her mother. She just felt proud of them for her own sake. But now, as she looked at her mother from across the table, she felt strangely aware of the bond between them. Her mum wasn't a bad person, she'd just messed up, like everyone else did.

'So,' Jess said, 'what do you want to talk about?'

Abby took a deep breath. It was now or never. 'I know it's impossible for you to understand, Jess, why I did what I did and, to be honest, I can't explain or excuse it. I love your dad. I've spent my life telling you how important love is and that you have to respect other people. And then . . .' Abby looked down at her place mat sadly. 'I messed up because I didn't respect your dad. For a little while, I forgot about him and thought only about myself. I'll never stop regretting that; I'll never stop regretting hurting your dad and hurting you.'

She looked back up at Jess, the heartfelt plea in her eyes. 'I'd do anything if I could turn the clock back, Jess, but I can't and that's why we have to go forwards. Your dad wants a divorce.'

'Has he asked you for a divorce?' asked Jess.

'No,' admitted her mother, 'but he's going to. He's so hurt and devastated by what I've done. Men and women are different, that's a fact,' she added wryly. 'I think women can get over affairs more easily than men can. When their pride is hurt, there's no going back for them. That's what's happened with your dad and me. I'd have him back in an instant,' she said truthfully. 'I want you to understand that. If we could be a family again, I'd do anything to make it work.'

On the other side of the table, Jess's eyes filled with tears and she looked away, desperate not to let her mother see how upset she was. There was nothing she wanted more in the whole world than for her parents to get back together, but it wasn't going to happen, was it?

Abby didn't seem to have noticed the tears pooling in her daughter's eyes. She too was staring off into the middle distance, trying to find the right words to explain to Jess how their family had broken down and couldn't be fixed. 'I have to consider the possibility that your dad might meet somebody else and want to marry her,' Abby said slowly.

The idea horrified her but she had to bring it up. It wasn't fair otherwise. What if Tom did meet someone else and the only thing stopping him having a proper relationship was the fact that his teenage daughter would disapprove, would still hope that her parents could get back together? Abby owed it to Tom to set him free, if that's what he wanted. It wasn't fair to cling to him when she was responsible for the split. And she had to make sure Jess understood that her father's life would go on.

'We'll have to sell the house,' Abby went on. 'I know you hated moving to Dunmore in the first place, so at least you won't miss it.'

Jess thought about Oliver. For months she'd hated Dunmore, hated the fact that she had no friends there and hated the fact that she had to take the train out from Cork every evening after school. For so long, Dunmore had felt like a wasteland in the back of beyond where she knew nobody. And then she had fallen in love with Oliver: Oliver, who lived in Dunmore. She said nothing.

'With the money we get from selling the house, your dad can buy a new home where you can stay with him. You and I will have a home of our own: you, me and Wilbur.' She smiled at Jess, hoping to make her daughter smile back at the mention of her beloved tabby cat.

'So I'd stay with Dad sometimes and you other times?' Jess asked slowly.

A terrible thought struck Abby. What if Jess didn't want to stay with her? What if she wanted to live with Tom, after all?

'I thought you'd want to live with me,' Abby said hesitantly. 'That's what normally happens – the children stay with their mum – not that you're a child or anything . . .'

Her voice trailed off miserably. Kids might want to stay with their mum if their mum hadn't been the person who had broken up the marriage in the first place. It might be different in this case.

'No, that's OK. I'll stay with you,' Jess said. 'It's just going to be weird having two homes. Where do you think we're going to live?'

The waitress, in full medieval serving wench costume, arrived with two pizzas. 'And that's one vegetarian pizza for you,' she said cheerfully, putting an enormous pizza down in front of Jess, 'and one four seasons for you, ma'am.' She placed an equally enormous pizza down in front of Abby. 'Can I get you anything else?'

Abby looked at the huge pizza and wondered how she was ever going to eat it. Her appetite had totally vanished. But politeness took over.

'No, thank you, that's fine. We've got everything, thank you very much.' She found herself saying thank you even more than normal in Florida because all the serving staff were so incredibly polite. It seemed churlish not to be three times as polite back. The waitress left and the Barton women surveyed their food.

'Do you ever feel as if you've ordered too much?' Jess asked.

'At every single meal,' her mother replied grimly.

Jess laughed. 'Steph would really hate these sorts of meals,' she said lightly. 'She's always on a diet these days – not that she needs to because she's totally skinny, but she's always going on about her weight.'

'You don't worry about your weight, do you?' asked her mother anxiously, fearing that Jess was going to get caught up in the teenage diet syndrome.

Jess shook her head. 'I can't wait to get my train tracks off and I'd love to have, well, proper boobs.' She blushed a little bit. 'But I can honestly say I don't think I'm fat. Although I'm probably the only girl in the class who doesn't think she is,' she added thoughtfully.

'Thank God for that,' Abby said, grateful for small mercies.

'Hey, I'll probably need therapy when I'm older to help me cope with having had braces and glasses,' Jess said, and then she laughed to show she was joking.

They made an attempt to eat some of their pizzas, and began to talk about issues like women who thought they were too fat and people like Steph who were permanently on a diet. It was a good conversation and, for a little while, it felt to Abby like she was talking to a friend and not her daughter, after all. Jess really was so clever and could talk about anything. Funny how her mother had never seemed to realise that before.

Jess was not a child any more, she was a young woman. They ate, talked, laughed, and Abby decided that she couldn't bring herself to mention the whole notion of leaving Dunmore.

It wasn't as if anything was decided, she reflected. Just because she'd done a really good audition for the TV chat show didn't mean the whole thing was going to happen. She'd wait and see. For now it was enough that she and Jess had shared this evening.

It was nearly ten by the time they'd finished their meal and began to walk back to their room. They still had to do some last-minute packing before tomorrow morning's early flight.

Abby knew she wouldn't sleep – she never did before a flight. She always got so wound up about whether she'd wake up in time and whether she'd remembered the passports and the tickets.

'I think I'll have a bath when we go up,' Jess said companionably as they got into the lift.

'Good idea,' said her mother. 'It'll take me ages to finish packing anyway and then we can try and get some sleep.'

On their floor, they got out of the lift and began the walk to their room.

'Mum,' began Jess carefully, 'do you think Dad knows that

you'd take him back and have everything go back to the way it was before, if he could forget what had happened? Do you think that he knows that you want to forget it all and try again?'

Tears pricked Abby's eyes. Oh poor, poor Jess.

'Yes,' she said slowly. 'I think he knows. I've certainly told him so. But I don't think I could ask him to come back to me and be married to me if he didn't want to. Do you understand that?'

She wanted to tell Jess that she *had* tried but that Tom hadn't been interested. As far as he was concerned, it was over. Abby had hoped that perhaps it had been Tom's pride speaking that day when she'd asked him to reconsider ending their marriage. But as time had gone by and he still hadn't made some move towards reconciliation, it seemed as if she was wrong. Tom had made his mind up and he didn't want to be married to Abby any more.

'You can't make someone love you when they've stopped, can you?' Abby said sadly.

Jess nodded. She was afraid to speak. Abby unlocked their room and they went inside. Instantly, Jess went into the bathroom and began to run the bath, the noise of the water blocking out any chance of further conversation.

'I'll be in here for a while,' she called to her mother.

'OK,' Abby replied.

Jess shut the bathroom door, sat on the edge of the bath and finally let herself cry. Outside the bathroom, her mother sat on the edge of the bed and did exactly the same thing.

CHAPTER TWENTY-NINE

Rested and relaxed after her holiday, Abby flew home on Sunday to find herself in the eye of a storm. Somehow the news of Abby's audition with the 727 Network had just reached Roxie's ears and she was furious. Even worse, Brian was furious too. Roxie had left one and Brian had left three outraged messages on Abby's answering machine that morning, screeching that if Beech hadn't taken up her idea of the show in the first place, she'd be a nobody today. Abby listened to the rantings of the Beech MD for a few minutes, before pressing the delete button. Let Brian rant and rave, she decided. There was more to life than work. On holiday, she and Jess had managed to regain some of their old closeness and that was far more important than a stupid bloody job. And, she told herself, she hadn't ranted and raved when Roxie had hired two new presenters for the TV show. She'd behaved like a professional at all times and her reward was to listen to Brian screeching like an overgrown schoolboy on the phone.

She clicked the answering machine back on and phoned Mike Horowitz's mobile. It was a Sunday but, what the hell, this couldn't wait. Mike, who turned out to be in Paris on business, wasn't unduly worried over Brian's rage. But then he was not the sort of guy to get upset just because one TV company had the hump with one of his clients – especially when he had irons in the fire for that particular client.

'Don't worry about Brian,' he said. 'He'll get over it. He'd have to find out sometime. Besides, the Seven Two Seven

Network guys are really keen – the news has obviously got out.'

'But nothing has been agreed,' Abby protested. 'Nobody's shown us a contract or anything. It's not as though the job is in the bag.'

'True,' admitted Mike, 'but I happen to know that they've auditioned three other people for the job and none of them was anywhere near as good as you. Inside information,' he added happily. 'They even talked to Candy whatshername, although I believe she was hopeless – too brittle.'

Abby couldn't resist a satisfied smile. So Candy had gone for the same job and performed badly? Abby's mother might have taught her that it was wrong to find pleasure in other people's misfortune, but today she just couldn't help it.

'Are they going to make us an offer, then?' she asked Mike.

'I'm meeting the producer and the executive producer for lunch tomorrow when I get back and if they don't make us an offer, I'll go into a milliner's shop and eat all the stock,' Mike said, sounding justifiably self-satisfied. 'We could look for big money, you know.'

Abby thought of where big money had got her in the past. It had moved her family out of Gartland Avenue, where they had been happy, despite everything. It had bought them this glorious old house, a house where they were now miserable and which they were now going to have to sell. Money had brought nothing but trouble to the Barton family. Or perhaps it wasn't the money, after all – having it had merely highlighted problems that had been there all along. Either way, cash didn't solve everything.

'Look, Mike, I'm not out for huge money,' she said. 'If Tom and I do get divorced, obviously I'm going to need to make a reasonable living. But I'm no Ivana Trump. I don't need a fortune to spend in designer shops.' She could sense Mike's hesitation even over the phone.

'Abby, don't forget that you're the bigger earner in your

marriage. Tom would be perfectly within his rights to look for alimony and a settlement from you.'

Abby laughed mirthlessly before she could stop herself. 'Mike, you've never met Tom and it's clear that you really don't know that much about him,' she said. 'Tom would rather live in a box than take a penny off me.'

'Sorry,' Mike apologised. 'I didn't mean to interfere. That's your business.'

The following day was Monday and, despite the fact that she should have been jet-lagged after her flight from Florida, Abby woke early and felt full of energy. She got up, made herself a fruit smoothie, and then went for a speedy four-mile walk, listening to the radio on her Discman as she went. She got back at half-past nine, fresh-faced and energised, expecting to see a sleepy Jess emerging from her bedroom. But Jess was already up and she didn't look in the least sleepy.

'Dad phoned looking for you,' Jess said grimly.

Abby didn't know why but she had a feeling it was bad news. 'What's wrong?' she asked anxiously.

'Some journalist phoned him a few minutes ago looking for a comment about how the two of you were getting a divorce,' Jess said. 'Someone rang here too, but I let it go to answerphone.'

Abby's heart sank into her trainers. That was all she needed. She'd bet a month's salary that Roxie was behind this. The vengeance of a woman scorned was nothing to the vengeance of a commissioning director who saw a TV presenter getting the better of her. Who else could have revealed the status of their marriage? Roxie might not have known about the split for definite, but she was obviously sufficiently furious to act on the basis of strong rumour. It would be just her style to let the information slip out to a journalist when Abby was back in the country.

'Dad thinks you tipped them off because the new show is coming out and you'll be looking for publicity,' Jess added slowly.

Abby was horrified. 'It's not like that, Jess,' she said. 'You know I'd do anything not to hurt your dad. Before we went away I had an interview with a journalist and I was so anxious that the news of our separation would get out that I lied through my teeth. I don't want people to know any more than your dad does.'

She felt terrible to see the caged look on Jess's face. The happy, open expression that her daughter had worn throughout the holiday was suddenly gone. It was back to real life. She sighed. A chat with Jess would have to wait. She started to dial Tom's number.

Tom answered the phone on the first ring. He sounded rattled and immediately launched into an attack: 'How dare you talk about our private lives to all and sundry? I suppose you're desperately trying to publicise your stupid television show, but I don't want my name dragged into it – or Jess's name either. You can find some other way to get yourself into the papers. How did they get the number, anyhow?'

If Abby was shocked by the depth of his venom, she didn't show it. She knew that Tom couldn't forgive her for breaking up their marriage, so it was hardly surprising that he was going to blame her for everything that went wrong in the future.

'I didn't tell anyone about the separation, and I don't know how they got your number,' she said calmly, although she didn't expect him to believe her. Roxie must have found Tom's number in Abby's contact details in the office. 'I like my life private too, and if you think it's of any benefit to me to have news of our split splashed all over the papers, then you're wrong.'

'Wrong?' he demanded angrily. 'I'll tell you where I went wrong, Abby. I was wrong to believe in you for all those years. I was wrong to think I actually knew you. I didn't know you at all. You're just publicity hungry and you don't give a damn about me or Jess.'

Abby was about to say that this wasn't fair criticism but she stopped. Perhaps it was fair. So, she hadn't told anyone about their separation, and she'd done everything she could to keep it out of the papers. But she had slept with another man; she'd been responsible for the break-up. Everything went back to that.

'I didn't tell anyone anything,' she said, 'but if you want to believe I did, you're entitled to your opinion. You don't have to make any comment to the papers. I'll get my publicity people to deal with it.'

As soon as she'd said it, she knew that speaking about publicity people was a mistake. All of a sudden, she'd stopped sounding like Abby Barton, Tom's estranged wife, and was talking like some Hollywood movie star, exactly the sort of person Tom hated. *Her publicity people.*

They'd come full circle, hadn't they? No matter how much she protested to the contrary, Tom would believe that she had turned into everything he hated.

'I'm sorry about all of this, Tom,' she said. 'I'll try and sort it out, but there will be some publicity.'

She paused. It was now or never. Get your retaliation in first: 'I'll get my solicitor to ring you later in the week. We need to discuss formalities like the finances, selling the house, seeing Jess.'

'Fine,' he rapped back.

She hung up and found that her hands were shaking. The phone rang again and she ignored it. She heard the oily tones of a well-known gossip columnist on the answerphone and was glad she had. Her mobile rang lustily and when she recognised her assistant's phone number she picked it up.

'Hi, Katya. What's up?' she asked, although she knew the answer.

Katya sounded embarrassed. 'Well, Abby, em . . . it's just that I've just had a couple of people ringing me and I didn't want to bother you because I knew you had just got back from holiday but . . . well . . . they seem to know that you and Tom have split up and they want to do stories on it. I didn't know what to do.'

In the midst of her misery, Abby felt sorry for Katya. She

sounded out of her depth. 'Who was looking for me?' she asked, opening a fresh page on an A4 pad. 'What exactly do they know?'

Slowly, Katya began to fill her in.

Selina phoned next, and Abby could tell that she wasn't really able to talk freely.

'How are things at your end?' Selina said. 'Lots of phone calls this morning?'

'You can't talk, can you?' Abby asked quietly.

'No, not really,' said Selina cryptically. 'I'd love to meet up with you for a coffee but perhaps you could phone our mutual friend and talk about this.'

Mike.

'I will,' Abby replied.

By the time she'd managed to speak to Mike, Abby was aware that this wasn't just a bad dream. Both Katya and Selina had phoned back with more messages from interested journalists, and one or two had managed to get her home number from somewhere. Still in her sweaty walking gear, Abby sat in the study with the phone beside her and looked at the long line of names now written on her paper.

Mike, who had just stepped off the plane from Paris, said he knew one of the best PR people in the country, Nadia Wilson. He'd contact her and ask her to deal with all the press queries and to try to put a decent spin on the separation.

How could you put a decent spin on a divorce? Abby wondered glumly. But Mike told her not to be so negative.

'This too will pass,' he said, with the air of an all-seeing guru who'd witnessed more break-ups than a divorce lawyer. 'Look after yourself, Abby,' he advised. 'There's more to this than presenting your side of the story to the press. You've got to look after yourself and Jess. It'll be very hard on her when she sees the story in the papers. And it'll be very hard on you too. Why don't you go see a therapist or a counsellor to get you over the bad part?'

Mike was always surprising her, Abby realised. He really

483

did worry about her wellbeing, and not just about his twenty per cent.

'You're a good man,' she said, grateful for his support.

'You mean I'm a good man for an agent,' he joked back. 'I'm a shark, really, you know that, Abby. Let's face it, if you have a breakdown, what's twenty per cent of nothing?'

When they hung up, they were both laughing. But Abby's cheerfulness vanished when she went into the kitchen and found Jess sitting at the kitchen table, staring gloomily into an untouched bowl of cereal.

'I know this is hard for you –' began Abby.

'Hard for me?' Jess cried, not letting her finish. 'You've no idea how hard it is for me. You don't understand the slightest bit. Or how hard it is for Dad, for that matter. You know how proud he is – how's it going to look to everyone in his school when they've read that you and he have split up because you went off with somebody else?' Her voice cracked.

'They won't know that,' Abby said in horror. 'All they know is that we've split up. We're hardly going to tell them why.'

But Jess was right. That was a fresh worry – that some enterprising reporter would work out that adultery had ended the Bartons' so-called perfect marriage. Even worse, what if Jay came out of the woodwork to say that he was the third person in the Bartons' split? Abby paled at the thought. She looked at Jess to find her daughter watching her intensely, as if she knew exactly what was going on in Abby's mind. It was a look of disgust.

'Don't hate me, please, Jess,' begged Abby tiredly. 'Please don't hate me. We've got to stick together to get through this. I didn't want this to happen, you know I didn't. Please try and understand a little . . .'

Jess got up, emptied her untouched cereal into the bin and threw the empty dish and spoon into the dishwasher. She stormed out of the kitchen and Abby knew there was no point in going after her. Not long afterwards, she heard the front door slam.

Television certainly worked in mysterious ways, Abby realised. Instead of being put off by the news that their as-yet unsigned new chat show host's private life was going to be splashed all over the papers with grisly details of her marriage breakdown, the 727 Network were even keener to sign up Abby.

'It's the human element,' explained Nadia Wilson, the high-priced PR lady Mike had hired to take care of Abby at this difficult time, and who had insisted on coming over straight away to talk to her new client. 'You've got the right touch of empathy now. They'll be queuing up to appear on the show because you've been through the mill yourself. Stars like being interviewed by people who can see things from their side of the fence. That's why the Seven Two Seven Network don't want to hire the usual nineteen-year-old supermodel who's never been in love or had children or done anything. They want you: Abby Barton, real woman, mother and soon-to-be divorcée. Everything you've been through adds pathos and human emotion to the whole story. And,' Nadia grinned, 'the publicity won't be bad for the show. Let's face it, everybody is going to know about it now. The chat show, that is.'

Nadia was nothing like Abby had expected. She'd imagined that a high-flying PR person who masterminded publicity campaigns for the rich and famous would be a scary dame with a heavy eyeliner habit, long manicured talons and sharp designer suits. Instead, Nadia was a serene woman in her late thirties, who didn't need make-up to emphasise her shrewd dark eyes, and who looked as though she'd just dropped into a meeting on her way back from the grocery run. Her uniform consisted of jeans, a simple white shirt, flat boots and a man's diving watch. Her long dark hair was tied back in a ponytail.

'Saves trouble in the morning,' was Nadia's explanation

of her uncomplicated wardrobe choices. 'I just get up and put on a pair of jeans and another shirt. Simple.'

Nadia's straightforward approach to life also extended to publicity. She advised Abby to do one big interview where she actually talked about her marriage breakdown.

'Ostensibly the talk will be about *Declutter*, and leaving Beech, along with the new TV chat show. But you have to mention the break-up,' she counselled. 'Nothing too much but enough to get the reporters off your back. If we do the interview with a tame newspaper, then they'll let us see the copy before they go to print. Copy approval is everything. Everyone else will rip your quotes off from that interview but at least you'll have given your side of the story and be able to emerge with some grace.'

Abby, hollow-eyed from lack of sleep, stared at Nadia. 'What about Tom?' she asked. 'When does he get to give his side of the story?' It seemed so wrong that people would want to hear her view but not Tom's. Not that Tom wanted to talk to anyone about his private life, but that wasn't the point.

Nadia was matter-of-fact. 'He doesn't. You're the famous one: it's your story. Unfair, but there it is. I know you don't want to do anything to hurt him, so it's not as if your story is going to be too painful for him.'

'No, I suppose not,' Abby said. She thought about what she could say – how she had loved her husband, that they had drifted apart. Anything except that there was anyone else involved.

'So the actual part of the interview where I talk about our relationship isn't going to be very big?' asked Abby.

'Not a big part of the interview, no, but it probably will be a big part of the article,' replied Nadia, who believed that her clients needed to hear the truth, however painful. 'Keep it short and sweet. Just give them enough to feel they've got something to write about. When you know what you're going to say, we'll go over it a few times to make sure you're not revealing too much or leaving yourself open to criticism.' Nadia picked up her briefcase and prepared to leave. 'Don't beat yourself up over it, Abby,' she added. 'You're not the first couple to split up and you won't be the last. In a month, somebody else's life will be the *cause célèbre* and everyone will have forgotten about yours.'

When Nadia was gone, Abby allowed herself to sit down at the kitchen table and cry. Jess was still out, Abby didn't know where, and suddenly, now the calls had stopped, it was so quiet in the house. Abby felt lonely. She didn't know who to talk to. She badly needed a friend. If only Sally had been around.

Sally would have understood, for all that she loved Tom. She was a realist and knew that sometimes marriages went wrong. There weren't many people like Sally: people who'd listen to your side of the story without moralising. Lizzie Shanahan was a bit like that too, Abby suddenly realised.

Lizzie was one of life's genuinely kind people who'd been through enough pain herself to see that nothing was simple. But Abby hadn't spoken to Lizzie for ages. She'd been so tied up in her own misery that she hadn't made the effort to see her, or Erin for that matter. And now she was paying the price for neglect.

She thought of her sister, Viv, in Australia. They hadn't spoken for months. Abby hadn't told Viv that she and Tom had separated. Abby had hoped that she mightn't have to tell Viv at all, holding out in the vain hope that they'd get back together. Some hope. She couldn't land all this on Viv now.

But she did need someone to talk to. Hauling out the phone directory, she began to look through the listings for counsellors. It was a sad thing when she had to pay someone to listen to her side of the story.

Although Abby read the papers first thing every morning, dreading a gossip piece about her and Tom, nothing appeared. A bigger story about a sex scandal and a squeaky boyband star had broken, and everyone was interested in that, Nadia explained.

Jess was still barely speaking to her mother and Abby didn't know which was worse: being ignored or being shouted at by a distraught daughter.

Nadia set up the interview with the *Sunday Sentinel* for Friday, and Abby was dreading it. Nearly as much as she was dreading meeting the therapist on Thursday. When she'd made the appointment she'd felt eager to spill out how she felt but now that the meeting was imminent, the idea of talking to a complete stranger about the breakdown of her marriage just filled her with horror. Was there to be no privacy left in her life?

On Thursday, Jess and Steph went into town for the day. Abby felt guilty at resorting to the age-old tactic of cheering her daughter up by giving her money for treats but it had seemed like a good idea at the time. At least it would get Jess out of the house and off having fun with Steph. Since Monday, Jess hadn't even cycled off to the animal refuge, preferring to sit in her room with the door shut and the music on loud. If only she'd talk to me, Abby thought miserably. But Jess clearly had no intention of talking to anyone about how she felt. If she was like this now, Abby wondered what she'd be like when her mother had done the interview and it had appeared in the paper. Jess was going back to school in a week and the exam results were due in two, which added to the sense of general tension.

Abby's favourite magazine carried a big article on the strains of school for teenagers, complete with a piece on how to cope with waiting for exam results.

'Teenagers need to know you fully support them, no matter what their results are like,' advised the article.

Exam results were the least of their worries, Abby thought grimly. Jess could fail everything and Abby wouldn't have dreamed of saying a word to her. Why was it that, these days, life was like walking on a tightrope in high heels?

Tom had barely been civil to Abby when she'd phoned to discuss the interview with him.

'I don't want to know,' he'd snapped. 'I don't see why you have to say anything at all.'

Abby tried explaining that the story wouldn't go away until she talked about it, but Tom wasn't interested. The only thing he did want to talk about was taking Jess away for a week until all the fuss died down.

'For her sake, and mine,' he'd said harshly.

'Of course,' Abby replied.

Now she sat in the therapist's waiting room and read all the posters stuck to the walls about family therapy, marriage breakdown and mediation. Mediation was the trick to family breakdown these days, apparently. Trained mediators would meet the warring couple and help them split their belongings, their money and access to the children.

'Talking is good for the family,' cooed one poster.

Abby glared at it, as if it personally was responsible for the mess her life was in. She was the only person in the waiting room and as she looked around at the shabby collection of furniture, she reflected that break-ups were never like this in the movies. There, it was wham bam thank you, ma'am and, before you knew it, everyone had new lives, new homes and the only arguments were over who got the precious CD collection. Real life was different. This room spoke of real life, and real families who had sat in the mismatched chairs and tried to sort out what was going on with their lives. The memory of tears and fierce arguments lingered in the air, along with a faint smell of cigarettes. Abby could imagine red-eyed people ignoring the no-smoking signs and lighting up to banish the nerves and anxiety.

This was the other end of the marriage trail, a far cry from the hopeful excitement of engagement parties and white weddings. Would people be so eager to rush up the aisle and get married in front of four hundred of their close friends if they knew that this was where it could all end up, in this doomed room with its dismal posters?

At exactly one o'clock, the office door opened and the previous client emerged.

Paul Doherty, psychologist, smiled at Abby and ushered her in. She'd been watching *Frasier* too much, Abby realised, as she sat down in his comfortable office. After years of looking at the antics of the Crane brothers, she'd half imagined that all therapists were just like them – intellectual, cultured types who could engage in long discussions about how many angels could dance on the head of a pin.

By contrast, Paul Doherty looked quite like a family doctor: tired around the eyes and a little rumpled. There was a big desk in the room but he didn't sit behind it; instead he sat in an armchair opposite Abby with a fresh notepad on his lap.

'Hello, Abby. Do you want to tell me why you're here?' he said in a low soft voice.

Abby toyed with the idea of saying 'not really', but she knew that would be wasting both of their time. So she started to tell the story of her marriage to Tom: how her job and new salary had come between them; how she'd felt lonely and unloved. She couldn't let Tom off the hook for that; she knew that his behaviour had certainly contributed to making their marriage worse. But when it came to talking about Jay and how he'd made her feel and how she'd committed adultery with him, her voice faltered. That was nobody's fault but her own.

'I don't know why I'm here really,' she said suddenly, breaking off her story. 'I shouldn't be looking for help or absolution because it's all my fault. It was my fault my husband left me and it's my fault that my daughter won't talk to me. I did it. One stupid action and the whole house of cards has come tumbling down.' She waited for Paul to say something.

But he said nothing and just looked at her, his face expectant.

'I have to do all the talking, don't I?' Abby asked.

The glimmer of a smile touched the psychologist's lips. 'I'm afraid you do need to do most of the talking,' he said. 'That's how it works. Words can unburden us. I'm not saying that by talking about what happened you'll be able to magic it all better. Nothing can do that. But if you can work out why you did what you did, you can learn from that and you can move on with your life.'

It made sense, Abby realised. She just wished it could happen quickly, that she didn't have to go through all this pain and self-flagellation. Getting over what she'd done stretched out in front of her like a desert road with no water in sight. But she fixed the cushion behind her back to make it more comfortable and began to talk.

The interview with the *Sunday Sentinel* was a nightmare. The journalist was lovely, a far cry from the sharp-eyed Maria Carroll, who'd probed Abby's personal life so relentlessly. But despite that, Abby found the whole experience horribly painful.

At least she was able to speak positively about her career and the new opportunities coming up. The first episode of the new series of *Declutter* had just gone out, and both the critics and the public loved it. They liked the new format, they liked the inclusion of the twins, and they still loved Abby.

'Abby Barton is still the best thing about this show,' one television critic had said.

Strangely enough, this accolade didn't thrill Abby the way it once would have done. There was more to life than getting a good review in the papers. But she did feel a sense of relief. And she fielded the questions about the rumour of her moving to the new chat show with ease. Nothing had been signed, she said, truthfully, although she'd love to work on the show. She liked new challenges, she added.

She knew she looked well too. Nerves had helped her lose the extra five pounds she was always desperately trying to shift. Now her clothes hung even better on her frame than before. Another one of Ruby's magical facials had made her skin look bright and youthful, and she'd had her hair highlighted just before the interview.

But these were all surface things. Abby knew now that

they weren't the really important aspects of life, and it was very hard hiding her devastation at the break-up of her family from someone who was gently but firmly trying to get her to divulge her innermost secrets in an interview. By the time it was over, Abby felt stripped of her defences and exhausted.

On Sunday, the day the article was to be printed, Abby woke early. It was still too soon to go down to the newsagent's and, besides, she didn't want to buy the paper in her local shop. So she drove to a twenty-four-hour garage outside town where she knew she would get her hands on the earliest edition.

Sitting in the car in the garage forecourt, she cringed at the front-page headline flagging the article: 'The secret misery behind Abby Barton's bright smile, see pages 6 and 7', and riffled through the paper until she found it.

Nadia had insisted on copy approval and had read the article to Abby over the phone the night before. There was a difference, however, between hearing it read and seeing it in full colour, with unflattering photographs of herself and Tom.

Her hands shaking, she read. It was a balanced article and talked about her career success, merely mentioning the fact that her marriage had recently broken down. Everything she said had been faithfully reported, but to Abby's eyes it still looked like a horror story.

Tom had taken Jess away for the weekend to London, but some well-meaning person would be sure to keep a copy of the paper for Tom. They'd see it when they got back all right, and they'd be hurt by it. Abby turned the car for home. She was too sad even to cry. She'd never felt lonelier or lower in her life.

Lizzie got the Sunday papers on her way back from ten o'clock Mass. She'd been feeling a bit low and had hoped that a spiritual hour in God's presence might cheer her up and distract her from thoughts of Simon but it hadn't quite worked out that way. Instead of communing with a higher power, she'd found herself fascinated by the two small children in the pew in front of her. Adorable twin girls, they'd spent the entire service playing incey wincey spider with their parents, making it absolutely impossible for Lizzie to concentrate on the ceremony. Mass was over before she knew it, and Lizzie felt hideously guilty for having gone with the intention of praying and ended up doing nothing but amusing herself. Honestly, what was she like? Her concentration was shot to hell. She vowed to go again during the week to make up for it. Lord knew, she'd prayed enough for God's help in sorting out the whole problem of Debra and Barry – the least she could do was actually listen when she was in His house.

At home, she dumped the bag containing the papers and the makings of Debra's breakfast on the kitchen table. Debra was very fond of a proper cooked breakfast and Lizzie, who normally had nothing more than toast and tea, had got into the habit of providing a full fry-up for her daughter and eating some herself. All those bacon and eggs were doing nothing for her figure, Lizzie thought ruefully. Debra was still slim as a reed and never put any weight on. Lizzie wished she could say the same thing about herself. She'd have to go back on her diet soon.

When the breakfast goodies were stowed away in the fridge – Lizzie wouldn't dream of cooking anything until Debra decided to get up – she sat down at the table and scanned the *Sentinel* quickly.

'Oh no,' she breathed when she came upon the big double-page article on Abby Barton. Poor Abby. Her heart went out to the other woman.

Lizzie would never forget the pain and trauma of her own break-up – imagine if she'd had to talk about it in the newspapers? She thought back to the first time she'd really talked to Abby, the night of Sally and Steve Richardson's party. They'd got on so well, but the trouble between Abby and her husband had been obvious even then.

Perhaps their marriage had been bad for years, Lizzie thought sadly. You never knew with other people's relationships, did you? They could look perfectly all right on the surface and, underneath it all, be a hotbed of hate and resentment.

The reverse was also true: look at her own marriage. She had assumed it was all perfect, while everyone else seemed to realise it wasn't. Lizzie jerked herself out of her bout of self-pity. Enough wallowing in the past, she ordered. You've moved on, you have a new life and you're not going to get maudlin about your marriage, right?

But had she really moved on, she wondered.

She flicked through the article again, wincing as she read the journalist's description of Abby: 'On the television, Abby Barton is bubbly, lively and like your best friend. You'd trust her to de-junk your house and sort out your life at the same time. But, in the flesh, Abby is quieter and there's sorrow in her eyes. She's got the career every woman dreams of, but it hasn't been without its price. Over the past few months, Abby and her husband, teacher Tom Barton, a deputy headmaster at an exclusive all-boys Cork school, have separated. It was nobody's fault, Abby told the *Sunday Sentinel*. They were both devastated by the break-up. But Abby Barton is a realist and she knows that when it's over, it's over.'

Lizzie read on. The journalist described Abby's new career prospects and there were some funny quotes from Abby about how hard it was to be the nation's favourite de-junker, and still be hopeless at filing paperwork. Lizzie imagined how hard it must have been for Abby to make those jokes, when she would be feeling so miserable.

On impulse, Lizzie picked up the phone and dialled Abby's number. If she stopped to think about it, she would lose the courage to do it. Abby must have millions of friends who'd rally round at a time like this, offering support and consolation. But Lizzie could add her voice.

Abby's answering machine clicked in and Lizzie left a

message: 'Hi, Abby, it's Lizzie Shanahan, and I was just phoning to say that if you're feeling a bit blue after the article in the paper, well, I'm around if you fancy a cup of coffee or anything. It's hard enough when your marriage ends without having to talk about it, you poor thing.'

A thought suddenly struck Lizzie – what if Abby thought she was phoning up only to pry? 'Oh, Abby, I'm not ringing because I want to hear things, honestly,' she stammered. 'I just thought I'd be there to talk if you felt like it because, like I said, I've been there. Bye.' Lizzie hung up, not knowing if she'd done the right thing. That was the story of her life, wasn't it?

When they'd first moved to Dunmore, Greg and Erin had often gone for a Sunday-morning stroll down the town, meandering along the streets, admiring their beautiful new home. They'd buy the Sunday papers and pop into a café to enjoy brunch. It was a habit they'd acquired when they lived in Chicago, although the scenery there had been somewhat different. But at this point in Erin's pregnancy, despite swimming four times a week at the local pool, she no longer had the energy for long walks, so these days they drove into the town, parked the car and strolled all of fifteen yards to Molly's Coffee Shop, which was their favourite hangout. Greg had coffee, and Erin had copious cups of tea. As they both indulged in big fat breakfast muffins, Greg read the papers at high speed, flicking through the supplements and discarding them on a spare chair as he went. Erin preferred to read at a more leisurely pace, really taking in articles and enjoying the turn of phrase of writers she liked.

It was Greg who gave a sudden expletive of surprise.

'There's an interview here with Abby,' he said. 'It talks about her marriage. I didn't know she and Tom had broken up . . .' He scanned through the article rapidly.

'Gimme a look,' demanded Erin.

She read through the article carefully and her heart went out to Abby. Erin had suspected there was something wrong in the Barton household for a long time, but Abby had kept very quiet about it.

'I should phone her,' Erin said decisively.

'Are you sure?' Greg asked. 'I didn't think she was that close a friend of yours.'

'She wasn't at first,' Erin admitted, 'but she's a nice woman. I like her. Besides, I bet everyone's too nervous of going near her today and that is exactly when she needs some support.'

Greg looked at his wife admiringly. Erin had so much courage and energy. He loved her for that. Anyone else might shy away from contacting Abby today of all days, but not Erin. She understood more than most people that sometimes you needed to hear a friendly voice.

Erin was halfway through leaving the message when Abby picked up the phone.

'Oh, hello, Abby, you're there,' said Erin in surprise.

'Yes, I'm here,' said Abby wearily. 'I'm afraid to go out in case somebody spots me on the street and points and says, "There's that woman from the telly who split up from her husband."'

Erin laughed out loud, which somehow gave Abby the courage to laugh too.

'I know,' Abby groaned, 'it sounds ridiculous, doesn't it?'

'It doesn't sound ridiculous at all,' Erin replied. 'If I were you, I'd probably feel exactly the same and be considering how to dye my hair so no one could recognise me. Fame, huh? It's not all it's cracked up to be.'

'You said it,' replied Abby with relish.

'So,' Erin went on, 'do you fancy coming out today then? We could confound all the critics by doing something really public – unless you're busy,' she added.

Abby was so touched that for a moment she could barely speak. She'd had messages of both sympathy and encouragement from a variety of people, including Selina, Nadia, Mike and, surprisingly, Steph Anderson's mother, Lisa. But nobody had suggested actually doing anything. Apart from Lizzie Shanahan, that was.

'I'm not doing anything,' Abby began. 'Jess is with Tom, but I'm sure you normally spend Sundays with Greg.'

'Greg can do without me for one afternoon,' Erin said cheerily. 'He's fed up looking at me and my big bump and having to go out at all hours to buy ice cream and corn on the cob so I can eat the two together.'

Greg, who was listening to every word, laughed at this. 'Don't forget to tell her about the midnight trips to the garage,' he interrupted. 'The guys at the garage shop can't understand why I don't have an ulcer, what with all the weird food combinations I buy.'

'Did you hear that?' demanded Erin. 'Honestly, men! They have it so easy. Right, Abby, where will we go and what will we do?'

Abby didn't know. 'Lizzie left a message earlier and suggested I could meet her for a coffee, so perhaps we could do that.'

'I've a better idea,' said Erin with enthusiasm. 'Why don't we drop round to Lizzie's, pick her up and go out for lunch? I can be designated driver and you pair can get smashed out of your heads on cocktails and scandalise everyone in the neighbourhood. What do you think?'

'Sounds great,' said Abby, and was surprised to realise that she had tears in her eyes.

Lizzie was halfway through cooking Debra's breakfast when Abby rang. Lizzie was thrilled when she heard the plan.

'What a brilliant idea. I'd love that, and it'll get you out of the house, Abby. There's nothing worse than sitting at home thinking things over on a day like today.'

'Erin's going to pick me up in half an hour and then we'll swing by your house,' Abby said. 'Does that sound OK?'

'Great,' Lizzie replied. 'That'll give me a chance to beautify myself.'

Debra was not impressed with this change to her Sunday-morning routine. She liked having a leisurely breakfast with her mother, knowing that if she wanted another fried egg or a piece of toast, Mum would hop up and make it instantly. It was like being a kid again: comforting and homely.

However, she was marginally impressed when she learned that one of the visitors was going to be Abby Barton, the same Abby whose marriage breakdown details were splashed all over the *Sunday Sentinel*.

'Do you think she'll tell us the inside story?' Debra asked with excitement.

Her mother glared at her.

'Obviously I'm not going to *say* that, Mum,' Debra protested. 'I was just thinking, you know, seeing as how she is a friend of yours and everything, that she could tell us what really happened. I bet they always leave juicy stuff out in the papers.'

'I can't believe you've just said that, Debra,' Lizzie said crossly. 'We're talking about a marriage breaking down here. You, of all people, should know how serious and distressing that is.'

Debra just shrugged. 'Well, if I can get over Barry, she can get over Tom or whatever his name is, can't she?'

Lizzie began to wonder if there was really any future for Barry and Debra. She'd hoped the row would blow over but from the cold way Debra spoke of him, it was clear that she meant the split to be for good. Lizzie was shocked that her daughter could be so callous about the man she'd been so desperate to marry. Was Debra just pretending to be hard to hide the fact that her heart was breaking or did she really feel nothing for Barry? If she didn't feel any emotion for him, then that was the scariest thing of all.

For the first time ever, Lizzie began to wonder if she'd done something wrong in bringing up Debra. Her own mother, though loving, had been so tough on her daughters, and Lizzie had desperately tried not to be that sort of parent. She'd thought that encouraging her children was the way forward. They knew they were loved and adored, and were daily told how clever and talented they were.

This method seemed to have worked with Joe, who was clever and funny, and yet still managed to be kind, despite all his wit and intelligence. But it didn't seem to have worked so well with Debra, Lizzie reflected. In fact, the more time they spent together, the more Debra reminded Lizzie of her own mother: always ready to speak her mind, no matter how painful it was for the person listening.

'Debra, there's a big difference between splitting up after seventeen years and splitting up after a few months of marriage,' Lizzie said mildly. She wanted to add that it didn't seem that Debra was exactly heartbroken by the split with Barry but she didn't.

'I suppose . . .' Debra admitted, buttering a piece of toast. 'I bet you that Abby will get loads of money out of her husband, won't she? They've got a big house on Briar Lane too. That'll go for millions.'

'I don't think money is the most important thing on her mind at the moment,' said Lizzie coldly.

Thoroughly disillusioned with her daughter, she went upstairs to get ready.

'Erin, this was a brilliant choice of restaurant,' said Lizzie in admiration as they walked into a noisy, glamorous eaterie full of stylish people who made Lizzie feel underdressed. Despite being in the country for only six months, Erin had somehow figured out the best place in Cork to have Sunday lunch.

Lizzie's idea of the most glamorous place you could lunch on a Sunday had been the big hotel in Dunmore where you sat amid the sedate portraits and heavy brocade curtains and ate a formal meal, talking in hushed tones while the staff looked as if they wouldn't know which muscles to use to smile. This place looked like much more fun, with friendly waiters and waitresses zipping around at high speed and a lively hum of conversation. The fabulous seafood buffet, displayed like a work of art, looked much more exciting than the Dunmore hotel's traditional roast beef and broccoli.

'Greg and I come here sometimes,' Erin said. 'It's fun and the food's great. I just thought it would be good today to get out of Dunmore.'

'I just hope Greg doesn't mind us taking you away from him today,' Abby said.

'Not at all,' replied Erin. 'He has the place to himself and can watch sports on the TV all afternoon. He's thrilled.'

'This is a gorgeous treat for a Sunday,' said Lizzie in appreciation as she looked at the menu. 'I never go out for Sunday lunch normally.'

'You and Debra should come here,' Erin said carefully. 'It's sad about her and Barry but it must be nice for you having her at home nowadays.'

Lizzie didn't reply for a moment or two. Was it nice having Debra at home these days? It certainly wasn't how she'd expected it. Lizzie had got used to living by herself now, used to being her own boss and doing what she wanted when she wanted.

But she couldn't admit that to anyone, not even to Erin and Abby, to whom she had been very honest on other occasions.

'Yes,' she agreed loyally. 'It's wonderful having Debra around.'

Abby was listening to the conversation but was barely taking part. She was so aware of what a public place this was and how many of the diners there must recognise her. What would they be thinking? That she was a very brazen hussy indeed to appear out for lunch, looking so carefree, on the day when her marriage breakdown had been splashed all over the papers?

She'd done her best to look presentable but knew her face was white and strained, both from stress and lack of sleep.

'How's Jess?' asked Lizzie, and then instantly knew she'd said the wrong thing because of the haunted look that came over Abby's face. She cast around frantically to change the subject, but Erin had a better idea. Erin realised that it was important for Abby to talk about what had been happening and get it off her chest.

'I bet she's really upset about all this newspaper stuff,' Erin said.

'She's in bits,' admitted Abby. 'Tom's taken her away for the weekend. She's upset over how what's happened is affecting her father and she'll be upset over everything that's in the paper and, oh . . . I feel like such a bad mother,' she said miserably.

'You? A bad mother?' said Erin incredulously. 'Don't be ridiculous, Abby, you're a great mum. This is just a blip: normal, messy life intruding into the fantasy world we all think we should be living in. You're too hard on yourself. We probably all are. I keep thinking I'm going to be a bad mother because I'm doing something wrong with the pregnancy and not eating enough calcium or I'm having too much tuna fish. But that's what motherhood is all about, according to my sister, Kerry: sheer guilt.'

Lizzie gave a great peel of laughter at this. 'You're so right,' she said. In Lizzie's mental parenting manual, it was all her fault that Debra was hard, not Debra's.

'Anyway,' continued Erin, 'if you want to talk about dysfunctional mothers, let me tell you about mine.'

So as food and drink were delivered to the table, Abby and Lizzie listened enthralled to Erin's story about meeting her birth mother for the first time.

Erin told it all in a very matter-of-fact manner, without self-pity, but, even though she did her best not to sound as though she blamed Shannon for what had happened, she couldn't help herself. Shannon *was* to blame. Erin would have loved another meeting with her, just to say all the things that had been rattling angrily round in her head since the last time.

'She's just different,' Erin said at the end, trying to convince herself as much as the others. 'I can't explain it any other way. She's not like any other sort of mum, and I suppose I shouldn't have expected her to be either.'

It really was the most amazing story, Abby thought, worthy of several magazine articles. It made her own tawdry marriage breakdown seem commonplace in comparison. Somehow, hearing Erin explain the whole saga made Abby feel more normal, more grounded. Everybody had secrets and skeletons in the closet: it was just that, with most people, the rest of the world didn't get to hear about them.

Lizzie felt honoured that Erin had confided in them. 'Don't worry,' she reassured her, 'we won't breathe a word of this to anyone else.'

But Erin didn't feel the need for secrecy any more. 'It's strangely cathartic talking about it,' she admitted. 'It was such a big secret for so long and I didn't tell anybody when I lived in America. But now, forgive me for sounding like a clichéd phone advert, but it's good to talk about these things. Bottling stuff up doesn't get anyone anywhere.'

'I went to a psychologist to talk about the breakdown,' volunteered Abby suddenly.

The other two looked at her, willing her to keep telling the story because they knew it would be good for her to get it out into the open.

'And what did he or she say?' prompted Erin.

'He didn't say very much at all. I did all the talking. It wasn't what I'd expected, to be frank. I wouldn't have gone to see anyone but I feel so guilty about everything, especially about Jess and how hard it must be for her. You talk about your birth mum being messed up,' Abby went on, 'but I've been just as bad a mother.'

'No you haven't,' insisted Erin. 'Having your marriage break up doesn't move you from the good mum to the bad mum pile.'

Miserably, Abby thought that if the two women knew why her marriage had broken up, they might think just that.

'I shouldn't criticise Shannon,' Erin continued, although that's exactly what she wanted to do. 'That's not fair. She didn't want to be a mother, but what's wrong with that? Lots of people don't want to be parents and they're not hauled over the coals for it. Not wanting kids doesn't make you a bad person but,' she looked down at her plate, 'I've spent years imagining that absent mother equals bad person and that was wrong.' If she said it often enough, Erin hoped that maybe she'd believe this herself.

'She was very young when she had you,' interrupted Lizzie gently. 'I was just twenty-two when I got pregnant, and I have to admit it was scary. For a few days until I told people, it felt like the end of my life as I knew it. You feel so alone. I can understand how your mum wanted to run away from all that.'

'You're right,' agreed Erin. 'I've really got to forgive Shannon and move on.' She would manage it, she told herself, she *would*. 'There's no point crying over the past,' she added. 'I should look to the future.'

'Do you know, that's exactly the sort of thing Sally would have said,' Abby remarked.

In the midst of the noisy restaurant, they were all silent for a moment, thinking about their friend and what she'd brought to their lives.

Lizzie knew that she had tried to move on, especially after Myles had found new love with Sabine, but all her plans for a new, improved life hadn't quite worked out. She was still stuck at home all the time, thinking about the sort of life she could have if only she got off her fat bum and did something about it. And what was stopping her going out and getting that life?

Debra, said a little voice in her head. *Debra's stopping you from moving on. She wants you to be the same old mum, as if nothing has changed, as if she was still going out to school every day and coming home to a happy family life, cooked dinners and reliable old mum sitting there every evening. Men, like Simon, are not an option in Debra's eyes.*

Things had moved on, the whole family's lives had changed and they had all grown older. Debra couldn't seem to see that, and because Lizzie didn't want to hurt her, she didn't want to force Debra to see the truth either. And how could she? Debra needed her and Lizzie knew that she had to be there. Mothers could never let their daughters down.

Abby remembered how, when she'd first met Sally, Sally used to treat her a bit like a grown-up older sister and ask her advice. In later years, Sally's wisdom had been obvious to everyone and she had become the sort of person other people went to for advice. But what sort of advice would she give Abby now?

Sally and Tom had been friends before he introduced her to Abby. Would she have taken his side in the break-up, become Tom's friend in future instead of Abby's? Abby hoped not. Surely Sally would have tried to keep them both as her friends.

For all her inherent goodness, or perhaps because of it, Sally had not been the sort of person who would moralise or choose sides. She was a realist, who appreciated her good fortune in life. If she'd still been around, would she have persuaded Tom and Abby to talk to one another, acting as a go-between to help them get back together? Who knew?

'Lizzie, you know you were asking us for ideas about remembering Sally?' Erin said slowly. 'Well, I've been thinking about the fund-raising you've been doing in Sally's name. I don't know what you think, but I had an idea about that when I was visiting my mum and dad. It was more something my sister, Kerry, said actually. She's involved in a health centre where people who are ill get complementary therapies like massage. It's linked to the Life Beats Cancer organisation, although they don't only treat people with cancer.'

'Oh,' said Lizzie excitedly, 'they're the people I talked to when I wanted to raise money for charity with my parachute jump!'

'Then you'll know all about them,' Erin said with enthusiasm. 'The thing is, Kerry had breast cancer herself and that's how she got into the complementary therapy area.

She learned how to meditate and had regular massages, and said it was such an incredible help to her when she was going through it all. She said she'd never forget how great it was just to have somewhere to go and talk to other people, a place where she felt normal and not like some sort of a freak.'

The others were looking at her with interest and Erin went on: 'This set me thinking. Imagine if we had a centre like that in Dunmore, dedicated to anyone with cancer and maybe their families, where people could get massages, healing, learn meditation, have counselling, whatever. It's not in place of normal medicine or anything, but it could be a help with getting through it all.' Her voice was enthusiastic. 'When Sally was sick we didn't know what to say to her, but going to a healing centre could have really helped her. And I kept wondering how Steve was going to cope and what I'd be like if Greg was the one who was ill or what he'd be like if I was ill and who we'd go to for support. Kerry said that people just don't know what to say to you – they either avoid the subject altogether or they treat you like some sort of tragic victim, which isn't what you want when you're trying to beat a disease. So that's when I had the idea.

'Kerry says that the Life Beats Cancer people have a research wing, but they've also set up a couple of complementary health centres round the country and they want to set up many more. We could link up with them and learn the right way to do it. OK, it's going to take time because I'm sure something like that would take a lot of money to run, but we could do it, couldn't we?'

Lizzie's eyes shone. 'What a fantastic idea,' she exclaimed. 'When I was trying to raise money for the parachute jump, I was astonished at how many people remembered Sally and would have done anything to help. There's so much goodwill out there and it's all down to her. I'm sure we could get a lot of people interested in the scheme, important people, people with contacts, people who could get us state funding. We could set up the Dunmore branch of Life Beats Cancer.'

'And I could use my contacts in newspapers and magazines,' interrupted Abby. 'We could easily drum up publicity that way because, let's face it, after this weekend, the whole country knows who I am,' she added ruefully.

'And if we could get Steve involved just a little bit, that would be fantastic,' Erin added. 'I know it must be very painful for him right now, but wouldn't he love something set up in Sally's name, something that would help other people who are going through what she went through?'

Suddenly, the lethargy was gone and they talked animatedly about their new plans. Ever organised, Erin had a notepad in her handbag and began drawing up lists. The first things, obviously, were to talk to Steve, and then to the people at LBC to discuss the proposal.

'We could get a lot of people to do charity parachute jumps,' Lizzie said. 'That really appeals to younger people – it's fun and they're doing something good at the same time. I made friends with the people who run the jump centre and they'd be sure to help us set up a weekend solely for our charity.' And she'd get to talk to Simon again, she thought eagerly.

Abby knew someone who'd done a lot of charity work for autism and could possibly give her hints on the best ways of raising money. Erin said she didn't know very much about charity fund-raising but she was a good organiser.

'Just imagine if Dunmore had its own Life Beats Cancer centre – wouldn't that be brilliant? It could be somewhere friendly and supportive and helpful in all sorts of ways,' Erin enthused.

'And somewhere that people could access accurate information so it wouldn't all be so terribly scary in the beginning,' Lizzie said, remembering the Penders and how terrified they'd been when Mr Pender had been told about his prostate cancer. 'I see it in the surgery all the time. People are so petrified about the word "cancer" that they often don't bother to consider the cure rates and how successful modern medicine is today. And that's half the battle, isn't it? Being able to be positive and knowing that there is hope out there.'

'Kerry would help us,' Erin said. 'I'll ring her as soon as I get home and ask her advice and what she thinks has worked.'

'Yes,' said Abby enthusiastically, 'and I'll ring my autism friend when I get home to pick her brains. I've got to do a few more interviews for *Declutter*, and it would be great if I could get publicity for Life Beats Cancer too while I was at it.'

Erin and Lizzie grinned at the enthusiasm in their friend's voice. Fifteen minutes ago, she'd been despairing. Now she was full of life and vigour.

'It's Sally,' Erin remarked. 'She's still looking out for us, isn't she?'

For the first time since Sally's death, Abby didn't feel the usual sense of terrible loss and powerlessness when she thought of her friend. This was something they could do to make the world better in Sally's name.

'We should call it after her,' she suggested. 'The Sally Richardson Health Centre or something like that. It has to have Sally's name in the title. We're doing it for her.'

Abby looked around at the other two, who nodded in agreement.

CHAPTER THIRTY

Jess hated going to stay with Aunt Caroline and Uncle Phil. However, she couldn't say anything to Dad: he needed to get away and be with his family, and he'd asked her to come with him. The article about him and Mum splitting up was due to appear in the paper on Sunday and Dad said he didn't want to be around when it came out.

'A weekend away is just what the doctor ordered,' he'd said to Jess, trying to sound cheerful when she knew he wasn't. 'We'll go to see Caroline and Phil.' He announced it as if going to see his sister and brother-in-law in Kent was a great treat. 'That will be fun, won't it?'

Jess didn't have the heart to tell him that no, it most definitely would not be fun. She wasn't sure how this visit would help, seeing as Aunt Caroline wasn't a calming person to be around, but he needed her and she was going to support him.

Sometimes Jess wondered what it would be like to have brothers and sisters, people you could go to when you were in trouble and who'd understand everything in your head because they'd grown up the same way.

Brothers and sisters weren't all they were cracked up to be, Oliver said. He had a younger brother and sister, but they were kids, both under ten, and while they were fun, you couldn't really talk to them.

And Steph had a younger sister, Natasha, who was thirteen, and they fought all the time. Steph said she couldn't imagine ever telling Natasha anything. To be honest, Jess couldn't imagine her dad confiding in Aunt Caroline either.

Aunt Caroline wasn't anything like Dad. She was three or four years older and she'd lived in Kent for as long as Jess could remember. Sometimes Aunt Caroline and Uncle Phil had visited Cork but they had never stayed with Mum and Dad. They always stayed with Granny and Granddad Barton until first Granddad, then Granny died.

Jess hadn't seen them since Granny Barton's funeral, nearly two years ago. Uncle Phil was OK, but Jess found Aunt Caroline hard going. Mum didn't like her much either, Jess knew, but Mum had somehow managed to hide this from Dad for years because she didn't want to hurt him.

Jess herself was doing a lot of things to make sure Dad wasn't hurt – going on this trip was a particularly irritating addition to the list. And she felt bad about leaving Mum, even though she hadn't been able to say this to Abby.

Jess didn't know what it was, but sometimes, when she wanted to say something comforting to Mum, she just couldn't manage it. It was like she had to let off steam with her mother, and there was no room for her to hear how hurt and upset Mum was back.

Then, Jess would feel guilty and mean for not supporting Mum. She'd looked so sad when she dropped Jess over to Dad's place on Friday, like she was going to cry or something, and when she'd driven off, Jess had been overcome with this desire to phone Mum on her mobile and say, 'I'm really sorry, I know you're upset but I had to go away with Dad this weekend and I'll be back soon.' But she hadn't. Then as soon as she got inside Dad's front door, he was all businesslike, checking their travel documents, and the chance to phone had passed.

They were flying to London and then they'd rent a car to drive to Kent. Dad loved organising holidays, sorting out tickets and money. And Mum was so dreadful at that type of thing. That was why it always worked so well when they went on holidays as a threesome – Dad would do the boring things like tickets, and Mum and Jess could just have fun. But that wasn't going to happen ever again.

On the plane, Dad flicked through the duty-free brochure. 'Is there anything you want in here?' he asked Jess.

'Dad, just because you and Mum have split up, you don't have to keep buying me stuff,' she said. 'Mum bought me a really expensive pair of sunglasses in Florida and now you want to buy me something else. I'm not a stupid kid, you know. I understand that divorce can be expensive.'

Her father looked crestfallen.

'I don't mean to be horrible,' Jess went on. 'It's just that I am sixteen and I do know about money. We won't have as much, I know.'

'You're not to worry about money,' Dad said then. 'We'll have enough, I promise.'

Jess rolled her eyes. Dad just didn't listen, did he?

Travelling was tiring, Jess decided later that evening as they crawled along the motorway in a tailback that looked as if it was hundreds of miles long. Or maybe travelling was only tiring when you were going somewhere you didn't want to go. She'd loved going to Florida, but getting to Aunt Caroline's was definitely exhausting, though Dad had been chirpy for the whole trip, as if it was all great fun.

'It's great to get away for a weekend,' he said, seemingly unperturbed by the fact that the car was going at about five miles an hour. 'And it will be good for you and me to spend time together,' he added.

Jess thought that they probably wouldn't get that much time on their own together at all – Aunt Caroline tended to monopolise Dad when she got the chance.

'I wonder, will the boys be home for the weekend?' Dad asked out loud. He was talking about David and Ross, Jess's cousins. They were both a lot older than her, in their early twenties, and she didn't know them very well. 'Although I think Caroline said they weren't going to be there,' Dad added.

At least that was something, Jess thought with relief. There would have been nothing worse than having to spend the weekend with her cousins being expected to mind her the whole time.

Aunt Caroline and Uncle Phil lived in an old terraced house in a bustling town just off the motorway. Dad parked the car, and he and Jess were just stretching after their long drive when Aunt Caroline raced out of the house and flung her arms first around Jess and then around Dad. Aunt Caroline was tall like Dad, but there the similarity ended. Big and bustling, she wore what Jess felt were horrible granny clothes and had a velvet hairband holding back her dark hair.

'How are you both?' she cried, as if they were survivors from some terrible accident. 'I was so worried about you getting here tonight. Come on in, come on in,' she rattled off. 'I've supper ready, if it's not burned to a crisp in the oven. Oh, you poor, poor things. The traffic is dreadful, isn't it?'

Jess remembered what was so irritating about her Aunt Caroline. She never knew when to shut up. She meant well but her constant stream of conversation was instantly annoying.

Inside the house, there were more hugs and probing 'How are you, Tom?' comments from Caroline before she showed Dad and Jess to their rooms.

Jess's bed was in a tiny boxroom that was obviously also used as a study because it had a desk and a computer stuck in one corner. Situated right at the top of the house, the room was cosy and at least away from everyone else. Grateful for that, Jess finally shut the door on Caroline and plonked herself down on the bed.

Peace at last. But it wasn't for long. Jess had barely had a chance to change her T-shirt when Caroline was roaring up the stairs that dinner was on the table and girls who wanted some had better rush downstairs quickly and wash their hands. Jess grimaced at her reflection in the wall mirror. Did Aunt Caroline think she was still ten? *Girls who wanted dinner had better wash their hands* indeed!

Jess hadn't planned to bother with make-up, but now she

drew in a fat brown line of the eyeliner Steph had given her for her birthday and added mascara just to make the point to her aunt that this girl had grown up.

Downstairs in the big kitchen, Dad was sitting in a comfortable seat with a glass of wine in his hand, while Uncle Phil carved a joint of roast beef and Aunt Caroline fussed about with vegetables, gravy and trimmings. Caroline really didn't look like Dad. She looked like a different generation altogether with her long cardigans, her silky blouses, her pearl earrings and her fondness for long plaid skirts. Jess thought of Mum, who wore funky modern clothes and never looked her age. Mum would have used Aunt Caroline's beige silky blouse for a duster.

She slipped into a chair and Caroline put a big plate of roast beef in front of her.

'I don't eat meat, Aunt Caroline,' Jess said politely.

'Nonsense,' said her aunt. 'A growing girl like you needs red meat. Eat up, we don't have any of that vegetarian nonsense in this house.'

Jess looked to her dad for back-up as she didn't want to be rude. She hadn't eaten meat for nearly three years, and she wasn't about to start now. But Dad gave her an apologetic look across the table, as if to say, 'Go on, eat it, don't upset your aunt.'

Jess stared back down at the plate. She couldn't eat meat and she didn't want to eat vegetables that had touched meat. Why hadn't Dad said anything to Aunt Caroline? Mum would have: Mum would have told her straight off.

Jess was hungry, but she only allowed herself to nibble the vegetables that hadn't been near the offending roast beef. Aunt Caroline kept shooting her disapproving glances, her lips pursed like a prune. To make up for all the food she couldn't eat, Jess ate lots of garlic bread. If Aunt Caroline said one word to Jess, she'd tell her in no uncertain terms that she didn't eat meat and that was it.

Luckily, Caroline said nothing about the untouched food on her niece's plate. Instead, she directed most of her talk to Dad, which was fine with Jess because it meant she didn't have to answer questions. A lot of Aunt Caroline's conversation revolved around what she called 'the you-know-what'.

Jess figured out that this meant divorce or separation. It was as if Caroline didn't want to actually say the words with Jess present. Did she think Jess was six instead of sixteen?

'It's not the end of the world and you just have to look forward to the future,' Aunt Caroline said several times. 'Lots of people get on with their lives and are perfectly happy, Tom.' She patted Dad's arm a lot. He'd have a bruise in the morning, Jess thought to herself. Aunt Caroline was a big woman.

Jess helped tidy up, and then Aunt Caroline brought out a huge syllabub-type thing from the fridge. Pale pink and glistening, it wobbled horribly in its bowl and Jess thought she'd be sick if she had to eat any of it.

'I don't really like desserts,' she said quickly, in case she was forced to eat some.

'That's all right then,' said Aunt Caroline in the sort of voice people used when they were trying to humour difficult children. 'Would you like to run along and watch some television?'

Grateful for the reprieve, Jess ignored the patronising way her aunt had said it, and smiled 'yes'.

She asked if she could get herself a glass of orange juice from the fridge, then headed for the living room. From the comfort of a big armchair, she could hear the buzz of conversation from the kitchen, and she knew that Aunt Caroline was really talking about the divorce now.

Sometimes, fragments of conversation drifted across the hall into the living room.

'I always knew you shouldn't have married her,' Aunt Caroline said in a distraught, tipsy voice. 'I always knew she wasn't the woman for you. Mother knew it too, but would you listen to us? No.'

Jess flicked around with the television zapper until she

found something she liked watching. She turned the volume up. She didn't want to listen to Aunt Caroline running down her mother. And it didn't sound as if Dad was standing up for Mum, either. Jess knew that it was Mum's fault that they'd split up. She knew that Mum had done a terrible thing but she was sorry for it. She would have loved Dad to come back. But Dad wasn't giving her a chance, was he?

Even with the TV loud, she could still hear some of the conversation from the kitchen. Now Caroline was going on about Mum's career and how that had ruined the family. That wasn't a fair thing to say, Jess thought. Mum worked really hard and her money had meant a lot to the family. So, Dad had found it difficult when Mum was earning more money than he was, but men were funny about money, Jess knew – she read *Cosmopolitan* magazine sometimes – but guys had to deal with this, didn't they? Surely what was important was that the family as a unit was making a living, not who was making most of the money. And Jess was proud of Mum for what she'd done with her life. None of her friends' mums had ever achieved anything like Mum had. Jess used to say that having a famous mother wasn't anything to write home about, but that didn't mean she wasn't secretly proud of her.

And Dad needed to understand that. If ever they got a chance to talk during the weekend, Jess promised herself that she'd tell him so.

She turned the TV up even louder. Aunt Caroline would probably complain but tough titty. By the sounds of it, they were getting through plenty of wine in the kitchen. They probably couldn't hear themselves any more, never mind the TV.

The next morning after breakfast, Steph rang Jess on her mobile.

'How's it going, babes?' she asked perkily.

'Don't ask,' Jess said.

Aunt Caroline had actually provided Coco Pops for her

for breakfast, which was nice, in that it meant her aunt was trying to be thoughtful, but irritating because she'd got it wrong.

'They still think I'm a kid,' she told Steph angrily. 'I'm surprised Aunt Caroline didn't go out and buy some *Thomas, the Tank Engine* books and leave them in my room along with some crayons and a join-the-dots pad.'

'Ouch, Coco Pops, that's bad,' said Steph. 'You should have borrowed my Wonderbra and black chiffon top, *then* they'd know you weren't a kid.'

Jess laughed. 'You know I don't have anything to put in your Wonderbra, so I'd look even more of a loser then – just someone who wanted tits and didn't have them.'

'Why don't you go out, buy some cigarettes and hang around the back garden smoking and looking moody,' Steph suggested. 'That's what I do whenever any of my rellies carry on like I'm a kid. That soon makes them see that I am a woman.' She pronounced the word 'woman' with a twang. 'That and my see-through chiffon shirt.'

Jess smiled at the thought. 'Aunt Caroline would probably have me carted off by social services if I turned up with a packet of fags. She'd also have whoever sold them to me arrested. I hate being here,' she added gloomily. 'She keeps making remarks about Mum all the time. At least last night she waited until I was out of the room, but this morning she said several things when I was there, really hurtful stuff.'

'I just don't understand it,' her aunt had said as she cooked breakfast for her brother. 'How could any mother live with herself when she's using her family to get cheap publicity for some hopeless tabloid television show. Disgraceful, that's what I call it.'

Jess waited for her dad to stand up for Mum but he didn't.

'You don't know what you're talking about, Aunt Caroline,' Jess said coldly. 'Mum isn't like that. She didn't want to talk to anyone about what was happening. The papers are interested in her because she's famous. If you want to bitch about her, please don't do it when I'm here.'

She left the room feeling so angry she could barely see straight. She knew Aunt Caroline would be pissed off with her for the whole of the rest of the weekend and probably Dad would be too, but she didn't care. Abby was her mother and she expected Caroline at least to respect her.

'Old people have no sensitivity,' Steph agreed, when she heard the story. 'Just ignore the bitch. She's probably jealous 'cos your mum is kicking and she's an old crone. What sort of town is it anyway? Can you go out shopping and spend the day ignoring them?'

'Good idea,' said Jess.

She slammed the front door deliberately when she left. She didn't care. Let them see that she was angry. She walked down the main street and began to wander in and out of clothes shops, thinking of how much more fun she'd have had if Steph was with her. Nobody could shop like Steph. At least she had some money. Mum had given her some before the weekend, saying that she knew that Jess might like to get away on her own for a while. Mum had been right about that.

She'd been gone about an hour when Dad rang.

'Hi, Jess, is everything OK?' he asked anxiously.

'Everything is fine,' Jess said in cool measured tones.

'Listen,' Dad said hesitantly, 'I'm sorry about earlier. Caroline didn't mean to say those things about your mum –'

'Yes, she did,' Jess said firmly, 'and, what's worse, you didn't correct her. I didn't come over here to listen to people bitch about Mum all the time. I thought you were both going to act like adults about this break-up.' There was silence at the other end of the phone.

'And you're the only one who really is acting like an adult in all of this,' Dad said ruefully. 'I am sorry, Jess. Caroline means well. She's sticking up for me in the only way she knows how. But she shouldn't have said anything about your mum in front of you.'

'No, she shouldn't,' said Jess. She kept walking, looking for a coffee shop.

'What are you up to?'

'Going to have a coffee,' Jess replied.

'Can I come and join you?' he asked.

Jess thought about it. 'OK,' she said. 'Come down the main street and go past Mango and Tesco. There's a small coffee shop with a big green sign out in front. It's called Have A Break. I'll be in there.'

He got there in ten minutes. Thankfully, he was alone. Jess had had a horrible vision of Aunt Caroline coming too, ready to apologise before offering to buy Jess an ice cream or a new dolly to make up.

'Do you want another cappuccino?' Dad asked.

Jess nodded. She'd really got into the habit of drinking coffee with Oliver.

'I'm sorry about earlier,' Dad said again when he came back with their coffees.

'Slagging off Mum is against the rules,' Jess informed him. 'As the child of the breaking-up parents, I'm not supposed to play one off against the other and you're not supposed to slag off Mum in my presence. Also, she's not supposed to slag you off. And she doesn't, by the way.'

Her father looked slightly ashamed. 'I'm sorry,' he repeated. 'I didn't mean to do that. I shouldn't have done that.'

'Well, *you* weren't slagging Mum off,' Jess conceded, 'but Aunt Caroline certainly was and you weren't standing up for her. I know Mum did a terrible thing but it doesn't mean she's a bad person and that you have to hate her for the rest of your life. I'm going to be living with Mum and seeing you too, so the two of you are going to have to try and get on or it's going to be impossible for me.'

'Wherever did we get you from?' asked her father, shaking his head. 'I thought you were my little girl and it turns out you're the most grown up of the lot of us.'

'It's the new human relations class in school,' Jess explained, smiling to show she was joking. 'I'm going to get a degree in it. Seriously, though, we do a lot about relationships and it's good. And magazines are full of stuff too, so you can't avoid

517

it. That's the problem for boys – they don't ever read about relationships and emotions so they don't know how to get on with girls or how to communicate.'

This wasn't strictly true. Oliver mightn't be the sort of person to read women's magazines, but he was pretty good at communicating. But then, he was naturally an intuitive and sensitive person. Jess knew her dad well enough to admit that, however flatteringly you could describe him, sensitive wasn't one of the words you'd use.

'We should talk about the future, you know,' Jess said. Her dad looked startled but she went on. 'Are you and Mum going to get a divorce? I'm not trying to pry but I'd like to know. Mum says that you'd like a divorce but that she'd try again if you wanted to.'

Tom grimaced. 'It's not that simple, Jess,' he said.

'Why not?' asked Jess. 'You're always telling me that the most complex problems are simple at the back of it all.'

'Ah yes,' said her father, 'but this is –'

'Different?' said Jess with a hint of sarcasm. 'It's not that different after all. Why can't you make it work again? You got on and you loved each other, and fine, so you fought sometimes and you used to be cross when she was working away a lot, but you can get over that. I know you didn't like her earning lots of money too, but you could sort those things out.'

Tom's face was a picture as he looked at his daughter. 'What do you mean about money?' he asked hesitantly.

'I'm talking about you and Mum and her money,' Jess said. 'I read in *Cosmo* that it's hard for men when their wives are earning more money than they do, but we should be proud of Mum for what she's done.'

'I was proud, I am proud,' Tom protested, 'and there was no problem with the money,' he added.

'Oh, get real, Dad,' said Jess, sounding a bit irritated. 'I'm not a child, remember?'

'I didn't say you were,' her father said.

'You think it and you treat me like I am,' Jess said. 'Don't forget, Dad, I was there when you and Mum argued that time that she bought the Jeep. Remember you said the family had managed perfectly well on your salary before and we didn't need a big fancy four-wheeler. I *heard* you. Then Mum said that it was her money and she'd do what she wanted with it. And I heard you argue about the new house in Dunmore.' Jess sighed. 'I mean, I know I didn't want to move but neither did you. I didn't want to be away from Steph but you just didn't want to move because it was going to be mainly Mum's money buying the house. So you can't say you didn't argue about money, can you?'

Years afterwards, Tom would look back and try to remember exactly when he'd felt that Jess had grown up, and he would think of that moment. Suddenly, she spoke like an adult, albeit a young adult, but an adult none the less.

She'd been able to look at her parents' marriage, consider what was going on and come to some perceptive conclusions. Tom hadn't managed to do that himself, he realised shamefacedly. He'd been so busy blaming Abby for everything that had gone wrong in their marriage that he hadn't seen that he was at fault too. The realisation hit him like a blinding flash of light. He had a lot to be ashamed of too. He hadn't slept with somebody else, but then there were many types of betrayal, weren't there?

Jess had said that she was proud of her mother and what she'd achieved, but Tom knew that in his heart of hearts he'd felt jealous of Abby's achievements. He'd never been able to admit that before – not even to himself. But it was true. When she'd worked part time, he'd been able to feel comfortable in the knowledge that he was the breadwinner and the head of the family. But with her success, the lines were shakier. He'd been the brilliant one at college; all his friends had looked up to him, thought Tom Barton was a pretty bright guy. His brains had earned him a reasonably good job. He was a good deputy headmaster, although he reckoned he'd be an even better headmaster. But then, in a flash, Abby's career had eclipsed his.

He was smarter but she was earning more money and he saw the effects of that money every day. Better clothes, better food, more expensive bottles of wine: all the subtle things that had come into their lives.

'Don't let all of this change you,' he'd warned Abby. But the person it had changed hadn't been Abby – it had been him. He was the one who felt diminished by it.

He thought back guiltily to that ten-year anniversary party for Beech earlier in the year, when he'd let those two girls flirt with him shamelessly. Abby had been furious, he'd seen that and he didn't care. He'd hated being at the party as her consort, not Tom Barton, renowned deputy headmaster, but Tom Barton, husband to the famous Abby.

'Do you think I pushed your mother away?' he asked Jess suddenly.

It was a question he would never have asked her before today. He had thought of her as a kid and wouldn't have dreamed of asking for her opinion on his marriage. But now he could see that Jess was not only a young adult, she was the most important witness to the disintegration of the relationship. If anybody knew what had happened, she did.

Jess shrugged. 'I don't know. I suppose Mum wasn't happy and that's why she did it. But she doesn't blame you, she blames herself.'

Tom knew that was true. He knew that Abby had taken the burden of guilt onto herself because that was the way she was. Some people blamed themselves for everything; others blamed themselves for nothing. She was in the former category and he was in the latter. But he'd had his part to play in the breakdown. She'd blamed herself for not being able to communicate with Jess too, and Tom knew he hadn't helped matters either. He remembered guiltily how he'd snapped at Abby so many times and told her that teenagers were just difficult, making it sound as though *he* was the expert because of his experience at work, while she knew nothing.

'Do you want to meet somebody else?' asked Jess.

'No, don't be ridiculous,' said Tom quickly. He was always astonished by the speed with which Jess's mind flipped from one topic to another. 'That wasn't why I left.'

And he realised then with painful clarity why he *had* left – because he'd felt overshadowed by Abby in so many ways and she'd put the final nail in the coffin by sleeping with another man.

How to emasculate your husband in one easy lesson – have sex with somebody else. Even if it was a one-off, never-to-be-repeated occasion, your husband will be devastated because if he's not the best at sex, then what is he the best at?

'I don't want to meet anyone else,' Tom repeated. 'Your mum and I have been together a long time. We didn't split up because we both wanted other people.'

'Well, then, why don't you get back together?' Jess said, as if it was the most obvious thing in the world. 'You could have counselling and talk about your problems,' she suggested.

Tom allowed himself to grin at his daughter. How could he have thought of her as a kid? She was sixteen going on sixty. 'So that's the advice they're giving in *Cosmo*, is it?' he asked.

'Talking is good for problems,' Jess pointed out loftily. 'If you were a new man you'd understand that, but seeing as you're an old man . . .' she teased.

'Can you teach an old man new tricks?' Tom asked.

'I don't know,' Jess said, 'but we could always try.'

Tom thought about Abby at home in Dunmore, alone and coping with the fallout of the newspaper article. He hadn't been fair to her when she had tried to talk to him about that. He knew in his heart that Abby wasn't the sort of person to sell their story for publicity: he knew she'd been pushed into a corner where she'd had to talk. But because he was hurt and angry, because he wanted to hurt her back, he'd pretended that she was that tell-all sort of person. When they got back, he'd apologise to her. Even if it was too late to save their marriage, he could always tell her the truth and admit that he'd been to blame too. It wouldn't get them back to the way they'd been before but it would be a start.

CHAPTER THIRTY-ONE

For years, Erin had thought that charity work was the preserve of bored housewives. Now that she was actually involved in fund-raising, she found out that the opposite was true – it was very hard work and took a lot of organisation and commitment. Determined to do her research properly, she'd started by investigating how to set up a charity legally. Then, she'd made contact with the Life Beats Cancer people and they'd been thrilled with her idea. They pointed out that what she was planning was a long-term project and that, in their experience, it could take anything from eighteen months to two years to get the centre running – and that was only if the fund-raising went smoothly.

The next thing to do was to discuss the idea with Sally's family.

Abby said that she hadn't seen much of Steve during the summer because he genuinely didn't seem to want to talk to people.

'Maybe it's just me,' she added. 'He might hate me for splitting up with Tom.'

'Nonsense,' said Erin stoutly. 'Think of what he's been through – I'm sure he just can't face the world; it's nothing to do with you and Tom. Greg sees Steve every day at work and that's what he thinks is happening. Greg's asked him out with us a few times but Steve says no. Wouldn't we all be the same?'

'I suppose,' admitted Abby.

In the end, Erin managed to meet Steve during his lunch break.

'I don't have much time,' he said to her when they met in a pub near the office.

Erin took one look at his too-thin face with its haunted eyes, and felt a fresh wave of pity wash over her. If she'd been through what Steve had been through, she didn't think she'd have wanted to face the world either.

'How are Jack and Daniel?' she asked, knowing there was no point asking how Steve himself was. That was apparent: he was suffering pain beyond measure.

'They're good,' Steve said, the fierce tension leaving his face briefly. 'We've got this wonderful nanny, Andrea, and they love her. Delia moved in for a while after . . . you know, but she's moved back out now. I wanted to make things as normal as possible, if you see what I mean.'

Erin nodded. She really felt as if she might cry. She cried at the least things now.

'Daniel talks about Sally all the time but Jack doesn't,' Steve went on. 'He has nightmares, though. I didn't think small children got nightmares but they do, apparently. I keep asking myself if it was a good idea to have them in the church for the funeral. I wanted them to be able to say goodbye so they'd have that memory when they were older, but now . . .' He stared off into the middle distance. 'Sorry,' he said. 'You wanted to talk to me about something, Erin, didn't you?'

'I wanted to run an idea by you,' she said, gulping. She couldn't cry now. She began to explain about the Life Beats Cancer centres and the plan to raise funds for one in Dunmore, in Sally's name. Steve said nothing for the whole time she was explaining it to him and, at first, Erin thought she'd made an incredible mistake and that he hated the idea.

'It was just a thought,' she stammered. 'I didn't mean to upset you.'

'You haven't.' Briefly, Steve smiled and he looked like the handsome man Sally had spoken about when Erin had first met her. 'It's a beautiful idea. Thank you, she'd have loved that.'

'We don't expect you to help,' Erin said hurriedly, her relief evident. 'We know you've so much on.' Like raising two small boys without their mother.

Steve nodded. 'I'd like to be involved at some point but not yet. It's too soon for me.'

'I understand.'

Steve got up. 'Sorry, I have to rush back,' he said. 'Busy time at work.'

Erin nodded and he said goodbye. He'd eaten about a quarter of his sandwich. Erin looked down at hers. She wasn't hungry either.

Next, she talked to Abby and Abby's friend, trying to find out what sort of fund-raising events worked for them and which ones didn't. She visited Kerry and spent many hours laughing and talking about their childhood, as well as hearing Kerry's advice on what cancer patients really wanted.

Greg was delighted to see her so excited about something, particularly as she had been a bit subdued since her ill-fated meeting with Shannon. But he was worried that she was taking on too much when she was so heavily pregnant.

'I don't want you overdoing it, love,' he said. 'I know that "rest" isn't a word in your vocabulary but you've got to have a few hours off every day.'

'Don't worry about me,' Erin said. 'I like being busy. I'm only doing two days at the beauty salon as it is, so I need something else to keep me occupied. It's either that or spend every penny we have buying new baby clothes.' She already had quite a selection of baby clothes – all white because they didn't know what sex the baby was going to be – and both Mum and Kerry were knitting furiously. Erin thought the notion of Kerry knitting at all was absolutely hilarious.

'I just can't see you with wool and needles,' she said in amusement one day on the phone when Kerry told her she was halfway through a tiny white matinée jacket.

'Ha bloody ha,' retorted Kerry. 'Course I know how to

knit. Just because your vision of me is that of a wild party animal from ten years ago doesn't mean I don't know how to do domestic things, I'll have you know. I can make cookies and garden too,' Kerry said indignantly.

'You sound just like one of the Waltons,' giggled Erin. She hadn't realised how much she'd missed her sister all these years. 'It's great to be back, Kerry,' she said impulsively. 'Really great. Thank you, thanks for everything.'

'You mightn't thank me when you see this matinée jacket,' Kerry said dubiously. 'I know I can knit but I'm not exactly brilliant, and doing sleeves is very hard . . .'

'I wasn't talking about the matinée jacket,' Erin replied.

The following weekend the whole family were coming to Dunmore to spend quality time with Greg and Erin. Erin had set them up in an excellent bed and breakfast nearby.

'Somebody has to make sure you're getting enough rest,' Mum had fussed over the phone. 'I know you're all tied up in that Life Beats Cancer work now, Erin, but you need your rest – babies need rested mothers. You'll be sorry you didn't have more sleep when the baby is born and you're run off your feet.'

'Oh, Mum, aren't you and Kerry coming down to help me when I have the baby?' Erin said mischievously. 'You know I won't have a clue. I'm not planning to do a tap of work – the pair of you can do it all!'

Her mother laughed, a joyous, musical sound that Erin had almost forgotten.

'You're a right brat, Erin Flynn,' her mother said cheerfully. 'I'm too old to be looking after another baby.'

'You'll never be too old, Mum,' said Erin fondly. Neither of them mentioned that this would be the fourth-generation Flynn child. They didn't have to. Erin's baby would be an adored member of the family, whether she or he was a grandchild or great-grandchild or whatever.

'So get your feet off the floor,' Mum insisted. 'Lying down with your feet up is vital.'

'Yes, Mum,' said Erin obediently. It was like old times. And she loved it.

The following Thursday was one of Erin's days working in The Beauty Spot. She was perched behind the reception counter, carefully looking through the appointments book and trying to find a cancellation for a customer who'd phoned to beg to be fitted in for a bikini wax for her holidays. Business was good and the salon was permanently busy.

Today, the place hummed with activity and all the treatment rooms were full. Ruby, whose facial had just cancelled, had popped out on an afternoon latte-and-muffin shopping run and was due back any second. Erin couldn't wait. In the last few weeks, her appetite had suddenly increased and she felt as if she was eating for three, never mind two. She'd phoned the grateful bikini wax lady back with an appointment, and was just flicking through a sheet of papers to find the figures she planned to go over later, when the door of the salon opened. Erin looked up and her mouth fell open in astonishment. It wasn't Ruby with the familiar coffee shop bags.

Instead, there stood Shannon, her long copper hair secured in a haphazard ponytail, a flowing caftan-style garment in shades of yellow worn over her jeans. She carried a big army rucksack in one hand and a carton of juice in the other.

At the sight of Erin, Shannon's face lit up.

'Hello. I didn't know if you'd be here or not,' she said as casually as if she and Erin were friends always occasionally popping into each other's places of work.

After a moment, Erin found her voice. 'What are you doing here?' she demanded.

'I wanted to see you,' Shannon said, with child-like simplicity. She set her big rucksack down on the floor. 'I felt bad about the last time – Kerry said it upset you.'

Erin looked in amazement at a woman so lacking in normal intuition that it had taken another person to tell her their meeting hadn't gone well. Only someone like Shannon, someone completely on another planet, could have failed to notice this all by herself.

'When were you talking to Kerry?' asked Erin bluntly.

'The other day.' Shannon was vague. 'It was a shock for me, seeing you and the fact that you're all grown up. And pregnant,' she added, gesturing to Erin's belly, almost as if this was the first time she'd noticed.

The salon door tinkled, heralding the arrival of Ruby and her fragrant haul of goodies.

'Herbal tea that smells like horrible old socks for you, Erin,' she said, placing a paper cup down on the counter in front of Erin, 'and a blueberry muffin. I know you've been dying for that,' Ruby went on, then stopped, suddenly aware of the strained atmosphere.

'Ruby, this is a . . .' Erin paused, 'a relative of mine who's dropped in to see me. I'm just going to nip out and have a cup of tea with her. Will you have time to keep an eye on everything here while I'm gone?'

If Ruby thought it was strange that Erin a) hadn't introduced her to this relative by name and b) possessed a relative who looked as frankly unusual as Shannon, then Ruby was far too polite to say anything.

'Sure thing, girl,' she said easily. 'I'm free for the next three-quarters of an hour.'

Three-quarters of an hour should certainly do, Erin thought as she got her handbag and led Shannon out the door and into the coffee shop across the street. In fact, three-quarters of an hour was probably too much time. She was curious as to why Shannon was here in the first place. Dunmore was a long way from Shannon's home in Wexford, particularly as she didn't have a car and had to rely on public transport, so why was she here? Erin hoped that she wasn't looking for money – Kerry had said that Shannon was always broke and on the scrounge, however innocently. It would have been the final nail in the coffin of their relationship for Erin if Shannon had turned up just to borrow.

'What do you want?' she said as they stood at the counter

in the coffee shop, conscious that her voice was a little sharp.

Shannon gave this question great consideration and spent ages looking at the board behind the counter where all the various teas and coffees were listed. Finally, she settled for blackcurrant and apple tea. Erin went for ordinary tea, paid, and they sat down at a small table in the corner, as far away from people as possible.

Erin decided to let Shannon speak first, but Shannon showed no inclination to actually say anything – instead she sat there happily, staring around her as if the small café was the most interesting place she'd ever been. Erin was not the sort of person given to filling in every conversational gap with chatter, but even so, she found Shannon's quietness unsettling.

'What are you doing here?' she asked finally.

'Oh, I've got these friends who live in West Cork and I thought I might go and see them,' Shannon said. 'They've got this lovely cottage and a bit of a farm and it's paradise. Then I thought of you being here in Dunmore and I decided it'd be great to drop in and visit, get to know you a bit better.' She beamed at Erin as if this innocent little plan was the cleverest thing she'd ever come up with in her whole life. Going to West Cork to see friends – why not drop in on her long-lost daughter and kill two birds with one stone? Erin thought bitterly.

'And what time are your friends in West Cork expecting you to arrive?' enquired Erin, with the sneaking suspicion that she already knew the answer to that question.

Shannon's youthful face was carefree. 'Ah sure, they're not really expecting me at any particular time,' she said. 'I can roll up when I please. I thought I might spend the night with you. You've got a spare bed or an old sofa I could kip down on, don't you?'

Shannon was quite happy to sit in the car while Erin whizzed around the supermarket to buy groceries for their dinner. As she shoved the small trolley down the aisles with haste, Erin phoned Greg.

'What are we going to do?' she hissed. 'She expects to stay the night. What are we going to talk about?' She threw all sorts of unnecessary food into the trolley without stopping to think.

Greg sounded unperturbed. 'You did want to get to know her better,' he said reasonably.

'Yes, but I didn't expect her to turn up out of the blue and say she was going to stay, did I?' said Erin. 'That's hardly normal behaviour.'

'I don't think Shannon is exactly normal, from what you've told me,' Greg pointed out. 'Anyway, it might be good for the two of you to spend some time together. I can make myself scarce tonight . . .'

'Don't you dare,' said Erin, shocked. 'I don't want to be left on my own with her.'

Next she phoned Kerry.

'She asked where you lived and I knew she'd go there eventually,' Kerry said, sounding remarkably laid-back about it all, as if Shannon turning up out of the blue was perfectly natural. And it probably was, for Shannon.

'But I don't even know what to say to her, how to talk to her,' protested Erin as she threw a couple of supermarket ready meals into the trolley.

'You were the one who wanted to get to know her,' Kerry pointed out.

'That was before I'd met her,' Erin said. 'I thought we could bond. I didn't know she was going to be the hippie from hell.'

'Well, bond with her tonight,' Kerry said. 'Look,' she added, 'forget that she gave birth to you. Imagine she's your sister; a long-lost very eccentric sister, whom you don't know very well. It's the mother thing that's messing it all up in your head. Try and forget that she's your natural mother at all and imagine she's just dippy Shannon, the forgotten sister who ran off years ago. Because that's what she is, after all.'

'I suppose,' Erin said slowly. She was so thrown by Shannon's reappearance that she didn't know what to think. But maybe Kerry was right: she should treat Shannon like a long-lost sister, and stop tying herself up in knots thinking that Shannon really was her mum and had left her all those years ago.

'Right,' she said with a confidence that she didn't really feel. 'That's what I'll do. I'll phone you tomorrow and tell you how we got on.'

Greg was there when they got home and Erin was really relieved to see him.

'Thank God you're here,' she whispered to him as they hugged.

'Are you sure you don't want me to go out and leave you two alone?' Greg whispered back.

'No way,' hissed Erin.

Shannon seemed pleased to see Greg, shook his hand politely, and wandered into the big, airy living room.

'Wow, this is really nice,' she said, meandering around, picking up pictures, books and knick-knacks, admiring things.

Erin felt the knot in her stomach tighten. She didn't know how to react, but what was it Kerry had said earlier? Imagine she's your eccentric older sister, the one you don't know very well. Sister, right. Erin could do that.

'Do you like those malachite platters?' she said, seeing Shannon admiring the two rich green carved discs that hung on one wall. 'We bought them in Mexico when we were on holiday there. We drove through at Nogales and then we went a little further in country, stayed for a few nights and bought those. There's something nice about getting a memento of where you've been on holiday, isn't there?'

'Yeah.' Shannon sounded wistful. 'I never got to Mexico. I always meant to because myself and some of the gang were living in New Mexico for a while, but we never made it over the border.'

'Oh,' said Erin cheerfully. 'Why ever not?'

Shannon looked a bit shifty. 'Oh, some hassle with documents, you know . . .'

Erin could work out what had happened. She and Greg exchanged a glance. If Shannon's friends had been people who regularly protested outside military bases, then perhaps some of them were in trouble with the law and travelling into a different country would involve being noticed by the authorities. Time to change to a different subject, Erin decided.

'You must have picked up some great stuff from your travels around the world. Tell us, where have you been?'

It was the right question to ask. With a glass of water in front of her – Shannon didn't drink, said she didn't want to pollute her body with alcohol – she talked about some of the places she'd been over the years, starting with the anti-nuclear protests in America. She'd certainly travelled a great deal in her life. Erin and Greg were astonished at how many places she'd visited, and Erin was particularly surprised at how movingly Shannon talked about the various protests she'd been on.

It was clear that the lifestyle had held many charms for Shannon: normal responsibilities like paying the rent or the electricity bill didn't appear to matter in the free-wheeling group with whom she'd travelled the world. But it was equally clear that she genuinely believed in the causes she'd fought for. There was no doubt that when Shannon talked about the dangers of war, she meant what she was saying.

As the evening progressed, Erin knew she couldn't have coped without Greg there to keep the conversation flowing. She would have found Shannon's presence too difficult, because Shannon never talked to Erin as if there was anything but the most tenuous link between them. There were no references to 'when you were a baby', no mention of the Flynn family at all. And Erin found that hurtful.

Instead, Shannon regarded the people she'd travelled with as her family, a sprawling group of friends she'd picked up over the years who now lived in the four corners of the globe, like the people she was travelling to meet in West Cork.

'And how did you manage financially when you were travelling around?' Greg was genuinely interested in this.

Shannon smiled happily. 'We did a bit of everything,' she said. 'Farming in some places. I was a terrible farmer, I can tell you. I hadn't been brought up with animals and it was very difficult. But in some places we had a bit of land and we grew vegetables to feed ourselves and to make a bit of money. In other places we helped farmers out, that was how we survived.'

Erin thought of how she had fantasised Shannon's life to be. Shannon living an expatriate life in some tiny village in France, so much a part of the scenery and fluent in the language that the locals had even forgotten that she wasn't a native. Or else Shannon settled down somewhere in America, talking longingly of Ireland but firmly rooted in her local community.

'And sometimes we did a bit of housework, you know, cleaning or chambermaiding in hotels,' Shannon went on. 'Ironing was the worst. We lived above an ironing shop once and worked instead of paying rent. I hated ironing but we had to do what we did to survive.'

'When I heard you were my mother and that you'd left home to travel, I imagined you had a totally different sort of life,' Erin said abruptly. 'I thought it must be so wonderful and that's why you'd never come back to see me. I never thought you'd be doing other people's ironing or pulling up vegetables to make your living. That wasn't the picture in my head at all.'

'I'm sorry about the other day,' Shannon said suddenly, 'when you came to see me and Ciara turned up. I got a bit of a shock, that was all. I knew you'd come and find me eventually, I just hadn't expected you to be so grown up.' The innocent smile was there on her face again. 'I always thought of you as a child and there you were, a woman with her own baby coming.'

Erin didn't want to let anger ruin things this time. 'But you must have known I'd be grown up by now,' she said. 'I'm twenty-seven, Shannon; it's twenty-seven years since you had me.'

'Time goes very quickly,' Shannon said helplessly. 'And when we were out on the road and I had friends with babies, I liked to imagine that you were a small child at home and that Mam was looking after you. It made me happy to think of you there. She was a good mother and I knew she'd take care of you.'

'And that was why you left me, was it?' asked Erin. 'Because you knew that I would be better off with Mum than with you?'

'I suppose,' said Shannon slowly. 'When I was first pregnant, I didn't want you. I was scared, Erin. And then when I was older, well, you were better off where you were.'

'Who gave me my name?' Erin asked suddenly. It had felt strange when Shannon called her Erin for the first time. The name hadn't tripped lightly off Shannon's tongue; it didn't sound like a word Shannon had thought long and hard about.

'Oh, Mam called you that,' Shannon said. 'Isn't it obvious? She loves all those Irish names: Shannon, Kerry, Erin. I liked Spring Flower myself, but Mam said you couldn't call a child that, it would be stupid.'

Erin and Greg both failed to hide their amusement. Greg burst out laughing.

'Ah, Shannon,' he said, 'come on, Spring Flower? You couldn't call a child Spring Flower.'

Shannon laughed too. 'Lots of people have mad names for babies. That was a nice one. I know a woman called Turmeric; now that's bad.'

'Spring Flower Flynn.' Erin tried the name out loud. 'No,' she said, 'I'm glad Mum went for Erin after all.'

When it was time to cook dinner, Shannon surprised them both and said could she help?

'Well,' Erin said, 'I was just going to stick these ready-made dinners into the oven, to be honest. I'm a bit tired and I don't feel up to cooking at the end of the day.'

'Leave it to me,' Shannon said. 'I love cooking and it's not often I get to do it in such a nice kitchen as this. Most of the places I've lived in haven't been high on cooking equipment or incredible ovens.'

She wasn't looking for sympathy as she said this, Erin realised. It was just a statement of fact. Shannon had chosen to live her life a particular way and she had no regrets about it. She mightn't have had a big bank balance, but she seemed happy about the way she lived. Erin sat down at the small kitchen table and watched. Cooking obviously relaxed Shannon and, as she worked, she talked about the different places she'd lived and the recipes she'd picked up there. She talked about cooking on the tightest budget imaginable, when she'd had to make meat loaf for thirty from a small bit of ground beef and whatever vegetables they could grow themselves. And she talked about great banquets when the gang were in funds and made up for the hard times with veritable feasts.

'Now, you really need fresh herbs for this,' Shannon advised as she made up a marinade with all the skill of a TV chef. 'But we'll make do with what you have.'

'Tell me, is there anyone special in your life?' Erin asked, moving the conversation onto different ground. 'I noticed that you had "Shannon and William" written up on your doorbell in Wexford.'

'The real William and I didn't last very long,' Shannon revealed, keeping her eye on her cooking. 'We split up about six months ago but then this stray cat came to live with me and I called him William too, William the second. Although he didn't hang around long either,' she added thoughtfully. 'I must have bad luck with Williams. That must be it. I should have given him a different name like . . .' She concentrated on finding another name, as if it was the most important thing in the world.

'Michael,' suggested Erin, trying to get into the whole cat-naming business.

'Ah no, Michael isn't a good name for a cat,' Shannon said seriously. 'You'd never see a cat called Michael, would you?'

Erin thought that there weren't too many felines around answering to the name of William either, but she didn't say anything.

It was strange talking to Shannon. Her mind didn't work in a conventional way and there were none of the usual conversational markers to go by. Shannon wasn't interested in talking about her job – she was working part-time in the launderette to pay the rent. Nor had she any interest in discussing family. She'd only mentioned Erin's pregnancy once, in the beginning. Erin realised that it was up to her to keep the conversation going.

'Will I tell you about the baby?' she asked.

'Oh yes, please,' said Shannon, as if she'd been only dying to know all the ins and outs of Erin's pregnancy but hadn't wanted to ask.

So Erin told her everything and even took out the scan pictures for Shannon to look at. Shannon held the grainy black-and-white photos with something approaching awe, her fingers tracing over the curled-up shape of the baby.

'Isn't she wonderful?' Greg said proudly. 'I think it's going to be a girl although we don't know for definite.'

'Your grandchild,' Erin said softly. 'Your grandson or your granddaughter.'

Shannon looked up at both of them, her eyes wide in astonishment, as if the thought had never occurred to her before. This baby was going to make her a grandmother.

'Imagine,' she breathed. 'I don't have to be called Granny, though, do I?'

Dinner was a great success. Shannon's Chicken New Mexico managed to be hot, spicy and utterly delicious all at the same time. Erin finally felt relaxed around Shannon. Kerry had been right: it was easier to treat Shannon like some long-lost relative than to obsess over the fact that she was really Erin's mother.

Shannon wasn't cut out to be anyone's mother. She was too like a child herself: a combination of selfishness and self-interest mixed up with enthusiasm to get involved in some great plan to save the world. Saving herself had never even occurred to her.

Greg carefully made up the sofa bed in the living room for her at about half ten.

'I don't know how comfortable you're going to be there, Shannon,' Erin said. 'Nobody's ever slept on it before. It's new.'

'You'd want to have seen some of the places I've slept,' Shannon said cheerfully. 'This is a bed fit for a queen, thanks,' she added.

Suddenly she leaned over and put her arms around Erin, who was utterly astonished at this gesture of affection. Shannon had never touched her before.

This is my mother hugging me, Erin thought to herself. She put her arms around Shannon's waist and hugged back. No, she decided, this wasn't her mother, not really. Shannon had carried Erin for nine months, but she was still better as a big sister. Erin had a mum already.

Erin slept well that night and woke the next morning with a strange feeling of lightness in her head. It was as if a burden had been lifted from her. She stretched luxuriously in the bed and was just wondering where Greg was, when he appeared with a tray containing tea, toast and some fresh fruit he'd cut carefully into a juicy fruit salad.

'So you're awake, sleepy head,' he said good-humouredly as he put the tray on the bed.

'I know, it's disgraceful,' Erin said, peering at the clock. It was five to eight. 'I haven't slept this long in ages. Is Shannon up yet?'

'Yes,' he replied. 'She was up before me and she's out on the balcony now, meditating.'

'Good for her,' said Erin, sitting up so that Greg could put the tray on her lap.

'Bye, love. I'm heading off to work now,' Greg said, kissing his wife gently on the lips. 'Will you be OK on your own?'

Erin nodded. 'We'll be fine.'

After breakfast and showering, she went to find Shannon.

'Morning, Shannon,' she said cheerfully. 'What are your plans for the day?'

She decided that this was the best way to deal with Shannon – to give the other woman the chance to do her own thing and not to crowd her or expect Shannon to hang around anywhere she didn't want to. In fact, Erin had time to herself as it wasn't one of her days at The Beauty Spot and she'd planned nothing more taxing than to make some phone calls about the charity project and to do a little shopping. But saying she was free might put pressure on Shannon.

'Isn't it a wonderful day?' Shannon said, staring out at the beautiful morning. 'It's a good day to be alive. I think I might head off down to West Cork today, you know: take a nice drive through the countryside and enjoy myself.'

'Oh, you want me to drive you?' asked Erin in surprise.

Shannon shook her head. Today, she looked fresh and laid-back in loose coolie trousers and a simple linen shirt. 'I'll hitch. I hate the bus and the train. Hitching is great – you get a chance to meet people and see a bit of the countryside.'

'Hitching is dangerous.' Erin was horrified that anybody would hitch in this day of serial killings and nutters.

'It's not dangerous,' Shannon said. 'You wouldn't believe the adventures I've had when I've been hitching.'

'Oh, yes I would,' Erin said. 'I can't believe you still hitch.'

'It's like life,' Shannon explained. 'You get out what you put into it.'

There really was nothing Erin could say to that. Eventually, they agreed on a compromise. Erin would drive Shannon a little way along the road to a small village where she could pick up a ride into West Cork. Erin still thought that hitching

537

was a ridiculous way to travel, but Shannon was determined. She wouldn't dream of getting on a bus or a train, not when there were lots of drivers meandering around the country, only too eager to have someone new to talk to.

As they drove out of Dunmore, it began to rain, and Erin hoped that Shannon would give up her hare-brained scheme and decide to get a bus after all. But no, Shannon was prepared. She had her rain slicker, an ancient see-through thing, veteran of many a protest march in the pouring rain. At a tiny hamlet, Erin stopped and they went into a pub for refreshment. Erin could already feel Shannon moving away from her: it was almost a physical thing, as if the woman had begun to distance herself as soon as she'd decided to set off on the road. That was how she lived her life, obviously – everything had its own place, friends in one box, family in another. Shannon was well able to close the door on one compartment and open another. Who knew when Erin would see her again?

Erin realised that if they were to stay in touch this was the way it would be, with Shannon always ready to take off to the next place, to the next party, to the next protest. She'd be happy to leave everyone behind, knowing that she could always come back to them. That was probably how she was able to leave Erin behind twenty-seven years ago, knowing that Erin was safe and looked after, and that if Shannon needed a place to stay, she could go home to her family.

As Mum had said so wisely, if you wanted to stay close to Shannon, you had to accept the way she wanted to live her life. Erin understood that now.

There was only one more question she had to ask, and as they sat in the tiny pub, while a barman rushed around getting the place ready for the proper drinkers, Erin asked it.

'Tell me about my father,' she said. 'I want to know who he is.'

Shannon didn't look surprised at the question but she didn't look too pleased at it either.

'I was hoping you wouldn't ask me that,' she said, sounding mildly irritated, as if Erin had asked her some anodyne question about whether she dyed her hair or not.

'It's not unreasonable to want to know.' Erin couldn't prevent the slight edge from entering her voice.

'I know,' said Shannon, 'but it's in the past . . .'

'Oh, come on,' said Erin. She rarely lost her temper but this could just be the time. 'Just because my conception was some one-night stand with somebody you can barely remember doesn't mean that I don't have a right to hear about it.' Erin almost spat the words out and Shannon seemed shocked out of her habitual languor for the first time since Erin had met her.

'It wasn't like that,' Shannon protested. 'It wasn't a one-night thing. He was a friend.'

Erin sat back in her chair, trying to get comfortable. 'Go on,' she said.

'He was a friend of mine. We'd grown up together, been in school together,' Shannon continued. 'He wasn't my boyfriend or anything and he knew I wasn't going to hang around Kilbarrett for very long. We were just good pals.'

Erin, who had always assumed her father was one of the anti-war/anti-nuclear protesters that Shannon had been with at the time, said nothing but just listened.

'His name was Paul,' Shannon said, 'Paul Whelan. He wanted to go to university and study arts but there was no money. His dad had a butcher's shop, so he went into that. We'd always been friends – nothing like boyfriend and girlfriend, but we got together a couple of times. You know how it is. Then we both got on with our lives. He was working in the shop and he began seeing this girl who worked there too. I had other things in my life and then I found out I was pregnant. I couldn't tell him.'

'So he never knew that you were going to have a baby?' Erin asked quietly.

'He did in the end,' Shannon pointed out. 'I was as big as

a house and when he asked me, I told him it wasn't his. It was the easiest thing to do. His mother was very religious; she would have killed him. He didn't need to know. I told him it was someone else.'

'Did you ever see him again afterwards?' Erin asked.

'No,' Shannon said blithely. 'He was clever, though. He should have gone to university, that was for sure. If only there'd been the money, if only his father had thought university was a good plan. He probably has a whole fleet of butcher shops now, you never know.'

Suddenly Shannon looked worried. 'You're not going to go off and find him and tell him he's your dad, are you?' she asked.

Erin knew there was no point in trying to explain. Mum and Dad were her real parents: they were the ones who had been there for her when she had been growing up. But that didn't mean she didn't feel this burning need to find her true dad either. He would never replace her dear old father, but she needed to know where she'd come from.

'The whole family knew this guy, Paul?' Erin said his name for the first time. 'Why didn't you tell them he was the father?'

'Because Mum and Dad would have wanted me to do the sensible thing and settle down with him, try and make a go of being together and bringing you up. I didn't want to do that; that wasn't the way I wanted to live my life. You can't blame me for that,' Shannon said. 'I wouldn't have been much good as a mother, anyway. I gave you the best start I could, didn't I?'

She was eager to be forgiven and Erin knew there was no point in denying Shannon that forgiveness. She thought about what life would have been like if Shannon had brought her up – a lifetime of travelling, with no security, no money, and Shannon scrabbling round, trying to make a living for herself and her child. It wouldn't have been any sort of life, Erin knew. Whatever Shannon's motives for leaving Erin behind, it had turned out for the best.

'Yes, you did the right thing,' she said now. 'Mum and Dad were great parents.'

Shannon beamed at her and finally Erin smiled back. 'You did the right thing,' she repeated.

CHAPTER THIRTY-TWO

By the time three weeks had passed since Debra and Barry had split up, Lizzie began to abandon hopes of them ever getting back together again. There had been one or two phone calls between the newlyweds, but they had always ended with shouted recriminations. The situation was at stalemate.

It wasn't that Debra was morose – if anything, she seemed quite happy, enjoying her freedom and clearly loving being fussed over at home by Lizzie. Since Lizzie had promised her daughter that she wasn't interested in men – meaning Simon – they'd been getting on brilliantly. Gwen, ever the doom merchant, said that was largely because Lizzie had given her daughter free rein with Lizzie's credit card.

Lizzie hadn't mentioned the scene with Simon to her sister for a long while. It was too humiliating, and she couldn't have faced it if Gwen had been as disgusted as Debra over Lizzie's behaviour. She was relieved when she was sympathetic. Simon had phoned the next day but Lizzie, the memory of the night before in her mind, had explained that Debra was going through a difficult time and would he mind if they took a raincheck on another date?

'Fine,' said Simon evenly. 'I'd love to see you again but you call me when things have calmed down.'

Lizzie hadn't called. That was easier with Debra on full alert for any signs of a man phoning, and anyway, maybe Debra had been right: men did complicate matters.

At least Debra was easier to live with – as long as Lizzie

didn't make any other plans in the evenings. But her mother worried that if the split went on any longer, it would be irreparable, and she hated to think of what that would do to Debra.

The problem, Lizzie felt, was that Debra was still utterly confident that Barry would come crawling back to her, saying he was sorry, and that they could start all over again, with Debra having the upper hand. Yet this scenario was growing more unlikely by the day.

Then Myles came up with the idea of having a conference between both families, to give Debra and Barry a chance to talk on neutral territory. 'Perhaps if she sees us all there, then she might come to her senses and realise what family and marriage are all about,' he said hopefully.

Lizzie suspected the hand of Sabine in all of this. It was unlikely that Myles would ever have come up with this idea on his own.

Joe thought a family conference was ridiculous. 'If Debra has decided not to go back with Barry, then she's unlikely to change her mind just because you and Dad and Barry's parents and Uncle Tom Cobbley and all turn up to talk to her about it,' he pointed out to his mother on the phone.

'Yes, but we have to try,' said Lizzie.

'Mum,' said Joe, 'the only thing you've got to try and do is stop treating Debra like a child. She's a grown-up and if she wants to leave Barry after five minutes of marriage, then that's her business.'

'I know it's her business –' his mother protested, but Joe interrupted her.

'Well then, why don't you leave her to sort it out by herself? If she was truly an adult, then she'd have to find somewhere else to live and get on with her own life. Because you and Dad are mollycoddling her, she doesn't have to do that. She can run to either of you when things get rough.'

That wasn't absolutely accurate, Lizzie thought. Debra couldn't really run to Myles any more, as had been proved the night of Lizzie's parachute jump. Debra had fled to her father's apartment and had ended up back with Lizzie the following day. Sabine's influence had changed his relationship with his daughter. Myles now treated Debra more like an adult than an adored young daughter, and clearly expected her to get on with her life in the way that he was getting on with his. Naturally, Debra chose to see his behaviour as casting her off in favour of another woman. Suddenly, Debra didn't like Sabine any more.

'I don't know why I invited her to the wedding in the first place,' Debra said. She still hadn't forgiven Sabine for making it clear that night in her father's apartment that she disapproved of Debra's juvenile behaviour.

Lizzie held her tongue, while privately asking what did it matter who had been to the wedding, seeing how the marriage hadn't lasted? She had become very good at holding her tongue. Joe was the only person who seemed to realise this. Everyone else thought it was sad that the newlyweds had teething troubles, but that until these were sorted out it was wonderful for Debra and Lizzie to be living together. They appeared to think that Lizzie was bored and lonely on her own and that having her daughter around was a treat.

'Mum, you've got to tell her to move out and make her own way,' Joe said. 'You've taken care of her long enough.'

Lizzie hadn't told Joe about Simon either. Lizzie still shuddered to think of that evening. The embarrassment haunted her in the middle of the night.

In her heart, she knew that Joe was right. She'd come a long way since the divorce, even though she mightn't have realised it before. But she had got used to living on her own and not having to order her life around someone else's. Perhaps there was another reason for not looking for romance.

'I can't tell her to leave, Joe,' Lizzie told her son. 'It wouldn't be right. I'm her mother.'

'Mother smother,' said Joe, doing his best Jewish momma impersonation. 'You have to let go, Mum, or she'll take over your life. I'm not just saying this for you, I'm saying this for her too.'

'Well, then, you tell her,' Lizzie said, getting cross. She was fed up with everyone else telling her how to act. Why did nobody discuss this with Debra?

'All right, I will,' said Joe. 'Get her for me.'

Lizzie didn't know exactly what Joe was going to say to his sister, but when Debra walked back into the kitchen after the conversation, her pretty face was set with rage.

'Who the hell does Joe think he is?' she demanded at the top of her voice.

'What's wrong? What did he say?' asked Lizzie, hating herself for being a coward and pretending she hadn't the slightest idea.

'He said I should either go back to Barry or move out,' Debra said furiously. 'He said if Barry and I were serious about splitting up, we should just sell the house and set about getting a divorce, and that I shouldn't stay here any longer because you have your life to lead. As if he knows what he's talking about!'

Debra went straight for her packet of cigarettes and lit one furiously. Lizzie didn't like her smoking in the house but there was no point saying anything. Debra did what Debra wanted to do.

'I told him you liked having me here, that it was a comfort for you to have someone to come home to at night after years on your own,' Debra said. 'Wasn't I right to say that?'

'Oh yes,' said Lizzie weakly, feeling even more of a coward than ever.

'And then . . .' Debra inhaled heavily, 'he said what if you got a boyfriend, how would that work out? How ridiculous, I told him. Mum never loved anyone except Dad.'

Lizzie realised with a pang that part of the reason Debra had been so furious that night she'd discovered Simon and Lizzie together was because she couldn't cope with the idea of her mother with any man other than her father. It was obviously hard enough for her to accept Myles having someone else in his life; but it was impossible for her to deal with Lizzie doing the same thing. Debra might have been in her early twenties but when it came to her mum, she was still a kid. Mums shouldn't have boyfriends.

In the end, it was Barry's mother, Flossie, who took action. She phoned Lizzie one day at work and said they had to do something about the kids.

Lizzie got quite a shock when she heard Flossie's voice, partly because she wasn't sure if Flossie considered the whole split to be Debra's fault. If that was the case, Flossie might have been phoning to rage about her, and Lizzie wasn't prepared for such a confrontation.

But assigning blame seemed to be the last thing on Flossie's mind. All she wanted was for Barry to be happy and he wasn't happy right now, was he? 'Stuck in that house on his own, miserable without Debra, coming home for his supper sometimes – we have to get them to sort it out, Lizzie,' Flossie said sincerely. 'Poor Barry's in bits. I hate to see him like this, and the problem is they're just so young, they don't know how to talk about things and get all the arguments out in the open, do they?'

'No, they don't,' agreed Lizzie, thinking of her own marriage and how she obviously hadn't been able to get all the arguments out in the open, either. If she had, maybe she might still be married. 'Myles suggested we have a family conference,' she said. 'That way they wouldn't be able to shout and scream at each other because we'd all be there.'

'That's a great idea,' said Flossie enthusiastically. 'You know, at the moment they're just too stubborn to meet up and discuss it all. That's what this is about: stubbornness.'

The plan was made there and then: Lizzie would get Debra to a certain restaurant at a certain time next Sunday while Flossie would inveigle Barry there too. Given time and opportunity, surely the hapless couple could work things out?

Only Joe and Gwen thought this was a bad idea, but then Gwen and Debra had never seen eye to eye. Gwen thought her niece was a smart little madam who only cared for herself. Debra, on the other hand, regarded her aunt as old-fashioned and bossy – nothing like her soft old mum.

'I suppose, no matter what happens, you'll end up paying for a big dinner,' Gwen said when she heard of the plan.

'It's not about money or who pays for dinner,' Lizzie pointed out impatiently.

'I beg to differ,' said Gwen, 'but it is about money. Think of all you and Myles spent on that bloody wedding. If Debra knew that she and Barry were totally incompatible in the first place, then you wouldn't have needed to shell out all that cash on the most expensive day that the whole of County Cork has ever seen.'

'Oh, for God's sake,' said Lizzie, finally losing her temper. First, Joe never stopped telling her how to live her life, and now Gwen was at it too. 'I wish everyone would just leave me alone.'

'It's not me you should be getting angry with, Lizzie,' Gwen pointed out. 'It's Debra. That daughter of yours needs to hear a few home truths, and one of these days I'll let her have them,' Gwen added with grim relish.

The venue for the big reconciliation was a large family restaurant in Dunmore, cleverly picked by Flossie on the grounds that there'd be so much noise anyway, nobody would notice the odd raised voice from the Shanahan/Cronin table. Lizzie was sick with nerves, thinking about the whole thing. It was her job to get Debra there looking her best, and the ploy she'd used was to tell her daughter that they deserved a nice Sunday lunch out and why didn't they both dress up for a glamorous lunch?

'Glamorous Sunday lunch? Here?' said Debra in disbelief when they pulled up outside the restaurant. The Hungry Hunter was indeed not known for its style, but had a reputation instead for being the sort of place where small children could throw chips on the floor without the waiters minding.

'Er, well, you know, they get a different crowd in at lunchtime on Sundays,' lied Lizzie, terrified that Debra would pull out. 'Oh, come on, Debra, it'll be fun.'

Grudgingly, Debra followed her mother inside. Lizzie just hoped that everyone else was there already because, if the waitress seated them at a table with empty spaces for four other people, she'd smell a rat. Then, Lizzie spotted Barry and his family, and relief washed over her. She'd done her bit; the rest was up to the newlyweds.

She wondered what lie had been told to get Barry there, although he looked happy enough, sinking a pint of beer. There was no sign of Myles, though. Lizzie hoped it was just that he was hiding until the opportune moment. He was.

'Lizzie! Debra!' Myles hopped out from behind a pillar, threw his arms round his daughter and started to lead her towards the big table where Barry sat.

'This is a set-up,' Debra said furiously, glaring at her husband.

But still, she sat down directly opposite Barry, shooting him another fierce glare as she did so.

'Was this your idea?' she demanded.

'I was going to ask you the same thing,' retorted Barry sharply. 'I told you the last time we spoke that I wasn't going to apologise because I hadn't done anything wrong, understand?'.

'What do you mean, you haven't done anything wrong? The whole thing's your fault,' screeched Debra, so loudly that all the other diners looked up.

Small children screaming at the top of their voices were quite common in this restaurant but grown-ups doing the same thing were a little more unusual. Real-life cabaret was always fun, and the other diners began to pay attention to the Shanahan table.

'So that's the way you're going to play it, is it?' demanded Barry, as oblivious as Debra to the interested gaze of the onlookers. 'Little Miss Never-Does-Anything-Wrong.'

Lizzie had been wondering if there was any point in her sitting down or not, but now she sank down wearily beside Flossie and the two women looked at each other in sympathy. This was not going according to plan.

Myles looked across at her impotently and she felt a wave of anger. This had been his idea in the first place and, now they were all here, he wasn't doing anything to stop Barry and Debra fighting.

It was Barry's father who intervened. 'Now look here, you pair,' Stan said firmly, in the tones of someone who was used to being obeyed. 'We've all made an effort to get you both here because we think you were made for each other. We don't want to see your marriage going down the tubes. You've only been married six weeks. You've got to understand that marriage isn't about splitting up every time the going gets tough. If that was the case, none of us would stay together!'

Flossie shot an embarrassed look at Lizzie, as though to apologise that her husband had forgotten that Lizzie and Myles were divorced. But Stan was going full speed ahead now and tact was a forgotten country.

'Marriage is a journey,' Stan said. 'It's a voyage, like a big liner going off onto the ocean . . .'

'Like the *Titanic*,' suggested Barry wryly.

'Not like the *Titanic*,' said Stan. 'Every time you hit a bit of trouble, you can't bale out.'

'I bet you told them it was all my fault,' Debra said furiously to Barry, interrupting Stan.

'No, but I told them you were a spoilt bitch,' Barry said. 'And you are. I don't know why I bothered turning up at the altar at all that day – if Dad hadn't forced me to, told me it would kill my mother if I let you down, I wouldn't have showed up at the church at all.'

There was a silence, then: a silence so intense that even the people at the tables around them sat still, listening. Though there were times when Lizzie wanted to slap Debra and make her realise what she was throwing away, she felt hugely sorry for her daughter at that moment. Debra's mouth was an oval of shock as she stared at Barry, disbelieving.

'What?' she breathed.

Lizzie tried to pull her away. 'Come on, Debra, it's time

549

we went. There's no point having a full-scale argument here. You and Barry have to sort this out in private. This was a mistake . . .'

But Debra would not be moved. She stood her ground and stared at Barry. 'You didn't want to marry me?' she said.

'What do you think?' Barry snapped back. 'It's a pity I listened to Dad and went ahead with it. Think of the money we'd have saved.'

As the colour drained out of Debra's face, Lizzie made another attempt to pull her daughter away. 'Come on, Debra . . .'

'I knew we shouldn't get married,' Barry snapped. 'You were just pushing and pushing all the time to do it because it was the next step after we'd been together so long. The ultimate commitment, you said it was. You don't know what commitment is all about, Debra Shanahan. You're the most selfish person I've ever met. It's all "me, me, me" with you. Nothing I ever did was good enough for you, was it?'

'Don't talk to me like that,' said Debra in a pained whisper.

'I couldn't do anything right on the honeymoon, I couldn't do anything right when we got home, so what was the point of staying together?' said Barry bitterly. 'You didn't want me, Debra. You simply wanted a husband, any husband, and I was the poor sap who was standing in the wrong place at the wrong time. The worm has turned, Debra. You spent years making me feel as if I wasn't good enough for you, as though I'd been so lucky to get you. Now I know I'm too good for you!'

Lizzie would have gone through her own divorce ten times if she could have just taken the pain out of Debra's eyes. 'Come on, Debra,' she shouted, desperate to get her daughter to go.

This time, Debra allowed herself to be pulled away. Lizzie led her stumbling out of the restaurant. They stood outside, Lizzie with her arms round her daughter. Debra was clearly in a state of shock. At first Lizzie couldn't work out what the girl was saying.

'Why?' moaned Debra. 'Why did he say those things? I love him, I didn't mean to hurt him. It's just I never wanted him to take me for granted, like Dad did with you. If we'd started off that way, we'd have been stuck like that for ever and then, twenty years down the road, I'd have been dumped, like Dad dumped you. And I didn't want that.'

She was silent all the way home in the car, and that was almost worse. If she'd been raging against Barry, calling him every name under the sun, then Lizzie would have known that Debra was going to get better. But the anguish and misery on Debra's face told its own story.

Lizzie knew how she felt. Debra thought she'd been loved and that love had given her power – the power to leave Barry, knowing that he'd want her back and would eventually give in to all her demands. She was the powerful one in the relationship. Suddenly, all that had changed. Barry had admitted that he hadn't wanted to marry Debra and now she had to face the truth – that he didn't love her enough, that he could do without her. The fairy-tale marriage was over and Lizzie felt guilty that her and Myles's dysfunctional marriage had obviously contributed to its demise.

At home, the phone was ringing but Lizzie didn't pick it up. She knew it was probably Myles, Stan or Flossie, all trying to find out how Debra was. Nobody could have missed the look of shocked horror on her face; nobody could have been in doubt as to what Barry really meant when he said all those things. It was over.

'I'm sorry, Mum, I think I'll go upstairs to bed,' Debra said in a low voice, as if it was perfectly normal to go to bed at lunchtime on a Sunday.

'Do you want me to bring you up some tea or anything?' Lizzie asked worriedly, wishing she could offer more comfort than mere tea.

But Debra shook her head. 'I'm better off on my own, thanks.'

Lizzie thought she might ring Joe to fill him in on what had happened. It seemed now as if Joe was the only one of the Shanahans with any sense at all. He'd seen that Debra and Barry were totally unsuited to each other. Lizzie, Myles and Debra herself had been the idiots who'd thought that it could all work out. And we should have known, Lizzie told herself angrily.

Of all people, she should have realised that this marriage wasn't going to work. She should have learned the lesson from her own marriage, she thought miserably. What was that awful thing Debra had said just now? That she hadn't wanted Barry to take her for granted the way Myles had taken Lizzie for granted. What a legacy to give her daughter, Lizzie thought sadly.

The cute fridge magnets said you should give your children two things: roots and wings. She'd added her own offering: a screwed-up sense of what marriage was all about. Well done, Lizzie.

She picked up the phone and dialled. One of the many nice things about Joe was he never said 'I told you so.'

CHAPTER THIRTY-THREE

September arrived in a haze of sunshine and it didn't make going back to school any easier for Jess Barton. It had rained solidly for the last week of the holidays and now, now that she had to drag on her uniform and schlep back to school to wait for her Junior Cert exam results, the sun was shining at Greek-island-in-August level.

Jess could have just about coped with her life, including the fact that her mother was permanently miserable – Dad obviously hadn't made an effort to speak to Mum after Jess's pep talk – if it hadn't been for her mother's bombshell about the new chat show. It wasn't that Jess hadn't known the chat show job was on the cards. The problem was that Mum was now seriously discussing moving from Dunmore to Dublin to fit in with it.

'We have to leave Lyonnais anyhow,' Jess overheard her saying on the phone one night. 'I think a fresh start in a new city might be the way forward. With my share of the money we get for this place, Jess and I could have a lovely place in Dublin, maybe an apartment because I'm fed up with gardening.'

Jess could barely believe what she was hearing. She didn't know who her mother was talking to but this person was being given more information about Jess's future than Jess was.

'Yeah, Mike, I don't mind holding on while you negotiate the best deal – I'm not in any rush to sign the contract,' her mother went on. 'I still don't know if it's the right thing to do or not. Jess might hate to leave Cork, you never know. She's under a lot of stress right now because the exam results are out soon and I know she's focusing on that.'

From her earwigging position at the top of the stairs, Jess felt furious. How did her mother know if she'd like to leave Cork or not if she didn't ask her?

'OK,' finished her mother. 'I could come up next week to meet them and perhaps have a look at some apartments to get a feel for what we could afford. Near good schools, definitely. No, I don't want to mention it to anyone, not until we've made a definite decision to do the show.'

Jess waited for her mother to inform her of any of the great relocation plan but she didn't. The exam stress was nothing compared to the stress of waiting to see if they were going to up sticks and move, Jess thought furiously.

But the thing that really destroyed Jess's fragile self-confidence was the behaviour of Saffron Walsh.

Jess's classmate Saffron had returned from holidays with a permatan ('sunbed', snorted Steph scathingly) and a renewed determination to carry on her grudge against Jess.

'She's never forgiven you for saying she had the individuality of a sheep in English class,' Steph sighed on the first day back, when Saffron and her gang banged into Jess one by one in the fifth-year locker room, murmuring 'ugly bitch' under their breath.

'What do I care?' said Jess, but she did. She might have lost her train tracks – she'd almost kissed the orthodontist when he'd said they could come off – and she might be dating gorgeous Oliver from sixth year, but she was still easy prey for the vindictive Saffron.

It didn't matter that Steph pointed out that Saffron only had it in for people she felt threatened by.

'Why should she be threatened by me?' grumbled Jess.

'You're smarter than her, you're dating a pretty cool guy, you look great without your train tracks, and you've got a famous mother. Not to mention the fact that she's going to get zip in her exams. In Saffron's eyes, you're competition, so she hates you.'

Jess was just about able to put up with Saffron hating her – after all, she didn't think much of Saffron either. What she couldn't deal with was the sudden influx of horrible text messages on her mobile, all from a withheld number. 'U thnk ur smthn special – ur not!' was the cleanest of them. Then, her new trainers were pulled from her gym locker and doused with nail varnish. Jess didn't know why, but seeing the pristine, new, blue and white trainers all smeared with horrible blood-red polish really upset her. What hurt wasn't so much that they were ruined, it was the fact that anybody could hate her enough to do this to her.

'You know it's Bitch Walsh,' Steph said after the incident with the trainers. 'Report her to Docker.' All the students called the headmistress, Mrs Doherty, by the nickname of Docker.

'I can't,' Jess said. 'She'd have no proof and Saffron would really have it in for me.'

'Well, tell Oliver or, better still, your mum.'

But Jess stubbornly refused to tell Oliver. He'd got so serious and intense since he'd gone into sixth year.

'It's the Leaving Cert in nine months: this is the most important year of my life,' he kept repeating anxiously. 'I'm going to have to study hard this year, Jess. We won't have as much time together, you know.'

'Yeah, I know,' she said off-handedly to hide how hurt she was.

Jess knew that Oliver was ambitious and needed to do well in his exams so he could do science at university, but she didn't see why he had to get so fired up the first week back at school.

The party, a big one held by an older friend of Zach's, on the first weekend back in school, turned out to be the last straw. Jess had been so excited about it. She hoped that she and Oliver would have such a great time that he'd get over his just-back-to-school studying frenzy, and realise that fun wasn't outlawed once you got to sixth year.

It was also the first party she'd been to with Oliver since the visit to the orthodontist. She felt more than halfway decent for the first time in her life.

'You'll look fabulous,' Steph had ordained after a lengthy trawl through her wardrobe to find something suitable for Jess to wear. In the end, they'd decided on Jess's own jeans and a silver mesh top with a black spindly-strap camisole underneath. Steph's mother had a knobbly cardigan that looked like something from a designer label and Steph swiped it as a final cover-up 'in case it's cold when you're snogging outside'.

'We won't be snogging outside,' Jess grinned. 'We can snog perfectly well inside. It's only thrill-seekers like you and Zach who feel the need to get down and dirty at bus stops and on park benches.'

'That's only 'cos we don't have anywhere else to go,' protested Steph. 'If we had a free house all the time like you, we could be at it there.'

'I don't have a free house and we're not at it,' Jess pointed out.

'You're the only one who isn't,' Steph said loftily. 'It's fantastic,' she added.

'You won't think that if you end up pregnant.'

'Ugh, don't be so negative,' Steph said with a shudder.

'You shouldn't have rushed into it,' Jess went on. She knew that Zach had put fierce pressure on Steph to sleep with him and she disapproved. 'I hate all that "if you loved me you would" shit.'

'Oh, gimme a break. I'm old enough,' retorted Steph. 'We both are. It's not as if we're kids or anything. I mean, there was a time in history when we'd have been married at sixteen, you know.'

'And you think that's a good option?' demanded Jess crossly. 'Women were treated like chattels then. They couldn't vote or own property, they were like bloody cows. Would you like that?'

'I'm only saying . . .' Steph protested. She scowled at her friend and stuck her tongue out. 'You're well up on history for someone who couldn't wait to get out of studying it.'

'Very funny,' growled Jess.

'Bet you if Oliver asked you to have sex with him, you wouldn't say no,' Steph added.

'He knows I'd say no,' Jess said, then, looking at Steph's disbelieving face, she collapsed into giggles.

'Slapper,' said Steph, then collapsed into giggles too.

The truth was that Jess wasn't sure what she'd do if Oliver asked her to sleep with him. She was pretty sure he'd never try the Zach trick of emotional blackmail. Oliver was too straight for that. So if he did ask her to have sex, it would be because he loved her and really wanted to, and Jess didn't know how she'd react.

Everything had changed so much during the summer. Sometimes, she still couldn't believe that he was going out with her. He could have had anyone in their year or his year, for that matter, and yet he wanted to go out with her. She felt both wildly flattered – and a little scared that one day it would all be over. But that anxiety still didn't mean she'd say yes if he did want sex.

The night of the party, Steph told her mother she was staying with the Bartons out in Dunmore. This was a lie. In fact, she and Zach were part of the huge crew staying over in the house where the party was being held. The guy whose party it was said his parents were away and, unless the music was so loud that somebody called the cops, they were safe.

'My mother won't check,' Steph said confidently. 'She says she feels so awful about your parents splitting up that she doesn't know what to say to your mother.'

'Handy, that,' said Jess, feeling more and more like a grumpy elderly relative. She had been looking forward to the party but now, with Steph planning a complicated night of deception, she felt as if everything was running out of her control. What if Mrs Anderson phoned the next morning to speak to Steph? Jess had visions of herself going puce and stuttering hopeless lies about Steph being in the shower.

'Tell her that,' Steph said, 'then phone me on my mobile and I'll phone her right back.'

'What if she doesn't believe me?' demanded Jess. 'Or if my mother picks up the phone?'

'God,' groaned Steph, 'I just want one night with Zach. Improvise! Take your phone off the hook until I phone your mobile and tell you I've talked to my mum.'

'OK,' said Jess reluctantly. She didn't know why but she had a bad feeling about everything.

Worse, Zach let it slip that Ian Green and his gang were coming, meaning Saffron would be there too.

Abby dropped Oliver and Jess at the party, telling Oliver sternly that she expected her daughter home by half eleven.

'No problem, Mrs Barton,' Oliver said. 'I'm going to book a taxi in loads of time.'

'Good,' said Abby. 'And don't take a lift home with anyone who's been drinking. Phone me for a lift rather than do that. At least seventy-five per cent of all fatal accidents are caused by young, inexperienced drivers . . .'

'Mum!' said Jess. 'We're getting a taxi, OK?'

She only hoped her mother wouldn't bump into Steph's mum now lest the false sleep-over arrangements were revealed.

Jess needn't have worried. It was after ten and the party was going full blast before Steph and Zach turned up with half a bottle of vodka and a six-pack of alcopops. They both smelled of a mixture of cigarettes and whiskey, no doubt filched from Steph's dad's drinks cabinet.

To make matters worse, Zach produced two beautifully rolled spliffs from his denim jacket pocket.

'Isn't he a good boy?' cooed Steph, wrapping herself round her boyfriend.

'Steph, what are you doing?' Jess hissed. 'If you get caught –'

'Who's going to catch me? They've got a free house tonight.'

Jess knew Steph was right but she couldn't help worrying

for her friend. This was not normal Steph behaviour.

Steph wasn't the only one who wasn't acting quite normally. Oliver seemed unnaturally quiet all evening, and when Jess asked him what was up, he said he'd had a big talking to from his dad about how important this year was in school, how he had to work hard and how it didn't look good that Oliver had only been back in school a week and was already out partying.

'Your dad can't be piling the pressure on yet,' protested Jess. 'The exams aren't until next June and nobody works harder than you!'

'Yeah, well, my dad says I've got to get into uni this time round, he can't afford to send me back to repeat my exams. If I don't get what I want in college this time, I'd have to go to one of the crammer schools and they're so expensive. He can't afford it.' Oliver looked stressed. 'This is a one-off deal. What a great year this is going to be.' He got up abruptly. 'I think I'll get another drink. Want one?'

She shook her head and watched him amble over to the table laden down with cans and bottles.

A girl in a skimpy halter top and a tiny miniskirt instantly sidled over to him and began chatting him up. One of Saffron's cronies, a real cow named Sherry, Jess thought sourly, although Oliver didn't appear to be unduly upset by the attention. Soon, he was chatting away with Sherry and it didn't look as if he was moaning about studying now.

Irritated, Jess went off in search of Steph, who was just on her way to the loo for a lipstick, eyeliner and hair session. Steph wasn't walking very steadily and Jess knew her friend was drunk.

'Are you all right?' she asked, worriedly. 'You're a bit wasted, Steph. Sure you don't want to go home?'

'Chill,' said Steph. 'You don't have to take care of me, Jess.' There was no talking to her when she was in this mood, so Jess headed back down the stairs. On the landing, she met Saffron coming up. As usual, Saffron looked about twenty in an expensive sequinned top worn with low-rise jeans. She was alone.

'Hello, baby girl,' she sneered. 'Did your mummy let you out?'

'Fuck off, Saffron,' said Jess, trying to get past.

'Ooh, bad language,' taunted Saffron. 'From what I hear, talking about fucking is as bad as it gets with you. Because you won't actually do it. Afraid, baby girl? Afraid of sex?'

'Leave me alone,' said Jess, confused. How did Saffron know that she and Oliver hadn't had sex?

'He's going to dump you, by the way. Oliver's not interested in a kid like you,' hissed Saffron. 'If you're too much of a kid to have sex, why would he hang around?'

Stung, Jess stared at Saffron. Oliver wouldn't have told anyone, couldn't . . .

But Saffron had some evil sixth sense for Jess's thought processes. 'Think he wouldn't talk about it, do you?' she taunted. 'They all talk about it, don't you understand? Guys like sex and they think about it, like, every ten seconds. It's all they talk about. Oliver's a cool guy. He needs someone who understands him.'

Jess found her voice. 'Like you, I suppose?'

Saffron's eyes were like diamond chips. 'No, I've got a man, baby girl. But he does like my friend Sherry. He was with her at the party in August, when you were away on holiday with your mummy. Didn't anybody mention that to you?'

Jess stared at Saffron. She had to be lying, she *had* to be.

Saffron dealt the trump card. 'Yeah. He knows your friend Steph is staying over tonight with Zach and he can't understand why you won't do the same. Goody Two-Shoes wouldn't do that, would she? You think you're so clever, with your TV star mum, but we all can see through you. You're just a stupid kid, aren't you?'

Jess fled. She rushed downstairs and went to find Oliver.

He'd been near the CD player when she'd left, and now he was standing in the archway between the kitchen and the den, laughing and talking to someone. It was Ian Green, Saffron's boyfriend. Whatever they were talking about, it was cracking them both up and Oliver's head was thrown back in a roar of laughter. Sherry was with them, laughing too, and sliding her hands up and down her mini skirt so nobody could miss glancing down at her long, long bare legs.

Bastard! Jess didn't even want to confront him, she hated him so much. Instead, she grabbed her cardigan and was out the door in seconds. As she walked down the drive, crying, she texted Oliver: 'Had to go home. Don't follow me. Ever.'

It took her twenty minutes to flag down a taxi and in all that time, Oliver never phoned or texted her back – proof that Saffron was right and he wasn't interested in her. He was probably snogging horrible Sherry now, thrilled that Saffron had done his dirty work for him and got rid of Jess.

Wiping away the stinging tears, Jess sat in the back of the cab and felt as if her heart would break. She switched off her phone. She didn't want to talk to him now, even if he did ring.

At home she couldn't sleep. Even when she'd made her bed as comfortable as possible with the pillows squished just the way she liked them, and had got some chocolate from the kitchen, she found herself lying there in the dark, thinking. Mum wanted to move and she hadn't bothered to mention it to Jess; Oliver wanted to break it off with her and he'd picked the coward's way out; Saffron was ruining her life by being such a bully and nobody had noticed. Even Steph hadn't been there for her, Jess thought, feeling suddenly sorry for herself. She was totally alone.

Curling up in a foetal position in her bed, she cried herself to sleep.

She was due to spend Sunday with Dad, so she got up early and phoned him. Dad sounded thrilled to hear from her but he said that their plan to go for a long walk had to be postponed.

'I've got a ton of work to do on the school extension,' he said apologetically. 'I'll pick you up and you can watch TV or a video until I'm finished and then we can go out for something to eat or a movie, OK?'

Jess felt too worn out after a sleepless night for any walk so she said yes, that was fine. She wanted to be out all day so she didn't have to talk to Steph or Oliver or anyone, and she might as well spend it with her father. Just in case anyone tried to contact her, she left her mobile phone behind. If nobody had wanted to talk to her the night before, then they couldn't talk to her now.

In the end, Dad spent so long poring over architect's documents and engineer's reports that it was too late for the movie Jess wanted to see.

'We can order a takeaway,' Dad said hopefully.

'Yeah, great,' said Jess, feeling even more sorry for herself. Was it too much to hope that she might come first for *any* of the people in her life?

The idea to run away came to Jess as she sat on the train on Monday morning, nose up against the grubby window, watching the countryside speed past in a haze of rain. She wished with all her heart that she was going somewhere else, away from Dunmore, away from home, away from the bullying of school – and, most of all, away from the humiliation of knowing that Oliver didn't care for her any more. She'd even got a later train this morning to avoid bumping into him. And now, she had to face Saffron in school. Who knew what fresh torture Saffron would have ready for her? Her locker emptied out all over the floor or more vicious text messages?

She could have coped with everything else, she'd got used to coping, if it hadn't been for Oliver.

She knew he'd phoned her: she'd checked her mobile

for messages and his number came up several times from Saturday night and Sunday, but she hadn't listened to his messages. It would kill her to hear him tell her what she already knew – that it was over. So she deleted everything. Like he'd deleted her from his life, she thought furiously.

Steph had phoned late on Sunday and she'd sounded hung over on her message. Jess hadn't phoned back. She knew she'd cry if she talked to Steph and she couldn't bear to hear what might have happened at the party after she'd rushed off.

Nobody would miss her if she did run away, she decided. Mum and Dad didn't really notice her any more. They were too busy locked in their own private misery.

Mum went through her day like a person who'd had her brain replaced by a robot's. She talked to Jess and went to work, all on automatic pilot. The only thing that made her just a bit animated was this charity thing she was involved with in Sally's name. Even then, she would constantly mutter about how awful it was that poor Sally was gone when other people, who didn't appreciate what they had, were left.

Dad wasn't much better. Jess decided that giving him some home truths when they'd been at Aunt Caroline's had been a complete waste of time. Instead of going to see Mum, he would miserably ask Jess how she was, like he wanted to know but didn't have the courage to phone Mum up herself. Yesterday, he'd asked stiffly after Mum and when Jess had snapped, 'Why don't you ask her yourself?' he'd clammed up.

Her parents didn't seem to realise that she was stuck in the middle, taking misery from both sides and trying to get on with her life. Well, she was fed up with it.

The fields gave way to suburbs, which in turn gave way to the city sprawl and the gloom of the approaching station. As the train chugged lethargically on, Jess almost wished it would stop before it got to the station, so that she would never have to get off and face school again and that bitch Saffron. Thinking about Saturday night gave her a tense, jumpy feeling deep inside now, like Wilbur behaved before thunder. At school, all the teachers were on a high waiting for the Junior Cert results, and all the Junior Cert pupils were in the depths of depression for the same reason.

Exam trouble, boyfriend trouble, parent trouble, bitch at school trouble – Jess had it all.

But why was she relying on the train stopping to keep her from school? The idea was so startling in its simplicity that she wondered how she hadn't thought of it before. She wouldn't go to school at all. Everyone else was behaving badly, so she would too.

She'd go away somewhere and let everyone sort out their own stupid problems because nobody cared about her. Bunking off school was something Jess had never done before. But today, Jess would join the ranks of the bunkers-off. At the station, she got off the train long enough to buy a soda from the shop. Then, once it was empty, she got back on and let it take her back to Dunmore. At home, she let herself in quietly, though knowing her mother wouldn't be there.

The idea about where to go had come to her on the journey back to Dunmore. In the animal refuge, she'd read about a fantastic new animal rehoming centre outside Galway city, where people interested in careers with animals could train. Jess was sure she'd read that you didn't need lots of exams to get in – all you had to do was demonstrate a love of animals and a willingness to work hard. That was where she'd go to see if she might get a job there in the future. Everyone else was worrying about their future – Jess would worry about hers. She'd visit and ask about working there when she finished school, or maybe doing shifts there in the holidays. It wasn't as if anybody would care where she was on her holidays – they all had so many other things to worry about, they seemed perfectly happy to ignore her.

Mum could go to Dublin, Dad could obsess about his precious school extension, and Oliver, Saffron and Sherry could go to hell.

Jess couldn't remember all the details of the new centre

but a few minutes' Internet surfing would reveal all, and she could check out somewhere to stay. She wasn't exactly in funds and there had to be a hostel or cheap bed and breakfast she could stay in for a couple of days. Jean would give a reference over the phone if they needed one; surely they'd be keen to offer her a job in the future because she was young, enthusiastic and cheap.

It didn't take her long to track down the refuge and find a hostel nearby. Pleased that she'd managed to plan all this ahead of time, she shoved a few things into her rucksack and changed her school uniform for her jeans, a sweater and her new cord jacket that Steph said made her look at least eighteen. Good, she'd need to look older if her plan was to work.

Her purse with her bank card, her mobile phone and her address book completed the kit. On impulse, she took the brown beanbag puppy she'd had for years too. He was faded and a bit bedraggled, but he might be company for the trip.

Wilbur was nestled up on a towel on the radiator in the main bathroom. He protested as Jess picked him up from his cosy nest, but she held him close and told him she was going away for a while but she wouldn't be long.

'You'll miss me, won't you, Wilbur?' she murmured into his warm fur. In reply, the cat wriggled from her grasp, digging his claws into her arm as he made his getaway.

'You could have been sweet just this once,' said Jess tearfully.

In the kitchen, she took two small bottles of orange juice, some granola bars and thirty euros from the wooden teabox where her mother kept cash for people like the window cleaner. Then, she wrote a note. They hadn't bothered keeping her informed about stuff like getting divorced, she thought grimly, but she at least would behave properly. She propped the note up by her mother's calendar, took one last look round the homely kitchen, and left by the back door, taking her old light windcheater and an umbrella as a last-minute thought. There was another train in half an hour and she wanted to be at her destination by nightfall.

The phone was ringing that afternoon when Abby arrived home after a day working on a private commission. It was Katya to discuss some messages she'd taken, and although Abby noticed the message light winking on the answering machine, she hardly thought it was urgent. When she'd finished talking to Katya, she switched the answering machine off and went into the kitchen to pour herself a glass of water. Then she set the oven for dinner before going back to listen to her messages. The last one startled her.

'Mrs Barton, this is Rebecca Tierney from Bradley Secondary School. It's midday on Monday and I'm phoning because Jess hasn't come to school today. If a student is ill or has to take time off, it's school policy that the parent phone and tell us so we can mark them as "absent with permission" or "ill" on the register. We'd appreciate it if you could adhere to this policy.' The voice drilled out a phone number and hung up.

Abby had to play the message again to get the number and her hand shook as she wrote the digits down. She dialled hurriedly and the phone rang out without anybody picking it up. There was no facility to leave a message either.

Shit. She looked at the time. It was after five and there was probably nobody to answer the phone in the school office. She dialled Jess's mobile but it was switched off.

'Jess, it's Mum. Can you give me a buzz back when you get my message, love?'

Grabbing the phone directory from the hall table drawer, Abby found the school's listing and dialled every number, but no one answered. Abby felt panic begin to set in.

From her address book, Abby found Steph's mobile number but another recorded voice told her the number she'd dialled had been changed. So she rang Steph's home and found herself talking to Lisa Anderson, who clearly thought Abby had called for a chat.

'It's about Jess, actually,' Abby interrupted. 'I'm worried about her. She didn't go to school today, her mobile is off and when I phoned Steph's phone, it says the number has changed. Has she got a new number?' Even as she said it, she felt like an utter failure again. She didn't have the phone number of her daughter's closest friend. How uncaring was that?

'I'll murder the pair of them if they bunked off school,' said Lisa. 'Although it is unlike them. They're good girls, really. Well, we don't see Jess as much now, of course, and she's so involved in that animal place, isn't she? Steph says Jess loves going there. You've raised a good kid, Abby. Nobody could say she doesn't care about anything but herself or that your fame or money have changed her.'

Abby felt sick to her stomach to think that Jess hadn't changed but she had. Lisa rattled off Steph's new phone number. 'Ring me back if you can't reach them,' Lisa continued. 'Steph's been driving me mad to give her the money for a new pair of trousers, so ten to one the pair of them are in town trailing through every shop on Patrick Street. We'll track them down.'

Abby hung up, aware that she'd felt so down since she and Jess had come back from Florida that she wouldn't have had a clue if Jess had needed new clothes.

And why had she been feeling down? For so many reasons that seemed inconsequential compared to Jess being missing.

She'd felt down because Tom still spoke to her on the phone as if she could transmit the plague through the receiver, and because there was no hope for her marriage and she'd finally had to face it. She'd felt miserable because Roxie in Beech was behaving like a prize bitch now that it was almost certain that Abby was leaving. Even when Mike had leaked a story to a favoured few contacts in the press, saying that Beech had realised too late that they'd treated their star badly, Abby hadn't cheered up. Brian, faced with a few snide television comments about how Abby had been

567

the true star of *Declutter*, was back-pedalling furiously and trying to get Abby back, but it was too late. Anyhow, Brian being hypocritically nice to her didn't stop Roxie from being as poisonous as ever, so that had upset Abby.

But none of these things mattered really, did they?

What selfishness had made her think that her own problems were more important than communicating with Jess, Abby asked herself over and over again. She'd been so tied up with her career and her marital problems with Tom that she'd forgotten her daughter.

Steph was indeed trailing round shops in Patrick Street when Abby phoned her, but she was on her own.

'No, Jess didn't come to school today and I've texted her about twenty times asking her where she is,' Steph said indignantly, 'but she never texted me back. I thought she must be holed up in her room feeling sick 'cos she didn't phone me back on Sunday, either.'

'She isn't sick.' It was Abby who was feeling bad now.

'She's never done that before, not ever.' The mild indignation was gone from Steph's voice and she now sounded worried. 'Do you think it's because of Saffron and the hassle she's been getting? I did tell her to talk to someone about it but Jess said teachers were clueless about bullying.'

'Bullying?' Abby was glad she was near the stairs so she had something to sink onto when her legs would no longer hold her upright. 'I . . . I didn't know. What bullying, Steph?'

She could hear the hesitation in Steph's long-drawn-out 'Well . . .'

'Please tell me. It's important, Steph. Jess is missing, that's serious.'

'It's . . . Jess pissed Saffron off last term, and this one, for some reason, Saffron is in real bitchy form. Since we got back last week, Jess has been getting these nasty texts on her mobile and someone's been mucking with her things. There was nail varnish spilled all over her new trainers last week. We figured it was Saffron and I think she had a go at

Jess at that party at the weekend too. Horrible bitch.' The grapevine meant Steph had heard that Saffron had fought with Jess, but over what, nobody knew. She had learned one or two interesting things about Saffron, though. Steph decided it was about time that lying, cheating Ms Walsh got her comeuppance. When Jess got back, they'd sort out Saffron once and for all, Steph vowed.

'What did the text messages say?' asked Abby, rage growing inside her.

'They just called her names and said she was a waste of space. I said she should tell Docker, Mrs Doherty, I mean,' Steph said. 'But Jess said she couldn't prove anything 'cos Saffron blocked her number on the texts and, anyhow, she reckoned Saffron would get bored with it eventually. I'd have taken Saffron on but Jess isn't like that. She hates confrontation. Didn't she tell you anything about it, Mrs Barton?'

'No, I wish she had. Steph, Jess wouldn't do anything to harm herself, would she?'

'Fuck no!' said Steph, startled. 'Oh God, sorry, Mrs Barton, I didn't mean to swear but Jess would never do that. If she was going, she'd leave a note, wouldn't she?'

Abby took the stairs two at a time. In Jess's room, her uniform was lying on the bed, but apart from that, the room was exactly the same as normal. There was no note to be seen. She checked her own room but there was nothing anywhere there, either. Back downstairs, she ran into the kitchen and scanned the room hurriedly. Beside her calendar was a folded-up piece of paper.

Mum, I'm taking a few days away. Don't worry about me, I'll be fine. I've got money and my phone. I'll call.
Jess.

After getting no joy from Oliver, except for learning that there'd been some misunderstanding and that Jess hadn't phoned Oliver back despite him leaving endless messages on her mobile, the first place Abby thought that Jess might go if she really wanted to get away was the animal refuge.

As she drove against the traffic out into the countryside, the rain began to fall again and Abby thought of Jess possibly wet and miserable, instead of safe and dry at home. By the time she followed the sign up the second road on the left, Abby had never seen so much mud. Old Farm Road was axle-deep in a thick blancmange of it, and she wondered how someone without a four-wheel drive – let alone on a bicycle – could ever reach the refuge. Fifth gate to your left, a man walking a dog had told her. Abby kept a wary eye out for the fifth gate but, even in the evening gloom, she had no trouble spotting it.

A wooden sign swung jauntily on a post, with 'Dunmore Animal Refuge' inscribed in poker work. The gate was shut and Abby had to brave the deluge to open it.

The 'Keep the Gate Shut' sign looked like an order rather than a request. The sound of dogs barking brought a woman out of a large barn to survey Abby. She was tall, very thin, possibly in her late forties and dressed for flood in ancient waterproofs. Her hair was completely hidden by a large knitted cap covered in turn by the sort of see-through plastic rainscarf Abby hadn't seen since her grandmother was alive.

'Hello,' the woman said.

'I'm Abby Barton,' said Abby. 'I'm looking for Jess.'

'Jean,' said the woman, holding out a hand. 'She's not here.'

'Oh no,' said Abby, and burst into tears.

Jess reached the hostel in Galway at four in the afternoon. After the train, it had taken a bus journey and a half-hour walk to get to it but now that she was there, Jess wondered if it had been such a good place to stay. The on-line site had mentioned a bright, friendly place with modern accommodation and a rec room for residents. In reality, the dorm she was shown into was very shabby and the bunk beds were practically antiques. But she wasn't there for a luxury holiday, she reminded herself, investigating her upper bunk. The hostel was useful because it was just a mile away from the Galway Bay Animal Centre.

She phoned the animal centre from the hostel and got talking to a very nice man who said they were always looking for carers, but that they had their quota at the moment and were full for holiday work for the foreseeable future too.

'We might have a holiday placement in about a year, but if you're still in school, that'll be no good to you,' he said. 'Why don't you phone the refuge in Kildare? I hear they're looking for holiday workers.'

That threw Jess. 'But . . . I'm here now,' she said, thinking of how far she'd travelled.

'Sorry, you should have phoned first,' the man said.

That wasn't what she was hoping to hear, Jess thought in despair. She needed some sort of positive response after coming all this way. They couldn't turn her away without talking to her. Maybe then they'd see how much she loved animals and how perfect she'd be for a place there in the future. 'Please can I come and see you?' she begged. 'I'm really good with animals and if somebody dropped out of the Christmas holiday work, I'd fill in.'

The man hesitated. 'Phone again tomorrow to talk to Kenny. He runs the place,' he said. 'I'm not promising anything, mind, but Kenny might be able to put you on the cancellation list.'

'Great,' said Jess. But when she'd put the phone down, she thought maybe this hadn't been such a great idea after all.

It was one of the hardest phone calls Abby had ever had to make. Jean had offered her a cup of tea to combat shock, but Abby had said no, she had to get home and wait in case Jess phoned. And she had to tell Jess's father what had happened.

She dialled Tom's number. He answered on the second ring.

'Jess is missing. I don't know where she is and she left a note, but there's no sign of her. Steph doesn't know where she is and she's not answering her mobile phone.' Abby blurted it all out in an instant.

'Hold on,' said Tom, trying to pick up the salient points. 'Jess is missing since when? Are you sure she's not just bunking off school or something, or down at that animal refuge?'

'No,' said Abby, her voice breaking. 'I've been there and they haven't seen her. She's definitely gone. I talked to Steph and she said that Jess hadn't been in school today. The school rang me to inform me – that's how I found out in the first place. She's been gone all day and I had no idea. I talked to Oliver's mother and she gave me his number. He's at school, but I think he and Jess had a falling-out. He hasn't seen her since the party and he sounded really upset about it. He says he rang and rang on Sunday and she never answered.'

'Have you contacted the police?' said Tom, instantly acting like the professional teacher.

'No,' cried Abby. 'I thought I'd ring you and ask you first what you thought.'

'I'll phone the police and then I'll come on over,' said Tom decisively.

Within half an hour both Tom and a kindly policewoman called Anna Dunne were sitting in the kitchen in Lyonnais.

As soon as Tom had arrived, Abby had thrown herself into his arms, hugging him and crying at the same time.

'It's all my fault. If I'd been here, I'd have known that she wasn't at school today and we could have started looking earlier and, oh my God, Tom, *anything* could have happened to her.'

It was as if they'd never been apart, Tom thought, holding Abby tightly in his arms. He stroked her hair and murmured comforting noises into her ear. 'It's all right,' he said, 'it's all right. We're going to sort it out. She can't have gone far. She knows we love her and that we'll be worried. She'll phone.'

He'd dealt with runaways before through his work, but it was a different kettle of fish when it was your child who'd run away.

Somehow, the policewoman's factual information about how many teenagers ran away and were found quickly afterwards didn't seem to comfort quite so much when you were talking about your teenage daughter.

Because Jess was under the age of eighteen, she was considered a high-risk category, Sergeant Dunne explained. The fact that she'd left a note was a positive thing, but the usual police search procedures would take place regardless.

'If you agree to publicity, we can try to have Jess's picture on the news tonight. The papers will probably carry her description and the fact that she's missing tomorrow.'

Abby clung to Tom's hand. This was all so frightening. 'Yes,' she said, 'we want publicity. Anything to find her.'

'Did you have a row with Jess?' asked Sergeant Dunne, taking notes.

Abby shook her head. 'Not today or yesterday.' She wanted to say that there had been so many rows in the household over the past few months that it would be impossible to pin Jess's actions on any one row. 'Tom and I are separated,' she sighed, 'and that's been very difficult for Jess. But we have been working through it and we're all getting on. I think she may have had a row with her boyfriend. They were at a party on Saturday night and she left early to come home and hasn't spoken to him since. And she's being bullied at school too,' she added.

Tom looked horrified. 'Bullied at school?' he asked.

Abby nodded. 'I didn't know either,' she admitted to the policewoman. 'Her best friend, Steph, told me today. One of the girls in her class has been picking on her, sending text messages and just generally being a bitch. Steph said they couldn't prove where the messages were coming from but they both figured out it was this girl. I don't know if that's what pushed her over the edge or whether it was Oliver.'

Abby started to cry and Tom put his arms around her

again. He thought of the times he'd had parents in his office in school who were shocked and astonished when he told them that their sons had been bullied or were bullies themselves. Tom had always wondered how they didn't know what was going on in their children's lives, but now he understood that all too well. He'd been so tied up in his own problems that he'd neglected Jess. He'd spent Sunday with her and she'd seemed fine – a bit quiet, yes, but he hadn't noticed anything else. And apart from that weekend in Kent when she'd stunned him by her mature awareness of what had gone on with him and Abby, he hadn't really asked her about how she felt. He'd assumed that she was able to deal with everything, but he was wrong.

Anna Dunne spent an hour with them, talking about all Jess's friends, the places she went, what she did in her spare time. Abby told her about the refuge.

'I'd never been there,' Abby sobbed. 'When she started working there, I rang and I talked to Jean, but Jess didn't want me to go. She wanted it to be her own place. I should have realised that there had to be something wrong.'

'The fact that she didn't want you going to the refuge doesn't necessarily mean anything,' said the sergeant calmly. 'She volunteered there, so she wasn't keeping that from you. Teenagers are always pushing the boundaries. They want lives away from their parents and this could have been just that for Jess. But the bullying is something we have to look into, and we'll need to talk to her friends and the boyfriend.'

'I'll kill that bitch Saffron Walsh when I get my hands on her,' Abby vowed. 'How dare she do that to Jess?'

'There's a lot of it about,' Sergeant Dunne pointed out. 'Mobile phone bullying is endemic. Lots of kids get bullied and they don't tell their parents. Schools find it hard to cope with it and plenty of parents don't want to believe it when they hear that their kids are bullies.'

Tom was about to point out that his school had a good programme on bullying, but he stopped himself. What was the point of telling everyone how marvellously his school had dealt with the problem when all along his daughter was trying to deal with the same thing and he hadn't even noticed?

Sergeant Dunne took a photo of Jess and said the national and regional radio and press would be contacted that evening, although it was up to individual news organisations as to whether they ran with the story or not. She, as the family's liaison officer, would be in constant contact.

'Let us know if she gets in touch, obviously,' said Sergeant Dunne.

When she'd left, Tom and Abby sat together in the kitchen holding hands, as if the close contact could somehow protect them from bad news.

'She's not the sort of person to run away just for the sake of it, just to worry us,' Abby said. 'I can't bear to think of her alone . . .' She couldn't continue the sentence. The world was full of sick and twisted people. If only Jess would phone. 'How could I not have known she was being bullied?' Abby fretted. 'I should have known. She's been so quiet since last weekend and I just thought it was over you and me and the divorce and everything. Why didn't I ask her?'

'Why didn't *I* ask her?' Tom said. 'If she had a row with Oliver on Saturday, she must have been upset about it on Sunday and I never realised.'

Tom and Abby Barton didn't sleep that night. They lay down together in the big bed they used to share, fully dressed and holding hands for comfort. They talked about what it had been like when Jess was a child, the funny things she used to do, how they loved her so much, how she was growing up so quickly. Sleep was out of the question.

At half-past five, Tom got up and went downstairs to make some tea. Abby, shattered from lack of sleep, walked into Jess's room and lay down on the bed.

'Where are you, Jess?' she begged, her eyes closed as if in

prayer. 'I know you're hurting, Jess, but please, please come back to us. We miss you and we're so worried.'

Many miles away, in the uncomfortable bunk bed of the hostel room, Jess lay awake and listened to the snores of the girl sleeping in the bunk below. She held on to her mobile phone tightly. She'd woken half an hour ago and suddenly felt scared because she hadn't known where she was. Then she remembered running away and leaving the note, not caring what effect it would have on anyone. And now, too late, she did care. She thought of her mum finding the note and being terrified; she thought of her dad. He was always warning her about strange guys who tried to get teenage girls into cars.

'Dad,' Jess used to say in exasperation, 'that sort of thing only happens in movies.' Honestly, he worried so much. But Jess knew Dad believed that sort of stuff. And he might think that was what had happened to her now. She should have phoned.

And she thought of Oliver. She didn't know why, but she felt guilty. She hadn't given him a chance to talk to her and explain things. She'd been so angry and hurt on Saturday night that she'd acted on impulse, but now she understood that the Oliver Saffron described wasn't the Oliver she knew. Saffron was evil. She'd twist anything to upset Jess. She switched her phone on, her fingers lightly touching the buttons. The phone beeped loudly, telling her she had messages, but Jess didn't want to access them. Oliver could have left one and she couldn't bear to hear his voice. And Mum would have left one, or many more than one, probably. Jess definitely didn't want to listen to that.

She *could* send a text message, maybe, to let Mum and Dad know she was OK but then they'd want to come and get her, and they'd be angry. Jess couldn't cope with a row; there had been so many rows.

Her eyes got used to the dark and she looked around the

small dormitory room. Maybe if they came and got her, it wouldn't be such a bad idea, after all. This place wasn't exactly the Ritz. She should have phoned the animal refuge before she'd come here – how dumb was that just to rush onto the train without checking if there was a job vacancy? Oliver would have checked. She missed him, she thought suddenly. She wished she hadn't erased his messages, then she could listen to his voice. She pushed a button on the phone and the display lit up, showing her the time: it was a quarter to six. It was too early to send a text or phone. Everyone would still be asleep. Anyway, they knew she wouldn't do anything silly. She'd give it a little bit longer before she phoned.

Tom came into Jess's bedroom with two cups of tea. He hadn't bothered to bring anything to eat. There was no point. Neither he nor Abby had been able to eat a single thing the night before.

'Sit up and drink some tea,' he said to Abby gently.

Tom had put milk and sugar in it. She needed the sweetness.

'I thought she'd like this bedroom best of all,' Abby said, her voice far away. 'Do you remember when we looked at the house first, Tom, I thought she'd like this room because it looks out over the town and it's got the cherry trees outside the window? I thought it was like a bedroom in one of those books I used to love when I was a kid. I always wanted a bedroom like that myself.'

Tom thought about Abby's childhood home. He hadn't been there often – the last time was when Abby's mother had been dying and they'd come to take her to the hospital. It was a small, shabby house with no luxuries. Abby's father had drunk too much of the family's money for them ever to be able to afford anything better. There had been no cherry tree at the window of the room where Abby had grown up. Tom felt a pang of misery for his wife. She'd tried so hard to give Jess the things that she hadn't had when she was a child, and all he'd done was knock her for her efforts. She'd thought she was doing so well in earning the money to buy this beautiful home and, all the while, he'd silently resented her for it.

'I'm sorry, Abby,' he said, and he really meant it. 'I wasn't much of a husband to you, was I? You did your best, you tried to make us all happy, and I was so caught up in my own jealousy that I couldn't see it. I'm sorry, so sorry.'

'It's not your fault,' she said, in that same faraway voice. 'I should have seen what it was doing to you. I thought it was great if I earned more money, so we could go on better holidays, and have a bigger house, and everything. Because I didn't have those things when I was a kid, I thought they were important but they weren't. *We* were important; the family was important.'

'But we could have had it all,' Tom said. 'There's nothing to say we couldn't have been a happy family, and had the better life. I was the one who couldn't cope with that, not you.' He reached out, took her hand and held on tightly. 'We could try again, Abby, we could. Jess would love that. The weekend we were over in Kent with Caroline and Phil, she asked me why we weren't getting back together. If only I'd said we would,' he said in anguish, 'then maybe we wouldn't be in this position now.'

Abby raised exhausted eyes to his. 'You weren't the one who broke the family up in the first place,' she said.

'But it didn't really mean anything, did it?' Tom asked.

Despite the pain and fear she was going through, Abby knew this was a question she had to answer seriously. 'No,' she said in heartfelt tones. 'No, it didn't mean anything. I told you that before and you didn't believe me, but it's true. And I love you, Tom. I've always loved you. I suppose I forgot it a bit when we were going through bad times and we were too stupid to see that,' she said.

'I was too stupid to see it,' Tom said, 'but I love you too, Abby. We can get through it, can't we?'

Abby looked at him sadly. 'We have to get through this

first, Tom, before we think of anything else.' But she kept her hand clasped in his and squeezed it more tightly.

To think she'd been worried and upset about people knowing that she and Tom had broken up. That was just a drop in the ocean compared to the pain of thinking of Jess alone and scared somewhere. The fear of not knowing was the worst.

'Will I make you some breakfast?' asked Tom. 'I could fix you a fruit smoothie.'

Abby smiled at him. 'That's kind of you,' she said, 'but I couldn't eat a thing.'

'I know,' he said. 'I'm the same but we should keep our strength up.'

'I think I'll go outside,' Abby said, although she didn't know why she had this desire to sit out in the garden. It was a beautiful sunny morning and the walls of the house seemed to be closing in on her. She might feel better if she was outside.

She sat on the steps leading down to the patio and Tom joined her. They sat hip to hip, staring into the garden. Dew sparkled on the grass, making the garden seem lit with diamonds. Abby thought of all the mornings she'd looked out of the kitchen window on this scene and not appreciated all the good things in her life.

'Are we bad parents?' she asked Tom.

He shook his head. 'We're not,' he said. 'We took our eye off the ball because we'd got so caught up with our own problems.'

'If only we could turn the clock back,' Abby sighed.

Tom put his arm around her and held her close. 'We've got to be hopeful,' he said. 'She's been gone less than twenty-four hours. She might be absolutely fine; we've got to keep hoping.'

'That's what we kept saying about Sally,' Abby said slowly.

Wilbur wandered out through the patio doors and stalked in front of them, his furry tail held aloft, his huge grey eyes wide as if to say, 'What's going on here?' Abby could barely cope with looking at the cat. He was such a reminder of Jess.

'She wanted us to take that puppy from the refuge,' Abby said slowly. 'I thought it would be too much trouble and she'd get bored with it, that I'd have to look after it, or you would, and I said no. Oh, Tom.' She turned and buried her face in his chest, weeping. 'Why did I say no?'

She was sobbing so loudly that, at first, she didn't hear the sound of a text message coming through on her mobile, which was on the kitchen table. She and Tom both leaped to their feet, and raced into the kitchen. A text message had just come in. Her fingers shaking, she accessed it.

'Oh my God,' she said, 'oh my God, Tom. It's Jess.'

'Hi, Mum,' said the message. 'Sorry I left. I'm OK. I just needed to get away. Phone me and we can talk. Love Jess.'

'Oh, Tom,' said Abby, her voice tremulous.

'Here, give it to me.' He took the phone from her and quickly dialled Jess's mobile number.

A sleepy voice answered hello.

'Jess,' he said, trying to hold the phone so that Abby could hear too.

'Hi, Dad,' said Jess. She'd felt better when she'd sent the text message and had thought she might go back to sleep. 'What are you doing phoning me?'

Tom laughed.

'Darling, are you all right?' asked Abby anxiously.

'Yes, Mum, I'm fine,' said Jess. 'I'm sorry I went away. I just needed time on my own and –'

'It doesn't matter,' interrupted her mother. 'Nothing matters as long as you're OK. Where are you? We want to come and get you.' Tom pulled the phone back to him.

'Oh, I can get the bus back to Cork and the train home to Dunmore,' suggested Jess. 'That's how I got here.'

'You'll do no such thing. Your mother and I are coming to pick you up. Tell me where you are,' Tom said.

'You won't be cross with me, will you?' said Jess in a wobbly voice.

Tom, who hadn't cried for a very long time, felt the tears come to his eyes. 'No, love, we won't be cross with you. We're just so happy that you're safe.'

A few hours of blissful sleep later, Jess called Steph in school break time.

'My parents would completely murder me if I pulled a stunt like that,' Steph said, when Jess had explained everything. 'I mean, the police were involved and everything. And,' she paused, 'you're going to kill me for this, Jess, but I told your mom about Saffron and the text messages.'

'I wish you hadn't,' sighed Jess.

'I thought maybe that was why you'd gone,' Steph pointed out.

'It wasn't,' Jess said. 'It was lots of things, but it was Oliver at the party that really did it. Saffron told me he was only going out with me because he was bored and he thought I was a kid because I didn't want to have sex with him, and didn't I know that?'

'Oh, Jess, you big moron,' Steph said angrily. 'You know better than to listen to a word Saffron says. Anyway, she's jealous of you. Zach found out that she's always really liked Oliver and he's never been interested in her. I think she's getting a bit bored with the lovely Ian, basically because he's as thick as a plank. I'm sure she thought that if she could break you and Oliver up she was in with a chance.'

'You're not serious?' asked Jess, hope rising in her heart.

'Did you ask Oliver any of this before you ran out on him that night?' Steph said. 'Or did you just take Saffron's word for it?'

Jess felt ashamed to admit that she had taken Saffron's word for it. Why had she believed Saffron, a girl who bullied her, instead of believing Oliver?

'Paranoia is a terrible thing,' Steph said gravely. 'There are drugs for people like you, Jess, proper ones you get from the doctor –'

'I feel such an idiot,' Jess groaned, interrupting. 'And Mum and Dad really contacted the police? Why? I left them a note and everything.'

'A note? You leave home and bunk off school without telling anyone where you're going, and you expect them to get happy over a note? Jess, hello! The cops were round my house last night. My mother went mental when she heard about Saffron and the texts. She said we both should have told your mum what was going on. I told her we couldn't tell her *everything* or she'd, like, have a heart attack.'

Jess giggled. 'You didn't say that, did you?' she said.

'Well, I was upset,' protested Steph. 'I was worried about you. I kept phoning you all day and you never answered. Where are you anyway?'

Jess told her.

'And your mum and dad are coming to pick you up?' Steph asked.

'Yeah,' said Jess. 'You're probably right – they will kill me or ground me for the rest of my life.'

'Did you phone Oliver?' asked Steph.

'How can I after everything?' Jess said.

'Because if the police were round my house yesterday, they were probably round Oliver's too, so he knows you're missing and he'll be worried about you too,' Steph pointed out.

Jess cringed. 'I never thought of that,' she admitted. 'I left a note to avoid all this hassle,' she added. 'I said I was just going to go away for a little while. I didn't think they'd do all this.'

'Phone Oliver now,' advised Steph. 'Because when your mum and dad get hold of you, all phone privileges will be revoked and you'll never be able to talk to him again to apologise. Actually, I'll buy you a pigeon, 'cos that'll be the only way you'll ever be able to communicate with the outside world.'

'This is not cheering me up,' Jess warned.

'That's what friends are for,' Steph said happily. 'I'd better go, the bell's just gone.'

Jess knew Oliver's timetable as well as she knew her own. At this time of the day, he had applied maths. She rang his phone, assuming that it would be off and that she could leave a message for him. She wasn't sure what she was going to say, but sorry was going to be a big part of it.

To her surprise, Oliver answered the phone on the second ring.

'Jess!' he said.

Taken aback, Jess stammered, 'Er . . . hello, Oliver. I didn't think you'd answer. You've applied maths now, don't you?'

'How can I sit in applied maths when you're missing?' Oliver demanded.

'I'm not missing any more,' Jess said. 'I just went away for a little time on my own.' It sounded a bit lame put that way. 'I'm sorry, Oliver,' she said, 'sorry for the other night. I was a stupid bitch, I know I was.'

'You're OK, though, aren't you?' he asked.

'Fine,' Jess replied. 'Did you have the police round your house last night too?'

'Yes,' he said. 'If you'd stayed missing, I'm sure they would have come back and searched the place. And if they'd found that baseball bat with all the blood on it, then I'd really have been in trouble,' he joked.

'Oh, Oliver, I'm so sorry,' Jess said. This running away thing made for a lot of apologising. 'I'll make it up to you. Well,' she added, 'I will if I'm ever allowed out of the house again. Steph reckons my parents are going to completely kill me or ground me for ever for this.'

'Bet you they won't,' Oliver said. 'They'll be so glad to have you home. Like I will,' he added.

Jess felt herself go pink with pleasure. 'You'll still be glad to have me home, after everything?' she asked.

'What do you think? But you'll have to tell me what happened the other night, anyway. I was going mad when

I couldn't find you and all I had was this daft text message. I got a taxi to your mum's, but all the lights were off and I didn't want to ring the doorbell and wake everyone. I didn't know what to do – I was so worried in case you hadn't got home.'

'You came to my house on Saturday night?'

'Yeah.'

'Oh, Oliver,' she said, a lump in her throat. 'That's so sweet. I can't wait to see you.'

At the hostel gate, there was an old tree stump that made a surprisingly good seat. Jess sat down upon it and waited for her parents to arrive. She'd idled away an hour and a half making herself breakfast in the shabby hostel kitchen and now she thought she'd like to sit outside. Steph was right: they *would* kill her, she thought. How could she explain that it seemed like a good idea at the time, that she hadn't planned to frighten them by running off but that everything had seemed so awful and getting away had felt like the only sensible plan? Neither Mum nor Dad would understand.

Steph kept sending texts on Jess's mobile: 'Are they there yet?' 'Be brave. Text me when you've seen them.' 'Did you talk to hunky Oliver?'

None of the messages made Jess feel too confident. The police had gone round to all her friends' houses to see if they might know where she'd gone. Imagine how upset Mum and Dad must have been to get the police involved.

But in spite of her misery, there was an oasis of happiness in Jess's heart – Oliver had forgiven her and she couldn't wait to see him. She felt so stupid when she thought of the party and how she'd jumped to conclusions. Steph had been right: the only way to deal with the likes of Saffron was to ignore her. She'd hate that.

Jess was busily thinking of just how she'd stare right through the other girl whenever she saw her, when she realised that her mum's Jeep was coming up the road.

'Oh God, how am I going to cope with this?' Jess muttered to herself. They would kill her.

The Jeep pulled to a stop right beside her. Dad was driving, and almost before he'd turned the engine off, the passenger door opened and Mum leaped out.

'Oh, Jess, Jess,' gasped Abby. 'Thank God you're safe. We've been so worried about you. Come here, let me look at you. Are you all right? Are you sure you're all right?'

She threw her arms round Jess and held her tightly. Jess allowed herself to sink into her mother's embrace and suddenly, feeling her mother shaking with emotion, she realised the full weight of what she'd put her parents through.

'I'm really sorry, Mum,' she said and started to cry. 'I didn't mean to hurt you. I just needed to get away on my own for a while because . . . because of so many things.'

Suddenly Dad was there too, with his arms around both Mum and Jess, hugging them.

'We're sorry, Jess,' he said, and his voice sounded all weird and croaky. 'We're sorry for what *we've* put you through. We've been so selfish, thinking of ourselves and not of you, but you should have told us how you felt and you should have told us about the bullying.'

'Yes,' interrupted Abby fiercely, 'if I get that girl Saffron, I'll bloody kill her! In fact, we're going round to her house to confront her and her parents, I can tell you that.'

'No, don't,' said Jess quickly. 'It wasn't really Saffron's fault that I ran away. It was just – everything. Everything got on top of me.'

'Well, we're going to sort it all out,' her mother said firmly, wiping her eyes.

'But the police . . .' began Jess, wondering how much trouble she was in.

'They're glad you're safe,' said Tom. 'We phoned the family liaison officer after you phoned us and they're just relieved. I said you hadn't meant to cause any upset and that we'd talk to you.'

'Sorry, sorry,' said Jess, feeling even worse now.

'There was a tiny bit about you in some of the papers,' Dad said, 'but you didn't actually make last night's TV news.'

'The TV news?' asked Jess, shocked.

'You disappeared,' her mother explained. 'The police took it very seriously, thank God.'

'But that's why I left the note,' Jess groaned. 'I told you I'd be all right and I'd phone.'

'You're under eighteen,' her father said. 'That's enough to get the police searching for you, and I'm glad they did. I don't know how your mother and I would have coped if we hadn't had their back-up.'

'I am so sorry,' Jess said again.

'We all are,' Dad said. 'We know you're under a lot of pressure and that's our fault too.' He put Jess's rucksack in the back of the Jeep and they all climbed in. 'How about some lunch?' he suggested. 'I'm ravenous. Your mum and I haven't eaten for ages.'

'That sounds like a brilliant idea,' said Jess. She was hungry too, which was odd, because, earlier, she'd felt all nervy and like she was going to lose her breakfast. Now, strangely enough, she felt as if she could eat.

'Where to?' asked Mum cheerfully.

In the back seat, Jess watched in astonishment as her dad reached out and grasped her mum's hand.

And they exchanged the sort of glance Jess hadn't seen in a very long time. She sat back and said nothing, afraid that speaking might break this magical moment. Could Mum and Dad be getting back together? She hardly dared to hope. They found a cheap and cheerful restaurant not far from the hostel and the three of them piled in. Immediately, the smell of chips filled the air. The three of them sat down, and Jess noticed that her mum's hand found her dad's under the table. She had to say something.

'I know I'm in terrible trouble and I'm going to be grounded for ever and have my pocket money taken away and have my kneecaps nailed to the floor,' she joked, 'but could you treat me like an adult long enough to tell me something?' She looked meaningfully at her parents' clasped hands.

Abby's other hand reached over the table and grabbed her daughter's.

'We've been the stupid ones, Jess,' she said. 'Not you. All you did was run away when things got a bit tough. We ran away for a lot longer. You were only gone twenty-four hours. Your dad and I ran away from each other and from reality for months.'

'And it's thanks to you that we've realised it, Jess,' said Dad soberly. 'I've been thinking so hard about what you told me at Caroline's – I haven't exactly been the perfect husband, have I?'

Abby listened quietly.

'She told me some home truths,' he went on, speaking to Abby now, 'about how I'd resented your career, Abby. You told me the same thing and you're both right. I did and I'm sorry. You were working for all of us to have a better life and I got caught up in my own petty jealousies over that.'

He looked over at her mother and Jess was thrilled to see that it was the loving way he used to. For so long, they'd glared at each other, with Mum giving Dad her laser eyes and Dad staring angrily back, his face taut and cynical. It was different now – he looked the way he used to look years ago. He looked like he loved Mum again.

'So, it's all down to me?' Jess enquired cheekily.

Her mother laughed loudly. Jess hadn't heard that sound for a long time either.

'It's all down to you,' repeated her mum, 'but don't think you're going to get off the hook, madam,' she added, waggling her index finger at her daughter in a pretend menacing manner. 'You've no idea how worried we were. Just think: in a few hours, we were going to have an alert on all the news bulletins saying you were missing.'

Jess cringed at the thought. 'I didn't want you to go to all that bother of calling the police or anything.'

'I know you didn't,' said her mother, 'and I know you're

587

sixteen and capable of looking after yourself but you've never been away from home on your own like that without us knowing exactly where you were, so we were worried, really worried. Please don't ever do it again.'

'I won't, I promise,' said Jess, 'but only if you guys promise not to stress me out, either!'

'Peace, peace,' begged Tom. 'Let's order.'

But Jess wanted to be sure that things were going back to normal. 'Are you moving back home, Dad?' she asked bluntly. 'You're not getting a divorce any more?'

Her parents looked at each other. In the time they'd spent together worrying about Jess, they hadn't actually talked about Tom moving back in or about calling the lawyers off. During the night, it was enough that they were close again, talking the way they used to. Abby waited to see what Tom would say. She remembered how he'd behaved before when she'd asked him to move back. She'd never forget how painful that had been. He'd thrown her suggestion back in her face and more or less told her that hell would freeze over before he'd do such a thing. Worse, he'd refused to take any responsibility for the problems in their marriage.

Until now. She could barely believe the admission of guilt he'd made but it was still up to him to make the move. She'd let him know that she loved him and that she'd love to have their marriage back. But he still had to realise that it took two people to break up a marriage – and two to fix it.

Abby could see the waitress bearing down on them. In a moment she'd be there, ready to break the spell.

'I'd love to move back in,' Tom said, adding, more hesitantly, 'if your mother will have me. Will you, Abby?' he asked quietly.

'Are youse ready to order?' asked the waitress.

Abby looked at her husband and daughter, her exhausted face split with a wonderful smile.

'Yes,' she said, from the heart.

'Well, what do you want?' the waitress went on, pen poised over her pad.

The three members of the Barton family grinned at each other. Jess realised that her parents were too choked to speak, so she did it for them.

'Chips all round,' she said, 'and three vegetarian pizzas.'

CHAPTER THIRTY-FOUR

Lizzie was finding that living with Debra was not getting any easier. Since the disastrous meeting of the two families, there didn't appear to be any hope of a reconciliation between Debra and Barry, and Lizzie was learning the hard way that even mentioning him caused tears.

'I just think you ought to meet him, that's all I'm saying,' she would soothe. 'Not that he was right and you were wrong.'

'You don't understand,' sobbed Debra. 'He lied to me. He told me he loved me on our wedding day and now it turns out he didn't even want to be there. I can't forgive him for that. He betrayed me and he did it publicly. How can we go back now? Tell me that.'

Her mother couldn't answer.

The only things that would cheer Debra up were shopping and going out in the evenings. Her mother, though usually tired after work and with the fund-raising she was doing with Erin in memory of Sally, was expected to provide both the entertainment – whether it was going to a pub or a restaurant, or just getting in a takeaway and a video – and the finance. As their hectic social life went on Lizzie found her bank balance suffered correspondingly. The night-time cosmetic party sales looked increasingly like her only option to make ends meet – either that, or sell her body, and she couldn't imagine that being a particularly lucrative business, given the state of it.

Worse, her fiftieth birthday was looming at the end of

September and she'd done hardly any of the life-changing 'Things to Do . . .' things she'd planned. So much for chatting men up just for the hell of it or doing something mad. The parachute jump had been her one and only dash for excitement, and she hadn't been back. Gorgeous Simon would think she'd been teasing him. She knew she ought to ring him, but she just couldn't pluck up the courage. He'd have been perfectly justified in slamming down the phone, seeing as how she'd ignored him so spectacularly for ages. And what was the point of phoning him to apologise or make up when Debra obviously still needed her? So she tried not to think about him at all, because if she did, if she remembered how they'd got on so brilliantly and how she'd felt so attracted to him, then she felt overwhelmed by a sense of loss.

After years of thinking she'd never meet a man she fancied or who fancied her, she had, and she'd managed to screw it up.

'We could go to the new restaurant on Castle Street tonight,' suggested Debra one Thursday evening when Lizzie had had a particularly long day and wanted nothing more than to collapse in front of the soaps. 'I believe the food's gorgeous.'

'OK,' said her mother, who'd just got home after a speedy after-work trip to the supermarket to stock up. She shoved the chicken pieces she'd bought for that evening's dinner into the fridge and stowed the rest of the shopping, wondering how she was going to squash her feet back into her shoes to go out. The postman had delivered two bills that morning: one a jaw-dropping phone bill, and the other an outrageous electricity demand.

The phone rang and Debra leaped at it. As it was so rarely for her nowadays, Lizzie kept unpacking shopping and was almost surprised when Debra yelled, 'It's Aunt Gwen for you.'

Gwen didn't usually phone twice in one day, thought Lizzie, who'd spoken to her sister earlier from work. Gwen was a very comforting person to talk to these days. There were none of the heavy silences there were with Debra where Lizzie weighed up every word in case she said the wrong thing. With Gwen, if you said something tactless, she'd shout with laughter and never take offence.

'Shay's gone to his poker night and I thought I might drop in to see you and cheer you up,' said Gwen. 'You said you were staying in.'

'Well, we're going out to dinner in town, now, actually,' Lizzie said, hating herself for being shown to be such a wimp. Earlier, she'd told Gwen how exhausted she was, and about the murderous bills.

There was a silence at the other end of the phone, a Gwen silence that Lizzie could translate easily after forty-nine years of practice: You're tired, you're broke and now you're going out because Debra wants to and you won't say no to her, it went.

'I might come along myself,' Gwen announced.

Piggy in the middle, thought Lizzie with a groan. That was all she needed.

The new restaurant was booked out, so Gwen led the way into the pub next door, the Rock's Tavern, a spit-and-sawdust venue with an American ranch theme – waitresses dressed in cowgirl outfits, and plenty of country music playing in the background.

'What a lovely place,' Gwen said, settling herself down happily at a table. She then went on to commit what were in Debra's eyes two enormous social solecisms: one, by slipping her tired feet out of their flat shoes and putting them up on the bars of a nearby chair, and two, by ordering a glass of stout.

Debra, whose current shoe fetish meant she was sporting yet another pair of new sandals in honour of the posh new restaurant, stared at her aunt in horror. Debra would never have dreamed of ordering something like a glass of Murphys, and as for sticking slightly swollen, unmanicured toes out in public, well . . . she was horrified.

But Gwen didn't appear to notice her niece's discontent – or if she did, she didn't give a damn.

'Isn't this the life?' sighed Gwen, sitting back and taking a deep slug of her stout. 'I don't get out on my own often enough, do you know that, girls?' she said. 'Maybe I should take a leaf out of your book, Debra, and leave poor ould Shay so I could go off on girls' nights out.'

Lizzie stifled a giggle at the thought of Shay abandoned while Gwen embraced the single life. Debra, on the other hand, looked disgusted at the thought of her aunt considering acting like a twenty-something.

Gwen and Lizzie both ordered chips and sausages in a basket, but Debra found there was nothing on the menu that she wanted to eat. Perfectly happy to eat big fried breakfasts at home, she liked healthier, trendier food when she was out.

'There's nothing here I like,' she said, a tad petulantly, as she scanned through a menu made up of steak sandwiches and deep-fried everything with chips. 'This is all swimming in cholesterol,' she complained. 'I don't know why we had to come here instead of a proper restaurant.'

Gwen took another meditative sip of her drink. 'It's far from fancy restaurants you were reared, my girl. Are you the same one who expects her mother to make her big cooked breakfasts every weekend?'

Lizzie gulped. She hadn't meant to bitch to Gwen about Debra's childish insistence on a weekend fry-up routine but she must have done. Now Debra would sulk and the evening would be ruined.

But Debra was smart enough to take more criticism from her aunt than she would have from her mother. 'Once a week it's all right to eat that sort of junk,' she said loftily.

'So you'll wolf down fried food if your poor mother buys it *and* cooks it, but you're too posh to eat it on a night out, is that it?' demanded Gwen.

'No,' began Debra.

'And while we're on the subject of buying food,' said

Gwen, getting into her stride, 'when are you going to start paying your mother for staying with her? She's feeding you, and you eat like a prize pig for all your moaning about cholesterol.'

Lizzie winced, but there was no stopping her sister when she'd started.

'She's paying the electricity bill, the heating bill, the mortgage, you name it, and you still expect her to get up out of her bed on a Sunday morning and cook you your breakfast. When is that going to change, Debra?'

'Oh . . . I . . .' stammered Debra.

'Well, you might say "Oh, I",' retorted Gwen. 'It's about time somebody had this out with you, my girl. I'd be ashamed if you were my child. You have your poor mother run into the ground looking after you, and she's broke. Do you know she's been thinking of taking a second job just to make ends meet? And why is that?' Gwen paused for dramatic effect. 'Because she spent every penny she owned on your bloody wedding and now she's letting you leech off her when you earn a good wage.'

Lizzie couldn't bear to do more than glance at Debra. Her daughter looked the same way she had at the disastrous Cronin/Shanahan reconciliation dinner.

'Ah, Gwen, don't say anything more,' Lizzie begged her sister.

'You're too soft on her, Lizzie,' Gwen said sharply. 'I'm saying all this for your own good too. I've held my tongue for months now but something has to be done. Look at her here tonight, sitting like Lady Muck, not even able to put her hand in her pocket and buy us a drink, and then turning her nose up at the food here.'

'I didn't,' protested Debra.

'You did,' said Gwen. 'You're spoilt, Debra, that's your trouble. You're upset over Barry and you want to make sure everyone else is upset too. Isn't that why you threw a tantrum when your poor mother brought her new man back to the house?'

Lizzie held her breath, waiting for Debra to attack her and demand to know why Gwen had heard about this. But Debra was silent.

'I shouldn't have done that,' she admitted slowly.

'No, you bloody well shouldn't,' snapped Gwen. 'How dare you interfere in your mother's life? Doesn't she deserve some happiness of her own?'

'I was upset and worried –'

'. . . About yourself. If your mother had a man, you wouldn't be numero uno in her life any more, that's more like it,' Gwen said. 'It's about time you grew up, Debra. Your mother never says a word against you and you're using her. It's got to stop. What if you got back with Barry? I bet you'd rush off and not bother to think that you were leaving your mother alone, having scuppered her chance to have a life with this man.'

'I didn't –' began Debra.

'Why is it that all your sentences begin with "I"?' said Gwen with chilling accuracy. 'I, I, I. You never think of anyone else.'

'I'm sorry, Mum,' said Debra, beginning to cry.

'Cut the tears out,' warned Gwen. 'Stop treating your mother like a doormat or you'll have me to answer to.'

'But I am sorry.'

'Being sorry is about more than just saying it,' her aunt said. 'It's about demonstrating it.'

'But she's never said anything to me,' Debra went on.

'Because she loves you and she doesn't want to hurt you,' Gwen said. 'And because you love only yourself, you let her.'

'I'm sorry, Mum, I'm really sorry. I didn't think,' sobbed Debra, and for once it sounded heartfelt. 'I love you and I'd never hurt you.' She got up, tears falling down her pretty face. 'I'm going to the loo.'

Lizzie went to get up with her but Gwen held her back. 'Let her go,' she said. 'You can't protect her from everything, Lizzie, especially not herself. She has to grow up and realise that other people have to be treated with respect.'

Lizzie sat down again and sighed. 'You were too hard on her,' she said.

'I wasn't. You're too soft on her, Lizzie. God rest our poor departed mother, but she has a lot to answer for. She made you so scared of being tough that you've let Debra get away with everything her whole life. That's just as bad as being too hard on her. There's a happy medium.'

'She's so upset,' Lizzie went on unhappily.

'Debra's a lot tougher than you give her credit for, Lizzie. She's young enough to change and if she doesn't learn now, she never will. If she's hard and selfish her whole life, is that going to make her happy?'

'No,' admitted Lizzie.

Debra came back to the table after a few minutes, her face still tear-stained. 'This isn't going to be much of a girls' night out if we're all arguing,' she said shakily. She squeezed her mother's hand and managed to smile at her aunt. 'Are you ready for another round?'

'You're paying?' enquired Gwen.

Debra had the grace to blush. 'Yes,' she said.

Life Beats Cancer had been very encouraging about Lizzie's idea to get lots of people to do parachute jumps in aid of the charity, so Erin arranged a meeting with the co-ordinator at the Santa Monica airfield to organise it.

She had planned to go along with Lizzie, who was feeling very nervous about possibly bumping into Simon, on one of Lizzie's Wednesday afternoons off but, at the last minute, Erin had to cry off.

'My blood pressure's only a teeny bit up,' she told Lizzie on the phone, 'so I don't know why the doctor wants me to stay in bed.'

'Should I phone Greg and tell him to nail the duvet to the floor with you stuck in the bed?' teased Lizzie, who knew just how hard Erin found it to sit still.

'I've so much to do,' wailed Erin, thinking of the sheaf of papers she'd been working on so diligently and all the plans that required careful nurturing. Thankfully, someone had now been found to cover Erin's maternity leave in the beauty salon, so at least that wasn't taking up her energy now.

'We're in this charity business for the long haul,' Lizzie reminded her. 'You lying in bed for a couple of days won't put the kibosh on everything.'

'I know, but I'm leaving you to do so much of it all, Lizzie,' Erin pointed out.

And it was true: Erin's energy levels meant she was confined to making phone calls rather than trekking round visiting the great and good of Dunmore, trying to get them involved in the proposed Sally Richardson Centre. And since both Jess and Tom had returned to Lyonnais, Abby had understandably been spending a lot of time with her family.

'I'll be back helping soon, I promise,' she vowed to both Erin and Lizzie, 'but we could do with this time as a family. It's so lovely to wake up in the mornings and know that they're both there with me.'

The one thing Abby wasn't too busy to do was help Erin with organising a surprise fiftieth birthday party for Lizzie, although she didn't mention that bit of planning to Lizzie. Anyhow, organising a party was hardly hard work, and she was having fun bouncing ideas for it off Tom and Jess.

Lizzie totally understood that Abby had other things on her mind. Looking after your family – no matter what that meant exactly, Lizzie thought ruefully, thinking about Gwen getting tough with Debra – was a number-one priority.

But the fact that Erin and Abby were otherwise engaged meant that the donkey work was falling to Lizzie. Fortunately she loved it.

For this job, her natural empathy and kindness were the perfect assets. Nobody could look into Lizzie's warm eyes as she told them about the plans for the centre and then tell her that their company or business didn't want to get involved.

'Once you wedge your foot in the door, Lizzie, they can't say no to you,' said Abby gleefully when Lizzie reported back about an interview with the legendarily stony manager of Dunmore's Victorian Hotel. It had somehow ended up with Lizzie getting a tour of the banqueting facilities and a commitment to give the Sally Richardson/LBC charity a seventy-five per cent discount on the ballroom hire for their first big event.

'How did you manage it?' asked Erin in awe. 'That guy is supposed to be as hard as nails. I was advised not to bother even talking to him and to try one of the other hotels instead.'

'Lizzie has charm, eyes nobody can say no to, and she's gorgeous,' teased Abby. 'That's her secret.'

'Stop it,' retorted Lizzie good-naturedly.

'They all fall for her, Erin,' Abby went on. 'None of these captains of industry can quite believe it when lovely Lizzie appears before them and they'd sell their grannies to please her.'

'They wouldn't,' said Lizzie, who was flattered that someone as glamorous as Abby would even think such a thing, but who didn't for one second believe that her success with men on the fund-raising trail was anything to do with her personally.

'I'm only teasing,' Abby added. 'But that guy in the Victorian is well known for being a tough cookie, so well done. You're brilliant at convincing people to help us.'

Lizzie smiled. There was no way she was going to tell the girls that the man had held her hand slightly longer than necessary when saying goodbye, or that he'd pointedly said it might be an idea if she came to the hotel one night for dinner so they could talk over the event.

She wasn't even a teeny bit interested in him. She sighed. There was only one man she was keen on seeing again and she hoped, when she went out to the Santa Monica flying school, that she would.

On the Wednesday concerned she took ages getting ready. It was a business meeting, after all, but there was nothing wrong with looking nice, was there? She changed into a pink silky sweater over slim navy trousers, hoping she'd managed to combine professional with approachable. Her hair was a bit sticky-out, though: some of Debra's anti-frizz stuff might work.

In Debra's room, a pile of nearly packed suitcases and a cardboard box full of odds and ends were testimony that her daughter planned to move out at the weekend. Her friend Frieda's flatmate had got a six-month job abroad, so Debra was taking her room in the interim.

Debra and Barry's beautiful town house was to be rented out. It was more sensible that way, Debra said, as they'd never make any money selling it yet and it would be an investment for both of them.

'I'd hate to get rid of it, anyhow – does that sound silly?' Debra had said when she'd told her mother of the plan.

Lizzie had shaken her head. It made perfect sense. She was proud of the way Debra was facing up to things nowadays, but she still had a private hope that time and distance would help her daughter and Barry to sort out their differences.

Barry had even come round one night to talk about renting the house out, and the atmosphere of his visit had been light years away from that of the last time he and Debra had met. Debra had managed to be polite and businesslike with him, although she'd cried in her mother's arms after he'd left.

'I'm sorry, Mum,' she'd said, wiping her eyes. 'I didn't mean to let you and Dad down by all of this. I'm so sorry.'

In the midst of her anguish for the pain Debra was going through, Lizzie felt irritation at herself for how she'd dealt with her daughter over the years. If only she and Myles hadn't indulged Debra so much, then things might be different. It was a pity that Debra was having to grow up now, at the age of twenty-three. Gwen's savage talking–to hadn't devastated Debra in the way Lizzie had been scared it would; instead, it had made the girl sit up and take notice of how she had been behaving.

'She won't change overnight,' Gwen had said when Lizzie

reported back how much easier it was living with her daughter since that night in the Rock's Tavern. But the new, improved Debra was a far cry from the moody, childish version of the past couple of months.

In a big bag of cosmetics on Debra's dressing table, Lizzie found the anti-frizz stuff and did her best to flatten her tortoiseshell mop into some semblance of sobriety.

She added lipgloss that went with the sweater, then rubbed it off in case it looked too obvious.

Of course, she mightn't see Simon at all, but if she did, she wanted to look nice – though not as if she'd tried too hard.

Gwen rang just as she was rushing out of the door.

'Hi, Lizzie,' said Gwen. 'What are you up to?'

'I'm doing a bit of research for our charity,' Lizzie said, fudging it a bit.

'Oh, what?' said Gwen with interest. She was fascinated by the whole plan and had already offered her services.

'Erm . . . I'm going out to talk to the parachute centre people about setting up a weekend solely for our charity,' Lizzie admitted, knowing full well that Gwen would make the connection.

'Oh,' said Gwen, naughtiness in her voice. 'That's where that delicious Simon fellow works, isn't it? Have you got your full war paint on?'

'Stop it, Gwen,' warned Lizzie, glad her sister couldn't see her, because Lizzie's face was going a becoming shade of pink to match her sweater. 'He's just someone I met, it doesn't mean anything. Today's about the charity. Anyway,' she added, as if this was the final clincher, 'I'm too old to be going out on dates.'

'Is that Debra speaking or Lizzie?' asked Gwen intuitively.

'It's common sense speaking,' said Lizzie crossly, sorry that she'd ever told Gwen about Simon and their abortive date.

'Common sense my backside,' said Gwen pithily.

Lizzie was shocked. Gwen was not a woman to veer into the lexicon of rudeness.

'What's wrong with a woman of your age going on a date?' demanded Gwen. 'You've got all your faculties, all your own teeth, and they aren't holding a bed for you in the old folk's home yet, as far as I know. Not that that's any indication, either,' she added. 'Look at Myra who used to live beside me. She went into Shady Pines home full of misery about her poor departed Howard and how she wouldn't be long following him into the next world, and I just heard she's getting married next month to Oswald, this man she met in basket weaving. You're never too old,' Gwen finished her homily.

'How lovely for Myra,' said Lizzie. 'I must send her a card.'

'Don't let Debra's views cloud yours,' Gwen went on. 'Anyway, if she is a changed woman, she's big enough and ugly enough to look after herself and leave you to your own life.'

'She is,' protested Lizzie. 'It's this weekend she's moving out and she's apologised for everything. She really has turned over a new leaf.'

'Hmmph,' snorted Gwen. 'I hope so, or she's going to get another lecture from me. Is this Simon going to be there today?'

'I doubt it,' said Lizzie nonchalantly, as if she hadn't dressed up for the express purpose of seeing him.

'Well, if you see him, apologise for not ever phoning him back and ask him out.'

'Ask him out?' The whole world had gone mad, Lizzie decided, when her respectable sister Gwen was telling her to ask men out. 'I can't do that,' Lizzie said. Then, she remembered her 'Things to Do . . .' list still crumpled up in her handbag. Asking a man out was on the list. Mind you, so was buying yourself expensive jewellery and she hadn't managed to do that either. She supposed she *could* ask him out but he probably wouldn't be interested. He'd been keen before but she'd ruined it all by backing off. It was unlikely that he'd even want to talk to her.

Two people carriers with business logos and a bus were parked in the flying school car park when she got there. Probably a corporate parachute day, she decided. There was lots of noise coming from the big hangar, which was where the students learned how to jump in harness. There were delighted screams and laughter every few moments as another person leaped from the platform thirty feet off the ground, practising the right way to flex their knees and break their fall. Lizzie felt a pang of envy for all that day's students – they were going to have the incredible experience of their first parachute jump. Lizzie would never forget that magical feeling of floating through the air like a bird. She'd love to do it all over again. Simon had said he'd do a tandem jump with her, but that was before the embarrassing encounter with Debra. What guy in his right mind would want to hook up with a woman whose family life was so awry that she couldn't even stand up for herself in front of her daughter?

When she went into the office, a small balding man she didn't recognise was behind the desk. He introduced himself as Trevor, and Lizzie explained about Erin not being able to come.

Trevor was all business and, over a cup of coffee, he outlined the way the centre operated group charity jumps. It was all very informative and, by the end of half an hour, Lizzie had found out everything she needed. But there had been no sign of any instructor she recognised.

'Thanks, Trevor,' she said as he walked her out to her car. 'We'll be in touch about the wording of the sponsorship cards and to agree a date that suits all of us.'

They said goodbye and, deflated, Lizzie got into her car and pulled the seat belt on. So much for beautifying herself. If destiny had anything to do with dating, then it was obvious that she wasn't meant to meet Simon again.

A tap on the window made her look up, expecting to see Trevor with some last-minute point to make. Instead, it was Simon.

He looked just the same as she remembered: the lean,

smiling face, and the eyes that glittered with some private amusement. Lizzie rolled down the window.

'Hi,' said Simon.

'Hello, how are you?' gasped Lizzie in return.

'Oh, fine,' he said, 'fine. You never got back to me.'

'Sorry,' said Lizzie penitently. 'It's just . . .'

'A difficult situation?' he asked. 'I got that feeling. I don't think your daughter was too pleased to find me there.'

'No,' agreed Lizzie. 'She wasn't. She was a bit out of her depth.'

'I hope I didn't make things difficult for you.'

'Oh, you didn't,' protested Lizzie. She felt so ashamed of herself because Simon hadn't made things difficult – Debra had done that. But because Lizzie hadn't had the courage to confront her daughter, she'd messed up things with this lovely man.

'It was all my fault,' she said abruptly. 'Debra couldn't cope with her father and me getting divorced and she couldn't cope with me seeing anybody either. Not that I have seen anybody else,' she added hastily, lest Simon think that she had a stream of strange men running through the house all the time.

The glimmer of a smile touched Simon's mouth – his sexy mouth, Lizzie thought, an unfamiliar tingle starting deep in her belly. 'Anyway,' she went on before her courage failed her, 'I'm really sorry I didn't ring. It wasn't that I didn't want to – it was just I was so engulfed by family problems. Things are much better now, but I felt embarrassed to phone after so long.'

'I understand,' he said easily. 'I didn't want to phone and hassle you.'

She beamed up at him. 'And I thought you'd gone off me,' she said in a teasing voice.

He shook his head and looked right at her. 'Not at all.'

'I came out here today to talk to Trevor about a group charity jump,' Lizzie went on, 'and I have to confess, I hoped I'd see you here.' There, she'd said it: she had told him the truth.

Simon slouched comfortably against the car. 'I was just leaving for the day,' he said. 'Do you fancy a return trip to Jimmy's Seafood Shack for a quick bite to eat?'

'I can't think of anything I'd like more,' Lizzie said. 'Why don't we go in my car?'

As they drove to Jimmy's, Lizzie felt she owed Simon more of an explanation. 'Debra's been through a lot,' she sighed. 'She broke up with her husband, Barry, and I suppose I didn't want to push her too far by introducing a man into the mix. You got caught in the middle, Simon. I'm really sorry.'

'Hey, you don't have to apologise to me,' he said. 'We had our problems with Adam, my son . . . Families can be tricky things.'

'Yeah,' said Lizzie.

They talked some more, with Lizzie briefly assuring him that things were OK with Debra now. What Lizzie really liked was the fact that Simon just listened and didn't try to give her unasked-for advice on what she should or shouldn't have done with Debra, her life, or anything. He had his son, Adam, and could probably have offered some ideas of his own on children and divorce, but he seemed to understand that Lizzie was fed up with other people's opinions.

'You're very easy to be with,' she said as they reached Jimmy's Seafood Shack. 'You don't tell me what to do like everyone else does.'

'Do you like people telling you what to do?' he asked.

'No,' Lizzie said, 'actually I don't. I've had a lifetime of it but I can't stand it.'

'That's good then,' he replied. 'We should get on like a house on fire.'

Jimmy's was busy even though it was early, but Jimmy himself found a cosy corner for Lizzie and Simon.

'You're a regular customer?' Lizzie asked idly, wondering if Simon brought lots of women here.

'A big gang of us from the club come here most weekends,'

he said, obviously understanding what she was getting at. 'If Jimmy's eyes are out on stalks looking at you, it's because he's never seen me here with a woman on my own before.'

'And I thought I'd managed to be subtle,' laughed Lizzie.

'Subtlety is overrated,' he replied, smiling back at her.

At that moment, Lizzie's mobile rang. 'Sorry,' she apologised as she fished it out of her bag. She looked at the display pad: Debra.

'Hello,' she said.

'Hi, Mum, I was just wondering where you are,' said Debra. 'I went to the supermarket and got some of that mushroom pasta you like. I thought we could have a nice dinner with me cooking for a change.'

'I'm afraid I won't be home,' Lizzie said, staring at Simon. 'I'm out for dinner with Simon, remember, from the parachute jump centre?'

There was a pause. 'Go for it, Mum,' said Debra.

The tension left Lizzie's face and her eyes sparkled as she looked across at Simon.

'Thanks, love,' she said.

CHAPTER THIRTY-FIVE

On the day of Lizzie's surprise fiftieth birthday party, Erin began to worry that the whole affair wouldn't have quite the sparkle that Sally and Steve's legendary parties used to have.

'Ruby keeps getting all misty-eyed telling me about them,' she said to Abby. 'That one where you all did the conga and the police were called sounds great. Some people have the knack of giving parties effortlessly. Me, I keep waking up in the middle of the night worrying about it all – should we have just gone for a dinner party instead of a huge bash here? Not that I'm saying a word against the house, Abby: it's gorgeous, it's just . . . I'm anxious . . .'

They were taking a quick break in the kitchen at Lyonnais, where all day Saturday the combined talents of Abby, Tom, Erin, Greg, Jess, Steph, Oliver, Ruby and Gwen had transformed the huge downstairs of the house into a balloon- and fairy-light-filled bower with a giant banner (carefully painted by Steph who was the most artistic among them) proclaiming 'Happy Birthday Lizzie' in pink letters. The terrace was going to be pressed into service too, but because the late September weather couldn't be relied upon, Abby had begged patio heaters and a terrace canopy from friends. Tom was in charge of drinks and was treating the utility room like his own personal fiefdom, complete with a borrowed freezer jammed with ice, a keg of beer, boxes of wine, and a whole case of champagne paid for by Lizzie's son, Joe, who was flying over from London with his girlfriend later that afternoon.

'Nonsense, Erin,' said Abby calmly. 'If you're worried, it's just pregnancy, I promise you. No wonder you can't sleep with that bouncing baby wriggling away inside you as soon as you lie down! Everything is going to be fine and this is going to be a party to remember.'

And she meant it. Since the whole trauma of Jess running away, Abby found that her ability to worry had miraculously decreased. It was as if the genuine terror of Jess being missing had shown her what real anxiety was all about.

Tom was the same. Like survivors of some near-catastrophe, they could appreciate every moment of calm for what it was and didn't obsess any more about what might happen. Of course, the air of tranquillity also owed a lot to her reconciliation with Tom.

Nothing was like it had been before, but then it hadn't been perfect before, Abby now realised. Their relationship was deeper, stronger and more honest than it had been for years. They didn't just go through the motions of discussing how they felt: instead, they really talked.

She and Tom had gone to see her psychologist together and, somehow, the waiting room with its posters about family mediation didn't seem the dismal, hopeless place she'd thought it was now that she had Tom by her side.

To her utter surprise, Tom had entered into the whole marriage counselling thing with relish. After the first couple of sessions, where he'd sat as stiffly as if he was anticipating a wisdom tooth extraction without a shot of novocaine, he'd begun to open up until, suddenly, it was as if he'd suggested counselling.

'You're turning into Woody Allen,' she teased him one evening after a session when he wanted to continue talking about how his own family set-up – deeply traditional, working father, home-maker mother – had fixed his mental goalposts on what marriage should be.

'I have more hair than Woody Allen,' said Tom smugly.

'Not hard, that,' Abby joked, ruffling his abundant mop.

'What if Simon can't get Lizzie here on time tonight, or if

she works it out and the surprise is ruined?' said Erin to Abby now, hating herself for sounding like a moaning Minnie.

The whole plan to surprise Lizzie was a delicate piece of engineering. It depended on a series of events working out, culminating in Simon and Lizzie dropping in to Lyonnais to see Jess's new puppy, a baby Jack Russell named Kim, before they went out to dinner with a small group of family and friends. Anything could go wrong, Erin thought.

Honestly, she never used to be like this. She'd been a highly paid human resources executive once, and most of the time she was an organised woman who was planning the Dunmore Life Beats Cancer centre fund-raising with military precision. For the past few days, she'd been jittery and anxious, and she and Greg had even argued about the grouting in the shower of the main bathroom, which had gone all grey, despite Erin scrubbing at it the night before with an old toothbrush.

'This is a new apartment,' she'd said, hot and bothered from crouching in the bath, scrubbing. 'This is an absolute disgrace.'

'Erin, honey, you don't have to do this,' Greg tried to tell her. 'I'll do it,' he added, although he couldn't really see much difference between the supposedly dirty grouting and the clean stuff.

'No, I'll do it,' said Erin fiercely.

'OK,' he said.

He'd read the chapters in their book about the last month of pregnancy but he still felt it didn't give half enough warning about how pregnancy could affect a woman. He'd talked to Kerry about it because he'd been so worried about this moody new Erin, but she'd told him to relax and that wild irritation was part and parcel of the whole process.

'Wait till she's had the baby and you're concentrating on three a.m. feeds,' Kerry had said soothingly.

'You mean it'll be easier then?' Greg had asked hopefully.

Kerry laughed. 'No, you big eejit, it'll be worse. But the

happiness will rub out the exhaustion, the sleep deprivation and the feeling that nothing you can do is right.'

'Thanks, Kerry,' groaned Greg. 'Boy, can you tell it like it is.'

'Sit down and mind Kim,' ordered Abby now, putting the tiny, wriggling Jack Russell puppy into Erin's arms. 'Practise soothing him.'

'Babies don't wriggle like puppies,' Erin said, as Kim struggled manfully to nibble her earlobes.

'Oh yes they do,' Abby laughed.

'Black bra or pink bra?' asked Steph, swivelling to see herself in Jess's mirror.

Jess, sitting cross-legged on the bed painting her toenails, looked up and examined her best friend critically.

'Pink is cooler, black looks a bit slutty.'

They both looked at the effect of the pink bra under the skinny pink rib top.

'OK, you can wear the black one and I'll wear the pink,' suggested Steph. 'Zach's used to seeing me in full slut gear but Oliver needs to see the hot and sexy side of you.'

'No, he doesn't,' retorted Jess, but she still tried on the black bra. Oliver had gone home to change before the party but it would still be nice if she could show him a more grown-up version of herself. She wasn't ready for anything else, though, and Oliver knew it.

'What's the story on this chat show job they want your mum to do?' Steph asked, seeing that Jess didn't want to talk about her and Oliver in that way.

'Mum says she'll only do it if Dad and I want her to.'

'Cool,' said Steph. 'So, d'ya want her to do it?'

'Yeah, she'd be good at it,' Jess said. 'Only she doesn't want to have to leave me and Dad here for the three days every week she'll need to be in Dublin.'

'I'd jump at the chance,' said Steph dreamily. 'Imagine that sort of TV show. She'd be really, really famous then.'

'There's more to life than being famous,' pointed out Jess.

'Like what?' demanded Steph.

They heard the doorbell ring.

'That'll be the first guests arriving,' said Jess, leaping off the bed and racing to the door. She was on door duty until Oliver and Zach turned up. 'Some day I'll tell you all the zillions of things that are more important than fame.'

'I won't believe you,' Steph called at her as Jess took the stairs two at a time. 'Fame is everything,' she sighed.

Opening the door, Jess grinned. She would never forget Steph's loyalty to her. Before Jess had returned to school, Steph had gone to the headmistress and spilled the beans on Saffron Walsh's behaviour. Mrs Doherty had been furious, particularly since the bullying had led to Jess running away and the police being called, and now Saffron's school career was hanging on the thread of future good behaviour. The once-untouchable Saffron was deeply shaken by it all and when she'd apologised to Jess, she actually seemed to mean it.

Steph was a great friend, Jess reflected, but she had mad ideas sometimes. If she thought that fame was everything, then Steph had a lot to learn.

Debra noticed the ring on Nina's left hand when Nina put her arms around Myles in the airport to greet him hello. Three diamonds on a band of white gold, it was delicately beautiful, just perfect for Nina's equally delicate hand.

'You're engaged!' exclaimed Debra, who was still having to work on what her Aunt Gwen caustically called her habit of speaking first and thinking afterwards.

'You're wasted in double glazing, sis,' said Joe wryly, giving his sister a hug. 'With your powers of observation, would you not think of joining the police?'

Debra gave him a mock punch on the shoulder. 'Hello to you too, big brother. Sorry, I didn't mean to ruin the surprise,' she added.

She was learning, slowly, not to take herself so seriously and to be more careful of others' feelings.

'Congratulations!' said Myles in delight, hugging Nina even more tightly. 'Show me this ring. Oh, it's beautiful, just beautiful. You're a dark horse,' he added proudly to his son.

'We didn't want to say anything tonight because this is Mum's night,' Joe pointed out.

'I'm going to take the ring off for the party because it would be awful to steal Lizzie's thunder on her birthday,' Nina said quickly. She'd meant to take it off on the plane but had forgotten – it amazed her that, after only a week, the ring and all it represented felt like such a part of her.

Myles shook his head. 'Don't,' he said. 'Lizzie's not a bit like that. She's the least prima donna-ish and most loving person I know. She'll be so thrilled for you both.'

Joe and Nina linked their fingers and beamed at each other.

Debra quenched a pang of envy. It wasn't their fault that she'd messed up her own marriage. She thought back to her engagement and wedding with more than a hint of guilt: it would never have occurred to her to remove her engagement ring at any point to save her mother from anything. She thought too of how she'd asked to invite Sabine to the wedding. That must have been hard on her mother, but Mum had dealt with it for Debra's sake.

Everyone in the big hall of Lyonnais was holding their breath, all except Kim, who didn't see why he couldn't yap happily. Just because Tom and Abby were welcoming Lizzie and Simon at the front door didn't mean he couldn't make some noise, and why were all these people standing silently, eyes glued to the porch door?

'Shush,' said Jess, kissing Kim's adorably soft little head. She loved his velvety chestnut-coloured ears. When he lay upside down, he looked like a naughty little bat, shining eyes full of mischief and bat ears dangling down.

Oliver tickled Kim's tummy and the puppy squirmed in delight.

Jack and Daniel Richardson stood beside Jess. They'd been promised sole charge of Kim once the surprise bit was over and the party was in full swing.

Steve's hand was on Jack's shoulder and on his other side was Ruby, who was determined not to leave Steve's side all evening. Parties must be hell for him, she'd said to Erin and Abby. She owed it to dear Sally to keep an eye on him.

'He was really good to come,' Erin agreed, but she knew Steve had been trying to make an effort to get out a little bit, and that Lizzie's surprise party was his first foray into the real world since Sally's death.

'You, Lizzie and Abby have been so good setting up this charity in Sally's name,' he'd told Erin when she'd invited him to the party. 'I'll drop in with the boys. We probably won't stay long but . . .'

'Stay for as long or as little as you want,' Erin said. 'We'll all be thrilled to see you.'

'Can you hear anything?' whispered Greg to Erin.

Through the glass doors separating the porch from the hall, everyone could see the tall figures of Tom and Simon coming into view.

'Where's Lizzie?' asked Clare Morgan, putting on her glasses to peer through the glass doors.

'She's behind them, I think. Get ready,' whispered Erin.

'. . . and he's just the cutest little devil of a thing,' Tom was saying, as the porch door was opened and suddenly Lizzie and Simon were in the hall with at least sixty people screaming 'Happy Birthday, Lizzie' at the top of their voices.

Speechless, Lizzie felt for Simon's hand, turned to look in astonishment at Abby, and then looked back into the smiling faces of all her friends and family raising glasses to her. Balloons, lights and a huge banner decorated the hall.

'Oh, it's perfect,' she breathed, 'perfect.'

Lizzie Shanahan's surprise fiftieth was certainly a hell of a party, as any of the people of Dunmore who weren't invited would have said if they could have peered in through the windows at the laughter-filled scene in Lyonnais. And despite the loud music, laughter, and vast quantities of drink whizzing around, it was very civilised.

The Shanahans really were people to admire, because of the way Myles and Lizzie had moved seamlessly on from their broken marriage to forge new relationships, and yet remained true to their family. Because that's what it was all about: family, blending new families and old families but keeping it all on an even keel. Myles was there with his new partner, Sabine, and she and Lizzie had talked for ages, laughing no less, while Lizzie's new man, a tall, handsome fellow called Simon, was stuck in a corner having great chats with Lizzie's son, Joe. Of course, it was a pity that young Debra's marriage to Barry Cronin hadn't lasted, but all families had their burden, and certainly Joe Shanahan seemed deliriously happy with that lovely London girl who worked in the art gallery.

Gwen Hoban, Lizzie's sister, and always the first person to call a spade a spade, was telling that lovely Dr Morgan that Debra had settled down a lot since the wedding and added that she wouldn't be surprised if Barry and Debra managed to make it up after all. They hadn't sold their house, Gwen said, tapping her nose as if this was an important clue to what might happen in the future.

The Shanahans weren't the only ones enjoying themselves. Greg and Erin Kennedy were squashed up on one armchair and Erin was tearfully telling Greg that she was sorry she'd been such a crosspatch and she didn't know what had come over her. They'd certainly settled in well after moving from Chicago. He was doing well in the telecoms company and all the staff had nothing but good to say about him, while Erin had thrown herself into the community, helping out in The Beauty Spot when poor Sally Richardson had passed away. And now she was energetically setting up some sort of cancer centre in the town in Sally's name, somehow managing the neat trick of getting everyone else just as enthusiastic as she was, without making them feel guilty for not having thought of it first.

She'd sounded very American when they'd first arrived, but it turned out she was Irish after all, and her family often came to visit her from Wexford and Portlaoise. She often walked down the pier with a woman with streaked blonde hair who was obviously her sister, two little girls in tow. One was a dote of a thing with poker-straight dark hair, about six, who skipped along, holding her aunty's hand and talking nineteen to the dozen. The other was a little angel in a pushchair with shining dark eyes in a tiny face. Erin would have her own pushchair soon – she was as big as a house with her pregnant belly and she couldn't walk too far, so the sister made her sit with the older child while she pushed the little one so she'd drop off to sleep.

And the Bartons, well, they were quite the success story of the town. There had been some talk in the papers of a split but from the way they were arm in arm as they talked to that nice Steve Richardson, it was difficult to believe that the journalist had got it right. That marriage was rock solid: anyone with half a brain could see that.

Their daughter was a nice girl too; done really well in her exams, apparently. She was doing a great job minding those two little Richardson boys, bringing them outside into the garden to play with the puppy, a tall, smiling young lad accompanying them.

Yes, it definitely looked like the party of the year in Dunmore, a party where nobody had a care in the world. It was a pity that poor Sally Richardson wasn't around to see it: she'd always been a great one for marvellous parties, but sure, she was bound to be sitting on a cloud somewhere smiling fondly down at them all, getting the other angels to hurry up with the nectar punch and cranking up the celestial choir so there'd be some music. If ever there was a woman who'd known the value of laughter and enjoying life, it was Sally.

AFTERWORD

Writing this book, I was painfully aware that the character with breast cancer was going to die and hated to think that this would upset anybody who is fighting cancer. As around one in eleven women develop the disease, every one of us knows brave and courageous women who are successfully fighting breast cancer. The severity and speed of Sally's cancer are very rare and represent the worst-case scenario possible. The fact is that the vast majority (75%) of women with metastatic breast cancer are still alive five years after diagnosis and the percentages are getting higher all the time.

Life Beats Cancer is my fictional invention, but there are, of course, a huge number of genuine cancer charities that deserve our support.

Thanks to Lucy Kelly and Deborah Hutchings of Cancer Research UK for their advice. Needless to say, all mistakes in the novel are mine.